Valentin

MW00614035

Hope you enjoy

the "Legacy.

God Bless,

Bruce T Clark

The

Custer

Legacy

By

Bruce T. Clark

THE CUSTER LEGACY

Copyright Bruce T. Clark 1997

ISBN: 978-1-60704-010-1

Library of Congress Catalog Number
97-60852

Cover Design by Patrick Diemer

Reprinted in 2008
Seton Press
1350 Progress Drive
Front Royal, VA 22630
(540) 636-9990

Printed in the United States

Dedication

One soft and starry evening, in the spring of 1956, I met a lovely young lady named Mary Kay. Five years later she became my bride and, ultimately, the mother of our seven sons. Like many other young husbands, I spent the early years of our marriage trying to become my wife's hero. Then one day I suddenly discovered that she had become mine. For she is far more than a wife, a mother, or even a hero; she is an inspiration to everyone who knows her.

One of the nicest rewards of writing "The Custer Legacy" is the ability to dedicate my first novel to my first love, with profound affection, and an ever-increasing admiration for all that she has done and everything that she has accomplished; but most of all, for everything that she has helped the rest of us to become. She truly is the wind beneath our wings.

CONTENTS

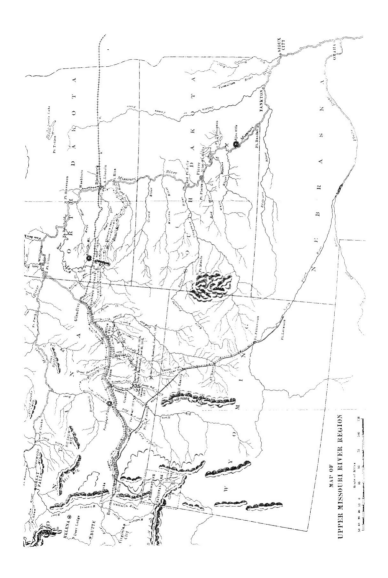

MAP OF
UPPER MISSOURI RIVER REGION

xi

Prologue
➢
Man Of Mystery

St. Peter's Square
Vatican City
June 25, 1999

He limped cautiously along the rough, uneven cobblestone street. He did not seem to be an old man, yet he moved with the halting, arthritic gait so common to the elderly. As he neared the end of the street, he paused in the shadows of an ancient building and looked about furtively. He was glad to stop, even for a moment. The pain emanating from the wound he had suffered two days earlier was becoming unbearable.

Thank God, he thought, once I cross the square, I'll be safe.

He was a man of medium height and indeterminate years. Over the past few weeks, the travel and the pain, but most of all the stress from constant danger, had stripped away much of his excess flesh, giving him a gaunt, almost cadaverous appearance. A broad-brimmed hat, together with the equally dark cloak that hung so loosely about him, might have attracted attention anywhere else in the world, but now served only to mark him as one who belonged in this place. His anguished eyes, looking out of a face ashen with fatigue, peered nervously at each stranger approaching along the narrow thoroughfare.

How curious, he mused, that his journey should end on this day of all days. How strange that June 25 had been important in so many other years, since the very beginning of the mystery on June 25, 1520. Long ago, when he accepted the assignment and began fitting the pieces of scant haphazard information together, it had seemed like an impossible challenge. As he unearthed scores of additional facts, he discovered that not a single one of his predecessors had ever returned, or even been heard from again. Had it not been for God's guidance, he would surely have met a similar fate and the secret might have remained hidden forever, just as the Old Ones intended. He wondered if any of the others had survived long enough to learn the ancient secret. It will bring great good to the world, he thought, just as in the wrong hands; it has wrought such terrible suffering.

When he found the second treasure, he believed it was a great stroke of good fortune, but the discovery had brought a new force of vicious enemies into the chase. Several times in the past few weeks, both his enemies, as eager to foil each other as they were to stop him, had nearly succeeded in their attempts to learn the secrets that only he possessed, or failing that, to simply kill him. Each time he had managed to escape and elude pursuit.

To reassure himself, he reached into his heavy canvas pack and touched an object that held the key to a centuries-old enigma. As he withdrew his hand, a cold chill of foreboding made him shiver. How foolish, he thought; premonitions of impending doom should be reserved for superstitious old women.

By sheer force of will, he pushed himself erect, shouldered his bag, and leaving the security of the shadows, resumed his painful trudging walk, still glancing fretfully about him as he crossed the crowded, sunlit square. After what seemed to him a very long way, he reached the opposite side and paused beside a gate, a gate that meant the end of his long but successful journey.

He reached forward to ring the bell, but as he did, he saw an ominous shadow and suddenly felt a sharp pain rip into his back. Filled with utter disappointment and frustration, he pitched forward as the remaining strength drained from his tortured body, his arms too weak to cushion his fall. In an instant, his pack was roughly ripped from his shoulder. Over the thunderous roaring in his ears, he heard a new sound, the rush of approaching footsteps. With his last ounce of strength, he turned his head and looked up into the concerned face of a Swiss Guard. With his last conscious breath, Antonio Garza whispered, "Tell the Cardinal I found it."

PART ONE

GOD, GOLD AND GLORY

Chapter I

➢

The Feathered Serpent

The Pagan Empire of Montezuma
Tenochtitlan, Mexico
June 25, 1520

Padre Diego Garza looked quizzically up at the large crucifix, mounted upon a rough stone wall, which still bore countless stains of human blood, despite repeated efforts to scrub them away.

"Why do Your followers sometimes act in such harsh and brutal ways?" he asked the lovingly carved figure of Christ that looked down at him from the old wooden cross. His words echoed in the cavernous chamber. "You died to atone for the sins of man. Yet a soldier who professes to be a Christian, one of Your sons, has committed a vile and murderous act—the merciless act of a madman."

For the past seven months, all of them, Don Hernando Cortez, Padre Olmedo, the Conquistadors and he, in his own humble way, had made slow, tortuous progress. Now it seemed that everything they had accomplished would be swept away by one irrational act of bloodthirsty violence.

He crossed himself and rose from his knees. As he did so, he sensed an alien presence. His sandal-clad feet caught momentarily on the uneven floor as he turned, but he was still in time to glimpse shadows on the opposite wall. Clutching his robes about him, he hurried to the entrance in time to see four natives as they rounded a corner of the temple-pyramid and disappeared.

As he stood on the temple balcony, his anguished gaze swept across the city's vast expanse. It was a place of pagan deities. For hundreds of years it had been the devil's playground. He longed to block the pervasive stench of moral decay from his nostrils and the blatant signs of golden avarice from his eyes.

He had come to this savage land at the request of his old friend, Padre Olmedo, from the land of Estremadura, a part of Spain famous for brave bulls, stalwart soldiers, and sagacious saints. When Padre Olmedo had taken him to meet the leader of the expedition, Don Hernando Cortez, he saw a bright blue banner on a wall, which proclaimed: "Friends, let us follow the Cross. Under this sign, if we have faith, we shall conquer."

The first words Padre Garza heard the great Captain from Castille utter solidified his faith in Don Hernando Cortez.

"Holy Fathers," said Cortez, "we are going to the land of infidels to teach them the way of the Cross. But in our company will be many who do not share our motives. Every army has its seekers of fortune and seizers of opportunity. It will be my job to mold them into soldiers and yours to enlist them in the ranks of our Blessed Lord. I pray that we may be worthy of those tasks. I fear neither worldly force nor reprisal, but I remind you that messengers of God are often waylaid by disciples of the devil." Cortez rose from his chair, crossed the large room, and laid a steady hand on a shoulder of each of them before he continued.

"Holy Fathers, I ask now, will you come and march beside me in the shadow of the Holy Cross of Christ?"

How could anyone refuse to follow this servant of the Lord? wondered Padre Garza. How could anyone bear to disappoint him? Yet Lieutenant Pedro de Alvarado had been foolish enough to undo all that had been done. He stood transfixed, recalling everything that had happened during the months since their arrival.

He well remembered the day they had left the ships and come ashore. The following morning, they began the long trek westward toward the capital city. During the march from the sea, a steady procession of messengers arrived from the Emperor Montezuma. "You must stop now!" they commanded. "Go back at once!" they ordered. Soon the messages softened dramatically, and the couriers pleaded with the Spaniards not to come any closer.

They received bribes in the form of pagan statues and other golden ingots. Messengers arrived daily. None came empty-handed. Yet the relentless invasion continued. At first they thought the Aztecs' intense fear was caused only by the fact that they were strange-looking men with bearded faces, riding on alien animals, and carrying long sticks which spat out fire and smoke. But they soon discovered that the natives' terror was far deeper than they had even imagined.

Their very first convert in the pagan land was a bright young Tabascan Indian woman whose Christian name was Doña Martina. She became a confidante and interpreter. She told them why Montezuma was frightened, and why he did not attack them. When they landed in 1519, it was the year of ce acatl, a special festival which occurred every fifty-two years: in 1415, 1467, and again in 1519. The legend of ce acatl warned the Aztecs that during one of those ce acatl years, the great emperor, Quetzalcoatl, would rise from his grave and return from the East, together with many other pale-skinned men. They would come mounted upon fearsome four-legged beasts, and would be clothed in radiant attire. Montezuma had every reason to believe that the Conquistadors, with their white skins and shining armor, were the warriors of a risen Quetzalcoatl. The Spaniards also learned that Quetzalcoatl had hated human sacrifice so much that, before he went away, he vowed to return and wreak havoc upon anyone who ever again practiced the despicable ritual.

Padre Garza shuddered as he remembered his revulsion when he learned that Montezuma presided over an empire which, at festival times, sacrificed as many as ten thousand victims to bloodthirsty gods. Experienced Aztec priests became so quick and proficient in these sacrificial rituals, that they were often able to cleave the chest of the trembling victim and seize his frantically beating heart in their hands, before ripping it from his terror-stricken body and casting it down upon a pagan altar of bloody stones.

In some years as many as a hundred thousand human hearts were fed to the insatiable devil-gods of the Aztecs.

Doña Martina told them that Quetzalcoatl's personal symbol had been a feathered serpent. Tradition warned Montezuma that he must fear that sign above all others, lest the feathered serpent destroy him in reprisal for his human sacrifices and blood lust.

"Little does Montezuma know," Padre Garza told his young friend Curco, "that his immoral empire will one day be replaced by an immortal empire. A symbol, but not one of hatred and revenge will destroy the Aztec Empire. The Holy Cross—the symbol of love and redemption, will defeat it. Whether we win or lose, here and now, is unimportant. Eventually, God will win His ageless battle with the devil. Someday the bodies and blood of human sacrifices will be replaced by the Body and Blood of Our Lord."

He looked down from his vantagepoint high up on the steps of the temple-pyramid, and saw an approaching column of marching soldiers and mounted men. Don Hernando Cortez and his men had returned from an encounter with the rebel Panfilo Narvaez. Some weeks before, Narvaez and a number of his followers had landed in the wake of Cortez and advanced on the Aztec capital. Their quest was not for God, but for gold. Now, Padre Garza saw Narvaez riding boldly along beside Cortez. Obviously, the Captain's powers of persuasion had converted yet another to his cause.

Far below his high perch, the foot soldiers halted and the riders dismounted, just as the sun sank behind the volcano of Popocatapetl. As if by magic, the blooming fields and gleaming buildings of Tenochtitlan were instantly bathed in a rosy glow.

Padre Garza descended a long flight of steps and entered the section of the temple that served as the expedition headquarters. Padre Olmedo would be present when Lieutenant Alvarado reported to Captain Cortez on the deteriorating situation. When he did, Don Hernando might wish to speak with both of his priests.

He entered, crossed the room, and stood beside his friend, Padre Olmedo. A moment later, a furious Hernando Cortez was followed into the room by a crestfallen and worried-looking Pedro de Alvarado. Cortez was in a black rage as he shook his fist and thundered at Alvarado.

"Your conduct has been that of a madman. How could you violate my orders? How could you have been so stupid? Didn't you realize there would be reprisals? How many of us will die because you behaved like a fool?"

Alvarado may have been a fool, but he was not foolish enough to interrupt the Captain or to offer any excuses.

Cortez turned to the priests.

"Buenos noches, Padres. A hundred thousand pardons for my outburst. But I regret to say that this man may well have killed us all. What is the attitude of the people?"

It was Padre Olmedo who answered.

"I fear that you are right, Patron. Since Lieutenant Alvarado slaughtered the worshipers at the festival, there has been great unrest, even among our allies."

"Padre Garza," queried Cortez, "what about your students, your young people?"

"I have seen none of them, except Curco, since the night of the massacre at their temple, Patron."

"Padre Garza saved Curco's life," Padre Olmedo added. "As you know, Curco is the son of the High Priest. This morning, the boy visited the chapel after Mass and asked Padre Garza to attend a meeting with his father tomorrow at sunset. Perhaps, then, we may discover the intentions of the Aztec priests."

"Perhaps," replied Cortez. "However, I want the guard around Montezuma doubled. Also, we must let him know that if he tries to escape again, we will not be as gentle as we were the last time.

"Alvarado, I will decide on disciplinary sanctions against you after I determine a course of action. I want you to go to the barracks room and select a double squad of soldiers. You are to form them in column order and march to the Emperor's quarters. They are to remain there, two hours on watch and two hours off, until they are relieved sometime tomorrow afternoon. When they are in position, return here and report compliance. After that, you will confine yourself to arrest in your quarters. You are fortunate, Alvarado, that I am a patient man. You are dismissed."

As he finished speaking, the two other conquistador officers entered, bowed to the priests, and retreated to the far end of the room where they were soon engrossed in an earnest conversation with the Captain.

The two padres prayed briefly for God's guidance, then busied themselves straightening the altar covering, preparing vestments for the following day's Masses, and reading their offices. All the while, the Captain and his officers remained at the end of the long chamber, and continued an animated and often heated discussion.

Suddenly from the corridor came a frightened scream, followed by the sound of running footsteps. The five men rushed from the room, but were too late to catch any glimpse of the runner. In the light of a wall torch, they saw the figure of a man, lying near the temple doorway. From the victim's chest protruded a ceremonial Aztec dagger. Encircling the hilt was an intricate carving of a feathered serpent. The position of the body and the large pool of blood were ample proof that Pedro de Alvarado had made his last mistake.

Late that night, after the padres had said a Mass for the dead, Pedro de Alvarado was buried in a secret, unmarked grave.

Captain Cortez ordered them to say nothing of the incident to anyone. There was no proof that an Aztec had murdered Alvarado, Cortez reasoned. It could have been one of the Spaniards. If so, silence might induce the culprit, by word or action, to reveal his identity. If the murder had been committed as an act of Aztec revenge, silence was the best policy for that as well.

Padre Garza returned to his cubicle well after midnight, and wearily lay down upon his thin pallet of straw, but he could not sleep. He thought about the body of Pedro de Alvarado in a lonely grave and said a prayer for the repose of the foolish man's soul.

But it was another problem that gnawed at his conscience and jolted his mind back to a state of alertness each time he dozed off. Each morning after Mass, he distributed Holy Communion to the sick in the infirmary and to the outlying guard posts. Now that a Spaniard had been killed, he felt a premonition that he, and perhaps many others, might soon die. He gave no thought to himself, but felt an immense fear for the sacred Host that was under his protection. The thought of the Host being desecrated by Aztec pagans filled him with fear and loathing.

The answer to his dilemma suddenly came to him. The sword! Of course! The perfect hiding place! He arose and went to the cedar chest which held his vestments and Mass kit, as well as a number of personal possessions. From the bottom of the chest he removed a beautiful sword in a jeweled scabbard and carried it to his table. He lit an additional candle and sat for a long time, holding the magnificent weapon, and remembering.

➤

His grandfather, the first Diego Garza, had been born into a Castillian military family on December 12, 1432. Dedicated to a military life at birth, Diego graduated from the Royal Academy of Toledo the week before his twenty-first birthday, in 1453, and was assigned to the palace guard of the new King of Castille, Henry IV, who would be crowned early the following year.

Before he left Toledo, Diego Garza went to the foremost sword makers in Spain, Espadas Españas, and commissioned them to craft a fine sword for him. He wanted the best that money could buy. Diego spent several hours in the shop with Jose Mendoza, the expert craftsman who would actually design and forge the weapon. He would make a sword, Mendoza guaranteed Diego, that would be the envy of every young caballero who saw it.

When Diego returned to the shop, five weeks later, his joy knew no bounds. The sword far exceeded his wildest expectations. The weapon was so perfectly balanced that it almost came alive in his hand as he drew it from the scabbard. Amazingly, the hidden compartment that Mendoza had built into the hilt was undetectable. The chance of anyone finding and opening it without guidance was virtually nonexistent. Jose Mendoza assured him that anything hidden within the slender chamber would not be found for a thousand years. His beautiful sword was identified by an inscription, which had been engraved along one side of the blade. It began one-third of the way from the tip and extended upward, toward the hilt.

DIEGO GARZA - ESPADAS ESPAÑAS - TOLEDO ESPAÑA - MCDLIV

His grandfather had served his sovereign, King Henry, for the next fifteen years. They were difficult, nearly impossible years, because Henry IV was a weak king. To avoid trouble, he made many concessions to the Moors, as well as anyone else who threatened to disturb the tenuous peace. He brought his kingdom to the very brink of annihilation many times during his reign.

Then, late in 1469, General Diego Garza's troops quelled a bloody uprising and saved Henry's life once again. The morning after the last battle, the king summoned him. As he entered the royal chambers, a gentle lady, a blond-haired, green-eyed young woman, diverted his attention. Moments later, he was presented to Henry's heir, Isabel, and given the formidable task of protecting her.

In less than a week, Diego learned that the eighteen-year-old Isabel was everything that Henry would never be. She was unassuming, but iron-willed, and highly intelligent. She was also an extremely devout Catholic. Diego was convinced that she would, one day, lead her people out of their prolonged darkness. He would willingly have died to protect her.

During that first month, Isabel came to admire and respect Don Diego as well. One day, as they rode in her carriage, she confided in him.

"Don Diego, I am troubled. I need your help."

"My Lady, you know I am yours to command."

"Very well. King Henry wants to give me in marriage to King Alfonso of Portugal. But that will serve no good purpose. I must marry Ferdinand, Prince of Aragon. Our marriage will be best for all of Spain. He is a year younger than I am, but he is strong. He agrees with my proposal, but says he must, at this time, lead the armies of Aragon. Don Diego, you must go to him and persuade him to return with you at once. Otherwise, all may be lost."

Diego was surprised by the political awareness of one so young, but he felt compelled to remind her of his duty.

"My Lady, I am needed here to protect you. Only three days ago, another attempt was made on your life."

"My life is already lost if I cannot, with Fernando, unite our floundering land. Could not Lieutenant Vargas command the troops until your return?"

"If you feel that strongly about it, My Lady, I will make the necessary arrangements and leave as soon as possible."

The next morning, Isabel gave him a letter for Ferdinand that said: "Come, come, for the love of God."

Diego's mission was successful. He reached Ferdinand without incident and convinced the young prince to return with him. To ensure their safety on the journey to

Valladolid, where Isabel waited, Ferdinand and his two friends disguised themselves as merchants. On October 11, 1469, they all reached Isabel's side.

One week later, on October 18, the young couple were married.

Three years later, on the eve of Diego's fortieth birthday, King Henry IV died and Isabel and Ferdinand ascended the throne.

The armies of King Alfonso of Portugal immediately threatened the young rulers. Queen Isabel rode about the countryside persuading young men to join an army which King Ferdinand and Don Diego trained and led. Alfonso's forces were repulsed! It was the first step in the dynamic couple's long and successful reign.

They led their subjects toward peace, prosperity, and freedom, which finally came to fruition in 1492 when the last of the Moors were expelled from Spain after nearly 800 years of occupation. On the second day of the New Year, Boabdil, the last Moslem ruler in Spain, surrendered to Doña Isabel and Don Fernando.

In the spring of that year, Don Diego, nearing his sixtieth birthday, asked for permission to retire after his lifetime of service to Los Reyes Catolicos (The Royal Catholic Sovereigns). His wish was reluctantly, but gratefully, granted.

On the day that Don Diego left her side for the last time, after twenty-three years of allegiance, Queen Isabel arranged a great celebration to honor and reward her oldest friend and most valiant protector. Don Diego stood before the throne and became a peer of the realm. He was knighted and made a Grandee of Spain, an honorary position that provided him with an ample retirement income. As he took his leave, tears rolled, unabated, down the cheeks of Doña Isabel. The eyes of Don Fernando and Don Diego were misty as well.

Hundreds of Diego's former troops, dear friends, and ardent admirers lined the exit halls to thank him and to wish him well. One of the last to step forward and grasp his hand was a stranger in dusty traveling clothes.

"May God go always with you, Don Diego," said the man.

"Do I know you, Señor? Are you from this city?"

"No, Don Diego. I have come here to seek the help of El Rey y La Reina. A great man like you has no need to know the likes of me. I am just a humble sailor from Genoa. My name is Cristobal Colon."

➢

Padre Garza awakened from the dream about his grandfather as the first light of day crept into his cubicle. The anguish in his back, neck, and shoulders, which he had suffered since a serious boyhood injury, was far worse than usual. The intense stabs of pain were explained when he realized that he was still seated in the chair by the table. He had spent the night there with his head resting on the cushion of his arms. His eyes fell on the sword and he thought once more about his grandfather. Last year, when the expedition sailed from Cadiz, the courtly old gentleman had come to see them off. In his late eighties, he still made no concession to the years as he stood upon the quay, watching their ship disappear from sight.

Before his departure for the New World, Diego had gone to stay with the Grandee for a fortnight. On their final day together, realizing that it might well be their very last visit, they had strolled in the garden among the roses and statuary, and talked of many things. Late that afternoon, as the sun waned and the shadows lengthened, they rested on a white marble bench beside a bubbling fountain and quietly watched a dozen goldfish swimming lazily in and out amongst the miniature nooks and crannies of their watery home. At last, the Grandee broke the silence.

"Diego, I have a gift for you. The sword I have used to serve God and protect Spain for the past sixty-five years."

"I'm a priest, Grandfather, not a warrior! I have no need for a sword."

"Diego, sometimes a priest must be a warrior in order to be a priest. As a representative of God, you inherit His enemies. Placing malice and snares in the path of ones like you is the devil's joy. You cannot begin to imagine the difficulties that you may encounter in that strange, savage land across the sea. Your mission is to bring souls to Christ. How do you plan to accomplish that if you are dead? My son, you must survive to perpetuate the Faith."

The Grandee arose and assumed an "on guard" position.

"Surely you have not forgotten everything that I taught you about swordplay. I'm sure your arm is still strong and your wrist still steady. Besides, my old Toledo blade is too fine to lay idly in an old man's rack, while it and I both collect a layer of dust. Let us talk no more of this; please do as I wish."

Thank God for the Grandee's foresightedness, Padre Garza thought. Grandfather was as wise as always.

He arose and donned his cassock. Then for the first time, he cinched the sword belt around his waist. The long sword, bumping against his leg, felt strange as he descended a steep flight of stairs to the fountain that the members of the expedition used for bathing.

He stopped near the cascading water and removed most of his clothing, carefully hiding the sword under his folded robe before wading into the shallow pool. As he cleansed his body, he kept careful watch on his possessions. He finished his bath quickly and dried himself. When he was clad, he once again belted the sword about his waist, then climbed the long flight of steps and went to join Padre Olmedo in the celebration of Mass.

Before entering the chapel, he removed the weapon and carried it back to the sacristy where Padre Olmedo waited. As he entered the chapel to begin Mass, it seemed to him that every man who was not on duty was in attendance.

When the Mass ended, Padre Olmedo stayed in the chapel to hear the confessions of a dozen or more Conquistadors.

Padre Garza returned to the sacristy and prepared everything he needed to distribute Holy Communion to the soldiers who had remained at their posts. He counted out a sufficient number of Hosts, then took up the sword. He had to sit down and use both hands in order to release the ingenious catches that locked the hidden compartment. If they were not unlocked in precise order, the compartment would remain tightly shut. He carefully completed the sequence and found that there was ample space for the Hosts.

He went forth to perform his duties with renewed vigor and confidence. For now he could defend the Host, and even if he were overwhelmed or killed, they would be safe forever in the hiding place. Before reaching each guard post, he stopped in a secluded place and removed enough Hosts for the men on duty. In about an hour, he returned to the chapel where he removed the remaining Hosts and sealed them safely within the tabernacle.

For the rest of the day, remembering his grandfather's admonition, he wore the sword everywhere he went, except in the chapel. Now as twilight descended and the others were gathering together for the evening meal, he excused himself and descended the temple steps to meet Curco, who would take him to the Temple of the High Priest of the Aztecs. As he reached the last flight of stairs, Curco stepped from the shadows and greeted him. The boy's eyes opened wide when he saw the sword, but he made no comment. A moment later, they were on their way, talking as they walked in their strange and special language, a mixture of the Spanish words Curco knew and Aztec ones the Padre had learned.

Chapter II

➤

Secret of the Aztecs

Main Aztec Temple
Tenochtitlan, Mexico
The Same Evening

Curco led Padre Garza along a wide boulevard to the city's center. One entire side of the large plaza was occupied by the main temple-pyramid of the Aztecs. Padre Garza shuddered as they entered this building which, he realized, for hundreds of years had been the scene of so many horrible, ritualistic murders.

The first time he saw this maleficent mausoleum, all the walls were splashed with red. The odor of fresh blood was unmistakable. It was reminiscent of freshly sheared copper. The smell stirred unpleasant memories of his first and only time on a battlefield. As he went about ministering to the dying and dead, a strange cloying smell seemed to follow him. Not until a veteran soldier identified the source did the horror strike home. Now he was in a pagan land where blood flowed like an endless red river.

His grandfather said soldiers could smell a battlefield for weeks, find evidence of it for years, and feel the spirit of its victims for centuries. "The aftermath of this evil empire will endure in infamy," he told Curco and his other young students, "but the evil must be stopped now. We must stamp out this blood lust and misery for all time and teach your people about Christ. To accomplish that, no sacrifice on my part would be too great."

They entered the living quarters of the High Priest and his family, and after Curco's introductions, they all sat down for a cordial meal consisting of native fruits and vegetables, which Padre Garza found to be as delicious as they were refreshing.

When the dinner was over, the High Priest, Attapa, using signs and gestures, tried to thank Padre Garza for saving the life of his eldest son. As his father stepped out of the room, Curco, also using signs to supplement his few Spanish words, invited the Padre to select anything he saw in the dwelling as a gift. While Curco was explaining this, Attapa returned to the room, straining under the weight of a golden statue, which he placed in Padre Garza's hands.

For its size, the object was extremely heavy. Padre Garza realized that it was not a hollow shell as he had suspected, but a solid gold ingot, worth a small fortune to the metal dealers in Spain. "This is for you," Curco told the Padre.

Before the Padre could explain his reasons for refusing any reward, there was a loud commotion outside in the main temple. Curco went to the entrance and returned with two young men, about his own age. They bowed to the High Priest and the Padre, then began to speak far faster than the Padre could follow. Almost at once, Attapa interrupted them, and hurried out the door, followed closely by his two young visitors.

Curco explained that four young men had gone hunting for tigres, that is, jaguars, and bad fortune had befallen them. One had been attacked by a big cat and badly clawed. The second man, intent on aiding his friend, had fallen from a tree. One was bleeding and the other appeared to be dead. Their friends had brought them to the High Priest for help.

Curco and Padre Garza left the living quarters and hurried into the main temple where the young men had been laid on two of the side altars. The upper leg and forearm of one hunter had been opened to the bone by the sharp claws of the jaguar. The other victim's face and body had lost all color. Padre Garza had seen men turn blue before they died, but this young man was pale.

He decided that the second man could not be saved. But the jaguar's victim might be if the rapid bleeding could be stopped soon enough. He turned to Curco with a request for materials to make tourniquets and bandages. But before he could speak, Attapa descended from the high altar carrying an earthen container.

He quickly took from his robes a small ladle, which he used to remove a thick liquid from the large container. He poured this substance directly into the bloody wounds in the arm and leg and then, without waiting to observe the result, turned his attention to the lifeless young man. Again he dipped the slender spoon into the container, but this time he removed a very small quantity. Then, with Curco's assistance, he pried open the slack jaw of his patient, dripped about a dozen drops of the liquid into the man's mouth, and stepped back.

Padre Garza's gaze shifted back to the bleeding man's gaping wounds. He could not believe his eyes. The blood, which only moments before had been gushing forth, had stopped completely.

Then he returned his attention to the dead man. What was this? The color had disappeared. The skin was now a shade of rosy pink. How was this possible? A few minutes earlier, this man had been one heartbeat from death. Now he had recovered enough to speak! It was obvious that he had sustained a number of broken bones, but it was also obvious that he would live. This magical liquid had saved his life!

"Either I am dreaming or this is a miracle cure!" Padre Garza thought to himself. "It is a great gift from God! If it can restore consciousness to a young man that I thought was dead, that is truly miraculous. It is more precious than all the gold that will ever be found. I must learn this secret!"

Attapa summoned several of his assistants to the temple. When they arrived, they were bearing litters. The recovering patients were gently placed upon these stretchers and carried off for further care.

By now, Padre Garza was totally mystified.

"What did your father use?" he whispered to Curco.

"It is an Aztec secret made known to every High Priest by his predecessor." The Padre was eager to ask many more questions about the mysterious substance, but was forestalled by Attapa.

"Do you have any pain in your body?" asked the High Priest.

"Yes I do!"

"Where is the pain?"

"I have pain in my back, neck, and shoulders, from an accident I suffered long ago."

"Let us remove your tunic and try to ease the pain," the High Priest said by signs.

Curco and Attapa helped him to remove the clothing from his upper body, exposing the painful areas. Attapa brought forth the earthen container and small ladle, and applied a small quantity of the medicine to the painful areas. He used his hands to spread the substance about, then washed them at once. Almost immediately the Padre's neck and back began to feel warm, and then very hot, but it was a comfortable hot. Within a few minutes the pain, for the first time in many years, was gone. Completely gone!

"This is wonderful medicine," declared Padre Garza. "A great gift from God! Would I still be permitted to select the gift of my choice?"

"Certainly," Curco assured him.

"Then," pleaded the Padre, "share the secret of this wondrous medicine with me and allow me to share it with others."

When Curco translated this request, Attapa hesitated, perhaps in surprise, but more likely because he realized the great danger he and his family would face if anyone learned that a Spaniard possessed this great Aztec secret. After a long silence, he resignedly nodded his head in assent.

They led him to a small chamber behind the main altar, where a great number of earthen jars of various sizes were assembled, and explained that these containers held the six unusual ingredients from which the wondrous formula was blended. This area was also the drying room, where various components were dehydrated before being ground up into powdered form. Eventually, all the materials would be carefully measured, combined, and allowed to ferment.

From a storage shelf, Attapa removed a small golden scroll. Padre Garza noted that it had been hammered down until the sheet of gold leaf was no thicker than a similar piece of parchment. In Attapa's other hand was a sharp writing implement, which resembled a stylus. He handed these things to Curco and removed ingredients from various jars, one at a time. He patiently identified and described each one of them to the Padre. As he did so, Curco drew a pictograph of each object, and how it could be identified as it grew or existed in nature. He also indicated the amount of each material that was required in relation to the others in the final potion.

When the drawing was finished, Padre Garza carefully examined it and discovered that the pictographs were simple to understand, since each ingredient was very clearly identified. The formula contained specific amounts of six different components. Using Attapa's stylus, Padre Garza carefully etched the Spanish name next to each ingredient on the list.

He was astonished by the medicine's simplicity. The first five items were common plants or herbs, which could be found growing in most fields or bogs. When he identified the main ingredient, he turned to Curco and smiled. "That's incredible," he said. "My mother's kitchen is never without this! Small wonder we were always so healthy. It also explains the instant feeling of heat."

The final section of instructions described the mixing and blending of the materials. Once prepared, the solution had to be thoroughly shaken each day for three full months. Only then would natural fermentation bring the elixir to its full potency.

Padre Garza carefully rolled the golden scroll and placed it inside his robes. Just before they left the small room, the High Priest spoke earnestly to Curco, who translated, with the aid of sign language, his father's words.

"You are in great danger! Many of the Aztec warriors want to kill all of you! Very soon, I think, they will attack. Although you have mighty weapons, you are few while they are many. Be careful! You are not like us, but you are our friend. You are a good man. To keep you safe, we will walk back with you."

Together with Attapa and Curco, Padre Garza strolled back across the plaza and along the wide boulevard toward the temple-pyramid of the Spanish expedition. When they arrived, he blessed them both and bid them good night.

The Padre climbed the steps, entered his room, and closed the curtain, then withdrew his sword from its scabbard and worked the intricate mechanism, which opened the small secret compartment. He measured the available space inside the cylinder and trimmed the scroll to fit as tightly as possible. When he inserted it, he was pleased to see that the scroll was now exactly the right length and fit snugly against each end of the hidden cylinder. When he allowed the scroll to unroll slightly, it welded itself against the walls of the chamber. He closed the compartment, snapped the mechanism shut, then shook the sword violently about, listening intently for telltale sounds of movement from within. He heard nothing! Satisfied that the contents were safe from detection, he returned the weapon to its scabbard and hung the sword belt over the back of the chair next to his pallet. Finally, he knelt and said prayers of thanksgiving for the foresightedness of his grandfather, and for the wonderful medicine that he would soon share with all of suffering mankind. As he fell asleep a short time later, he concluded that it would be wise to leave the Aztec scroll in its hiding place until the present danger had passed.

➢

The next morning after Mass, Padre Garza discussed the Aztec's warning with Padre Olmedo, and they decided to go to the Patron with the new information.

"Padres," said Don Hernando, "I am not surprised by this. It confirms all of the other signs I see. Did the High Priest indicate how soon this attack may come?"

"No, Patron, I think he does not know. Perhaps no one really knows. But they greatly fear our weapons."

"Should the Aztecs attack, we will give them even more reasons to fear our weapons. Since Alvarado is dead, I have been forced to promote Lieutenant Narvaez to my second-in-command. My other two officers are brave and willing enough, but they lack experience.

"I spoke with Narvaez last night," he continued, "and worked out a plan for retreat. I intend to drive the horses away and fight on foot. Picture a phalanx. It is a fighting formation shaped like an equal triangle. Now, picture another one directly behind the first, but facing the opposite way. Together they form a large diamond shape. That formation maximizes our ability to move equally well in every direction, since each point can, at once, become the front point of the phalanx.

"When we form this wedge, I will command the front half and Narvaez the rear. Padre Olmedo, stay beside me. Padre Garza, please march as close to Panfilo Narvaez as possible. There are many Aztecs, and they are likely to be fanatical. We will suffer a fair number of casualties, but most of us will get through. I pray that both of you will be among those who do.

"If one or both of you do not live through this ordeal, I swear that you will look down from Heaven and see us return to conquer this land in the Name of Christ. Someday we will expel the devil and his evil forever."

➢

Two days later, in the early evening, the attacks began. They continued for the next forty-eight hours. During the hand-to-hand battles, a great many Aztecs and several Spaniards were slain. On one occasion, the feathered warriors fought their way up to the temple platform directly below the one held by the Conquistadors. Cortez himself led the charge, which drove them off that platform, down the temple steps, and out into the plaza. When he returned from this sortie, ten of the soldiers who had fought beside him did not.

During the lull that followed, the Patron called a strategy conference with the padres and his three officers.

"Friends," he said, holding a bloody rag to his forehead, "it is time to retreat. We are low on food, and the troops are losing their resolve. Therefore, we will form the phalanx at midnight.

"Padres," he continued, "I will split the command into two divisions. Lieutenant Narvaez and his men will leave their posts and convene for Mass with Padre Garza at ten o'clock. When that Mass ends, they will relieve my second section. We will attend Mass with Padre Olmedo. Nuñez, you will second Narvaez and Padilla will assist me. Questions? Very well. May God be with all of us."

➤

It was now midnight. Padre Olmedo's second Mass had ended a few minutes earlier and the second section was assembling on the temple's lowest platform. On the terrace above, Narvaez and his troops stood in the bright moonlight, awaiting the Patron's orders.

As Padre Garza rested near the temple wall, the second unit's subaltern, whose unlikely name was Alvar Nuñez, Cabeza de Vaca, which means Head of the Cow, approached him. Nuñez came to a halt before Padre Garza.

"Padre, would you give me your blessing?"

"Of course, my friend."

Nuñez knelt and received the Padre's blessing. As he rose to his feet, the young conquistador noticed the sword.

"I am glad to see your sword, Padre. We may need every weapon we have tonight."

"Alvar," began the Padre, "I have something important to tell you about the sword."

At that moment, Cortez ordered Narvaez to bring his division into position.

"Tell me later, Padre. As we march."

It took only a few minutes to form the soldiers in the double phalanx, but staying in formation proved to be more difficult. Padre Garza, marching in the middle of the group, guessed they had come about half a league before Alvar Nuñez came to his side.

"What did you want to tell me, Padre?"

He withdrew the sword to explain to Nuñez, but before he could speak, the underbrush along both sides of the road erupted with Aztec warriors, brandishing war clubs and thrusting with spears.

"Use the sword now!" shouted Nuñez. "Talk about it later!"

After that, Nuñez and the other soldiers were busy fighting the insane mob of Aztecs that swirled around them. A short time later, most of the Aztecs lay dead and the rest had been driven away; but the price of victory had been high. Along with dozens of wounded, more than twenty Spaniards lay dead. Among them was the gentle Padre Diego Garza.

A young Aztec lad, wild with fury and fear, had rushed at him with a club poised high in the air. Padre Garza could have killed the boy, but such a thought never occurred to him. Holding the sword at both ends, he had raised it to protect his head. Had he held it with the razor-sharp edge up, the fine Toledo steel might well have severed the wooden club. But in his inexperience, he held the sword with its flat side exposed. The rapidly descending club struck the blade a foot below the hilt and snapped it off.

The second blow, following closely on the heels of the first, shattered the kindly priest's head and killed him instantly.

Alvar Nuñez, who had suffered two minor wounds in the melee, ran to the Padre's side — filled with grief and dismay — unwilling to believe that his beloved Padre was dead. A few moments later, he was assigned the task of assisting Padre Olmedo in the burial of all the Spanish dead. With a heavy heart, Padre Olmedo said prayers for the dead over their fallen comrades and prepared the body of Padre Garza for burial.

After Padre Garza had been lowered into his shallow grave, Nuñez reached down and placed the broken portion of the sword blade beside him, where he hoped it would remain forever. He wondered what the Padre had been going to tell him about the sword. It was strange that the portion of the blade now lying beside the Padre bore his name.

DIEGO GARZA - ESPADAS ESPAÑAS -

The section of the blade still attached to the hilt said:

TOLEDO ESPAÑA - MCDLIV

Noche de Triste, the Night of Sorrow, ended with Alvar Nuñez standing beside the grave, clutching a remnant of the Grandee's sword, weeping and wondering why a good man like his dear friend, Padre Garza, had to die.

Although the Night of Sorrow was over, the campaign was not. Hernando Cortez returned to the coast with the survivors.

The following year, Cortez received reinforcements from Spain and again marched on the capital city. This time there was no retreat. This time victory was achieved. This time the city was evacuated and every blood-splattered temple was burned to the ground. This time, Christ entered the front door as the devil bolted out the back.

23

Padre Olmedo celebrated Mass the day after the pagan temples were destroyed, and then a procession, which included Alvar Nuñez, wound its way back toward the main plaza. Leading the parade were Narvaez, carrying the flag of Spain, the Patron, Don Hernando Cortez, who carried a statue of the Blessed Virgin, and in the middle walked Padre Olmedo, who carried a huge cross. For such a large crucifix, it certainly wasn't very heavy, thought Padre Olmedo. Then tears came to his eyes as he realized that, somehow, his dear friend, Padre Diego Garza, was still sharing his load.

Chapter III

➤

Cabeza de Vaca

Arid & Desolate Plains
The Future State of Texas
June 25, 1530

It was 1530. He was certain of that. The primitive calendar, which he had tried to keep for the past three years, indicated that it was late in June, but he could not be sure. Worst of all, Alvar Nuñez, Cabeza de Vaca, was lost. He hoped the other ten men in his party did not know that he was lost. He shook his head violently from side to side in an effort to focus his mind. The sun-baked plains of this alien land had already scorched their skins, turning them as black as the devil's heart. Now the cursed heat might fry their brains before it killed them all.

Through bleary eyes, he thought he saw a small grove of trees far off in the distance. He called the site to the attention of the others, in hopes that it might renew their resolve to plod wearily ahead. Where trees grew, water was usually present. As he trudged along, forcing one foot in front of the other, he thought back over the past several years.

He had joined the conquering force, which Cortez brought back to subdue the Aztec Empire in 1521, and had remained on duty in Tenochtitlan for the next three years. Finally, in December 1524, he resigned his commission and sailed back to Cuba. During the Feast of the Nativity and throughout the rest of a pleasant winter, he relaxed and enjoyed a welcome release from the stress and danger he had endured for the past several years. But he soon became bored with the inactivity, and entered the service of the Captain-General in the early spring.

One of the first things he had done upon his arrival in Cuba was to take Padre Garza's sword to the island's best metalsmith. By grinding and reshaping the portion of the blade that remained, the clever craftsman had taken a broken sword and created a fine fighting knife. The redesigned blade was razor-sharp along one entire edge, while the newly reinforced opposite side was honed for only the first few inches above the point. Finally, the tip had been curved upward, adding a new and formidable dimension to the knife's capabilities. Now, after the blade had inflicted a gaping entrance wound, the curved tip, acting in the fashion of a shallow hook, imparted another internal wound as the knife was extracted, causing additional shock and trauma.

When Nuñez returned to the shop, the knife-maker's fee seemed high, until he saw the finished product. Then he would gladly have paid much more. For close combat, Nuñez had never held a deadlier weapon. From the knife-maker's shop, he went straight to a boot maker, and spent the rest of that afternoon watching him cobble a sheath to hold the knife and a fine sharpening stone securely. From that day, the weapon was never far from his hand.

Two years later his friend, Panfilo Narvaez, returned from Spain and again recruited Nuñez into service. The year before, Ponce de Leon came back to Spain from the Florida peninsula, and caused wild hysteria with tales of a fountain of youth and great quantities of gold. Narvaez had been sent to find those wonders.

The expedition sailed to the tip of Florida, where they landed on the first day of May 1527. Narvaez sent his ships to explore the coastal areas, while he and two hundred fifty other men struck off across country. Several weeks later, when the land party reached their prearranged rendezvous, the ships were not there. They waited for over a month, but never saw the vessels again. Without the ships, Nuñez and his party were isolated in a strange country amongst hordes of hostile savages. Fierce natives who turned out to be cannibals. They lost men in battles with the natives and others to marauding wild beasts; but the worst enemies of all were the tropical diseases.

The party moved slowly northward along a great length of land beside the sea (Florida), then westward across many hundreds of leagues (Louisiana and Texas). Each week more men were lost. They were killed fighting fierce savages. They drowned fording rain-swollen rivers. One man was even struck and killed by lightning. But most of them were the victims of raging fevers.

Narvaez had died of one such fever over a year ago. All of the other officers were also dead, as were nearly all of the men. Now Alvar Nuñez, Cabeza de Vaca, led the ten survivors.

➢

They finally reached the few scraggly trees, which were growing at the bottom of a high hill. They sat beneath them, grateful for even the meager relief provided by the sparse shade.

Suddenly one of the men screamed. Nuñez spun around to look at him and saw an arrow protruding from the man's back. He rushed to the victim's side.

"Garcia, don't move! I will help you! The rest of you watch the crest of the hill! They may charge down upon us!"

He turned back to help Garcia just as the soldier coughed up several great gobs of frothy blood, indicating a pierced lung. Garcia coughed once more, issued forth one final, stuttering rattle, then died.

Now, with shrill war whoops, a dozen Indians whom Nuñez, from earlier encounters, recognized as Comanches, charged forward and stormed down upon the bearded, skeletal, wasted wanderers.

Any Comanche who was fooled by appearances, or overestimated his ability to kill these strangers and take their scalps, soon regretted his rash presumption. It was a silent, deadly, brutal, hand-to-hand struggle, with no quarter given or expected. Nuñez saw man after man, red and white, go down, to rise no more.

His final antagonist was a tall, scar-faced, hatchet-wielding warrior, whose facial flaws were all covered with blue paint. The lethal blows, which he and the Comanche intended for each other, were delivered simultaneously. He buried the Spanish knife in his enemy's heart just as a blow from the hatchet exploded inside his head. He sank to the ground, ready to accept death.

He was flabbergasted several hours later when he regained consciousness. As feeling returned to his tortured body, he wished that he were dead. The pain in his head was unbearable. He revived enough to see that he had been moved away from the battle site. Beside him, moaning in his sleep, lay one of his men. The only other two men in sight sat beside a small pool of water.

"Mis amigos," he asked, "what happened?"

"When the fight ended all the Indios were dead. But, in the distance we saw a much larger force coming toward us. Juan and myself were the only ones still standing. We examined each of our compadres. Seven of them were dead. Only you and Sanchez were alive. We carried you to this place. We were fearful that the Indios would follow us, but they did not."

"How is Sanchez, now?"

"We don't know. He is barely breathing."

"How badly am I hurt?"

"You were stabbed in the shoulder and the blue Comanche's hatchet chopped off your left ear. We stopped along the way and sealed both of your wounds with a hot iron. We were able to stop the bleeding, Alvar."

"You saved my life, mis amigos. I am grateful."

"You have saved our lives many times. Rest now, Alvar."

"One more question, Ramon. Did you recover my knife?"

"We could not. The Comanches were too close. I am sorry."

"I understand. But I am sorry too. It was a wonderful knife."

"Maybe the blue warrior will be buried with it."

"No, Ramon. It is a war weapon, which will claim many more lives. Now we must rest. Tomorrow we will decide what to do."

➢

Both the Spaniards recovered and the small party continued to wander about the American Southwest. They discovered many wonders and made friends with dozens of Indian tribes, most of whom were quite cordial and extremely helpful. Then in the summer of 1536, long after being given up for dead, the four men wandered into Mexico City. By then, they had spent nine grueling but exciting years, walking across thousands of miles that no white man had ever seen before.

The journals of Alvar Nuñez, Cabeza de Vaca, were published in 1542, and read, not only in Spain, but in many other European nations as well. The stories of his journeys played a major part in the exploration of the Americas, for they inspired Coronado, De Soto, and hundreds of others to walk again where he and his companions had gone before.

In the early 1540's, Cabeza de Vaca returned to Spain and lived there for many more years. After his exciting life, he had earned a rest — and a right to dream of tall glistening mountains, and vast sunlit plains. It was time to sit beside cozy fireplaces on crisp winter evenings, and conjure up visions of deadly blue Comanches, and faraway rippling streams, bathed in the light of a million twinkling stars. Most of all, it was a time to remember his beloved friend, Padre Diego Garza, and wonder what had become of a never-to-be-forgotten, almost magical knife, that he had lost so long ago.

PART TWO

GATEWAY WEST

Chapter IV

The Immigrant

Post Civil War
St. Louis, Missouri
October 16, 1866

The first thing that the patrons of the plush Princess Hotel noticed that evening, as they entered the main lounge, was a man in worn traveling clothes, perched on a high stool. He sat near the end of the long mahogany bar, drinking slowly from a large tankard of ale. His attire, as well as the dark stubble that obscured the lower half of his face, convinced the steady stream of well-dressed passersby that he could be dismissed as a budding inebriate; or at best, one of the seemingly endless string of aimless veterans whose lives had been altered by the horrors of war. Most of these wretched men would never amount to much, the affluent denizens of the Princess Hotel had decided long ago. Itinerants of that ilk were completely unworthy of a well-to-do gentleman's attention. And so they scarcely spared more than a glance for the young man, as he sat pondering his future.

He had been born on April 12, 1840, in County Cork, Ireland, the fourth child of Patrick and Shannon McCarthy, but the first to survive beyond his first few weeks of life.

Those were black days in Ireland. The potato famine was taking its toll, as were the diseases and misfortunes that always seem to come with the bad times. Shannon McCarthy was only twenty-three when, ten days after the birth of her last child; she was lowered into the flinty, barren soil. Her difficult life and stressful death made her appear to be a woman closer to forty than to twenty. Before she died, Shannon extracted two solemn vows from Patrick. He somehow had to escape from the miseries of Ireland and seek the bounty of America. He also had to remain strong in the Catholic Faith for her and for the sake of the baby, whom she had proudly named Kevin Shannon McCarthy.

Not until years later did Kevin learn that his father had acquired their twenty pounds passage money by promising to pay back five pounds each year for the next ten years. This unfair arrangement had been forced upon Patrick by the only available money source, the English landowners for whom the McCarthys had labored for the past two hundred years.

➤

There were few jobs open to a hot-blooded bog Irishman in the New York City of the 1840's, particularly one who had an infant son. Patrick took the only job that was available to him. He joined the U.S. Army. It was only a few dollars a month, but you couldn't be fired, you wouldn't starve, there were people to help care for Kevin, and most importantly, there was always a nearby church. It was not an easy life for either of them, and there were many hardships to be shared as the next twenty years rolled by.

Kevin grew into a tall, dark-haired, ruggedly handsome lad while he learned to cope with the rough-and-tumble life of the frontier at a dozen different army posts. As he reached maturity, the sour fruits of war were ripening, and feelings of discontent were sweeping across the land. Ironically, Fort Sumter was fired upon the morning of Kevin's twenty-first birthday, and the Civil War began. The next day, Private Kevin McCarthy joined Sgt. Major Patrick McCarthy's 69th New York Regiment, the Irish Brigade.

➤

The war ended, four long years later, on April 9, 1865, three days before Kevin's twenty-fifth birthday, when Robert E. Lee rode his horse, Traveler, along a dusty Virginia lane on Palm Sunday and laid down his sword for the very last time.

Unlike some of his comrades, notably the flamboyant George A. Custer, a man often described as a modern D'Artagnan, or Kevin's best friend, the wild-eyed Myles Keogh, Kevin had learned to hate war more with each passing day. His father had lasted through two and a half years of the brutal conflict, and lived to see Kevin and Myles Keogh receive battlefield commissions on the same day at Chickamauga, before dying in Kevin's arms at the Battle of Missionary Ridge.

He died one cold November morning on those fire-swept slopes, at a place picked by God, perhaps to acknowledge the deeds of this good and faithful servant who had been a warrior in His army far longer than in the Armies of the Potomac or Tennessee. A true missionary who had brought many souls home to the Lord, despite the enduring grief and empty loneliness that had haunted him every day of his life after the death of his beloved Shannon a quarter of a century before.

During those dreadful years of conflict Kevin had learned to love the West as much as he had learned to hate the war. He was mustered out of the Grand Army in late spring, and since he had no family, no ties from the past or plans for the future, he drifted slowly westward as 1865 ended and 1866 began. He spent the fall and winter working for the Bock Brewery in Cincinnati, where he hauled beer by day and enjoyed the city by night. After four years of war, it was relaxing to unwind amid the big city's lights and to be excited by its temptations. As a result of his virtuous Catholic upbringing, Kevin seldom got drunk, and avoided the women who abounded in the city's waterfront saloons.

By the middle of 1866, most of the Queen City's luster had faded and Kevin was ready to move on once again. In no particular hurry, he purchased a half interest in a flatboat, one of the endless string of such craft which floated slowly down the Ohio River to Cairo, Illinois, where the lazy Ohio meandered into the mighty Mississippi.

For over fifty years, flatboats carried America's pioneers, together with all of their worldly possessions, from Pittsburgh's three rivers, southwestward to the mouth of the Ohio. Just a short distance north of Cairo was the sprawling metropolis of St. Louis, gateway to the West. There, each year, thousands of innocent pilgrims were spewed forth to fend for themselves, to live or die in a pitiless wilderness.

Kevin had invested 200 dollars for his half share in the keelboat, convinced that it could be sold for a handsome profit in Cairo, to the keelboaters floating on down the Mississippi to Natchez and New Orleans. The huge number of boats, which they encountered on the Ohio River each day after leaving Cincinnati, soon made him wonder if he bought a foolish dream rather than a keelboat. Fifty miles east of the Mississippi, his suspicions were confirmed. Boats of every size and description were anchored, or swung from tethers along both banks. It was even worse in Cairo. Boats could not be given away. The night before, Kevin and his partner had been forced to convert their 400-dollar keelboat into a 20-dollar pile of firewood. A far poorer, but much wiser Kevin McCarthy had arrived in St. Louis early this morning.

He had spent most of the day searching for work. At one point he even thought about reenlisting. All of the frontier regiments were busy in the city, recruiting for anticipated action against the Plains Indians. Posters hung on every corner lamppost, urging men to volunteer for security in the plodding infantry divisions, or adventure in the more glamorous cavalry regiments. Late in the afternoon, he had met John Handley, a friend from his teen years in New

York. Eager to talk, after so many years, they arranged to meet for dinner this evening, here at the Princess Hotel.

➤

Kevin had just ordered a second drink, when Handley arrived and sat down across from him.

For the next hour Johnny talked about the Ninth and Tenth Cavalry Regiments. Units composed totally of former slaves. Negro troopers under the command of white officers. Lieutenant Handley exuded enthusiasm about the great potential of the black soldiers.

"Kevin, they're going to become two great cavalry regiments. I'll bet they'll be goin' strong fifty years from now. For now, all the troopers will be Negroes, and the officers will all be white. Quite a few of 'em are former Confederate officers. Good men who have sworn allegiance to the Union. We're callin' them Galvanized Yankees."

"I read a story about the new regiments in the Cincinnati newspaper. Aren't a couple of the troops already on station?"

"They sure are! Buffalo Soldiers are guarding the railroad construction crews in western Kansas. I'll be going out to the 'end of track' in a couple of days. I was waiting for them at Fort Leavenworth when they reported, wearing those old-fashioned coats made from buffalo robes. The agency Indians camped around the fort gave them the name, Buffalo Soldiers. Now they're all so proud of that name, they're callin' themselves Buffalo Soldiers. But I'll guarantee one thing; most of those men are a whole lot sharper than any of us ever imagined they would be. Many of them will be damned fine Non-Coms as soon as we can train 'em. I was happy to get a commission in the Tenth Cav, and I'm damned proud to be serving under Colonel Grierson. You remember John Grierson, don't you?"

"I've never met him, but I remember the raid he led through the Confederacy from La Grange, Tennessee, all the way to Baton Rouge."

"I'd be glad to speak to Colonel Grierson about you, Kevin. I'm sure he could arrange for a direct commission if you wanted one."

"I appreciate your offer, Johnny, and I'd like to hold it in reserve for a few days. But I honestly think I've had my fill of military regimentation."

They finished their drinks and strolled into the hotel's excellent restaurant, which offered a spectacular view of the St. Louis waterfront.

Over a fine dinner and good wine, Handley brought Kevin up to date on news of their mutual friends and former comrades.

"Did you hear that George Custer is scheduled to report to Fort Riley as second-in-command of the Seventh Cavalry? He'll be serving under Colonel 'Andy' Smith. I'll bet the 'Boy General' is hopping mad about not being given command of the regiment. I'll also bet that if Custer has anything to say about it, at least three of our war buddies will be joining him as troop commanders. His brother, Tom, of course. He'll probably request Fred Benteen and, if he can wrangle it, your old friend, Myles Keogh."

They parted late that evening, with Kevin assuring Handley that he would stay in touch.

➢

In the days that followed, Kevin firmly rejected another army hitch. He considered the possibility of becoming a buffalo hunter, and even interviewed for a job as town marshal. But a hunter never stopped killing and a lawman never stopped worrying about getting killed.

His problem solved itself one night in late October at the Paradise Café. The restaurant, famous for its excellent food, was as usual heavily crowded. New arrivals who lacked reservations were compelled to find places wherever there was an empty chair. Kevin chanced to sit beside a tall, heavyset man with a thick black beard. The rough clothing he wore, and the bullwhip coiled beneath his seat, marked him as a "mule skinner."

His name was Harry Bronson and, together with his brother Curt, he owned and operated the B Bar B Freight Line. Their heavy wagons carried supplies to the mining towns in the backcountry and brought out high-grade ore to the foundries along the river. Business had been growing at a fantastic rate since the end of the war. B Bar B now owned ten wagons and sixty mules and was adding another team and wagon nearly every month. What he needed right now, Bronson told him, was a man to come in to help him and to learn a bit about the freight business. He would need to drive a six-mule hitch, as well as take care of the office accounts.

Harry said it was proving difficult to find the right man for two reasons: first, because nobody in town seemed able to handle both parts of the job and second, because the work would last for only a few months until Curt arrived from Indiana with his family.

Kevin mentioned that as a boy, he had earned extra money driving mule teams for a railroad during the three years that he and his father spent at Fort Erie. He had driven six-horse hitches during his time with Bock's in Cincinnati. His experience with accounts had come as a result of his adjutant duty during his army service.

Before the meal ended, the new friends had struck a deal. For Kevin, it offered an opportunity to learn about a business, which would continue to prosper throughout the West for many years to come, while avoiding a long-term commitment. In Kevin McCarthy, Harry Bronson found an employee who seemed to be eager, intelligent, and honest. A young man whose attitude indicated that he would not hesitate to do his share and who could be counted on when the going got tough.

The relationship they forged that evening was everything that either man could have expected. By the time Curt Bronson and his family arrived from the East in May, Kevin was well versed in all aspects of the freight business.

On a pleasant evening in June, the two friends again sat at a table in the Paradise Café. The following morning, Kevin would board a riverboat and begin his journey up the Missouri toward the gold fields of Montana. The men were discussing the problems Kevin might encounter at the end of his journey.

"Kevin," Harry said, "before you make a commitment on wagons and mules, regardless of how good the prices seem, you should check things out in Omaha or Independence. As a matter of fact, I've heard of some good deals upriver, in Bismarck."

"I've been giving that some thought, Harry. If I can find a willing wagonwright in any of the outlying towns, I'd be willing to give him part of my business in return for his supplying the wagons. What do you think?"

"I don't think it'll work," Harry said flatly. "Those people have heard the same offer over and over. You need an investor who knows you and believes in you. Someone like Kerry Kelly. But your biggest problem will be the same as ever, hiring reliable drivers and guards. A lot of strange things can happen in wild country, and most of them are bad. Take it one step at a time until you hit your stride. The more you know about everything from here to Montana, the better off you're bound to be."

Kevin's face crinkled in amusement as he spoke. "There are some great advantages to operating in the wilderness. The men won't find any whiskey or women in the hundreds of miles between the gold fields and Bismarck. There's no temptation to leave. And even if a man were fool enough to want to, the threat of hostile Indians would make him think twice."

"Probably so, but don't plan your trips too close together. Danger pays big dividends, but it also makes a man thirsty. You're going to have to give those boys time to drink up every dollar before you head them out again."

"You suppose there's any truth to the rumor that Jed Willis is working on a six-ton ore wagon? Good grief, that's twelve thousand pounds! Two million dollars in pure gold!"

"Don't get your Irish blood up, Kevin. Outside of the mint, there's never been that much gold in one place at one time."

"You're probably right, but it sure would be a sight to see!"

The conversation ended as several friends joined them, and the rest of the evening was spent in a festive mood.

The next morning, they shook hands on the dock, and then Kevin climbed aboard the Titus B. Turner, a riverboat propelled by a paddle wheel on each side, for the trip upriver and the start of his eagerly anticipated adventures in the Great American West.

Chapter V

Emerald Eyes

St. Louis, Missouri
Aboard the riverboat
Titus B. Turner
June 10, 1867

Kevin stowed his luggage and equipment in his cabin and then made his way forward to the purser's office, where he arranged to deposit his surplus cash in the ship's imposing safe. The purser was much too busy to provide any up-to-date information about the river towns ahead. He did, however, invite Kevin to return early the following morning, and cautioned him against becoming involved with any of the professional gamblers and cardsharps who earned their living in the upper-deck card rooms. The concerned man's advice made Kevin think about his friend, Kerry.

Shortly after he began working for the B Bar B, Harry Bronson introduced him to one of the company's principal investors; a man named Kerry Kelly, who made an excellent income playing poker on the riverboats. As Irish as the Blarney Stone, he was a jolly, red-faced giant whom everyone instinctively liked.

At first, Kevin thought his carefree attitude might just be a facade, used to conceal a scoundrel who victimized other players by cheating. But as the months went by and Kevin came to know the big Irishman better, he discovered that Kerry Kelly was a completely honest man.

One night, as they sat at the Paradise Café enjoying a late supper, Kevin found out why Kelly was such a successful gambler.

"I'm not really a gambler," he said. "I'm actually a traveling investment banker."

Kevin was perplexed. Kelly sensed that and continued.

"To me, poker's not a card game, it's a money management business. Like every other enterprise, it requires an initial investment, a continuing outlay of capital for advertising and a complete knowledge of how to sell your product. Most importantly, you must be concerned with the potential of your competitors and have an ability to forecast their probable moves.

"Kevin, let me ask you three questions. If eight men play poker for eight hours, would you agree that they'd finish one hand about every seven or eight minutes? Roughly eight deals per hour?"

When Kevin acknowledged the probability, Kelly continued.

"Then in eight hours, they'll be dealt about sixty-five hands. Is it safe to assume that each of the players will be dealt a nearly equal number of good, fair, and poor hands?"

"Over that many hands, I think we can safely say that," Kevin agreed. "But the players who usually win are thought of as lucky, while those who lose think they're unlucky. You're saying that there's no such thing as luck in poker?"

"Not exactly," Kerry replied, "but I am saying that anyone who relies on luck will lose far more than he will win. A lucky man is one who knows how much to leave to chance. An amateur leaves everything to luck. A professional leaves nothing to chance. To him it's a business, not a hobby. Let's say a storekeeper runs a sale on an item or items to encourage the townspeople to shop at his emporium. He often sells some products at cost in order to make a profit on the rest of his merchandise. Would you shop at a store which you knew was making a huge profit on every one of the goods it sold?"

"You're right. Unhappy customers leave and spend their money somewhere else."

"Unhappy poker players do the same," Kelly assured him, "and the player who runs first is the one who feels overmatched. When everyone wins, everyone's happy. In that eight-player game we were talking about earlier, I'm going to bluff in about a dozen of the sixty-odd hands. That's my advertising budget. If I manage to win two of those twelve hands, my advertising's free. But if you don't bet on a few losers, nobody will play along on your winners. It would be foolish."

Kerry picked up a slice of steak with his fork, inserted it in his mouth and chewed it thoroughly before continuing.

"On board the riverboats, in the average eight-handed game, a player wagers about three greenbacks on each hand. That means a profit of around twenty dollars every time you win. If a player wins one hand each hour, he winds up even. But in an eight hour game, if I win two hands every other hour, while one man fails to win any, at the end of the game all of the other players will have an average loss of only a dollar and a quarter an hour, but my profit is eighty dollars. A cheap night of fun for them and a very profitable night for me. Of course, it seldom works out exactly that way, because the players are never evenly matched.

"The one person no one wants in a card game," Kerry explained, "is a compulsive loser or an uncontrolled drinker. They're bad for business as well as downright dangerous. I want everyone to leave that table thinking that next time, with a little better luck, it's going to be different. Now you know why I smile whenever I'm described as a professional gambler. That statement is absurd, but I wouldn't change it for the world, since it conveys elements of risk and chance. The secret to success in gambling is never to gamble. Calculate carefully. Take no chances. Put nothing at risk which you're unwilling to lose! And remember that old adage: 'Taking advantage of an opponent's weaknesses multiplies your own strengths.'"

"That," his friend agreed, "is a good way to insure success in any kind of endeavor."

Kevin left the purser's busy office, climbed the steps to the ship's open, windy top deck, and then strolled back toward the stern. The farther one could get from the rhythmic vibrations of the two powerful steam engines and the deafening grating sound they created, the better. Once the Turner was underway and free of her docking tether, the worst of the vibrations would stop; but the clanking would continue for as long as they fought against the currents of the mighty Mississippi and the muddy Missouri.

As he neared the end of the promenade deck, now crowded with excited river travelers, he was surprised to see Geoffrey Gerot, an old comrade from the 69th Brigade, bedecked in the uniform of an army Captain, leaning against the aft rail. Kevin could spare no more than a glance for his friend. The next moment his entire attention riveted upon the most beautiful young woman he had ever seen, who stood at Gerot's side.

Geoffrey's voice boomed across the deck in a perverse greeting they had used in combat to relieve a bit of the pressure.

"I thought you were dead!"

Kevin's response was automatic. "That'll be the day! It's great to see you again, GeeGee."

"For me as well, Mac. Come and meet my sister, Catherine."

Kevin strode forward to accept the delicate hand, which she offered.

"Cat, this is the great Kevin McCarthy."

"This is indeed a pleasure, Miss Gerot."

"I feel as though I already know you, Captain McCarthy. My brother believes that, except for himself, you and Myles Keogh were the most awesome weapons the Union ever put into the field."

She's as charming as she is beautiful, thought Kevin, whose spirits had soared from the moment he heard the word "sister."

"GeeGee tends to be overly enthusiastic, Miss Gerot."

"Only about himself. Please call me Catherine, and allow me to call you Kevin. GeeGee is the only one who dares to call me Cat."

"With the greatest of pleasure, Catherine," Kevin replied, thinking how difficult it would be to deny her anything.

She was slender and above average in height. Her dark blond, shoulder length hair moved gently in the light breeze, which luffed across the wide river. Her large, luminous eyes, a lovely shade of emerald green, almost matched her silk dress and cape. Loose-fitting traveling clothes permitted only speculation, but he had been aware of her grace of action as she came forward to offer her hand. Admittedly ignorant of feminine fashion and apparel, Kevin decided that she looked wonderful.

"How far are you and GeeGee going, Catherine?"

"GeeGee's been assigned to duty at Fort Phil Kearny, so we'll be leaving the boat at Omaha. An army supply train goes out to the Bozeman Trail forts three or four times each month, so we'll be safe. How far are you going?"

"I'm not really sure. I'm going to start an overland freight business, but the location of the eastern terminal is still questionable. Omaha is one of the towns I want to check on."

"Then I'll look forward to your company for a few days in Omaha," Catherine said, favoring him with her radiant smile.

Kevin grinned in return.

The first overnight stop for paddle wheelers on the Missouri was Jefferson City, about a hundred and fifty miles upstream from St. Louis. It was a passage that the powerful riverboats normally made with relative ease. But this year the winter had been harsh and the spring rains unusually heavy. Now, in the late spring, the last of the snow was melting out of the high valleys of the Rockies, adding evermore volume to the already dangerously high Missouri. Every river, stream, and creek seemed to be overflowing its banks, and roaring, tumbling, or trickling down its own steep or shallow hillside in a sustained effort to swell the Big Muddy's debris-choked torrent to a record level.

Progress against the power of the awesome river was tortuously slow. The Turner's engines fought the current while the pilot carefully avoided the many huge floating tree trunks which were capable of doing severe damage to the boat, or rendering one of the side wheels inoperative. On three separate occasions during the trip, warm winds of early summer whirled across river waters still as icy cold as the glaciers that had spawned them, and blanketed the Missouri in a thick, blinding fog. As soon as the mist began to creep in, the master would call out to the pilot, "It's time to strangle a sycamore," then the packet would be nosed slowly up onto one of the gently sloping mud banks, and spring lines would be tied to a pair of the mighty giants that grew along the shore. Because of these difficult conditions, and the frequent stops at various river towns for passengers and freight, as well as to continually replenish the supply of wood which the packet's furnaces quickly devoured, it was late on the afternoon of the second day before the Turner was safely tied up at Jefferson City's cobblestone wharf.

Kevin invited GeeGee and Catherine to join him for a tour of the town, followed by dinner at Riverside Tavern, a restaurant recommended by Harry Bronson and Kerry Kelly. Jefferson City was interesting but, as Kevin suspected, completely unsuited for his purposes, lying as it did within a hundred miles of St. Louis.

Dinner was enjoyable for all of them, as GeeGee recalled a few of his more comical military experiences, Kevin reminisced about the many misadventures he and his dad had shared at various army posts, and Catherine joined in with genteel humor about convent school education in Philadelphia. Most of all, Kevin enjoyed Catherine's radiant beauty and her merry laugh. It was so bright, rich and full of fun that her mirth seemed to embrace and transform everyone around her. She is quite a lady, marveled Kevin, numerous times during the evening.

They returned to the riverboat shortly after eleven. GeeGee headed straight for his cabin, having consumed his usual drink or six too many. Catherine and Kevin stood together beside the rail for a few minutes, each enjoying the closeness of the other and sharing a sight of the majestic river slipping past them, bathed in an eerie light cast by the silvery, shimmery moonlight. Their romantic mood was enhanced even more by melodies from banjos and mandolins being strummed by crewmembers on the foredeck.

The strings' mellow sounds were joined by a majestic bass voice that sang a plaintive song of sweet red wines and tall Georgia pines. I sure would like to kiss her, thought Kevin. I wonder if I should? But in the instant Kevin pondered, the moment was lost and would have to wait for another time. They enjoyed the serenade until it finally ended, then arm in arm they strolled leisurely back to her cabin and reluctantly parted.

Kevin went forward around the pilothouse to his tiny cabin on the side of the vessel. He found a note tacked to his door. "Join me for a drink in the Ace of Spades. Fred Benteen."

The Ace of Spades was the gaming room on board the riverboat. It was also a men's lounge since ladies were not permitted to sit in the room or to loiter near by. Women were allowed to frequent saloons on some of the less reputable side-wheelers. But to refer to those who did so, as "ladies" would not have been accurate.

As he entered the gaming room Kevin decided that the lounge's decor would do credit to the finest hotel in St. Louis. With the exception of the passageways, which ran along the outer rails on both sides of the boat, the lounge straddled the entire width of the Turner's middle deck. A huge, horseshoe-shaped bar stocked with a vast array of liquors and excellent wines, and manned by three busy bartenders, was the centerpiece. Around the outer perimeter of the room were large octagonal card tables. Each of the eight sides was wide enough to accommodate a comfortable armchair and an ample poker chip tray. A long string of windows, in the shapes of spades, hearts, diamonds and clubs, had been built into the top section of the lounge's bulkheads. Their height prohibited casual passersby from peering into the lounge, while allowing warm soft light, from green and gold Oriental lanterns positioned along the rails, to shine into the room.

Kerry Kelly had told him of being aboard on stormy nights during spring and summer, when a restless river began tossing the boat about. The lounge became a special place from which to view nature display her awesome power. The storms, which began with heavy pelting rains, were soon joined by window-shaking thunder and jagged blue lightning streaks that tore open the western skies. St. Elmo's fire lent a mystical dimension to the spectacular display by gliding up the rigging and dancing across the spars. These dazzling tempests provided sights, which remained forever engraved upon the memories of the beholders. "It would be a callous gambler," Kerry exclaimed, "who chose to continue his game and ignore the spectacle of nature's pyrotechnics!"

Kevin entered the lounge and paused for a moment to savor the aroma of vintage wine and aromatic cigars. As his eyes adjusted to the lights, he saw that the former Colonel Benteen was now wearing captain's bars. Nonetheless, he filled the room with his presence as he had always done.

He was one of the many officers who had been elevated to high temporary rank during the War Between the States. Some officers had been promoted far beyond their level of capability, but the silent and steady Fred Benteen had worn his colonel's eagles with dignity and extraordinary ability. Thought of as a martinet by many, he and Kevin had not been close friends during the war. But then, most colonels and captains were not. Particularly when the colonel was as aloof and standoffish as Frederick Benteen. The only thing the two had in common was their mutual admiration and respect for Kevin's father, the 69th's Sergeant Major.

"Good evening, Colonel Benteen. It's good to see you again."

"Belated congratulations on your field commission, Captain McCarthy. I'm sure the Sergeant Major was very proud."

"I hope he was, sir."

"I know he was. He was one of the finest soldiers and best men I ever knew. Where are you headed?"

"I'm not really sure. I'm determined to start a long-haul freighting business between the river and the mountains, but my station locations are still undecided."

"There are a lot of trouble spots from here to the mountains. My sister's husband, who manages the Overland Freight Line depot here in town, thinks operations soon will be suspended between the river and Forts Phil Kearny, Smith, and Reno, as well as the other isolated army posts, until things cool off a bit." He sipped his drink and frowned. "Sioux and Cheyenne are still rampaging down the Bozeman Trail and along the Platte River. Last December they butchered that fool, Bill Fetterman, and his whole command."

"What's the real story behind the massacre, Colonel?"

"Stop calling me colonel or sir. Call me Fred. I'm only a captain now and besides, I hope you and I can be friends. I don't have that many!"

"We are friends and I will try, but calling you Fred just doesn't seem right."

"Getting back to Bill Fetterman, did you ever meet him?"

"I met him a couple of times, but I didn't really know him."

"Fetterman was one of Phil Sheridan's boys, along with Tom and George Custer and the rest of those crazy egotists who rode through the Shenandoah Valley in sixty-two. They all had the same goals. Ride to the sound of the cannon, have a horse shot out from under you once a month, get a lot of banner headlines, and make Brevet General at twenty-three."

"And Custer was the worst of them all," Kevin acknowledged.

"He was in a class by himself!" Benteen spat out bitterly.

"Remember the last big parade for the Grand Army in Washington, the month after Bobby Lee surrendered? Who got the biggest headlines the next day? Andy Johnson? Sam Grant? Uncle Billy Sherman? Hell, no, they went to D'Artagnan Custer! And why? Because that showy bay horse that he brought in from Kentucky to ride in the parade, the one he called Don Juan, supposedly got away from him, directly in front of the reviewing stand, and cavorted all over Pennsylvania Avenue before he calmed down.

"Custer loses control of his temper a dozen times a day, but he never loses control of a horse! Hell, Kevin, centaurs couldn't ride that well. The photographs in the Washington newspapers said it all a lot better than words. There perched the Daring Dandy, astride Don Juan's back, trying to regain control with one hand on the reins, waving his gaily plumed cavalier's hat to a bevy of beauties with the other, grinning from ear to ear and, all the while, his spurs are buried deep enough in that poor animal's flanks to make him jump over the moon. And finally, with a clatter of hooves, he thundered off down the avenue, yellow sash streaming, golden curls dancing, amid the adulation of thousands of his frantic fans. It was quite a circus!

"Bill Fetterman was cast from the same mold. He came out to Fort Phil Kearny last year and took command of B Troop. Rash and opinionated, but a good officer. Within three months, he had one of the best, most proficient troops on the post, but he made two big mistakes. He listened to the people who knew nothing about Indians and he disregarded the ones that did. Before they came West, Phil Sheridan told his whole staff that the only good Indians were dead ones and that Indians were lousy fighters. Fetterman believed that rot!

"When Forts Phil Kearny, Smith, and Reno were built along the Bozeman Trail, to protect freighters and miners, all of the trees, for over a half mile in every direction, were cut down. No one can get any closer without being seen. It gives us a large, clear field of fire, but at Fort Phil Kearny, once you go beyond that perimeter, you're surrounded by thick stands of trees, huge rocks, and deep gullies. It's real ambush territory. And all three of those forts sit right in the heart of Sioux country.

"During the winter, a wood-cutting detail goes into those stands of trees about four times a week to cut logs for our heating and cooking fires. Each time, they cut the trees back a bit more in the same area. That way it's easier for them to get wagons in there and also a lot safer, because it diminishes the cover for the hostile Indians.

"We had several skirmishes last year from late summer on. Nothing serious. Just the young bucks letting off steam. Then, one morning in the middle of December, a short time after the cutters went out, we heard heavy, sustained rifle and pistol fire. When it continued for several minutes, the call to boots and saddles was sounded. Lieutenant York rode out with his platoon from D Troop to investigate. The hostiles began to drift away as soon as York and his troopers approached, but by that time Corporal Daniels had been killed and Sergeant Mulcaddy badly wounded. There's a path through the hills up there, called Lodge Pole Trail, that's well hidden from the Fort. The war party came down the Lodge Pole Trail during the night and laid an ambush for the cutters. Mulcaddy and his people walked right into it.

"That night, Colonel Henry Carrington called a meeting at headquarters to decide on a course of action. At that meeting, that fool Fetterman was indignant because, according to him, 'a few digger Indians embarrassed the entire United States Cavalry.' He went on to question Jack York's courage, then York questioned the legitimacy of the captain and his various ancestors. Both men were ready to strip their tunics and fight it out! Right on the spot! It was all we could do to separate them, but the bad blood remained. 'I'm not scared of a few Red Sticks,' Fetterman shouted as he left. 'Give me eighty good men and I'll ride through the whole Sioux Nation.' Exactly one week later, Fetterman got his chance. Kevin, excuse me for a few minutes. I'm going down to my cabin for some fresh cigars."

Kevin decided to wait for Benteen out on deck. As he enjoyed the crisp night air, he thought about all he had learned from one of Harry Bronson's veteran freight drivers who had grown up on the western frontier.

In most years, by mid-December, the Indian trouble on the frontier was over; but last December, in 1866, the week before Christmas, although the temperatures were hovering near zero, no snow had yet fallen. The small bands of cut-slash-and-run Sioux warriors, and their Cheyenne allies, were still free to roam and plunder. Since early summer of the year, they had raided all the way down the Bozeman Trail and eastward along the Platte River.

Although one of America's least glamorous rivers, the banks of the gentle waterway were a highway to the West for many immigrant trains and the northern route of the Overland Stage and Freight Line. So many wagons followed the Platte Trail that the deep ruts, grooved by their wheels, would still be visible a hundred years later.

The Platte River was also a Mecca for farmers who irrigated their land with its limited water supply. The river was often described as a mile wide and an inch deep; but in an area with an annual rainfall of less than fifteen inches, it was a ribbon of life to those who settled along its length. They prospered by raising winter wheat, potatoes, and sugar beets, as well as fine beef cattle and horses.

The horses which were raised by the settlers, and the horses kept by the operators of the freight stations and the Overland Stage's relay depots, were highly coveted by the red marauders. Horses were not only a means of transportation to a Plains Indian; they were also his sign of wealth and his currency. A raid on a settlement for a Cheyenne warrior was like a trip to the bank for a St. Louis merchant, only better. To the Indian, a raid meant making a profit, pursuing his hobby, and having fun. To a white man, war was hell; war was a place where he might die. To a red man, war was recreational; war was a place where he could die bravely. War had been the Indian way of life for many centuries. Who could stop them, Kevin wondered? For that matter, who could even catch them? They were the finest light cavalry in the world!

The Bozeman Trail, which led northwestward toward the Montana gold fields, wound its way through a portion of the two sacred areas of the Sioux, the Bighorn Mountains and the Black Hills.

Along this entire long route, forts had been established to insure the uninterrupted westward expansion of a nation committed to the concept of Manifest Destiny.

Benteen returned with his fresh supply of cigars. Once again they seated themselves at a table in the lounge, where Benteen ordered two more brandies and resumed his story.

"Four times in the next ten days, Fetterman had his company ready to ride at the crack of dawn, whenever the woodcutters left the fort. He ordered them to turn back at the first sign of danger and hightail it back to the fort, regardless of the number of hostiles they saw.

"Just after dawn on Dec. 21, as soon as the cutters reached the woods, we heard a staccato of shots and war whoops. The woodcutters' wagons came hurtling back past the first line of trees and out into the open! Half a dozen Sioux and Cheyennes followed them for a short distance before they stopped. They sat on their war ponies within 500 yards of the palisades, waving their rifles and shouting in defiance.

"To catch the Indians off-guard, Fetterman waited until the gates of the fort swung open to admit the wagons. Then he charged pell-mell into action. When he left the fort that morning with B Troop, Mark Post, a reporter from one of Colorado's leading newspapers, went with him. Also, two Crow trackers and Clayton Forrester, a civilian scout. Ironically, the total number in Fetterman's command was eighty, the exact number that he bragged he would need to fight his way through the whole Sioux Nation.

"A few minutes after Fetterman's company disappeared from sight, furious firing began. We mounted a relief column composed of my H Troop, along with Charley Bascom's A's, but just as we started, the firing stopped as abruptly as it had begun.

"We rode out and I sent my scouts ahead to look for any signs of an ambush, but by then the Indians had carried off their dead and disappeared. From the position of the bodies, as well as the tracks and signs, we were able to reconstruct the fight. The six or eight hostiles we saw from the fort had drawn Fetterman in by moving slowly through the trees, just beyond carbine range, until they had the whole patrol strung out along a deep, narrow ravine on the Lodge Pole Trail.

"The main body of Indians had dismounted and left their ponies farther back up the Trail and infiltrated down on foot. From the spent cartridges we found there must have been several hundred of those sneaky bastards. The Sioux and Cheyenne were lying in ambush behind every rock and fallen log. It was easier than shooting fish in a barrel! We found very little blood or other signs in the Indians' positions to indicate casualties. Those hostiles probably didn't have more than a handful of killed or wounded! Thanks to Bill Fetterman's foolishness, we lost a hell of a lot of good men for no reason!

"That ambush was laid as skillfully as any we studied at West Point! Whoever planned their strategy is very good. All we could do was collect the bodies of our troopers;

most of them pretty badly mutilated, and give them a decent burial. Bill Fetterman got his eighty men, but was able to ride less than a mile through the Sioux Nation."

"Were you able to recover all the bodies?"

"All, but one. We didn't find the body of the civilian scout, Clayton Forrester. Clay rode with Jeb Stuart's cavalry during the war, Kevin. He was in charge of Jeb's skirmishers, until he got shot up at Yellow Tavern, the same day that Stuart was mortally wounded. I got to know him pretty well before he disappeared. He graduated from the Virginia Military Institute in 1858 and described himself as an old-fashioned Virginia Cavalier.

"Clay is a fine gentleman, Kevin, and a gallant soldier. I was proud to call him my friend. He is absolutely fearless and a dead shot with a pistol, held in either hand. Near Fetterman's body, we found over fifty .44-40 caliber cartridge cases. Clay was the only man at Fort Phil Kearny who carried weapons of that caliber. His Henry rifle, as well as his Colt revolvers, fired .44-40's."

"If he was still alive after the fight, I hope they didn't torture him to death," Kevin said.

"Amen to that, Kevin! But for some reason my instincts tell me we haven't seen or heard the last of Clayton Forrester."

"I hope you're right, Fred."

"By the way, Kevin, I came to Jefferson City to escort a shipment of test rifles back to the fort. They're the new lever-action, Winchester Model 1866. The army wants us to field-test them. They seem to be better than the Henry. The new metallic cartridges certainly will be more reliable. I'll show you one in the morning."

"Great! I'd like that. I've heard a lot about them."

They finished their drinks and parted. It had been a long day, filled with excitement, camaraderie, tales of tragedy, and a good deal of gratefully consumed brandy and cigars.

Kevin dozed fitfully throughout the night and dreamed of white men dying in furious battles, red men in war paint, and smoking Winchester rifles. But his most persistent and lingering visions were of Catherine and her sparkling emerald eyes.

PART THREE

THE PRISONER

Chapter VI

➤

In Enemy Hands

A Sioux Winter War Camp
Little Bighorn River
Wyoming Territory
December 25, 1866

As he struggled upward through the black murkiness, back into the world of consciousness, Clayton Forrester's first sensation was that of lying on his back, seeing a patch of blue sky through a small circular hole, crisscrossed by a spider web of poles.

For some reason, he couldn't seem to focus his vision or his brain. Then he realized that he couldn't open his right eye. In an abstract, almost disinterested way, he concluded that it was swollen shut. He began searching his memory in an effort to reconstruct the ambush.

He remembered the men and the horses screaming in anguish. He remembered moans of pain from the ones who were no longer able to scream. Most of all, he clearly remembered the grimaces of agony and disbelief on the faces of those that death had silenced. It sure had been one hell of a fight. Almost as bloody as the Battle of Yellow Tavern had been.

He had seen Fetterman go down along with most of the others. He pictured Blarney Quinn, next to him, firing his carbine into a horde of fleeting targets. He remembered Pasha falling under him, pinning his leg to the ground. He recalled, with gratification, the last shot he had fired, the one that peeled off the top of a tall Indian's head. And he remembered thinking at the time that he would be dead very soon. Then nothing.

He tried to reach upward to feel his head, only to discover that his right arm wasn't working either. He slowly and carefully drew his left hand up along the length of his right arm. It was bound from wrist to shoulder with soft bandages and immobilized by a rough splint. He winced as his hand caught in a fold of the bandages, and realized that the ring and little fingers on his left hand were also encased in splints. He felt another bandage covering a wound on the right side of his chest and noted that it was encrusted with dried blood. The last exploration he made, before gingerly lowering his hand, was to check his beard. In his Confederate cavalry days, he learned to keep track of the passage of time by the length of his whiskers, accurately described as a "Confederate calendar."

As he took stock of his situation, Forrester decided that wherever he was, he had been there for several days. He also reasoned that since his wounds had been dressed, he was not going to be killed, at least not for a while. Someone had made an obvious effort to keep him warm and to make him comfortable.

The question was why? Why hadn't they just killed him when they had the chance? Maybe they planned something special for him. After all, they were vicious heathens. He recalled reading about the Black Robes who were captured and tortured. Jesuit priests like Jean Brebeuf and Isaac Jogues, had their fingers chewed off and were forced to run the gauntlet. He prayed that if that were his lot, he would bear the pain well, until God saw fit to end his misery. He lost his train of thought and absently wondered why his leg wouldn't move, but soon lost interest in his surroundings and slept restlessly throughout the balance of the peaceful winter afternoon.

He was hurtled sharply back into consciousness by a vicious pounding inside his head and a thousand agonies, which cut like red-hot daggers through the rest of his tortured body. It was night. His view through the network of poles disclosed only a few twinkling stars in the crisp, wintry sky. He sensed the presence of another human being and a moment later felt a soft arm slip gently beneath his neck.

"You must try to eat," he heard a woman's soft voice say in surprisingly good English.

The arm tenderly cradled his head and raised his face toward a tiny patch of moonlight, which had invaded the darkness. With her other hand, she held a buffalo-horn spoon to his lips. The hot, savory broth was delicious. She patiently fed him, until the last morsel had been emptied from the wooden bowl. Then she carefully lowered his head and withdrew her arm.

"Who are you?" Forrester whispered through cracked lips.

"I am called Little Fawn," she replied.

"Where are we?"

"We are camped in the village of Tushunca Witco, on the banks of the Greasy Grass, in the shadow of the Bighorn Mountains."

"How far have we come from Fort Phil Kearny?"

"It is a ride of two suns."

"How long have I been unconscious?"

"You have wandered in the Land of Shadows for four suns. Sleep now."

The broth did little to ease his pain, but much to soothe him. He dozed fitfully, awakening often as various pains jarred him back to consciousness. During one of his conscious moments, he reflected that it must be December 25. During the Christmas holidays in 1860, he had been in a civilian clinic. Christmas of 1864 had been spent recovering from wounds in an army hospital, and now, in 1866, it seemed that he was in an Indian infirmary.

Several times during the night, he perceived that someone else was nearby, and twice he was aware of fresh wood being fed into the fire. Finally, his pain seemed to ebb, and he was able to sleep in relative peace for several hours.

When he next awakened, a pretty woman, probably in her mid-twenties, dressed in white buckskin, was leaning over him, examining the wound in his chest.

"I seem to have a lot of wounds, Little Fawn," he said, trying to smile up at her.

"Wounds that would kill most men," she replied with a smile, obviously pleased that he had remembered her name. "White Wolf would not believe that your spirit had left the Land of Shadows until he came to my lodge and saw you for himself."

While they talked, she began to remove the bandages from his other wounds, being careful not to pull the healing areas open. Twice she took water from a nearby gourd and soaked the adhesions before gingerly working the dressings free. Her easy competence was so reassuring that Forrester relaxed.

"Who is White Wolf?"

"He is a great warrior of the Oglala Sioux. It was he who was brave enough to crack your head with his coup stick and send you to the Land of Dreams."

"Why didn't he just shoot me? It would have been much easier."

"A Sioux gains no respect by shooting a brave enemy, but earns much honor by striking him with his hand or coup stick. Besides, Tushunca Witco said you deserved to live."

Forrester wondered exactly what it was he was being kept alive to do. Would he die a spectacular death later?

"What is a coup stick, Little Fawn?" he asked.

"A short stick or club used to touch or strike the body or head of a still-dangerous enemy. The 'coup,' or brave deed, is commemorated with an eagle feather in the war bonnet and a painting on the warrior's lodge. Blue Leaf, the woman of White Wolf, has already painted the picture of his victory over you."

"Where did you learn to speak English so well?"

"I am not Sioux. I am Mandan. I was a student at a mission school until I was captured by the Sioux in my sixteenth summer."

"Are you now married to a Sioux warrior?"

"I am a White Sun Woman, a medicine woman, a healer. To the Sioux, I am a sacred person. I will never be permitted to marry."

"You mentioned the name Tushunca Witco. Is he a chief?"

"Tushunca Witco is the greatest war chief of the Sioux Nation, since the Great Spirit brought forth the land and the water and the sky in the Great Shower of Stars. Your people call him Crazy Horse. Makhpiyaluta, Red Cloud, is the Sioux's father. Tanka Yotanka, Sitting Bull, is their uncle. But Crazy Horse is every Sioux's hero. He is a great man and a great leader. This is his village."

"One more question, Little Fawn. Do you know what happened to Pasha, my horse?"

"He received two very bad wounds in the shoulder and flank, as well as some other small wounds and bruises during the fight. I fear that he will never be able to run hard again. But, like a tame dog, he walked between the poles of your travois, the horse-drawn litter that carried you here. The great number of scars that you and your war pony bear tell me that you both heal well. You will do so again."

"We've been through a lot together."

Forrester drifted back to sleep and rested peacefully until the White Sun Woman returned to help him with his midday meal. Sounds of a crackling fire and the appetizing aroma of sizzling meat welcomed him back from Little Fawn's Land of Shadows. A moment later she entered the wickiup, followed by three Sioux warriors. All of them appeared to be in their late twenties or early thirties, about the same age as Forrester.

The first, a man of medium height and weight, was dressed in black wolfskins. Even the winter cape that he wore was made from the entire pelt of a black wolf. The craftsmanship and care, which had been spent in curing and sewing the skins, was obvious. Forrester's attention was drawn to this warrior's eyes. They were large, very dark, and widely spaced. They gazed unflinchingly back into his own with a mixture of curiosity and respect. He seemed to exude an aura that Forrester had encountered only twice before. It was the same feeling that he and others felt in the presence of Stonewall Jackson and Robert E. Lee. No one had ever been able to describe it, but everyone knew it was there. Each of the three warriors spoke little English, so the conversation, aside from a smattering of sign language, was translated by Little Fawn.

"This is the great war chief, Tushunca Witco," began Little Fawn. "He would have me say that his village is honored at the presence of so great a warrior. His heart is glad to see that your wounds are healing."

Still seeking a logical motive for this friendly attitude, Forrester replied, "Please say to the mighty chief that I am honored to be in the camp of so worthy an enemy."

When this was translated, Crazy Horse bowed his head slightly and then touched first his forehead, and then his heart. Little Fawn seemed surprised by the gesture. She told Forrester that it indicated thanks, but was used only among close friends.

Crazy Horse spoke again and then gestured, in turn, to his two companions. Through his good eye, Forrester could see that one of them was exceedingly large, while the other man looked extremely villainous because of the scar running along the left side of his face, from his hairline to the point of his chin. As Crazy Horse spoke, this fierce-looking visage broke into a grin.

"Crazy Horse tells you that the big warrior is Tall Bull. He is the real nephew of our uncle, Sitting Bull. This other warrior is White Wolf, who Crazy Horse says should no longer try to crack eggs without waiting for help from his woman."

"Please tell White Wolf that I know all about his strong arm. My head buzzes like a swarm of bees from the crack he gave me."

When this was relayed to White Wolf, he grinned and pointed at Forrester's head before replying.

"White Wolf says there is not an arm in the whole Sioux Nation that is strong enough to dent your head. He wants you to know that he did his best."

"Tell him that I believe him. I hope he never feels compelled to try again." Little Fawn and all of the men smiled.

Forrester was puzzled by the attitude of these warriors. He was an enemy. He had killed many of their friends and would kill many more if he could find a way to escape. Yet he saw that they did not hate him. On the contrary, they held him in high esteem. Curiosity overcame caution as he studied each of them carefully. Tall Bull smiled often, but seldom spoke. White Wolf, in addition to being a fearsome warrior, was a born mimic and storyteller. But it was Crazy Horse who dominated the gathering, though not by words or gestures. His presence alone was enough.

After a short stay, Crazy Horse and Tall Bull left, but White Wolf stayed. With Little Fawn translating, White Wolf spent the balance of the afternoon telling them about one of his recent adventures.

➢

A short time before the fight on the Lodge Pole Trail, White Wolf said he had led a war party of ten young warriors north to the Missouri River with the intention of raiding for horses. The raid had been very successful. They captured more than forty fine ponies from outlying ranches and a large Pawnee village. White Wolf described one of the ponies, a magnificent young chestnut stallion, as the finest horse he had ever ridden.

One night, shortly before their planned return, they camped near the river. Just before dark, a small keelboat crammed with trade goods was poled to the shore by four white men. Confronted by the painted faces of White Wolf and his companions, the wise traders quickly laid aside their weapons and made peace signs.

Fortunately for the white men, the Sioux had just gorged themselves with buffalo tongue and hump meat and were in an unusually friendly mood. To strengthen this somewhat tenuous truce, the traders bestowed numerous gifts upon the Indians, who were able to curl up for the night with full bellies and wrapped in the folds of new, warm, gaily colored blankets.

Perhaps believing that their escape would be easier if the Sioux were drunk, the traders included two kegs of whiskey. Trade whiskey was almost always a vile concoction of a gallon of grain alcohol, a cup of molasses for flavor, a tobacco plug for taste, a cup of coal oil for kick, and any other liquid, such as Missouri River water, that might be at hand to stretch the concoctor's profits. Luckily for the traders, White Wolf would not allow his men to drink the liquor until they were safely out of hostile territory.

It was not until the triumphant warriors returned to their village, and a great victory dance was held in their honor, that White Wolf allowed the whiskey to be distributed. One of the kegs was contaminated. Everyone who drank from it became violently ill. The next morning, Leaping Elk and Snapping Turtle were dead.

As the party's leader and war chief, White Wolf swore revenge on the traders. Although nearly everyone in the village tried to convince him that his chances of finding the culprits were poor, he would not be dissuaded. In company with his friend, Gall, he set out for the Missouri. As they rode northward, White Wolf admitted to Gall that he knew they probably would never find the evil, bald-headed white trader with the enormous mustache who had poisoned his men, but they would return with white men's scalps.

White Wolf led Gall back through the same hills and across the same prairies that he had followed with the war party. When they arrived on the banks of the Missouri, it was close to the place where he had met the riverboat before. After examining the area along the riverbank, they discovered that this spot was used frequently by the rivermen, since a great shelf of outcropping rock provided a natural dock for the boats. Trunks of two nearby giant live oak trees were scarred and grooved by the thousands of ropes, which had secured vessels over the years.

They decided to camp a short distance from the landing spot and ambush the crew of the next boat, which was unfortunate enough to happen along. For the next three days, they secured drinking water from a small spring rather than approach the river for fear of leaving signs, which might betray their presence.

In the late afternoon of the third day, their patience and caution were rewarded. They heard the sound of voices drifting across the water, and a short time later, a keelboat glided into view. Peering through the thick foliage that lined the riverbank, White Wolf could scarcely believe his good fortune, for there, on the prow of the boat, with the bowline in his hand, crouched the white man with the baldhead and huge mustache. The Sioux could see that the bald man had only two companions on this trip. Gall and White Wolf waited until the boat had been tethered to the oak trees, then shot and killed the bald man's helpers.

The Bald One had just reached his rifle when White Wolf leaped aboard and knocked the weapon from the trader's trembling hands. The maleficent smile on the warrior's painted face and the large, deadly knife, which he held in his hand left little doubt about either his competence or the eventual outcome. The trader's eyes rolled back in terror and a shudder coursed through his body as he suddenly realized that the rest of his life could be measured in seconds. The scream of panic which started deep within the Bald One's chest died in his throat, as White Wolf's heavy blade split him from groin to breastbone and continued on into his heart, which exploded in a gory shower of crimson.

Since he didn't want anyone to question their victory, and since he had no desire to transport a body back to the village, White Wolf carefully severed the trader's head, placed it in a handy canvas sack, and tied the top tightly with a length of the ship's anchor rope. He then splintered several casks of coal oil with his tomahawk and splashed the contents across the deck. Finally, he set fire to the boat and pushed it out into the river, where it was quickly swept away by the current.

Elated by his enemy's death and his own good fortune, White Wolf washed the blood and gore from his skin and hair, and then reapplied his war paint. Before leaving the riverbank, he lovingly removed all the stains from the blade and hilt of his unique knife and carefully wiped it with a bit of soft doeskin. He had taken the knife from the hand of the first man he ever killed in battle, a Comanche warrior who, with his companions from far to the south, had foolishly raided into the country of the Sioux.

Forrester and Little Fawn could clearly see the reflected rage in White Wolf's dark eyes as he recalled the Comanche war party coming silently in the night and stampeding the village pony herd, after butchering the young boys who were guarding it. Since each Sioux warrior slept with his best war-horse staked out beside his teepee, pursuit had been swift. The flight, and the fight, ended several days later and many miles away. In later years, the bleached bones of their dead could trace the trail of the Comanches' retreat.

The final fight took place between White Wolf and a tall, rangy, sinewy Comanche, one half of whose face was painted black and the other half red. In the best traditions of the Plains Indians, the fight had been tomahawk against tomahawk and knife against knife. It soon became apparent to White Wolf that the Comanche was a much better knife fighter than he. Almost before the fight began, his opponent slashed his face from forehead to chin, missing his left eye by the tiniest of margins. Knowing that he had to end the fight as quickly as possible, he feinted a blow with his own knife. When his adversary moved to parry it, he was off-balance for one instant, but in that moment, White Wolf was able to sweep his tomahawk beneath the Comanche's guard and deliver a fatal blow to the warrior's chest. The fight had been, however, anything but one-sided. For the next ten winters, the ache in his thigh and the pain in White Wolf's shoulder, as well as his facial scar, would give mute testimony to the black-and-red warrior's skill.

After his companions treated his wounds, White Wolf examined the Comanche's exotic knife for the first time. To illustrate his words, White Wolf withdrew the knife from its sheath and held it up for Little Fawn and Forrester to see. The blade was almost as long as a man's forearm, and appeared to be sharp down the entire length of the bottom edge, while the top edge was sharp for only the width of a hand. The blade was curved slightly upward at the tip, allowing it to hook and rip into an opponent's flesh. The knife's hilt was made from an unknown material which, White Wolf said, kept his hand from slipping even when it was covered by water or blood. Between the blade and the hilt, a guard of soft metal, about the size of a forefinger, protected the hand by catching the enemy's blade on its soft surface and turning it aside. Finally, from the base of this guard to the tang at the top of the hilt, ran two parallel pieces of curved steel, which acted as a barrier to any blows directed at his arm or body. White Wolf said he had often used these twin protectors as weapons to ram into an unsuspecting opponent's body or head.

Forrester could see letters that had long ago been etched into the blade of this wondrous weapon which proclaimed:

TOLEDO ESPAÑA - MCDLIV

The knife was clearly White Wolf's proudest possession.

When Gall and he had returned to the village, White Wolf continued, they proudly displayed the trader's head for several days, while carefully concealing it from the women. When everyone had lost interest in the gruesome trophy, White Wolf discarded the head in the river near the village.

The next morning, White Wolf's seven-year-old son, Jumping Frog, was swimming in the river with the other boys, when he discovered the head bobbing near the bank amongst a tangle of driftwood. Intrigued by the endless possibilities and delights, which this unique prize offered, Jumping Frog and his friend, Chipmunk recovered the waterlogged object and set it out in the sun to dry.

Later that day, the lads returned to the task of beautifying the head. They fitted it with a headband and then placed a pair of ragged feathers inside the band. Finally, they propped open the eyelids and mouth, placed streaks of war paint on the cheeks and forehead, arranged the feathers at jaunty angles and stood back to admire their handiwork. Thrilled by their own artistry, they were, of course, eager to show off this masterpiece. With each boy grasping an ear, they lifted the head and set off for the village.

The boys soon realized that this system was not going to work. They were simply not strong enough to bear the weight with only a thumb and two fingertips. Then Jumping Frog had a wonderful idea. They searched along the riverbank until they found a dead branch just the right size, then sharpened it at both ends, and pounded the stick into the head until it came to rest against the skull. An ideal means of transport had been created. Now either of them could carry the trophy with comparative ease.

They took turns carrying the prize as they skirted around the village, carefully staying out of sight at the edge of the woods. At last they arrived at a dense copse of pine trees, a short distance behind Jumping Frog's teepee.

They crawled beneath the low-hanging branches, well into this maze of foliage, and discovered a tiny clearing. There they forced the stick into the soft earth and left the head to its lonely, sightless vigil.

Since the last of the daylight was quickly disappearing from the western sky, Jumping Frog and Chipmunk raced back to the creek and rinsed the paint, blood, and grime from their bodies. Then each hurried to his lodge, since the time of the evening meal was at hand. Jumping Frog was never late for meals when his mother served the pemmican which she made with finely chopped venison, wild onions, sage and other savory seasonings, all of which were held together by rich buffalo tallow. It was Jumping Frog's favorite food.

He entered the lodge and accepted a container of hot herb tea from his mother. Satisfied that all was well with her son, Blue Leaf returned her attention to the preparation of the family's evening meal. A few minutes later, White Wolf arrived.

As they enjoyed their supper, he announced to his family that Crazy Horse was taking a large war party to the big log fort of the Yellow Legs. The principal warriors would be himself, Gall, American Horse, He Dog, Roan Calf, High Cloud, Many Kills and Young-Man-Afraid-Of-His-Horses. (This fierce warrior was so-named because young men from other tribes were so frightened by even the presence of his horses that they cowered in fear.) It would be the best war party in many winters.

After the meal was finished, White Wolf taught his son to fashion a short hunting bow from the wood of an osage orange and how to reinforce it with strips of rawhide. Blue Leaf watched them from the corner of her eye, while she worked dyed porcupine quills into the white buckskin ceremonial shirt, which she was making for her husband.

Sitting in the warm comfortable lodge, richly decorated with sleeping couches and luxurious animal pelts, his small belly stuffed with good food, Jumping Frog soon began to feel very tired. When he toppled over, White Wolf gently laid him on his couch and watched Blue Leaf pull a buffalo robe over him.

As she returned to the fire, her husband's arm encircled her shoulders, while his other hand touched her thickening waist.

"Soon our little Frog will have a brother."

"Are you so sure that we cannot make girls?" she teased.

"No girl this time," he guaranteed. "Now I must go to Medicine Raven's lodge with the other leaders of the war party."

"Since all of you will be there, I will go to the wickiup of Crazy Horse and help Black Shawl to prepare."

They embraced outside the teepee and then walked in opposite directions. All the while, Jumping Frog slept soundly.

He later told White Wolf and Blue Leaf that when he had been awakened by a howling coyote, close to the back of the teepee, he immediately thought of the head. What if the coyote or some other animal discovered it? The thought of leaving his warm comfortable bed and crawling around on the freezing ground at this hour made him shiver, but he had to rescue the head. Reluctantly, he arose and dressed in warm clothing, then stealthily left the lodge.

The full moon provided ample light, and he moved quickly to the grove of pine trees. He circled the area in an effort to find an opening. Finding none, he was forced to drop to the ground and crawl forward toward the clearing. The head was just as they had left it hours before. Carefully shielding the trophy with his own body, he knelt down and began crawling backwards, pushing his way through low hanging branches which scratched him unmercifully. When he finally emerged with the head intact, he decided that a few cuts and scratches were a small price to pay for his success.

He carried the trophy back to the teepee and stood pondering. If he left the head outside, one of the village dogs could drag it away, or a small animal might gnaw on it. The only thing to do was take it inside where it would be safe. He carried the head to the far side of his sleeping couch and drove the stake into the ground. He looked at it when he finished and was delighted to discover that his handsome prize was bathed in a patch of bright moonlight which was coming in through the lodge's smoke hole. He fell asleep smiling up at the head and savoring his good fortune.

A short time later, his parents returned. White Wolf paused to secure Chestnut's tether, while Blue Leaf entered the wickiup alone. She bent down over her son's couch and pulled his covers back over him. As she started to straighten up, she was startled to suddenly come eye to eye with a grinning, feathered, war-painted head. Her loud scream of fright and outrage woke half the village. When White Wolf burst through the doorway, his Spanish knife poised to kill enemy or animal, all she could do was point at the horrible head. White Wolf's relieved bellowing laughter awakened the other half of the sleeping village!

Clayton Forrester was very troubled by White Wolf's gruesome story. The fact that a seven-year-old boy could find pleasure in decorating and playing with a human head demonstrated the great gulf that existed between traditional cultures and the primitive one of the Sioux. To desecrate part of a human body was, to him, unthinkable. Yet to the Indians it was not only acceptable, but also rather humorous. Small wonder that civilized people called them brutal, savage heathens.

Chapter VII
➢
War Weapons

Sioux War Camp
Little Bighorn River
Wyoming Territory
April 21, 1867

Forrester's wounds continued to heal slowly as the months of winter passed and the deep snow melted away. By the Moon of Green Grass, he had recovered enough of his strength to move cautiously about the village, although he still needed to lean on a forked walking stick. It had been fashioned for him by White Wolf from a stout cottonwood bough and presented by Jumping Frog with great joy and ceremony. Since then, his only accident had come one day as he hobbled past the village's horse herd. From their midst had burst a scarred old campaigner, who rushed toward him, nickering wildly. It was Pasha, his distinctive Turkish forelock dangling in front of his eyes. The animal was so overjoyed to see Forrester that he bowled him over.

His restored mobility brought with it many advantages and one disadvantage. It was good to move around again and to regain some measure of independence, but his advancing state of convalescence also meant that he would have to leave the lodge of Little Fawn. She had cared for him for four months and his feelings for her now went far beyond simple gratitude.

The night before he went to live in the lodge of Many Kills, whose son, Iron Shirt, had been killed in the fight with the Yellow Legs, he and Little Fawn spoke of many things.

As she removed the bandage from his nearly healed arm, he spoke with great emotion.

"You have done wondrous things to heal my mind as well as my body, Little Fawn."

"I only help the Great Spirit."

"I'm grateful to you both."

The smile left her face and she said wistfully, "My lodge will be empty without you."

He pulled her gently toward him and whispered.

"You know that I love you very much, don't you?"

"On the morning that you returned from the Land of Shadows, I told you that I was a White Sun Woman and that I may never marry. Now, for the only time, I will tell you this. I love you with all of the heart that is not mine to give." She paused and added softly, "And now, my love, we must never speak of this again."

"Is there no way to change this rule, Little Fawn?"

"I have taken a vow from which no White Sun Woman has ever been released."

"Have any of them ever tried?"

"I don't know."

"If you could be released, would you marry me?"

"Again, my answer must be the same—I don't know. This has been my life for eight summers. It is the one I expected to live for the rest of my days."

"Will you think about it?"

"I think of little else."

"Will you still teach me to speak in the tongue of the Sioux?"

"For now, that would not be wise. We must try to put aside our feelings. Besides, Many Kills' woman, Night Wind, can teach you. Please, help me to do what is best, whatever that may be. Give me time to think. I cannot do that when you are close to me."

"I'll do as you ask, but my heart will never change."

"Clayton, I will welcome the sight of you every day.

Please do not avoid me. We can be friends, but we cannot be alone. Let us put away this talk and enjoy our evening together."

He lay awake that night for several hours after he rolled up in his blankets. He had found love in this winter camp on the banks of the Little Bighorn, that was true, but he had found much more. For here there existed simplicity he had not known since his childhood. Indian society was far from Utopian, but there was certain honesty about it. Honesty that had all but disappeared from a strife-riddled American nation during the war. These past four months amongst people that he had always thought of as savages had truly caused a renewal of his faith in mankind.

In talks with Crazy Horse and White Wolf, as he learned more of their language, he had begun to understand more about the problems, which the Indians faced. Many of them, which the Sioux thought of as clear-cut, were to him a bit clouded, while some others were crystal clear. Like the senseless slaughter of the animal which the Sioux thought of as a brother, an animal he counted on for his continued survival, an animal that provided food, shelter, and clothing, an animal he called "Pte," the buffalo. When the buffalo disappeared, the Sioux would disappear with him.

In the very early hours of morning, Clayton Forrester made some hard decisions. He would stay with the Sioux for as long as they would let him. He would stay near Little Fawn, and he would help these people who had been good to him. He would not fight for them against his former friends, but he would teach them whatever he could, and be their voice in powwows with white men. He looked across the lodge toward the sleeping Little Fawn and silently pledged, "I cannot promise you forever, unless we one day wed, but until that time, I will be as good for you as I can be, and your people will be my people, my love."

Early the next day, soon after the morning meal, Little Fawn announced that there were visitors waiting outside the wickiup. As Forrester emerged from the lodge, he was surprised to see a formal gathering of Crazy Horse, White Wolf, Medicine Raven, and several other village leaders. All were bedecked in their finest beaded, quilled, and fringed buckskins. Most wore headdresses made from eagle feathers. Each feather, he knew, symbolized a brave deed or coup. In some of these, more than a hundred bright feathers, dyed vivid vermillion, bright blue, or coal black, streamed in two long parallel lines down the backs of their owners. The war bonnets worn by Crazy Horse, White Wolf, and a few others contained so many feathers that the lowest ones bumped against their heels.

Little Fawn had taught Forrester enough sign language and he had learned enough Sioux words to understand the importance of this ceremony. He was being escorted to the lodge of his new "foster" or "step" parents. At first, he thought that he had misunderstood the words, but they were repeated. Little Fawn had explained that the Sioux exercised three options with captives. They were killed, became slaves, or were adopted into the tribe.

When one was adopted, two sponsors were required. One was his tribal father, who was responsible for his "son's" future conduct; the other was his "special friend," who would provide him with horses and weapons and instruct him in the warrior's arts. Any misconduct would bring great shame upon both of the sponsors. Until now, Forrester had assumed that Many Kills would be his tribal father, but now it seemed that he would not.

When Little Fawn explained the ceremony, she refused to speculate about the identity of the sponsors. However, she did say that Sitting Bull had an adopted son, a white man named Frank Grouard. His Sioux name meant Sitting-With-Upraised-Hands, but he was usually called the Grabber. Crazy Horse had neither adopted, nor sponsored anyone into the Oglala tribe. Little Fawn concluded that he probably never would.

They left the wickiup of Little Fawn and with the shaman, Medicine Raven, in the lead; they proceeded to the lodge of

Many Kills. It was a large, impressive teepee, colored gold and blue, and pitched in one of the places of honor along a high bank overlooking the river. As the procession drew near, Many Kills and Night Wind came out of the doorway to welcome them. Many Kills explained to those who had gathered that they were happy to welcome their new stepson to their lodge and into their lives and asked him to accept their gifts. Night Wind disappeared inside the teepee and returned moments later with a luxurious, thick buffalo sleeping robe, which she presented to Forrester.

As she finished speaking, a clatter arose from the area behind the lodge, and a moment later Jumping Frog and Chipmunk came into view leading a small brown-and-white pinto mare and a beautiful iron and black Appaloosa stallion. The boys came to a stop a short distance behind Many Kills, and stood waiting. The warrior took the reins of the pinto in one hand, while with the other he lifted the feathers of his headdress, which otherwise would have dragged on the ground, and led the animal to Little Fawn.

"Accept this pony, White Sun Woman, as a small token of the debt we owe for the care you have given our stepson."

"There is no debt, Great Warrior, but I will cherish my new pinto pony."

"To our stepson, Night Wind and I give this swift war pony."

Many Kills led the fiery stallion to Forrester and then, placing one hand on his heart and the other on Forrester's, he said, "It is our hope that this pony will be as brave as our stepson."

Forrester examined the Appaloosa carefully. He was obviously a young horse, a good deal taller and sturdier than most Indian ponies. His small head seemed to indicate either Arabian or Spanish bloodlines. The stallion's body was the color of gun metal, with characteristic Appaloosa markings, black stockings on all four of his slim legs, as well as a thick black mane and tail. The most unique coloring was on his hindquarters. They looked as though someone had taken a thick patch of stars from a dark wintry sky and thrown them, like a blanket, across his haunches. A perfect name for the horse immediately came to him.

He took the reins from Many Kills and then, imitating the warrior's gesture, placed one hand on his heart and the other on the Indian's. He inclined his head to Night Wind and said,

"I am grateful for this gift, Mighty Warrior. In honor of the deeds of my stepfather and the graciousness of my stepmother, the war-horse will be called Star Walker. With him to carry me, I will always try to be a good son and make you both proud."

➤

Two weeks later, Forrester sat with White Wolf in front of his lodge, enjoying the sounds of a spring evening. They listened as a concert of crickets performed in the woods, accompanied by a chorus of riverfrogs who added their throaty songs to the prairie serenade. A short time earlier, Many Kills and Night Wind had departed, after feasting on buffalo ribs and hump meat. Jumping Frog had gone to sleep and Blue Leaf, whose time was near, had decided to rest.

White Wolf stretched and yawned. "It is a lazy night, my brother."

Forrester smiled. "Blue Leaf is such a good cook that we all ate too much."

"That is true," his friend mused, "but I grow tired of buffalo meat. I would enjoy eating a few elk steaks."

"I didn't know there were any elk nearby."

"Oh, there are not, but hunger makes the way short. We should hold an elk hunt before we return to the Yellow Legs' fort. Gall will go with us, and Touches-The-Clouds loves elk meat. Your wounds will allow you to ride, will they not?"

"I am ready to ride Pasha, but my leg is not yet strong enough for Star Walker. Besides, Pasha seems ready to run. He would like to be on the go again."

"My brother, your war pony was badly hurt in the battle. He is old and tired. If you are not ready to ride Star Walker, I will give you another animal."

"No, White Wolf. If you think it is wise, we will take another pony along, but I owe Pasha a chance."

"Then that is what we will do."

"White Wolf, you promised to tell me about the fight on the Lodge Pole Trail where I was captured. Will you do that now?"

"If it is my brother's wish. In the Moon of the Popping Trees, we moved our village to the Medicine Creek, below the Sand Hills, near the alkali flats, five suns before the fight. We had raided along the river that white men call the Platte, and the trail they call the Bozeman, for many moons. We fired at the forts to draw out the Yellow Legs and their wagons each time. We knew the soldiers would not expect us to do more than fire our weapons and then ride slowly away as we had always done before. But this time, it was not the same.

"Many moons ago, when Red Cloud and Two Moons went to the Peace Council at Fort Laramie, the men who spoke for the Great White Father told them that the Yellow Legs' forts would keep my people safe from evil white men. But their hearts were bad. They spoke false words with a snake's forked tongue, my brother. Now they kill our friend, Pte, the buffalo, and leave him to rot in the dust. They kill my people with poisoned firewater. They kill us because we are not like them. They rape our women and kill them after they have satisfied their lust. Many of these men are devils, my brother.

"Ten suns before we moved the village, we were camped on the Creek of the Beaver. Two young girls, Shining Path and Blue Bird, left the camp to collect buffalo chips for the cooking fires. We found them stripped, raped, and murdered. Everywhere on the ground were the tracks of shod ponies, white man's ponies. The Yellow Legs who died on the Lodge Pole Trail paid for the murders of our children."

Forrester was stunned by White Wolf's words. He did not for a moment doubt them, but they recounted atrocities, which he had been told were only committed by savage Indians. He remembered another time in his life when he had seen the aftermath of rape and pillage. His mind drifted back to a day in Georgia, a spring morning along Peach Tree Creek, when twelve deserters had been hanged for a similar offense. "No," he thought, "no race of men is blameless, and the pain they inflict is always bitter and lasting to the victims and their loved ones."

White Wolf continued. "Crazy Horse organized a big war party. Gall, Many Kills, He Dog, American Horse, Roan Calf, High Cloud, Young-Man-Afraid, and myself. Each led more than fifty warriors. Our Cheyenne brother, Bobtail Horse, led a small band of decoys. If the log cutters came, they would skirmish with them; otherwise they would taunt the Yellow Legs inside the fort, until they came out.

"Since the Moon of Winter was bright, our war party traveled only at night. Long before the moon set on the third night of our journey, we stopped high up on the Lodge Pole Trail. From each chief's group, one pony holder was chosen, and the warriors' horses were strung out on a picket line. Although they would be allowed to graze, the pony holder could quickly lead his whole string of animals down the trail at the first sound of firing from below. Crazy Horse stopped too far from the fort for any pony sounds to carry to the ears of the Yellow Legs. There were no morning meals or fires. There would be no telltale wisps of smoke against the morning sun.

"We moved quietly down the trail to the place of the ambush that Bobtail Horse had told us about. At the end of the first long steep hill, which rises from the prairie in front of the fort, the trail drops back down into a long deep gully before it rises again and slopes sharply up toward the summit. Between those hills, the trail runs along the bottom of a canyon, which is shaped like one of Blue Leaf's iron kettles. You remember, my brother, it is steep on every side and covered with fallen trees and large boulders.

"Just before we arrived at the ambush spot, Crazy Horse divided the war party into four groups. Two of the groups climbed to the top of the side hills then descended to places of concealment from which they could fire down onto the trail. The Yellow Legs saw no signs of our presence or passage, because we never came near the trail. Crazy Horse, together with Man-Afraid, American Horse, and their warriors, prepared to stop the head of the column as soon as the last of the Yellow Legs had ridden into the trap. I, together with Gall, Many Kills, his son Iron Shirt, and our men, took up places where we could stop any attempted retreat."

"Did your people walk through the entire gorge, White Wolf?"

"Yes, with Crazy Horse and Man-Afraid."

"How was it that the Crow trackers did not find any signs?"

"There were no signs to find, my brother."

"How can that be?"

"Crazy Horse and Man-Afraid walked all the way to the other end of the trap and looked up on both slopes for any hint of the ambush. As they walked, they used clumps of sagebrush to erase their footprints along with all the others."

"Was it still dark?"

"Yes. But they waited with us until the rising sun allowed them to see, then Bobtail Horse and his warriors went down to bait the trap."

"And we came after them like a wolf chasing a field mouse."

"Bobtail Horse is very good at luring people along. He waited for the cutters of logs to return to the fort, certain that a Yellow Leg war party would come out. We heard the shots from the fort and were happy to hear the sound of a bugle. It told us the soldiers were coming.

"Bobtail Horse waited so long to run that the Bluecoats were almost on his pony's heels as he came thundering past us and on through the warriors with Crazy Horse. You saw it, my brother. Once the Yellow Legs entered the canyon, there was no escape. Their ponies could not climb up the sides of the canyon, and the rain of bullets stopped you from going forward or back. Most of the Yellow Legs died quickly. All except you and the red-haired soldier with the stripes on his arms."

From the description, Forrester identified the soldier as Master Sergeant Blarney Quinn, an old friend who had joined the army when he was sixteen and risen through the ranks.

"Many shots were fired at you, but you were hard to hit, my brother, since your pony kept dancing and moving. Even when we shot him out from under you and your right leg and arm were pinned beneath him, you continued firing with your left hand until I struck your head with my war club. Even as the blow sent you to the Land of Shadows, you fired the bullet that killed Many Kills' son, Iron Shirt."

"Does Many Kills know that I killed his son?" Forrester asked.

"Many Kills knows, but he is grateful that his son died well at the hands of a brave warrior. We were all proud of the way you fought my brother. Crazy Horse made medicine and asked the Great Spirit for your life and that of the red-haired soldier, but he was dead when we went to him. You were the only one left alive. We placed you on a travois and rode back to our village. We scalped the other white men, but not the red-haired soldier."

"To me, White Wolf, war is a terrible thing. It makes my heart sad because so many good men on both sides were killed. In your world, it is good to die to protect your beliefs.

In the world I came from, it is better to live to perpetuate them. That world holds life to be sacred. But I'm grateful that Sergeant Quinn was not scalped. He was my brother then, as you are my brother now."

"I am glad. Your brother died well. Tomorrow you begin your preparation for the Giving of War Weapons and to learn the ways of a Sioux warrior. But I think there are many things you can teach us, as well. Let us talk more of this as we share a pipeful of tobacco."

➤

Several weeks later, Forrester and White Wolf were once again seated beside a small cooking fire, preparing to enjoy the reward of a successful elk hunt. Together with Gall, they were eagerly anticipating the pleasure of devouring the four huge steaks, which hung, sizzling, over the fire. Touches-The-Clouds could not wait. He sat contentedly munching on the raw elk liver, which had barely been warmed over the flames. As he tore each bite away with his strong teeth, blood trickled down his chin and spattered his chest.

"Cloud," said Gall, "why don't you cut the meat instead of gnawing it like a coyote?"

"Half the pleasure is in the gnawing!" Cloud grinned.

"Perhaps our white brother could teach you the customs and language of the Sioux. He now speaks better than you do."

"In return I could teach him the art of gnawing," sputtered Touches-The-Clouds.

Gall is right, thought Forrester. In the past six months he had learned a great deal about the Sioux. In many ways, they lived a savage, cold-blooded existence. But in other ways, their society was far better than the one which white men call genteel and civilized. Immoral acts, such as theft and adultery, almost never occur. Special warriors, called the "Shirt Wearers," were responsible for the welfare of all other tribal members. There were no slums here on the plains, and no poverty. Almost every Indian he had met had been open, helpful, and friendly. No one was ever reviled. And yet, he had witnessed appalling things as well.

With sadness, he remembered one morning during the winter. The village's oldest war chief, White Antelope, died suddenly. He was "buried" on a small platform, which was built in the branches of a large cottonwood tree. Since he was a revered warrior, weapons, which he had long, since been too weak to use were laid out beside him. His favorite old war pony, which he had been unable to ride for many years, was slain beneath his platform so that he could ride on his journey to the Great Spirit. Substantial rations of food and water were also provided. Finally, his woman, Red Fern, chopped off two of her fingers to show her grief and sorrow. The "funeral" was a great success.

The mourners returned to the village and immediately began to dismantle the teepee in which White Antelope and Red Fern had lived happily for many years. One family claimed the handsome green-and-yellow buffalo hide covering; another took the long, straight Aspen lodge poles, which they had obviously coveted for many years; yet another seized the iron cooking pots and woven sleeping couches. Within minutes, the trade blankets, buffalo robes, weapons, and every other item of value had disappeared.

"Why have they torn her home apart?" the astonished Forrester demanded of White Wolf.

"She has no right to a home with us anymore. The death of her husband took that right away. Look at her standing over there. She knows that our ways are harsh, but she does not grieve for herself because she has known that this day would come for many years. She also knows that she will die if no one takes her in."

Red Fern sought refuge and shelter with her younger brother, but was refused a place in his lodge. Having nothing left to keep her warm, except her thin doeskin dress, she slept that night amongst the pony herd. The night turned bitterly cold as a fierce winter wind hurtled over the high mountain peaks of the Rockies and howled across the prairie.

By dawn, Red Fern was dead. From one morning to the next, she had gone from loving wife, to rich widow, to unwanted beggar, to frozen corpse.

➢

Forrester's thoughts returned to the present as White Wolf tossed him a huge hunk of meat, which claimed his attention. Although he regarded his three companions as friends, he still did not feel like a peer, because he was unarmed, and would remain so until the "Giving of War Weapons" ceremony. As he ate the big, tasty steak, he asked White Wolf about his immediate future.

"When we return, my brother, you will spend three suns in the medicine lodge, being purified. Then a feast will be held and you will become a Sioux. Someone will present you to Crazy Horse and pledge his own honor that you will always be true to the Sioux Nation. He will give you a Sioux name, mix his blood with yours, and become your Sioux father.

"Then someone else will mix his blood with yours and become your tribal brother. He will give you your war weapons, which will be blessed by Medicine Raven. Then your brother will pledge to hunt you down and kill you with those weapons, should you ever bring disgrace upon your new people."

"Who will these two warriors be?"

"Never fear," White Wolf said. "There are always at least two fools in every village!" All three of the Sioux laughed heartily. Even Forrester was compelled to grin.

All the way back to the village on the Little Bighorn, he pondered the possible identities of his sponsors. He was fairly certain that Many Kills would not be his father, but perhaps he would be his sponsor. White Wolf had become his best friend; perhaps he would be the one, but somehow White Wolf didn't fit the tribal father role. The warrior for whom he had the greatest respect was, of course, Crazy Horse. But he would be presented to Crazy Horse. It was all quite confusing.

His relationship with Little Fawn weighed even more heavily on his mind. Each day, he loved her more deeply. But he respected her wishes and did not mention marriage again. He felt certain that the enforced separation was just as difficult for her. He hoped that his new status as a warrior might pave the way to their being together.

The morning after they returned from the elk hunt, Forrester went to the lodge of Medicine Raven, where the old man explained the ceremonies which Forrester would undergo during the next three days.

"First," said the wise medicine man, "many stones will be heated in a large fire. Then hot stones will be rolled into a small medicine lodge. Sprinkling them with water will make steam. For the next three suns, you must wait for an omen. Each time the rocks grow cold, my helper, Bending Tree, will exchange them for new hot ones from the fire and pour more water over them.

"During the days that you are inside the lodge, you will have no food and only small sips of water. Soon you will receive a vision from your 'spirit guide.' Your guide can be any type of creature or object. A horse, a wolf, or," the old man chuckled, "even a raven. In the vision you will learn your warrior's name. If you do not receive a vision or sign during the three days, I will speak with your tribal father and we will give you a name."

Medicine Raven handed him a new breechclout and sent him to bathe in the cool waters of the river. When he returned, the old medicine man placed a necklace of sacred snake rattles around his neck and applied a variety of paints to his body.

"Bending Tree has prepared the medicine lodge. It is time to begin your medicine quest."

He raised the small square of buckskin that covered the tiny opening into the medicine lodge, and Forrester slipped quickly into the small, steaming, unbearably hot enclosure.

By mid-afternoon, despite small sips of water, Forrester was beginning to dehydrate. The intense heat and blistering steam were taking their toll. His newly healed wounds began to throb anew as he slipped in and out of consciousness. Each hour his delirium deepened and he dreamed of events long past.

He saw himself as a small boy, fishing with his father, Glenn, on the Rappahannock River near their Virginia plantation. Then he was a cadet on the drill field of V.M.I. He pictured his first sweetheart, Mary Morgan, the great-granddaughter of the famous Revolutionary War general, Daniel Morgan. He remembered his grief when he came home at the end of his plebe year and learned of her death, a few days earlier, in a freak riding accident. She was laid to rest on the morning of his return. For many months after that, he thought his heart would break each time he thought of the vivacious young lady that he had loved so much, for far too short a time. He recalled another sad morning when he had ridden off to war on the beautiful black gelding he had named Sable, and how the gallant animal had died at the Seven Days' Battles.

He relived the firefights, the skirmishes, and the battles of old and saw the friends whom he had lost. He thought of the great raid the Confederate Cavalry had made into the Union stronghold of Pennsylvania in the fall of 1862. Then he was at Yellow Tavern in 1864 with the impetuous leader that he and all the others had followed so willingly and loved so much. There was Jeb Stuart, waving his yellow-plumed hat and urging them on. Once again, he felt the great pain and sorrow when he vividly saw his hero shot down into the dust. He saw himself rushing forward to Jeb's side and once again felt himself being blown out of his saddle by a well-aimed Minie ball, lying in the dirt, writhing in pain.

Throughout these days and nights of delirium Forrester relived his life. He saw himself returning from the fight at Petersburg, the dying Confederacy's last-ditch effort to protect the capital of Richmond. He saw the devastation that had descended upon his home at Forest Glen — and learning from neighbors that during the preceding winter his father had been killed by a Union patrol while trying to stop their foraging — and discovering that his mother had died a few weeks later, as much from a broken heart as from the pneumonia. His last heartrending view of the rubble that had been his loving family's home made him vow to leave and never return again.

In his dreams, Forrester began to see bird's-eye views of the plantation, and the battles, and the other events of his life. He saw himself in them, and yet he was not in them. He was hovering over them, able to fly like the wind from one scene to the next. Now he was soaring high above the earth, racing toward the sun. He seemed to see himself from a great distance. He was riding a giant hawk, which swooped down on their mutual foes. Forrester saw himself firing his pistols at many enemies and the hawk crushing others in his powerful talons. Suddenly he felt the hawk shudder in flight, and then drop like a falling stone onto the rocks far below. Forrester's vision exploded into blackness.

He slowly returned to consciousness on the third morning and recognized the interior of Medicine Raven's wickiup. While Bending Tree went to get him food from the lodge of Many Kills, Forrester drank small sips of water and recounted his dreams for the medicine man.

"I am very confused by my visions, Medicine Raven. What do they mean?"

"I am not fully clear about them. But soon I will speak with the other wise men of the tribe and we will know the answer. At the ceremony of war weapons, your new name and war sign will give you the answers to your vision. Never fear!"

➢

After his meal, Forrester bathed and swam in the river before returning to the lodge of his foster family. Many Kills and Night Wind talked and joked with him throughout the rest of the morning but provided no hint about the evening's events. Night Wind's excellent venison stew and the ordeal he had undergone during the preceding three days made him so drowsy that he fell asleep soon after the noonday meal.

He awoke in the late afternoon to the sounds of ceremonial drums. Many Kills stood in the doorway, engaged in a conversation with someone just outside the lodge. A moment later he turned and entered, followed by Gall and Touches-The-Clouds. The usually jovial Gall spoke solemnly.

"We have come to prepare our brother for the ceremony."

Touches-The-Clouds handed Forrester a beautifully decorated breechclout. Porcupine quills and colored beads had been laboriously sewn on the soft doeskin.

"This will replace your old buckskins," he said. "It is a gift from Little Fawn. She sends you word that her heart, which is filled with love for you, is now swelled with pride."

Forrester was encouraged by Little Fawn's open admission. She was seldom out of his thoughts. He hoped for the hundredth time that his new status would make it possible to share a lifetime of love, after all.

Many Kills brought forth an array of paints and handed them to Gall. Across Forrester's shoulders and chest, high up where the recipient could not see them, Gall painted five different signs, starting on the left shoulder.

"This is the sign of your foster father, Many Kills," he said. "It gives you goodness and signifies that you have replaced the son that he lost."

Over Forrester's heart, he painted another emblem and said, "This sign is for your tribal father. It gives you leadership. Next is the sign of your tribal brother; it stands for justice.

This sign on the right side of your chest is for your friend, Touches-The-Clouds. It stands for loyalty." Last of all, Gall painted his own sign on Forrester's right shoulder. "The sign of Gall gives you strength. May you always be worthy of these gifts, my brother."

They emerged from the lodge and were confronted by an honor guard of warriors. Among them were Tall Bull of the Hunkpapa Sioux; the Sans Arc chief, Broken Pipe; and the Brule warrior, Two Arrows. Their two great leaders, Bright Moon and Bobtail Horse represented the Cheyenne.

With Forrester walking between two columns of warriors, they moved toward the center of the village where the ceremony would take place. Facing away from the approaching group was a raised dais upon which sat a chief, wearing a magnificent war bonnet, whom Forrester assumed to be Crazy Horse.

For the last time, Forrester wondered who his tribal father would be. The procession wound through the teepees and finally came to a stop before the chief. Forrester looked into his face and saw not the young Crazy Horse, but the aging Sitting Bull.

Off to the side of the platform, the crowd suddenly parted and Forrester was surprised to see a regal figure advancing through their midst. It was Crazy Horse. But on this occasion, he wore no black wolfskins or war bonnet. He was dressed, as was Forrester, in a ceremonial breechclout. A single black-and-white feather decorated his long, black hair. Stopping beside Forrester, he asked in a booming voice, "Is your heart now a Sioux heart? Is your body now a Sioux body? Is your mind now a Sioux mind? And do you wish Sioux blood to run in your veins?"

"I do!" Forrester replied.

He wondered why fate had decreed that he would always fight for noble, but unwinnable causes, first for the sovereign rights of Virginia, and now for the human rights of his adopted people.

"Is it your wish to become my true son?"

"It is, my father," he said to this great chief and guardian of his people, who had earned Forrester's respect as a warrior and a leader.

Crazy Horse turned Forrester toward him, placed one hand on his own heart and the other upon that of his true son, who duplicated the chief's gesture. Forrester was reassured as the eyes of Crazy Horse smiled into his own.

Medicine Raven came forward and cut a small gash in each of their left wrists. When blood from each wound was flowing freely, he held them together and chanted, asking the Great Spirit to allow Sioux blood to flow into the body of this new warrior.

Then Crazy Horse faced Sitting Bull and proclaimed, in a loud voice, "On my honor, mighty chief of the Hunkpapa, I swear that my son will do great deeds and will always be loyal to his Sioux parents and brothers. The great white warrior, Clayton Forrester, is gone. In his place stands the great Sioux warrior, Fire Hawk."

From his place of honor, Many Kills came forward and held up the sign of Fire Hawk, which had been painted on a buffalo hide shield. It was a black hawk with outspread wings and talons. In each claw, the hawk held a pistol, which spouted red fire.

"It is time for my son, Fire Hawk, to receive war weapons from the hand of his brother, White Wolf," Crazy Horse declared.

As White Wolf came forward, several other warriors accompanied him. If Fire Hawk had been expecting primitive weapons, he was pleasantly surprised. For White Wolf was carrying Fire Hawk's own pistol belt, which held an ample supply of ammunition in addition to the pair of .44-40 Colt revolvers. White Wolf buckled these around Fire Hawk's waist and then brought forward his Henry rifle, which he presented. Next came a beautifully crafted tomahawk from Crazy Horse. But it was the final weapon he received which Fire Hawk could not believe. From his own hip, where it had hung for many years and served him well in so many encounters, White Wolf withdrew the possession that he prized above all others, the Spanish knife, and placed it in Fire Hawk's hands.

Stunned by White Wolf's generosity, Fire Hawk looked down at the shimmering blade as it gleamed in the firelight. He wondered about the many men who had owned the weapon for the past four hundred years. But then his thoughts changed to a hope that this instrument of war and death might somehow help him to become a purveyor of peace and an insurer of life for his adopted people.

Medicine Raven came forward to bless the weapons and receive White Wolf's pledge. White Wolf swore that should Fire Hawk ever betray the trust that had been placed in him, he would cheerfully cut out Fire Hawk's contemptible heart.

When the ritual ended, White Wolf, in an uncharacteristic display of emotion, squeezed Fire Hawk's shoulder.

"For the rest of our days, we will truly be brothers! We will live as brothers and, if need be, we will die as brothers!"

And so, the former Confederate soldier and army scout named Clayton Forrester ceased to exist, and in his place now stood a Sioux warrior called Fire Hawk. A just man, he had recognized in a very short time the desperate need of his adopted people for the counsel and leadership that only he could provide. Once that decision had been made, he courageously accepted responsibility for his future actions, whatever the consequences.

For regardless of the nobility of his purpose, or the compelling nature of his cause, most members of the white race would never accept such a defection by one who had been their own. Shocked "civilized men" in every corner of the land were entitled to, nay expected to, exhibit furious hatred and outraged indignation. They would, moreover, see Forrester as a white man who had turned his back on his own race. A man who had disavowed his heritage, discarded his birthright, and chosen to live in the wilderness like "any other ordinary savage."

To almost every American, this one vile act of treason linked Clayton Forrester's name forever with those of Benedict Arnold and Simon Girty. He had committed an unforgivable act! All of his former virtues would now be wrapped inside a blanket of shame!

For the rest of recorded history, if indeed history chose to remember him at all, Clayton Forrester would bear the brand of — **RENEGADE!**

PART FOUR

WAR PAINT AND WINCHESTERS

Chapter VIII

➤

Two Different Worlds

Statehood Day
Omaha, Nebraska
July 4, 1867

It had been a day of great celebration and jubilation, as it should have been. Today was not only America's 91st birthday; it was also the day on which Nebraska had entered the Union as the thirty-seventh state. The "Cornhuskers" had finally arrived. The festivities were still in full swing an hour past sunset as Kevin McCarthy and Catherine Gerot strolled down River Street toward Omaha's Grand Hotel, where they planned to join GeeGee and Fred Benteen for supper.

"Some of the batters could certainly hit the ball a long way," Catherine exclaimed excitedly. "Did you ever play baseball?"

"A few times. Baseball was a popular game during the war, but I never got the hang of it."

"Hitting a ball coming right toward your head as hard as a man can throw it must be awfully difficult."

"I found it nearly impossible."

"Well, I want to try. I'm sure GeeGee will say it's unladylike, but I want to try anyway."

"If I can buy the proper gear, let's try it and just forget to tell him."

"Do you mean it?"

"Sure. I'll try to find the things we need tomorrow."

They arrived at the hotel and turned into the lobby. As they entered, Fred and GeeGee rose to meet them.

"Well, Cat, how was the baseball game?"

"It was fun. So were the fireworks. There were hundreds of them! More than I thought I would ever see at one time. Did you two enjoy your shooting?"

"I can't speak for Fred, but I sure did! These new Winchesters are the fastest loading, best handling, most accurate weapons I've ever held in my hands! You can load one up on a Sunday and shoot it for the rest of the week."

"One thing's for sure," added Benteen. "There will be a lot of surprised Indians out there the first time they run into a storm of lead from these guns. Kevin, have you decided to continue upriver in the morning?"

"No, I'm going out to the Bozeman Trail with all of you and scout around a bit. Maybe Myles hasn't left for Fort Riley yet."

"That'll depend on the Boy General," Benteen declared grimly.

"Mac, Fred's giving each of us one of the new Winchesters. I already have mine," GeeGee said with a broad smile.

"How can you do that? Weren't they all consigned to the army?"

"All but six," Fred answered. "They'll go to marksmen, in and out of the military, who will put them through a real test. Your only obligation is to write a report and send it to the factory at the end of one full year, describing the rifle's performance."

"Well, I sure can't turn down that deal. No doubt I'll have plenty of chances to use it."

➢

The next morning, after breakfast, Kevin took Catherine to a store that sold sports equipment, and purchased a baseball and bat for her. Kevin hid the items away in his room, and then spent the rest of the morning outfitting himself for the trail.

Since his new rifle was a .45-55 caliber, he searched until he found a Colt pistol that would fire the same metallic cartridges. He purchased a warm bedroll and a strong waterproof ground cloth to spread out under it. Cooking and camping gear followed. Then his two saddles. The lightweight two-sided packsaddle was large enough to haul everything he would need. He could scarcely believe his good luck when he found a sturdy, well-worn saddle, which fit him perfectly. Nothing made long days on horseback more uncomfortable and tedious than a poor-fitting saddle.

Leaving his most important purchases until the afternoon, he returned to the hotel for lunch with Catherine. She was waiting for him in the dining room as he entered.

"Did you find everything you needed?"

"Pretty much. I only need to find a couple more items."

"Oh! What?"

"Horses. A saddle mount and a pack animal. Since I need 'em by tomorrow morning, finding a good pair might not be so easy."

"May I come horse hunting with you?"

"It's pretty hot out there today! Are you sure you want to?"

"I'd love to."

He reached across the table and took her hand.

"In that case, nothing would give me greater pleasure."

They both enjoyed the delicious lunch of broiled brook trout and fresh vegetables. A sparkling burgundy wine complemented the meal, as did the fresh fruit dessert.

When they finished, Kevin went to the livery stable. There he hired a horse and a surrey with a top, which would ward off the hot sun. Not only would the rig be more comfortable, but also it would allow them to cover more territory in a shorter period of time.

Since Omaha was one of the terminals of the Overland

Trail, there were dozens of horse dealers and traders in the immediate area. Buying a packhorse proved to be much easier than Kevin had anticipated. At the third corral they visited, he found a brown, five-year-old mare.

"She's only about fourteen hands high," he said to Catherine, "a bit too small to be ridden regularly, but she looks strong and she's well proportioned. Look at that deep chest and those sturdy legs. I think she'll be an ideal packhorse, and I could certainly ride her in an emergency."

"She seems to be a very gentle little animal," Catherine observed. "She has such a sweet face."

Kevin haggled briefly with the dealer over the price of the mare, but quickly agreed when the man offered to have her shod as part of the agreement.

She stood very patiently while the blacksmith fitted her with new iron shoes.

"She's so calm and demure," Kevin said to Catherine, "that she almost seems shy."

"She's one o' them hosses the cavalry brung in from an Injun village. A week ago she was a sure enough Cheyenne pony."

Before he finished speaking, Catherine and Kevin were both smiling at the coincidence. The mare was instantly named Shy Ann.

Finding a saddle horse proved to be much more difficult. Kevin had been warned about the folly of taking a stallion into Indian country; but he still wanted a high-spirited gelding — sixteen or more hands tall — young, strong, and quick, with an easy-to-ride, mile-eating lope. Most of all, he did not want a flashy animal. Several horses came close to fitting those requirements, but time and again he rejected them for various reasons.

It was nearly sundown when they arrived at "Jackson Horse Dealers and Traders." As they neared the stables, Catherine grabbed Kevin's arm. "Look at that golden palomino. Isn't he one of the most beautiful animals you've ever seen?"

"He sure is. Custer would love to have him for parades. But taking a horse like that into Indian country would be like waving a red banner in a bullring."

"Well," she acknowledged, "you're the expert."

"I suppose it wouldn't hurt to look at him."

On closer inspection, Kevin found the animal to be everything he was looking for. The palomino was young, big, and strong. And he was pleasantly surprised by the horse's price. When he rode the animal, Kevin found one of the palomino's gaits to be an easy rolling canter, which reminded him of sitting in a rocking chair. The only problem was the palomino's appearance. Any young Indian warrior who saw that horse would want to steal him.

Catherine smiled wistfully as the palomino was led away.

"I suppose you'll marry a drab and unattractive woman for the same reason, won't you? You certainly could never be expected to go around waving a banner, could you? No sir! Ugly is the best!"

Kevin could not help laughing.

"All right! I'll buy the horse! Catherine, you could get me to do anything, couldn't you?"

"I wondered when you would discover that," she said softly, placing her hand behind his head and bringing his lips gently down to meet her own.

An hour later, the beautiful palomino, Banner, was stabled next to Shy Ann in the hotel barn, and Catherine had gone in to dinner with a far wiser and much happier Kevin.

The next morning, together with the other travelers bound for the Bozeman Trail, they left on the first stage of their journey.

➤

That same morning, four hundred miles farther west, Fire Hawk and White Wolf were preparing to camp near the mouth of Crazy Woman Creek, where it emptied into the North Platte River. The Sioux warriors were returning from a raid on a Shoshone village. White Wolf spoke to his companion.

"Since we have ridden all night, I think it is safe for us to rest."

"I agree. The pursuit is likely over. This string of ponies is ours."

"The Shoshones were fools to chase us so far, anyway. How could they hope to catch the best ponies in their herd when they were carrying no weight?"

"I suppose you would have let them go if they had stolen your ponies?"

"Of course not! Remember the flight of the Comanches?"

"So the Shoshones were right to try."

"You know as well as I, Hawk, that they could catch a moonbeam easier than they could outrun Star Walker and Chestnut. Sometimes you are very slow to understand! Will you watch first or sleep?"

Fire Hawk could not suppress a grin. "You sleep, I'll watch."

They decided to keep the dozen Shoshone horses on the lead lines which had held them together for the past two nights and a day, but which allowed them to graze. Although the Shoshones had probably given up the pursuit, it was possible that a determined leader might still be pushing them ahead. White Wolf fell asleep at once, while his companion took the first watch.

Fire Hawk climbed to a spot just below the crest of a low ridge, which overlooked their campsite. Shielded behind a clump of low bushes, he could remain concealed while observing their back trail as well as the prairie in all directions. The sun was just rising behind him as he took up his position. If there were any persistent pursuers left, the sun's glare would blind them and offer him additional protection from detection. The Shoshones might still come. The horses were not the raiders' only prizes; two fresh scalps dangled from White Wolf's belt.

Almost constantly for the past thirty hours, they had galloped with the captured horses strung out between them. During the long run, Fire Hawk had, more than once, marveled at Star Walker's power and speed. Of all the horses he had ever ridden, this one was the best, although Pasha was a close second. He watched the captured horses as they grazed in the valley below him. All of them were prime animals, but two in particular caught his attention. One of them, a coal black stallion, had the same small head and short back as Star Walker, suggesting Spanish or Arabian bloodlines. Only slightly smaller than the Appaloosa, if White Wolf agreed, the black would make a fine war pony for Crazy Horse. The other special pony was a dark red sorrel filly with a white face and matching mane and tail. She was so full of energy that she constantly danced and frisked about. The red filly would make a wonderful gift for Many Kills.

He thought back over his first eight months with the Sioux. He had met a good number of them who had been victimized by the White man's continuing encroachment and greed. A short time after he received his war weapons, four teenaged boys had gone fishing a short distance from the village on Goose Creek. When they did not return at sunset, Forked Tail went to look for them. When he found his son and the other lads, they were all dead. They had been hanged from the branches of a tree. A sign was nailed to the tree. It read: "A good Injun is a dead Injun."

This incident was a turning point for Fire Hawk. He had known and liked all four of the youngsters. But the lost acquaintances were not the primary reason for his change of heart. He had always hated human beasts who made war on women and children. They were a scourge on the earth and every one of them deserved to die, regardless of the color of their skins, or the color of the uniforms they wore.

101

He knew that his four years of military service and hardship had made him bitter. The death of his father and the loss of so many of his good friends had convinced him that there were no winners in wars. Just survivors and casualties. But he had also learned that just and moral men must, at some point, draw a line and stand firm against injustice. He was still not certain that the Civil War had been a completely honest conflict, but he was sure that someone had to take up the cause of the Sioux. He was not sure of the role that he might play. He would never fight former friends in the army, soldiers like Fred Benteen, whom he knew to be good men. That line was clearly drawn for him as well. But short of killing, he would do everything he could to aid the Indian's right to live freely. For now, he decided, he would be a teacher and a guide to the future.

His thoughts drifted back to a day when he and White Wolf had gone with the war party of retaliation, which struck three relay stations along the North Platte River a week after the young boys were murdered. All three of the station keepers had been killed and the buildings were burned to the ground.

The third station the war party attacked was the one closest to Fort Laramie. By then, word of the other raids had filtered back to the army post. Sensing this, Crazy Horse sent scouts to watch every possible route that an approaching cavalry unit might follow. Thick black smoke from the burning buildings and stock pens, billowing straight up into the bright cloudless sky on that windless day, served as a beacon to effectively beckon the eager young troopers to their deaths. Scouts soon returned and reported the location and size of a fast-approaching patrol.

Crazy Horse, an expert tactician, split his band of sixty plus warriors into three elements. White Wolf and Gall each led groups to positions a mile closer to the cavalry. Once there, they found concealment on opposite sides of the trail. Then the wise war chief spread out the balance of his force just below the brow of a small hill, half a mile from the burning buildings. Fire Hawk immediately saw the wisdom of this deployment. The cavalry leader would be eager to gain a vantagepoint overlooking the burning station before he slowed his detachment's pace and began to exercise full-scale caution.

We studied this strategy at V.M.I., he thought. It's a double envelopment trap. Hannibal invented it in 216 B.C. at the Battle of Cannae. Daniel Morgan employed it at the Battle of Cowpens in 1781. And I was there when General Lee and Stonewall Jackson used it against "Fightin' Joe" Hooker at Chancellorsville, in May '63. Crazy Horse simply knows that it will work.

And work it did.

As the head of the column reached the base of the hill, the Sioux on the hilltop cut them down with a withering fire. The riders at the rear of the army unit swung around to escape the fusillade, but by then Gall and White Wolf's warriors had closed in for the kill. The outcome was preordained. Minutes after the first shot was fired forty cavalry officers and men lay dead.

Unwilling to participate against former friends, Fire Hawk had watched from a high hill. The troopers had not panicked and had, given the existing conditions, performed very well. Three Sioux warriors were dead and several were wounded.

He lost two good friends in this small but deadly battle. One was a tough; young, devil-may-care white warrior named Jack York of the U.S. Cavalry. The other was a strong, young, steel-nerved red warrior named Touches-The-Clouds. Jack would no longer swing the ladies at the dances and Cloud would no longer gnaw his meat. Each had died while fighting bravely. As Fire Hawk looked down at them, lying side by side, he was sad, but he was also very proud.

➢

Yes, the past few months had been a time filled with danger and adventure, as well as with many surprises.

White Wolf awakened him at midmorning and announced that the Shoshone "women" who had been pretending to be warriors must have gone home, because they were nowhere to be seen.

"The village will be back on Medicine Creek by now, Wolf."

"Since the Yellow Legs' forts are so close to the village, I will take in a war party. By now the cutters of wood will think we have forgotten them. Will you go, Hawk?"

"With reluctance, but I will not take part in the attack."

"I would not ask you to fight your old brothers, Fire Hawk."

"White Wolf is wise."

"Perhaps. But I know that before we die, all of my enemies will also be your enemies."

They kept the captive ponies on long picket ropes throughout the day as they warily moved along the southern bank of the North Platte River. Since the area through which they rode was a much traveled part of the Overland Trail, one of them constantly scouted ahead while the other led the two strings of ponies. It was good to have the dozen extra horses. Their presence permitted Fire Hawk and White Wolf to switch to a different horse every few miles and keep all of them fresh. Since their own mounts had run hard during the initial flight from the Shoshones, they were both permitted to rest and amble along for most of the day without the burden of a rider.

Fire Hawk rode the bald-faced filly in the morning, and she confirmed his first impression. She would make a fine mount for Many Kills. When White Wolf returned from scouting ahead in the early afternoon and took over the task of leading the ponies, Fire Hawk returned the filly to the lead line and mounted the black stallion.

He moved at a steady canter along the trail until he was about two miles ahead of White Wolf and the herd. Suddenly, far ahead, he noticed a pair of hawks circling high up in the bright sky, intent upon something far below them. The soaring birds triggered the same prickly sensation on the back of his neck that he used to get when Yankee columns were nearby. During the war, he had noticed that feathered hunters often patrolled in the wake of such columns, searching for food scraps the soldiers might drop.

Cautiously, he moved off the trail and rode toward a high ridge, which paralleled the Platte about a half-mile to the south.

When he reached it, he dismounted and climbed the steep bank on foot. Along the crest, the trees were so thick that he could not see through them for more than a few feet in any direction. He searched carefully along the summit until he found a towering old ponderosa pine tree, whose spire towered forty or fifty feet over that of its neighbors. He scaled this giant until he had a clear view of the trail ahead.

Stretching out toward the horizon and moving slowly into this hostile no-man's-land was a long line of prairie schooners. At this distance, the weathered wagons and the earthen colors of the plodding oxen blended so well with the background that they were almost invisible; but the big sun-bleached, white canvas covers stretched between bowed wagon frames stood out as brightly as polished silver. The land voyagers' patient progress over the gently rolling hills, coupled with the motion of the rippling river behind them, created an illusion of phantom merchant ships carried along by gentle trade winds. The defensive formation the wagon train employed was also reminiscent of ships on the high seas, huddling ever closer together, trying to maximize firepower in dangerous sections of the ocean where pirates were likely to be lurking.

Although very little of Clayton Forrester still remained in Fire Hawk's mind, when caught off guard, his first reaction was to tell himself that there was nothing to fear. But the next instant, the part of his mind that had become Sioux decided that these people would kill him without a moment's hesitation.

He scrambled from his high perch and clambered down the tree in such haste that he skinned his hands and knees. He slid down the hillside some distance from the black stallion, so as not to alarm him, then rode at a dead run toward White Wolf and the pony herd. The big black horse proved to be nimble and extremely fast, confirming Fire Hawk's decision to give him to Crazy Horse.

To avoid the wagon train, they forded the wide, shallow Platte and moved the horses to a large stand of juniper trees about a mile north of the river. Once the danger passed, they continued cautiously along the northern bank until late afternoon, before recrossing the stream and riding south. Despite the detour and the slower pace, they were back in the village by nightfall.

As always, Blue Leaf had prepared an excellent meal, to which she and White Wolf invited Fire Hawk and Little Fawn, as well as Many Kills, Night Wind, Crazy Horse, and Black Shawl.

White Wolf heaped praise upon Fire Hawk for his skill in capturing the ponies and for sensing the presence of the wagon train. Crazy Horse and Many Kills beamed as much at the success of their adopted son as they did a short time later when they were presented with magnificent new ponies. White Wolf enjoyed himself so much that he failed to mention his plans for another attack on the forts along the Bozeman Trail. As they walked back toward her wickiup, Fire Hawk assured Little Fawn that the whole village would hear of White Wolf's plan very soon.

➢

The following morning, as soon as the sun had peeped above the horizon, White Wolf strolled through the village, inviting about thirty selected friends to join him on the warpath.

At noon, a number of the principal warriors gathered near the wickiup of White Wolf to enjoy a midday meal and to discuss the foray. Fire Hawk and Many Kills were, of course, present. They were joined by Gall, Man Afraid, American Horse, High Cloud, Roan Calf, He Dog and his son, Bull Elk. The last to arrive, in the company of two braves unknown to Fire Hawk, was Crazy Horse. All three accepted food from Blue Leaf, then sat down in the midst of the gathering.

"My brothers," said Crazy Horse, "Black Moccasin and Growling Bear have just come from our Uncle, Sitting Bull, with good news. A great herd of buffalo is grazing on the high plains above the chalk cliffs. Our Uncle asks us to come and help stampede this herd over the high cliffs. The women can butcher them all in one place, instead of having to follow the herd over several miles as they do when we hunt Pte in the usual way. All the meat can be smoked there instead of being carried back to camp. We will have enough to last us until the snow melts in the Green Grass Moon. I ask that you wait until after we do this before going to the fort of the Yellow Legs."

It was White Wolf's place to answer.

"We will do as you ask. The high chalk cliffs are not much farther from the White Eyes' forts anyway." And they all laughed.

So it was decided that all present would raid the fort after Pte had been stampeded over the precipice.

As they walked back toward their own lodge, Fire Hawk asked Many Kills if this type of buffalo stampede happened often.

"It has been done ever since the Great Spirit brought forth the Great Shower of Stars. But since the time I was a small boy, my son, I have seen it done only a few times. Pte is not often so good to us and does not stay near these high cliffs."

➢

Early the next morning, more than fifty lodges were struck, and all the worldly possessions of their inhabitants were packed upon horses and stowed aboard travois. Nearly three hundred people and over seven hundred horses, together with dozens of skinny, mangy, yelping dogs, were strung out in a long line which stretched out over a mile of prairie. The procession quartered into the morning sun as it moved northeastward toward the Sand Hills.

It was not a good day to travel, and normally they would have waited for conditions to improve, but they could not count on the restless herd to graze near the sheer cliffs for very long.

When they left the vicinity of Medicine Creek, all vestiges of moisture disappeared from the soil. A mere hundred yards from the water, the earth was bone-dry and chalk-soft. Unfortunately, it was a completely calm day, without the hint of a breeze to carry away the heavy blanket of alkaline dust, which clung to humans and animals alike. Anything that moved through this cloud was quickly coated with acrid mineral salt, which irritated the eyes, invaded the mouth, and burned the throat.

Within five miles it was impossible to tell if the procession was comprised of the same band of war-bonneted Sioux who had left a refreshing river an hour before, or if, somehow, they had been transformed into a ghostly gathering of Macedonian warriors, bedecked once more in full battle array after moldering in their graves for two thousand years — now intent upon joining Alexander in a macabre march to the ends of the earth.

Although they were traveling within the large triangle formed by Deer and Medicine Creeks and the Platte River, it was July in the heart of America's dry lands, where the annual rainfall rarely exceeded fifteen inches.

Even at the slowest pace, three thousand restless hooves threw a gigantic cloud of dust thousands of feet into the air, which could be seen for many miles. If the travelers had been a small war party whose main strength lay in stealth tactics, the towering pillar would have been cause for great alarm. However, this cloud was so huge that it acted as a protective device for the Sioux rather than a locating beacon for any potential enemy.

If a cavalry patrol approached, the cloud would serve the troopers as an early warning signal, since the size and density of the cloud would indicate too many horses to be caused by another military patrol. The direction of the cloud, moving as it was toward the northeast, eliminated any possibility that it might be generated by a group of westbound Oregon immigrants. The speed, at which the cloud moved, although slow, was still appreciably faster than that of one caused by slow, plodding oxen. Finally, on a day unfit for travel, the dust cloud's very existence was, in itself, significant. Adding all of these factors together would have convinced any prudent military commander, unprepared for a fierce battle against at least one hundred determined hostiles, that his best course was to steer a wide berth around the telltale dust.

Fortunately, the arid alkali flats were only a few miles wide, and by early afternoon they had been left behind. The Platte was hardly more than a meandering trickle in the oppressing heat of the summer, but the Sioux were grateful nonetheless to be able to take full advantage of its meager waters on this afternoon. As a precaution, White Wolf dispatched three sentinels to keep watch. As they left to take up their posts, every other living creature stood, sat, or lay in the shallow stream. As soon as they had an opportunity to rinse some of the grime from their own bodies, White Wolf, Fire Hawk, and Many Kills went to relieve the dusty and beleaguered guards.

Fire Hawk and Many Kills rode to the top of a low bluff, which commanded a view of the trail along the river for well over a mile. Many Kills was riding the sorrel filly which Fire Hawk and White Wolf had captured from the Shoshones. The old warrior was patiently teaching her to stand quietly, but Fire Hawk could see her muscles quivering under the strain of enforced inactivity.

Fire Hawk grinned at his foster father.

"Is my father happy with his new pony?"

"Cistinna Dancer makes me feel like a young man again!"

Fire Hawk puzzled over the word cistinna. Then he remembered a time several months before, as he lay wounded in the wickiup of Little Fawn, when she had gone to treat a cistinna with a broken arm. It meant little girl.

"Cistinna Dancer could not be handled by anyone other than a young man, my father."

"My son's words are too generous, but they are welcome. I thank you for them, and for Cistinna Dancer."

Fire Hawk looked back toward the river bivouac and spotted a diminutive rider approaching on a slowly moving bay horse, who favored his off hind leg. Fire Hawk smiled as Jumping Frog and Pasha drew nearer. They made an ideal combination. It was time for the small boy to learn to ride, as well as how to groom and care for animals. Also, Jumping Frog spent a part of each day exercising Pasha without putting himself at risk.

Although his scars would always remain, Pasha's wounds were completely healed. However, he still limped, not as much from necessity as from habit. Also, he had decided that he would do no more running. His standard gait was a calm walk, but with a great deal of encouragement he would occasionally break into a slow, ambling trot. Whenever Jumping Frog tried to make Pasha quicken his gait beyond the trot, the old horse slowed back down to his normal walk. If the lad's hard heels continued to beat their rhythmic tattoo upon his ribs, Pasha stopped completely and maintained a stubborn disinterest until he was again ready to move forward at his own preselected pace.

Jumping Frog was grinning as Pasha stopped beside them.

"We almost got lost in the dust, Fire Hawk. It was good to jump into the river."

"The alkali flats are bad, all right. But by camping behind them, we discourage attackers who might come from that direction. It's a lot easier to guard three sides than four."

"When will we ride again?"

"Very soon, Frog. We must reach the village of Tanka Yotanka before sunset in order to stampede Pte at first light."

"Can I help?"

"Pasha is no longer able to run fast enough. But we will count on you to help us with the meat and hides. Perhaps we could even persuade you to eat some of the hump meat and tongue."

The lad laughed and rubbed his small belly. "If eating Pte will help you, I promise to do my best."

➢

The caravan left the Platte and continued on into the Sand Hills. A few miles from the Hunkpapa camp, Growling Bear and Black Moccasin rode ahead and alerted the village to the Oglala's presence. As the new arrivals approached, they saw the reflection of many large fires in the darkening sky. A short time later, they were close enough to determine the reason for those fires.

They had been built in a great half circle across the widest portion of a narrow plateau in front of a large herd of grazing and milling buffalo. The animals' fear of the bright, crackling flames was the Sioux' insurance that none of the restless beasts would attempt to break out of the immediate area. The high mesa, about a mile wide at the point where the fires had been built, gradually funneled

111

into a much narrower area, no more than a quarter of a mile in width, before it ended abruptly at the brink of a sheer cliff. Between the edge of this high rimrock and the floor of the valley below was a vertical drop of nearly two hundred feet. It was over this steep precipice that the Sioux intended to stampede the herd the following morning.

As they entered the village, Crazy Horse rode up beside Fire Hawk. He was mounted on his black war pony, which he had named Nighthawk because of the color and to honor his son. "We are invited to eat and smoke with Sitting Bull, my son."

"It will be good to see the Uncle again, my father."

Crazy Horse and Fire Hawk rode toward the center of the camp and dismounted in front of a large red-and-yellow teepee. Almost at once, a middle-aged, gray-haired man, whose face was carved with deep, weathered grooves, came out to meet them. "I thank my brother for coming so quickly."

"My Uncle need never fear for my delay," replied Crazy Horse. He placed his hand upon Fire Hawk's shoulder. "Tanka Yotanka, you have met my son, Fire Hawk. I ask that he be welcomed into your village."

"The son of Tushunca Witco is welcome in my heart as well as in my camp," Sitting Bull replied solemnly.

Fire Hawk nodded his head slightly to Sitting Bull. "My wish is that it might always be so, Uncle."

They were joined for the evening meal by the Oglalas, White Wolf, Many Kills, and Man Afraid. Gall was there, happy to be back among his own Hunkpapas once again. Sitting Bull had also invited his nephews, Tall Bull and One Bull. They greeted Fire Hawk and the others warmly, and enjoyed the feast. The final guest was the Uncle's adopted son, Frank Grouard, The Grabber, who said nothing and looked sullen throughout the festive meal.

When they had finished eating, Sitting Bull took a very special medicine pipe from a heavy buffalo-hide pouch and filled it with tobacco. He puffed on the pipe and blew smoke to the four winds in prayer and supplication before passing it on to his primary guest, Tushunca Witco. The war chief imitated the medicine man's gestures and then passed the ancient pipe to Fire Hawk.

"This is the sacred pipe of the Sioux, my son. I have not seen it for many years. It is only smoked at very important times." He indicated the delicate carving on the pipe stem. "Written on the sacred pipe are the words, 'Peace Without Slavery.' We smoke this night to ask the Great Spirit that it would always be so."

The pipe made the circuit of the suddenly solemn circle and was returned, at last, to Tanka Yotanka, who stored it away once more. It was the only time that Fire Hawk would ever see the famous medicine pipe.

The rest of the evening was spent devising a plan, which would string all available riders across the back and along both sides of the large herd. Each warrior was assigned a place in the long, semicircular line, so that there would be no confusion the next morning.

➢

Sunrise illuminated the silhouettes of more than two hundred warriors, mounted on their horses, in their assigned positions.

The mesa ran from east to west, with the cliffs at the western end. Dawn brought with it a strong west wind, which crested the cliffs and carried the scent of the Sioux away from the herd. The horsemen, moving onto the plateau between the fires, were able to get within a hundred yards of the dozen old bulls who were acting as sentinels for the herd, before they were detected. Then the riders charged forward, waving blankets or buffalo robes and shouting at the top of their voices. The sentinels turned tail and sped toward the rest of the herd, snorting, bellowing, and spurring their lethargic mates into motion.

Once the huge herd was moving, the only remaining task was to make certain that they kept going and that the animals on the outer fringes did not double back and escape. Crazy Horse, Fire Hawk, White Wolf, Many Kills, and a dozen others were riding along the outermost tip of the right wing. Several times during this headlong dash, small groups or individual buffaloes tried to break through the Sioux hard-riding cordon, but were always pinched back and forced to run with the rest. As the animals neared their brink of doom, after a run of over three miles, the dust raised by several thousand pounding hooves became so thick that a few of the creatures did manage to elude the determined drovers and go thundering back along the mesa to safety.

The vast majority of the herd, however, was packed so closely together that there was no possibility of escape. Whenever one of the behemoths tripped and fell, it never regained its feet. Other members of the herd, unable to avoid or jump over their stricken mate, tripped and fell as well. Often a dozen or more of the huge creatures were crushed or badly maimed before those behind were able to split and slide off to one side or the other, like a raging torrent confronted by an immovable object in its path. When one of the tiny calves fell victim to this onslaught, it was instantly pounded into the ground.

Although the many dead and dying animals strewn along the entire length of the mesa gave mute testimony to Pte's passage, well over a thousand of the terrified beasts ran until they were swept over the precipice and plunged into the depths below. At the base of the cliffs, nearly a hundred women and half as many teenage girls and boys, in an effort to end the suffering in the aftermath, searched for animals that had not perished in the fall and slit their throats. Meanwhile, back on the high mesa, another team of skinners and butchers were already at work on the animals that had fallen along the way.

Near the far end of the mesa, just short of the cliffs, a

group of tired but jubilant drovers were gathered around a large spring. As they rested, they chewed on strips of fresh raw meat.

"I wish Touches-The-Clouds were here," mused White Wolf. "How he loved fresh liver. My heart has been heavy since his death."

"It always hurts us when good friends die," Fire Hawk said, thinking of the comrades he had lost in the past years. "Have you seen Many Kills?"

"He was behind us when the chase began, Hawk. I did not see him after we started."

Nearly three dozen ponies, belonging to warriors who encircled the spring, were resting in the shade of some tall rocks. Fire Hawk's eyes searched for Cistinna Dancer, but she was not among the ponies. Suddenly, his heart sank within him.

"My father is not here, my brothers. Let us search for him."

All of the men moved swiftly to their horses, quickly mounted, and spread out across the plateau.

It was Fire Hawk who first saw a splash of alien color on the ground a few hundred yards from the end of the mesa. It was a small red sorrel pony with a white mane and tail. Nearby lay a badly battered human body. Many Kills had ridden his final trail, and the high-spirited Cistinna Dancer would dance no more. They were left where they had fallen, and cairns of rocks were piled over them. Then Fire Hawk found Night Wind and broke the news of her husband's death.

Since all the buffalo carcasses had to be butchered and smoked before they spoiled in the hot sun, no ceremony for Many Kills could take place for the next three days. But on the evening of the third day, a memorial ceremony was held for the great warrior.

Several of Many Kills' friends offered fitting and generous tributes to this good and brave man, but it was the final two speakers who completely captivated the many listeners.

The people from both villages, who had gathered together in a large circle, were hushed and respectful as Tushunca Witco began to speak.

"My brothers, the Sioux Nation has lost a great man. Our Oglala people have lost a great leader. I have lost a great friend. We are all sad because Many Kills is gone, but we must be grateful that such a warrior lived among us. We will all see Many Kills again some day. He will be on guard along the Star Road of the Great Spirit. My brothers, I will miss Many Kills for many reasons. He was my sponsor at the Giving of War Weapons. He has ridden beside me on many warpaths. He has fought next to me in many battles. He has shared with me his great wisdom in times of trouble. Perhaps it was the Great Spirit's plan to send to us a warrior to be the adopted son of Many Kills, a warrior who will stand beside me in the future, as Many Kills did in the past. Again, my brothers, I tell you, Many Kills will never die. He will live forever in our hearts."

His eulogy was heartfelt and emotional, and the crowd's mood reflected their great leader's ability to capture their attention and hold them spellbound. As Tushunca Witco sat down, another warrior arose. It was Fire Hawk. His powerful voice shook with emotion as he spoke.

"In my life, I have been greatly blessed by the Great Spirit. For in my life, my brothers, I have had three fathers. The first was Glenn Forrester. The second was Many Kills. Both of them were mighty warriors. Both of them died helping and protecting their people. I loved them both dearly, and will always remember them with great respect. I will always try to bring honor to them. My third father, Tushunca Witco, I respect and admire more than any other man. He honors me by sponsoring me and allowing me to walk beside him.

"From this moment on, I will protect and care for my mother, Night Wind, for as long as she or I may live. The feet of my father, Many Kills, are on the trail of the rainbow, but his lodge will remain active. For in that lodge, the spirit of Many Kills will continue to live beside the Sioux warrior, Fire Hawk, and his mother. And for as many years as I have left, I will help the Sioux people. I will be your worker and your advisor, as well as your warrior. For as long as my father, Tushunca Witco, needs me, I will be a right arm that will help him to safeguard the way of life you have always known. Together, we will fight to make the pledge on the sacred pipe come true. Together we will fight to establish 'Peace Without Slavery.'"

Chapter IX

➤

Dream Lover

Fort Phil Kearny
Wyoming Territory
August 15, 1867

It was nearly dusk, but Catherine and Kevin continued to linger under the clear, cooling spray from a miniature cataract, which cascaded down next to them from the rocks above. They had arrived before noon and shared a picnic lunch. The hottest part of the day had been spent swimming, lolling in the crystalline pool, and enjoying the waterfall as it tumbled down over weatherworn stones. Now as they watched, fading light from the setting sun reflected upon the dancing waters and created a rainbow of colors.

It was evident from the watermarks on the rocks, which impounded the pool that the level had been much higher on other occasions. A prolonged drought in the region had caused some of the smaller streams to dry up completely, now that the searing hot days of summer had arrived. This tiny brook, with its glittering cataract and inviting catchment, owed its existence to several natural springs, which Kevin had discovered on the uppermost portion of the hillside. The springs were, in all probability, part of a large artesian system, which was not entirely dependent on rainfall for its existence.

Myles Keogh had discovered this oasis, located about ten miles north of Fort Phil Kearny, during one of his patrols. Subsequently, it had become a frequent retreat for Myles and his wife, Megan. When he had gone to his friend this morning to seek directions, Kevin had been duty bound to invite the Keoghs along; but since Myles was the Officer of the Day, they were forced to decline. Kevin had been relieved. Deep down, he really wanted to be alone with Catherine.

He rented a horse and a surrey with a top from the Sutler's store, similar to the one he had shared with Catherine in Omaha; but when he arrived at the Gerot quarters, she came out in riding clothes and a broad-brimmed straw hat. "I had hoped we could ride instead of taking a buggy."

"It's pretty warm already, and it feels like it's going to get a whole lot hotter," he cautioned.

"You're starting to be as overprotective as GeeGee. I promise you that I won't melt. Besides, from Megan's description, there's a wonderful pond that we'll appreciate even more after a ride in the hot sun. Megan and Myles always go on horseback and, so far, they've survived. Although we'll be swimming in bathing attire, I'm sure we will too," she said, blushing slightly.

Kevin's eyebrows shot up.

"What do the Keoghs wear for swimming?"

"For goodness' sake, McCarthy, don't be so Puritanical and naive. Use your imagination!"

Kevin felt a trickle of perspiration start to course down his spine that was not generated by the heat of the sun. He looked at her and saw her mouth curl up in a small demure smile, while her lovely emerald eyes looked back at him coyly. In the time he had known her, Kevin had learned never to be surprised by Catherine's spontaneity. A short time later, mounted upon Banner and Shy Ann, they rode off to their picnic at the spring.

➢

The area surrounding the pool was far removed from normal travel routes and was, as yet, unsettled. Nonetheless, during their ride, Kevin remained alert for dust clouds, which would indicate approaching riders. Later, when they arrived at the waterfall, he reconnoitered the entire perimeter. At the end of his reconnaissance, he decided that anyone who approached would, almost certainly, come across the prairies that lay in front of him, rather than try to come through the rough, broken, rocky country on the mesa above him. Feeling comfortable and secure, they settled down to enjoy a day in their pleasant hideaway.

Catherine placed an oversized red-and-white-checkered tablecloth on a large flat rock and laid out a fine picnic lunch of fried chicken, cucumber salad, biscuits with honey, and a magnum of excellent claret. The blackberry pie that she had baked for dessert was also superb — very tart and tasty. As a special treat she had brought along a gallon of buttermilk, in a mason jar with a long cord, allowing it to be lowered into the water to cool. Buttermilk was Catherine's favorite beverage, and, in spite of himself, Kevin was developing a taste for it as well.

Soon after they finished their meal, they removed the outer clothing they had worn over their swimwear and waded into the cool, bracing water. Before entering the pool, Catherine had rearranged her lovely ash blonde hair into two long braids, which she deftly pinned on top of her head in an effort to keep her hair dry. The pigtails made her look like a schoolgirl. But even a dull, black, unattractive, full-length bathing smock could not conceal the fact that a mature female — most definitely not a child, was wearing it. They stayed in the pleasant surroundings for nearly an hour before clambering back to a place on the sunny rocks. Catherine reclined on her back, while Kevin sat cross-legged beside her and smiled into her eyes.

"I'm glad we were able to come out here by ourselves today, Sweetheart, because I have so many things to tell you. Let me begin by saying I love you."

Catherine returned his smile, and waited expectantly.

"You are the most beautiful and desirable woman I have ever known — and my love for you knows no limits. For a while, those two factors worked against each other. Since I never felt this way before, I thought I was reacting to my strong desire for you, rather than recognizing my feelings as true love. Of course physical attraction is a part of our relationship, but affection and friendship have become far more important. I know that I want to marry you and share my life with you." He grinned and added, "Then we can swim like Megan and Myles."

"My darling Kevin, I love you very much. More than I thought I could ever love anyone. And I want to please you and be everything to you. You were smiling when you said you would like to swim as the Keoghs do. At this moment, my Beloved, there is nothing I would rather do than tear off this ugly-duckling costume, make love with you, and forget all about our faith and responsibilities. But we both know that can never happen. We must not defy God, and we must not break GeeGee's heart. We must not disgrace each other or ourselves. I love you deeply and completely. Becoming your wife and sharing your life is the purpose of my life, but I have had another dream as well, for a very long time. I want to share that dream with you.

"My parents came from France. My father, Maurice, was born in 1793, on the same day that Louis XVI was guillotined. Both of his parents met the same fate soon after he was born. Arrangements were made to send him to live with my grandmother's brother, who was a teacher at the University of Tours, a beautiful, medieval city that overlooks the Loire River. He lived with his uncle and learned from him until the spring of 1811, when he was eighteen and ready to enter the university. But one day a squad of conscription agents, acting on behalf of the Emperor Napoleon, descended on the city and carted off the older boys, including my father, to become soldiers in the Grand Army.

Bruce T. Clark

"You remember from history, that in 1811, the Emperor's armies were completely successful in battle. They captured many areas of Europe. Father was assigned to the force that conquered Northern Italy. He told us that the following year, when Napoleon invaded Russia, he continued to use the same military tactics, which had worked so well throughout all of his European campaigns. Imperial armies always moved faster than their enemies did because they were not dependent on a line of supply. They foraged and lived off the land. But in Russia, because of the scorched earth policy, they could not live off the land. The entire army was stranded and forced to retreat in the dead of winter. Most of them perished! Only thirty thousand soldiers, out of several hundred thousand, survived. Father was so terribly frostbitten on the return march that his feet eventually had to be amputated. He lost a good deal in the awful cold of that bitter Russian winter on the outskirts of Moscow. But he abandoned none of his dreams.

"He returned to his studies three years after his departure with two artificial feet, but also with a renewed determination to become a teacher of great literature. To prepare for an academic career in one of the world's finest universities, he worked diligently for nine years, and earned his master teaching credentials. Then, in 1823, at the age of thirty, he and my mother, Monique, who was five years younger, married and took ship for their new home in Canada.

"For the next seventeen years my parents remained childless. Father became head of the Literature Department at the University of Montreal, and mother pursued her own career as a lithographic art illustrator. Then, in 1840, GeeGee was born, and three years later it was my turn. Father always said I was a present for his fiftieth birthday. Mother and GeeGee were very close, but I was always Father's little girl.

"My earliest recollections are of him cuddling me in his lap, and captivating my imagination with stories of places and things that he had dreamed of seeing, but never would.

122

He let me see the Loire Valley through his eyes and made me want to see it through my own.

"One day, when I was eleven, a priest from the university came to the door with sad news. While he was teaching a morning class, Father had suddenly clutched his chest, gasped once, then toppled over. Before a doctor could be summoned, he was dead. Mother had never been a strong person, and she died a year later. Only then did GeeGee and I finally realize that although Father had often sought Mother's solace, it was really she who leaned on him.

"When Mother died in 1855, GeeGee, who was fifteen, enrolled at L'Ecole a La Militaire de Quebec and I was sent to the Sisters of Charity Academy in Philadelphia. I spent the next five years with the Sisters and then returned to the University of Montreal to take up a scholarship which my father had arranged as part of his stipend. I graduated four years later with honors. I received an excellent foundation in my Catholic Faith from the Sisters and a fine education at the University of Montreal, where I majored in Romance languages, but spent a great deal of time studying the literature and works of great authors and poets.

"Almost every Sunday, after Mass and dinner at the Academy, we girls were taken on tours to various places in Philadelphia. When it was possible, I elected to visit the docks along the Delaware River, to see the sailing ships. As I stood watching them, on the Sunday that I knew would mark my final visit, I wrote about my dreams. They seemed so sentimental, once they had been set down on paper, that I have never shared them with anyone."

She took an old, dented, waterproof folder from the bottom of the picnic hamper and lovingly withdrew a tattered, well-worn paper. She carefully unfolded and smoothed it, then slowly began to read. At times her voice shook with emotion.

"Tall ships moving briskly before the wind. Stately ships which ply their fortunes around the globe. Swift ships that fly before the trade winds that take them to fabled ports of

123

call and bring them back again with exotic cargoes from the seven seas. Silks and spices from the Orient, laces from Ceylon, fragrant wood from the mysterious isles of the Pacific. They provide us with marvelous mangoes from Bombay, Guyana pineapples from the coastal plains of South America, and a plethora of other wonders from all the lands of the Earth. Today, I was able to buy some beautiful, tiny, scrimshaw handcrafts made by sailors from the bones of whales. Whenever I watch a clipper ship, with its anchor aweigh, free itself from the embrace of the land and go forth before the fickle winds, to match its frail timbers against the powers of nature and the whims of the sea, my spirit takes wing as well, and I carefully recover my father's dreams from distant corners of my mind where they have been stored, and start anew to build more dreams of my own next to his."

As she returned the paper to the protective cave, which held many more of her treasures, Catherine's eyes were misty.

"My Love, until I met you, those sights and sounds that Father instilled in my memory were a very important part of my dreams. The money from father's estate makes it financially possible for me to travel and realize my dreams before I settle down. Am I being selfish? Or foolish? If you tell me that I am, I will think of them no more."

"I don't think you're being selfish or foolish. You're an intelligent, mature woman. My only wish is for your happiness! But would a major trip like that be safe for you?"

"Every five years, the University of Montreal takes a limited number of faculty members, students, and graduates on an eighteen-month tour of Europe. The trip is chaperoned and perfectly safe. Before GeeGee and I left to come West, a letter arrived from the University inviting me on this year's tour. If I accept, I can meet them in New York City, instead of going to Montreal, but I'd have to leave at the end of next week."

"In that case, I think you should go."

"You won't be angry?"

"Of course not. While you're away, I can get my freighting business started. We can get married when you return. Being in love with you is wonderful, but I'll have to earn a fine living to support the big brood of children we're bound to have."

"I accept," said Catherine as she threw herself on Kevin and began planting kisses all over his face.

➢

Ten days later, early in the morning, Catherine kissed Kevin and GeeGee goodbye and left for Omaha with the weekly patrol.

The two old friends stood talking for a few moments after her wagon disappeared from sight. But since Lt. Colonel Custer was due to arrive at any time, Captain Gerot quickly excused himself and returned to his troop's bivouac area. All three of the companies slated to join Custer's regiment had stepped up their training schedules in order to impress their demanding new commander.

As GeeGee departed, Kevin was approached by Captain Benteen, whose stern frown indicated his agitation.

"If you're still determined to do this, I've made out all of the necessary paperwork. Sign it at the bottom."

McCarthy did as Benteen requested and returned the forms to him. A moment later, a strange looking wagon stopped beside them and McCarthy climbed up on the seat beside two burly soldiers.

"Don't worry, Captain Benteen Darlin'," chuckled the burlier of the two troopers. "I'll bring him back all safe and sound."

➢

So it was that an Irish immigrant named Kevin McCarthy, and a Sioux warrior, educated at the Virginia Military Institute, a man now called Fire Hawk, rode forth to do battle for a second time.

Although the two men would never meet face-to-face, fate had chosen to intertwine their destinies. Two very different men, but each committed to protecting the way of life he had chosen.

Their first confrontation had occurred one bright July morning on the rolling hills of Pennsylvania near a small town called Gettysburg. In that mammoth battle, one had worn blue and the other. Now they were about to meet again, in a minor but bloody skirmish.

After this encounter, more than nine years would pass before they met for a third and last time — and faced their final tests of courage. Terrible ordeals which both would pass, on a day when one man would live and the other would die.

Chapter X

➤

Indian Summer

Fort Phil Kearny
Wyoming Territory
August, 1867

Hostile eyes watched the wagon train as it disappeared from sight that morning. A short distance from the fort, within the fringe of some thick woods, three Indian warriors sat astride their ponies. One was the Cheyenne, Bobtail Horse. The others were the Hunkpapa Sioux, Growling Bear and Black Moccasin. They, along with several others, had decided to join White Wolf and his Oglala collaborators in their latest assault against the soldiers at Fort Phil Kearny. They had been sent ahead by the war chief to reconnoiter the fort and to report any unusual occurrences.

Long before sunrise, under the stealthy cloak of darkness, they had stolen down the Lodge Pole Trail, together with the Cheyenne, Two Moons. Walking their ponies slowly and carefully, they skirted around the fort, being careful not to disturb any birds or animals that, by a call of panic or flight, might alert the sleepy sentinels that patrolled the parapets. By first light, they were nearly a mile beyond the fort, on the eastern side, from which the weekly supply trains approached.

In the faint glow of dawn, Bobtail Horse detected several unusual sets of wagon tracks — parallel grooves made by very wide rims, but closer together than those of a normal freight wagon. For some unknown reason, the wheels on one side of each wagon cut deeply into the surface of the trail, while those on the opposite side did not. The warrior wondered how anything could penetrate this surface which, in the past few months, had been compacted to granite hardness by a multitude of rolling wheels.

Intrigued by the uneven tracks, the party followed them eastward toward the rising sun. They had not far to travel. Five miles from the fort, the tracks abruptly left the trail along the riverbank and turned sharply toward the south. The new trail followed a natural bench of smooth stone for a half mile and ended at an extremely large clearing, in the middle of dense pinewoods.

It was evident from the tree stumps and the many piles of cut, trimmed, and stacked logs, that the fort's woodcutters had spent a great deal of time clearing this area. With the exception of a few blackberry bushes, every other growing thing, down to the smallest sapling, had been felled for several hundred yards in every direction. In the center of the clearing, eight seven-foot-high piles of logs had been stacked in four pairs of two, which were laid at right angles to each other. Each stack of logs had been carefully bound together by stout stakes and heavy bindings.

Bobtail Horse made sure that his pony's hooves stayed on the stony trail and cautioned each of the others to do the same, lest any signs of their passage be left in the soft earth. He then studied the terrain around the clearing. Years of experience in analyzing trail signs convinced him that four of the strange wagons, each pulled by four horses and manned by three workers, had been here the last time a work detail visited the area.

All things considered, Bobtail Horse decided that he had never seen a better site for an ambush. Here was a huge clearing with no natural barriers or obstructions to hinder or trip up the war ponies. There was plenty of room to form a large and deadly moving circle around the pitifully small group of soldiers, then pick them off one by one, with only a slight risk to themselves.

Each member of the war party could hang down on the far side of his racing pony and shoot under its neck, by anchoring himself in position with a handful of mane and one heel clutching the animal's back. That foot, flattened along the spine of a swiftly galloping horse, was the defenders' single, tiny target. Every rotation of the ever-tightening circle would bring the whooping antagonists fractionally closer to their intended victims. Best of all, reasoned Bobtail Horse, the attackers would be facing fire from only twelve, slow-to-load, inaccurate, short-barreled muskets.

The scouts left the clearing, warily retracing their steps to a vantagepoint from which they could maintain a constant vigil on the stockade. Bobtail Horse sent Two Moons back to White Wolf with a suggestion that the war party attack the soldiers as soon as they returned to their logging camp. Their superior numbers would overwhelm the pathetic handful of helpless White Eyes, capture all of their ponies and guns, and take a fair number of scalps as well. Ambushing them would be child's play.

Minutes after Two Moon's departure, the gates of the fort swung open and the wagons of the weekly supply train emerged. Bobtail Horse was close enough to hear the laughter of a tall, fair-haired woman in a calico dress, who embraced first a soldier, and then another man, before scampering nimbly up to the high seat of the lead wagon, where she perched next to the blue-coated driver.

Now, as he waited for the rest of the war party to arrive, Bobtail Horse knew that their medicine was good. At the rear of the supply train, as it left the fort, were the four cumbersome, high-sided logging wagons. As soon as the caravan and their cavalry escort disappeared from sight, Bobtail Horse sent Growling Bear scurrying back up the Lodge Pole Trail to summon the war party, while he and Black Moccasin followed the White Eyes at a safe distance. As they ambled along, both men were confident that before sunset fresh scalps would be dangling from their belts.

They followed the tracks of the horses and wagons until they separated at the logging site cutoff. There, the main contingent continued eastward, and the four special wagons turned off toward the south. Once they were sure of the woodcutters' whereabouts, the two warriors backtracked and were now shielded from both the main trail and the loggers' clearing by a small stand of trees.

While they watched the woods along the far side of a narrow, shallow creek for the first signs of the approaching war party, they prepared for the upcoming battle by carefully applying war paint to themselves and their ponies, which they took from the war bags hanging around the horses' necks.

Minutes later, their vigilance was rewarded. Watching intently through a small break in the trees along the opposite bank, they glimpsed over eighty horsemen, in single file, pass through this minute opening before being lost to sight once again in the dense woods. As they watched, two riders detached themselves from the trees and splashed across the stream. The horses were a chestnut and an Appaloosa. Moments later, White Wolf and Fire Hawk drew rein and dismounted beside them. They too were painted for war.

"What have you learned, my brothers?" asked White Wolf.

"As you know, there are three Yellow Legs on each of the four wagons. There are no spare horses for any of them to use. There will be no escape," responded Bobtail Horse.

"We will send in a small group of warriors to encircle the wagons and draw the fire of the White Eyes," decided White Wolf. "If they think we are few in number, they may shoot all of their guns at once and not hold any shots in reserve. While they are reloading their weapons, the rest of the war party can ride into position and form a large circle around them. Since we are many and they are few, our fight with the wagon soldiers will be over quickly. This night there will be a scalp dance."

The four men forded the river and rode quietly for a short distance. They came to a small secluded valley, which was almost completely surrounded by towering red rocks. Within this natural fortress, they found the other members of the war party awaiting their return near a large refreshing spring. Close by, two dozen war ponies drank greedily from other springs which seeped through the rocks, while the remaining horses stood contentedly, munching lush, green, knee-deep grass.

White Wolf dismounted near a small grassy knoll, climbed to the top, and addressed the warriors as they gathered below him.

"My brothers," he said, "it is a good day to fight the Yellow Legs. It is a good day to drive them from our hunting grounds. If need be, it is a good day to die. All the woodcutters are in the center of a large, clear pasture. Except for the side that opens to the river, the rest of the area has been stripped of its thick woods. Many trees still stand on the borders of the clearing and will shield us from the Yellow Legs' eyes while we surround them.

"I will divide our warriors into two long lines and one small group of attackers. Each member of those long lines, which will be led by Gall and Man Afraid, must walk his pony quickly and quietly around the edge of the woods and string out along the east and west sides of the clearing. When the ends of the lines meet on the south side and everyone is in place, Almighty Voice will give the call of a lynx, and my strike force will attack the wagons. Thinking we are few, the soldiers may all fire at us and empty all of their rifles. If they do, every warrior must ride like the wind from the woods and overrun the wagon soldiers while they reload their weapons. If they are still firing, ride in a circle inside the clearing and continue firing while you shorten the distance. Does everyone understand?"

"War Chief, may I speak?" asked the son of He Dog.

"Speak, Bull Elk."

"I speak for myself and twelve other young warriors, including my brother, Pale Horse. We ask that you let us form the attack force and have the honor of drawing the fire of the Yellow Legs and counting coup on them. It is a fine day to take scalps and to win feathers for our warbonnets."

"What do Bull Elk and his friends plan to do?"

"Just what you and other great warriors, like our father, have taught us. We will ride toward the wagon soldiers until they lift their rifles, then we will quickly drop down to the far side of our ponies until they fire. If all of them shoot at once and empty their weapons, we will ride into their camp and kill them with our knives and tomahawks before they can reload. Otherwise we will continue to taunt them."

"It is a good plan, Bull Elk, worthy of those who showed you the ways of the warpath. Very well, you may draw the weasel's teeth. Fire Hawk, Bobtail Horse, and the rest of us will join Gall and Man Afraid, while you younger warriors bait the trap."

➢

Earlier that morning, shortly after breakfast mess and the trooping-of-the-colors ceremony, a special squad of soldiers had assembled in the fort's armory — a windowless room which contained a long string of rifle racks, all of which held obsolete, single-shot Springfield rifles. Most of these weapons had seen extended service in the hands of Union soldiers during the war.

Along one end wall were several stands, which held the sabers of the rank-and-file troopers. Next to these stands were racks especially designed to accommodate and store the Winchester Model 1866 repeating rifles which Captain Benteen and his detail had brought back from St. Louis the month before.

It was Captain Benteen who now stood at a slate board, which hung on the end wall near the saber stands. Before him, on both sides of a long weapon-repairing table, sat twelve troopers. Ten of them were privates. The others were non-commissioned officers. One was the special squad's leader, Staff Sergeant Toby Shaddick, a wily old veteran of two earlier wars. The remaining man was the fort's foremost marksman and trainer, Corporal Dickie

O'Herron. For the past six weeks, he had been assisting Shaddick with the special unit's preparation. Although they were exact opposites, the pair worked very well together.

Dickie O'Herron was very tall and as thin as a rapier. The soft brown hair, which hung down around his shoulders, failed to hide an exceptionally long neck. His physical appearance, coupled with his surname, accounted for most people referring to him as the Stork. He had grown up in the hills of Kentucky and was a deadly rifleman. He rarely spoke, and when he did, his words came forth in a slow, exasperating nasal twang. He insisted that his proficiency with a rifle was so well-known that once a grizzly bear, over two miles away, had stopped eating honey and raised a paw in salute the minute he saw the Stork. Then he raced up and surrendered on the spot, knowing that if the Stork could see him, the Stork could kill him.

Toby Shaddick, on the other hand, was short and very round. Not fat, just round! Huge burly shoulders, extending out from an almost nonexistent neck, were wreathed by long, black, curly hair, which reached below the level of his collar. His wide chin and upper lip were concealed by a grand growth of whiskers, which had been molded into a handsome beard and full, wide mustache. His appearance would have been foreboding and sinister had it not been relieved by a pair of sparkling, bright blue eyes, and a huge, red-veined, frequently broken, putty-soft nose — a proboscis that appeared to have been dabbed on by God as a humorous afterthought. It could safely be said that his unique Irish mug would never be duplicated.

His friends, who were numbered in the hundreds, called him Villain. He had just finished his twentieth year in the military. For more than a dozen of those years, Villain had been the boxing champion of his various regiments. He was still a man of awesome power and legendary determination. He had three weaknesses in life: small children, soft women, and most of all, hard liquor. On hot summer days, Villain sweated alcohol. But in a fistfight, or a shooting war, he was the man everyone wanted to have next to him.

Captain Benteen, the squad's commandant, finished reviewing their mission and diagramming probable tactics on the board, then turned to face the troopers.

"Any questions?"

"Captain," asked Shaddick, "how sure are Raven Wing and the other scout that there are hostiles in the area?"

"They're convinced of it, Sergeant, and so am I. According to last night's duty officer, Lieutenant Harris, a rain that was heavy enough to erase all the old marks and signs fell for a short time around 3:00 A.M. This morning, an hour after sunrise, Raven Wing and Crawling Cat found four fresh sets of unshod pony tracks coming down from the Lodge Pole Trail. There was only one set going back. We must assume that at least three hostiles are still close by."

"Could they be a hunting party, sir?" queried a trooper named O'Leary.

"Raven Wing says no. A four-man hunting party would have no reason to send one of their number back up the trail. Four men are not enough for an effective nuisance raid. No, O'Leary, I'm convinced that they're advance scouts for a major war party. They haven't hit us since they got Fetterman. It's time. Besides, if they are just troublemakers, there's very little we can do about it. But we can do a lot about a war party, and we will! Anything else? Very well, the mission is on! Set it in motion, Sergeant."

"Right ye are, sir. Well now, me buckos, let's be hitching the lovely animals to the fine wagons and be going out to harass the heathens."

Corporal O'Herron took charge as the troopers shouldered their packs and weapons. Eight of them paired off. Each grasped an end handle and helped to lift one of four large, identical trunks. They left the armory, staggering under the enormous weight of the loads, crossed the parade ground to the area where their special vehicles were parked, and gratefully loaded one trunk into each of the wagons.

While this was happening, Villain, in company with Troopers O'Leary and Fahey, headed for the Sutler's store to replenish their supply of tobacco and sweets. They still had money enough in the squad fund to buy a few things for them all. Small treats that would help them endure what promised to be a long, hot day.

As they entered the store, Shaddick spotted an old friend.

"And how are ye, this fine mornin', Captain, darlin'?"

"I'm fine, Villain. How are Sally and Carrie?" responded Kevin McCarthy.

"The Missus is as grand as ever she was, and Carrie's gone off to school in St. Louis. She's going to be a teacher, she is."

"It doesn't seem possible. I still think of her as the tiny girl that I used to watch over when Sally got so sick, back at Fort Defiance. I was only nine or ten years old at the time."

"I don't know what we would have done without you and your Pa in those days. God rest his blessed soul."

"I'm sorry I missed Carrie. When did she leave?"

"Just a month past. She'll be home for a while at Christmas. Well, Captain, darlin', we're off to harass the heathen."

"Really?" asked McCarthy. "What's on tap?"

"Ah! There's a word that sets me mouth to waterin'. But we're going off to a big brouhaha, and that's for certain."

Kevin drew a full explanation about the mission from Sergeant Shaddick, who, seeing the mounting excitement in his old friend's eyes, invited him along if he could get permission from Captain Benteen. But Kevin found the Captain adamant in his refusal.

"I will not accept the responsibility!" he told McCarthy. "If anything happened to you, I would be court-martialed. I think you're trying to forget about Catherine being gone by creating an exciting diversion for yourself."

"Without any doubt, Fred, that's a part of it. But I also want to go because Villain asked me to. Besides, I'm pretty good at laying out ambushes. I've sure been involved in enough of them."

"As long as you are a civilian, Kevin, you can forget it!"

But permission was finally, if reluctantly, granted when Kevin enlisted as a special army scout for a term of twenty-four hours.

➢

And so it was that a short time later, a white strike force, composed of a traditionally unlucky number of thirteen members, set out to ambush members of a red strike force whose first wave of attackers would, ironically, also number thirteen. On this day, they unwittingly carved out an adventure that would transcend time and space. For Shaddick's sharpshooters and White Wolf's warriors were about to clash in a brief but bitter battle which history would forever remember as the Wagon Box Fight.

Chapter XI

➤

The Wagon Box Fight

Sioux Hunting Grounds
Wyoming Territory
August, 1867

Before they left their sanctuary in the sheltered valley, White Wolf and his warriors split into three groups. As they emerged, Gall and his party rode off toward the southeast in order to intercept and cross the creek a mile upstream from the loggers' position. Since a strong east wind was blowing, they were forced to move slowly toward the clearing, lest they raise a dust cloud, which might alert the cutters. Man Afraid's column, which now included White Wolf, Fire Hawk, and the original group of decoys, angled out toward the southwest for an anticipated crossing well beyond the tree line on the clearing's opposite side. Bull Elk, Pale Horse, and their friends would wait until they heard Almighty Voice's lynx, then ford the stream and move forward at once to the attack.

Meanwhile, at the logging area, no one was cutting, stacking, or doing anything with logs. Each of the four wagons, with its crew of three, had been pulled into the openings between the high piles of logs. The logs and wagons, which had seemed so innocent when viewed separately, took on a far different appearance when seen together.

Now, the eight impenetrable stacks of logs, laid out as they were in right-angled pairs, formed four corners of an ingenious stockade. The specially constructed wagons became the fort walls. One side of each wagon was built with a double-ply construction. The inner wall slid upward to become an upper wall. When this sliding section was secured into position on top of the wagon's original sides, a seven-foot-high wall was created. It not only shielded the wagon's occupants, but also formed a safe corral for the teams of horses.

The final inventive touches were equally clever. Two custom-fitted, paper-thin sheets of metal, painted to resemble canvas and stored in the wagons during transit, were moved into position. One sheet formed a protective roof, while the other hung down over the side of the wagon that faced the enemy. The purpose of these coverings was to ward off any flaming arrows that might be fired at the mobile fortress.

The mystery of wheel tracks being deeper on one side than the other was explained. The outer walls were made from heavy, four-inch-thick slabs of oak, which no bullet could penetrate. Into these outside walls, rows of loopholes had been cut. The riflemen inside could open them to shoot, or close them up for protection. The reason the tracks were not consistently deeper on the left or right was also apparent. Two of the wagons had thick walls on the right, while the thick walls of the other two were on the left. They were designed to be used singly or in pairs. This was the military thrashing machine that awaited the jubilant Sioux and Cheyenne who were, at that moment, moving in covert fashion to ambush "a pathetic handful of helpless White Eyes."

As he rode Star Walker slowly behind White Wolf's Chestnut, Fire Hawk felt an overwhelming surge of uneasiness. Not for himself, but for his companions. His agreement with Crazy Horse and White Wolf was straightforward and simple. He would not take part in fights against white men that he knew. Since he had spent a good deal of time at Fort Phil Kearny, this was one of those occasions. All the same, the farther they rode, the stronger his feelings of uneasiness became.

Then he realized what was missing. He had heard no sounds of chopping since their circuit of the woods began. Surely, at this hour of the morning, no noncommissioned officer would allow his entire work force to rest. Then another possible solution came to mind. They could be using two-man buck saws rather than axes. The softer sounds of the coarse-toothed blades biting into the wood would not be audible for a very great distance.

Momentarily that thought allowed him to relax, before another disquieting one took its place. Why did one set of wagon wheels always bear so much more weight than the other? Obviously, some type of small, but very heavy loads were being hauled back and forth. What kind of cargo was small enough to be carried on one side of a wagon, but heavy enough to cut through a road surface? The most perplexing problem was why did the tracks indicate the same weight distribution, coming out and going back in? Neither the axes and saws, nor even the hauling block and tackle would weigh enough to make a difference in the tracks. Of course, all the ruts would be deeper on return trips, because then the wagons were hauling heavy logs. The more he puzzled over the enigma, the more confused he became.

These profound reflections, however, did not affect his vigilance, as a short distance ahead he detected movements which heralded the arrival of Gall's detachment. The clearing's encirclement had been completed.

As soon as White Wolf was certain everyone was in position and ready to go, he gave the prearranged signal to Almighty Voice. A moment later the scream of a hunting cougar split the air. Before the echo of the big cat's eerie cry had died away, a clatter of hooves and a chorus of war whoops came rolling up from the creek. The chiefs who were in charge of the various groups of warriors surrounding the clearing's perimeter moved out of the trees to positions which allowed a line-of-sight view of each other, and also of Bull Elk's band as it thundered down upon the four wagons and the piles of logs.

Fire Hawk and White Wolf sat astride their restless mounts and watched as the young warriors raced in toward the wagons, still two hundred yards away. They could see them bobbing up and down, constantly weaving their hard-running ponies from side to side, encouraging the animals to move forward in an erratic manner. They fired almost continually while jerking their bodies about in violent contortions. Each man was intent on presenting as poor a target as possible while offering fleeting, yet inviting, shots to the marksmen within the circle.

All at once, the wagons erupted in a blaze of rifle fire and a cloud of smoke. Trying to count the shots, White Wolf and Fire Hawk estimated ten or twelve. Riding much closer to the action, Bull Elk, Pale Horse and their allies were counting as well. It had been a wild and ragged volley of fire. Not a single shot had found its mark. Every rifle within the circle of wagons must now be empty. Bull Elk smiled at the foolishness of the Yellow Legs and at his own good fortune. Now he could rush forward, leading the young warriors who followed him, count coup, slaughter the White Eyes, and become a great hero.

He pictured his triumphant return to the village with strings of new ponies and dangling scalps. He could imagine the respect in Yellow Bird's eyes as she came out of her father's lodge to welcome him, pleased at the prospect of becoming his woman.

Since empty rifles did not need to be feared, Bull Elk pulled himself erect on his buckskin mustang's back, beckoned to his followers, and charged directly at the now defenseless wagon soldiers.

Suddenly he felt as though a war club had been rammed into his ribs! It was such a violent blow that a wave of dizziness engulfed him and made it difficult to maintain his seat on the racing pony. He bent far forward, striving to recover his balance by pressing his chest against the horse's straining neck. He twined his fingers into the buckskin's flowing mane and gripped the heaving shoulders as tightly as possible with his knees.

He felt an alien wetness on his neck and shoulder, and thought for a moment that a stray bullet might have struck the pony. He looked down and noticed with detached curiosity an ever-widening streak of crimson as it coursed across his chest. Since there was no sensation of pain, he tried to remain calm and solve his dilemma. This makes no sense, he reasoned; empty guns can't shoot me. That was his last thought! The next instant a heavy rifle bullet struck the bridge of his nose and tore away the top of his head. Bull Elk was dead before his tense muscles relaxed enough to allow his limp, mutilated body to topple to the ground.

He lay there among the corpses of his followers, as their now riderless ponies, screaming in confused panic, momentarily milled about in frightened groups of twos and threes, before they fled from the circle of death.

The wagon soldiers' first ragged volley had been a deliberate ruse, designed to encourage the brave young warriors to abandon their defensive tactics and charge forward. The subsequent fusillades that shredded the Sioux ranks had been well-executed and deadly.

As echoes from the final rain of death died away and a busy wind lifted the heavy curtains of gun smoke from the brutal stage, bright sunlight suddenly peeped through the clouds and smiled a silent salute down upon this field of honor and place of pride, a tribute to those who lay upon newly hallowed ground, who could see no more through sightless eyes.

Inside the wagon fortress, amid the predictable smiles of success, all else remained calm and expectant. During the Indians' first charge, shots had rained down upon the walls of the armored wagons, but none had penetrated the thick sides. In the first lull, Shaddick spoke to the squad that had gathered in the middle of the quadrangle.

"Well, laddies, we surprised them and we've hurt them, but they'll be back, right enough."

"Is it time to send up the signal, Sarge?" asked O'Herron.

141

"No! Let's see what we're up against before we deal another hand into the game. We can defend against a force ten times our own number. We have a clear field of fire in all directions, and they may allow us to give them another lesson before they run. All right, to yer posts and keep a sharp eye."

"What kind of signal was Stork talking about, Villain?" asked Kevin McCarthy as they climbed back into their war wagon.

"Colonel Carrington has placed the three companies that are going with Custer on alert. Captain Keogh's, Captain Gerot's, and Captain Benteen's. That's nearly a hundred and fifty men. A third of the force at the fort. If we need their help, our orders are to light that mound of logs, a hundred yards off to our right, in front of Dickie's wagon. They've been covered with pitch and they'll raise the devil's own cloud of black smoke. Short minutes after they're lit, our own lads will come ridin' in to save us, and in a twinklin', the good times will be over."

"It's too dangerous for anyone to go out to those logs, Villain."

"Ah, but there's no need, Captain darlin'. Can ye see the wee red rag hangin' in the logs from here?" When Kevin nodded, the Sergeant continued.

"Right behind it is a small keg of gunpowder. When Stork's bullet hits that powder keg, the fire will spring up to high heaven. The lads at the fort will have no trouble seein' that."

"Do you think the Indians will be back soon?" McCarthy asked.

"I know they'll be back soon. They're out there right now, makin' up a plan."

Shaddick turned toward the other men who shared the command wagon and spoke to a trooper with a mop of carrot-colored hair and freckles to match. "Red, you'd better open up that armory trunk and get things ready.

Kevin watched with interest as the youngster jumped to obey his sergeant's order.

Shaddick was correct about the war party. A short distance away a strategy meeting was underway. The participants were White Wolf, Gall, Man Afraid, American Horse, Tall Bull, Bobtail Horse, and Fire Hawk, who said; "Those troopers are armed with repeating rifles. Before I left the fort, there was much talk about them. Like this Henry rifle I hold, those new weapons will fire many times without being reloaded."

"The new weapons defeated Bull Elk and his warriors. They did nothing wrong in their attack," said White Wolf. "If I had been the leader, I would be lying on the ground where he lies now."

Gall spun his pinto pony around to face White Wolf. Fire Hawk noticed that the Hunkpapa's war-painted face had twisted up to resemble a gargoyle. Gall's struggle to control his voice and temper were obvious as he spoke.

"What is your plan now, war chief?"

"We must drive the White Eyes out of their wagons and kill them in the open."

"What would make them come out?" asked Bobtail Horse.

"We must set the wagons on fire." said the leader. "We will shoot flaming arrows into them and set them ablaze. The stacks of green logs will not burn, but the heat from the burning wagon wood will drive the Yellow Legs out."

"Bull Elk proved that drawing near the wagon circle means death," pointed out Gall. "And burning arrows cannot reach the wagons from the trees."

"You are right about both of those things, my brother," acknowledged White Wolf. "But we can send in a long line of warriors with one burning arrow each. They can shoot short buffalo bows from under their ponies' necks and drive them into the sides of the wagons, or over the top of the walls, to the inside of the wagons."

Fire Hawk spoke.

143

"Your plan is good, but it can be even better."

"How, my brother?"

"Stagger the bowmen with riflemen."

White Wolf looked puzzled, so Fire Hawk continued.

"Between every two riflemen rides a bowman. The riflemen can lay down a heavy fire to protect the fire makers. You have over eighty warriors. Divide them up into two groups. Let those who are the best shooters of arrows use bows, and everyone else can carry rifles."

White Wolf and the others saw the wisdom in his plan and agreed instantly.

➢

[Since most people are naturally right-handed, soldiers of every army are taught to shoot from the right shoulder. Plains Indians were no different. They shot rifles right-handed and fired their short buffalo bows the same way, holding the bow in their left hands, along with a handful of pony mane, and pulling back the bowstring with their right or strong hands. Arrows were then launched over or under the neck of a wildly galloping pony. To accommodate these firing procedures they usually circled an objective in a counterclockwise manner. That is, approaching from the defender's right and going away to his left.

The soldiers of the Great Plains regiments also shot from the right shoulder, clutched the pistol grips of their rifle stocks with right hands, pulled triggers with the right forefingers, and used their right eyes to aim through iron sights positioned along the tops of the rifle barrels.

This "right side preoccupation" tended to minimize the view of anything coming across the field of vision from the right side to the left. Sometimes a target was directly in front of them before it could be seen clearly. This afforded little time to properly aim and fire. The riflemen's left eyes had an unobstructed view of a disappearing danger that their right eyes found difficult to detect during its approach.

The era of single-shot breechloading rifles had little effect on firing procedures, which had been employed since the advent of muzzle-loaders, hundreds of years before. The rifles still had to be removed from the shoulder and reloaded with single cartridges. And spent cartridges still had to be ejected from the chamber before fresh ones could be inserted into firing position. Breechloaders were, of course, easier and faster, since black powder no longer needed to be measured and poured into the muzzle; round bullets no longer had to be held in place with a greased patch and rammed down the length of the barrel with a ramrod; and the rifle no longer required priming with a cap before each shot.

Even with the advent of breech-loading weapons, very few riflemen were capable of performing all the necessary functions without looking. Therefore, most lost all visual contact with the tactical situation during those precious seconds which reloading required. When the rifle was finally ready, the user returned the heavy weapon to his shoulder, located a new target, and tried to align the rear sight with the front one, holding the rifle steady for long enough to hit a moving target, which in many cases was bobbing about on the back of a dancing war pony.

Is it surprising, then, that for every shot that found its mark, ten others did not? Or that the Plains Indians were so disdainful of the enemy that they willingly offered themselves as targets? Bull Elk had every right to be surprised!

On this hot August day in 1867, many things conspired against White Wolf and his fellow attackers. The Winchester Model 1866 repeating rifle was much lighter than the old Civil War weapons. They now had "built-in magazines" which could store a dozen or more cartridges in the rifle's receiver until such time as they were needed.

After each shot, a lever under the pistol grip was thrust down and then pulled back into the firing position. On the downstroke a spent cartridge was expelled, and on the upstroke a new one was removed from storage within the magazine and moved up to the firing chamber.

Most of all, the riflemen had been coached by Dickie O'Herron. His training had produced a squad of experts. His system was as simple as it was ingenious. After each shot, the butt of the rifle was removed from the shoulder and lowered toward the hip, while a fresh round was being levered into position. This permitted a clear, unobstructed view of the entire killing zone. As soon as he selected his next target, usually from the approaching enemies on his right, the shooter aimed his front sight directly at that target. When the re-levering stroke was completed he raised the rifle to his shoulder, and as soon as his rear sight aligned with the base of his front sight, he squeezed the trigger without any further aiming. This system completely stopped the wavering and shaking so common to earlier systems. Each squad member had been taught to hit a man-sized moving target, seventy-five yards away, eight times out of ten. Every bullet found a target when Bull Elk and his warriors closed to a distance of only thirty yards.

Now as the Sioux and Cheyenne raiders, their plans completed, assembled for the next attack, they were about to be confronted by many formidable problems. Their arrow fires would fail because of the metal coverings. The rifle fire would not succeed because of the thick, bulletproof walls. And if that was not enough, yet another surprise awaited them in the armory trunks. A number of new tactics would be tried during the balance of this skirmish, and the success of each would be measured in Indian lives.]

➢

Five hundred yards from the wagons, White Wolf's division awaited Almighty Voice's signal. He had sent Man Afraid, Gall, and their half of the force through the woods on the east side of the clearing to a position past the wagons. From there, riding in single file, they would attack the north and west sides of the wagon fort. White Wolf and his warriors would charge in from the south end of the clearing, and attack the wagons on the south and east sides. They would continue this deadly circle of fire until the White Eyes were driven from their wagons.

Realizing that the Yellow Legs at Fort Phil Kearny might hear sounds from the fight with the wagon soldiers, White Wolf sent He Dog back along the trail to watch for any approaching forces. Fire Hawk was dispatched to find a circuitous line of retreat around the fort. By the time this skirmish ended, the Lodge Pole Trail almost certainly would be blocked by military patrols, eager for revenge.

At that moment the signal cougar screamed. Seconds later, White Wolf had Chestnut in a dead run, leading a line of whooping warriors, thirty strong, that charged across the meadow in united resolve.

Since he led the charge, the war chief did not see the first, dismal results as they occurred behind him. As each arrow hit a wagon's metal side or top, it fell harmlessly to the ground. The intervening rifle fire was no more effective. Meanwhile, the return fire from the wagon stockade had a devastating effect.

Knowing from experience that the warriors would be clinging to the far sides of their mounts, O'Herron trained his sharpshooters to concentrate fire on the only available target, the rider's left leg. That leg, clamped tightly against the pony's spine, along with a handful of the mane, was all that held these gifted horsemen in position. The swiftly moving targets, legs from knee to toes, were less than two feet long and extended only a few inches above the animal's back. Nevertheless, during the first complete circle, nearly a third of the warriors were unhorsed by the uncanny marksmanship of the riflemen. Once they were on the ground, another well-aimed bullet killed them within seconds.

Looking back over Chestnut's haunches, White Wolf realized that his war party had been decimated. A dozen

147

ponies lay in grotesque positions, writhing in pain, and nearly half of the warriors who had left the hidden valley a few hours before, now lay dead and still.

Realizing that another circuit would bring about more death and tragedy, White Wolf broke off the circle and charged back down the meadow, followed by the now-silent survivors. He halted the limping Chestnut at the end of the clearing, two hundred fifty yards from the wagons, beyond the range of the deadly rifles.

As he looked back, he noticed blood on his horse's hip. He dismounted to examine Chestnut's wounds more closely and felt severe pains shooting through his own foot and up his leg.

Chestnut had suffered two wounds, on his hip and upper leg. The leg wound was minor, but the one on his haunch would take some time to heal. It would not impair his ability to run, since no muscles had been torn, but it was both deep and painful.

White Wolf had not been as fortunate. He had been shot through the fleshy part of his left calf and another bullet had torn away two of his middle toes. From his medicine pouch, he took salves and unguents, which would stop the flow of blood and promote the healing process. He applied these to Chestnut's wounds, then smeared them liberally on his own. All around him, others were tending their own wounds and those of their ponies.

Minutes later, just as the first aid was being completed, they heard strange whirling sounds overhead. Before anyone could move, four mortar shells exploded near them. Three of these, grapeshot-filled canisters, inflicted a few minor wounds to nearby warriors and their horses. But the fourth mortar exploded directly between Growling Bear and Two Moons, killing them instantly. Before any more mortars could be fired, the bowed and bloodied attackers jumped on their ponies and raced away. As they galloped along the woods on the eastern side of the clearing, an explosion from a small pile of logs near the middle of the open area startled them. The timbers began burning fiercely and sent a towering column of thick black smoke into the air.

As they neared the creek, the warriors halted their mounts and waited as two riders pounded toward them on hard-charging horses. White Wolf recognized Star Walker, and moments later Fire Hawk and He Dog stopped beside them.

"I have found a way around the fort," Fire Hawk told White Wolf, "and He Dog says the black smoke was a signal for many soldiers to come here quickly."

"We will return to the hidden valley, my brother," responded White Wolf, "and wait until the White Eyes go back. After dark, we will return and recover the bodies of our dead. They were brave and deserve to be given warriors' burials. This is a sad day for our nation."

"White Wolf," replied Fire Hawk, "a chief who can win every battle has yet to be born. We will fight again, on other days."

➢

Back at the wagons, the troopers were preparing to harness the teams and load their equipment.

"A successful day, Villain," said McCarthy.

"It was that. But sad as well. I hate to see brave men die."

"They've killed plenty of us!" said the private called Red. "Remember the boys with Captain Fetterman?"

"We've killed plenty of them, too, lad. They may not quit until they're all dead. And by then, most of us may be dead as well," he added prophetically.

A short time later, the wagons were loaded and ready to go. As McCarthy and Shaddick sat waiting on the high seat of the lead wagon, they were astonished to hear the sound of a military band. Minutes later, at the end of the clearing, the advance elements of the relief column hove into view. It was the troop of Captain Myles Keogh.

Behind this unit came the band, their brass instruments gleaming in the sun. McCarthy and Shaddick remembered the band's lilting tune as the Garyowen.

Between Captain Keogh and his company were two color bearers, holding aloft Old Glory and the proud regimental banner. In the van, beside Keogh's drab claybank sorrel, danced a big, beautiful blood bay stallion. Astride this magnificent animal sat a truly magnificent officer, regaled in an eloquent gold-braided uniform. His gold-laced hat and gold-hilted sword fittingly complemented his flowing, golden hair.

Brevet (Temporary Rank) Major General, now Lt. Colonel George Armstrong Custer, had come to the Great Plains.

➢

Not far away, a painful procession was approaching the hidden valley. Covering their retreat, Fire Hawk heard the music, too. He had last heard the Garyowen played at Appomattox Court House in Virginia. The band of the First Michigan Cavalry was playing it. It had meant Custer then and it meant Custer now. It also meant trouble for friend and foe alike.

Fire Hawk made certain that there would be no pursuit and rode toward the valley. Inside the natural fortress, he dismounted next to White Wolf, who was leaning against a large rock, trying to ignore his pain.

"I am sorry about your wounds, Wolf. If you will allow me, I will bandage them."

"As you wish, Hawk. They will remind me of a terrible day."

"When they heal, they will remind you of deeds to be done and fights to be won."

Fire Hawk took the Spanish knife from its sheath and cut a soft doeskin into strips. He cleansed the wounds and bound up White Wolf's leg securely. Next he packed green mulberry leaves against the stumps of the toes, before covering and cushioning them with thick pads, made by folding over several layers of the same doeskin. These he tied in place with wet rawhide. When the rawhide dried, it would harden and form a firm, protective cast over White Wolf's foot and toes. Jolting from riding horseback would still be painful, but at least it would now be bearable.

"You are truly my brother, Hawk," said White Wolf.

"Did you not say it would be so, the night you gave me this Spanish knife, Wolf?"

He held up the knife and studied the inscription.

TOLEDO ESPAÑA - MCDLIV

What a fascinating history this marvelous old weapon must have after so many years, he thought. Having been forged in Spain, in 1454, it might even have been brought to America by one of the Conquistadors, as far back as the 1520's. He wondered about the many hands that had wielded the knife before it eventually came into the possession of the Comanche from whom White Wolf had won it.

He smiled as he returned the weapon to its sheath on his belt, then turned to White Wolf and said: "On my way back to the valley I saw an old enemy from my last war. While we wait for darkness, I will tell you about him. His name is George Custer."

PART FIVE

"THE ONLY GOOD INDIANS ..."

Chapter XII

➤

Harbingers

Montana Territory
August 25, 1868

Kevin McCarthy left his riverfront freight office in the late morning and strolled slowly down to the docks. His timing was excellent. The Titus B. Turner was just beginning to breast the current and move in toward the dock. His partner was coming in on the riverboat, and they were meeting for lunch in the finest restaurant afloat. Actually, the only good one. It was enjoying such success that the other river packets would soon follow suit. Appropriately, it was called the Harbinger. A very clever name, thought Kevin.

As soon as the gangplank was lowered, he made his way to the main deck and then aft toward the spacious dining room.

An impressive voice announced an equally impressive presence.

"Right this way, Kevin me lad," roared Kerry Kelly. "And take the edge off your terrible thirst."

Kevin approached his partner with an outstretched hand, but as usual, that was an insufficient greeting for the big Irishman, who enveloped McCarthy in a burly bear hug.

"How are you, Mule Skinner?"

"Good, Kerry. How was your trip?"

"Very profitable."

"Aren't they all?"

"Not like this one. But I may have some trouble with one of the losers."

"What's his problem?"

"He makes dumb bets, then curses his bad luck. Typical loser!"

"Well, all of my news is good. The Big Bart Mine has awarded us the hauling contract. For a full year! In the first six months, we'll be able to pay for the additional equipment that we'll need to meet the terms of the contract. That means a nice profit in the final six months. Of course, any extension of the contract will hinge on our overall performance."

"McCarthy and Kelly Freight Express is turning a better profit than Harry and Curt at the B-Bar-B," Kerry announced happily.

"It's a far different business out here. We have an element of danger much greater than Harry and Curt's. Back there, they use one driver on a run and once in a while a guard goes along. Out here, I have to use one or two shotgun guards on every trip. Because of the rough terrain, our mule teams need six or eight animals, not the usual four. Higher expenses are reflected in higher charges. Because of those conditions our employees are paid more, but we realize a slightly better profit margin."

"Well, Partner, as long as we're solvent."

"We're much more than that. I transacted our first contract ten months ago, and last week McCarthy and Kelly showed a net profit for the year."

"You mean our entire investment has been recovered?"

"That's right. We've paid for the mules, the wagons, and all of our initial start-up expenses. We are now showing a profit."

Kelly gave him a hearty slap on the back and said, "Kevin that's great! You've done a first-rate job."

"Thanks, Kerry, but it was easy. Remember the lesson you gave me, long ago, about playing winning poker? Well, most of the business principles I've employed are part of your poker table wisdom. I just converted them to the freight business."

"Well, in that case, let's order a bottle of champagne! We'll celebrate my brilliance and your adaptability!"

Inside the Harbinger, they selected a table on the side away from the dock, which provided a panoramic view of the river. They ordered lunch, then sat sipping excellent vintage champagne.

"What's the latest news from Catherine?" Kerry asked.

"She'll be in Paris until the end of August, then they're going to Geneva. She seems to be enjoying herself very much."

"When is she scheduled to return?"

"I'm going to New York to meet her, next May 18."

Just then a disheveled, red-faced man staggered up to their table. His rocking stance and bloodshot eyes gave mute testimony to his alcoholic condition. Kevin assumed this was the man Kerry expected to cause trouble. As he mouthed slurred words, his caustic breath made the partners recoil in their seats.

"Kelly," he slurred, "someone in that game last night cheated me."

"Mr. Terhune, you are absolutely correct," Kelly responded. "You cheated yourself by playing."

"Whaddya mean?" slobbered Mr. Terhune.

"At eight o'clock last night, Bill Shaw dealt a hand of draw poker and announced that a pair of jacks or better were required to open. Four of us drew cards, Mr. Terhune, and you called every bet, to the very end of the game. You didn't raise in order to bluff us out; you merely stayed in because you seemed to think your cards might win. All you had at the end was a pair of nines. You threw your money away by staying in a game where the man who opened had you beaten, even before he drew any cards. If that's not cheating yourself, I don't know what is!"

Mr. Terhune, unable to remain standing under his own power any longer, slumped into a chair, as Kerry Kelly continued.

"At half past eight, you fell asleep on the table. A short time later, two of the porters carried you down to your cabin. At nine o'clock you were back, insisting that you be allowed to play. For the next hour, we tried to ignore you. Finally, you passed out. To keep you from being robbed, Shaw and I emptied your pockets and turned your cash over to the purser. You had twenty-two dollars. Does that sound like someone cheated you?"

"I dun't b'leve ya," stammered Mr. Terhune. "I lost close to a hunner dodgers and I'm gonna take 'em outer yer hide."

"Mr. Terhune," Kelly said stonily, "you distress me. You need a keeper, but never again will I be tempted to perform that servile task."

"I'll git even wiz ya," simpered Mr. Terhune.

Kevin had finally had enough. He exploded out of his chair, braved Terhune's toxic exhalations, and seized the quivering man's collar in an iron grip, nearly throttling him in the process.

"Mr. Terhune, you are a nuisance, a menace, and a stench in my nostrils. But since you might, at some point, become dangerous, I am forced to speak to you. You don't have the courage to face Kerry Kelly because you are a sniveling coward. However, you might be tempted to bushwhack him. In case you ever consider that, remember this. Kerry Kelly is my friend, my partner, and one of the most honest men I have ever known. You better start praying for his future every night and crossing your fingers for luck to shine on him every day.

"Mr. Terhune, if my friend is killed, or if he dies, or if he has an accident, or if lightning comes down from a stormy summer sky and strikes him dead, I'm going to blow your alcohol-soaked head clean off! It won't make one damned bit of difference to me if you're in China when that lightning strikes! I'm going to blow your head clear off! Do you understand me?"

Suddenly much more alert, Terhune nodded.

"Mr. Terhune," intoned Kevin, "if you understand me, you had better say so."

"I understand," came a far more intelligible reply.

"Good! Please remember that I saved your life here today. I hope you will always be grateful. Now, you may go. Mr. Terhune."

The crestfallen, would-be troublemaker's rubbery legs carried him out the door faster than the laughing friends could believe.

"Kevin, I'm glad you're my friend, because I sure wouldn't want you for an enemy."

"Kerry, you are handicapped by some sort of romantic code. I suffer no such scruples. When someone I care about is threatened, I come at that threat by the shortest possible route, fast as a striking snake, carrying the most dangerous weapon I can find. One day, you're going to try sweet-talking some dangerous man and he's going to kill you." He stopped and clapped his friend on the shoulder. "You know I only holler at people I care about, don't you?"

"I know, Kevin, and I do appreciate your friendship. I'm just not a warrior."

"My friend, every one of us needs to be a warrior sometimes."

Chapter XIII

➢

The Ghosts of Battles Past

Sioux Hunting Camp
Sand Creek
Colorado Territory
August 25, 1868

On the same afternoon that Kevin and Kerry had lunch, nearly six hundred miles away, in the southeast corner of the Colorado Territory, were gathered a hundred men who were always warriors.

Outside the wickiup of Fire Hawk and his mother, Night Wind, more than a dozen warriors sat and rested after consuming an enormous meal of hump meat and tongue. The great northern herd of buffalo, for some unknown reason, had not come to their normal summer range this year. Even the oldest people in the tribe could not remember this ever happening before. Since Pte had not come to the Sioux, it had been necessary for them to travel far to the south to seek good hunting. Now, Crazy Horse's village of Oglalas was camped next to Dull Knife's Northern Cheyennes.

The huge herd had stopped to graze on the grassy plains along the banks of Sand Creek, and it was here that the two camps had been pitched. The numerous teepees, painted every hue that nature could conjure, splashed a panorama of color along the river's edge for nearly a mile. In the twinkling twilight, as those colors were reflected in the lazy, rippling stream, the display offered by the watery rainbow should have created a festive mood. But this was a place of great sadness, where even the laughter of children was rarely heard.

➢

[Four years before, Chief Black Kettle and 500 Cheyennes had been camped at this exact spot when they were attacked, suddenly and viciously, by Colonel J. M. Chivington and members of the Third Colorado Territorial Militia. Swooping in before dawn, the militiamen claimed to have scored a colossal victory. And it was, numerically. These "courageous men," fighting to protect Colorado from a "howling horde of vicious savages," slaughtered two hundred seventy "dangerous aborigines" on that heroic morning in 1864.

The mighty militia did not suffer one single casualty.

Late in 1863, Black Kettle had agreed to peace terms and had accepted an American flag as a symbol of his new allegiance. On the day of the Sand Creek Massacre, that banner was proudly flying over his lodge. Chivington's militia members, many of whom had been gathered from the bars and brothels of Denver, ignored the flag. They rode through the village, shooting anything that moved. Black Kettle was fortunate. He escaped, unharmed. His wife was not as lucky. Although she managed to elude pursuit, she was shot several times during her flight. Seventy elderly Southern Cheyenne men were killed that day, along with two hundred women and children, many of them tiny babies held in their mothers' bloody arms. The heartless murderers even killed a six-year-old girl who carried a white flag of surrender. The white men scalped a large number of these helpless, yet somehow dangerous Indian insurgents. Many others suffered worse humiliations and mutilations. Dozens of women underwent crude mastectomies. Fingers and ears were cleft from the living as well as the dead. Most were kept as mementos, but others were sold as commemorative souvenirs of the militia's great victory.

Colorado's leading newspapers called it a great victory and proclaimed that "the heart of the Cheyenne resistance has been cut away." They should have added that if the "heart" had not "been cut away," it was the only organ that hadn't been. Sand Creek would always be a place of sadness for just and moral men of every race, a place to grieve and sense the restless souls of many innocent victims who would forever wander, and wonder why.

When news of this merciless slaughter reached Sioux ears, they began attacking every wagon train foolish enough to venture into their territory. For the next dozen years, the Cheyenne and Sioux fought the White Eyes, and three new names were written in blood across the frontier: Red Cloud, Sitting Bull, and Crazy Horse.

Being older and perhaps a bit less energetic than the others, Red Cloud eventually surrendered and embraced the white man's ways. But appeasement and surrender were not the route chosen by the others. Sitting Bull and Crazy Horse never surrendered. They fought for justice until they were murdered. Heroes to the end.]

➢

In the last of the twilight, Fire Hawk watched a beloved figure approaching. It was Little Fawn, in company with a Cheyenne Dog Soldier unknown to Fire Hawk. He rose and walked toward them.

"Fire Hawk," she said, "this is Striking Eagle. He comes with a message from our Cheyenne brother, Black Kettle."

"Striking Eagle is welcome in my lodge. Have you had meat?"

"Not since early this day, warrior."

"Come then and eat of hump meat and tongue while we speak."

They returned to the cooking fire and were greeted by those present. Many of the Sioux, including Crazy Horse, White Wolf, Gall, and Man Afraid, knew Striking Eagle and welcomed him with gestures of friendship. Night Wind came out of her wickiup to greet Little Fawn. Fire Hawk suspected his foster mother of playing matchmaker between himself and this White Sun Woman for whom he yearned so. In the past year, Little Fawn had not again spoken of marriage. But her affectionate gestures and the wistful looks of love and longing in her eyes made words unnecessary.

After Striking Eagle and Little Fawn had finished their food, she turned to Fire Hawk and spoke.

"There is sickness in the camp of Black Kettle. He asks that I come and heal those who now walk in the Land of Shadows."

"Do not our Cheyenne brothers have healers, Striking Eagle?"

"We do, Fire Hawk. Both of them walk in the Land of Shadows."

"Where is the camp of Black Kettle?"

"It is far to the south, on the Washita River."

Fire Hawk visualized the area in his mind and estimated a ride of over two hundred miles. The Washita River was in Indian Territory, a thin, narrow strip of land at the northwest corner of the Oklahoma Territory.

"I feel that I must go, Fire Hawk. Will you come with me?"

"Of course you must go, and of course I'll come with you."

Her radiant smile awarded his quick assent.

"How soon can we leave?"

"In the morning, if you wish, Little Fawn."

"Good. I will prepare my things and be ready to leave at first light."

"Striking Eagle, your pony is probably worn out from your long ride. Before dark, let us go out to the pony herd so that you can select a new mount. Meanwhile, Little Fawn, while you get started on your preparations, I'll round up your pinto, Sugarfoot, along with Star Walker and Gray Ghost. Ready, Striking Eagle?"

White Wolf joined them as they started to walk through the village toward the pony herd, which was grazing along the riverbank. As they passed his lodge, Jumping Frog raced out to meet them. White Wolf stopped and ruffled his son's hair.

"I thought you were taking care of your baby brother."

"Mother's here and Tadpole is asleep. Can I come?"

"Yes. For a little while."

As they approached the horses, Pasha left the herd and shuffled toward them. As his legs had grown stiffer, and his scars whiter, his vision and hearing seemed to have improved. He moved directly toward Jumping Frog and nuzzled him until the lad relinquished a few of the sweet treats he always had with him.

Fire Hawk pursed his lips and emitted a shrill whistle. At once, two of the ponies separated themselves from the others and trotted toward him. One of them was Star Walker. His companion, with the exception of the Appaloosa markings, looked like his twin brother. His coat was unrelieved, gunmetal . One morning, soon after Fire Hawk took him from the Pawnee, a dense fog had come rolling off the river. The pony blended so perfectly into the mist that he was nearly invisible. He looks, Fire Hawk thought, like a gray ghost. And that became his name. The horses were so well matched that they were perfect running mates.

Fire Hawk attached lead ropes to each of their halters and handed the ends to Jumping Frog. Then he moved slowly through the big herd until he located the pinto Little Fawn called Sugarfoot, and her other paint horse named Pogo. He snapped lead lines on the two ponies and led them out of the herd.

Striking Eagle came toward him leading a tall, buckskin horse.

"Fire Hawk, will you trade this buckskin for my claybank?"

"He looks like a good one, Striking Eagle. He is yours. But you'd better take your own pony, too, and let him loaf along the way. I won't take Little Fawn that far without spare horses."

"Good! When we reach Black Kettle's camp, look over my ponies and make your choice."

Not to be outdone, Jumping Frog led Pasha back to the camp. Since there were now seven horses to be tethered, Fire Hawk ran a stout rope between two trees and tied all the animals up short.

White Wolf and Jumping Frog went back to their lodge, and a short time later Striking Eagle left to visit his friend, Bobtail Horse. Finally, Night Wind came out and told him she was going to help Black Shawl. By the light of the moon, Fire Hawk sat for some time in front of the wickiup, smoking his pipe and honing his Spanish knife — as always, wondering about its origin, and wishing that somehow he could have known all of the weapon's owners. Suddenly, a shadow obscured the moon. He looked up to find Little Fawn standing there. She sat down very close to him.

"You have been patient with me for many moons," she began. "I can hold back that which is in my heart no longer. You know that I love you. I love you much more than I loved you yesterday, but far less than I will love you tomorrow. I know that because each day it is the same. You are a great warrior because you can be fearless and ferocious, but you are also kind, and tender, and considerate. I know I am blessed to have your love. I have spoken to Medicine Raven and Crazy Horse and told them of our feelings. They have both said that if you agree, we may wed, and that I can continue as a healer, although I would no longer be a White Sun Woman. If that is your wish, that is what we will do."

He pulled her close to him.

"Is there even a small doubt in your mind about my answer?"

"I hope not, warrior."

"You know not, woman! What will happen now?"

"When we return from the village of Black Kettle, Crazy Horse will call a tribal council. At that powwow, he will speak for us. So will Medicine Raven. I think we will receive the council's permission. Then we will be married and go to Blue Valley for our first moon together. There, we will learn to love each other."

"I have been sad a long time, Little Fawn, but tonight, you have made me happier than I have been since I was a child. Let us hurry to the Washita and hurry even more coming home."

"This is a happy home for you now, is it not, my love?"

"Home and happiness are where you are; sadness and unhappiness come when you go. I never want to feel cold emptiness again."

"I must go now and prepare for tomorrow," she said as she rose. "Tonight I will dream of us together in Blue Valley."

They kissed tenderly and parted beneath the smiling moon.

The following morning, they rose at the first light of dawn. An hour later, they had eaten and were ready to ride. As they mounted their ponies, a grinning White Wolf approached.

"I see my brother is happy today. Did you sleep well, Hawk?"

"If you see so much this morning, you should know whether I slept well or not, Wolf."

"Oh, I was just curious because I heard someone wandering about in the night and thought it might be you."

"Why would I be wandering about in the night?"

"Oh, perhaps because you are going on a long journey."

"You and I have been on many long journeys. Have you ever seen me restless before any of those?"

"No, but this is different."

"Why is it different, Wolf?"

"I just think it is."

"Would you stop talking in circles and tell me what you want?"

"I just thought you might bring back some fine new lodge poles from Blue Valley," said White Wolf, with a knowing smile. When they rode out of sight, he was still grinning.

➢

It was now late afternoon of their third day on the trail, and the weary travelers were over two-thirds of the way toward their destination. So far, the trip had been smooth and uneventful, but all of them were beginning to show signs of fatigue. A short distance ahead, according to Striking Eagle, was an excellent campsite beside a clear-water creek and impounds, around which were several groves of large trees. The three riders, as well as the horses, would welcome the pleasant shade and cool water.

As they rode, the three riders maintained a constant vigil on different portions of their limited horizon. They were far from their normal range and riding through an ever-changing frontier. Even in familiar locations, when the day-to-day situation was in flux, danger might be lurking anywhere. And this assuredly was not friendly country. Only a short distance ahead lay an area called Indian Territory. It was, however, far more than that. Those who knew it best referred to it as Badman's Territory, because of the lawlessness.

Fire Hawk remembered the many newspaper accounts he had read. During the Civil War, Border Raiders, men who darted across the border between the slave state of Missouri and the free state of Kansas, had developed some hard-to-break habits. They learned that it was far easier to make money at the end of a gun than at the end of a shovel. Others discovered that pistol points were more convincing than pencil points and much longer lasting. So it was that even after the war had ended, the raids continued. But now, all of the proceeds were rerouted. They no longer went into the coffers of a needy Confederacy, but found their way into the pockets of greedy lawbreakers. The happy outlaws called it six-gun justice. The frightened victims called it mayhem and murder.

The killers and the spoilers who preyed upon peaceful settlers in the postwar towns of Kansas, Colorado, New Mexico, and Texas required a nearby sanctuary. They found that ready-made hideaway in Indian Territory. Outlaw towns sprang up, where the price of admission was a price on your head. Ruthless vigilante law was established, which provided quick, if questionable, justice.

Most real lawmen did not enter the Indian Territory, Fire Hawk reflected grimly. Those who did often settled down and sank deep roots. Small landholdings were readily available for them in new developments with picturesque names like Boot Hill, where tiny plots of land, six feet long and three feet wide, were deeded to them forever.

➢

Fire Hawk was jolted out of his reverie by the sight of several vultures, about a mile off to his right, silhouetted against the sky. In this rolling hill country, where vision was limited by the crest of the next rise, he could not determine the reason for the scavengers' interest. He called a temporary halt and reined Gray Ghost around to face Little Fawn and Striking Eagle.

"I want you to remain here until I return. If you hear shots, go back the way we came. If I do not return soon, wait until you feel it is safe, and then go on to the Washita."

"Be careful, my love," Little Fawn said softly.

He handed her Gray Ghost's reins and slid from his back. He then whistled for Star Walker, who was fresher than his running mate after lazing along all day. Also, he could be trusted to follow instructions. His steel nerves matched his steel color.

Fire Hawk rode cautiously forward. Vultures meant death. But when they hovered and did not land, it meant some form of life amid the death. He topped a rise and saw two bodies stretched out on the ground being circled by a small pack of coyotes. The vultures were reluctant to land because of them, and the animals were unwilling to turn their backs on the birds.

Fire Hawk urged Star Walker into a canter and frightened the cowardly beasts away. The birds continued to circle, reluctant to abandon a meal.

The victims were Southern Cheyenne Dog Soldiers. Their arms were banded in the Cheyenne tribal colors of red, yellow, and white. Both were tattooed with the sign of the dog. They had been dead for several hours. Their bodies were bloated, and blowflies were crawling in and out of their wounds.

These two young men had died hard. Fire Hawk found no gunshot wounds. They had both been slashed many times and finally gutted. Their systematic executioners had been expert and creative in the art of agony. It was obvious that the torturers wanted answers and that they had engaged in this type of questioning before. The puzzler was, what did they want to know so badly that they would willingly deal out this kind of punishment?

From the signs, Fire Hawk determined that four shod horses had left the arroyo along with the two barefoot ponies ridden here by the Dog Soldiers. The shod horses, in all probability, belonged to white men, although three of the men had been wearing moccasins, and only one a pair of boots. The boot tracks were very interesting. In each heel print he could see the outlines of three tiny horseshoes. All the tracks led away to the north.

Fire Hawk, using a shovel-shaped rock, scraped out a shallow but adequate grave and laid the warriors in it, side-by-side. He covered them with the dirt he had removed and then piled as many rocks over the bodies as he could find in an effort to protect the corpses from the scavengers that still lurked in the shadows and in the air.

As he worked, Fire Hawk fought to control his overwhelming feelings of revulsion and horror that always welled up in the face of brutal and senseless victimization. How could anyone treat another human being with such a monstrous lack of respect and ruthless disdain for justice? He had discovered that diabolical savagery was not confined to primitive societies, as he had once supposed. Compassion and concern came as naturally to most of them, he had learned, as to the people of more "genteel" cultures.

Conversely, he had seen a perverse compulsion to inflict terror and pain upon defenseless people, by individuals from the most refined backgrounds and highest classes. Perhaps it was the strain of combat that brought about such Attila-like behavior, he had rationalized at first. But he had now learned, to his dismay, that most cases of inhuman behavior were triggered solely by opportunities to terrorize and brutalize without fear of reprisal — in the tradition of Nero and all other Coliseum voyeurists. The participants' identities changed, but the robust spirit of evil seemed to go on forever.

His grim tasks completed, Fire Hawk remounted Star Walker, glanced once more at the cairn, and urged the pony into a gallop. Returning to his companions, he recounted his experience, but eliminated all references to the torturing of the victims.

They continued their journey toward the nearby water hole, and as expected, saw the prairie glade from the crest of the next ridge. They also saw a great deal they did not expect to see.

Along the north side of the creek milled a restless herd of horses, at least five hundred of them. Within the circle of trees were a number of warriors that Fire Hawk recognized as Arapahoes, but the vast preponderance were Southern Cheyenne Dog Soldiers.

As yet, no lodges had been erected, but for some reason the village looked strange. He suddenly realized why. He did not see a single woman, child, or dog. This was not a village, it was a war camp. A mammoth war camp! He turned to Striking Eagle and asked, "Do you know them?"

"Most of them. But this many warriors must come from many villages. I see the man who leads them. He is war chief of the Southern Cheyenne and leader of the Society of Dog Soldiers. Since Black Kettle became a peace chief, unwilling to fight for Cheyenne rights, this man is now chief of most of the Southern Cheyenne. He is to them what Crazy Horse is to our brothers, the Sioux. He is Roman Nose."

"I met him several years ago," added Little Fawn. "I treated his broken wrist. He is truly a great man."

They moved slowly down the slope into the encampment. As they proceeded, Striking Eagle led the way and nodded gravely to many warriors that he knew.

They stopped and dismounted in the shade of the trees near a small knot of warriors. One of them left the group and came to meet them.

This man, thought Fire Hawk, would be impressive in any setting. He was very tall and well built. His muscles rippled under a smooth skin that resembled polished copper. In his hand he carried a Henry repeating rifle, while in his belt reposed a wicked looking knife and equally impressive tomahawk. But it was his warbonnet that captured and held Fire Hawk's attention. Like Crazy Horse's, there were so many feathers cascading down Roman Nose's back that the lowest ones bumped his heels as he walked. This man was a prototypical Plains Indian warrior.

He stopped before them and welcomed Striking Eagle, then turned to Little Fawn.

"White Sun Woman, I am honored to have you in my camp."

"Your wrist healed well, mighty chief?"

"It is as strong as the Great Spirit made it. I am grateful, Little Fawn."

"I was glad for the chance to help. Roman Nose, this is my warrior, the son of your friend, Crazy Horse. In the next moon, Fire Hawk and I will wed."

"I have heard much of you, Fire Hawk. The White Eyes' great loss has been our great gain."

He came to stand directly before Fire Hawk and placed his hand on the other's heart.

"Few men I have known would be worthy of Little Fawn. You are one of those men. I am honored to welcome the son of Crazy Horse to my camp and call him my brother."

"There are also few men whose friendship would do me such a great honor," responded Fire Hawk.

They stood in silence for a moment, then Fire Hawk asked, "Why have you assembled such a large war party, my brother?"

"Across the plains, there is much killing. The White Eyes say it must stop. We make treaties with them, but it does not stop. We hold peace councils with them, but it does not stop. Last year, I went with Black Kettle to meet the Great White Father's Chief Howard. The great, one-armed warrior spoke kindly to us, as if we were children. I think he is a good man. He said the killing must stop. But as we returned from that peace powwow, white men killed two of my warriors. They were killed as easily as you and I would kill a rabbit. The killing does not stop. Of course, we killed those white men. The killing goes on! It does not stop!

"Now our scouts tell us that many white men ride the warpath against us. The Horse Killer [Sheridan] comes after us. Yellow Hair [Custer] looks for us. The Big Scout [Forsyth] seeks us. When they find us, maybe they will be sorry that they did. There are many White Eye war parties, large and small, roaming the prairie. There are more coming out. We are riding to seek the help of your father, Crazy Horse, and your uncle, Sitting Bull.

"We will only defend ourselves, as we ride to the lands of the Sioux. But then we will search out and destroy as many of our enemies as we can find. Early this morning, I sent scouts out in every direction to be my eyes and ears. I have learned much of the enemies' intentions. Soon I will know the rest. Two of my scouts who traveled toward the setting sun will return soon. Running Horse and Young Otter have been gone longer than the others. They may have much to tell us."

"My brother," said Fire Hawk sadly, "Running Horse and Young Otter will not return. I buried them an hour ago, less than a mile from here. Four white men, or at least men riding shod ponies killed them. The signs around the bodies were moccasin tracks, except for one set of boot prints. If I ever see those tracks again, I will know them. In each heel are the marks of three tiny horseshoes."

"The tracks of those boots are well known to me," responded Roman Nose. "They seem to be everywhere there is trouble."

Fire Hawk and his companions consumed a Spartan meal of buffalo jerky and pemmican, refreshed themselves by swimming and floating in the pond, then spent the early evening visiting with Roman Nose and others. Shortly after moonrise they went to sleep.

The next morning, they bid farewell to their hosts and rode on toward Indian Territory and the camp on the Washita. They arrived shortly before dark and were welcomed by Black Kettle.

Little Fawn visited more than a dozen of the sick Cheyennes and treated them with herbs that she had brought. The children seemed to respond more quickly than the adults do. By midnight, several of the young ones were sitting up begging for food.

Little Fawn prepared a thin but savory broth from three sage hens that Fire Hawk had snared earlier. He sat beside her as she fed the nourishing liquid to her last patient. Then they walked back to the wickiup to which she had been assigned. They stood outside the lodge for several minutes, holding each other tightly and sharing whispered endearments.

"If we are ever separated, always remember how important you are to me and how much I love you," she sighed.

"I want you to tell me that every day for the rest of our many years together."

"Oh, I will! I will! Thank you for sharing such wonderful happiness with me, my beloved."

They embraced once more. Then smiling, she left him.

Fire Hawk checked the horses and then, for some reason he was never able to explain, he led Star Walker and Gray Ghost back to Black Kettle's lodge and tied them beside the doorway. When he entered the wickiup, his host was already asleep.

A short time later, he too was deep in slumber and dreaming of the happiness he had finally found.

➢

He was jolted awake by the sounds of cannon and bugles, just as the first rays of the rising sun crept into the teepee. What was going on? This was a peace camp! Everyone knew that! Why would anyone shoot into any camp that was filled with old men, women and children? Suddenly, he remembered Sand Creek, and his heart was filled with horror and dread.

Cannon balls were exploding amidst the teepees, and everyone from the oldest man to the youngest toddler was trying to flee from this dreadful, deadly menace. The little girl, whom he had last seen enjoying broth at midnight, ran past. Just then a shell blast lifted the tiny, helpless child from her feet and a second later replaced her with a bloody bundle of tattered rags.

Grateful for having the horses so near, he leaped astride Gray Ghost. Leading Star Walker, he raced down the long row of teepees. The waiting Little Fawn clambered up onto the patient pony's back, and together they sped toward the far edge of the village. They flashed across the bare, open ground, intent on reaching the dense woods, which lay just beyond. They nearly made it. Scant yards from the thick cover's safety, Little Fawn was suddenly hurtled forward against Star Walker's straining neck. Moments later, she fell limply to the ground as the Appaloosa raced on into the trees.

Fire Hawk spun Gray Ghost around to confront Little Fawn's attackers. There were three, and they were racing toward him, shouting and firing their carbines. He started toward them, committed to protecting Little Fawn, when Gray Ghost toppled like a stone, shot through the head. Fire Hawk sprang clear as the horse fell and took refuge behind his quivering body.

He lifted his rifle and shot the first trooper in the chest and the next one through the head. Hurrying to fire his third bullet, he rammed a fresh cartridge into the chamber before the spent one was fully ejected, temporarily jamming the weapon.

By then the last soldier was upon him, leveling a Dragoon pistol. Fire Hawk bounded forward to the blue-shirted man's side and, using his rifle as a club knocked the surprised cavalryman from his saddle with one well-aimed blow. The trooper quickly recovered his feet, drew his bayonet, and spun around to meet the advancing Fire Hawk.

"I ain't scared o' you, Red Stick!"

"You will be before you die, you blue-bellied bastard!" vowed Fire Hawk.

"You ain't a Red Stick, you're a Reb!"

"That's right, you murdering son of a bitch. But where you're going, it won't make one damned bit of difference."

They circled each other warily. Using the tactics that White Wolf had taught him, Fire Hawk waited for just the right moment. It came as the soldier attempted to slash him. He parried the thrust with his deadly Spanish knife, then drove the blade inward and upward, well into the forearm of his antagonist who dropped his weapon and suddenly turned chalk white. Fire Hawk wasted no more time. He drove the tempered steel into the trembling man's belly, temporarily impaling him.

"Now scream loud enough for Jeb Stuart to hear, you Yankee trash."

The man gurgled as Fire Hawk, applying every ounce of strength and energy he could muster, drove the end of the blade upward into his heart.

As the dead man slid to the ground, Fire Hawk turned and raced toward Little Fawn, who had not stirred since she had fallen.

He slipped his arm beneath her shoulders and cradled her small body against his chest. He felt a bare flicker of life. Her eyes opened and she tried to smile up at him.

"I am sorry, Beloved, that I must leave you. We will never be together in Blue Valley. But I promise to wait for you beside the Star Road of the Great Spirit. We will walk on it together."

Her final act was to raise her hand and tenderly brush a tear from his cheek.

"Do not weep. Next time we are together, it will be forever. Goodbye for a little while, my love."

He squeezed her hand gently, and smiled down at her. She returned his smile, and then she died.

Carefully, lovingly, Fire Hawk wrapped Little Fawn inside an army blanket that he had taken from one of the dead trooper's horses. Using an entrenching tool, which was also attached to the saddle, he buried her in a deep, unmarked grave in the middle of the dense woods she had tried so valiantly to reach. Beside her still body, he left a portion of his heart that he would never need again. For to him, her lonely grave was a melancholy abyss, a mournful place where part of his spirit would dwell for the rest of his empty days. Her death was even more painful than those of others whom he had loved were. She had trusted him with her life, and he had failed her. For a long time he sat hunched beside her grave, wracked by misery and despair.

He finally quit the woods and was surprised to hear sporadic firing from the river. He removed the least bloody uniform he could find from the body of its former owner and found that he could just squeeze into it. Then, mounting one of the cavalry horses, he rode slowly back along the edge of the village, where soldiers were in the process of stripping the bodies and burning the lodges.

In the distance he saw the long yellow hair of Custer, sitting astride a dancing horse and gesturing about as he issued orders. Custer was Little Fawn's real killer! He pulled out his Spanish knife, held it up and said, "As God is my judge, some day I will sink this blade into his black heart!"

Fire Hawk pulled the wide-brimmed hat far down over his eyes as he continued to circle the village perimeter for the balance of the afternoon. On four different occasions, he caught soldiers in isolated areas and killed each of them with one quick, lethal thrust of the Spanish knife. The fifth man was standing alone on the outer fringe of some dense woods as Fire Hawk approached him. He reined his mount close to the soldier. Then, carefully using the horse's body to shield his movement, he hurtled himself onto the man's shoulders and bore him to the ground. Obscured by the thick trees, he straddled his helpless victim's chest and drew back the knife to deliver the fatal blow. As he did so, he recognized his friend, Fred Benteen. He maintained his grip, but whispered, "This is your lucky day. Fred. I'm going to let you live."

It took several seconds for Benteen to realize who it was. Forrester had been naturally dark complexioned, but now the skin of the man he had known as a friend had been turned a brownish red by the sun. Also, dirt and dried blood, except for the streaks beneath his eyes covered his face where his tears had washed the grime away.

Benteen recovered enough of his breath to pant out a question.

"Clay Forrester, is it really you?"

"Not anymore, Fred! The last vestige of Clayton Forrester died this morning and was buried with the woman he loved. I have quit your world! Every bit of me is now the Sioux warrior, Fire Hawk."

He held the knife close to Benteen's face.

"If you ever see this knife again, it will be buried in the heart of that bastard, Custer. You tell him he better sleep with one eye open from now on. As of today, this knife will be called Widow Maker. One widow that I swear it will make is Libbie Custer. I'm going to walk away now, Fred. If you raise the alarm before I disappear, I'll put a pistol bullet in your head. I can no longer afford the luxury of having white men for friends."

With that warning, he rose and melted into the thick shadows.

A badly shaken Fred Benteen walked back to the river, feeling as though he had just attended Clayton Forrester's funeral and realizing how close he had come to needing one of his own.

Fire Hawk moved back through the woods and stopped for the last time beside the final resting place of his beloved. He sat there for the rest of the day, thinking and brooding about Little Fawn and their unfulfilled promise of wedded happiness. Meanwhile, the cavalrymen rounded up the Cheyenne survivors and took them away.

Black Kettle had not been a survivor, nor had Striking Eagle. He had seen both of their bodies as he circled the village. As darkness fell, on a hunch, he whistled for Star Walker. Moments later, with a clatter of hooves, the faithful pony arrived at his side. As darkness closed in, he turned the animal toward the North Star and started back to find Roman Nose and his avengers.

It had been the worst day he had ever endured. It would be a long time before he knew another happy day. It was the first day of his personal war with Custer, a war that would end only when one or both of them were dead. He thought again of Little Fawn and could scarcely see the stars through his tear-filled eyes.

Lost in deep reverie, he rode along for several hours. It was well past midnight when he finally pulled Star Walker to a halt beside a small creek. He dozed restlessly under the cover of darkness and allowed the horse to graze, rest, and recover his strength. Fire Hawk rose just after sunrise and rigged several snares before going to bathe in the creek.

When he returned and checked the snares, two of them held unwary sage hens or prairie chickens. A further search revealed several nests, containing a fair number of eggs. He looked along the creek bank until he found a thin, nearly flat rock, with a depression in the center. He built a small fire around this rock and, when it was hot enough, fried the sage hens. After he removed the meat, enough grease remained in the rocky recess to fry six eggs. Sadness had stripped away his appetite, but he knew he must eat. He mustn't die! There was too much left to do!

An hour later, he mounted and rode until late afternoon. He began to remember certain landmarks and realized he was nearing the oasis where he had last seen Roman Nose. Fearing that the campsite might already have visitors, he approached it with an extra measure of caution. Peering over the crest of the final hill, he saw that his suspicions were correct. Three ponies were grazing next to the pool. Suddenly, Star Walker whinnied. His call was answered, immediately, by one of the horses below. Fire Hawk realized why. He knew all three of those ponies. The one who had answered was White Wolf's Chestnut. The others were Man Afraid's roan and Gall's pinto. For the first time since the bombardment, Fire Hawk relaxed.

He remounted Star Walker and walked him slowly down the hill.

By now, the others had recognized him as well. They rose from their small cooking fire and came to meet him, words of greeting on their lips.

White Wolf looked at him and knew that something was terribly wrong.

"What has happened, Hawk?"

177

"The worst possible calamity, my brother. Yellow Hair and his men have wiped out Black Kettle's village. Many of the Cheyenne are dead, including Black Kettle and Striking Eagle. Nearly all the rest are captives; very few escaped." He paused and sighed a huge sigh before he continued in a halting voice.

"Little Fawn is also dead. I got her out of the village and nearly to the woods, but the soldiers shot her in the back. I could not save her, Wolf."

In an uncharacteristic gesture, White Wolf came to his friend and placed a hand upon each of his shoulders, then whispered to him so softly that the others could not hear.

"You are the finest warrior and the bravest man I have ever known. You are also the best friend I have ever had. I know you would have died to save her if it had been possible. I know you are sad and will grieve for many moons, for you loved her. Many more of us will be sad and grieve for many moons because we also loved her. Come now, my brother, and rest. Then we will talk."

They had come to escort him and Little Fawn home after hearing about the rampaging White Eyes. On the way they had encountered Roman Nose and the Cheyennes and learned his plan.

"Did the Cheyennes kill any of the soldiers?" asked Gall.

"I saw only two soldiers' bodies in the wagons."

"Did you kill any of them, Hawk?" White Wolf asked hopefully.

"I shot two and killed five others with my Spanish knife, the Widow Maker."

"That's a perfect name!" exclaimed the knife's former owner.

"What do you wish to do now, Hawk?" asked Man Afraid.

"We must hurry and catch up with Roman Nose," said Fire Hawk, "before he can kill all the Yellow Legs. Maybe we can even corner Yellow Hair and allow him to feel the Widow Maker's caress."

"I want to be with you on that day!" proclaimed White Wolf.

➢

The following morning they left early and rode northwestward throughout the day. Along the way, they saw signs of many large parties of horsemen. Often the prints of barefoot ponies were found beside those of ironshod cavalry mounts, indicating the presence of Crow and Arikara scouts, as well as a few traitorous Sioux.

Studying the tracks at one recently used campsite, Fire Hawk discovered another imprint of the strange boot with the three tiny horseshoes which he had first seen next to the bodies of the two Cheyenne Dog Soldiers. Things are getting interesting, he thought bitterly. Enemies seem to be sprouting up as quickly as blades of grass in springtime.

Chapter XIV
➤
War Chief

Sioux War Camp
Sand Creek
Colorado Territory
September, 1868

It was noon three days later, and the four warriors were relaxing beside a gurgling spring in a pleasant, shady glen. They sat, picking the last of the succulent meat from the bones of a wild turkey which Gall had snared and cooked the night before.

Fire Hawk was beginning to feel a little less miserable, after suffering in silence through the first bitter days of melancholy sorrow. He knew that only time would blunt his misery. During some of the other occasions, when sadness had nearly overwhelmed him, he had not had the good fortune to be surrounded by good and caring friends. It was strange, he thought; in all of his thirty-two years, he had enjoyed fewer than a dozen close friendships. His roommates at V.M.I., his scout team members during the war. And now these three Sioux warriors. Though they were fierce and formidable, they were also sincere and supportive companions.

Satisfied that all the meat and marrow had been stripped away, Fire Hawk discarded the bones and rose to his feet. He washed his hands in the spring, splashed his face with cool refreshing water, and filled the canteens he had taken from the dead soldiers.

He had picked up several of them, since each trooper carried two. White Wolf and Gall each had canteens; Man

Afraid, however, declared that he would die of thirst rather than use any object a white man had owned. Fire Hawk had been on the verge of reminding the stocky warrior that the strawberry roan he rode once belonged to a white man, but thought better of it.

Star Walker moved in beside him and thrust his muzzle deeply into the water. He was still warm from his morning exertions. For the first week of September, it was very hot. The midday sun beat down unmercifully from a cloudless sky. There was not even a breath of wind to move a leaf. These were days to seek out the cool high mountain glades like Blue Valley, he thought, with a new pang of regret. A dozen times each day, small things reminded him of Little Fawn and caused his heart to ache. Those feelings would continue, he knew, for a long, long time. A few minutes later, the warriors reluctantly left the oasis and continued northward.

The country was no longer empty. On every high hilltop could be seen a pair of sentinels. Running Horse and Young Otter had not died in vain, thought Fire Hawk. Roman Nose has learned a very valuable lesson. When fighting highly mobile forces, send pairs of messengers to the highest ground to watch for dust trails. When dust appears, one messenger reports the activity, and the other stays in place. If the lookouts are strategically located on every high mesa across a twenty-mile line, they can trace the movements of anything larger than a jack rabbit for hundreds of square miles. A large and ready striking force can then intercept and annihilate every weaker enemy.

They were still several miles from the camp on Sand Creek when Man Afraid, who possessed extraordinary vision, saw an immense amount of smoke on the horizon. A short time later, it was visible to all of them. It was not intermittent and dark, as from a fire as it consumes a building or an old log structure. This smoke was uniformly light blue, clean, and steady.

"It's the smoke from cooking fires," claimed Gall.

181

"There is too much smoke for that," observed Man Afraid.

"No," insisted Gall, "it is cook smoke."

A short time later they sat overlooking the camp on Sand Creek and saw that Gall had been correct. The four friends stared down into the valley in amazement at over a thousand lodges. They saw Oglala, Brule, Sans Arc, Hunkpapa, and Blackfoot Sioux. Northern and Southern Cheyenne. Even a few wickiups belonging to Arapahoe.

As they started down the slope, they had to skirt around some high rocks. Three of them went to one side while White Wolf rode the opposite way. Having a slightly shorter distance to traverse, he was waiting for them on the far side of the broken ground as they approached. He beckoned them over and pointed at the ground.

A heel print with three tiny horseshoes was plainly visible.

➢

Fire Hawk and his companions soon discovered that the entire southeastern portion of the sprawling encampment contained all of the Oglala and Hunkpapa lodges. Their teepees, along with those of the other principal Sioux leaders, had been erected in one of the four long double rows. In this same row, side-by-side, stood the wickiups of Sitting Bull and Crazy Horse. Next to them were his own and Little Fawn's. At the sight, Fire Hawk's heart, already heavy with grief, ached anew.

The other three men went directly to greet their families while Fire Hawk continued on to the wickiup of Crazy Horse, who was sitting in front of it, speaking with Sitting Bull.

He guided the tired Star Walker to an area behind the teepees where he would be able to obtain water and graze, and dismounted. He removed the pony's hackamore, draped it over his arm, and left the animal to contentedly chomp grass. As he walked back toward the two Sioux leaders, Fire Hawk lovingly stroked the halter. Little Fawn had braided it from black and silver horsehair, especially for Star Walker. As with everything she had done, her workmanship was exquisite. Each day a hundred different things reminded him of their wonderful times together, and he missed her desperately!

As he emerged at the front of the teepee, both chiefs stood to greet him. Sitting Bull smiled and nodded and Crazy Horse gently squeezed his arm.

"Welcome back, my son."

He looked closely at Fire Hawk and knew something was wrong.

"What has happened?" Crazy Horse asked with concern.

Fire Hawk related the story of the journey, of Custer's sneak attack on the sleeping village, of his desperate attempt to get Little Fawn and the others out of danger, and of his subsequent revenge on the seven cavalry troopers. He omitted nothing except his final words with Little Fawn.

"I have sworn to kill Yellow Hair before I die," he concluded.

"We will help you, my son. Even now, we are making plans to go after the Yellow Legs."

"Good. If we are to survive, for even a little while, we must hunt down as many as possible and kill them. But you must know, my father, that in the end, there can be no victory for us. All we can buy is time."

"A time of freedom, my son. If we can buy for our people even one extra day of time, we must fight to win that day."

"Then, my father, from this moment on, I will fight next to you to earn that day for them!"

"You are blessed, Tushunca Witco, to have a brave and loyal son," said Sitting Bull. "My son, the Grabber, is a traitor. He has turned his back upon our people and fled to the White Eyes. Perhaps as you look for Yellow Hair, Fire Hawk, you can look for the Grabber as well and kill them both."

"I promise to try, Uncle."

Fire Hawk walked back to his lodge and told Night Wind of Little Fawn's death. She sobbed and wailed and could not stop.

"I am sad beyond words," her adopted son told the grieving woman. "I wish that she had lived and I had died. But that was not meant to be. You and I must live and be strong, mother, to protect and fight for our people. That is what Little Fawn would have asked of us. We cannot allow her death to be in vain."

➢

That night, a great council of all the tribes was called. On the north side of Sand Creek was a large, natural, bowl-shaped hollow, with gently rising slopes on three sides. It was there that the conclave was convened. Because of the contour, and the tiers of listeners staring down upon the speakers, it reminded Fire Hawk of the auditorium at V.M.I. Because of the unique shape of this natural bowl, the acoustics here were nearly as good as those of the indoor amphitheater had been.

Roman Nose began the meeting by reciting a litany of broken promises and outrages. His indictment went on to include the latest massacre on the Washita. He ended by urging every able-bodied warrior to ride with him, at once, in search of Custer. The order of the day was revenge. He stirred his listeners to a fever pitch with his oratorical eloquence. A ripple of eagerness swept through the conclave. Only a universal respect for Crazy Horse held the angry avengers in place to await his words.

Crazy Horse had spent the early evening discussing strategy and tactics with Sitting Bull and Fire Hawk. He came away from these sessions with a good plan of action and absolute trust in his foster son's military prowess.

When he rose to speak, Crazy Horse did so with complete faith in his own ability to shape the outcome of this conference.

"Brothers, hear me. Roman Nose speaks well. There is no more need for talk of peace. No, brothers, it is time for the action of war. Hear me, brothers. In this place, in this time, we have assembled a great striking force. From this valley, we can send forth enough warriors to paint this country red with blood. But what of our villages, if we go and hunt down the White Eyes? We have seen what they do to villages that are not ready for them!

"Hear me! We must not trade the lives of our families for the deaths of the White Eyes. It is not our way. But there is a way. We must split this great force into two parts. I will stay here with half of our warriors, to safeguard the women and children, while Roman Nose leads the others in pursuit of the White Eyes. Each Sioux and Cheyenne tribe should decide which warriors will stay with me and which will go with my brother, Roman Nose."

He paused to let his plan take root, then continued.

"Since I will remain here to defend this great village, I am appointing my son, Fire Hawk, to lead the Oglalas. With him will go three groups of Sioux warriors, led by White Wolf, Man Afraid, and Gall. It is for Roman Nose to say how his force is to be used and where they are to go."

Knowing that he had won the assembled warriors to his side, Crazy Horse sat down.

Now Roman Nose reclaimed the crowd's attention.

"At dawn, let every tribe send their war chiefs to me. We will make plans and prepare. I ask Crazy Horse to help us to do this."

Since everyone seemed to agree that his ideas were good, the participants left and returned to their respective camps.

At daybreak, twenty war chiefs, representing over a thousand warriors, returned to the site of the previous night's conclave. Those thousand warriors would form a new and mighty strike force.

They decided to spread the force out, and surround a huge area under the cover of darkness. A slice of territory

185

so large, that three nights would be required to complete the infiltration. Then on the fourth morning, they would begin riding slowly back toward the center, driving everything before them that was caught within the jaws of the trap. They would close that trap at the Arickaree River in ten days. It was like the fishnets he had devised as a boy, thought Fire Hawk; there was plenty of room to swim in, but none to swim out.

➢

It was late the same afternoon, and the principal warriors of the Oglala had just concluded a council of war. Roman Nose had assigned them an area from Sand Creek, southeastward toward the Washita, the place from which Fire Hawk and his friends had just returned. It was a smart assignment because of their familiarity with that territory, and because it was a beehive of activity.

The Sioux leaders decided to split their strike force of four hundred warriors into three groups. The first two, commanded by Gall and Man Afraid, would be composed of one hundred fifty men each. The third, with White Wolf in charge, would be made up of the final hundred.

Gall's group would leave at midnight and ride due east until dawn. By then, they would be twenty-five miles from Sand Creek. They would remain hidden throughout the day. Then, the next day at dusk, Gall would lead his group south, leaving a sentry posted every quarter of a mile. After traveling twenty-five miles, one hundred warriors would be strung out in one long line, each in sight of the men nearest to him. They would then constitute the eastern side of an enormous square. Gall would then turn west, with the rest of his force, and start to form the southern side.

Also at dark on the same day, the groups of Man Afraid and White Wolf would begin. Man Afraid would parallel Gall and form the western side. After his twenty-five mile leg to the south, he would turn eastward and rendezvous with Gall in the middle of the southern grid line of the square.

White Wolf would lead his warriors directly east until he joined up with the northern end of Gall's line, while Fire Hawk stayed on the northwestern corner and anchored the formation.

When they were all finally in place, every enemy within six hundred square miles would be trapped. At dawn on the third day, Fire Hawk would begin tightening the noose. Since each man could see the next, every warrior around the entire perimeter would be in motion within a few minutes. Each member of the circle moving toward its center. Anyone within the closing wings would have to run or fight! There should be no place to hide!

Fire Hawk had carefully instructed his warriors to walk their ponies in order to prevent dust clouds; to quicken the pace only if they heard gunfire; to keep proper intervals; and to remain alert as they rode forward. Otherwise, concealed enemies might slip through any area that was left unprotected. He was certain that everyone would obey.

Fire Hawk had been somewhat surprised when Crazy Horse made him war chief of the huge strike force. He had watched the other warriors who might ordinarily have led the Sioux war party but detected no animosity. He was certain that they were relying on Crazy Horse's judgment. If he proved to be a good leader, they would follow him willingly. If he did not, they would refuse. It's the same deal Jeb Stuart gave me, he thought.

Since his orders were given and his subordinates could be counted on, there was little to do. Therefore, on behalf of Night Wind and himself, he accepted an invitation from White Wolf and Blue Leaf for dinner. His mother was still in mourning, and the time away from her own lodge would certainly help. For his part, he knew that he must concentrate on the action ahead. It would benefit no one if he were unworthy of this task. He knew in his heart that he could be a real asset to his adopted people. Crazy Horse was instinctively a brilliant strategist and tactician, but now the Sioux and their allies would be fighting book soldiers. At Virginia Military Institute, they had made every single cadet memorize the book. Fire Hawk decided that Crazy Horse and he would make a great team.

➢

Thirty hours later, the team leaders sat on their horses and waited for the sun to burst over the eastern horizon.

The previous afternoon, Crazy Horse had sent pairs of scouts out to each quadrant. Before nightfall, they had taken up preselected observation posts that provided clear views of large surrounding areas. Next, he had divided his huge force into three parts. Should the sentinels detect any suspicious movements, the first section would ride out and intercept any enemy aggressors who might threaten the encampment. The second, and by far the largest unit, would encircle the lodges and assume the mission of perimeter defense. The third, a highly mobile group, composed of hard-core, seasoned warriors, led by Bobtail Horse, would remain in reserve until they were needed. It was an excellent plan. For the second time in as many days, Fire Hawk concluded that Crazy Horse and he made a great team.

With a sudden flash, the sun appeared and began its climb across the skies. Fire Hawk touched Crazy Horse's arm.

"I won't disappoint you, now or ever, my father."

"I have no such fear, war chief," the Sioux leader affirmed, smiling broadly as he turned Nighthawk toward the village.

Motioning his assistant to a position beside him, Fire Hawk urged Star Walker forward. He grinned to himself as he covertly watched his young aide who was on his first warpath. Black Shield, the teenaged grandson of Many

Kills and Night Wind, was the only son of Iron Shirt, one of the warriors that Fire Hawk had slain during the Fetterman fight. Two nights ago, as Night Wind and Fire Hawk were returning to their wickiup, the lad had approached them with an urgent request.

He embraced his grandmother, then turned to Fire Hawk.

"I request the war chief's permission to speak."

Fire Hawk suddenly felt that he had been remiss in his duties. He was this young man's uncle and more than a little responsible for his orphan status. It was time to make amends.

"My nephew, Black Shield, is free to speak to me at any time. He is as welcome in my lodge as he is in my heart."

"Thank you, Uncle. I am ready to receive my war weapons and take the warpath. To receive them from you would be a great honor. My grandmother, Night Wind, is holding some weapons that belonged to my father and grandfather. Will you sponsor me?"

"Black Shield does me great honor with his request."

"Fire Hawk does me greater honor by his acceptance."

The ceremony had been conducted the previous evening. White Wolf and Fire Hawk had applied his war paint and Crazy Horse had welcomed the young man into the Oglala Bad Face warrior society. Then Fire Hawk had presented the newest Sioux fighting man with Iron Shirt's tomahawk and Many Kills' knife. To these traditional weapons, he added a Springfield rifle and a Colt pistol that he had taken from the soldiers at the Washita. His final gift had been a prancing young paint horse. He knew the choice had been a good one when he saw the pride shining in the lad's eyes.

This morning, Black Shield was riding into battle for the first time beside the warrior that he most admired. He grinned at his mentor and received a big smile in return. Fire Hawk reflected that only in a society where the courage to die well was prized above all else could a scene such as this have happened.

They rode south, veering slightly toward the east for over an hour. During their passage, they disturbed numerous rabbits, and several pheasants were forced into flight. Once a pair of black-tailed deer jumped out of a thicket where they had been concealed and bounded away in terror. The net was tight, and it was working. They maintained constant visual contact with the end riders of both lines to the south and east but saw no sign of any alien humans. Not even tracks.

Suddenly the silence was broken by a staccato of gunfire, coming from some distance off to the south. Moments later, they heard additional firing and saw a dust cloud moving toward them. A third set of shots erupted, very close at hand.

Fire Hawk could identify a rifle being answered by a pistol. Seconds later, a well-mounted, uniformed cavalry soldier burst over the rise directly ahead of them, intent on breaking through the tight Sioux cordon. The rider galloped toward them, leaning far over to the opposite side of his mount, firing as he came.

Fire Hawk heard one chunk of lead scream past, dangerously close to his ear. He waited, expecting Black Shield to fire, but the young man did not. Finally, with one well-aimed bullet, Fire Hawk knocked the fleeing trooper headlong from his saddle and watched his body go skidding and tumbling across the prairie.

He dispatched Black Shield to capture the runaway cavalry horse while he went to confirm its rider's death. The lanky, tow-haired soldier was dead. If Fire Hawk's bullet in his chest had started it, a broken neck had finished it. He breathed a silent prayer for the dead trooper and then spoke aloud.

"It wasn't your fault that you died, boy! You did your best. I'm just better at it than you, 'cause I've done it for a hell of a lot longer. Seven years and no end in sight."

The problem here, he thought, is not a white boy who died, in spite of fighting well. It's an Indian boy who lived, in spite of not fighting at all. Had the young warrior been alone, this savvy blue-shirted trooper almost certainly would have broken free, and Black Shield would be the one who now lay crumpled in the dust.

Hell's fire, he thought. The first time under hostile fire is riveting for anyone. I understand that. But the boy must never freeze up again. In combat, if you fail to kill an enemy you can kill, you not only fail yourself; you fail the men around you. If you died needlessly, others often did too. Whatever it took, the boy's buck fever, or fear, had to be stopped at once. For good!

Black Shield returned leading the trooper's mount—a short, stocky, blood bay gelding, with the typical black mane and tail, as well as four short black stockings. He was one of the best cavalry horses Fire Hawk had ever seen. In spite of his small body and short legs, the little horse had flown over the ground during the pursuit. He would make an excellent replacement for Gray Ghost. I'll call this little fellow "Socks," he decided.

He was surprised to see a Winchester repeating rifle in the saddle scabbard. He was surprised also not to see a dispatch case. Whatever the message was, it was too important to commit to written form. He plucked the Winchester from the saddle, spun around to face Black Shield, and thrust the weapon at him.

"This is a very valuable repeating rifle, Boy! It's yours now. Learn to hit whatever you shoot at. Now, you hear me and you hear me good. The next time I think you should fire and you don't, I'm going to break this rifle over your head. Do you understand me?"

"Yes, Fire Hawk."

"What happened here today is over! Never repeat it!"

Chapter XV

➤

Siege At Beecher's Island

Siege Site
Arikaree River
Colorado Territory
September, 1868

Throughout the remainder of the day, they continued to tighten the huge formation. Fire Hawk and Black Shield did not flush out further quarry, but other members of the cordon did.

It was late afternoon by the time the encirclement ended. The results had been very good. During the morning they had captured three supply wagons and six soldiers. The big wagons were hauling large quantities of food staples, as well as two dozen Winchester repeating rifles and a thousand rounds of ammunition. A short time later Gall's warriors had fought a running battle with a reconnaissance patrol, composed of eight troopers and a grizzled sergeant. Three of the troopers had died in the fight, and the rest had just been brought to Fire Hawk for questioning, along with the six wagon soldiers who had been captured earlier.

"Who are you, Sergeant?" the war chief asked.

"Sergeant Sean Flynn. U.S. Seventh Cavalry," replied Sergeant Flynn stiffly.

"I'm not blind! I can see your insignia! Which troop?"

"C Troop. Captain Tom Custer."

"What was your mission?"

"Go to hell, Forrester. I ain't gonna tell you nothin'."

"So, you recognize me? From where?"

"Villain talked about you one night at the Sutler's store."

"Villain's a good man."

"He said you was too. He said you wouldn't never turn on your friends."

"These Sioux are my friends, Flynn. What was your mission?"

"I ain't tellin' you squat, Reb, and nary a damned thing kin you do about it," Flynn spit out emphatically.

"I have people in my command, Flynn, who could make you beg to talk. But I don't think that will be necessary."

Without further comment, he turned his back on the soldier and strode toward White Wolf and Gall.

"Hawk, if you wish," said White Wolf, "I will make the Yellow Leg with striped sleeves sing like a bird."

"There is no need, Wolf. Soon they will all sing like a flock of birds. First, let the young ones tremble for a while."

The three friends waited for nearly an hour. Then Fire Hawk said to the others, "Go among the warriors, choose twelve of the fiercest looking, most intimidating ones, and send them to me."

When the painted dozen had assembled, he issued instructions, then led them toward the cluster of frightened troopers. Each Sioux singled out a captive, grasped his hair with one hand to reduce the trembling, brandished a scalping knife with the other, and smiled down at the victim with his most malevolent grimace.

It took all of Fire Hawk's willpower to keep from bursting into laughter.

"Now," he said in his most authoritative voice, "you prisoners are faced with a choice. You are going to be with us for quite a long time. How pleasant your stay will be depends on you. In one minute, my men are going to cut every stitch of clothing from your bodies. You will remain naked from now on, whatever the weather may be. When we return to our villages, your dignity, as well as your skins, will be bared to the scorn of our women and children. They will revile you and use you as pack animals. The choice is yours. The price of your comfort is your cooperation. If you help me, I'll help you. You have one minute to agree to my terms, and to raise your hands, indicating acceptance."

Very slowly every hand rose into the air. The last of them belonged to Sergeant Flynn.

"Very well, but remember, if you lie to me, the alternative is still available. Sergeant Flynn, front and center."

Flynn's entire body shook with fury as he approached the war chief. He had decided to cooperate for the sake of his men, but the idea of capitulation made his blood boil. If I were alone, he thought, this war-painted, turncoated rebel bastard would wait for hell to freeze over before I told him one damned thing!

"Tell me the truth, Flynn. Or it will go hard for your men."

"Well, it's like this," the old soldier began. "There's better than twenty squads out lookin' for yer villages. All the way from the Missouri to the Washita. The regiment is split up inta six parts, with two reinforced companies to a part. We're ordered to skedaddle back to the regimental camp on Mission Creek if'n we spot any hostiles, but no later than six days from today."

That was interesting, thought Fire Hawk; their rendezvous is the same day as ours, but fifty miles toward the northwest.

"What's the strength of the Seventh now, Flynn?"

"We're up to the mark. We're runnin' more of a short brigade than a regular regiment. Beside his twelve companies o' cavalry, Custer got hisself six companies o' infantry and a hull platoon o' mortarmen. All told, well o'er a thousand men. That ain't counting Colonel Forsyth's company o' scouts, or the band."

"We can't forget the band, Flynn. If Custer could go to Heaven by himself, or go to perdition and take the band, he would order them to strike up the Garryowen and march happily off to hell."

"You know the General well?"

"Just this well, Flynn. I don't know about the band, but I am personally going to make sure Custer gets to hell."

Flynn looked at the dark, smoldering eyes, glistening with hatred that peered out of the war-painted face, and shuddered.

"Tell me about George Forsyth's outfit, Flynn."

"Him 'n Fred Beecher recruited about fifty scouts. Most of 'em is squaw men, or old-time trappers that has been around forever. They know which end o' the crick the beaver is at. Them fellers is big trouble. Them old boys will learn ya how to dance, Reb! If'n you painted bastards tangle with them, they'll put a hull lot 'o Injun livers inta their war bags! Ya kin count on that!"

Fire Hawk grinned as he turned away filled with new respect for the feisty old sergeant. Men like him had been the hearts of military units ever since Caesar's Legions had roamed the earth.

Now that Fire Hawk had the knowledge he needed, he sent teams of couriers to Crazy Horse and Roman Nose with a summary of the information he had obtained from Flynn. Then he called the other leaders to a council of war.

Since they were in possession of Flynn's orders, they decided to re-form the three-division war party into two large groups. One half, with Man Afraid and Gall in charge, would ride east for about twenty miles, then south toward the Washita and finally west to Black Butte. There they would meet the forces of Fire Hawk and White Wolf, who would start by riding west and then duplicate all the other movements in reverse.

Again, the warriors would drop off at appropriate intervals and create a long picket line. As before, they would offer the enemy an option of immediate battle or of being herded toward the waiting clutches of the stalkers along the Arikaree River.

Six days from now, the Sioux and Cheyenne would assemble over a thousand warriors there. Fire Hawk hoped Custer would get wind of the buildup and come out in force.

➢

It was now the afternoon of that sixth day. Only a short time and a few miles remained until the meeting on the Arikaree. The war party had ridden all the way down to Black Butte, which was just a few miles from the Washita River, and had been riding north for the past three days. They had seen no large enemy units but had picked off three more cavalry patrols. The prisoner count was up to thirty-one. Several of the new captives willingly confirmed the information that Sergeant Flynn had provided.

In one of these skirmishes, Black Shield was a participant and had acquitted himself well. He was in the party that pursued ten fleeing soldiers. One of the troopers spun his horse around and attempted to break out through the line by riding directly at the young warrior, throwing up a hail of bullets as he came. Black Shield waited calmly until he was certain of his target, then dropped the soldier from his saddle with one shot.

He never mentioned the deed, nor did Fire Hawk. They didn't need to. They both knew that the slate had been wiped clean. He was now a warrior who could be counted upon.

A short time later, still several miles south of the Arikaree River, a rider appeared on the horizon. He came on at a lusty gallop, hesitated beside the riders in the vanguard, and then came straight toward Fire Hawk. As the rider approached, the war chief recognized Bobtail Horse, the warrior who had been left in charge of the reserve force. The new arrival pulled his pony back on its haunches and slid to a halt a few feet from Star Walker, who shied quickly away from him.

"Roman Nose and his warriors drove a big party of army scouts out into the Arikaree," gasped Bobtail Horse, his shortness of breath obvious. "Just as they did, another group of our warriors came down from the other direction. Now the scouts are trapped on a small sandy island in the middle of the river."

"How far is the island from the riverbanks, Bobtail Horse?"

"It is inside the distance an arrow can fly."

"What is the plan of Roman Nose?"

"He will keep them there until they are all dead, or we are."

They quickened their pace and arrived at the Arikaree a short time later. As they rode along the bank, Fire Hawk looked across at the island and saw a great deal of furious activity. The men, using butcher knives and tin plates, were digging rifle pits in the sand to conceal themselves from snipers along the shores. When those pits were finished, their defensive position would be excellent. Surrounded by fresh water, if they had carried ample supplies of food and ammunition, the siege would be a long one.

He remembered the rule of attack from assault tactics classes at V.M.I., which roughly translated said: An attacking force can never have a comfortable margin of superiority when storming a strong defensive position. This well-fortified island, sitting in the middle of this churning river, certainly fit that definition. It was as strong a position as one could hope to find.

Much to the relief of the Indians, the scouts had chosen to swim their horses across to the island with them. Perhaps they could not have reached the refuge without them. Bobtail Horse said that a small party of scouts had stayed behind on the riverbank to form a rear guard. It was their intense fusillade that allowed the others to gain the safety of the island. Once across, the island's occupants had laid down a reciprocal volley, under which the rearguard had then crossed. Two or three of this group were wounded before they could breast the river.

Fire Hawk sought out Bobtail Horse and asked to be guided to the spot where the rearguard action had been fought.

The signs indicated that about ten men had been part of the fierce little fight. Although many of the tracks were nearly obliterated and difficult to read, one was perfectly clear. A boot heel with three tiny horseshoes. The boot's owner was on the island.

➢

Fire Hawk was correct. The man was on the island. So were fifty-one other men. One of them was dead, and four others were wounded. The dead man was the party's second-in-command, Lieutenant F.H. Beecher. A few minutes earlier, he had been buried in a place that would immortalize his name in the pages of history. This spit of land would forever be known as Beecher's Island. While the other defenders were digging, four men were formulating a plan. The scout leader, Colonel George A. Forsyth, spoke.

"Our options seem to be limited, gentlemen."

"They are, Colonel, but they're pretty good," said Jack.

"It's their play," opined Harry. "They kin charge or sit."

"That big bunch that just rode in are Oglalas. If Crazy Horse is in charge, they'll sit," declared Frank. "If'n it's White Wolf or Man Afraid, they'll charge. The parcel that jumped us was all Cheyennes. That tall, copper-colored Injun that's leadin' 'em is Roman Nose. First thing tomorrow, he'll charge for certain. Next thing tomorrow, I'm goin' to blow him off'n his horse and kill him dead. I'll drop him in this river, 'en that's for certain."

"Since we have plenty of food and ammunition, if we stay under cover as much as possible, we're going to be tough to dislodge," decided Colonel Forsyth.

"They can't get us with thirst and we've got three weeks worth of rations, plus plenty of bullets," agreed Jack, "but they could still force us out, Colonel."

"How?" asked Forsyth.

"By killin' the horses and lettin' them rot," advised Jack. "There are fifty animals who make fine targets out here on this island in the middle of September. As soon as they die, the heat will go to work on their carcasses.

Within hours, they'll begin to smell, bloat, and invite infectious vermin from miles around. If that happens, Colonel, we better start thinking about somebody getting ashore and going for help before we die of the plague."

"Hell, Jack," exploded Frank. "Any Injun would rather kill his own family than kill a hoss. They ain't never goin' to kill good hosses and that's for certain."

"Well," concluded Jack, "if they do, we're in deep trouble, and that's for certain. I wonder what's goin' on over there?

A powwow was going on. A half-mile from the river, behind a small row of low hills, a war camp had been set up. In the middle of the camp, a spirited discussion was underway.

"I am a Cheyenne Dog Soldier, not an old woman. I do not need to spend a month waiting for the White Eyes to turn to dust," bellowed Roman Nose. "I will lead a charge against them after the sun comes up and kill them all."

"Roman Nose, my brother," replied Fire Hawk, "I do not counsel cowardice; I counsel caution. The days when our people could draw the fire of the White Eyes, fighting with single-shot rifles, and then send in a second and third and even fourth wave before the weapons could be reloaded, are over. At this moment, you sit here with a Winchester rifle in your hands that can be loaded and then fired more times than you have fingers, before you need feed it fresh cartridges. My plan will work, my brother; let us try it."

"I do not say that Fire Hawk's plan is bad. It is good, but it is slow. My plan will also work, and it is not slow."

Braving the wrath of the feisty Dog Soldier, Fire Hawk said, "My brother, at sunrise, a dozen of us can fire our rifles at the island and kill every animal out there before you finish your morning meal. Seven suns from now, the scouts will wish they were dead. Twenty suns from now, they will be dead. There is no need for any of us to die."

"Tomorrow will be a good day to die for my people, Fire Hawk."

"Tomorrow will be an even better day to live for them! Black Kettle is already dead! Who will lead the Southern Cheyenne?"

"Tomorrow, I will! I will rout the White Eyes from the island. I know you mean well, my brother, but speak to me no more of this."

As a last resort, Fire Hawk asked White Wolf, Man Afraid, and Gall to go with him to speak to Roman Nose's friend and subchief, Black Bear. Fire Hawk presented his plan and added a plea that he speak to Roman Nose. Black Bear would not consider it.

➢

Early the next day, more than two hundred Cheyenne warriors fanned out along the riverbank behind their legendary leader, determined to drive the hated White Eyes from their perilous sanctuary. At their head rode a war chief anxious to prove that his self-proclaimed myth of invincibility was really true.

The defenders allowed the Cheyenne to reach a point halfway between the shore and the island before they opened fire, then they sent volley after volley crashing into the horde of Indian horsemen, toppling rider after rider from his pony and into a river that soon ran red with blood.

The first to fall was Roman Nose, but a hundred others died before the heroic charge was blunted, and half a hundred more before they could regain the sanctuary of the far distant bank.

Roman Nose and many of his dedicated band proved that day that they could indeed die well. But it was a hollow and forlorn gesture in the face of fifty defenders who proved that they could live well, and win. First round to the White Eyes. That was for certain.

The enormous number of casualties suffered by the Cheyenne was a crushing blow, but it accounted for only one part of their devastating defeat. Even more damaging was the loss of Roman Nose, a leader his people truly thought of as invincible, if not immortal. When Roman Nose died, so did their dreams of a great victory.

The third and final setback was the reversal of roles that the first encounter had brought about. The attackers had become the underdogs. Their confidence was wavering. For the first time, they actually believed that they might lose, while the opposite was true of the defenders. Their resolve had stiffened, and they were even more confident of victory. An hour later, their morale was given an even bigger boost, for it was then that Black Bear led a new assault on Beecher's Island.

Roman Nose's successor split his remaining two hundred plus warriors into two long columns and led another charge. This time, however, they did not start on the riverbanks directly across from the island, nor attempt to attack the entire length of the sandy ait. Instead, they began upstream in the middle of the river and, in double file, swept down upon the narrow tip of the island.

When the two columns finally reached this log-jammed jutland, after struggling through the shallow river's swift and hampering current, every rider had to rein his struggling, protesting pony toward one side of the island and follow in the watery wake of the warriors who had preceded him on the perilous journey along an entire length of bloody beach, bristling with gun barrels.

During that ride, each warrior concealed as much of his body as possible behind his horse, fired rapidly at his enemies from beneath the animal's neck, and hoped to survive the defenders' deadly barrage of whistling lead.

Observing from a distance, Fire Hawk decided that this might well be one of history's most courageous attacks. Not one man hung back or shirked his duty. Most of the riders did not live to reach the end of the island, and those who did had tragically little effect on the well-prepared and proficient defenders. The Cheyenne paid a fearsome price to achieve a terrible defeat.

Black Bear's plan was only slightly more successful than that of his predecessor. Roman Nose lost three-quarters of his men; Black Bear's dead numbered two-thirds. At dawn, more than four hundred Cheyenne warriors had been in the attack force. Now it was noon, and less than one hundred thirty remained alive. Black Bear was wounded but still survived. Bobtail Horse had emerged without a scratch. Fire Hawk was grateful. He had lost enough good friends for one day.

He returned to the war camp and called White Wolf, Gall, and Black Shield to him and explained his plan. A short time later, the four warriors left the camp and walked to a small hillock which overlooked the river and the island. Their mission was distasteful, but necessary. Fire Hawk gave final instructions to Black Shield.

"Before each shot at an animal, try to find a human target. All right, let's begin."

The four marksmen opened fire on the scouts' horses, which could not be hidden on the small island. At almost every shot, another of the unfortunate beasts fell to the ground and lay still.

Temporarily, the animals that fell offered additional cover and concealment, but very soon the defenders would begin to wish the horses were far away.

From the corner of his eye, Fire Hawk saw one scout rise up slightly to aim at them. Before the man could fire, Fire Hawk shifted his rifle and put a bullet through the forehead of the careless defender. This was war, he thought, as much as the big one I fought in. Less than an hour later, all of the horses were dead and two more White Eyes had been wounded.

202

As they bellied down off the hill, Fire Hawk decided to position two carefully-chosen sharpshooters, one on this low crest and the other on the opposite side of the river. It made sense to continue harassing the defenders. In the days ahead, they might get a killing shot, as constant pressure and fatigue made the scouts grow weary.

Sometime in the next forty-eight hours, the hot sun and warm, humid air would make the dead horses begin to rot and bloat. The stench from that decay would soon make the sand-spit a horrible place to be. The poor wretches who occupied it would soon become miserable, hot, dirty, tired, careless men. Weary, careless men soon became desperate men. Desperate men soon became dead men.

Surely, he mused, Forsyth and his men must know their already-deplorable conditions will continue to deteriorate. To intensify their misery, he decided to fire sporadic, random rifle shots. Increasing tension and discomfort may force a few of them to go for help. Undoubtedly, messengers will try to go up or downstream for some distance before they leave the safety of the river. Our warriors, posted on both banks, can nab them as they come ashore.

➤

On the island, another meeting was underway. It was being held within a barricade made up of the bodies of dead horses. The four plotters were the same ones who had met earlier; however, their appearances had changed. Colonel Forsyth's shoulder bore a blood-soaked bandage, and a similar protective device now encircled Harry's head.

"Colonel," said Jack, "in a couple of days, this island will be one of two things. A living hell, or a dying hell. We need to send for help."

"I think you're right, Jack, but tonight and tomorrow, they'll be expecting us to try a breakout. Of course, they'll have sentries posted each night, but those men will grow more restless and less watchful as time goes by. What do you think, Frank?"

"I think two or three nights is the limit. Remember, our men will get restless, too."

"All right," said Forsyth. "We'll set it up for three nights from now. Jack, what are your suggestions?"

Chief Scout Jack Trudeau pondered for several moments before answering. A short, wiry French Canadian in his mid-thirties, Jack was famous for his trapping and tracking skills, but was best known for his great running ability. In a short race, many men could beat him. If the race went on all day and all night, some might bring him to earth. But in a twenty- or thirty-mile race, no one could catch him. At least, no one had for the past dozen years, although many men, both white and red, had tried.

"I think we should send out three two-man teams, Colonel. The two men wouldn't actually travel together. They would remain some distance apart. In that way, each could cover for the other, but if one got caught or killed, the other might still get away."

"I like it so far, Jack, but why only three teams?"

"Because we have three possible escape routes. We can go toward the far bank, across from their main camp, or we can go up or downstream. I think the team that goes to the far bank, or the one going downstream, will only wind up acting as live decoys. Those are the obvious three breakthrough points. If any of our men are discovered, they should create as big a commotion as possible to mask the other messengers. Fortunately, nearly every man on this island has the experience and ability to break out."

"Choose the team leaders," invited the Colonel.

"Me, Frank, and Harry, if he's able. If not, Brian O'Toole."

"I'm able, right enough!" asserted Harry.

"Then it's settled?" asked Forsyth.

"Not by a jugfull," countered Frank. "Let O'Toole lead a team and I'll go it alone."

"But we have only three directions to try," counseled Jack.

"I think you're wrong, Chief Scout," said Frank. "There are actually four. You forgot the one nobody else will even think of. The one that goes right through the middle of the Injuns' camp. That's where I'm goin'. That's the one place they won't look."

"At least you hope they won't," said the Chief of Scouts, with mixed emotions.

They spent the next few hours selecting the teams and making final plans. Harry Holloway and Ken James would attempt their escape over the far bank. Brian O'Toole and Tim Paul would float along with the current in the middle of the river for several miles, before approaching either bank. Jack Trudeau and John Daniel would move slowly and cautiously upstream for a short distance before seeking refuge in the shadows near the shore. Frank would "go it alone."

➢

As Forsyth's Scouts had ridden along the Arikaree the day before, Trudeau had taken note of two unusual sites that might aid them in their escape. The first one, about a mile upstream, was a great pile of buffalo bones.

White hunters usually carried off the meat and hides on their first trip to the marketplace, since they would be consumed or rendered useless by wild animals if left unattended. But they almost always left the bones and came back for them at another time. Bones could be ground down and used to manufacture a wide variety of products, ranging from soaps to fertilizers. Buffalo bones were valuable. That huge pile he had seen would be worth hundreds of dollars when hauled to the nearest town. For the present, they offered the fugitives an excellent sanctuary on an otherwise stark, flat prairie.

The second hiding place was three or four miles farther upstream. It was a small grove of cottonwood trees, in one of which was a recently erected Cheyenne burial platform. Since no Plains Indian would violate such sacred ground, they could hide throughout the entire day in the tiny copse of cottonwoods.

Yes, Jack thought, that's the best way to go. Also, it was good to know that Johnny Daniel had stuck to him like a shadow for more than twenty miles the last time they had raced. If he and Johnny could get out of the river without being seen, they would never be caught. Having reached that comforting conclusion, despite the cramped discomfort, the moaning of the wounded, and the gnawing of sand fleas, Jack Trudeau dozed off thinking to himself, "I've been in lots of worse places."

➢

Early the following morning, as soon he and the other Sioux leaders had eaten, Fire Hawk had Sergeant Flynn brought to him. He was hopeful that the sergeant might have been lulled into a cooperative frame of mind by the fair treatment he and his men had received since their capture.

"Good morning, Sergeant," he said good-naturedly.

"Mornin', Captain."

Well, thought the war chief, this is certainly an improvement.

"Sergeant, how much do you know about Forsyth's men?"

"Wadayamean?"

"For instance, are there any Indians in the Scout Company that you know of?"

"Red Sticks? Hell, no. None o' them. There may be a few Frenchies, like Trudeau and Longpre, but no Injuns or breeds."

"Breeds?"

"Half-breeds," clarified Flynn.

"All right, Sergeant, you may go."

"What are you thinking, Hawk?" asked White Wolf.

"Just this," replied the war chief. "If you were sitting on that island and wanted to get away, what would you do? Which way would you go?"

"I would wait until the moon set and float down the river."

"Now you are thinking like a white man, Wolf. Think like an Indian, or a white man who looks like an Indian, or somebody that knows our ways. Now what would you do?"

"Aiyee!" exclaimed White Wolf. "Of course. I would sneak across the river, kill the first warrior I saw and steal his clothes, then go straight through the war camp to the pony herd. Once there, I would just fade away."

"That's what I would do, too. The other day Sean Flynn said something he didn't repeat today. Most of Forsyth's Scouts have lived among the tribes for many years. They know our ways well. At least one of them will try going through our encampment."

"You sent unmounted warriors for a great distance along each bank in both directions. Why did you not let them ride?"

"For many reasons, Wolf. A pony's noise, at the wrong moment, might cover the sounds of someone in the river. A waiting man is silent. A pony offers a large, easy-to-see silhouette against the sky. A man, lying on the ground, is nearly invisible. Finally, if one of our sentries were to be overpowered, his horse would give a fleeing man more mobility and a much better chance to escape."

"Fire Hawk, you are a wise war chief."

"My last war taught me many things — like the surprise we set up downstream. By the way, how is your foot? I saw you limping."

"Sometimes the toes that are not there become very painful. But the wounds have healed well. Of course, I am no longer a feared runner."

207

"I didn't know that you were ever a feared runner, Wolf."

"I never was! But now I am less feared than ever before."

"Let me get your mind back onto the island for a while, Wolf. Let us suppose that the moon has gone down and it is very dark. You have managed to creep across the river without being seen. Where would you try to come ashore?"

"I would stay in the water, watching and listening until I was certain that no one lurked in that small clump of trees near the bank, then I would dart into them."

"Then, as you reached those trees, if you saw a wickiup just a short distance away, what would you do?"

"I would wait until it seemed safe and then run to the darkest side of the lodge and wait again in the shadows."

"Good!" said Fire Hawk. "Now, in those deep shadows you find the doorway and just inside you discover a medicine man's long robe and buffalo horn headdress. Remember now, you are a jittery, shaky fugitive who knows that being caught means certain death. What would you do?"

White Wolf could not contain a bellow of laughter. "I would give thanks to the Great Spirit, put on the robe, and pull the horn headdress as far down over my face as I could. Then walk slowly away, acting like every other medicine man acts."

"Let's find Black Shield and a few of his friends and give them three assignments. First, they will raise a lodge with the doorway in the proper location. Next, I want them to find the longest robe and the biggest horn headdress in camp. Finally, they must gather up all other similar costumes and take them far away. The next time we see someone walking around wearing buffalo horns, we'll have our man."

➢

The next three days on Beecher's Island were, as Jack Trudeau had forecast, a living and dying hell. Three men were dead and four times that many had been wounded. The bloated horses were giving off such a putrid, sickening stench, that it brought tears to the men's eyes. Many of them had stuffed chewing tobacco into their nostrils to quell their nausea. That had done very little except produce a large number of swollen and sore, red and raw noses, most of which were still sensitive enough to separate the equally wretched odors of vomit and rotting horseflesh.

Jack Trudeau's old friend, Pierre Longpre, had found a means of escape. He had risen for a look at the near bank and been greeted by a bullet in the head. Pierre had often ridiculed the Indians' poor marksmanship. At least one of them could certainly shoot, reflected the Chief Scout. Only a few seconds elapsed from the moment Pierre had lifted his head until he was dead.

➢

It was midevening of the escape night. In a little over three hours, they would make the break. If it went well, seven of them would get out of this hellhole. Jack Trudeau crawled over to a shallow trench where John Daniel lay and rolled in beside him.

"Johnny, I've been thinking about our escape for the past three days. I thought about leavin' our buckskins here on the island and just wearin' breechclouts, but our white bodies shinin' in the water would be like the sun shinin' in the sky. I think we better wear our clothes until we get onto the bank by that big pile o' buffa bones, upriver. By then, these damned buckskins will be so waterlogged; they'll weigh forty pounds. If the coast is clear, we kin strip down to clouts and run fer it. If we hide under the bones, our duds will be dry by mornin'."

"Them is good plans, Jack," Daniel agreed. "Lot o' them banks has that red dust. Reckon it won't hurt ta roll around in thet whist we was wet. Take our shine away and make us look more like Red Sticks, wouldn't it?"

"It sure would, Johnny. You ain't so dumb as ya look, are ya?" laughed the Chief Scout.

"No, and I ain't near so dumb as you look, Jack," joked his friend in return.

A short distance away, Frank was pondering similar questions, but since he was going it alone, he could do everything his own way. He had always preferred doing things his own way. He peered again at the small clump of trees on the opposite bank. He had watched the area around the trees since late afternoon and was certain that no guards lurked in the vicinity. Stupid Red Sticks, he thought. They would never suspect that anyone would try to escape right through their camp. Obviously, those trees would be his first goal.

Once I get there, he thought, I'll kill the first Red Stick who passes me wearin' either a robe or blanket, and head for the horse herd. He chuckled, thinking how easy it would be.

Three hours later, the seven messengers were in a final meeting with Colonel Forsyth.

"The closest friendly forces are fifty miles northwest of us, with Custer at Mission Creek," Forsyth told them. "If you get cut off from Custer, General Crook is camped across the badlands at Burning Wells. Also, you might encounter a patrol at any point; there are many of them out there. If someone gets through to Custer and he force-marches back to us, help could arrive as early as the 25th, five days from now. Well, men, good luck to you all. May God's blessings go with you."

Chapter XVI

➢

Escape

Siege At Beecher's Island
Arikaree River
Colorado Territory
September, 1868

As soon as the meeting ended, Harry Holloway and Ken James slithered down the bank of the island and began their slippery journey toward the far shore. Although the apparently sluggish current of the two-foot-deep river seemed unlikely to aid Brian O'Toole and Tim Paul in their attempt to float a heavy log downstream, Holloway and James' problem was entirely different. Shallow water proved to be a serious challenge for them as they tried to keep as much of their bodies submerged as possible. In many places, a current far stronger than they had anticipated surged against their struggling torsos and flailing legs.

They tried to hold themselves against the relentless force by grasping stones and rocks, but soon discovered that the larger rocks were impossible to hold, since they were covered with green moss and algae, while the smaller ones simply pulled out of the riverbed at the slightest touch. They fought to avoid being swept away by digging boot toes and fingertips into the gravel.

Several times they floundered into deep channels where the water pressure was much stronger. On those occasions they lost all control and were carried along, head over heels, until they reached the next shallow place.

Halfway toward their objective, the spraying and splashing in the river alerted the sentries on the far bank, who began firing at the fugitives. They were fortunate that the Indian riflemen on the distant bank were impatient. If they had waited, Holloway and James would certainly have perished. As it was, both men were able to regain the safety of the island with only a few bruises and superficial wounds. The escapees of the first team had been foiled in their attempt, but had succeeded in acting as decoys.

➢

Brian O'Toole and Tim Paul had crawled carefully to the upper tip of the island where a large log, swept downstream by the last big rainstorm, lay rocking gently back and forth in the shallow water. Jack Trudeau and John Daniel had helped them to dislodge it from its sandy cradle and had then held it against the current while O'Toole and Paul concealed themselves amongst the sparsely leafed branches. When both were in position, the four men levered the fallen giant away from its prison and pushed it well out into the deepest channel. But, as they had feared, even in its center, the river's sparse volume was inadequate to provide sufficient buoyancy to float the heavy log. It constantly bumped and scraped against the river bottom, and the men were forced to exert great pressure in an unremitting effort to coax the log into continuing its interrupted passage down the shallow, watery canyon. When the staccato of shots directed at Holloway and James began, the noise provided the fugitives with an opportunity to force their Trojan Horse past a bend in the river and find temporary sanctuary within the dense shadows of some low-hanging branches. Gratefully and silently, they rested.

➢

Frank, the scout who had decided to attempt an escape through the heart of the Indian village, was in the river near the bank when the volley of gunfire from the distant shore had erupted. Them fellers are right on cue, he thought. Since the shots were coming from downstream, several warriors, eager to get a better view, actually skirted around the small grove of trees where Frank planned to seek refuge.

Since it was a night with extremely thick cloud cover, the fugitives had not waited for the moon to set before venturing forth. At isolated times, when no clouds obscured the moon, the landscape was bathed in bright light, but those periods were widely spaced. Darkness prevailed almost constantly.

It was near the end of one of the dark spells when Frank reached the cover of the trees. As he peered out through the branches, the moon momentarily poked out from behind one cloud, before being swallowed up by another. In that instant of light, he saw a teepee only a short distance away.

A moment later, darkness once again covered the land and he darted forward into the deep shadows behind the lodge. Crouching there without moving or breathing, he listened for any sounds from within. Holding his knife in one hand, he reached out with the other and explored with his fingertips. Almost immediately his hand encountered a buffalo robe. Clinching his knife tightly, he prepared to strike out and kill whoever was wearing the robe; but he soon discovered that the garment was merely lying on the ground along with a ceremonial buffalo horn headdress.

This is the lodge of a medicine man, he decided. Perhaps he dropped these things here and rushed off to find out about the firing on the island. I had better not tarry in case he returns.

Frank donned the vestments just as the moonlight broke through the clouds once again. Instinctively, he ducked under the flap of the lodge into its interior. Inside he discovered three pots of paint: a red, a white, and a yellow.

Minutes later, when he emerged from the wickiup, he looked exactly like a Cheyenne medicine man. The robe nearly touched the ground, the horn headdress came down to the level of his eyes, and he was painted in the traditional fashion of a holy man. I have, he decided, found the perfect disguise. Even when the moon burst forth again, turning the night as bright as day, he could not help grinning as he walked toward the pony herd.

Back at the decoy lodge, two other men were also grinning.

"It is almost like he was following your directions, Hawk."

"He certainly is being cooperative, Wolf. Let's go get him. We can hold this refugee with Sean Flynn and the others."

Keeping the bogus medicine man in sight, they strolled after him. Suddenly Fire Hawk stiffened and knelt beside a fresh track left by the man they pursued. There, in the moonlight, they could clearly see the mark of his boot. In the center of the heel print were three tiny horseshoes.

All thoughts of capture and mercy quickly evaporated. They were replaced by the memory of two young Cheyenne Dog Soldiers, made to suffer terrible pain and humiliations in a lonely arroyo. Soon those thoughts were also crowded aside by the memory of a beautiful, loving, and tender young woman. A woman whom he had loved more than life itself. A woman waiting for him beside the Star Road of the Great Spirit.

"You, medicine man!" hailed Fire Hawk. "Stand where you are! If you try to run, I'll shoot you in both of your legs and leave you here, screaming in pain."

As they approached, the man turned to face them.

"Take off the robe and headdress, you murderous, torturing bastard," Fire Hawk said in a low, quavering voice.

As soon as he removed the headdress, both men recognized him as Frank Grouard, the Grabber, the treacherous adopted son of Sitting Bull.

"Grabber," asked White Wolf, "did you live among our people long enough to learn a death song? If you know one, sing it now."

"Two against one," protested the Grabber. "Is that what you noble warriors call fair?"

"Grabber," said White Wolf, "I would give my Chestnut pony for a chance to spill your blood. But I fear no bribe can tempt Fire Hawk away from his vow to kill you."

"You have to answer for many things," advised Fire Hawk. "First, for the pain you inflicted upon Running Horse and Young Otter. Second, you must be punished for betraying Sitting Bull, a man who trusted and befriended you. Most of all, you must pay for the murder of Little Fawn, a young woman who spent her life helping and healing, and bringing hope back to so many. You yourself are alive today only because of her knowledge and skill; yet you repaid her kindness by helping our enemies to put a bullet in her back. To pay for all of these things, you must die!"

Fire Hawk withdrew his Spanish knife and started toward his enemy.

"Come and dance with the Widow Maker, Grabber."

Surprisingly, the Grabber stood his ground, took a long-bladed knife from his belt, and replied in a voice loaded with venom.

"I didn't shoot your greasy red bitch, Hawk. I only wish I'd had that pleasure."

Fire Hawk was tempted to rush forward and end the insults with a thrust to the heart but realized that was exactly what the Grabber hoped he would do.

Fire Hawk was right. Now that he had been caught, the Grabber had no hope of survival. If he could provoke this other white man into a storm of rage, a quick death would be his reward. He had made too many others suffer the horror of slow and tedious deaths to harbor any illusions about his own ability to withstand great physical pain.

Glittering knives poised in hand, the bitter enemies began circling each other, searching for the all-important first opening of the fight.

As he studied the movements of his opponent, Fire Hawk realized that the Grabber was not a skillful knife

215

fighter. He doesn't react to my blade, thought the war chief. He responds only to my eye and head movements. To test his theory, Fire Hawk held his knife steady, but feinted slightly with his head and eyes. As anticipated, the Grabber immediately moved to counter.

Fire Hawk brought the Widow Maker to a position directly in front of his body, with both hands resting on the hilt. Suddenly, he transferred the deadly weapon to his left hand, but feinted with his head, eyes, and right hand toward the Grabber's heart. The long blade of the Arkansas Toothpick, which the Grabber held, jumped out to parry Fire Hawk's threatened blow, but encountered only empty air. Failing to feel an impact of steel against steel, the Grabber's facial expression became one of complete confusion.

Seconds later, his look of bewilderment was exchanged for a grimace of excruciating pain, as he discovered the whereabouts of the missing Spanish knife. Fire Hawk had thrust it deeply into the Grabber's lower groin. As it was withdrawn, the upturned tip inflicted even more damage. The result was a gory, vicious looking wound, a jagged gash from which blood spewed with each irregular heartbeat. The Grabber clutched his abdomen with his free hand, and emitted a blood-chilling shriek. As Fire Hawk bounded out of reach, the Grabber recovered slightly and stumbled toward his far more nimble antagonist in a crab-like, halting gait, his stiletto extended before him. As he came, he sliced desperate, menacing, but futile arcs through the empty air of a suddenly silent, expectant night.

His lurching walk ended abruptly. Merely standing had suddenly become an overwhelming challenge. His legs shook uncontrollably. His glassy eyes, in an ashen face, mirrored his abject frustration. The Grabber was dying from despair as well as from blood loss.

Every human being seems to have a built-in physical barometer that sends messages to his brain when his body has suffered too much damage to ever recover. It is then that the mind eagerly relishes the release from pain that only death can bring. Once that mental acceptance of non-recovery is reached, death, for the first time, becomes a man's best friend instead of his worst enemy. The Grabber had reached that point. Willingly he would have embraced death.

Fire Hawk was not enjoying this spectacle at all. He was not, by nature, a cruel man; but he did believe in an eye for an eye. The useless misery and death he had witnessed made him question the traditional philosophy of forgive and forget. For the present, he rejected his normal world of rationality. For these last few moments he had descended into a pit of hell. A dark and sinister place where fury and rage erased every human emotion. Fire Hawk was consumed with the idea that the Grabber had to suffer a measure of the pain and sense of futility that he had inflicted upon his many helpless victims.

As Fire Hawk turned to face the Grabber for the last time, his reason returned. This man might be a miserable wretch, but he was no coward. He was still doing his best to steady his stiletto and defend himself. Therefore, he was still very dangerous. Once more Fire Hawk feinted toward the heart and at the last moment changed targets. This time the knife's razor-sharp point entered the underside of his enemy's right forearm, just above the wrist. The long, slender-bladed stiletto slid out of the Grabber's powerless fingers and fell harmlessly into the dust.

"Now you know how your victims must have felt, Frank. It's a horrible, hopeless feeling, isn't it? Tonight, you have suffered for Running Horse, Young Otter, and others I know nothing about. Sitting Bull would want me to kill you slowly, extracting the last possible ounce of revenge. But Little Fawn, in her endless mercy, would want you to suffer no more. I have caused you great pain and you have borne it well. I will not rob you of your last bit of dignity. I hope neither of us winds up in hell, Frank!"

That strange prayer was the last thing the Grabber heard. For in the next second Fire Hawk rammed the Spanish knife into the Grabber's heart and ended his misery. Fire Hawk turned to White Wolf.

"Revenge is a terrible thing, Wolf!"

"Hawk, it was not revenge. It was justice. The Uncle took the Grabber in, trusted him, made him his son; and the sneaky weasel betrayed us all."

"All the same, he died a hard death."

"So did his victims. So did the Dog Soldiers. So did Little Fawn. So did you. Part of you died on the Washita, my brother. That part may never come back to life. Hawk, this was justice!"

"I killed him to warn all others about the price of treachery and to avenge Little Fawn. Still, he died a hard death!"

"You have taught an important lesson here tonight, my brother. Everyone must know that if they betray us, they will be punished!"

Just then, from far downstream, a string of shots rang out.

"It sounds like we've caught a rabbit in our snare, Wolf."

➤

Fire Hawk was half right. They had actually caught a pair of them. Brian O'Toole and Tim Paul were in the snare. They had kept the heavy log moving for over a mile. On countless occasions, when it ran aground, they freed it, using brute force. Suddenly their progress was stopped cold in the middle of a deep channel where the river ran between two high banks. Tim Paul, who was near the front end of the log, moved forward to investigate and made a most unhappy discovery.

"Brian, there are a pair of heavy ropes stretched across the river. The tree branches are tangled up in them. We'll have to hack our way through, but it'll take us a long time."

Brian opened his mouth to reply just as a storm of bullets, fired down from the high banks, blasted into them. One of them pierced O'Toole's throat. His last sounds were not words, only the gurgle and rattle of death.

Shielded by the log's foliage, Tim Paul was more fortunate. Only the right side of his body was visible and vulnerable to attack. Nonetheless, three bullets struck him. The first entered the back of his shoulder and passed on through, shredding the tissue and muscles but somehow missing the bones. The second punched a clean hole through his side, just above the hip. It was bloody and painful, but it was not serious.

The third wound was far worse. That hit must have come after the impact of the first two spun him around, for it entered the front of his lower leg, where it splintered and decimated his shinbone. Worst of all, the bullet did not exit but remained lodged within the wound. Had he been near a medical facility he might have lost only his leg; here in the wilderness, he almost certainly would lose his life as well.

The Sioux guard force did not climb down the slippery, steep bank to the river. Instead, they skirted around it to a gentler slope and then scampered back along a narrow beach to the log. They recovered the corpse of the first scout at once but were unable to find the other.

➢

The river carried Tim Paul's unconscious, battered body far downstream. Like a chunk of flotsam, it bounced off rocks and bungled its way through rapids and shoals before finally coming to rest on a low sandbar beneath a giant weeping willow tree which had grown beside the river's edge for many years.

Along the way, he had accrued even more damage. Once the current had carried him, face foremost, into a sharp rock, where he had suffered a gashed forehead, a blackened eye, and a broken nose. It was miraculous that any thread of life still remained.

Now he lay on his stomach, partly in and partly out of the river, his left side well up on the sand, while his badly damaged right side and leg were still exposed to the cooling waters.

High overhead the willow wept. Its long branches stretched protectively over him and bent down to caress the surface of the river in supplication, as if to say, "Help me to care for this poor man. He has suffered enough."

It was nearing dawn, and a thick gray mist hung over the river when he revived for the first time. He was thirsty. Although he was lying in fresh water, he was too weak to move his painfully broken body enough to drink. With his undamaged left hand, he scooped out a depression in the sand near his mouth. Soon the tiny hole filled with muddy, cloudy, precious water. He sucked it up greedily through cracked, parched lips. As he lapsed back into unconsciousness, he wondered how the others were doing.

➢

Several miles upstream, the only runners still in the race were approaching the big pile of buffalo bones.

"Past this little bend in the river and we'll be there," Jack Trudeau whispered to his companion. Just ahead of them, a pair of coyotes, apparently unaware of the scout's presence, came nimbly down the bank to drink. After quenching their thirst, the pair trotted back up to the top of the slope, but did not disappear totally from view. They remained silhouetted against the skyline, pulling and tugging at something that lay quite near the brink.

"Let's find out what they're up to," Jack whispered.

Silently the men crept toward the scavengers. They were nearly upon them when the coyotes caught their scent and scrambled away across the wide, flat prairie.

Jack peered over the rim of the high bank and saw, less than six feet away, the partially consumed carcass of a buffalo bull. Tracks around the huge beast indicated that it had apparently been brought down the previous night by a small pack of wolves that, after gorging themselves, abandoned the kill to the coyotes.

They had been able to eat very little before being frightened away. Fully two-thirds of the large carcass still remained.

Suddenly Jack felt a strange premonition. He slid down the embankment and whispered to Johnny Daniel.

"I got a hunch this here buffa bull is gonna save our skins."

Since they had only an hour until dawn, they worked quickly but quietly. Crouching as low as possible to the ground, they rolled the carcass over slightly and then, with Green River butcher knives and tin cups, began digging a hole big enough for them both to hide in. They were careful not to disturb the wolf and coyote tracks either by stepping on them or by digging where they were. They gathered all of the loose dirt in their buckskin shirts and then sprinkled it into the river where the current quickly swept it away, removing all evidence of their activities.

With their cups they scraped out a pair of barely perceptible, two-inch-high tunnels for air and vision, one faced the river, the other toward the pile of bones. Finally, they smoothed the soil to cover up any traces of their activities, assumed prone positions, and rolled the carcass slowly and carefully back over themselves. A short time later Jack Trudeau discovered that his strange premonition had been correct.

From his hiding place, he squinted at the pile of bones, which was about a quarter of a mile away. At first, there was nothing to see. But then, just after dawn lit up the eastern sky, he saw a stealthy movement behind the bone pile, on the side away from the river.

He continued to watch but saw nothing else for nearly an hour. Then, without the slightest warning, a pair of moccasin-clad feet blocked his view. The next moment he heard voices carrying on a soft conversation in Sioux dialect.

"I thought for sure some of them would head for this pile of bones, White Wolf."

"So did I, Gall! It's the first time Fire Hawk has been wrong."

"Maybe they started out and then turned back."

"Maybe. Well, they're not here. If anyone had tried to hide amongst the bones, Big Beaver and Running Fox would have gotten them. Do you think we should call them in?"

"No! They can sit in camp and do nothing, or sit here and do nothing. Out here, they might at least get us some fresh meat."

"If you want fresh meat, parts of this old buffalo bull aren't too badly chewed up," chuckled White Wolf.

"You are a good and considerate friend, but I think I will wait for something fresher."

"Gall, if anyone came upstream, maybe they bypassed the bones and went on to the clump of trees with the burial scaffold."

"If they did, they're dead by now. Fire Hawk sent Bobtail Horse, He Dog, and the son of Iron Shirt to guard the cottonwood grove early last night."

"He thinks of everything. Let us tell Big Beaver and Running Fox that one or the other of them must stay alert all day long. We'll relieve them before sunset and send out some fresh eyes."

"As soon as we do, we must hurry back to camp. My stomach is gnawing on my backbone."

Well, thought Jack Trudeau, whoever this Fire Hawk is, he has out-snookered me at every turn. Wonder why I ain't heard o' him before. I reckoned I knew all the big time Sioux and Cheyenne war chiefs. He must be a new 'un.

Trudeau watched the Sioux warriors walk toward the bone pile and stop next to it before he whispered to John Daniel.

"Let's try to sleep, or at least get some rest. An hour before sundown we'll make a break fer it. The Red Sticks behind the bone pile will be looking forward to hot grub by then and may not even see us when we go."

➢

It was a long, difficult wait. If the Indians at the bone pile had been alert, the scouts would have been discovered many times. Throughout the day they dozed fitfully while trying to ignore the ever increasing smell of the ripening buffalo carcass. On several occasions from midmorning on, small scavengers approached the tempting meal, only to turn away when they detected the presence of humans.

At one point, a vixen, with four kits, drew quite near before she gathered up her brood and hurried them away. Moments later, Jack saw a tall, rangy Sioux warrior start toward them, perhaps made suspicious by the sly fox's curious behavior. Just then, a bald eagle swooped down and landed atop the carcass. Satisfied that the vixen had seen the huge bird and had been alarmed about her kits' safety, the Indian returned to his bone pile vigil.

➢

About two hours before sunset, Trudeau decided that further delay would be foolhardy. Conditions were deteriorating rapidly, and their muscles were beginning to cramp. Cautiously, they both slid out from under the carcass, on the side closer to the river. They slipped silently down the bank and drank water quickly, but sparingly, quaffing just enough to slake their awful thirst. Then they moved slowly and carefully away from the river, keeping the bone pile between themselves and the Indians.

They were nearly a hundred yards from the river when they heard a shrill war whoop and saw the tall, rangy Sioux warrior coming after them, carrying a long spear. As he hurtled forward, he was grinning from ear to ear with eager anticipation.

The racing warrior closed the gap to less than fifty feet before the Scouts were able to accelerate to their best pace. After that, the Indian gained no further ground. If anything, the fugitives actually took back a bit of the lost distance. Furious that his initial burst of speed had not met with more success, the Sioux hurled his sharp tomahawk at the backs of the fleeing pair. It was a forlorn desperate gesture, born of frustration.

Running Fox, the Oglala Sioux who now pursued them, was known far and wide for his great running prowess. When he saw the two White Eyes, he was confident that he would quickly overtake and kill them with his spear. But as soon as the fugitives took a few racing strides, Running Fox realized that these men were capable of speed equal to, or perhaps even greater than, his own. It was this realization that compelled him to let fly with his hatchet at two nearly impossible targets.

As the lethal weapon spun toward his enemies, he saw that it would pass directly between them. A tiny distance, one direction or the other, thought the disgusted Running Fox, would have put one of them down. He watched as the tomahawk neared the end of its errant flight. In another second, it would miss its mark and fall harmlessly to earth.

At that very moment, John Daniel stumbled on the uneven ground and nearly fell. In a desperate effort to regain his balance, he flung his left arm violently outward, just in time to collide with the speeding hatchet. The blade struck with enormous force at the roots of his ring and little fingers and severed them both with surgical precision.

Still running at top speed, Daniel held up his mangled hand and stared stupidly at it, realizing that if the rapid flow of blood was not quickly staunched, he would bleed to death.

He foresaw a problem in closing the two gaping wounds. There were no stumps! Both fingers were sheared off at the palm. Tourniquets would be useless. He needed to stop running and cauterize these wounds properly. But he surely couldn't do that! Their buckskins had been left behind and now they wore only breechclouts. Daniel stripped off his clout, wadded up one end into a tight ball, then pressed it desperately against the spouting twin fissures.

Already he felt light-headed from blood loss and strain. Soon now, his legs would grow weak and force him to slow his pace.

"My hand's bleedin' bad, Jack. I can't keep goin' like this fer long."

"I know, Johnny. Let's separate a bit. You veer off to your right and see what he does. If'n he follers me, I'll lead him away from you and go on to Custer. If'n he follers you, come on back this way and we'll figger out somethin' else."

Daniel veered away from Trudeau, and for the next couple of miles, the distance between them continued to widen. Meanwhile, their pursuer stayed in the middle, loath to make a commitment until it was necessary. At length, he was forced to decide. He chose the blood trail. He left Jack and came after Johnny Daniel.

As soon as his purpose was clear, the Scouts once more veered toward each other and joined forces, a mile or so farther on.

"I'm near done in, Jack."

"I know, Johnny. Fetch me one more mile and then ya kin rest awhile. Gimme your tomahawk and then run on ahead. I'm gonna lag back and see if'n I kin snooker this here feller."

So it was that Jack began to run a bit slower, allowing his companion to pull ahead and the trailing Sioux to close the gap.

As the distance between them narrowed, Trudeau began to limp. Only a little at first, then more and more noticeably. Running Fox's confidence returned to full bloom. He would finish off this injured man, then quickly overtake the one who was bleeding.

Yard by yard he began to reel in his quarry. Fifty yards, then thirty, then ten. He could see the big veins in his enemy's neck, bulging out from the strain of his long run and the rivulets of sweat as they coursed down his heaving back.

Running Fox also noticed that his opponent's left leg buckled, ever so slightly, each time it pounded against the ground. He also watched the tomahawk that the white man carried in his right hand and the long knife he held clenched in his left.

The warrior was aware that the hatchet was the more dangerous weapon. At any moment, the man might spin around and throw the small hand ax at him; but Running Fox was convinced that the white man would not throw the knife. Once the hatchet was gone, the knife would be his only means of defense against the six-foot spear that the Oglala hefted in his hand. Yes, he decided, that tomahawk is the only thing that can harm me. Once he releases it, I will close in on him and run my spear through his body.

Suddenly the white man tripped and fell heavily to the ground, but quickly recovered and scurried up onto both knees, all the while retaining his grip on both of the weapons.

Running Fox did not rush toward his adversary. Instead, he circled carefully around him, watching the man's eyes and hands, confident that his great agility would allow him to dodge aside at the last moment and evade the tomahawk if it were cast.

When it came, the weapon was hurled so quickly and expertly that he barely managed to elude the deadly blade. If he had been even two steps closer, the hatchet would have buried itself in his body. As it was, he had to spin violently away and turn his back toward his enemy to keep his chest from being cleft in two.

He pivoted back around to face the white man and was greeted by a sharp pain in his lower forearm. He had been wrong; the man had thrown his knife. Had his arm not been accidentally shielding his body, the deadly blade would have pierced his heart.

More cautiously than ever, Running Fox moved slowly in for the kill; his long, sharp spear pointed toward the white man who had proven such a worthy warrior. He tried to ignore the pain in his arm and concentrate on his helpless enemy. The man had run and fought well; it was now time to make sure that he died well.

The white man made no attempt to regain his feet, but kept turning on his knees, always facing his adversary, his left hand, the one concealed behind his back, acting as a fulcrum with which the injured man levered his body painfully around. As he closed in for the fatal thrust, Running Fox watched his enemy's right hand, the fingers of which clutched a small red rock. No longer was there any need to watch the man's eyes. The Sioux's complete attention was riveted on the man's right hand and the red rock, as he moved slowly, but confidently, in for the kill...

...Then the entire world seemed to disintegrate around him! What was happening here, Running Fox wondered in alarm? Suddenly he could no longer stand. He found himself lying flat on his back, watching the darkening blue sky through narrowing and unfocused eyes. He heard a strange muffled sound in his ears and felt his body explode with pain. He tried to look toward the white man, but the shaft of a tomahawk protruding from his bloody chest blocked his blurry view. He struggled to reach it, but could not.

How can this be? The dying warrior wondered in his final moment of life. I watched him so carefully! I was so certain of victory! The white man never moved his hand!

Jack Trudeau stood looking down at the dead Sioux warrior.

"You sure was a good one," the Chief Scout thought,

"but I snookered you this time. Your back was turned when I threw the knife and you didn't see me fling it. You never guessed that I was left-handed!"

An hour later, a search party sent by Fire Hawk discovered the body of Running Fox and learned of the successful escape of his quarry. On this last evening of summer, the rock-hard, sunbaked prairie gave no clue as to the fugitives' whereabouts. Not even Bobtail Horse could find readable signs. It was as though the white men had sprouted wings and flown away.

They placed the body of Running Fox across the back of a pony and sadly returned to the war camp on the Arikaree, where they reported to Fire Hawk. After he had listened to them, he mounted Socks, rode to the lodge of Black Bear, and shared the news.

"Black Bear, I think we should send scouting parties out in every direction to watch for approaching soldiers. Also, we need to tell my father, Crazy Horse, what has happened. Last, we need to keep the White Eyes on the island under attack. We may still make them desperate enough to try to fight their way past us. They don't know that any of their messengers escaped."

"You are right, Fire Hawk. I will attend to it. I ask that you go to your father yourself and seek his wise counsel for us."

Early the next morning, leaving White Wolf in charge of the Sioux warriors on the Arikaree, Fire Hawk rode back to the main camp. With him went Black Shield and Big Beaver. Late that night, Fire Hawk sat with Crazy Horse outside his teepee.

"Roman Nose was foolish, my son. Our war with the White Eyes is no longer a game. You know far better than I that they are like the waters of a raging river. They will never stop."

He stopped to reflect and draw on his pipe, then continued.

"When I was a small boy, like Jumping Frog, I went with my father to the white man's Fort Laramie. They treated us with honor because then they were weak and we were strong. To cross our hunting grounds in peace and safety was all they asked.

"When they came to us then, we were like the leaves of a tree in summer. Now we are like a tree when the days grow short and the cold winds blow the leaves away. Soon we will be like a tree when snow covers the ground. There will be no more leaves.

"But that will not be enough for some white men, my son. They will not be satisfied until lightning strikes our tree and kills it. They will watch carefully to be certain that the leaves can never grow again. And then they will come again in peace and say, 'My poor red brothers, what has happened to your tree?'"

Fire Hawk remembered studying the plight of the Cherokees who, thirty years earlier, had walked their Trail of Tears, and knew that this wise leader was right.

"What must we do now, my father?"

"We must be wiser than they are. We must fight them only when we can win. We must all remember that when we kill a White Eyes soldier, another takes his place in the space of one moon. When they kill one of us, it takes us twenty winters to raise a new warrior. We must strike them and run before they can strike us back. We can never let them trap us as we trap them. And you, Fire Hawk, must share all your skills with us for as many moons as we have left. Help me to win these battles. Each victory will give our people a little more time and a little more freedom."

"What about the siege on the Arikaree?"

"You are right. The Yellow Legs will come from their camps. We must know where they come from and how many come. If they are few, you will ambush them. If they are many, you must pull back. With the new sun, I will break this large camp into small groups and send them off to the four winds. Then each one can avoid the Yellow Leg soldiers. I will lead the Oglala back toward the Muddy River and the Greasy Grass. If they follow, we will attack

229

every small group we find. If not, we will wait for another time."

"It is a good plan. I will return to Black Bear and White Wolf and tell them, then lead a scouting party toward the northeast. I think Yellow Hair will come from there with all his men. If he does, we'll pull back from the Arikaree and let the scouts go."

➤

It was midmorning, three days later. Fire Hawk and his scouts were forty miles northeast of Beecher's Island. From a hilltop high above a wide green valley, they watched as Custer's Seventh Cavalry moved along below them.

Sergeant Flynn had not exaggerated about the force Yellow Hair had assembled. Using the field glasses he had found on Socks' saddle, he counted twelve companies of cavalry, six of infantry, and four platoons of mortarmen. There were several ambulances and dozens of supply wagons. Fire Hawk estimated well over 1200 men in a column that stretched out for over a mile.

Sometime the next day, Custer's formidable force would arrive and relieve the island. He would charge in with flags flying, guidons flaring, and bugles blowing. The costly siege would be lifted.

Not since Gettysburg in '63, thought the former Virginia cavalier, have I seen so many killed so senselessly by so few.

➤

[How right he was. For in that decisive but little-remembered Siege of Beecher's Island, which began on September 17, 1868, and lasted for nine grueling days, over a thousand Sioux and Cheyenne besieged George Forsyth's fifty-two well-seasoned scouts. On the 25th, when they were rescued, only five of the island's defenders were dead and a mere eighteen were wounded. A thousand Indians took part in the battle and over four hundred were killed. Many others bore long-lasting wounds. Almost as serious was the fact that the Cheyenne nation lost both of its celebrated leaders in a very short time. After the deaths of Black Kettle and Roman Nose in the final months of 1868, the Southern Cheyenne would not return to their former place of prominence. Never again would the Dog Soldiers be the feared impact force they had been for so long. The warriors who perished in those sad months were their bravest and best. Crazy Horse had correctly observed that it would take nearly twenty years to raise their replacements. Only once more would the Southern Cheyenne go on the warpath: during the Red River Wars of 1874 and 1875. Those wars were their last-ditch efforts to resist being forced onto dismal reservations, which meant the end of their nomadic way of life. By 1890, all red men had been placed on reservations, and the great Indian Wars of the Old West were over. All that remained to be done was to exile the malcontents and to murder the remaining non-conformists.

During those years, far to the south in what is now Arizona, the Apache war chief, Geronimo, was finally cornered, in 1886, after many years of confounding the American and Mexican armies. Over ten thousand troops spent long, weary weeks and months in their saddles trying to capture this elusive Apache and his overachieving band of thirty-four men, women, and children. He was promised, by General George Crook, that if he surrendered, he would be sent away to Florida for "a little while," and then he would be permitted to come home. Geronimo was allowed to shake Theodore Roosevelt's hand in 1905, and even to march in Teddy's inaugural parade. But he was still waiting to come home when he died in 1909, wishing he were still running and raiding among the mountains and mesas of his beloved high desert, rather than suffering the wretched indignities of banishment and endless reprisals.

The two greatest Sioux chiefs were not exiled. They were both killed with the assistance of Sioux policemen they trusted: Crazy Horse in 1877, and Sitting Bull in 1890. By the Gay 90's, of course, many Americans agreed with General Sheridan, who years before had remarked, "... the only good Indian I ever saw was dead." This popular opinion had been spreading since the early months of 1876, when Crazy Horse and Sitting Bull, at the zenith of their power, decided to make the White Eyes howl one last time.]

PART SIX

FROM THIS DAY FORWARD

Chapter XVII
➤
To Have And To Hold

Catskill Mountains
New York State
May 25, 1869

Catherine sat smiling in the back seat of a fancy barouche. She kept saying over and over to herself, "Catherine McCarthy, Catherine McCarthy." She snuggled against the shoulder of her groom.

"I like the sound of it."

"The sound of what?" Kevin wondered.

"My new name. Catherine McCarthy."

"I would certainly hope so at this point of the game."

"Speaking of games, did you bring my baseball things?"

"Of course. They're stored at the hotel in the city. Do you expect to need them on our honeymoon?"

"No," she responded brightly, "I suspect we'll find other ways of staying busy."

A week earlier, Catherine had returned to New York City aboard the majestic Cunard steamship, Victoria. There to greet her were Kevin, GeeGee, Kerry Kelly, John Handley, Myles and Megan Keogh, Harry and Curt Bronson, and both of their families; also on hand were a number of Kevin's friends who had served in the Irish Brigade.

Kevin and his coterie had arrived the day before the ship docked. They had traveled cross-country aboard the very first transcontinental train to span the entire width of North America. In the station to welcome them were two of Sergeant Major Patrick McCarthy's oldest, dearest, and most influential friends. One of them was New York's senior U.S. Senator and majordomo of national Republican politics, Roscoe Conklin. The other was the kindly old chaplain of the Irish Brigade, Father Bemis Fitzgerald.

Thanks to Father Fitzgerald, they had had a wonderful nuptial Mass that morning. Thanks to the best man, Myles Keogh, and the brother of the bride, Geofrey Gerot, the wedding reception had been grand. And now, thanks to Senator Conklin, they were riding in this fine barouche and would be honeymooning at the Catskill Castle.

It was late in the evening when they finally arrived in the courtyard of a beautiful replica of a medieval castle. From the mountain road which led up to it, they observed the turrets and the moat shining in the bright moonlight. The drawbridge had to be lowered to allow them entrance to the inner keep.

The grand hall was richly furnished with tables and benches made from fine walnut, maple, and oak, all of which were polished, to a high luster. The floors were constructed from carefully fitted, dowel-and-peg hardwoods. Persian rugs were strewn about the gleaming planks in gay profusion. Colorful carpets offered a rainbow of scarlets and vermilions, indigos and ecrus, all of which enhanced the luxurious atmosphere.

Each wall was warmed and decorated with lovely, intricately patterned oriental tapestries. One of them, done in a dark, leaf green and a rich wine burgundy, reminded Kevin of the cranberry bogs on Cape Cod.

Catherine was pleased to see no signs of animal trophies, neither skins nor stuffed heads. There were, however, a large number of mounted fish, representing many different species and giving mute testimony to the region's well-earned reputation as an angler's paradise.

They approached a large stand-up desk, which stood near the center of the huge room, and Kevin spoke to the man behind it.

"Good evening, sir. We are Catherine and Kevin McCarthy."

"Good evening, folks, I'm Tony Castle. How may I help you?"

Tony Castle was a tall, almost reed-thin young man in his mid twenties. His large head and enormous hands seemed to be precariously balanced at the ends of his pipe-stem neck and arms. Because of the Castle's location in the Catskills, Tony often made visitors recall Washington Irving's description of Ichabod Crane.

"We hope you can accommodate us for a few days."

"Do you have reservations, Mr. McCarthy?"

"No, sir, we do not; but we do have a letter from one of your frequent guests."

Tony accepted and scanned Senator Conklin's letter. Not that it made the slightest difference. The rules of the hotel were quite clear. No reservations? No rooms! No exceptions!

"I am truly sorry, Mr. McCarthy, but we will be unable to accommodate you in the Castle for at least a month."

For the first time, he looked closely at them. They were in their late twenties or early thirties. A pleasant, clean-cut couple. Wholesomeness seemed to radiate from both of them.

He studied Catherine McCarthy and realized that she was an extremely beautiful and genteel young woman. Slender and graceful, with softly curled, dark blond shoulder-length hair, which framed her exquisite, oval-shaped face. Her delicate features and slim, gently curved neck combined to form a picture of classic beauty. She reminded Tony of a painting he had seen of Helen of Troy. The only things that seemed out of place were the tears that welled up in her large, luminous green eyes.

He knew his mother would refuse them lodgings. So would his father. Tony smiled to himself. More than that, his father would never have allowed the drawbridge to be lowered.

He noticed how stoically the McCarthys had accepted the bad news, in spite of Mrs. McCarthy's disappointment.

Well, decided Tony, I am not my mother, father, or anyone else. Maybe a lot of people could say no and turn them away, but I'm not one of them. I simply will not give her cause to cry.

"Since there is no more room in the Castle, perhaps you would be willing to stay in one of the small chalets along the lakeshore. Many couples actually prefer the privacy they afford."

A grin from Kevin and a big, beaming smile from Catherine that lit up her face rewarded his generosity. Just call me Santa Claus, he thought, grinning back at them.

He summoned a porter to carry their luggage and then led them along a narrow, winding, wooded path. At the end of this isolated lane sat a tiny, quaint, fieldstone cottage with a real thatched roof. It looked for all the world as though it had been built in Killarney and then magically transported across the sea by a legion of leprechauns, who, after lowering it into place amid the dense stands of spruce on the rocky shores of the mountain lake, had sprinkled it with stardust to add to its enchantment.

➢

Catherine and Kevin's idyllic honeymoon at the Castle lasted until the middle of June. During those days, they found complete fulfillment in each other and in their marriage. They both were honest, loving, and giving. In the past, people that had taken advantage of their generosity and goodwill, mistaking openness and cordiality for weakness had hurt them. As a result, both of them had become a bit reserved and less than candid in relationships. But now, in each other, they found a companionship that answered all of their needs. Never again would they need to be governed by an excess of caution.

During their three weeks in the Castle's cottage, Catherine discovered in her husband the male virtues that had appealed to her since childhood in her father and in GeeGee, but which she found in so few others. He was sensitive to her needs and moods, and constantly exhibited a great deal of tenderness and patience. In the past she had often thought about the intimacies which they would share after marriage and had been concerned. From the very beginning of their friendship, they felt an overpowering physical attraction toward each other, which became stronger as their love deepened. As the wedding drew near, Catherine desperately hoped she would always please him. In the first days of marriage, she discovered that all of her fears had been foolish. In each other they found an immediate, exciting, tingling pleasure, coupled with a total mutual respect.

During these lakeside days, Kevin learned that Catherine would attempt anything without complaining. On several occasions they rowed along the shore and fished. Every time she put a squirming worm on a hook, Catherine shuddered hard enough to rock the boat, but that never stopped her. She was a very game lady.

➢

Early one morning, she hooked a huge northern pike and pulled the giant fish close to the boat three different times. The first two times, Kevin tried to scoop the monster into a landing net in the conventional manner, but the pike was simply too large to fit into the mouth of the small net. The fish's broad back, Kevin estimated, was five or six inches wide.

The third time, Kevin placed the net in front of, rather than underneath the pike, and attempted to guide it toward the mesh. This was a big mistake. Since only one fluke of the treble hook was embedded in the fish's scaly jaw, that left the other two to become entangled in the strong cords of the net, which they did. The next time the fish moved its head, the hooks in the net held solidly and allowed the monster to break free.

Kevin was so angry with himself that he shook with fury. He had cost Catherine the best and biggest pike he had ever seen.

He looked at her as she sat there, excitedly crying, and smiling, and shaking, and looking unbelievably beautiful, and he loved her so much that he could not speak.

➤

On June 15, they reluctantly left the Castle and boarded a train to Philadelphia. There they enjoyed a visit with Mother Matilde and other teachers at the Sisters of Charity Academy, which Catherine had attended for several years. It was fun for her to show off her handsome new husband to the shy, admiring glances of the Sisters' new crop of impressionable students.

They spent the balance of the week touring the old city, sightseeing, and visiting its many historic buildings.

On their last day, they walked down to the waterfront along the Delaware River and enjoyed a picnic lunch while they watched several tall sailing ships slip their moorings and go forth on the tide. As always, the spectacle was exciting for Catherine. Kevin, watching her covertly, found the tiny lights dancing in her eyes more fascinating than the ships which danced about on the foam-flecked waves. How good the Lord had been to him, he thought for the thousandth time, to give him such a wonderful, kind, and glorious bride.

She turned toward him to say something about the ships or the ocean and saw him smiling at her. Her prior thoughts forgotten, she came to stand before him. Rising on tiptoe, she pulled his head gently toward her until she could reach his face. Tenderly she kissed each of his eyes and then his lips.

"Darling, I love you so much. When I am with you my heart is happy and full. When we are apart I am lonely and empty. Thank you for being you, and thank you most of all for loving me."

All he could do was hug her closely to him and again feel grateful.

➤

When they departed from Philadelphia, they journeyed north to Albany where they did more visiting. Then they traveled westward, down the length of the Mohawk Valley and along the shores of Lake Ontario, stopping at Niagara Falls to see its wonders, and at Fort Erie to see more old friends, before finally moving on to Chicago and a meeting with Jed Willis, the famous wagonmaker.

Chicago, in July of 1869, was really two different cities in one. The Lake Shore Drive area along Lake Michigan, which the McCarthys' hotel overlooked, was one city. Cooled by the strong offshore winds that wafted across its wide boulevards, Chicago's Loop spoke of energy, excess, and avarice. It was a world where the haves paid heed to neither the have-nots, nor the unlikely-to-gets.

The other city, the hot, sprawling metropolis, was one filled with squalor, wretchedness, and frail wooden shacks, all built so closely together that they seemed to lean on each other for support. This whole place is a firetrap, thought Kevin, as he journeyed to the Willis Coach and Carriage Works. If Nero were still alive, he would be humming in anticipation and tuning up his fiddle.

Kevin was not surprised, when two years later, on October 8, 1871, the Great Chicago Fire razed the city and eliminated the overcrowded conditions for more than 300,000 inhabitants.

Willis Coach and Carriage Works, proclaimed the huge sign. Builders of the Finest Coaches in the World, it continued. By Appointment to Prince Albert and Queen Victoria, it concluded.

Kevin entered a large reception area that was dominated by a luxurious vehicle. It was a low-slung, four-wheeled pleasure carriage for two, with a folding top and a high seat in front for the driver. The exterior was a deep, rich, iridescent silver, a color reminiscent of fine pewter. The shimmer and glow of the lustrous metal finish was unlike anything Kevin had ever seen, with the exception of a few fine hardwoods. The thick padded seats were covered in blood red leather. Inlaid, in both sides, was the Royal Crest and Seal of England. The handcrafted workmanship was flawless.

"The only one like it in the world," said a booming voice, "is at Buckingham Palace. It's called the Victoria. Prince Albert ordered the original one, back in 1862, to celebrate Queen Victoria's Silver Jubilee. As part of our fee, we were allowed to duplicate it for our lobby and inlay her royal crest."

"It's the most magnificent carriage I've ever seen," declared Kevin. "By the way, I'm Kevin McCarthy."

"I suspected that you were. I'm Jed Willis. Please call me Jed. I'm told that you're on your honeymoon?"

"A honeymoon that I think will last forever, Jed."

"Then you are as blessed as I am, Kevin. I hope that you and your bride will come up to Lake Forest for the weekend and give Ellen and me the pleasure of your company before you depart."

"I'd be delighted, and I'm sure Catherine would be also."

"Good. C'mon out to the factory and see how we operate," invited Jed.

The large factory was a marvel to behold. Although there was a great deal of modern machinery to make the more rigorous jobs a bit easier, the tasks which required intricate, handcrafted precision had not been affected. Wheelwrights still crafted the wheels, carriage designers the bodies, and trace makers, the draw poles. Seats were still produced by upholsterers and skilled leatherworkers. Illumination experts were on hand to design, build, and install gas night-lamps on each Willis carriage. The entire operation was a model of dedicated craftsmanship.

They visited an experimental department where new products were being developed. The employees there were working on a six-ton wagon. The wagon's gargantuan size and great weight caused most people to believe that the entire concept was impossible.

As they neared the back of the shop, Kevin saw a huge man lift a large, heavy wood-and-iron wheel and hurl it through the rear doorway onto a pile of discarded parts.

"Another bad one, Swede?" asked Willis.

"Boss, I thought for sure I had it dat time, but it vent to creepin' again. Vun of these days, I find da ansur."

They exited through the same rear doorway that Swede used for his discards and sat at one of several picnic tables which were scattered throughout a large grove of shady trees.

"Swede is Swen Larsen," explained Willis. "He's trying to find out why some wheels become creepers."

"That would be great, Jed. Creepers are a nuisance."

➢

[When a wheelwright made a wooden wheel, he fitted an iron strip or collar around the outside of the wood to protect it and keep it from wearing. Most of the time, the devices worked quite well and lasted for the life of the wheel. Other times, however, the iron strip would not stay in place. It moved off-center and crept to one side or the other, hence the name "creeper." If it crept to the inside of the wheel, it could encircle the axle and become disruptive. If it moved to the outside, it spun off and rolled away, or induced the entire wheel to creep off the axle. Even the best wagoneers in the world, from time to time, made creeper wheels. It seemed that once they started creeping, they could never be repaired. They simply kept creeping. Replacement wheels and parts were difficult, often impossible, to find. Owners of creepers who discarded them usually had duplicate wheels made by reliable blacksmiths; but in most cases they proved to be poor substitutes. Since the new wheel did not match its mates, the vehicle refused to roll

242

properly. When a man sold such a rig, he was honor-bound to tell a potential buyer that one of his wheels was "a damned creeper." Many years would pass before the concept of the production line and the advent of interchangeable parts finally standardized carriage making, and made the industry's products much more efficient and far less expensive. Until then, every wagon, cart, and carriage would be handmade, and each of them would be completely unique.]

➤

"As I wrote in my letter, Jed, I'm interested in purchasing a couple of your biggest wagons."

"The biggest wagon we currently manufacture is the three-ton high side. But, by next spring at the latest, we'll be ready to market a six-ton high side. Our big stumbling block was trying to stop rotating axles from wearing out under the enormous pressure produced by twelve thousand pounds of deadweight. Every axle we tested had to be pulled and replaced after a few hundred miles. We were almost ready to give up."

"Then you've solved the problem?"

"It's been solved for us. By Dorfmann wagoneers of Berlin, Germany. They invented a system that they guarantee to function, without problems, for a minimum of ten million revolutions. If it fails, they'll furnish a replacement assembly at no charge."

"Is Dorfmann reliable?

"Kevin, all of Queen Victoria's carriages are made by us or by Dorfmann. If they say it will work, it will work! If you plan to pull twelve thousand pounds for any distance, or cross difficult terrain, all possible friction must be eliminated; otherwise, your teams of animals will soon be too weak to move the heavy load."

"It seems like an unbelievable amount of weight to move."

"It is! We've had to redesign the T-6 from the ground up. The wheels are two feet farther apart than our standard heavy-duty wagon, and the big rig's center of gravity has been lowered. That will discourage tip-overs on steep trails in hill country."

"You certainly seem to have thought of everything, Jed!" exclaimed the enthusiastic Kevin.

"We sure have," joked Willis. "That's why they each cost a king's ransom."

Based on the production projections and his confidence in Jed Willis, Kevin ordered two of the T-6's for an April delivery in Bismarck, and took an option on two others at the same price, provided he purchased them within three years. He was pleasantly surprised by the financial terms Willis offered. They allowed him to pay most of the charges in installments and hold on to his cash.

➢

It was now late the following Sunday evening, or rather Monday morning, since it was hours past midnight. The McCarthys, aided by the light of a bright full moon, were picking their way down a long, steep flight of wooden steps to the Willis' private beach.

Accepting their host's invitation to come and spend a weekend, they drove northward along the shore of Lake Michigan, arriving in Lake Forest on Friday afternoon. Upon their arrival, the entire Willis family greeted them: the jocular Jed, his lovely and gracious wife, Ellen, and four enthusiastic Willis children. These were fifteen-year-old Tom, his sister Lisa, who was a year younger, and a pair of merry, twelve-year-old twins named Joyce and Don.

As they left their carriage in the long semicircular driveway and walked along the flagstone path that led toward the spacious veranda, Catherine's eyes were drawn to a bat and several balls that lay on the terrazzo. Excitedly, she asked Tom, "Do you play baseball?"

"Oh, sure! All of us play. Mom and Dad too."

"How interesting!" she trilled, winking at Kevin.

The Willis' home was a luxurious, twelve-room English Tudor, built on a high bluff overlooking the Great Lake. The view was a marvelous one of bright, sparkling azure water, reaching far out to a hazy blue horizon. Directly below the house and its large terrace, the lake had cut a deep bay, shaped like the letter U. Around the entire perimeter were high sand dunes, which afforded total privacy from the rest of the shoreline. Only from a boat on the lake could prying eyes peer into the sandy sanctuary.

Tied up at the Willis' dock were two splendid vessels: a plush thirty-two foot, mahogany-and-teak Trojan cruiser, which slept six; and a thirteen-foot Snipe, a jaunty little craft whose white hull and bright green trim begged the aspirant sailor to take the helm and whose towering white sail insured exciting scoots across long stretches of calm and clear glassy waters.

The Willises and their guests dined the first evening on the Great Lakes' finest offering, delectable yellow perch, or as many called them, walleye pike. Ellen mentioned that the firm, white, succulent flesh of this fish was ranked by many gourmets as the tastiest seafood of all. To complement the fish, crisp fried potatoes were served, along with fresh tomatoes, peppers, and corn on the cob. For dessert, they enjoyed a wonderfully tangy, wild cherry and cranberry cobbler.

After dinner, the children were left to their own devices while the adults retired to the back patio. Ellen and Catherine sipped sweet sherry, and the men enjoyed a full-bodied brandy, with aromatic Cuban cigars. In the day's final moments, they all watched, spellbound, as the ultimate Artist used the setting sun to paint new shades of pink and gold across the rippling waves. Finally, He tucked His world in for the night, beneath a midnight-blue, star-covered blanket.

"I think this is one of the most beautiful places in the whole world," Catherine sighed.

"There aren't many prettier ones," Kevin agreed.

"We were fortunate to find it and blessed by an opportunity to buy it," said their host. "Well, Catherine, if we had a baseball game tomorrow morning, could we, perhaps, coax you to play?"

"I might be so inclined," she laughingly agreed.

➢

As soon as breakfast was finished the next morning, the great game got underway. On one team were Catherine, Kevin, Tom, and Joyce. Their worthy opponents were Jed, Ellen, Lisa, and Don. They hit the ball, played hard, and ran around the bases until noon. By then, Kevin, Jed and Ellen, Lisa and the twins were all worn-out. Even Tom was ready to quit. But Catherine was still going strong. For her, there could never be enough baseball.

After lunch, they all donned their bathing togs and descended to the beach, where they enjoyed a wonderful afternoon. A strong east wind sprang up soon after they arrived, and before long whitecaps were leaping in the bay, and big waves came crashing onto the beach. This ended all efforts to swim peacefully, but the wild conditions were perfect for the more adventurous members of the party, led by Catherine.

Kevin lay on the hot golden sand and let the heat drain the soreness and fatigue from stiff, long unused, and nearly forgotten muscles that baseball had brought to his attention. He watched Catherine as she cavorted about with seeming disregard for her own welfare. She's in far better condition than I am, concluded Kevin ruefully. I'm going to start doing the same exercises that she does each morning. She returned and lay down beside him.

"You are a real wonder. Doesn't your energy ever deplete?"

246

"Not often! Hasn't it been a wonderful day, Darling? Swimming is always so much fun, except for this ugly duckling, Old Mother Hubbard bathing suit. I wish I could take it off."

"If you did, I could not be held responsible for my actions."

"Promises, McCarthy, nothing but idle promises."

The following day, Sunday, began with Mass and continued with a gargantuan breakfast of pork sausage and hotcakes. Yesterday's weather with its high winds, tossing whitecaps, and heaving waves had not abated. The lake, if anything, was even rougher. Because of the adverse conditions, thoughts of a smooth ride on the big cruiser had to be abandoned. However, Tom invited them to join him aboard the Snipe.

"What do you think, Jed?" asked the somewhat nervous Kevin.

"It's too rough for me, but Tommy goes out in weather like this whenever he can. He's our white-water sailor."

When Kevin saw the eager look of anticipation on his wife's face, he reluctantly agreed to the adventure.

With Tom at the tiller and the McCarthys struggling to follow his shouted instructions, they laid the Snipe on the port tack, cleared the bay, and beat their way to windward, into the teeth of a gusty east wind for two miles or more.

Throughout the entire run, the tiny craft would climb valiantly to the crest of each ensuing wave, then hang suspended on its brink for a moment, as though looking for a means of escape. Seeing none, she would eventually release her grip and plummet pell-mell down this new water slide into the whirling, gray-green maelstrom below. Often the Snipe disappeared completely. But soon she would reappear, shove her belligerent nose into the next wall of water and begin to claw her way out of the deep trough and rise upward toward the next whitecapped summit.

Several times on the outward voyage, rogue waves appeared from nowhere. Each seemed to pause with its imposing cornice hanging over the masthead, like the sharp blade of an ominous guillotine, before crashing down. But each time the Snipe met the challenge head-on and brushed it aside. Time and again, she rose like a buoyant cork and disdainfully pushed the suddenly impotent danger out through her scuppers and back to the sea.

Looking at Catherine's jubilant face, Kevin could see how much she was enjoying the wild, unpredictable ride. Well, he thought, Tom can handle the boat well, and worrying sure can't help much at this point. The voyage was definitely unlike anything they had ever experienced. At times it was fierce, as the pitching motion of the waves buffeted them about. On several occasions, in spite of the protection offered by their thick life preservers, they were bruised, as they slammed against the sides of the cockpit.

Tom Willis was bumped about, too, but to a much lesser extent, since he was held in place by his helmsman's harness. At length, he decided that they had come far enough from shore and put the nimble Snipe about.

Now they rode with the wind and the waves as well as the current. This combination of forces, coupled with the boat's streamlined hull and the large area of wet canvas sails, drove them along at an incredible pace. Catherine remembered a passage from a poem by Lord Byron in which he extolled the pleasures of "flying before the wind." As wonderful as the great poet was she decided he had not been able to capture the essence of the excitement and exhilaration produced by the actual experience.

For his part, Kevin had to admit that this part of the trip was fun. Maybe we can learn to sail and build a Snipe like this, or have one shipped out to Montana. There's no lack of space on the Missouri River. He looked at Catherine once again and decided that she liked sailing almost as much as baseball.

In a scant fraction of the time it had taken them to beat their way to windward, on the long, offshore reach, they darted back across the same stretch of pounding, pitching

248

waters. Kevin could scarcely believe his eyes when, through the bow wave's torrential spray, he suddenly saw the projecting arms of the bay looming ahead. Moments later they were in calmer waters but still being driven at breakneck speed toward the pier. He was certain that the boat would collide with the sturdy structure and be destroyed as a result. But Tom was extremely competent, as well as a bit reckless. At the last moment, he weathered his helm, dropped the sail, and slipped the Snipe neatly into place alongside the quay.

Aside from a slight mal de mer and an inability to walk in a straight line for a few minutes, the buoyant newlyweds were as good as new. The afternoon was spent on an abbreviated baseball game, followed by an hour of croquet on the spacious front lawn, and finally a long walk along the forested lakeshore that had given the quaint village its name.

As dusk approached, Jed, Tom, and Kevin prepared a fire in the outdoor cooking pit and roasted appetizing steaks over the open flames. It was nearly midnight when the festive party ended. But, according to Catherine, the weekend enjoyment was not quite over.

➢

Now, three hours later, the McCarthys were just reaching the foot of the Willis steps and spreading a blanket on the sand.

"Turn around while I get ready, please," requested Catherine.

Kevin, who had donned his bathing suit at the house, did as she asked and waited patiently through a series of female rustlings.

"I'm ready now," she finally said.

Kevin turned and beheld the beautiful Catherine. As often threatened, she had discarded the hated Old Mother Hubbard suit and stood before him in all her natural splendor. As she went bounding across the sand and into the surf, she tossed a laughing challenge back over her gleaming shoulder.

"I'll only be a moment. Then I hope you're going to make good on your promise."

Beautiful lady, Kevin thought, you can count on it!

➢

Late the next morning, they returned to Chicago and boarded a train for St. Louis. There they spent a few days visiting the Bronsons and Kerry Kelly and celebrating the Fourth of July with a picnic, fireworks, and, to Catherine's great joy, two baseball games, a new concept called a double-header.

They were both, perhaps, just the least bit glad to mount the gangplank and get aboard the Titus B. Turner two days later. It had been a great honeymoon and a wonderful way to start married life, but now they both were ready to settle down.

Throughout the homeward voyage their cabin was bedecked with flowers from the Bronsons. Wine was served at supper, courtesy of Kerry Kelly. Their time aboard flew by with excellent meals in the Harbinger, spectacular sunsets on deck, and dancing until midnight each evening in the tiny ballroom.

With mixed emotions, they disembarked at Great Falls, the paddlewheelers' final stop in Montana, and walked up the hill to their first home, a newly built house which had been completed the week before Kevin left for New York City.

Catherine loved it. She scampered from room to room and then outside again. It was perfect, from the white-and-blue trim, to the rose bushes, to the tiny crib in the nursery. She smiled and thought we'll need that soon. Then she knelt down beside it and thanked God for all their blessings...

Chapter XVIII

➢

For Better Or For Worse

Sioux Tribal Lands
The Powder River
Montana Territory
September, 1869

Nearly a year had passed since the night Fire Hawk killed the Grabber. The passage of time had dulled the sharp pain of Little Fawn's death, but the persistent, pervasive ache still remained. Whenever he saw something unusual, or had a thought he wished he could share with her, his heart sank into that deep, melancholy chasm that he had discovered near the banks of the Washita, and he mourned again, anew and alone.

During this long year of recovery, he learned several things for the first time, one of which was the probable reason for the slaughter on the Washita. The year before the attack, Yellow Hair [Custer] had been court-martialed for executing deserters without giving them a fair trial, and for deserting his command without authority. He was found guilty of all charges and sentenced to be cashiered from the army for one year, with loss of all pay and allowances. Another less popular officer might well have been sentenced to a long prison term, or even death, for such crimes.

Fire Hawk remembered the cruel and bizarre punishments Custer had meted out during the war. If a trooper was forced to straddle a wooden sawhorse for an entire day and then hobbled painfully about for the next week — or if a man was seen with half of his head shaved

— or a portion of his beard and mustache was missing — he could be readily identified as a Custer trooper.

The tyrannical George Armstrong "Autie" Custer was selfish, childish, and quite often foolish; but he won battles and made headlines. Because he did, several great eastern newspapers routinely assigned reporters to accompany him and chronicle his adventures whenever he set forth on a new campaign. He was rash and reckless, but he provided copy from which legends are made and folk heroes are forged. New York City journalists, together with his wife, Elizabeth Bacon Custer—a brilliant, beautiful, cultured, vivacious woman, known universally as "Libbie"— became the Boy General's chief drumbeaters. It was an impulsive wish to visit Libbie, which led Custer to desert his post and gallop across the entire width of Kansas.

The guilt from some of Custer's misdeeds even spread to his old friend and commander, Brevet General Winfield Scott Hancock. The gallant Hancock gained national prominence during the Civil War when he was gravely wounded during the Battle of Gettysburg, opposing the famous charge of Confederate General George Pickett. Partly because of his failure to control the flamboyant Custer, Hancock was removed from command along with his protégé.

To temporarily replace this brash brace of bonvivants, there came forth two senior generals: William Tecumseh "Uncle Billy" Sherman and Philip H. "Black Phil" Sheridan. Sherman had become famous for saying, "War is hell," and then proving it; Phil Sheridan for believing "...the only good Indian I ever saw was dead," then doing his best to make all Indians good and dead.

When the former General-in-Chief, Ulysses Simpson "Uncle Sam" Grant, was elected in 1868 as America's eighteenth president, the three principal generals of the Union army, the ones to whom most Unionists gave their unflagging loyalty, were reunited. Generals Sherman and Sheridan now ran the army, and President Grant ran the White House.

Custer had been restored to duty a few months before Grant's election, Fire Hawk discovered, and had resumed command of the Seventh Cavalry. He was now, of course, desperate to remove the stains from his badly tarnished reputation and justify General Sheridan's faith in him.

The quickest way to do that was to make headlines. The best way to earn those headlines was by killing Indians. On his first patrol, Custer had followed six young Cheyenne Dog Soldiers back to Black Kettle's village on the Washita and slaughtered as many men, women, and children as possible. Over two hundred Indians were killed, and fewer than sixty were taken prisoner. Prestige among his skeptical peers and adoring public may have been marginally increased, but the wanton carnage he ordered spelled his own death warrant in the villages of his victims and those of their allies.

The other news that drifted across the prairie involved life rather than death. It concerned Tim Paul, the scout who had been grievously wounded during his escape from Beecher's Island. He had been found by a patrol from the Tenth Cavalry. The Buffalo Soldiers transported him with all possible haste to Fort Wallace. Although his leg had been amputated below the knee, he was once again ambulatory and had returned to duty as a civilian scout.

Fire Hawk was glad. He had met Tim Paul in Dodge City in 1866. They had competed in the annual Fourth of July shooting contest in which he finished third, and Tim Paul, fourth. Second prize, that day, had gone to a young hunter who worked for the railroad. A man many were starting to call "Buffalo Bill." Honors in the match went to U.S. Marshall and former Union spy, James Butler Hickok, known far and wide as "Wild Bill" Hickok. The four of them spent the balance of that pleasant afternoon sitting in the Long Branch Saloon, buying each other drinks and reminiscing.

The third bit of news was also good. Sioux chief Red Cloud had met with General "Red Beard" Sherman to talk of peace.

"What must I do to have you stop your raids along the Bozeman Trail?" Sherman asked.

"Leave your forts and go away," Red Cloud replied. "Stop crossing our land, hunting our buffalo, and killing our people!"

"All right," Sherman responded. "As soon as the raids stop, we will leave our forts."

"No! There have already been too many broken promises," Red Cloud stormed at him. "I will sit high up in the mountains, and wait. Only when all Yellow Legs are gone from sight will we stop."

➤

[In an effort to halt the bloodshed at least temporarily, Sherman agreed, and the 1868 Treaty of Fort Laramie was signed. The following month, Forts C. F. Smith, Phil Kearny, and Reno were abandoned. The Sioux and the Cheyenne universally believed that Red Cloud had won a great victory, since the Bozeman Trail led through the Powder River Basin — land which stretched from the Black Hills to the Big Horn Mountains — traditional hunting grounds of the Teton Sioux and their Northern Cheyenne neighbors. Alas, the Laramie Treaty contained a provision that allowed the railroads to lay tracks across these and other tribal lands. Since the Northern Pacific Railroad would soon provide far easier access to northern Idaho and the western Montana goldfields than the Bozeman Trail ever had, Red Beard's concession was not as great as it seemed.

As soon as the troops vacated the hated forts, Sioux, Cheyenne, and Arapahoe warriors burned the stockades and buildings to the ground, leaving nothing except charred ruins. Fire Hawk himself put a torch to the quarters Clayton Forrester had once occupied. The fire quickly consumed the tinder-dry logs and left no trace of what had once been. Symbolically, the flames seemed to destroy the last thread that connected him to his former life.

A few months after the Yellow Legs' forts were burned down, Red Cloud and his powerful rival, Crazy Horse's uncle, Spotted Tail — a chief of the Brules — decided to take advantage of the general amnesty which Red Beard had offered. In the future, they would both live on land that had been set aside for cooperative Indians by the Laramie Treaty. The vast majority of the Sioux, as many as 15,000, tempted by free government rations and wishing to avoid further badgering by the military, joined them. They went to live on a very large, government-supervised reservation which contained many Indian agencies. Each of these agencies was named for either the area's leader or the agency's location. Red Cloud, Spotted Tail, Cheyenne River, and Grand River (or Standing Rock) were a few of the names that were employed. Actually the agencies were checkpoints, built to keep track of the wayward inhabitants.

Many others rejected the submissive way of life, preferring to roam freely across the wide prairies, in the majestic mountains, and along the pleasant streams. Three thousand Sioux and four hundred Cheyennes repudiated Red Cloud's leadership as well as that of all other "peacemakers" and pledged their allegiance to more aggressive chiefs who, like themselves, were willing to fight to retain their freedom. To answer the Oglalas' call for wisdom and leadership came Crazy Horse and Fire Hawk. From the Hunkpapa came Sitting Bull, Black Moon, Crow King, Four Horns, and Gall, who left with his Oglala wife and went to assist the other Hunkpapa. The Miniconjous had Hump and Lame Deer. The Sans Arc and Blackfoot Sioux were ably led by Black Eagle, Spotted Eagle, and Jumping Bear. The Northern Cheyenne leaders were Dull Knife and Little Wolf. Each of them was strong, devoted, and experienced. They had all proven to be good teachers; now it was time for them to become good students.]

➢

Late in the summer of 1869, these Indian leaders and their principal lieutenants held a powwow on the Rosebud River. The main strategist at the conclave was Fire Hawk.

"My brothers," he began, "we are now sure of many things and almost sure of others. We know that the White Eyes have far more warriors than do we. We are almost sure that they will never send a strong army against us at one time, because they think they are much better fighters than we are and they never expect to see a concentration of our warriors in one place. I think we can defeat them in every small battle and even in one or two large ones.

"This summer, I have seen many of our tribesmen who live on the White Eyes' treaty lands come out to us. For only here are they truly free. They will go back to be taken care of when the snows fly and the winds blow; but next year, and the next and the next, more of our kinsmen will come out and stay longer. Three or four years from now, 2,000 to 3,000 warriors will be available to fight the Yellow Legs, who do not believe that such a camp will ever exist. 2,000 warriors means 1,000 lodges and 10,000 ponies. No village of that size can endure for more than a few days. By then, the ponies will have no grass to eat and the big village will have hunted or trapped all the game. Yes, my brothers, such camps are hard to sustain, but not impossible. If one is needed in the future, we must find a way.

"Until then, we must separate and live in small bands. We must not remain in any one campsite for a long time. We must continue to move and be unpredictable. We must play coyote and rabbit with those who try to hunt us down, but we must be clever rabbits.

"I believe the day will come when Red Beard, Horse Killer, Yellow Hair, Bear Coat [General Nelson Miles] and the Gray Fox [General George Crook] will tire of being led around, and they will all come after us together. They will expect to catch each of our small bands alone. Then we will surprise them. That will be the day to gather 1,000 or 2,000 warriors and ride against them. That will be the day to split them into small groups — and kill them all.

"Before that day, we must teach our warriors to fight enemies in new ways. War can no longer be a game. It must become a deadly business. The time for coup sticks and brave deeds is past. We need smart live warriors, not brave dead ones. To live freely, we must know how and when to fight, and how and when to run. Let the White Eyes die for their cause! Let us live for ours!

"My father, Crazy Horse, bids me to travel to each village and teach our young men these new skills and tactics that will defeat the Yellow Legs. With me will go White Wolf, Man Afraid, Gall, and Black Shield.

"The first thing we must do is to set up communication lines between each of our villages. When you move your campsite or when something happens that needs to be shared, send out couriers. The warrior in charge of all scouts and messengers will be Bobtail Horse. Tomorrow we will leave for the first village."

➤

The chief of that first village was Chief Three Bears, one of Red Cloud's former followers. Three Bears was a respected warrior of great wealth, who for many years had raided into the lands of the Pawnee and had stolen hundreds of their ponies. But his best prize, he said, was a young, white female captive. Now a woman in her fifties, Calling Bird guessed she had been five or six when she was seized by the band of Pawnee raiders who had scalped and butchered her parents on their isolated homestead. For the next dozen years, she had been an abused Pawnee slave, forced to endure cruel treatment and eager to escape with Three Bears when given the chance.

Fire Hawk met them when he and the others were invited to a great feast in their honor. During the festive banquet, it was obvious that Three Bears and Calling Bird were very devoted to each other and proud of their beautiful daughter, Morning Dove.

As she and her mother served their distinguished guests that evening, Morning Dove favored Fire Hawk with several dazzling smiles. When the meal was finished and the last wisps of smoke curling from the pipes of friendship had disappeared; Fire Hawk rose to thank their gracious host and his family.

Although his words were directed toward Three Bears and both women, his eyes remained locked with those of Morning Dove.

➢

Sometime later, as moonlight danced upon the surface of the Powder River and a soft summer breeze sang through the pines, he left the lodge to which he had been assigned and strolled back along the riverbank toward the wickiup of Three Bears. He found Morning Dove waiting for him, as he knew she would be.

Tall, slender, and statuesque, she seemed to have inherited the best physical traits of each of her parents. The color of her smooth skin reminded Fire Hawk of cinnamon spice, mixed with cane sugar. Her deep-set, dark brown, almost black eyes, highlighted by prominent cheekbones, seemed to flash in the moonlight. Long, auburn hair, neatly coifed in a single, thick braid, hung down her back and nestled against a soft doeskin dress that emphasized the fact that this was a beautiful, provocative woman. Morning Dove stirred emotions within him that he had thought of as gone forever.

"I am glad you came to me, Fire Hawk."

"I had to come, Morning Dove."

"I know how you have grieved. Little Fawn and I were friends from the day she came to us from the Mandans. I loved her dearly. I too have been sad for many moons. My warrior, Bright Star, died during the fight on the Lodge Pole Trail that brought you to us."

"I know about Bright Star, Morning Dove. I know he was a brave warrior and a good man. No one can be more."

"Little Fawn said that of you. She loved you so very dearly."

"As I loved her. My heart broke on the day that she died."

"Fire Hawk, please do not think that I am bold for what I am going to say. As I prepared the body of my beloved for burial on that wintry day, my heart broke, too. Since then, the pain has never really left me, until tonight, when I saw you. For the first time since those sad days, my spirit soared and I knew some moments of happiness. I loved Bright Star. He will always have a special place in my heart; but I have lived for less than thirty winters, and I do not wish to mourn in lonely silence until the Great Spirit calls out to me. Are my feelings wrong?"

"No, they aren't wrong, Morning Dove. I feel the same way. No woman will ever replace Little Fawn in my heart, just as no man can take Bright Star's place in yours. But we cannot help the dead by living in constant torment. I have just met you; yet, I want to stay with you, learn all about you, and share with you the companionship I have to give and the time I have to live. Being close to you makes me feel alive again. You make me remember the joys that a family and the happy laughter of children can bring. That does not mean that I love Little Fawn any less. Perhaps I have learned to bear her loss, but I know I feel drawn to you."

"After such a short time, our feelings cannot be explained. But I feel the same. Let us walk along the riverbank and talk of our new joy and the wonderful gift we have been given."

➢

In the ensuing days, aside from the time Fire Hawk spent on the young men's training, the two of them were never apart. The attraction that each felt for the other intensified. At the end of the second week, Fire Hawk decided to test the communications network set up by Bobtail Horse, by sending messages to all the villages, inviting everyone to his wedding with Morning Dove.

The following month, Three Bears' camp on the Powder River was swelled to overflowing by representatives from almost every band of Sioux, Cheyenne, and Arapahoe on the Northern Great Plains who could find enough room to erect a lodge. If Red Beard Sherman and the others had known about the gathering, they could have swooped down on the revelers and annihilated every major hostile leader in one quick strike.

Fire Hawk spent the morning of his wedding day with White Wolf, Crazy Horse, Gall, Man Afraid, Black Shield, and several more of his friends, enjoying their jests and comradeship. And yet, despite his outward air of jubilation he was still troubled. Deep in his heart, one reservation about his union with Morning Dove still remained. Although his affection for her had deepened each day, and he was sure their marriage would be a happy one, he still felt as if he were deserting Little Fawn. It was a concern that frequently gnawed at his mind and emotions.

Late that afternoon, he and his friends went to the horse herd, placed halter ropes on a dozen of his best ponies, and led them to the lodge of Three Bears. It was the traditional token payment for his daughter. The others tarried beside the wickiup, but Fire Hawk left them and walked back along the riverbank by himself.

The path wound through many tall clumps of trees so that quite often the trail ahead was concealed. As he rounded one of these bends, a baby deer confronted him. The white spots on her back were still plainly visible. He stopped so as not to frighten the tiny creature. As he did so, her eyes opened wide, the tip of her tongue poked out between her teeth, and her head tilted to one side. These gestures were so reminiscent of his White Sun Woman that his breath caught in his throat. So many times she had used identical expressions to chide him for being foolish or obstinate. Fire Hawk smiled as the deer scampered off the trail and into the trees. Little Fawn's message of approval had been perfectly clear.

It was a good and satisfying marriage for them both. In the first four years, Morning Dove bore two stalwart sons whom they named Little Hawk and Fire Bird. Fire Hawk and his tacticians no longer went to different villages each month. The young men, as well as many seasoned warriors, now came to them.

It was not all practice. Skirmishes were frequently fought on the banks of the Platte River with determined settlers that had been compelled to move farther westward and along the old Bozeman Trail with gold miners heading for their northern diggings. Army supply trains could still be raided for arms, ammunition, hardtack, coffee, and sugar. Occasionally, a Missouri River paddle wheeler or a freight wagon could be waylaid. For four years, the weekly wars wore on.

In 1873, when Northern Pacific Railroad crews began laying tracks through the Yellowstone Valley, Fire Hawk and the others concentrated their attacks on these railroad workers and their equipment. Life expectancy for a rail jockey or a spike pounder was quite short, but the pay was excellent for the survivors.

Safeguarding valuable property and protecting the lives of his employees became every railroad builder's principal objective. The quickest and best way to achieve these goals was to hasten an end to the "Wild West." That could be done either by civilizing the nonconformist savages, or by killing them. To many nineteenth-century Westerners, the two choices were equally acceptable.

To aid in accomplishing one of these objectives, Fort Abraham Lincoln, a fine new army post, was built in the Dakota Territory on the west bank of the Missouri River, a bit downstream from the railhead town of Bismarck. To garrison this post came the Seventh Cavalry, under the command of Lt. Col. George Armstrong Custer. Of course, he was accompanied by Elizabeth "Libbie" Bacon Custer, who would provide a proper social climate, and by several newspapermen who were eager to drum up headlines and publicity. The first big chance came a month later when the Seventh Cavalry rode out to the Yellowstone Valley. Custer was after the hostiles.

The balance of 1873 and the better part of 1874 found Custer and the Seventh Cavalry wandering through the Yellowstone Country and the Black Hills. The Sioux and their allies seemed able to sweep down upon Yellow Hair's patrols whenever they wished, while the Yellow Legs discovered only those hostiles who wanted to be found.

To be sure, a few troopers lost their lives, but that seemed a small price to pay for those glorious months spent tramping in woods rich with game, and angling in streams choked with trophy-sized fish. But it was neither the creatures of the forest nor the denizens of the deep that riveted the attention of Custer's soldiers. It was the shiny yellow metal that lay gathering and glittering in many of the Black Hills' riverbeds. Custer's news hounds sent forth the word and banner headlines soon proclaimed:

RICH GOLD DEPOSITS FOUND IN THE BLACK HILLS

Before year's end, gold seekers were illegally sneaking into the Black Hills, hills which had been guaranteed forever to the Sioux by the 1868 Laramie Treaty. By the spring of 1875, a tiny trickle had become a giant torrent, as thousands of gold seekers poured onto the sacred ground.

The army tried to stop the headlong rush and failed miserably.

As a last resort, government agents tried to buy the Black Hills from Sitting Bull. Visited by a contingent of young warriors who promised to kill him if he agreed to the sale, the wise Sitting Bull refused to sign or even to acknowledge the proposed treaty.

In spite of the Sioux' adamant refusal to relinquish any of their territory, ever increasing numbers of trespassers continued to invade the Black Hills. To accommodate them, mining camps such as Deadwood and Custer City sprang up in many of the pristine valleys. Finally, President Grant took a hand.

Late in 1875, Grant issued the first part of a far-reaching proclamation. White settlers and miners, he said, were free to mine or settle on the open land to the west of the Black Hills. Reading between the lines, one could infer that federal officials would look the other way if anyone mistakenly crossed the boundaries and trespassed onto tribal lands.

The second part of the message was issued in December.

Runners were sent out by the Department of Indian Affairs to inform the hostile Sioux and Cheyenne that if they did not report to a reservation agency or an army post on or before January 31, 1876, they would be ferreted out and driven in.

Snowbound in the middle of a fierce winter, the tribes were disdainful of the message. Also, they were unfamiliar with the concept of an ultimatum. Even if it had been a matter of life and death, which they felt it, was not, the Indians could not possibly have complied with the unreasonable demand.

Of course, the government knew that to be true. The communiqué was not meant as an order or even as a challenge; it was simply a death warrant. On February 1, the day after the deadline, the Secretary of the Interior declared that any Indian who had failed to comply was a dangerous hostile. At that point, the Secretary of War was called upon to take appropriate action. He, in turn, ordered General Sheridan to subdue all the dangerous renegades as quickly as possible. Sheridan ordered his two principal

263

officers to prepare for extensive maneuvers against these dangerous native insurgents. Objective: Annihilation

The men to whom this odious mission fell were General Nelson (Bear Coat) Miles, Commander of the Department of Dakota, and General George (Gray Fox) Crook, commanding the Department of the Platte. The two were exact opposites. Miles was an outgoing, friendly commander. A lawyer prior to the Civil War, Miles was universally liked for his common sense, good judgment, humility, and kindness. Crook, who had just returned from a stint against the Apaches in Arizona, was reticent, drab as a mud fence, slow to anger, slower to talk, and slowest of all to confide in his subordinates. He was famous for wearing a one-piece canvas suit and braiding his long, forked blond beard. In an era when nearly every commander rode a showy, thoroughbred horse, Crook contented himself with a mule.

General Sheridan decided his best strategy was to converge on the Powder River Basin and to surround the hostiles as quickly as possible. To accomplish this he decided to send one column, under Crook, north along the old Bozeman Trail from Fort Fetterman in Wyoming. A second unit, led by Colonel John Gibbon, would move from Fort Ellis, in western Montana, eastward down both banks of the Yellowstone River. The Seventh Cavalry, under Custer, would leave from Fort Abraham Lincoln and move westward. They were the main force that would actually bring the hostiles to bay and snap the jaws of the trap shut.

Using the very latest information from the Indian Department, Sheridan assured his commanders that there were only about 500 or 600 hostiles currently camped out on the prairies or up in the mountains. When the snow melted enough to provide grass for the ponies, agency Indians would come out and swell that number by tenfold. Therefore, he urged them to take the field at once.

Only one column got under way before the end of winter. Early in March, the Gray Fox left Fort Fetterman and pushed northward through deep snow and bitter cold, with five hundred infantrymen, and six cavalry companies, commanded by Colonel Joseph Reynolds.

Late on the evening of March 16, Crook's two Arikara scouts were surprised to find the village of Three Bears, straddling the Powder River. (The Powder River's western bank was actually in Crow territory. The 1851 Fort Laramie Treaty had established this boundary for the Crow Nation.) Since the snowdrifts were too deep for his foot soldiers, Crook chose to send his cavalry to the attack early the next day.

The occupants of more than a hundred Oglala, Miniconjous, and Cheyenne lodges were still asleep when the Yellow Legs fell upon Three Bears' village on that bitterly cold, subzero morning. In the lodge he shared with Morning Dove and their two young sons, Fire Hawk was awakened by muffled sounds of rifle fire. At once he thought of the Washita; but this village was ready!

When the first blizzard lashed the village, Fire Hawk directed that a wall of wet snow be molded around the base of each teepee. Each storm provided ever more snow to be added to the walls. Once in place, the heat from within soon converted the snow to solid ice. All winter long these formidable ice walls grew thicker and higher, until at last they rose a third of the way up the sides of each lodge and created a hundred miniature fortresses. Similar defensive walls were constructed along both banks of the Powder. Regardless of which side of the river an attack might come from, the defenders were ready.

If the attack did come, instead of dashing out of their lodges as they usually did, the warriors had been trained to stay under cover and shoot from behind the protective ice walls. Fire Hawk had split the village into two halves to increase the firepower.

Chances of any force attacking along both banks of the river at the same time were remote. The warriors on the side that was not under attack would huddle behind the wall along the far bank, and pour heavy, demoralizing rifle fire into the attackers. Since the inhabitants in the other half of the camp would also be lying behind low protective walls, bullets would pass harmlessly over them and strike down their aggressors.

Fire Hawk's superb tactics and excellent training took a heavy and immediate toll on Reynolds and his surprised cavalrymen. Just moments after they wormed their way into this sleeping camp, the Yellow Legs, now with a swarm of angry lead hornets buzzing about their ears, rushed out again, licking their wounds and cursing the Arikara scouts for finding this deadly, inhospitable village.

Reynolds and his six companies of confused and demoralized soldiers scurried back to Crook's column, where their discontent and loss of resolve apparently spread rapidly and infected their commander. General Crook decided that the fighting was too hot, and the weather too cold, either to renew the attack or to maintain his present position. He ordered an immediate reversal of course and then hurried back to the warmth and safety of Fort Fetterman. He did not venture forth again until the end of May.

Fire Hawk and Three Bears met soon after the troopers' exodus and decided that since the exact location of their village was now known, it would be unsafe to remain. If a large force were to attack along both banks of the river at once, the entire village might well be wiped out.

Therefore, they struck the camp as quickly as possible and, despite the perilous traveling conditions, moved down the Powder and then cross-country to the eastern fork of the Little Powder, where the village of Crazy Horse was located.

Valuable lessons had been learned that morning. The warriors were now sure that Fire Hawk's strategies worked. They had been tested under fire, and the defenders had suffered not a single casualty. The second lesson was a dire one. The White Eyes had really declared war on them.

Crazy Horse, Three Bears, and Fire Hawk decided to move still farther north along the Powder and join Sitting Bull's village, doubling their size and strength. Fire Hawk's prediction of a powerful army of warriors was looming ever nearer.

➤

A week after the skirmish on the Powder River, Lt. Col. George Armstrong Custer was summoned to Washington to give testimony at the latest congressional investigation into widespread corruption on the frontier.

Opportunities for unscrupulous men in the burgeoning nation's remote outposts were nearly endless. The gambit ran from petty thimbleriggers in the seedier mining camps, who challenged the dupes to find tiny peas under walnut shells, to deadly, derringer-toting cardsharps who fleeced slightly smarter dupes, with slightly more sophisticated schemes, in slightly more progressive places like Deadwood or Custer City.

A more serious problem was posed by the Carpetbaggers, those unprincipled political vampires who had grown rich in the decade after the Civil War by sucking the lifeblood from the South and replacing it with equal measures of misery. As Reconstruction drew to a close and their illicit opportunities diminished, many of these callous provocateurs formed new allegiances with equally seedy federal officials and continued lining their collective pockets at the expense of a new set of unfortunates. This time they preyed upon the gullible reservation Indians, by supplying them with tainted meat, shoddy trinkets, and rotgut whiskey.

To all these abuses and more, Custer testified. He then went on to describe the illegal practices of a cartel known as the Indian Ring. By doing so, he incurred the undying and venomous wrath of President U.S. Grant, since many of the culprits Custer implicated were close friends or relatives of the President and his wife, Julia. As a punishment, President Grant decreed that Custer would be stripped of his command.

After a great deal of coaxing from Generals Sherman, Sheridan, and Terry, Grant restored Custer to his command of the Seventh Cavalry; but the President was adamant in his refusal to allow him to lead the Fort Lincoln contingent. Terry would remain in charge and, hopefully, keep a close rein on his unpredictable subordinate.

As he started out on this new campaign, Custer must have felt as though he were caught in a Washita deja vu. His reputation had again been sullied, and he had fallen from favor. Undoubtedly, he felt compelled to score a smashing victory just as he had against Black Kettle in 1868. Only then could he wipe the slate clean and return his precious ego to its proper state of luster.

We can be certain that as Custer left Fort Lincoln and headed west, leading the 600 officers and men that made up the twelve companies of 7th Cavalry, he was a desperate man indeed! For only by finding, facing, and defeating a large number of hostiles could he redeem himself. Killing Indians meant headlines, and headlines meant a return to glory. Any and all risks that might return him to his rightful place as America's Daring Dandy were justified. As he rode through the gates of Fort Lincoln, his only fear was that the renegades would run rather than stand and fight.

The other military commanders shared Custer's concern. They were fearful not only that the Indians would run away, but that their slower-moving troops would be unable to find or catch the extremely mobile hostiles. In a dispatch to Sherman, "Black Phil" Sheridan expressed his fears.

"We will never find anything like an Indian army," he wrote, "because no large gathering can feed themselves or their animals for more than three or four days at a time."

Sheridan forgot that a great deal can happen in three or four days, or even three or four hours, to an overconfident army led by an egotistical zealot, when they are fighting a well-trained and determined foe. This time Custer would not be facing timid old men and women, who crawled backwards, waving American flags. This time his adversaries would be eager young warriors, who charged forward, waving American scalps.

Fire Hawk wondered what the army commanders would have said had they known they were under surveillance by Bobtail Horse's scouts from the moment they left their forts. Knowing that they were at war, the Plains Indians were ready, willing, and waiting.

PART SEVEN

THE CHALLENGE

Chapter XIX

➢

For Richer Or For Poorer

Town of Great Falls
Montana Territory
May 25, 1876

Our seventh wedding anniversary thought Kevin McCarthy, as he sat in an elegant red-and-gold carriage, behind an impatient pair of beautifully matched black horses. While he waited for Catherine and the girls to join him, he reflected on the many gifts God had bestowed upon them during their marriage. They had been blessed with two wonderful daughters. Five-year-old Marie Monique, whom everyone called M's, and her sister, Kelly Arne, or Killarney, who was three. The previous year, Catherine had lost their third child.

Several weeks ago, they had decided to invite a group of close friends to help them celebrate this anniversary with a Mass of Thanksgiving. A solemn public devotion, thanking God for their bountiful marriage. But at this morning's Mass, they would be celebrating another, very special blessing. Yesterday they had confirmed that Catherine was carrying a tiny new life within her.

McCarthy and Kelly Freight Express was now the largest company of its kind in both the Montana and Dakota Territory. There were offices in Great Falls, Missoula, Bozeman, Fort Benton, Deadwood, and Bismarck. Four years ago, they had been awarded the U.S. Mail contract and proved that they merited that distinction. Now they owned eight T-6 ore wagons, as well as a large fleet of smaller rigs that were used to haul supplies to isolated settlements, mining camps, and army posts. Yes, Kevin reflected as he sat in the impressive coach, there was much to be grateful for.

His thoughts strayed to GeeGee, and Megan and Myles Keogh. They wouldn't be here today. All of them had been together a week ago at Fort Abraham Lincoln, in Bismarck. He had spent a pleasant evening visiting with them and many other old friends. He and GeeGee spent a couple of hours reminiscing, and singing campaign songs with several troop commanders—Myles Keogh; George Yeats, commander of F Troop, the Seventh Cavalry's most renowned spit-and-polish troop; Jim Calhoun, who was married to one of the Custer girls; Thomas McDougall; Ed Godfrey; Myles Moyland; and C Troop's distinguished commander, Captain Tom Custer, the general's younger brother, and the winner of two Medals of Honor during the Civil War.

He remembered others drifting in and out during the rowdy songfest. Troop commanders Tom French, Al Smith, Donald McIntosh, and Tom Weir had all stopped by. So had Doctor James DeWolf, and Chief Scout "Lonesome" Charley Reynolds. The ranking officer at the festival had been the Executive Officer, Major Marcus Reno.

Kevin thought the affable General Nelson Miles might make an appearance, but learned that he had quit the post and gone west to join Colonel Gibbon at Fort Ellis. George and Elizabeth Custer did not attend the party, nor did the socially aloof Captain Fred Benteen. Kevin had joined him for dinner, but did not see him thereafter.

It was nearly ten o'clock when Kevin and his brother-in-law met the Keoghs at their quarters, where they all enjoyed a late supper. Myles had been a Papal Guard in the Vatican during the reign of Pope Pius IX, prior to emigrating to America in 1862. Graced with Irish wit and charm, he amused them with comical stories about soldiers of fortune he had known, including their friend Lieutenant Charles De Rudio. They were all reluctant to end the party at midnight and admit that the wonderful evening was over.

The next morning, the regiment left Fort Abraham Lincoln and began a campaign designed to bring the hostiles to bay.

➢

M's and Killarney came skipping down the path and climbed into the carriage. Moments later, Catherine, beautiful and perfectly dressed as always, joined them, and Kevin thought no more of his friends.

That afternoon, after Mass, they attended an anniversary party that Kerry Kelly had arranged at Miles City's finest restaurant, a delightful place known as The Mother's. As he occasionally did on such special occasions, Kevin grew a bit tipsy. Consequently, when Big Bart Burley, owner of the Big Bart Mines approached him, he seriously considered a consignment that he ordinarily would have rejected as far too risky.

"I have a very serious problem," Bart Burley began. "I have a contract to deliver eighteen tons of gold dust and nuggets to the smelter in St. Louis, on or before July 10. Unfortunately, my miners at the Bozeman mine can't have the shipment ready until June 14. Ordinarily, that would leave ample time for delivery, by either railroad or riverboat; but the government has ordered all riverboats to stay in port, and trains to remain stationary until this damned Indian business is over.

"To insure 'on-time delivery,' the smelter owners insisted on a sizable performance bond when we negotiated the contract. They, in turn, are committed to the sponsors of the American Centennial Exposition. As you know, the Exposition begins in Philadelphia, in July. If the gold does not arrive by July 10, the Big Bart Mining Company will have to forfeit a great deal of money. So my question is this: If we made the handling easier by packing the gold in 900 small elkhide bags, weighing forty pounds each, would you be willing to haul it to St. Louis?"

"That's a hell of a long way to go, Bart! A hell of a long, dangerous way, with the tribes on the warpath. Just last week, Custer and the Seventh Cavalry left Fort Lincoln to join Terry and Crook and go after the hostiles in the Powder River Basin. In order to get your gold to St. Louis on time, I'd have to keep my wagons rolling for a major portion of each day, and go right through those hostiles. Any other route would take much too long. I'm sorry, but I think the whole idea is crazy."

"Perhaps it will seem less so when I explain my proposition."

"Go ahead."

"If you will undertake this project, and attempt to deliver the gold on time, I'll pay you $10,000, above and beyond your regular fee. That amount is less than the performance bond, and I'd sure rather spend money attempting to fulfill a contract, than pay a penalty for not fulfilling it. Defaulting on promises is the quickest possible way to lose valuable customers. Should you agree, I'll transfer the money to your bank account at once. I did not even consider the idea of tying your bonus to successful delivery, because I know that if you accept my proposal you will do your damnedest to succeed. For that very reason, as your friend, as well as your client, I ask you to consider carefully. Don't do this if you think the danger and risks are too great! You don't need the extra money enough to risk your life! If this delivery is impractical, I'll live with a forfeit. Folks in St. Louis and Philadelphia will simply have to understand and make allowances."

"I'll think it over, and give you my answer by morning, Bart."

They returned to the party and spoke no more of the contract.

Kevin spent a long pleasant afternoon dancing with Catherine and swinging M's and Killarney around the

274

room. In between times, he washed down a quart of Irish whiskey with a magnum of French champagne. He shared Bart Burley's proposition with Kerry, but made it seem far easier and less dangerous than it really was.

By the time supper was served, delivering the gold shipment didn't seem difficult at all. As he entered The Mother's dining room with Catherine on his arm and the girls scampering along behind, he felt almost invincible. If I don't seize this golden opportunity, he thought, I'll despise myself for the rest of my days. This is, he decided, a once-in-a-lifetime chance!

When they were seated, he looked down the long banquet table and attracted Bart's attention. He gave a nearly imperceptible nod, but it was enough. The gold mining entrepreneur raised his glass in salute and acknowledgment.

The next morning, the contracts were signed and the $10,000 transfer was made. On June 14, as scheduled, three huge T-6 wagons were loaded with a ransom in riches, and nine men set out on a great adventure. Although many wished them good luck, they counted more heavily on the Winchester repeating rifles and the brace of Colt Peacemakers each of them carried.

Chapter XX

➢

Until Death Do Us Part

Hostile Indian Country
Yellowstone River Trail
Montana Territory
June 16, 1876

Two days later, Kevin McCarthy sat high above the ground on the heaving seat of a straining freight wagon as it lurched along the south bank of the Yellowstone River. The trail began to ascend a slight grade, and the heavy wagon, laden as it was with six tons of gold, began to lose momentum. McCarthy's whip snaked out. A moment later the air above the ears of his mules crackled like a lightning bolt in a thunderstorm. Forced out of their placid indifference, the six weary animals threw their weight against the traces in reluctant response.

He turned in his high perch and peered back along the trail, watching as his other two wagons rounded the curve and began to slowly climb the slope. I must be a damned fool, he thought, to be risking so much on this trip. Sure, I'll make more in the next month than most folks earn in a lifetime, but I'd also like to live to enjoy it. A worried frown creased his forehead as he once again reflected that the likelihood of any of them staying alive, even to reach the Bighorn River, was diminishing with every passing mile. The chances of success had seemed pretty good when he made the deal. Things always seemed easier when you were a bit tipsy! Leave it to a blithering Irishman with a snootful of whiskey in his belly and a pretty girl on his arm, to brag about his ability and, worst of all, to believe his own tall tales!

Once again he cranked his head around to squint at the two "shotgun guards," snoozing like a pair of fat hogs atop the mass of elkhide bags that made up the heavy load. Their soft, contented breathing matched the tranquil, lazy afternoon. It's sure peaceful enough now, he thought, and easy enough to be lulled into a false complacency by the squeak of the wagon, the creak of the harness, and the sound of the river as it nibbled gently against the bank. But trouble has a bad habit of showing up all of a sudden if you aren't ready for it, especially in hostile country. And all the tribes were painted for war. That was for sure.

His gaze left the trail for a moment and rested briefly upon the Winchester repeating rifle that lay angled against his seat. His other drivers and all six guards carried Winchester 73's, as well as a pair of Colt Peacemakers. There's enough firepower in those twenty-seven guns, he thought, to turn a charge of Johnny Rebs, much less whip a few dozen Sioux and Cheyenne.

➢

A couple of hours later, the hundreds of unshod pony tracks he saw along the trail told him that they were in serious danger.

"We can forget about running off a couple of dozen hostiles, and start worrying about the Sioux lifting our scalps," Kevin told the two wagon guards, who were now wide awake.

I better figure a way out of this mess, he thought to himself. Catherine's too young to be a widow, and I sure don't want to be the target for a bunch of Indian arrows and bullets!

Another backward glance confirmed that the drivers and guards on both of his other wagons were vigilant and ready as they plodded slowly along in his wake. He withdrew a big military tactical map from its waterproof case, measured carefully, and estimated that they were within ten miles of the Bighorn River.

Although the trail was reasonably smooth, it took nearly two hours for the lumbering wagons to slowly and cautiously cover the distance. Every mile, they saw ever increasing numbers of unshod pony tracks. Some of them, according to his Seneca tracker Little Hatchet, were only an hour or two old. On two separate occasions, they heard the drumming of distant hoofbeats, and once a furious volley of shots broke the uneasy stillness.

Once again, Kevin began to doubt the wisdom of his decision to haul this gold. He hoped that his men's courage would not desert them during the night and that they, in turn, would not desert him. If they ran, he couldn't blame them. It sure was an awful place for anyone hoping to hang onto his scalp.

Suddenly, through the trees ahead, he beheld a sight that made his heart leap with joy. Anchored in the middle of the Yellowstone, near the mouth of the Bighorn River, was a long white riverboat. Across her sleek stern, Kevin could plainly see big black letters that proclaimed her to be the Far West.

A few minutes later, he reined the mules to a halt at the edge of the river opposite the vessel's anchorage. Jumping from the wagon seat, he hailed a man in an officer's cap who was standing on the top deck beside a pair of small cannons.

"Captain, may I come aboard?"

"I'm not the Master," came the reply. "I'm David Campbell, the pilot. I'll send the jolly boat over for you."

Kevin was rowed out to the big riverboat where he clambered up the boarding ladder and stepped gratefully onto the deck. There another officer met him.

"I'm Grant Marsh, the Master. I don't mind saying that you people are crazy to be rolling along this river in those three slow, cumbersome wagons."

"Captain Marsh, I'm Kevin McCarthy, and I totally agree. My men and I were prepared to fight off a couple of dozen Indians, but the trail signs indicate that there are hundreds of them in this area."

"McCarthy, if there is a more dangerous place on the American continent right now, I don't know where to suggest you look for it. Several army columns are in the field, intent on forcing as many hostiles as possible back into this area. Why are you here?"

"My wagons are loaded with eighteen tons of gold. We are bound for St. Louis. Perhaps you can help me out of a bad fix by taking my cargo as far as Bismarck."

"Ordinarily, that would be no problem, but I'm currently under contract to the army. The Far West is the support and supply ship for the squadrons of Terry, Crook, and Custer. If I receive no further orders by tomorrow, I've been directed to move along the Yellowstone to the mouth of the Rosebud and to remain at anchor until June 21. I may be in this region for a prolonged period of time. Does your cargo have a delivery deadline?"

"It does, Captain Marsh, but even the very latest delivery is far better than no delivery. I'm convinced that we are not going to live much longer if we continue with the wagons."

"If I take the gold aboard, what will you and your men do?"

"If we can't stay aboard, we'll conceal the wagons as well as possible and try to get away on the mules."

"McCarthy, what do you think your chances of survival are?"

"Not very good, Captain, but I see no alternative. Do you?"

"No, I'm afraid not. If it's any consolation, I'll guarantee the safety of your gold. I'll let no harm befall it."

"Hallelujah! That makes me feel a lot better. How do you plan to go about transferring the gold?"

"How is it packed?"

"Nine hundred sacks weighing forty pounds each. A total of eighteen tons."

"Far West is designed to carry up to 400 tons, using minimum draft, so the weight's no problem. However, the Department of the Army is paying $360 per day for her services; they have first priority. The bags will have to be spread out along the starboard deck from bow to stern. Every other bit of deck space is already being used. Fortunately, both cargo slings can lift a ton at a time. We'll move the Far West inshore and anchor close enough for the boom to reach your wagons, but it still means loading and unloading the nets eighteen times."

Captain Marsh immediately assembled the officers and crew on deck and explained what he wanted them to do. An hour later, the anchor was weighed, the vessel was snuggled against the bank, and the cargo booms were rigged.

Captain Marsh was right about needing every inch of space. They piled the unwieldy bags along the starboard side of the main deck, fore and aft, and still needed to use one side of the long interior companionway. It was after midnight when the gargantuan undertaking was completed and the dozen exhausted workers were able to get a few hours of much-needed sleep.

Only the two vigilant sentries, who stood watch near the pair of small, deck-mounted cannons, remained awake.

The following morning, not long after dawn, Captain Marsh came ashore and joined McCarthy and his men as they sat around a small cooking fire.

"I'm sorry I don't have my own packet, the Josephine, on this trip," Marsh told them. "She's capable of carrying many passengers. The Far West is simply not built to do that. What do you plan to do now, Kevin?"

"We're going to hide the wagons in that thick stand of pines back there. You can't see them from here, but there's a long line of thorn bushes around a major portion of the perimeter. Once the wagons are in the trees and we erase the wheel tracks, I think the chances of them remaining hidden are pretty good."

"What about the mules?"

"We'll try to ride away on the nine most tractable ones and turn the rest loose in this meadow. They'll probably stay here and eat all of the grass before they move on. Since that'll take them the best part of a month, I hope they'll still be here when we return. Even if the Sioux get them, it would be a small price to pay for our lives and the safe delivery of the gold."

"Which way will you head? Surely not the way you came."

"No, that would be suicidal! We'll head south and try to reach Fort Fetterman. I think that's our best chance. By the way, how much do I owe you?"

"$50.00 a ton. Guaranteed delivery to the dock in St Louis."

"Good. I can write out a bank draft or we can settle in gold."

"Either way is fine. Let's not worry about it until we get to St. Louis. Now, what more can I do to help you?"

"Just keep us covered with your deck cannon until we finish hiding the wagons and lining up the mules."

It was late morning, after the wagons were hidden, when Kevin came aboard to thank Captain Marsh and to say goodbye.

"Well, Grant, the next time we talk, I hope it will be over the two biggest steaks the Paradise Café can supply."

"I'll look forward to that, Kevin. Good luck, and may the good Lord take care of all of you."

Minutes later, Marsh stood on the deck and waved farewell as Kevin McCarthy and his men disappeared into the woods.

➢

At that very moment, less than forty miles to the south, on the upper Rosebud Creek, Crazy Horse, Fire Hawk, and White Wolf were preparing to lead a war party of seven hundred Sioux and Cheyenne against a much larger force of White Eyes, composed of over a thousand Yellow Leg cavalry and infantry, and nearly three hundred of their Shoshone, Arikara, and Crow allies. Ironically, this strong force was commanded by Gray Fox Crook and contained some of the same cavalry units which had been bloodied at Three Bear's village three months earlier.

Since then, the wary Sioux and Cheyenne had moved their camps about constantly, both north and south of the Yellowstone River, in an area between Sakakawea Lake to the east, and the Bighorn and Little Bighorn Rivers to the west. They lingered for short periods on the Powder, Little Powder, Tongue, and Musselshell rivers, and on Porcupine, Pumpkin, and Rosebud creeks, playing the game of coyote and rabbit in all these river valleys, and playing it well. All the while, they grew in strength as more and more agency Indians came out to join them.

Finally, in the last half of June, the Indian army that Fire Hawk had envisioned was in place. In Sitting Bull's huge village were over 1,000 Sioux and 120 Cheyenne lodges, over 7,000 Plains Indians, and nearly 2,000 eager warriors. Coming to look for them was a similar number of equally eager Yellow Legs.

For the past several weeks, ever since the columns left their forts, Bobtail Horse's scouts had watched these wandering and confused bands of White Eyes. As they drew nearer, Crazy Horse and Fire Hawk decided that the best course of action would be to ambush each of the columns separately, before they could unite.

As part of the preparation for these battles, three days were set aside to fast, to initiate new warriors at a Giving of War Weapons ceremony, and to hold a sacred Sun Dance festival. Fire Hawk had learned that even in the culture of the Plains Indians, where courage and ability to endure pain were cherished above all other virtues, very few men were brave enough to withstand the excruciating agony of the Sun Dance. This year, Black Shield had proclaimed his intention to be a Sun Dancer, and had asked Fire Hawk and White Wolf to be his sponsors.

At dawn, on the first day of the festival, four Sun Dancers and their sponsors assembled at the medicine lodge. Near it, a stout pole twice the height of a man had been erected and braced to keep it from being pulled over. From a groove near the top of this pole, eight thick, strong, rawhide thongs hung down to the ground. They were arranged so that two of them descended on each side and connected in such a way as to permit the rope to turn around in the groove without sliding up or down. Each dancer selected a different pair of rawhide straps, and the ritual began.

White Wolf drew his knife and cut two short, deep gashes on the right side of Black Shield's chest, which straddled his pectoral muscles. He jammed his fingers into one of the bleeding incisions and pulled the muscles far enough from the rib cage to insert a thick bone skewer into the first wound. Then he drew it under the muscles and out through the second slash. Finally, the rawhide thong was tied securely in place around the skewer.

When White Wolf finished, it was time for Fire Hawk, using his Spanish knife, to repeat the procedure on the left side. Not once during this entire terrible ordeal did Black Shield or any of the other Sun Dancers cry out or even flinch.

As soon as all four of the candidates were ready, they began moving and dancing around the pole. The Sun Dance would conclude at sunset, or perhaps earlier if the dancers were able to snap off the pole or topple it over. It could be uprooted if the four dancers, pulling their eight tethers out to full extension on the same side of the pole, were able to lean enough collective weight against the ropes. However, each time they attempted this, their strong, elastic pectoral muscles merely stretched a little bit more. The stake never moved, but additional flesh and sinews gave way and wounds opened still further.

The four resolute and determined warriors danced and staggered around the pole until the scorching sun went down. By then fierce pain and raging thirst brought on high fevers and delirium. When they were finally freed from their bindings, a mixture of salt and ashes was rubbed into the wounds. The salt retarded infection and the black ashes forever marked them as Sun Dancers, men who were truly the bravest and best.

Throughout that night and the following day, the four were watched carefully and nursed back to health. On the final day of the holy festival they would be honored for their great bravery.

Also on that third day, the boys who had fasted and received visions would become young men and take warriors' names at the Ceremony of War Weapons. This year was a special one for Fire Hawk. He was the sponsor of Jumping Frog, whom he had seen grow from a seven-year-old mischief-maker, into the awkward boy who loved and cared for Pasha until the old horse died the previous year, and finally into the tall, stalwart young man that he had become. The youngster had been an important part of Fire Hawk's life for ten years, and he was as proud of the lad as he knew White Wolf was.

The Giving of War Weapons was held on a warm, peaceful June evening. For many in attendance, it would be their last peaceful night on earth. The highlight of the ceremony, for most of the Oglalas, was the initiation of Jumping Frog into the warriors' society.

He stood before the warriors' dais of Crazy Horse, who rose to greet the young man. Next his father, White Wolf, approached, bringing the fine buckskin pony he had captured from Gray Fox's Crow scouts a few weeks before. Finally his sponsor, Fire Hawk, came forward bearing war weapons.

The rifle was a gleaming new Winchester Model 73, captured from one of Yellow Hair's civilian wagon masters after a running gun battle. The knife and tomahawk were both special weapons that had belonged to brave men in the past. The hatchet was the one the Forsyth Scout had used to kill Running Fox during the Siege of Beecher's Island. The knife was the Arkansas Toothpick that had belonged to the Grabber. Fire Hawk knew that both of these extraordinary weapons would serve his young friend well.

He withdrew the Widow Maker from its sheath, made a small cut in the new warrior's wrist and another in his own, then pressed them together, proclaiming, as he did, his trust in his protégé.

Now it was time for Crazy Horse to conduct the final part of the ceremony. He came forward and stood before the young man.

"What do you have to tell your people, warrior?" he asked.

"In my life," came the answer, "I have been blessed with two great teachers. But to me, they are much more than that. They are my heroes, and they are also the two finest men and most fearsome warriors I have ever known. One of them is my father, White Wolf. The other is my special friend and sponsor, Fire Hawk. Although I cannot repay them for their help, their love, or their devotion, I will tonight do them the greatest honor in my power as I take something from each of them with me forever. From this moment on I am the Oglala warrior, White Hawk, and I promise to make each of my namesakes proud of me."

➢

Two weeks later, White Hawk, together with seven hundred other Sioux and Cheyenne warriors, awaited Crazy Horse's signal to open fire and charge into Gray Fox Crook's bivouac on Rosebud Creek.

Bobtail Horse had discovered the encampment two days earlier. He estimated that over one thousand horse troopers and walk-a-heaps (the Sioux name for infantry soldiers) were in the temporary camp which had been there for several days. The night before, more than two hundred Indian scouts had joined Gray Fox. In the early morning, the troops were packing up their equipment and preparing to leave. This preoccupation produced a state of confusion and a complete lack of vigilance that seemed to offer Crazy Horse a perfect opportunity for his attack.

When the Sioux attacked, the soldiers were taken completely by surprise. It is probable that they would have been routed had it not been for the Crow and Shoshone scouts. As the shocked White Eyes were groping for unready weapons, their Indian allies rose to the occasion and fought off the eager attackers.

This Battle of the Rosebud, which produced many casualties on both sides, continued until midday when the Sioux and Cheyenne finally withdrew. By then, they had accomplished their mission of forcing Crook, once again, to turn tail and flee.

He retreated with one of the three forces that was scheduled to attack the Sioux and their allies in the days ahead. He gave no thought to the difficulty that his absence might cause the other two squadrons who did not know he was gone. His allies did not know Crook had quit the battle zone, but his enemies did!

Of equal importance was the fact that these Rosebud warriors had met a superior force and whipped them. Faith in their leaders and confidence in themselves would continue to grow for the next eight days and then — they would ride to meet Custer!

PART EIGHT

BULLETS, BUGLES, AND BLOOD

Chapter XXI
➢
Into The Valley Of Death

Rosebud & Bighorn River Valleys
Wyoming & Montana Territories
June, 1876

During the Sun Dance Festival, Sitting Bull fasted and prayed to the Great Spirit. The great Hunkpapa leader was "blessed" with a most welcome vision. He dreamed that he saw "many dead White Eyes falling into the Sioux camp."

Every Sioux man, woman, and child, and all their allies, were overjoyed to hear this news. No one questioned the sage medicine man's fortune-telling ability. He had demonstrated his strange and mystical powers many times in the past.

Some of the warriors thought the Battle on the Rosebud had fulfilled the dream. "No," their visionary leader had responded tartly, "I saw hundreds of Yellow Legs falling down, not mere dozens! Our big victory still lies ahead!"

Since Bobtail Horse and his scouts were still shadowing the columns of Bear Coat and Yellow Hair, Fire Hawk led the small war party that followed the defeated Gray Fox Crook and his troops back to their base camp on Goose Creek. Once he reached this zone of relative comfort and safety, it became apparent that Crook did not intend to venture forth again for a long time.

This was confirmed the following morning when the warriors intercepted a dispatch from Crook to Terry. It informed Bear Coat of the Rosebud fight and made Crook's resistance to orders quite clear. He would not break camp or rejoin the pursuit of hostiles until his troops were well rested and adequate replacements for his casualties arrived. Absolutely certain that Crook was out of the impending battle, and that his cohorts would remain ignorant about his decision, Fire Hawk led his warriors back toward the valley of the Little Bighorn, and their date with destiny.

➢

Meanwhile, aboard the Far West, Captain Marsh moved the vessel eastward and, on the morning of June 21st, dropped anchor at the mouth of the Rosebud. That afternoon, General Terry, along with Colonel Custer, Colonel Gibbon, and Major James "Grasshopper Jim" Brisbin, Gibbon's cavalry commander, came aboard to solidify final plans for the hostile warriors' capture or annihilation.

General Terry ordered Gibbon to march his slow-moving infantry back up the Yellowstone, to cross the river on the Far West, and to move along the Bighorn to the mouth of the Little Bighorn. Once there, his troopers were to dig in and prevent any hostiles from escaping.

Custer would lead his more mobile Seventh Cavalry up Rosebud Creek, try to rendezvous with Crook, and then march slowly across country to the upper reaches of the Little Bighorn. This large force would then fan out and push everything before them, down the river toward Gibbon's infantry. The hostiles would be caught between the three columns and forced to surrender or, if they were foolish enough, to fight. The punitive force's commanders' only real concern was that the Indians would filter through their trap and escape. As they left the Far West that afternoon, Terry decided to go with Gibbon and give Custer a free rein.

It is ironic that General Terry had deduced, so accurately, the approximate location of the big village but had so greatly underestimated its size. In mid-May and again at the end of the month, Lieutenant James Bradley's Crow scouts actually saw villages in the valleys of the Powder and the Tongue Rivers. Again in early June another patrol, this one led by Major Marcus Reno, chanced upon a village during the week of the Sun Dance while the Sioux were camped on the Rosebud.

On each occasion, the number of lodges was estimated at 350 to 400. Two warriors per lodge meant a total of 700 to 800 fighting men. That was the number the troopers expected to face. But when the villages were combined, a force three times that size would actually be arrayed against the soldiers.

The Custer cavalry that set forth on that June 22nd afternoon consisted of 31 officers, 585 enlisted men, 25 Arikaras and 6 Crow scouts, a handful of civilian scouts and wagoneers, and the newspaperman, Mark Kellogg.

Although these troop numbers represented only about half of his unit's authorized strength, when General Terry offered him four companies from the Second Cavalry, commanded by "Grasshopper Jim" Brisbin, Custer refused, convinced that his Seventh Cavalry alone "could whip all of the hostile Indians in the country."

In this supposedly invincible regiment were, in addition to George and Tom Custer, a third brother, called Boston or "Boss," and a nephew, Armstrong Reed, named for his famous uncle. Both these men were civilian attachés. The final Custer relative was brother-in-law Lieutenant James Calhoun, Commander of L Troop.

Apart from these relatives, Custer had few supporters. Two of them were regimental adjutant Lieutenant William Cooke, and the C.O. of spit-and-polish D Troop, Captain Thomas Weir. His two senior officers, Major Marcus Reno and Captain Fred Benteen led those who disliked Custer. All others were lukewarm at best. It was not a happy unit that rode forth that day to harass the hostiles.

As cavalry custom dictated, troopers were allowed some choice about their clothing, but each man carried a Springfield single-shot carbine with 100 rounds of ammunition and a Colt pistol with 24 rounds. This time, noisy sabers and swords had been forbidden.

According to the journals of K Troop commander, Lieutenant Edward S. Godfrey, who would eventually become General Godfrey, "Because of our late start on the 22nd, the regiment covered only a dozen miles and went into camp at 4:00 P.M., but we made up for the delay the next day by marching thirty-three miles and camped at 5:00 P.M. in the valley of the Rosebud. The 24th, we marched twenty-eight miles between sunrise and sunset with frequent halts and much scouting activity."

Noon on the 24th found them camped on the site where the Sioux Sun Dance had been held, nearly eighty miles from their starting point. Custer's Crow and Arikara scouts were troubled by the big medicine they sensed at this holy place and were reluctant to go on. In an effort to appease them, Custer delayed his departure and lingered for four hours over his midday meal while various bands of scouts fanned out in all directions. Yellow Hair was troubled by crisscrossed trails of travois poles that led off in a variety of directions.

"Those tricky Red Sticks are separating and preparing to scatter to the four winds," Custer confided to his adjutant, Lieutenant Cooke. "We have to corner them now, or get ready to chase them for a damned-long, hot summer."

He was somewhat reassured when his two best scouts, "Lonesome" Charley Reynolds and the part-Sioux Bloody Knife, determined that the crossing trails had been made by some of the agency Indians who were coming out to join their nomadic brethren. This was a good sign, they both proclaimed, because it meant that the main party of renegades was still together, not too far ahead.

➤

As Custer prepared to angle across country that afternoon toward the Little Bighorn, the Sioux and their allies, unaware of Yellow Hair's swift approach, were retracing their steps and again moving northward, back along the Little Bighorn, to hunt a large herd of antelope which their scouts had reported earlier in the day. Had it not been for these animals, the big village would have been exactly where Custer expected it to be. What might have happened then? We can only guess.

The village's new location was far different from the one they expected to find. Here the narrow valley of the upper stream had vanished. In its place was a vast open plain that stretched along the Little Bighorn for three miles or more. On the west bank of the river, huge meadows nearly a mile wide in places sloped up to gently rolling hills. The area offered the big pony herd ample space and sweet grass on which to graze. Beyond the eastern bank of this pretty meandering stream, a stream the Sioux called the Greasy Grass, towering cliffs rose abruptly and thrust their lofty, craggy parapets hundreds of feet into the skies.

Toward the south, where the hills were lower, a plethora of tiny rivulets gurgled along through groves of shady cottonwood trees and wandered leisurely down to the valley's floor. Although it was early summer, they were still being fed by the runoff from last winter's snows, which continued to cling desperately to the windswept summits of the Bighorn Mountains—majestic peaks that could clearly be seen shining on the southern horizon. To the north, nature had carved an infinite maze of coulees, canyons, and breaks, which lay concealed among an array of long, sharp, narrow ridges and provided endless places from which to swoop down and ambush a confused, outnumbered enemy.

When Fire Hawk returned from Crook's camp, he reconnoitered this rugged terrain on foot. Then he mounted Star Walker and rode down the Greasy Grass to the end of the valley. Along the way he passed more than a thousand Sioux, Cheyenne, and Arapahoe lodges that clustered along the invitingly wide western bank. Later, as he rode back toward his own wickiup, he remembered an advanced tactics professor at V.M.I. who had once described and diagramed the topography needed for a perfect ambush. He still remembered the drawings in detail and decided that this location could not be better.

His mind drifted back to the time he had spent at Fort Phil Kearny. He vividly recalled the disdain that many of the troopers had expressed for the Indians' fighting abilities. If the leaders of the pursuing forces still harbored similar foolish ideas about their own superiority, they would not live long enough to regret them.

The smashing victory over Crook on the Rosebud, coupled with Sitting Bull's prophecy of "many dead White Eyes falling into the Sioux camp," had made his warriors supremely confident. They were convinced that another, even greater victory was theirs for the taking. Also, the White Eyes' constant pressure, designed to make the Sioux abandon both their traditional hunting grounds and the sacred Black Hills, had created a feeling of desperation, the illusion of being cornered. And finally, no one could recall a village as huge as the one that now stretched along the banks of the Greasy Grass. Not only could it not be long maintained, but it would, in all likelihood, never again be duplicated. Once-in-a-lifetime circumstances had combined to create the overwhelming strike force of which Crazy Horse and Fire Hawk had long dreamed.

Tactically, Fire Hawk concluded, conditions were also perfect. Besides the ideal terrain, Crook's unprecedented retreat removed the usual danger of another force unexpectedly attacking their flank while they engaged the main body of troops. Warriors that he normally would hold in reserve to meet such a threat could now be released and thrust into the fray. Undoubtedly, here and now was their best and probably last chance to achieve a great victory.

Such were the thoughts of Yellow Hair and Fire Hawk on the eve of battle: a white leader believing that his opponents had every reason to run and hide; an Indian leader knowing they had every reason to stand, to fight, and to win.

➢

To make up for the prolonged midday layover, Custer and his troops pushed on until sunset before pitching a makeshift camp. There they waited for the return of the Indian scouts who had gone on ahead earlier in the afternoon. It was well past nine o'clock when they slipped back through the velvety darkness and rejoined the regiment. The scouts reported that a short distance ahead the hostiles' tracks crossed a summit ridge that separated the Little Bighorn and Rosebud valleys, and then headed westward toward the Little Bighorn. The trail was fresh. They were certain that the hostiles were nearby.

Custer was ecstatic! He decided to disregard Terry's order to ride up the Rosebud. Instead, the Seventh would make a forced night march in the wake of the fleeing Sioux. At dawn, he would order a halt and rest the troops throughout the remainder of the day, while the scouts attempted to ascertain the exact location of the village. Then at daybreak on the 26th, he would attack the hostiles with everything he had, kill as many as possible, and drive the rest down toward Crook and his battalion who would by then, Custer believed, be bivouacked at the mouth of the Little Bighorn. A short time later he summoned his officers and shared his new strategy with them. Since the plan made sense, nearly all of them agreed with it. But from that moment on, nothing seemed to go right.

The men were roused at midnight and in their saddles a short time later. The trail, which led up a steep, narrow, rock-strewn river valley, would have been difficult to negotiate in broad daylight; the thick, blinding darkness made it nearly impossible.

Two hours and six miles later, the exhausted horses and their weary, dust-coated riders were permitted to rest.

Some of the men even made coffee. Although the alkali dust in the water made the noxious smelling brew more wretched than refreshing, most of the parched troopers managed to choke some of it down.

At dawn, from a vantage point high atop a rocky peak called the Crow's Nest, Arikara scouts spotted, far off in the distance—an undulating movement that they identified as a huge pony herd. Back in camp, the scouts admitted that they had not actually seen any lodges, or for that matter any ponies, but they were sure the unique movement they had seen was a pony herd. Custer thought the scouts might only have seen waving grass, and could well have imagined the motion of horses; but if the Arikaras were correct, the camp was exactly where he had predicted it would be when he chose to disregard General Terry's orders.

Custer ordered Bloody Knife and his Arikaras to scout ahead, while the troopers ate a cold breakfast. It was fortunate that no fires were lighted, for only minutes later one of Bloody Knife's scouts rushed back into the bivouac with news of two hostile war parties that they had spotted nearby. Custer's nagging fear welled up once again. If his mighty Seventh Cavalry was seen, the renegades would be frightened and flee. He could not allow that to happen, not when he was this close to catching them.

For the second time, Custer changed his plans. He would not wait until dawn tomorrow; the regiment would attack immediately. He would hit them now, before they knew he was nearby.

➢

[If one reconstructs the circumstances surrounding the events on the Little Bighorn, aided by more than a century of hindsight, it is plausible to conclude that in his eagerness to attack and prevent the Sioux and their allies from escaping, Custer forgot or simply ignored three vital military rules he had been taught at the U.S. Military Academy. One: Rested troops win battles. His horses and men were exhausted; they had had no sleep and very little rest for the past thirty hours. Two: Know the disbursement of your enemy's troops. Custer had absolutely no knowledge about the size of the force that opposed him. Three: Visualize your objective. He did not yet know the exact location of the village or anything about the terrain that surrounded it. The only rule he seems to have remembered was one advanced by British Admiral Horatio Nelson who said: "A captain can never go far wrong by placing his ship next to that of his enemy." Of course, Nelson was speaking of the high seas where one's enemies could be seen, not of the high hills where they could hide.]

➢

At noon, the Seventh finally reached the top of the long slope, and Custer called the officers to a conference. To compensate for his complete lack of information, he decided to split his force into three component parts and allow the various divisions to operate in a reasonably independent fashion.

In charge of the first of these was the regiment's executive officer, Major Marcus Reno. It was composed of Troops M, A, and G, commanded by Captain French, Captain Moyland, and Lieutenant McIntosh.

A second detachment went to the senior captain, Fred Benteen. Together with his own H Troop, he had Captain Tom Weir's Troop D and Lieutenant Edward Godfrey's Troop K. Reno's and Benteen's groups each numbered approximately 130 officers and men.

Custer retained command of five companies and their 225 men but divided them into two battalions. Captain George Yeats, a Custer supporter, formed one with his own top-rated Troop F, and Troop E, the Gray Horse Troop, commanded by Lieutenant Algernon Smith.

Companies C, L, and I formed a division that Custer hoped would be the first to attack the hostiles. Tom Custer,

Jim Calhoun, and Myles Keogh were the troop captains. It is indicative of Custer's high regard for the skill and ability of Myles Keogh that Keogh was given command of this division in which Custer's own brother, Tom, and his brother-in-law, Jim Calhoun, held equal rank. Custer may have believed that the capable former papal guard was his best officer.

Captain Thomas McDougall's B Troop was detailed to guard the packtrain and to follow along at the best possible pace with the additional ammunition, rations, and other supplies. All of the regiment's civilian employees would accompany McDougall.

In order to remain concealed for as long as possible, Custer decided to ride toward the Indian camp through a narrow valley formed by a tributary of the Little Bighorn. However, since he could not see over the sharp ridges along his left flank while he was in the gorge, he ordered Captain Benteen and his division to scour the high bluffs and make certain that no Sioux force was lying in wait for them.

As Benteen's squadron struggled up toward the summit of this first line of ridges, the other two units started down the valley toward the village that they estimated to be about fifteen miles away, riding on both banks of a stream, now known as Reno Creek. As they rode, the scouts fanned out ahead of them.

Meanwhile, McDougall's packtrain, unable to sustain the pace, continued to drop farther and farther behind.

➤

By 2:30 P.M., the attack columns of Custer and Reno were about two-thirds of the way toward the Little Bighorn. It was then that the lead element of Reno's squadron rode into a deserted village on the eastern bank, where a lone lodge remained standing. Inside this teepee, troopers found the body of a young Oglala warrior. The Arikaras set fire to the lodge, and then the column rode on.

297

The body in the lodge was that of the warrior Bear Paw, who as a boy had been called Chipmunk. He had been severely wounded at the Battle on the Rosebud. Before he died, he had asked to be given the honor of being the first to face the Yellow Legs.

Watching closely as Yellow Hair's troops left the village was a party of about 40 warriors. Among them were Bobtail Horse, Black Shield, and Bear Paw's best friend, White Hawk. They had the responsibility of diverting one of the pursuing columns.

In accordance with their orders, they broke cover and dashed down the creek, slowly enough to be tantalizing but just beyond accurate firing range. At the same time, Fire Hawk's second bit of strategy went into effect. Parties of warriors began milling small pony herds around and around, beyond the ridges to the north and southeast, creating an illusion that the village's inhabitants were scattering and attempting to escape.

Custer ordered Reno to pursue the hostiles who were quickly disappearing down the creek — promising that his own column would follow in Reno's wake as soon as they could ford the stream. With that assurance, Reno formed his three companies into columns of four and, twelve abreast, they thundered down the valley.

About a mile downstream, the creek suddenly made a sharp bend around an outcropping of large trees that grew closely together, all the way to the water's edge. Reno could see nothing through these thick trees, but he did see a heavy dust cloud above them.

Convinced that horses of fleeing hostiles were raising the dust and believing that Custer was right at his heels, Reno charged ahead.

He was half right. Ponies of hard-riding Indians were indeed raising the dust, but they were not running away. As Reno rounded the wooded bend, more than two hundred warriors fell upon his outnumbered force. In the distance, he could see more Indians riding toward him in an effort to take part in the massacre.

Reno ordered a withdrawal to the protection of the thick copse of cottonwood trees, which at least offered some much needed cover from the deadly, withering fire. Within the woods, it soon became every man for himself, and Reno lost contact with most of his men.

The troopers' adversaries were White Wolf and a veteran force of canny warriors, all of whom were quite familiar with this grove of trees. As soon as Reno's purpose became clear, Sioux marksmen began to cautiously infiltrate, through the trees, toward several key locations that offered unobstructed views of the most likely hiding places. Their intense fire was so devastating that, thirty minutes after the fight in the grove began, and Major Reno was forced to order an evacuation.

He shouted a command to retreat, and in anticipation of this maneuver, Reno and his chief Indian scout, Bloody Knife, mounted their horses which stood nearby. Just as they did, a Sioux bullet tore away the top half of Bloody Knife's head and splattered the startled Major with bits of bone, blood, and brains.

Understandably shocked and confused, Reno slid off his horse. Many of his men dismounted as well while the slaughter continued unabated. Reno soon recovered his senses and decided, once again, that lingering in the trees meant certain annihilation. Hurriedly remounting his horse and ordering the survivors within earshot to do the same, he led them out of the woods and straight into a mass of Indians, which had doubled in size since the fight, began.

Through this savage horde, Reno and his troopers dashed back toward the river and the protection offered by the high bluffs beyond. Many of White Wolf's warriors rode with them. The panic-stricken soldiers were neither retreating nor withdrawing. They were not trying to defend themselves or each other. Most of them were not even firing their weapons. They were simply running away as fast as they could. The scene was one of chaos and bedlam.

White Wolf had orchestrated a complete rout!

Some of the Sioux rode close enough to their victims to hold the muzzles of their rifles against the bodies of the Yellow Legs before firing. Others simply pushed troopers out of their saddles and allowed them to be trampled under the hundreds of thundering hooves that drummed within this hellish inferno.

Before they reached the perilous safety of the cliffs, half of Reno's men were dead, wounded, or missing. One of the most heroic of these was Chief Scout "Lonesome" Charley Reynolds, who died a hero's death trying to protect Dr. Henry Porter as he ministered to the wounded in the grove. Other dead were Troop G's leader, Lieutenant Donald McIntosh; Lieutenant Ben Hodgson; and the regimental surgeon, Dr. James DeWolf. Missing were the Seventh Cavalry's Italian revolutionary and veteran of Garibaldi's legions, Lieutenant Charles De Rudio, as well as two squads from his platoon. More than a dozen badly wounded troopers clung to their saddles long enough to reach the heights, where they collapsed.

It was now 4:00 P.M.

➤

Reno ordered the troopers who were physically able to dig shallow trenches and prepare to repel the hostiles who were gathering below them. Meanwhile, Reno puzzled over Custer's disappearance. He had had no word from him since they separated at 2:30 P.M. Where in the hell can Custer be? he wondered. If he doesn't show up pretty soon, these Red Sticks will cut us to ribbons.

Suddenly, the Indians who were firing up at them stopped and began pulling back.

"Where do you suppose they're running off to?" the badly shaken, confused, and anguished Reno asked his friend, Myles Moyland.

"I think they're going to attack a force even weaker than we are, Marc. God help those poor devils, whoever they are."

➤

Soon after Reno's battalion dashed off after the Sioux decoys toward the southeast, Custer changed his mind and decided not to cross the creek and follow Reno after all. Instead, he decided to investigate the dust clouds that were still visible above the ridges to the north.

He ordered the five troop commanders to form their units into columns of two and then, ten abreast, they cantered up the long incline to the ridge summits. From that vantage point, they could look down and see the horrible sight of Reno's command, caught in the river's big bend, being cut to pieces by a horde of screaming, painted warriors.

Custer quickly called his brother Tom to his side.

"We've caught them flat-footed, Tom," he proclaimed. "It'll be a turkey shoot! Order McDougall to bring up the packtrain. We sure as hell can't afford to run out of ammunition."

The younger Custer did as he was instructed and dispatched a courier with a message for Captain McDougall.

"Come quick. Cross the high ground. Don't delay. Cut loose any pack that breaks. Come quick. Big village."

Custer, erroneously presuming that the entire hostile force was now in sight, and anxious to bring as much pressure as possible to bear on them, led his battalion off the summit and down into a ravine that ran at an angle toward the valley below. Wishing to get Benteen's division involved, Custer directed his adjutant to send a message to Benteen. Lieutenant Cooke scribbled a note on a page from his memo book and gave it to bugler John Martin. It said: "Benteen. Come on. Big village. Be quick. Bring packs. W.W. Cooke. P. Bring pacs," misspelling "packs" in his haste.

Martin reversed his course and started up the ravine toward the summit of the ridge. As he reached the crest, he met Boston Custer, who had left his packtrain assignment and was hurrying to help his more famous brothers slaughter Indians. Martin paused for a moment and watched the young man as he scurried down the ridge, eagerly rushing to keep his appointment with danger.

As Custer's battalion reached a point halfway down the ravine, now called Medicine Tail Coulee, Yellow Hair ordered Captain Yeats' two-company division to continue its descent, to ford the Little Bighorn, and proceed toward the big village. Meanwhile, Keogh's three companies would branch off and hold the high ground on the ridge to the north, now called Battle Ridge. It was by this route that Benteen was expected to approach.

The troops of Captain Yeats and Lieutenant Smith encountered no opposition as they descended to the river. However, as they prepared to cross the stream, four Cheyenne warriors appeared on the far bank and beckoned to them. Certain that they were riding into an ambush, Yeats ordered a halt.

On the opposite bank, Bobtail Horse sighed with relief. His tiny scouting party, composed of He Dog, White Dog, Roan Calf, and himself, were the only Indians in sight. If these Yellow Legs were able to ford the river, they could charge all the way to the village and cause real trouble. In an effort to freeze them where they were, Bobtail Horse and the others continued to shake their fists and shout at the confused troopers. Moments later Gall, with thirty warriors who had left the cornered Reno, joined them.

Shooting from cover, the new detachment of Hunkpapa Sioux laid down a devastating fire on Yeats' squadron, driving them back, away from the water's edge.

Fire Hawk and White Wolf soon rode up, accompanied by another fifty Sioux. Together, they all charged across the shallow river and forced the White Eyes to leave the ford and fight their way back up Medicine Tail Coulee to the crest of Battle Ridge, where they rejoined Keogh's division and Custer.

Unlike the earlier Reno rout, the soldiers of F Troop and the Gray Horse Troop performed brilliantly. They were well organized and never lost control. At the end, four troopers fought a rearguard action that allowed their comrades to escape and brought grunts of admiration from the attackers. All four of the rearguards were eventually killed, but the price they extracted was awesome. On the sand or in the shallows lay many dead warriors. Among the dead were He Dog, Roan Calf, and one of the Cheyenne's best scouts and warriors, the always reliable Bobtail Horse.

The warriors who survived the Battle at Medicine Tail Ford stormed up the hillsides and attacked the five companies that were now entrenched in defensive positions, stretching from the northern extremity of the Battle Ridge to the hill in the south, a hill that would one day be known as Calhoun Hill, in honor of L Troop's brave commander.

These continued and persistent attacks were taking their toll and inflicting ever mounting casualties on the Yellow Legs. They needed to gain a measure of mobility or find a stronger defensive position if they were to survive. Otherwise, all was lost.

While L Troop defended Calhoun Hill, Myles Keogh strung his own Troop I out along Battle Ridge and sent Troop C around the base of Calhoun Hill in an effort to relieve a bit of pressure by slowing down the infiltration of more and more warriors into the immediate battle zone.

C Troop soon discovered that the Indians were arriving too quickly to be stopped by one troop, or even a dozen troops. It was Tom Custer and his men who were forced to retreat and seek, once again, the temporary refuge of Battle Ridge.

Yeats and his two companies now began fighting their way up to the highest ground of all — to the northern end of Battle Ridge — a grassy knoll now called Custer Hill.

It seemed that things could not get much worse for the Seventh Cavalry, but they did. At that very moment, Crazy Horse and a new group of warriors arrived. He had crossed the Little Bighorn just below Medicine Tail Ford, skirted the battle zone, and swept down upon Battle Ridge from the north. Then he brought his warriors directly over the ridge's summit and caught many of the remaining Yellow Legs between his own men and those of Fire Hawk.

Dozens of troopers, caught in isolated outposts, were wiped out one by one. Finally, the last remaining group of Yellow Legs gathered on the crest of Custer Hill. In a last effort to bolster their chances, they shot the horses and used them as barricades.

Soon the gunfire directed at the warriors began to slacken. All of the rifle ammunition was gone. The only remaining weapons were service pistols and Custer's snub-nosed English revolvers.

For the next hour, Indian bullets found targets and whittled down the defenders of Custer Hill. Finally, only the three Custer brothers, Keogh, Yeats, Cooke, and Smith still lived. Five troops of the Seventh Cavalry now consisted of only seven men!

Then Boston Custer, Yeats, Cooke, and Smith were killed, and only three Yellow Legs remained. This was the moment Fire Hawk had savored since his day of torment on the Washita. This could not be done with hot lead; it had to be finished with cold steel.

He dug his heels into Star Walker's flanks and, with White Wolf at his side, led a charge toward the summit, a charge which included White Hawk, Black Shield, and a dozen others.

As they neared the hilltop, and its barricade, he felt Star Walker shudder as he was struck, first by one bullet and then by another. The gallant pony ran until he could run no more. When he finally collapsed, his forward momentum threw Fire Hawk into the enclosure where he came face-to-face with Yellow Hair. He knocked the empty pistols from Custer's hands, then slowly and carefully impaled his enemy on the eager blade of the Widow Maker.

"This is the payback for all the murders you committed on the Washita, you rotten bastard."

Custer's eyes showed a brief spark of recognition. Then they clouded over for the last time as he slumped to the ground.

Fire Hawk turned away from the dead general and stared down at White Wolf. His loyal friend lay motionless. A bullet had pierced his brave heart.

Suddenly Fire Hawk felt several hard blows. They hammered the base of his spine and smashed through his back. The front of his body also felt strange. He stared down and saw several jagged rib ends protruding from his own massive, gaping chest wounds.

He turned his head slightly and, through glazed eyes, beheld a still-smoking pistol in the hand of the last surviving Custer.

No longer able to stand, Fire Hawk collapsed upon the bloody battlefield. As he did, his hands grew limp, and the Widow Maker slipped from his grasp. Seconds later, a mortally wounded Myles Keogh tumbled down beside him, covering the ancient knife with his body. A moment later, Keogh shuddered and died.

Fire Hawk's last earthly sight was that of his warriors venting their rage on the mutilated body of Tom Custer.

➢

Now Fire Hawk could feel himself being lifted high above the wretched sights and sounds of the battlefield. He seemed to be floating upward and entering a world of peace and beauty, where pain and war and ugliness were never permitted to exist. Ahead of him, bathed in a comforting warm glow, he could see a beloved figure. He saw her smile as she came toward him along the Star Road. Enveloped in more comfort and tranquility than he had ever known,

305

Fire Hawk hurried forward to take the outstretched hands of Little Fawn.

➢

As the last shots and shouts from Custer Hill died away, Fred Benteen and his reconnaissance force had just completed their scouting mission and were entering the deserted village where Custer and Reno had separated. He ordered a halt before the lone, still-smoldering teepee, just as Tom Custer's messenger thundered into the clearing. Moments later, Trumpeter John Martin arrived with Cooke's scribbled note, which exhorted Benteen to bring the packs and to be quick. As Benteen gave the order to remount, Tom McDougall and the slow-moving packtrain were spotted coming down the trail on the far side of the village.

Ordering McDougall to follow along without delay, Benteen reformed his squadron and trotted on down the creek toward the Little Bighorn. Before they reached the river, they were met by one of Reno's Indian scouts who directed them up the slopes to the high bluffs beyond. As they reached the crest of the first hill, a hatless, nervous, disheveled Major Marcus Reno ran up to Captain Benteen.

"For God's sake, Benteen, halt your command and help me. I've lost half my men."

"Where is Custer?" Benteen demanded.

"We don't know. There was a lot of shooting a while back, but it slacked off."

Just then several ragged volleys of gunfire ripped across the valley, but neither of the commanders made any effort to see where they came from.

Captain Tom Weir of D Troop rushed up to them.

"That firing may mean that Custer has engaged the enemy. We must ride to the sound of those guns."

"My God, Tom, who in the hell do you think you are, Thaddeus Kosciusko?" asked Benteen. "The Revolutionary

War is over. There are only a few hundred Sioux out there. Custer can handle them."

"That's a smart-alecky response, Fred! It's also contrary to orders!"

Without further comment, Weir vaulted onto his horse and pounded down the steep trail toward the valley. Assuming that the Captain expected D Troop to follow him, Weir's executive officer, Lieutenant Winfield Edgerly, ordered the troop to mount, and then led a quick descent in the wake of his leader.

Weir galloped down the near slope, crossed a narrow ravine, and then ascended the far ridge to a high pinnacle, known ever after as Weir Point. From there he could survey much of the Little Bighorn Valley. To his left, he saw the teepees in the village, stretching out to the horizon. On his right was the Medicine Tail Coulee. In the distance low hills rose abruptly from the flat plains. All across the wide valley he could see Sioux and Cheyenne warriors, riding in every direction and firing down into objects on the ground.

Dozens of the alert warriors caught sight of him and charged forward. He quickly spun his horse around and came cantering back toward D Troop just as they reached the base of Weir Point. He ordered an immediate withdrawal and led them, in a calm, orderly fashion, back toward Reno's defensive position.

Moments later, McDougall and the packtrain arrived from the opposite direction. Lieutenant Godfrey expected Reno to order a support force to form up and protect the packtrain; but when he failed to do so, Godfrey took his own K Troop out, in two long lines of dismounted skirmishers, and held back the waves of scalp seekers until Weir's and McDougall's men had all reached safety.

Because more space was needed to accommodate these additional troops, many men were forced to seek cover beyond the original defensive perimeter, with its line of meager, shallow trenches. The heavy, continuous fire from the Indians made any form of further digging impossible.

Cover, on nearly all of the bluff, was woefully inadequate. Stealthy snipers moved forward throughout the remaining hours of daylight, while hundreds of men hugged the ground and prayed for deliverance. At nine o'clock, as a welcome darkness descended upon the beleaguered Yellow Legs, the victorious warriors slipped away. It was time to celebrate their great victory and to mourn their brave dead.

Behind them on the hill, officers tallied up their latest casualties. An additional eleven men were dead and a dozen more were wounded. But the defenders had had a successful afternoon. They had kept red aggressors from overrunning their positions.

For the next several hours, Indian drums sounded a eulogy to their honored dead, and the flickering flames from a hundred fires sent an eerie glow high into the night sky.

On Reno Hill, Henry Porter, civilian contract doctor and last surviving medic, had established a field hospital inside a shallow swale. Around the outer perimeter of this saucer-shaped depression, troopers dug trenches with all sorts of improvised implements. They used everything from the packtrain's meager supply of shovels to their own knives, spoons, and tin cups. They dragged dead horses and mules into position and then stacked saddles, boxes, and packs around the outer wall of the circle. Any object that might stop a bullet or deflect an arrow was added to the makeshift barricade.

More than three hundred men still lived within the confines of this escarpment, and every trooper capable of wielding a weapon became part of the perimeter defense force. Since the hostiles might come from any direction, at any moment, the defenders spent a restless night, braced and ready to repel an attack.

➢

Battle of the Little Bighorn — Day 2.

Shortly after sunrise, Trumpeter Martin sounded reveille. A moment later the first gunshot sounded from an Indian outpost.

Throughout the morning and early afternoon, bullets rattled through the camp and arrows showered down on it. All the while the defenders kept up a steady return fire.

On two occasions, bands of hostiles seemed ready to force their way onto the high ground but were successfully driven back each time. First by Reno's men and then by Benteen's.

At noon, Dr. Porter demanded water for the wounded. A brave party of troopers fought their way down to the river and back, getting only enough water to relieve the sufferings of the most critically wounded. Soon after the water patrol returned, the Indians' rate of fire seemed to slow. By late afternoon, it had all but stopped.

In the early evening, several warriors set fire to the prairie grass. This produced a thick, dense wall of smoke. Minutes later, a nearly endless procession of Indian men, women, and children, riding or walking along, carrying or dragging their possessions, emerged from the screen of smoke on the far side of the valley and climbed the first of the many slopes which lay between them and the Bighorn Mountains.

A relieved Major Reno, watching their exodus, remarked to his friend Captain Moyland, "That column is fully equal to the largest division of cavalry troops I have ever seen on the march."

What did this mass exodus mean? wondered the weary troops on Reno Hill. Were the hostiles really leaving? If so, why were they leaving? Was Custer coming? Were they about to see the comforting sight of regimental flags and guidons, proudly fluttering in the breeze? They cupped grimy hands behind straining ears and willed themselves to hear the soft sounds of squeaking saddles or even a bugler's clarion call. Could it really be Custer? Was it Terry? Or Crook? Or Gibbon?

Maybe, thought the pessimists among them, the hostiles were only moving their women and children out of danger. Once that mission was accomplished, they might return and kill everyone.

After a veritable eternity, deep darkness covered the land.

In the first hours of the sheltering darkness, the troopers buried their dead and moved down the slope, closer to the river, where the thirst that had consumed them for the past thirty-six hours could be slaked. During the night Lieutenant De Rudio, and some of the men left in the cottonwood grove, returned. Most of them had spent a gut-wrenching day and a half, hiding from hostiles and praying for deliverance.

➤

The following morning other prayers were answered when a long blue column of troopers hove into view. It was the 2nd Cavalry, led by General Terry. Moyland and McDougall rode out to meet the approaching column and, for the first time, learned the fate of Custer's command. The bodies of Yellow Hair and 209 of his men had been found four miles downstream.

Reno's casualties were also high—fifty-three dead and sixty wounded. On June 28, Reno's men assembled at the site of Custer's "Last Stand" and began the gruesome task of burying the dead, who were showing the effects of having lain in the hot sun for the better part of three days.

Nearly all of the dead were buried where they fell. Shallow graves were scooped out and corpses were covered with dirt, sod, and sagebrush. It was a sad day indeed. The spirit of the Seventh Cavalry had made this a close-knit unit. Gravediggers were not just burying bodies; they were also saying goodbye to friends.

Most of the troopers had been stripped of their clothing and scalped. Cheyenne victims could be identified by cut arms, the Sioux by the sliced throats. Nearly all of the troopers had been badly mutilated. Few were recognizable.

It was Lieutenant Charles De Rudio and his men who first ascended Custer Hill. They found Custer lying with both his hands curled around a blood-soaked chest wound above his heart. Also visible was a round black hole in his left temple, which had not bled at all. The knife thrust to his heart had killed him. The shot to the head had been delivered long after he died. Custer's body had been stripped but had not been scalped or badly mutilated.

While his men sadly dug graves, Lieutenant De Rudio examined two other bodies. One was so horribly mutilated that it was only after close scrutiny that he determined it to be the corpse of Captain Tom Custer. He had been hacked nearly to bits.

De Rudio turned his attention to the only body on the hilltop that had not been scalped or stripped: that of Myles Keogh. He had known and liked Myles since their first meeting in Italy in 1857. They had been fighting on opposite sides of a very bitter conflict in those days, De Rudio's faction dedicated to seizing Rome from Pope Pius IX, and Keogh's determined to stop them.

De Rudio reached down and gently rolled Keogh's body over. The expression on the dirt-smeared face was almost peaceful. Next, he carefully removed the soiled uniform with its two holes through the left breast, and rolled his friend's body in a woolen blanket.

With unashamed tears streaming down his beard-bristled cheeks, De Rudio looked down at the face of the jaunty, fun-loving Irishman for the last time. Then, as an afterthought, he reached down and snipped a lock of his friend's hair and put it inside his shirt pocket. He would give it to Megan Keogh at Fort Lincoln.

He helped the troopers to place the body in its grave, then gathered up Keogh's uniform and all the nearby weapons, including the knife dropped by Fire Hawk, and packed them in his saddlebags. When he visited Megan, he would suggest that all of these possessions, together with Myles' sword, the one inscribed with the papal guard's coat of arms, be shipped to Rome for display in the Vatican Museum. Myles would have liked that.

Late in the day, as they descended Custer Hill, De Rudio saw a familiar horse standing with drooping head and splayed legs. It was Myles Keogh's claybank sorrel, Comanche. De Rudio insisted that the animal's wounds be treated, and then Comanche was led gently away.

[Comanche recovered and for the next 15 years was a living symbol of the regiment's glory — the 7th's most famous survivor.]

➢

The dead had been buried; but there still remained sixty badly wounded men who needed medical attention that only a hospital could provide. On the morning of June 27, Terry sent a message to Captain Grant Marsh, aboard the Far West, informing him of the situation and requesting that he move the riverboat as close to the battlefield as possible. The courier found the vessel on the Yellowstone River at the mouth of the Bighorn. Marsh scanned the message and wrote a reply; then he sent the rider back to Terry.

Marsh went below to his cabin, where he removed a sheaf of maps from an overhead rack and quickly spread them out on his desk. They each contained his own careful and minute drawings of the Yellowstone's many tributaries and their various depths. Additionally, many of the streams and creeks, as well as some hills and valleys, were marked with coded symbols which he had made as he trekked around the countryside while the Far West waited at various anchorages throughout the entire area.

A few minutes later, his perusal completed, he summoned his pilot, Dave Campbell, and handed him General Terry's dispatch.

"Dave, we can close that gap to fifteen miles by working the Far West up the Bighorn to the mouth of the Little Bighorn, but the river is too shallow for us to make it with 18 tons of gold and all the rest of the cargo we have aboard. We'll have to off-load the gold and hide it in a safe place. Also, we had better remove the cavalry's store of oats. There'll be no room to carry the wounded with all of those sacks on deck."

"Skipper, twenty tons of oats aren't worth very much, but that is one hell of a lot of gold!"

"And one hell of a lot of hard work! But I have a plan."

He indicated an area on the map that he had studied earlier.

"Look how close we are to that spot at this very moment, Dave. It's less than a mile from here. I took a walk over there early this morning. It's the darndest place I ever saw. I wouldn't have discovered it at all if it hadn't been for a pair of coyotes. When I found it, I never dreamt I was looking at a place to hide tons of gold. Let's work out a timetable. Fortunately, all nine of McCarthy's mules are still grazing in the meadow next to us. If they weren't, my whole scheme would be impossible."

For nearly an hour, they worked out the details. Each of the nine brawny mules could carry five sacks of gold on each trip. Assuming that none of the animals were injured, the transfer would require twenty trips.

The two men left the cabin and returned to the main foredeck, where they summoned the crew. Several of the crewmen were sent to round up the mules while the rest began transferring the heavy load. Using both cargo booms, they were able to swing the entire golden hoard ashore and pile it along the river's edge shortly after the shore party returned with the pack animals.

Once a routine was established, they found the procedure to be far easier and less stressful than they had imagined. A mule was led into a loading area and two pairs of elkhide bags, connected by heavy rawhide thongs, were hung across his back; then a fifth bag was placed on his pack saddle. The entire process of loading each animal took less than a minute. The whole mule train was loaded and ready to go in ten minutes. It then required a little less than a half hour for the captain and the pilot to lead the beasts to the nearby hiding place. Once there, each of the surefooted animals was led up to the mouth of the ingenious gold cache, and his load was dropped straight down into one of the recesses. It took even less time to unload than it had to load.

➢

They labored until daybreak to complete the job. Before they left the hiding place for the last time, they hooked all nine of the mules together in tandem and performed two final tasks. Tasks that effectively sealed the cache. Finally, they dragged blankets over the ground to eliminate all signs of their activities.

"Skipper," declared Dave Campbell, "this is an unbelievable place to hide a treasure. The cache is absolutely invisible!"

"I was lucky to find the place, Dave. Since both entrances are now so well hidden, no one will ever find the gold. It's going to be a lot of work for somebody when they come back to get it. But that's McCarthy's problem, not ours. We'll bring him and his work party to the same anchorage we're at now, show him how to open the cache, and then watch them all break their backs."

They returned to the Far West and steamed carefully along the Bighorn to the Little Bighorn. There, on the morning of

June 30, the fifty-two wounded, who had been carried on litters from the battlefield, were brought aboard and laid on soft mounds of grass which the compassionate crew had piled on the decks.

As soon as the wounded men had been made as comfortable as possible, Grant Marsh raced the Far West down the Bighorn, down the Yellowstone, and finally down the Missouri, dropping anchor at Bismarck 54 hours later. Marsh made a run of 710 miles through treacherous shoals and shallows in record time, averaging more than thirteen miles per hour, a feat never duplicated before or since. When they arrived, the ship's flag flying at half-mast alerted everyone on shore that something was terribly wrong.

➢

A 15,000 word story was telegraphed to the New York Herald during the next twenty-two hours at a staggering cost of $3,000. By the following day, nearly everyone in America knew that wild, barbaric Plains Indians had massacred Custer and five of his companies. By the evening of the third day, nearly every outraged American was asking how such a horrid tragedy could have happened and demanding immediate retaliation.

It soon became evident that although the revenge for Custer would be complete, it would not be swiftly carried out.

Out on the Great Plains, convinced that the hostile forces were far larger and more powerful than they actually were, Terry and Crook waited for tardy reinforcements to arrive before going in pursuit. While they straddled campstools and procrastinated, the Sioux straddled their ponies and rode away.

➢

It wasn't until August 10 that the ultra cautious Terry and Crook finally joined forces and hit the trail. More

315

than 4,000 troopers set out in pursuit of one large group of hostiles who, six weeks earlier had disbanded and split up into many smaller groups — and then scattered to the four winds.

To say that the army's forces ran around in circles and looked foolish would be an overly generous statement. While the confused Yellow Legs wallowed through deep mud and forded flooded streams, conditions brought on by unusually heavy rains, Sitting Bull and his people were a hundred miles northeast of them, while Crazy Horse and his followers were a similar distance to the south.

After nearly a month in the field, Bear Coat Miles gave up and quit the chase. Not so the Gray Fox. Crook refused to give up. He forced his exhausted troops to persevere for five more weeks.

On October 9, his persistence finally paid off. At first light, a three-company battalion of cavalry, commanded by Captain Anson Mills, stumbled across the large village of American Horse and his band of Oglalas. They fired into the camp and held fifty plus warriors at bay until the rest of Crook's 2,000 men arrived. Although a few of the Sioux were taken prisoner, the great majority of the men, women, and children were killed. All of the teepees were burned down. Three hundred more "good Indians" for Sheridan!

Later the same afternoon, in response to the smoke from the blazing lodges, Crazy Horse and a war party of 200 fell upon the weary, nearly-starved soldiers and inflicted heavy casualties. That proved to be the final blow for Gray Fox. The next day he ordered a retreat and fled with all possible haste.

From a place high up in the Black Hills, Crazy Horse sat astride Nighthawk, and watched Crook's army as it disappeared in the distance.

"You taught us well, Fire Hawk," he whispered. "We cut, we slashed, and then we ran. We drove the Gray Fox away, and we earned a little more freedom and time for our people. You were a good and loyal son."

Crazy Horse looked up toward the heavens and sighed, realizing that the ancient prayer carved upon the Sacred Pipe of the Sioux would soon be lost. They would no longer enjoy "Peace Without Slavery." His people's days of peace had ended long ago. Loss of freedom would soon follow. Little more time could be bought for the Sioux at any price. He smiled wistfully, knowing in his heart that his own leadership would soon be lost to them forever.

As we leave the mighty Sioux chief for the last time, it is early morning, but it is actually twilight for his nation. The great victory over Custer would become a political pestilence for every Plains Indian. Crazy Horse had been right in his prophecy. The White Eyes would kill the Sioux tree of life and never allow it to bloom again. These adventurous days, filled with bullets, bugles, and blood, would end in tragedy for all the participants.

Chapter XXII

➢

A Deep and Sandy Silence

Aboard The Far West
Fort Abraham Lincoln
Bismarck, Dakota Territory
July, 1876

Grant Marsh and Dave Campbell sat on the foredeck of the Far West as she bobbed up and down beside a Bismarck quay. They had spent the afternoon drinking beer and enjoying the rhythm of the river as the muddy Missouri raced uninterrupted beneath the keel and rushed on to its rendezvous with the mighty Mississippi.

Two weeks had passed since the bloody afternoon on the Little Bighorn, and still another since Kevin McCarthy and his men had ridden away from the Yellowstone and made their desperate dash to the safety of the south. As yet, none of them had been seen.

"Dave, I'm ready to go back and pick up the gold."

"Don't you think we better wait til this Injun mess is over?"

"It's already over, Dave. The only ones who don't know it's over are all in the military. The Sioux have split up and run."

"Probably so, Skipper, but that gold ain't goin' anywhere."

"No matter. I made a deal with Kevin McCarthy to deliver his cargo to the St. Louis docks as soon as possible. It's time to follow through and get it done."

"Don't forget our other problem. We can't work the

Far West up the rivers by ourselves, and our whole crew has quit. They're all still scared stiff of the Injuns."

"I'm sure we can hire a half dozen rivermen who will crew the boat and help us recover the gold. We'll offer them top wages and bonuses to boot. The whole trip will take only a couple of weeks. C'mon, Dave, let's go round up a crew."

But Marsh was overly optimistic. The news of Custer was still too fresh. They visited sailors' haunts along the waterfront for the next three days without recruiting a single man.

Near midnight on the third evening, they decided to try one of the seedier riverfront taverns, a cabaret called The Channel. As they entered, two former members of their crew approached them.

"Evenin' Skipper. Howdy Dave," said a sailor known as Curly Bill. "Me 'n Jack the Beard wanna sign on again."

"We're going back upriver, Curly Bill."

"We know, Skipper. But me 'n the Beard think you're right. The Injun trouble ´s over."

"I'm glad you agree; but even with you and Jack, we're still at least four hands short."

"Maybe not. Me 'n the Beard has been sittin' here all night, and drinkin' wid a group o' rivermen. They be just what we need, we be thinkin'. Should we fetch one of ´em over?"

"Sure, Curly Bill. It can't hurt to talk."

Curly Bill returned with one of the most sinister looking men either of them had ever seen. His long, stringy black hair hung far down, partially obscuring a pair of half-closed, smoldering dark eyes. An angry looking red scar, starting at the hairline on the left side, ran diagonally across his forehead, round his eye, and then down his right cheek before disappearing at the end of his jaw. The blade which had done the damage must have clipped a part of his lower lip on the way past and severed a few of the nerves. The lip tended to flap when he spoke, making it difficult to understand his halting speech.

319

"Our new friends be tellin' us'ens you be needin' a new crew, Capt'n, ta sail da boat and ta bring in some gold. Me 'n my mates be ready to sign on wid ye. We ain't afraid to go upriver."

Marsh sent the man back to his friends and spent the next few minutes conferring with Dave, Curly Bill, and the Beard.

They all agreed that the applicants were a pack of rough river rats but felt that, together, they were more than a match for them. Under the circumstances, there was little choice.

"They're probably harmless enough," concluded Captain Marsh, "but we'll keep close tabs on them for a while, anyway. They sure are a scurvy looking lot."

Marsh filled out papers for his four new crew members which included good regular pay, as well as extremely generous bonuses.

The scar-faced man, whose name was Simon Dowdy, scrawled his signature proudly across the bottom of the page, while the other three had to be content with drawing their marks.

After making arrangements with Curly Bill and the Beard to bring the newcomers aboard in the morning, the Captain bought drinks for them all and then departed with Dave Campbell.

Since he did not wish to burden his friend with any further problems, Marsh kept up a lighthearted banter during their return trip to the Far West; but as they walked along the long, lonely wharf, he was overwhelmed by growing feelings of foreboding and uneasiness. He finally managed to shrug them off, deciding that the mood was the result of listening to the eerie echoes of his own footsteps resounding in the thickening fog.

➢

They were up and about early the next morning, long before the sun had popped over the eastern horizon. They quickly finished a few last-minute chores and were the first diners to enter the Pier Restaurant when it opened for business.

Knowing that they would be subsisting on shipboard fare for the next two weeks, both men thoroughly enjoyed the excellent food. A short time later, weighted down by a big breakfast of ham, eggs, and hotcakes, they returned to the Far West.

An hour later, the new men, led by Curly Bill and looking far less ominous in daylight, came strolling down the dock with their duffle bags. As soon as their meager possessions were stowed away in the crew's quarters, the mooring lines were cast off and the Far West pushed her nose out into the Missouri's swift current.

By the time they sailed past the Knife River, it was evident to Marsh that the newcomers were experienced riverboatmen. They performed their duties without hesitation or difficulty.

Since this journey was not a lifesaving mission, it took far longer to steam upriver than it had to race down. They even dropped anchor for a few hours and bought some last-minute items at the Fort Union Trading Post. Fort Union, which stood on a high bluff above the confluence of the Missouri and Yellowstone, had been a popular gathering spot since the earliest Mountain Men, braving the perils of the wilderness, came forth to trap in the beaver-rich streams and send the lush fur off to Europe's gentry.

It was evening of the fourth day when they nosed the Far West into the south bank of the Yellowstone near the mouth of the Bighorn. Landing was simple, despite the late hour, since hundreds of campfires blazed brightly along the shore for a mile or more.

On the bank above their anchorage, a large Silby tent had been erected. On twin staffs before it waved Old Glory and the colors of the 2nd Cavalry Regiment. It was General Terry's headquarters.

Bruce T. Clark

Marsh walked up the hill and stopped outside the tent's open flap. He bent down and peered into the gloomy canvas interior. Suddenly, his eyes opened wide in disbelief as he recognized a familiar figure, who now wore the insignia of the 2nd Cavalry. The dark countenance and huge putty nose were unmistakable. They belonged to First Sergeant Toby Shaddick. It was Villain.

"Villain!" yelped Marsh in delight. "I thought you were with Custer."

"I was, but I wasn't. At the end of May, Star Terry borrowed Captain Gerot, the Stork, and meself to teach marksmanship to the 2nd. A fortnight later, the headquarters troop managed to get itself ambushed. The commander and the first sergeant were both killed. Next day, Captain Gerot and meself took over the troop."

"I'm glad you weren't with Custer."

"I wouldn't have been with Custer anyway, but Captain Benteen and H Troop were badly banged up, too. By the way, a couple days ago we did a sweep to the south of here, toward the Rosebud, and found a friend of ours. He was near death when he turned up, but now he's feelin' better and talkin' about goin' to meet you."

"Kevin McCarthy?"

"The very same."

"What happened to him?"

"If you'll give me a few breaths to finish these reports for the General, I'll be taking ye over to see him for yerself."

"I'll do better than that, Villain. I'll go back to the boat and fetch Dave Campbell. We'll meet you back here in a half hour with a couple quarts of Irish whiskey and some applejack."

"Captain Darlin', I kin taste the heavenly brew already."

A short time later, Kevin McCarthy lay propped up with pillows in a hospital bed, while his three friends sat on field stools around him. All four of them were obviously enjoying the dark amber liquid they were sipping. The visitors settled back and listened as Kevin began his story.

322

"We didn't know it when we left the Far West that morning, but we were riding right into trouble. We heard shots several times during the early hours, but they were all far away. We kept moving at a steady pace, still hoping to reach Fort Fetterman. Since I got back here, Villain and several other troopers have helped me to reconstruct the reasons why things happened the way they did.

"We left on the same morning that the big war party of Sioux and Cheyenne crushed Crook and sent him packing. The hostiles pulled out late in the morning and split up. By then, we were only about twenty miles north of Crook's camp on the Rosebud. Less than two hours later, we were hit.

"About fifty Sioux came racing up the trail, whooping and firing their rifles at us. We were caught between a high hill on one side and a sheer precipice on the other. We never had a chance. I took two bullets, one in the left shoulder and one in my upper chest. My mule was shot in the head and tumbled down the slope into the deep ravine, carrying me along with him. I heard both of my legs break on the way down before I passed out.

"When I regained my senses it was dark and the Indians were gone. My right leg was caught under the mule and I couldn't move it. Fortunately, on the hillside a few feet above my head, a tiny spring was trickling out of the ground, so I was lying on soft, damp ground. My left shoulder was broken. Even with the soft ground, it took many hours to dig my way out from under the mule using my right hand. Once I got my leg loose, I was able to drag myself close enough to the spring to drink from it.

"I was mighty lucky the mule fell beside me, because I had packed two blankets behind the saddle and enough emergency rations to last for ten days. I made them last for twenty. On July 7, Villain and his patrol found me. If they hadn't come along when they did, I would have been eating mule meat."

323

"I assume no one else survived?" Marsh asked Villain.

"No. The whole lot o' em was stripped and scalped when we got there. We gave 'em all the best Christian burials that we could. Near the bodies there were a few dead mules and that was all. The whole place had been picked as clean as a chicken's gizzard."

Marsh rose from his chair and picked up McCarthy's empty canister. Then he went to the portable washstand that held the whiskey and applejack. He poured them both a substantial drink before he returned to Kevin, and handed him the libation.

"I had to off-load your cargo, Kevin."

"What did you say?" came the bellowed question.

"I had to cache the gold to provide space for Reno's wounded."

"Oh. Now what happens?" inquired the relieved freighter.

"Our crew will transport it back to the Far West and then take it, and you, down the river to St. Louis. But that's a lot of gold, and if you're eager to get it loaded, it would be a good idea to hire some additional help to bring it back aboard."

McCarthy turned to Villain.

"If the price were right, could you scare up a few dozen off-duty workers?"

"It'll be a sad day when I can't, Captain Darlin'," Villain called over his shoulder as he left to begin recruiting labor.

"I take it that the gold is close by and accessible?" Kevin asked Marsh.

"It's about a mile away, but it's hardly accessible. Let me tell you where it is and how cleverly we've hidden it."

Just then an army nurse came in to change the dressings on Kevin's wounds, and the conversation ended at once. Captain Marsh recovered his dark blue naval hat with its long yellow plume from its resting place at the foot of McCarthy's bed, and placed it firmly on his head.

"We'll tell you all about it at breakfast. For now, just relax and get some sleep. Nobody could find that gold in a hundred years. But just to make sure everything is all right, Dave and I will go out to the cache and check on things before we return to the Far West."

"My thanks to you both. I feel a lot better, knowing that things are shipshape."

Marsh and Campbell left the hospital and conversed for a moment before heading for the cache.

"Dave, were you watching that nurse when he heard the words gold and cache?" Marsh asked.

"I thought his eyes would pop out of his head, Skipper."

"We can't take any chances with McCarthy's gold. We'll start out in the opposite direction and go around in a big circle. If anybody follows us, we'll be able to double back and catch them. Only if we're sure nobody is behind us will we go to the cache."

They walked in a big circle, stopping frequently to listen for alien footsteps. An hour later they were more than two miles from the camp and well beyond the gold cache. When they stopped to catch their breath, Marsh said, "I guess we were wrong, Dave. There's no one near us. Let's check the cache and get back. We have a big day ahead of us."

To save time, they chose to cut across country instead of retracing their steps and proceeding by a more familiar route.

A short walk brought them to a shallow, wide arroyo, with a tiny trace of water running through the bottom. Since it would take many minutes to walk around this small canyon, they decided to jump down to the flat, sandy bottom and then climb up the far bank. In the moonlight, it appeared to be safe, since there were no bushes or rocks below on which to injure an ankle or knee.

Together, they jumped down to the inviting sand five or six feet below the bank. As they landed, the soft sand gave way, and they suddenly sank down to their knees. Dave Campbell, who had landed with his back to Marsh and some ten feet away from him, struggled for a few moments to free himself but succeeded only in forcing himself deeper and more firmly into the sand. He decided to stop squirming and ask for Marsh's help.

"Skipper," he called, "give me a hand. I'm stuck in the sand."

"I'm afraid I'm stuck as well, old friend. We've jumped into a quicksand bog. Our best chance is to call out as loudly as we can and hope that someone from the camp hears us. If they don't, we must remain as still as possible and try to stay on top of the sand until help arrives in the morning. Most importantly, we can pray for God's deliverance, in case my other ideas don't work."

For the next two hours, they remained as still as they could and shouted at the top of their lungs. But it was an attempt doomed to failure. They were stranded well over a mile from the camp and its drowsy inhabitants, on a night when a strong wind blew toward them from the river, a perverse wind that carried away their words and sealed their fate.

Far into the night, they reminisced about their good days and the people they had known. They worried about their families and how they would be missed. As the end drew near, they prayed together and said good-bye. Then they both met their final ordeals bravely. By daybreak, all that remained above the smooth, wet sand was a dark blue naval hat with a long, proud, yellow feather.

➢

Several hours later, after breakfasting with Kevin McCarthy, Geofrey Gerot left his brother-in-law's bedside, then strolled through camp until he reached the shore where the Far West was moored. He stopped at the bottom of the gangway and called up to a man with a livid scar who was replacing the aft chafing gear.

"Is Captain Marsh still aboard?"

"Da Captain hain't ben aboard since we tied up las' night," replied Simon Dowdy. "He cum bac ta fetch da pilot, den da bot went off tagether. We hain't seen neider o'dem since den."

"Thanks," said Gerot. "If he comes back, tell him Captain Gerot would like to see him, all right?"

"Sure, Captain, I be tellin' him, jus like you zay."

GeeGee hurried back to the hospital, keeping an eye out for Marsh or Campbell along the way. He went directly to McCarthy's cubicle and relayed the bad news.

"GeeGee, Grant said they would come up here for breakfast and tell me where they had hidden the gold. Also, I know that he and Dave were planning to check the cache before they headed back to the boat."

"Mac," replied GeeGee, "there are simply not a whole lot of places to get lost in this camp. And absolutely no temptations!"

"They're not lost and they're not in camp. Grant and Dave are either dead or too badly injured to move," Kevin said with foreboding.

"Tell me everything that you can remember about last night's conversation. Maybe we can figure out where they are." Gerot paused, then added, "Or where their bodies are."

The only additional piece of information Kevin could recall was Marsh's reference to the cache being about a mile from the camp. That was, he told Gerot, all that had been said about the location. It was not much, but it would allow the search party to limit their activities to that relatively small area.

GeeGee went directly to General Miles and obtained permission to use fifty men from his troop in the search party. Then, aided by the crew of the Far West, he formed them into a single line.

Since the Yellowstone bound the camp on one side, the sweep could be conducted in a half circle rather than a full one.

Gerot strung his men out along the riverbank at fifty-yard intervals. Curly Bill was the first man and would serve as the line's anchor. He was positioned next to the Far West, while Villain, the man on the opposite end, was over a mile downstream. When everyone was in place, Gerot fired a shot and the men in the long line began walking slowly away from the river and through the camp. When he reached the far edge of the bivouac, Curly Bill halted and fired a second shot. It was the signal for the line to begin pivoting on him, just as a garden gate swings on its fixed post and hinges.

Captain Gerot hoped that this time-honored military maneuver known as a sweep, a deployment normally used to seek out and destroy an enemy would aid his searchers to quickly locate the missing men in case they were badly injured.

About an hour after the sweep began, Corporal O'Herron, who was in line next to Sergeant Shaddick, called out to him.

"Villain, I think I've found 'em."

Shaddick hurried toward O'Herron, who was standing on top of a cut bank gazing intently down into a shallow arroyo. As Villain approached, Dickie O'Herron backed away and motioned for Shaddick to do the same.

"What have you found, Stork?"

"Walk back a ways with me and I'll show ya."

O'Herron led Shaddick along his backtrail for about fifty yards, carefully avoiding the two sets of footprints that were plainly visible in the soft earth.

"I first noticed the prints here. See, they swing around that long hollow log and then head straight down toward that bank. The prints weren't made by either army boots or moccasins, Villain, and they've been made since the heavy rain yesterday afternoon."

"You're right on both counts. They were made by boat shoes."

"I thought as much. There's somethin' else to see in that little canyon up ahead."

328

They followed the footprints back to the lip of the ravine, where they abruptly ended. It looked as though the men who made them had either flown away or vanished into thin air.

But as Villain and Stork stood looking sadly down at the deadly sand, a muddy blue hat with a long, limp yellow feather gave mute testimony to a third probability. Ironically, the hat Grant Marsh had worn with such great honor, pride, and devotion to duty was, for the moment, his tombstone.

The following day, the Second United States Cavalry conducted an Honors Ceremony for Captain Marsh and his loyal pilot. Later, the Catholic members of the regiment attended a requiem Mass. It was a fitting tribute to their exemplary lives and many heroic deeds.

➢

As soon as Kevin McCarthy recovered from his wounds, he hired a group of men to conduct a careful search of the area. Despite the fact that it was rough, broken country, McCarthy expected to find the cache very quickly. But as days dragged into weeks, he began to believe that the golden treasure might never be found.

Bart Burley descended on the site with another army of diggers and offered a fabulous reward for the golden hoard's recovery, but the cache had been too cleverly concealed. Finally, after nearly a year had passed, McCarthy and Burley, reluctantly and with deep regret, abandoned the futile search and returned to the operations of their companies. Although the loss of the gold shipment was a setback for them both, their businesses continued to prosper, and over the years the widespread publicity actually helped them to expand their corporations, and also to perpetuate their well-deserved reputations for honesty and integrity.

By far, the happiest of all the participants was Catherine McCarthy. For the rest of her life she thanked God a dozen times each day for the safe return of her husband.

But it was a reporter from a leading Colorado newspaper, observing the frenzied hunt with great interest, who had the most far-reaching and dramatic impact. He wrote a story about the lost hoard of gold and brought the treasure's existence to national attention.

In his article, he explained that Captain Marsh was forced to cache the gold in order to accommodate the Seventh Cavalry's wounded after their defeat at the Little Bighorn. He ended his report with an ironic proposition: that Custer was actually the person most responsible for the loss of the gold or, as the journalist referred to it, "the missing trove of riches." That being the case, the reporter continued, this great hoard of gold, and not his devastating defeat, should be remembered as the "Boy General's" final gift to his country. The writer concluded: "...even in death, this great general has added to his already lustrous legacy, by giving some lucky man the chance to live America's Golden Dream." And from that moment on, Burley's Gold would forever be known as the Custer Legacy.

For the next decade, droves of treasure seekers pounced upon the area each year, as eagerly as the hordes of Attila the Hun looking for new villages to plunder, each one convinced that an area so small could not conceal its treasure from someone as clever as he. But eventually, all admitted defeat and turned away.

In the late 1880's, rumors spread that the gold cache had been found, and for the next few years the numbers of hopeful hunters dwindled. Then in 1906, a strong tremor shook the valley and brought about some startling geographical changes. The earthquake caused a number of landslides to occur which sent thousands of tons of rock cascading down from cliff faces, where they covered many heretofore open areas, while other places that had long been hidden were laid bare. In a few locations, landslides actually altered the courses of streams, as the water, seeking the line of least resistance, jumped over the original banks and found new runoffs.

In some places, where two gullies ran side by side, divided by only a center ridge, the side that had lain barren for hundreds of years suddenly became the new riverbed and the former spillway became a wadi.

In nearly all of these locations, even though the topographical shifts and upheavals of the earth's surface were great, a moment after the tremor ended, things returned to normal and life went on as before. In this remote corner of the world's wilderness, the earthquake simply didn't matter. But in one place, it made a great deal of difference. A change occurred which one day would provide the key to a missing hoard of gold.

PART NINE

THE COVERT QUEST

Chapter XXIII

➢

Truth Shall Seek The Light

The Vatican
Rome, Italy
September 1, 1939

Emmanuel Questa had never been this depressed before, not at any time in his twenty plus years. He had come to attend the Pontifical College of Rome and study for the priesthood seven years ago, just before his fourteenth birthday. And this was a special day for which he had yearned since his arrival. It was the first day of his final year in college. Next September if all went well, he would enter the seminary and begin a new life, a life that would eventually lead to the priesthood. A life that had been his destiny since the first time he had assisted Padre Almonte at Mass on a summer morning in the Rio Grande Valley.

He stopped at the entrance to the college library and showed his identity card to the uniformed door guard. What a country this was for uniforms, a custom undoubtedly inspired by Il Duce, Benito Mussolini, the man who had been Italy's dictator since 1922.

Duce would be a comical figure, Emmanuel reflected, if he weren't so sinister. The people in Ethiopia certainly didn't think Duce was funny after he invaded their country in 1935, deposed their emperor, and crushed them under the heel of his Fascist boot in less than a year.

Manny recalled Italian newspapers hailing this unwarranted aggression as a great coup, just as they had when the German dictator, Adolf Hitler, renounced terms of the Versailles Treaty and invaded the Rhineland, the demilitarized zone between Germany and France.

The perpetually ineffective League of Nations passed a resolution branding both dictators' invasions as aggressive acts; but then showed their weakness by doing little else. After a long harangue, the League did pass economic sanctions against both aggressors, but petroleum products were not included on the list of contraband items. A strange way to register displeasure, Manny thought, since all mechanized armies ran on oil. It was the one thing that was indispensable. No fuel? No war!

On November 1, 1936, encouraged by the collective weaknesses of all the other European nations, Hitler and Mussolini formed a strong alliance by signing the Axis Pact. Mussolini had in the past been called the "Sawdust Caesar" by those who sought to ridicule him and his garish uniforms, and Adolf Hitler was often depicted as an "Austrian Paperhanger"; but now the world finally began to understand and acknowledge that they were not buffoons. They were cold-blooded killers, intent on total world domination.

As he ascended the library steps, Manny reflected on his new status. A great many things would change for him now that he was a senior. For the first time, he would be permitted to go beyond the fourth floor of the library. Only history students in their senior years and graduate scholars were permitted to enter the inner sanctum of the Vatican's archives, located on the upper floors. He had become one of the elite.

At last, he thought, I can delve into significant research on Hernando Cortez and his Conquistadors.

Again he wondered why this wonderful day had to be spoiled by Nazi troops storming across the borders of Poland and igniting a flame that would surely combust into another world war. Because of their treaty with Poland, England and France could not stand idly by while their ally fell victim to totalitarianism. They would be forced to declare war on Germany and her Axis partner.

Was it his fate, he wondered, to be associated with historical days? He had been born on November 11, 1918, Armistice Day. The day World War I ended. A day, people said, which would end war forever. A day, which led foolish men to decide that dignity and pride, should be taken away from a vanquished German people. A policy, which guaranteed the rise to power of someone, like Adolf Hitler and an ultimate course toward reprisal and revenge.

Manny stopped at the entrance to the archives, presented his pass to another uniformed personage, and went forward into the restricted area. On a rack, just inside the door, were pamphlets with detailed instructions for using the research facilities. He took one and walked toward one of the massive tables that were scattered around the enormous room.

These tables were so large that they were divided into four small, almost private study areas, by two-foot-high partitions that rose from the surface of each table. In front of every cubicle was an oversized, comfortable-looking captain's chair. Each table, and its four companion chairs, was constructed from a different exotic wood, emblematic of God's glorious forests throughout the world. The padded seats and armrests of each chair set were covered in finely grained, majestically-colored Moroccan leather. The set Manny chose was made from dark Spanish oak which blended well with the elegant, light teal leather.

He sank down gratefully into the chair and tried to peruse the paper, but the words seemed to swim before his eyes. Laying the document aside for the moment, he continued with his reverie.

He wondered how the day's events would affect America, which was, of course, still an isolationist country, proclaimed as such by the Neutrality Act of 1935 and a Second Neutrality Act passed in 1937. He smiled and thought, maybe they'll pass another one this year just to make sure no one misunderstands.

The Questa family had a special interest in national politics. For nearly a hundred years they had lived in Eagle Pass, Texas, on a small ranch near the big spread owned by the Garner family. For as long as they could remember, one of the Garners had been their congressional representative. John Nance Garner had gone on to become the U.S. Speaker of the House and for the past seven years had been America's Vice President. Everybody in the whole danged Rio Grande Valley was mighty proud of the Vice President!

If Mr. Garner hadn't helped him, Emmanuel reflected, he would be sitting in Eagle Pass at this moment and not in Rome. So, stop frettin', he told himself, remembering his Grandpappy's advice: "Work with zest, do your best, and let the good Lord take care of the rest."

As the next few weeks flew by, the fears of Emmanuel and his friends regarding the war in the outside world, and its potential effect on the Vatican, gradually dissipated.

By early November, all of the projections he had made on the first of September had come true. England and France dutifully declared war on the Axis Alliance; President Roosevelt once again declared America to be a neutral nation; and the conquest of Poland proceeded.

England, France, and their supporters, now known as the Allies, made every effort to bring the Soviet Union and her Communist boss, Josef Stalin, into their camp, but that was not to be. He chose to join Hitler in the sack and conflagration of Poland, rushing Red troops in from the East while the Germans poured in from the West. Poor Poland was crushed in the jaws of those two juggernauts who had joined together to form the Steel Pact.

Emmanuel and a number of his classmates volunteered to leave Vatican City and go to Poland to assist the victims and refugees. They quickly discovered that the Nazis would permit no such humanitarian intervention. The students were forced to vent their disappointment and righteous indignation by spending long, tiring hours on research and study.

➢

As he delved more deeply into his research, Emmanuel quickly discovered that some of the most interesting information about Cortez and his Conquistadors was provided by the observations and study notes left behind by earlier scholars, amid the library's plethora of logs, journals, and letters. Members of Cortez had penned most of these ancient documents' original company, but many others had been written by the troops of Narvaez, who followed in the Patron's wake a few months later. What a pity, he mused, that so much had been destroyed during La Noche de Triste.

Most of the correspondence and material gathered over the past four hundred years was fragmentary; but some was surprisingly well preserved. He found a brief letter written by Cortez to a Spanish Grandee named Don Diego Garza in late 1520. The note was solicitous of the addressee's health, and apologetic for the need to burden him with bad news. It concerned the Grandee's grandson and namesake, whom Captain Cortez referred to as Padre Garza.

Of course! Emmanuel remembered that Padre Garza had been another priest, who had served beside his more famous compatriot, Padre Olmedo.

At the very bottom of the letter, a shaking hand, probably the Grandee's, had written the number 7 and then inscribed:

"My gift did not save him. I wonder if its secret helped him?"

What gift? What secret? What did the 7 mean? It was really an enigma. What could a priest have that would save him, besides his faith? Obviously, that was not the type of saving to which the postscript referred. A weapon?

Probably not. Some type of armor? Absolute foolishness. It didn't save him! But did its secret help him? If he were dead, how could he be helped? Also, if he were dead, why would a secret matter? It certainly was a puzzlement.

➤

For the balance of the school year, while Emmanuel continued his careful research, the war in Europe escalated. In May 1940, Belgium, the Netherlands, and Luxembourg capitulated. A British Expeditionary Force of nearly 350,000 troops, which had rushed to France to help, was bottled up on the sandy beaches of Dunkirk, along the northern French coast. In early June, by the grace of God, they escaped. Every manner of floating craft, from luxury yacht to dugout canoe crossed the English Channel and whisked survivors back to safety.

Meanwhile, in the skies above, a new form of combat, staged between swift mechanical birds of war, reached a fever pitch, as the Battle of France ended and the Battle of Britain began. For the first time since the Normans came ashore at Hastings, in 1066, the English Bulldog was being threatened and preparing to meet an invasion force in his own fields, farms, and hedgerows.

Although the global situation continued to divert part of his attention as the world girded its political loins for additional terror, Emmanuel's long hours of diligence began to pay handsome dividends. Each month, as he amassed additional information on the Conquistadors and their famous days of yesteryear, his stock rose with his professors, and his grades soared correspondingly. Any and all doubts about his acceptance as a seminarian vanished.

For all that, he was no closer to solving the Padre Garza mystery. He had studied over a thousand ancient documents, some complete, but most fragmentary, and discovered three additional references to the Padre. One of them, written by Padre Olmedo, was very interesting.

Olmedo described both the burial of his colleague in the early morning hours of La Noche de Triste and the gathering of Padre Garza's possessions. They included his Bible and daily office, his Mass kit and crucifix, and finally a small vial, which, Padre Olmedo presumed, contained holy water. A few days later, the Padre used the contents of the vial to anoint one of the wounded soldiers. Moments later, the man began squirming about, proclaiming that the water had burned him. Padre Olmedo continued his narrative by explaining that he had spread a small amount of the liquid on his own hand and moments later felt a pervading heat. It was not an unpleasant sensation, he concluded, but a warm, reassuring tingle.

The final portion of Padre Olmedo's narrative was even more enlightening, as Emmanuel went on with his careful translation.

"The morning after his visit with Curco and his family," the journal continued, "Padre Garza was able to reach up and place his vestments on the highest shelf. That was something he had been unable to do before because of the intense pain in his upper arms and shoulders. When I asked him how it was now possible, he said Curco had given him something to relieve the pain, and that he did not feel it anymore.

"It was not until the episode with the wounded soldier that I wondered: 'Could the vial, which I had thought to be holy water, contain Curco's medicine?' I immediately tried some of the liquid on my own injured knee. Within minutes, I felt a warmth in the joint, and a short time later my pain disappeared.

"I questioned the soldiers, but learned nothing from them. I even presumed to inquire of Captain Cortez, the Patron himself, but to no avail. Perhaps when we retake the Aztec city, I can seek out Curco and learn the answer."

A week later, Emmanuel discovered another part of the missing puzzle.

He found a badly deteriorated parchment, written by Padre Olmedo in 1521, a week after the recapture of Tenochtitlan. So little of the original document remained that it was difficult to decipher. He arranged tiny fragments of fragile parchment together as if he were assembling the pieces of a delicate jigsaw puzzle. Unfortunately, many of the parts of this puzzle no longer existed.

After a great deal of time and exasperating effort, Emmanuel concluded that Curco and his entire family had been slain, along with many other inhabitants of Tenochtitlan, during the fierce fighting to re-establish control of the city.

It appeared that Padre Olmedo had attempted to interrogate a large number of the survivors about the medicine, but all of them had pleaded ignorance or maintained a stony silence.

"Perhaps," Padre Olmedo speculated, "nobody except Curco and his family really did know the secret. But, about one thing I am certain," he observed. "In all my years as a priest, I never knew anyone more committed to keeping good records than Padre Garza. If the information about the medicine is lost, it is not because he failed to safeguard it. I pray," the priest concluded, "that someday this wonderful healing agent will be rediscovered so that it may help all mankind."

➢

As the presidential election of 1940 approached, Manny read all of the available information concerning Franklin Roosevelt's campaign for an unprecedented third term in the White House. FDR dumped his former running mate, John Nance Garner, in favor of Henry Wallace, and beat his Republican opponent Wendell Willkie by 5,000,000 votes, overpowering him in the electoral college, 449 to 82. Manny felt sorry for Mr. Garner, but agreed with one Congressional observer who said: "Franklin Roosevelt was not running against Wendell Willkie. He was running against Adolf Hitler." That was good to hear, thought the young Texan, since it has become increasingly apparent that the goose-stepping Nazis and their Axis partners will never be stopped unless the United States comes to the aid of the Allies. How such a move would affect him and other American students at the Pontifical College remained to be seen.

➢

The week after this landslide election, Emmanuel celebrated his twenty-second birthday, and soon the season of Advent was upon them. So it was not until his first joyous Christmas as a seminarian that he was able to resume his diligent investigation and slide the final piece of the puzzle into place.

The day after Christmas, Emmanuel sat at the library table, which had, over the past year, become his favorite study area. The table and the wood of the chairs was Brazilian black mahogany. The primary color was such a deep dark brown that it appeared to be black. But the characteristic that made the table so beautiful was the bright yellow grain that coursed through the lustrous dark wood. The combination of colors always reminded him of a stalking tiger's fur. The matching set of chairs was covered with a rich, ebony leather.

The study area's other fascination was its location, next to a panoramic picture window that afforded an unparalleled view of the Vatican's legendary gardens. On this crisp winter's day, from his cozy perch on high, Emmanuel could either peer down at dozens of priceless, snow-draped statues or, if he chose, lift his gaze and look out at the distant hills, across the great expanse of the Eternal City. In every direction the view was magnificent.

He tore his gaze away from the magnetic lure of the ancient city and returned to the journals he had been perusing. Cabeza de Vaca had written them in 1542, after his seven years of wandering across the Great Plains of America. Although the tales of his journey and narrow escapes were extremely interesting, it was the letter which Emmanuel found tucked away between the pages of one of the thick logbooks which now claimed his attention.

Written long after the journals, the letter was directed to someone named Don Alejandro Mendoza. In it, de Vaca reminisced about his life, his many successes and his few failures, and then spent two rambling paragraphs bemoaning the loss of the "finest weapon I ever held." A weapon that he said had never failed him, "from the morning after that awful summer night in 1520, until it saved my life in the fight with the Blue Comanche many years later. I have always felt that I betrayed that good man's trust when I lost such a special weapon," Cabeza de Vaca concluded.

Manny remembered a reference to the Blue Comanche in the journals. He found the page quickly and reread the account.

Cabeza de Vaca detailed the duel in the roasting hot sun, the fear he felt, the injury to his shoulder, and the loss of his left ear to the Comanche's hatchet. He ended his description with a brief allusion to losing consciousness after burying his blade in the chest of his assailant and being saved by the quick action of two of his amigos.

Manny took a sheet of paper and jotted down all of the data that seemed to connect.

Q1. The morning after that awful night in 1520?

A. An obvious reference to La Noche de Triste.

Q2. The "finest weapon" had served him AFTER La Noche.

Why not DURING La Noche?

A. Because he didn't get it until AFTER the fight.

Q3. Then WHO did have it?

A. "That good man."

Q4. What good man?

A. Padre Garza? "My gift did not save him."

OF COURSE! The weapon did not save him.

Q5. "I wonder if its secret helped him?"

A. The Grandee, realizing that his grandson was dead, still asks the question. Therefore, the secret has nothing to do with the weapon's ability as a weapon, but as something else. Something that is not obvious to any observer.

Q6. Did Cabeza de Vaca lament the loss of the secret?

A. No! Only the loss of the weapon.

Q7. Why?

A. Because he is unaware of the "secret."

Q8. How could anyone have a cherished possession for ten years and not discover its secret?

A. Either I'm on the wrong track or the weapon has a built-in hidden compartment! There is no third possibility.

Q9. If such a hiding place were available to a man "committed to keeping good records," would he not conceal the Aztec secret within?

A. Without question.

Q10. What do I know about the weapon?

A. It was obviously of special design, probably made for the Grandee or one of his ancestors. It was the finest weapon de Vaca ever held. The weapon was a knife, not a sword.

(You run someone through with a sword, he reasoned, but you don't bury a sword in a person's chest.) Since the blade was strong, any hidden compartment must have been in the hilt. The hiding place was so ingeniously designed and brilliantly concealed that Cabeza de Vaca failed to discover it, although he used the knife on a daily basis for nearly ten years. The compartment was still a secret when Cabeza de Vaca left the weapon in the body of a Comanche who painted himself blue, sometime around 1530.

He looked at his notes and pondered an unanswerable question: Who was Don Alejandro Mendoza, and what was his special interest in the weapon? His identity might well be a key.

➢

Happy to have solved as much of the enigma as he had, Emmanuel finished up the last few days of the year studying and preparing for midterm exams, which were scheduled for the end of January.

During the first week of 1941, he took an afternoon off and walked across St Peter's square to the Vatican Museum. He sought out the curator of antiquities, Santino Nunza, and solicited his advice. He described his carefully reasoned scenario and asked, "Could such a weapon have been designed and constructed in the middle of the fifteenth century, Santino? Did such skill exist at that time?"

"Without doubt, my friend. Many weapons of superior quality, like the one you describe, were made at that time. However, the second part of your query is entirely different."

A strange, perplexed expression crept across Santino's face as he stated the paradox aloud.

"Could anyone have designed and built a secret compartment into the hilt of a sword or knife with such extraordinary skill that a man who used that weapon every day for ten years would not discover the hiding place?"

Hands folded behind back, fingers intertwined and head bowed, he paced slowly back and forth for several minutes, lost in deep thought. Once he came to a halt before Manny and poised himself to speak, while his friend waited expectantly. Seconds later, he shook his head, reclasped his hands, and resumed his pacing.

The next time he stopped beside Emmanuel, he did speak.

"Emmanuel, I don't believe it's possible! Cabeza de Vaca was a professional man of arms. He knew weapons well. They kept him alive. People constantly touch and caress the things they cherish the most. For example, your fingers often stray to the crucifix that hangs about your neck. That weapon would have been such a cherished object to that Conquistador. He depended on it for his very existence. It would have been as familiar to him as a part of his own body.

"Also," the curator continued, "to have a chance of remaining hidden, if such a compartment ever did exist, it would have had to be rigged with a multiple release locking mechanism, the only safeguard capable of preventing accidental triggering. To presume that such a concept existed 500 years ago is unreasonable."

"What is a multiple release mechanism, Santino?"

"It's a locking system that requires three or more different functions to be performed before a lock can be opened. For instance, a bank vault has a numbered dial built into the door. A series of numbers must be dialed before the locking bars or the tumblers release the lock and allow the door to swing open. A simple, one-stop, individual release would certainly have been discovered. Sometime in a span of ten years, even a double release would have been stumbled upon, but a triple release might never have been found. It's pretty hard to do three things with two hands."

"How would such a sequence be possible on something as simple as a knife, Santino?"

"Perhaps by squeezing one thing, pulling another, and pushing or turning a third."

"So are you saying that it's probable?" asked the enthusiastic seminarian.

"No, Emmanuel, I am not! I am saying that it is, at best, a very remote possibility. A one-in-a-million shot in the dark."

"But it's the only shot I have, Santino. Otherwise all hope of recovery is gone forever."

"You're right. I'm sorry. I know how important this project is to you. Before you go, come back to the Papal Guard's Room. I'm working on some new displays."

They walked toward the rear of the museum and entered a huge, marble-tiled room. This was the showplace where interesting artifacts of former papal guards were exhibited. Fascinating mementos seemed to cover every wall. On the main floor of the cavernous room, orderly rows of tall, glass-front display cases left only enough room for narrow walkways.

These well-lighted exhibits contained various uniforms that the Guards had gone on to wear after leaving the Vatican and the weapons that they had wielded in various wars and conflicts.

Each case also contained descriptive placards, giving a brief biography of the man that the display honored his years of papal service, and the circumstances of his death. The placards were printed in Italian, French, Spanish, German, and English.

As they walked down the room's long center aisle toward the storage and work area, Santino began telling Emmanuel about a unique sword that had just arrived from Lombardy, but before he could complete his explanation, he was summoned to the telephone.

Manny wandered about, peering at the numerous displays, and finally stopped in front of a double width display case which stood in a far corner. He read the information cards and was delighted to discover that the men who had worn the uniforms and wielded the weapons had played major roles in the history of the Great American West.

The young seminarian felt goose bumps rising on his skin as he read of Captain Myles Keogh and Lieutenant Charles De Rudio. Keogh, he saw, was killed at Custer's Last Stand. His friend De Rudio, who had fought with Garibaldi against the Papal Guards, had survived his harrowing experiences and survived until 1910.

The two Seventh Cavalry uniforms, which had been donated by Keogh's widow, were neatly hung on the compartment's back wall, looking for all the world as if they were waiting for their owners to return and claim them. Below the uniforms, at the bottom of the case, Santino, or one of his assistants, had laid out some of the weapons, which the cavalry officers and their antagonists used, in the famous battle.

Manny saw a Winchester lever-action repeating rifle, a single-shot Springfield rifle, a Colt Peacemaker revolver, and a Colt Navy Dragoon pistol. Both officers' dress swords were prominently featured, as were stone or steel Indian tomahawks and clubs. His gaze drifted from one object to the next, until his attention riveted on a most unusual knife. He examined it as closely as possible through the thick plate glass window.

The blade was about as long as his forearm and had been finely honed along one entire edge. The opposite side was sharpened for only the first three or four inches. Manny noticed that the blade curved up at the tip, conveying the impression of a hook. Above the blade and below the hilt, he could see a brass handguard about the length and width of his forefinger. From the base of this guard, upward to the triangular brass tang at the top of the hilt, ran a pair of semi-circular, parallel pieces of strong steel. Obviously, they had been set in place to protect the hand of the wielder as he clutched the dull material of unknown composition from which the hilt or handle was made.

It was one of the most unusual and fascinating weapons Manny had ever seen.

His prolonged examination was suddenly interrupted by Santino, who came toward him, mouthing an apology and carrying a large, strange-looking sword.

"Look at this, Emmanuel," he called excitedly.

Emmanuel hefted the huge, heavy weapon and decided that it was meant to be used with both hands.

"This weapon has a most interesting feature," explained the excited curator. "It's called a steel apple."

He pointed to the sword blade's broad upper edge, to which a clever craftsman had welded a hollow tube.

347

"As you can see," Santino continued, "the tube was sealed at both ends after a heavy, steel ball was inserted. When the sword is raised to strike a blow, this ball or "steel apple" rolls back toward the hilt. When the blade of the weapon is thrust outward and downward toward an enemy, the steel apple, careening along the tube, adds tremendous striking force to the blow. It is a most ingenious system," he concluded.

The museum's vast array of artifacts and Santino's wealth of knowledge claimed Emmanuel's attention for the balance of the afternoon, and he did not leave until suppertime. In an effort to compensate for the time away from his studies, he sat hunched over his books that night until long after midnight. For the rest of the month, looming midterm exams claimed his attention. When the results were posted, his hard work and effort had paid big dividends. He now ranked second in his class.

During the cool Roman spring, Emmanuel once again immersed himself in scholarly pursuits as he prepared the first draft of his thesis on Cortez and the Conquistadors. By the time it was ready to submit, his afternoon visit to the Papal Guard Hall was little more than a shadowy recollection.

➢

Spring of 1941 also brought on a heightening of international tensions and American involvement. In a January letter to F.D.R., Churchill proclaimed that the British treasury was empty. No cash remained to purchase U.S. arms and munitions.

"England," said Churchill, "will no longer be able to conduct operations against the Nazi forces."

"America," responded her president, "will become the great arsenal of democracy. We will lend or lease all of the materials you need to make our common cause succeed. It would be suicidal to wait until the war is in our front yard.

Our Bunker Hill of tomorrow may lie thousands of miles from Boston."

A pretty strong statement of commitment, coming as it did from the leader of the world's largest neutral country, thought an extremely concerned Emmanuel Questa.

In April, his fears increased when American forces began setting up military and naval bases in Greenland, and President Roosevelt declared "a state of national emergency."

On June 22, in spite of the Non-Aggression Pact signed by the two countries less than two years earlier, Hitler sent his German armies streaming into the Soviet Union. At the same time, in the Pacific, Japanese troops invaded oil-rich Indochina and shifted their war machine into high gear.

Meanwhile, in the quiet sanctuary of the Pontifical College, students from all parts of a world torn asunder by the ravages of global terror waited and wondered how long their safe haven would exist.

Many of the more timid Vatican denizens felt threatened, not only by the jack-booted Nazis and the pompous Fascists, but also because of the current actions of the Pope.

Eugenio Cardinal Pacelli had mounted the throne of St. Peter on March 2, 1939, and become Pope Pius XII. In all probability, thought Manny, he had been elected by his former peers because of his vast wealth of diplomatic experience and his days as Nuncio (Papal Representative of the Highest Order) in Hitler's Germany. He became the synod's last forlorn hope, their final desperate effort to forestall the uncontrollable conflagration that was ready to scorch the earth and consume her people in the fires of totalitarian aggression.

Not since the year 452, when Pope Leo the Great had stopped Attila the Hun at the gates of Rome, had such a scourge been known. But this pontiff's pleas had fallen on deaf ears and closed minds.

Six months later, as soon as the Nazis invaded Poland, the pope issued his encyclical, Summi Pontificantus, in which he denounced their actions. German Minister Heydrich forbade this papal decree to be read or circulated in any Nazi-held territory.

Within the borders of war-torn Poland, the Nazis retaliated by increasing their already horrible persecution, perhaps Heydrich's way of venting a small portion of his legendary rage.

Each new Nazi atrocity was immediately reported on Vatican radio and catalogued in L'Osservatore Romano, the official Papal newspaper. Heydrich countered by denying access to all the relief workers who requested permission to come to the aid of Poland's victims, and more and more innocent souls fell to the wrath of the godless aggressors.

Across the continents of Europe and Asia, doors of churches, convents, and chapels were thrown open to admit tortured masses of Jews, Catholics, and other fugitives who had incurred the spiteful wrath of tyrants simply by existing. Before the light of peace glowed once more, nearly half a million desperate fugitives would find refuge in these twentieth-century catacombs.

Certainly, Manny reflected, if the Axis Powers' past actions foreshadowed future events, the war would produce thousands of courageous martyrs in addition to millions of innocent victims.

➢

In spite of the tensions caused by the world's deplorable and ever worsening situation, as the days of summer approached and the final weeks of his first year as a seminarian drew near, Emmanuel's mind wandered once again to Padre Garza's Aztec cure. How wonderful it would be, he thought, if a miracle could somehow be wrought, and the medicine were available right now to end the suffering of so many in the war-ravaged world.

On June 25, eager to share the threads of the mystery with someone who might suggest a logical way to institute a search for the ancient medicine, Emmanuel requested an evening appointment with his academic counselor, Monsignor Dino Bettia. The elderly scholar greeted his young protégé warmly.

"I'm very proud of you, Emmanuel. You've had a wonderful year. What brings you to see me? Since you're carrying an attaché case, I presume that this is not a social call."

"Not entirely, Monsignor, although I am always honored to be in your presence."

The humble old priest dismissed the praise with a smile and a wave of his hand and motioned for Manny to continue.

"During my Conquistador research, Monsignor, I discovered that during Cortez' expedition, a very powerful medicine was given to one of his priests, Padre Diego Garza. The medicine took away his severe pain and began healing his body almost at once. The other priest, Padre Olmedo, used it on himself and felt instant relief, as did many others in the party. Ironically, only a small vial of the formula survived La Noche de Triste; but I have reasonably good proof that directions for producing the medicine were placed inside the hidden compartment of a knife hilt by Padre Garza just before his death. I've brought with me all my research materials that apply to the knife, as well as the mystery's other aspects. Unfortunately, I can't trace the weapon beyond 1530, when Cabeza de Vaca left it in the heart of a Comanche Indian somewhere on the plains of Texas. The chances of ever finding the knife seem remote, but how can we hope to reproduce the medicine if we don't find it?"

"As you yourself said, the knife's whereabouts have been unknown for over 400 years! Where would one begin to look?"

"I don't have the slightest idea, Monsignor, but I know the medicine can be a wonderful blessing for mankind, especially with this war raging out of control as it is."

"You're right, of course! Share your evidence with me."

Manny and the elderly cleric hunched over the research papers for the next hour before the Monsignor lifted his head.

"I'm convinced," he said, "that at some point the medicine did exist. And I agree with your conclusions about the knife. But I'm still no closer to formulating a viable course of action."

"Monsignor, I know that the Vatican frequently sends out mercy missions. For example, the one that was organized to aid people in Poland. Although that rescue mission was not permitted, many of us volunteered. Surely a search for the medicine would qualify as a mission of mercy, would it not?"

"If we knew where either the medicine, or significant knowledge about it, could be found, or even where it might be found, I think a search could be justified. Unfortunately, we do not know those things, Emmanuel. As far as Padre Garza's knife is concerned, we cannot assume that it still exists."

"If any hope of success exists, don't we owe the suffering masses of the world an effort?"

"Even if I totally agreed with your optimistic position, and shared your boundless enthusiasm, I have neither the ability to organize, nor the power to authorize such a search or mission."

"Who would have the ability and authority, Monsignor, assuming that he believed such a mission might succeed?"

"It would take a Prince of the Church, a Cardinal, to sponsor any such undertaking. Not one of them would endorse that type of risk unless he foresaw a good chance of success. Even so, we would have to find a very strong man, someone with great faith in his own judgment, and an almost overwhelming determination to persevere, in spite of the enormous odds against us."

"Monsignor, please consider the great relief that this Aztec medicine could bring to the war's victims," pleaded Emmanuel.

Monsignor Bettia rose and paced about the room, rubbing his chin thoughtfully, his forehead puckered by a deep frown.

"Very well, in spite of the very high probability of failure, I shall try to help you! Perhaps Our Blessed Lord will intervene and reward your strong faith in the project's success. Besides," he laughed, "you are one of my favorite students. I'll begin at once to inquire of my old friends and other sources. But please don't be too disappointed if I can't find a sponsor, Emmanuel. A Cardinal such as the one we seek may not even exist."

Chapter XXIV
➤
The Cardinal

A Restaurant In Rome, and The Residence
Of His Eminence, Luigi Cardinal Cabrini
Milan, Italy.
June 25, 1941

Such a Cardinal certainly did exist. At that very moment, he was enjoying a huge steak, Alfredo pasta, and a carafe of mellow, red wine at a bistro near the famous fountain of Trevi.

As he savored this ambrosial repast, he chatted amicably with a pair of Italian officers who sat at an adjacent table. The two men, as well as the maitre d' and waiters, respectfully addressed him as Segnori Crespo, little realizing that he was actually Luigi Cardinal Cabrini of Milano.

Luigi Cabrini was a worldly Cardinal. But that was not entirely surprising since he had been a worldly bishop and, prior to that, a worldly priest. He had spent several formative years in London after World War I—an experience that dictated his future style of living.

In almost all things, his conduct was beyond reproach. He was a totally chaste and honest man. He never lusted after women, or dreamt of unobtainable worldly possessions; but he did enjoy the finer things that life could provide. His body felt comfortable only when it was adorned in an expensive Savile Row suit, and what man of breeding clumped about in heavy brogans when featherweight, handcrafted Italian shoes glided so easily onto ones feet. In his own see, he was His Eminence, the Cardinal, unapproachable and austere, but on trips to distant places, or during ecclesiastical visits outside of Milano, he was quite often Segnori Crespo, the suave, silver-haired man-about-town.

He had come to Rome to see his friend Eugenio. Luigi Cardinal Cabrini never thought of the pope in terms of His Holiness, or Pius XII, but always as Eugenio. In 1939, the vote by the other Cardinals had been close. He had come within a whisker of being elected the prelate instead of Eugenio. Next time, he promised himself, it will be different. Before then, I'll do something that makes me the only logical candidate. I could have won the last time had it not been for Eugene's term as Nuncio to Berlin. Many of the members in the College of Cardinals hoped the Nazis would go easier on Catholics, and others as well, if a man they knew was selected as the new pope. Their dreams of reconciliation had gone up in smoke along with their ballots.

I did not expect any sort of compromise, mused Luigi Cabrini, but then I remember the day in 1938 when Hitler's goons threw the Austrian Cardinal's secretary out of a fifth-floor window at the German Chancery. Hitler had made threatening gestures toward the elderly churchman, and his young assistant had stepped forward to intervene. Just as quickly, the priest had been seized and hurled through the glass onto the cobblestone courtyard below.

All things considered, Cabrini decided, Eugenio is doing a good job. As well as anyone, myself included, could be expected to do under such trying circumstances. Nevertheless, he told himself, I must score some kind of special coup that will assure me of winning the next election.

Suddenly he shivered at the thought of needing another such election. Hurriedly, Luigi Cardinal Cabrini hastened to assure God that his reverie had not been wishful thinking. He loved Eugenio like a brother and would be content to have him rule the Church for many years. And, Cardinal Cabrini confided to Our Lord, he was grateful to be blessed with far more ability and talent than other men, a blessing that he felt was justified by his dedication to the greater honor and glory of God. Still, if the unthinkable happened, it certainly never hurt to be prepared.

He finished the final morsel of his sumptuous meal and reached out toward a silver reauchard, where an impressively-sculptured flagon containing one last half glass of flat wine protruded from a sea of tepid water and tiny shards of melting ice.

He poured the last drops into a fine crystal goblet and drank them, before withdrawing a heavy gold cigar case from an inside breast pocket. He opened the case and brought forth a large, West Indian cigar, an ornate gold lighter, and a small flat machine that resembled a miniature guillotine.

Using the palm of his hand, he rolled the cigar back and forth across the table several times before raising it to his nose. For a full half-minute, he inhaled the sweet, pungent aroma that emanated from the exotic tobacco and then inserted the end of the cigar into the opening of the guillotine. The tiny blade plunged downward and neatly severed the tip of the cigar. The lighter flicked and the happy cleric was soon engulfed in a thickening cloud of billowing smoke that wreathed about his head and obscured his smiling visage.

Without any further motions or requests from Signori Crespo, a waiter who was hovering just out of sight suddenly materialized and came forward with a small silver salver held on high. He stopped beside the guest's chair and with great pomp and flourish placed a brandy flute filled with fine Courvoisier on the table before him.

For the next hour, Luigi Cabrini savored his cigar and brandy.

As always, the satisfaction he derived from these indulgences served to remind him that, in this often savage world, exquisite pleasures were always available to those who could afford them.

➢

Late one morning, nearly a month later, Cardinal Cabrini's secretary placed a sealed letter, bearing the return address of one of his former professors, on the desk before him.

"Eminence," said the young priest, "knowing of your esteem for Monsignor Bettia, I brought his communication to you at once."

"Many thanks, Cisco," responded the Cardinal, reaching out to accept the letter.

As he opened the envelope, he thought, I have tried to gain the approval of this man for nearly forty years, yet this is the first time he has written to me outside of official channels.

The four-page letter apologized for presuming to intrude on His Eminence's busy schedule, inquired for his health, and then went on to mention the possible existence of an ancient Aztec medicine, reported to have great healing properties.

The only written record of the medicine's formula had been lost some time around 1530. However, the Cardinal's legendary love for intriguing mysteries, and the realization that such a cure could benefit so many of the world's suffering multitudes, had prompted the Monsignor to write to His Eminence. Also, the elderly cleric cautioned, if this information were to fall into the wrong hands, the medicine might be manufactured and marketed by unscrupulous and greedy men, eager to amass great fortunes and willing to withhold the cure from those who suffered the most. Therefore, he summarized; we must prevent anyone from using it for his own personal gain. The letter's final paragraph was a plea for His Eminence to formulate a plan and then to sponsor a search for this wonderful healing agent.

Cabrini laid the letter down and swung his red leather swivel chair around to face the window that overlooked his garden. You are right, my brother, he thought; we must safeguard the secret and ban any monetary profit. But there are other forms of profit!

He recalled Francisco to his office and dictated a short but very pleasant note to Monsignor Bettia, encouraging the elderly priest or any representatives of his choice to come to Milan and discuss strategy for the recovery of this medical treasure.

As he finished his dictation, Helena Musconi, Italian chef extraordinaire, came to the entrance and announced that luncheon was ready to be served on the shady side of the garden.

The Cardinal and Francisco rose at once and, exiting through double French doors, emerged on a horseshoe-shaped path which encircled the perimeter of the garden. They followed this gravel walkway for a short distance until they came to a thick grove of trees. There, beneath giant old oaks and elms, overhung with long strands of Spanish moss, they shared a sumptuous lunch consisting of veal scaloppini, eggplant parmesan, and a light Chianti.

His position with the Cardinal could be trying at times, Francisco reflected, but Helena's culinary mastery certainly made up for a great deal.

An hour later, they returned to work, and the Cardinal dictated a final paragraph to his reply, indicating that in view of the deteriorating state of world affairs, it might be wise to proceed with their project as soon as possible.

As was his custom at four o'clock, Cardinal Cabrini left his office and ascended to his private quarters for an hour's siesta.

He usually dozed off immediately, but today sleep did not come. Instead, he lay back and gazed up at the high, sculptured ceiling, lost in deep thought. A few minutes later, he suddenly sat bolt upright, swung his feet to the floor, and reached for his bedside telephone. Francisco answered at once.

"Yes, Eminence?"

"Cisco, call Emilio and ask him to come to my study this evening at nine o'clock. I would like you to be there as well."

"At once, Eminence."

At the appointed hour, the Cardinal was seated in a corner of his study upon a plush, gold, damask sofa, enjoying a snifter of Napoleon brandy. He heard a soft tap on the door just as the first of nine chimes sounded from his ornate grandfather clock.

He arose from his comfortably padded nest and advanced toward the center of the room before he responded to the knock. As soon as he did, the door swung open, and Father Francisco entered the softly lit room, accompanied by Emilio Duarte.

Duarte came to kneel before the Cardinal and receive his blessing prior to seating himself, tentatively, on the edge of one of the dark green leather chairs that fronted an enormous oak desk. As he strode back around the desk toward his custom-made high-backed chair, the cleric's soft, well-worn slippers made no sound on the beautiful parquet floor that completed the study's opulent elegance.

He settled into his chair and studied his guest for a few moments before speaking. Emilio Duarte was a barrel-chested, powerful looking man of less than medium height. If his legs had matched his long torso and arms, the Cardinal reflected, he would have been quite tall; however, they were unusually short.

His head was covered with a mass of long, black, stringy hair, which fell straight down on all sides. His small dark eyes were partially hooded by droopy eyelids that matched his long, black, equally droopy mustache. A casual observer might have expected him to fall asleep at any moment, but, as the Cardinal had beheld on many other occasions, the longer and closer one looked, the more dangerous and less innocent Emilio Duarte seemed to become.

If he were wearing a brace of revolvers and had a couple of bandoleers strung across his chest, thought Cabrini for the one hundredth time, he would look exactly like the Mexican Pistoleros in the American motion pictures. His conception of his guest was, he knew, greatly influenced by Emilio Duarte's actual adventures.

In April 1936, Duarte answered Francisco Franco's call to defend the Catholic Faith and the motherland at the outbreak of the Spanish Civil War. The Generalissimo called for 600 men. A volunteer army of 40,000 came forth.

Duarte had resigned from the constabulary of Navarra to become a Requete, one of the first of 100,000 fiercely loyal defenders of Church, Spain, and family, against the increasing onslaught of Communism.

He fought with Jose Moscardo at the Siege of the Alcazar in Toledo and stood with Franco as he rejected Adolf Hitler's offer of friendship and a portion of the tainted spoils of war.

Cardinal Cabrini had met Duarte in Madrid during the summer of 1940 and persuaded him to return to Milan and join his staff as bodyguard and chauffeur. Now, a year later, Emilio Duarte would gladly have died for his Cardinal as well as for his Faith or his country.

Cabrini began the small conference by inviting Emilio and Padre Francisco to prepare their own libations, anticipating that quite some time might be spent discussing this most unique problem.

When his conferees were once again seated, this time with drinks in hand, he presented the facts as Monsignor Bettia had outlined them and ended his summary with a question.

"Until 1936, when you became a Requete, much of your life was spent conducting police investigations. For Generals Moscardo and Franco, you did military intelligence work. Therefore, Emilio, I feel that you are the person best qualified to solve the mystery. Assuming that the Aztec medicine did exist at some point in time, where would you begin your search? Would you even bother looking for the knife with its secret compartment?"

"Before I attempt to answer your questions, Eminence, allow me to wonder and ponder about some things out loud," responded the former Requete. "The last person to acknowledge possession of the weapon was Cabeza de Vaca in 1530. Are we sure that the secret was inside some type of compartment at that time?"

"Reasonably certain, according to the Monsignor's researcher," responded Cabrini.

"Assuming validity, it means that not only would the weapon have to survive for more than 400 years, but that the secret compartment would have to remain undiscovered as well. The chance of either of those possibilities occurring is beyond calculation, Eminence. For both to happen is, I believe, impossible."

"Go on," urged Cardinal Cabrini impatiently.

"We don't really need the weapon to uncover the secret. Of course, it would provide a convenient key to the puzzle. But it has already served its principal purpose, merely by bringing the enigma to light. We may have to use a different key to unlock this ancient door of mystery."

"Where do we look for this new key, Emilio?" queried the cleric.

"At this moment, Eminence, I'm far more interested in finding a portal into the mystery than I am in discovering the key. The only logical place to begin is in the land of the Aztecs."

"Won't that be virtually impossible with the war going on?" asked the Cardinal.

"Difficult, Eminence, but the Americans have not yet entered the conflict, although I am certain they will do so before year's end. This war may be over before the people of Mexico's interior regions realize that it is underway. No, Eminence, the threat in Mexico's cities, villages, jungles, and mountains will not come from the outside world, but from los hombres malo, bad men who prey upon the inhabitants.

"When I lived in Navarra, I knew a man who went each year with a few of his amigos to a different part of the world to hunt for wild animals. One year they went to the Mexican jungles in search of los tigres. Jaguars. They were told these fierce animals had been hunted nearly to extinction in most parts of the country, but were seldom sought in the jungle areas where the men harvested the sap or chiclet from rubber trees. These men are called Chicleteers. The natives never venture into these sectors because they greatly fear the Chicleteers. People say that even the most ferocious tigres fear them. No creature is more dangerous.

"My friend and his compadres hired four local men to guide them to the tigres, but, although they heard the big cats howling many times, they never caught sight of them. Then one dark night, two of the guides came racing into camp and persuaded some of the hunters to go with them to where their friends had cornered a big jaguar. Neither hunters nor guides were ever seen again. They simply vanished into thin air. Los tigres are still out there in the back country, Your Eminence, and so are the Chicleteers."

"It appears that you will need to keep your wits about you and develop eyes in the back of your head," exclaimed the concerned Cardinal, "just to survive."

"Perhaps I paint a darker picture than necessary, Eminence, but treasure hunting is always a risky business, war or no war. Make no mistake. To multitudes of greedy men, this medicine we seek is not a great cure for many, but a treasure which will produce great riches for a few. Rest assured that wherever the search may lead me, I will ever remain cautious and alert."

"I will pray that Our Lord watches over you," responded the subdued cleric. "Very well, my friends, we will speak again of this situation when the Monsignor or his representatives arrive. For now, I will bid you both good night."

As soon as the door closed behind them, the Cardinal arose and began pacing about the room, ruminating as he moved and sipping from the ever-decreasing contents of his brandy snifter.

Emilio was, of course, correct. There was almost no hope of finding a weapon, which had disappeared, so long ago, much less any of its hidden contents. Also, Cardinal Cabrini wondered, if the Conquistadors themselves were unsuccessful in their search only a short time after the event, how can we hope to succeed now?

Even though Duarte had perhaps exaggerated the complexity and perils of a mission into the interior of Mexico, the journey would certainly be extremely dangerous. But this is such a unique opportunity to do good works and help so many troubled people, he told himself, that we must try. No stone can be left unturned.

Puzzled frowns intermittently creased his brow as he continued pacing about the room for the next hour, seeking solutions but finding none. Suddenly, he stopped the pacing in mid-stride and smiled to himself, realizing that his self-indulgent motivation had transformed itself into something of far greater importance.

Therefore, he concluded, draining his last drop of brandy, now that it has become a worthy cause, I will simply do what I have always done—give the problem to God. If He wants it to be solved, it will be, and if He does not, it doesn't matter.

➤

Ten days later, the Cardinal and four other men sat around a large circular patio table which had been positioned to allow warm sunlight to dart through thousands of tiny openings in the overhead foliage and dapple the diners as they enjoyed one of Helena Musconi's sumptuous breakfasts. The entire table was covered with mounds of poached salmon, eggs Benedict, great slabs of thickly sliced bacon, and a special treat that she called eggs Musconi, which consisted of Italian ham and soft scrambled eggs, laced with spinach and a multitude of spices. Food fit for either a king or a Cardinal observed Luigi Cabrini.

He smiled at the young seminarian seated opposite him.

"I am curious, Emmanuel, as to how you uncovered this great mystery?"

"It was more a matter of luck than of skill, Your Eminence. I found a number of clues while doing my research on the Conquistadors and merely put them together."

"In my more than six decades, I have eliminated luck as the source of most success. Monsignor Bettia told me of your class standing, your leadership abilities, and the perseverance you display in every task you undertake. I am certain that you will go far." He touched the red hat that was the symbol of his office as a Cardinal of the Catholic Church before adding, "Perhaps, someday, you will wear one of these."

The humble young seminarian was so embarrassed that his face suddenly became the same color as his host's hat.

An hour later, Emmanuel and the Cardinal sat on one side of a long, comfortable conference table. Facing them were Monsignor Bettia, Father Francisco, and Emilio Duarte.

Between them lay copies of the ancient documents Emmanuel had uncovered, together with his research notes and conclusions. Next to them were a number of maps of Mexico, steamship schedules, and various lists that Emilio had compiled in the past ten days.

The former Requete examined Emmanuel's question-and-answer sheet very carefully, before laying it aside.

"Emmanuel," Emilio began, "the priesthood is getting a great detective. Your investigative abilities and logical mind would be the envy of Sherlock Holmes. Your conclusions seem irrefutable. There can be little doubt."

Duarte stopped speaking and looked at the Cardinal, who nodded for his investigator to continue.

"I think we can safely conclude that no outsider has ever found the Aztec medicine."

"Why are you so certain of that, Emilio?" asked Francisco.

"For two different but similar reasons, Padre. If a benevolent source had turned it up, they would have given it to the people of the world. If a greedy group had found it, they would have sold it to the people of the world. Either way, its existence would be well known."

"What about those who are not outsiders?" asked the Monsignor. "The insiders and the local people. Are they aware of it?"

"There lies the problem, Monsignor. We can start with the safe premise that only a select few possess this knowledge, since only a small and tightly controlled group can possibly keep a secret, for even a limited amount of time. The fewer the confidants, the safer the secret remains. But from an investigative standpoint, the smaller the group, the lower our chances of success become. All things considered, it will be very difficult."

"What have you learned of the current conditions in Mexico?" asked the Cardinal.

"My sources tell me," responded the investigator, "that the German foreign office is filtering agents and spies into America through Mexico. The international boundary along the Rio Grande has become a hotbed of intrigue, but that shouldn't affect me in the interior or in the southern regions, so far from the border. Also, I'll have the diplomatic immunity provided by my Vatican passport and other credentials."

"My family are longtime residents of Eagle Pass, Texas, Señor Duarte," Emmanuel volunteered. "They would be honored to help you in any possible way. If need be, they can introduce you to the former U.S. Vice President, John Nance Garner, who lives nearby."

"Many thanks, young amigo. I will certainly appreciate any help they can give me. But I view this as a secret mission."

"How do you propose to proceed?" inquired the Cardinal.

"I think we are all agreed, Eminence, that since America will soon be forced into the war, time is of the essence. I can book passage on a tramp steamer, which sails from Genoa a week from today. Its first port of call on the Mexican coast is Campeche. That is, I believe, the area in which I should begin."

"Why there?" asked the Cardinal. "Why not in Vera Cruz, which would give you easier access to Mexico City?"

"Because this is a Mayan and Aztec secret, Eminence. If I am destined to find answers anywhere, it will not be in the modern cities, but rather in the old villages where the ancient customs still live. There, the Indian heritage may still flourish.

"Since this is not a twentieth-century mystery, we should not look for twentieth-century solutions. The urban barrio dwellers in every country are eager to modernize, not to protect their ancient cultures. It is not Mexico City which beckons to me, but rather the last bastion of ancient lore— the Yucatan Peninsula."

"Have you assembled everything you will need?"

"I have, Eminence, but there is no need to be burdened with a great deal of baggage or equipment. Aside from necessary papers and clothing, I'll be carrying one hundred U.S. $20 gold pieces, your letters of credit to obtain additional financing, and my credential documents to the officials of Mexico, which I would prefer not to use. I'll also carry a Model 1911 .45 caliber Colt automatic pistol, a weapon developed for the American army and guaranteed to stop any two-legged creature in the world."

"How did you happen to acquire such a weapon?" asked Emmanuel.

"It was presented to me by General Moscardo after the Siege of the Alcazar was lifted. It is one of my prized possessions."

For the next three hours, the men exchanged ideas and finalized plans. By the time the meeting ended and lunch was served, they felt certain that everything had been done that could be.

As the midday meal began, Cardinal Cabrini reminded everyone that although Emilio Duarte now bore the major burden, their daily prayers for his safety and success were still vitally important. For only by the grace of God would the medicine of the Aztecs ever become a source of salvation for the world's suffering.

Chapter XXV
➢
The Old Ones

Yucatan & Quintana Roo Provinces
Northern Yucatan Peninsula
Mexico
December 7, 1941

Three weeks before Christmas, it should be a lot closer to zero than to a hundred degrees, thought an extremely warm and weary Emilio Duarte as he struggled along the last hundred yards of the hot and dusty road. After four months of tramping around, he had decided that every road, trail, and lane on the Yucatan Peninsula was hot, dry, and dusty. Worse than that, until this morning none of them seemed to get him any closer to his goal.

It was the first Sunday in December, and he had just returned to the village of Tunkas, which was located several kilometers north of the ancient Mayan, later Aztec, city of Chichen Itza, to dine with his friend, Padre Pedro Constanzia.

He had met the Padre one sweltering afternoon in August at the ruins of Chichen Itza, a once magnificent Mayan cultural center. Although the young cleric had been born in Mexico City, he was as much a stranger to the Yucatan Peninsula as the Spaniard.

Padre Pedro, who had arrived three weeks earlier than Emilio, had been given the unenviable task of attempting to replace the recently deceased local priest who, for the past thirty years, had serviced an area which was apparently equally divided between staunch Catholicism and colossal superstition. Since this was his first independent mission, the Padre was as eager to accept the stranger's friendship and encouragement as Emilio was to receive the youthful priest's counsel and advice.

That first afternoon they scrambled around the fascinating ruins like a pair of schoolboys, exclaiming with excitement over each new and unique discovery. As nightfall approached, the Padre invited Emilio to return with him to the simple adobe parish house in Tunkas, where he lived, and to share his sparse evening meal of tortillas and frijoles.

"Forgive my boldness, Don Emilio," the Padre said as they ate, "but I think we are caught in the same dilemma. We are strangers trying to communicate with descendants of Mayas and Aztecs who are reluctant to talk even to their own friends. Why should they willingly speak with us?"

"You're right, Padre. Before either of us can accomplish his mission, we must be patient enough to allow them to get to know us and trust us. When they lose their fear and suspicion, they may begin to be friendly. Until then we must be helpful and solicitous, but never force ourselves upon them."

"It may take a very long time to earn that trust, Don Emilio."

"Perhaps, Padre, but we are doomed to failure if we do not. You, of course, have far more credibility than do I, by virtue of your collar. A priest is someone who is prone to be trusted by everyone. A foreigner, especially one who looks as sinister as I do, is apt to be mistrusted by nearly everyone. However, I think we can form an alliance which will help us both to speed up our acceptance with these people. Before I explain my plan, allow me to tell you of my quest and the great man I represent."

Emilio spent the next hour telling the story of Padre Garza's recently discovered secret and of his own mission to recover the medicine that the Padre had found so long ago. He told his host about his association with Cardinal Cabrini and concluded by showing the young pastor one of the Cardinal's letters. It was a brief note that assured the reader of the Cardinal's confidence in Emilio Duarte and requested any and all assistance he might require.

"Don Emilio, I will be honored to help you in any way I can."

"Thank you, Padre. You indicated earlier that although fevers and illness are very common in these parts, modern drugs which can cure such sicknesses, or at least reduce their severity, are extremely scarce."

"Mexico is a poor country, Don Emilio, inhabited by poor people."

"I can obtain large quantities of these so-called miracle drugs, Padre. Quinine, sulfa, and many others that are used to combat tropical fevers and illness. If the people see that we are helping them and their children, they will have a reason to trust us and welcome us."

"I sense there is even more to your plan, Amigo," smiled the insightful priest. "What is it?"

"Perhaps," responded his guest, "an exchange of medicines."

"I follow you, but how would you effect such an exchange?"

"I have a number of wounds in my body, put there by the knives and bullets of people who were not my admirers. I can think of nothing more natural, after a modern drug has helped one of the members of a local family, than to mention one of my wounds and wish out loud that I could find a medicine to relieve the pain. It seems to me that, out of gratitude, such a remedy might be offered if available, or at least alluded to, even if it is not."

"No wonder Cardinal Cabrini chose you for this mission. Your scheme is ingenious."

"I appreciate the accolade, Padre, but for the time being, please forget about my sponsor and my mission. I am merely here to assist you in easing the suffering of your flock."

Three weeks later, a large wooden crate filled with medicine and medical equipment was delivered to the Padre's rectory.

➢

For the balance of the summer and on into the fall, usually alone but occasionally with Padre Constanzia, Emilio rattled over the hills and across the plains in a rickety old Model T Ford, or on the back of an equally rickety old burro. In places where the Model T could not go, or the burro would not go, he walked. From Campeche to Cancun, wherever he went, he carried a heavy load of medicine and an unending supply of goodwill.

During those months, he became an angel of mercy to hundreds of poor families throughout the northern Yucatan Peninsula and earned for himself the title El Curandero, the Medicine Man.

One week he traveled to the extreme southern end of Yucatan and visited the ancient Mayan settlement of Monos, but to no avail. The following week he spent several equally unproductive days at a similar site in Eizna Tixmucuy. Finally, he decided to concentrate on the Yucatan's northern quadrant.

He became a frequent and welcome sight to the poor, suffering families who still lived on the sites of Mayapan, Uxmal, Sayil, Labna, Kabah, and Tulum, as well as those who dwelt near the ruins of Chichen Itza. Each location had been a place of pride to the Indian inhabitants during their days of glory, as much as half a millennium before Christ had walked beside the Sea of Galilee.

Each week Emilio Duarte's limps and lumps seemed to become more pronounced and visible, and the groans caused by the pain from his own old wounds grew longer and more audible as he patiently ministered to the needs of others.

Never did he complain, but only wished aloud that a medicine might be found to ease his pain and make his tasks a bit easier.

371

On two occasions, in dimly lit adobe dwellings, grateful mothers of feverish children had risen, obviously intent on performing an important service for Duarte. But in each case a stern look from their husbands had stopped them in their tracks and brought them sheepishly back to their seats.

➢

One morning, Emilio attended the early Mass in Merida. As he left the church and emerged into a bright, warm December sun, he was approached by a very frail old man who bore a message from a family that lived a few kilometers to the east, near the ancient city of Dzibilchaltun. The previous week, Emilio's medicine had brought their young daughter's extremely high temperature down to normal in a matter of two hours and had undoubtedly saved the youngster's life. Now they asked him to come to them once again.

Emilio rushed to the old Ford and, with grinding gears and screeching tires, hurried off, envisioning the child's relapse or a similar problem with one of the other villagers.

However, it was not an emergency to which he was bidden but a fiesta, in celebration of his young patient's sixth birthday. He watched her as she scampered about with her playmates, and decided that she had recovered completely from her recent illness.

As he looked around, it seemed to Emilio that every inhabitant of the village was here. They had undoubtedly pooled their meager resources in order to sponsor this joyous celebration. For once, food was abundant and tequila flowed freely. Emilio was careful to hold his consumption of the fiery liquor to a minimum. He had discovered that it had a kick like a mule and the aftertaste of an old riding boot.

A short time after his arrival, his grateful hosts, Don Julio and Doña Iñez Verrano, maneuvered him away from the other guests. When they were concealed from view, they presented him with a tiny stone vial encased in wicker.

"Por favor, Don Emilio," pleaded Don Julio. "Don't mention this to anyone else. Put it in your pocket for now. When you return to Tunkas, spread the unguent over the parts of your body that hurt. The pain will go away, almost at once."

"What is this medicine? Where does it come from?

"It is called the Tratamiento, Don Emilio," replied his host, "but we cannot tell you where it comes from."

"Don't you know?" queried the excited investigator, actually holding the legendary Tratamiento (treatment) in his hands for the first time.

"Don Emilio," replied a badly frightened Doña Iñez, "Los Viejos (the Old Ones) have placed a curse on anyone who reveals the secret of the Tratamiento. My husband and myself, as well as our daughter, Mercata, would die horrible deaths if we told you."

"I understand, my friends," responded El Curandero. "I will ask no more about the medicine. But can you tell me more about those you refer to as the Old Ones?"

"Los Viejos have always been with us. They are caretakers of the ancient secrets. They know things that very few others know, and they punish all those who dare to disobey or defy them."

"Have you ever seen one of these Old Ones?"

"Oh, no, Don Emilio, no one sees Los Viejos! Sometimes in the dark of night we hear them, but they are never seen. Only their messengers live among us. People chosen by Los Viejos to do their bidding. It is they who give us the Tratamiento when we need it."

"Where can I find one of these messengers, Don Julio?"

"A todos partes, sino en ninguana parte. They are everywhere, but they are nowhere. You cannot find them, but perhaps they will find you."

"That sounds very ominous, Don Julio."

"I know that I would not want them to find me, Señor Duarte."

Emilio realized that the ominous warning was generated by their genuine concern for him. He also recognized the futility of seeking any more information from them on the subject of the Old Ones. Superstitions ran too deeply. They were plainly frightened for their lives. Somewhere he had to find someone who would tell him all that he needed to know. They returned to the rollicking fiesta, where Emilio spent a short time visiting with the other villagers. Before leaving, he thanked his hosts again for their hospitality and praised their courage in providing him with such a wondrous but dangerous gift. Finally, he hugged little Mercata Verrano, wished her a happy birthday, bid good-bye to all, and took his leave.

He left the ancient village and drove westward for several miles before pulling off to the side of the road, stopping in the shade of a tall cactus. He withdrew the small stone vial from his pocket, removed the stopper, and spread a tiny portion on one of his most nagging injuries.

Marked by a jagged scar, the pain emanated from the joint of his left elbow, where a stiletto type bayonette had penetrated to the bone before ripping away a great gob of flesh as it exited. Although he had been fortunate enough to regain the complete use of the arm, he still had a large depression in the inner crook of the elbow, and had continued to experience a dull ache within the joint and the adjacent muscles ever since.

He was both hopeful and doubtful as he waited for the medicine to take effect. He did not have long to wait. Almost at once, he felt a warm glow as the soothing liniment penetrated the skin and invaded his injured muscles. Seconds later, the pain was gone.

Mystified by the medicine's rapid effect, but overjoyed by its result, Emilio thrashed the Ford's reluctant transmission into gear and continued on the journey toward Tunkas and his lunch with Padre Pedro.

Thirty minutes later he arrived at the end of the narrow road that led to the chapel and rectory. By then the engine was chugging and the red-hot radiator was emitting a dangerous, high-pitched whistling sound. Emilio quickly parked the old car and hurried along the lane, half expecting to hear an explosion from the road. He was almost surprised when it failed to come. By the time he reached the Padre's door, he felt as hot as the radiator.

As he entered the manse, Padre Pedro was bending over his ancient radio, straining to hear the announcer's words above the crackle of static that poured from the dilapidated speaker.

Emilio joined him and quickly discovered that the newscaster was describing an attack by Japanese forces on the American Naval Base at Pearl Harbor, Hawaii, earlier in the day. Although the information was still limited, it was abundantly clear to Emilio that this overt act of aggression would quickly bring the United States into the war. The broadcast ended, and Padre Pedro turned to Emilio.

"This means another world war, doesn't it, Don Emilio?"

"Without question, Padre. The Americans will declare war on Japan at once, and Japan's Axis partners will, in turn, declare war on the United States. Within a week, it will be a world war."

"How do you think this will affect you?"

"It won't hinder my mission here, but it may make my return to Italy more difficult unless I can book passage on a vessel from a neutral nation. Obviously, once war is declared, American surface ships and submarines will deny free passage upon the seas."

Emilio suddenly remembered something that only an hour earlier had consumed his entire attention.

From his pocket, he withdrew the small container with its precious contents, laid it casually on the table and said, "Rub some of this on your neck, Padre. See if it relieves your pain."

The young cleric's face lit up as he grasped the container.

"You found the medicine?" he asked excitedly.

"I believe so."

The Padre unbuttoned his collar and shrugged the shirt off the back of his neck. He pulled the cork stopper and coaxed a small amount of the thick liquid into the palm of his hand. This he carefully applied to the side of his throat and along the top of his left shoulder. Noticing that a small residue clung to his hand, he dabbed the remaining drops over a small but deep cut on his index finger which, a few minutes earlier, he had carelessly sliced open with a sharp bread knife. Although the wound was not a serious one, it was still bleeding profusely.

A moment later, the incredulous Padre sat staring in disbelief at a finger that bled no more. As he held his hand out toward Emilio to exhibit the speed with which the medicine had worked, he discovered the pain in his neck and shoulder had also stopped.

"This is incredible, Don Emilio! I have suffered constant pain since that loose tile blew off the chapel roof last week during the big storm and struck me. Now the pain is suddenly gone!"

"I know, Padre. I had a similar experience. After I left Dzibilchaltun, I applied the Tratamiento to the elbow that was so badly damaged several years ago, and have felt nothing since. Pain as severe as any I have ever experienced simply vanished."

"I wonder how long the relief lasts? And what makes it work so quickly?" pondered the Padre.

"The answer to the first question is one that we will know in the next hours, days, or weeks. What prompts it to work so quickly is something about which, for now, we can only speculate."

"I felt a sudden rush of warmth to the area," the Padre said, "before the pain left me. The warm feeling disappeared along with the pain and was replaced by a cool, pleasant sensation. When it touched my open cut, it felt almost like a bee sting for a few moments."

"Whatever it contains, Padre, it certainly works instantly. Small wonder Padre Garza was so impressed with it. Padre, have you ever heard anyone speak of Los Viejos?" (The Old Ones).

"Of course, Don Emilio. Everyone has heard of the Old Ones. From the time we are ninos, we hear of them. If we are not good children, we are told, they will come in the night and steal us."

"But do some people actually believe in them, Padre?"

"Certainly. Just as people in Ireland believe in leprechauns. At the university, I met an otherwise sensible young man from Ireland who claimed to have actually seen such a creature. He didn't look in his closet or search under his bed before he retired, but he was convinced that leprechauns really existed. All cultures seem to have their own superstitions."

"Padre, the Verranos are terrified of the Old Ones. To them, the Old Ones are far more sinister than any leprechaun. Supposedly, they're the guardians of the Tratamiento, and many other Aztec secrets. Secrets, it is said, they will kill to protect."

"I suppose similar threats have been heard since high priests of the Aztec Empire issued them five hundred years ago. Listeners readily believed the dire threats then, because they were being handed down from blood-drenched altars in pagan temples."

"Padre," responded Emilio, "five hundred years ago, the threats weren't idle and empty as they are now. The Aztec high priests were capable of enforcing their rules as brutally as they chose. The question is: How seriously should such threats be taken today?"

"Don Emilio, the threats and warnings are just as real today as they ever were if superstitious people believe them. Fear is the greatest enforcement agent in the world."

"It's hard for me to believe that people can be so naive."

"Only because you have always lived in a modern society, Don Emilio. Superstitions seem foolish to us because our knowledge gives us the ability to reason. Ignorance negates that great ability. And yet, simplicity is always preferable to excessive rationalism. In our own Catholic religion, the most devout are the ones whose strong faith permits absolute belief without any caution. One of my theology professors at the seminary told us that true faith would wither in an atmosphere predominantly composed of rationalism, but flourish in a garden of simplicity. Therefore, the meek of whom Our Lord speaks are the most pious of all. They deserve to inherit the earth. But since the beginning of the world the virtue of meekness has too often been confused with the handicap of weakness. This has been a sad truth since Cain slew Abel. Is it any wonder, then, that the Aztec high priests chose the meek as the most perfect sacrifices to their harsh gods? 'Meekness' was not rewarded by any inheritance of the earth. Instead, presumed weakness and innocence became the most precious gifts that could be placed upon the pagan altars."

"That's a paradoxical comparison, Padre."

"It's an invidious comparison, unless all of the premises are in place. Allow me to explain. Our religion is based on love. Our love for God and our love for others. But most of all, on God's love for man. Almighty God personifies justice and mercy. Aztec gods personified retaliation and retribution. Also, God gave us laws to live by. They are called the Ten Commandments. Hence, there are no surprises! But, as do all religions, we have sacrifices. The very core of our Faith is Christ's sacrifice on the Cross. Holy Communion, which we receive at each Mass, is an unbloody sacrifice re-presenting Our Lord's Passion on Calvary. Every day He demonstrates His eternal love for us by inviting His faithful children to partake of His sacred banquet.

"The Aztec paganism had no written rules and, therefore, many surprises. The Aztecs worshiped bloodthirsty gods who demanded sacrifices, as many as 10,000 helpless and innocent victims a day on special holidays. Human blood was the mortar that held their pagan system together, along with equal parts of fear, hatred, and uncertainty. People were not permitted to understand the requirements of the high priests or the gods because understanding might breed contempt and disobedience. Fear and uncertainty are still propagated by the practitioners of every ancient rite. It is only the people's irrational belief in the Old Ones that keeps them in a strangle-hold."

"How do you suppose the Old Ones grew to such prominence?" asked El Curandero, with a new, deep-seated respect for Padre Pedro.

"I can only speculate about that, Don Emilio. Perhaps it is like the majority of the world's secret societies. A handful of members form an executive tribunal and command the organization. Sometimes one strong individual becomes the sole dictator and rules until he is overthrown. In either case, the organization's rank and file do the bidding of their superiors to curry favor and to ascend to higher positions, hoping, of course, that one day they will become part of the elite or ruling class. Such a group can go on forever if the rulers are ruthless enough.

"I believe that no group can maintain total anonymity without a code of silence, similar to the Omerta of Sicily. If a member is suspected of breaking the code, or even contemplating such a transgression, he is eliminated immediately. Without mercy! In all probability, such executions are publicized among the other members to provide object lessons for all, as well as to silence the potential traitor. People simply disappear and are never seen again. Don Emilio, if they treat their own members with such open callousness, they would not hesitate to murder anyone else."

"So in essence, Padre," Emilio capsulized, "it would seem that the same callous bloodthirstiness that was so characteristic in the formation of the pagan society continues to play a vital part in perpetuating its worst evils."

"On a much smaller scale, Don Emilio, but just as frightening. As I said earlier, the advice you received from your friends in Dzibilchaltun was far from empty or idle."

"Don't worry, Padre, I'll be careful."

"More than that, mi amigo. Whenever you are away from here, sleep with one eye open, and with one hand on your pistol. As you know, desperate people often commit desperate acts."

➤

For the balance of the year, Emilio Duarte made short trips to the small towns and villages in the northern part of the Yucatan. Not once did he venture beyond a point that would preclude his return to Tunkas by nightfall. All the while he continued to make friends among the poor people who so badly needed and appreciated his modern medicine and growing medical skills.

Occasionally on these visits, he would slip in questions about the Tratamiento, Los Viejos, or anything else that might provoke an unguarded response. In many such instances, he saw a light of recognition flash in the eyes of his host, but each time it was just as quickly extinguished. Padre Pedro was right, Emilio often reflected; the fear of the bloodthirsty gods and their agents was still very much in evidence.

➤

One evening in early January, Padre Pedro's housekeeper knocked on Emilio's door and announced that a visitor wished to see him in the rectory parlor. As he entered the room, a very large man heaved himself off the uncomfortable couch and bowed.

"One hundred thousand pardons for imposing upon you without warning or invitation, Señor Duarte," said this strange-looking man with the chalk-like skin and pink eyes of an albino.

380

"No apology is necessary, Señor____? I'm sorry, but I don't know your name," responded Emilio.

"I am called El Blanco," replied the albino. "I have some information that you want."

"What information would that be, Señor Blanco?"

"If you will pay me a large sum of money, I will take you to a man who knows where to find one of the Old Ones' messengers."

Duarte forced himself to conceal his surprise and feelings of great interest. When he responded his voice was calm and steady.

"Will that man also expect a large payment?"

"But of course, Señor! Who can afford to work for nothing? Only the idle rich, who live on their ranchos grandes."

"Where do I find this man, Señor Blanco?"

"First things first, Señor Duarte. Let us decide on a fair price for my intercession and my friend's information. Let us not wander about in the darkness."

Emilio was pleased that payment was Blanco's main priority; otherwise, he would have suspected that Blanco might be plotting against him. Now that seemed unlikely.

"What kind of a reward do you want, Blanco?"

"Telling you about Los Viejos could be very dangerous, Señor Duarte. My friend and I are willing to do so only because we want to leave the Yucatan and go to live in Mexico City. To do that we must have 1,000 pesos — each."

Emilio began to haggle with the man in an attempt to get him to lower his demands; however, Blanco was adamant about the amount. The price was not really that high, but the prolonged discussion gave Emilio an additional opportunity to evaluate the strange man's motivation. An hour later, convinced that the 1,000 pesos were all that really mattered to Blanco, Emilio Duarte finally agreed.

"My friend," said Blanco, "lives amid the Pyramids of Coba."

"The Pyramids of Coba are a hundred miles away. Surely you don't intend to make such a journey tonight?" queried Emilio.

"Oh no, Señor Duarte, the trip requires several hours. If you wish, we can meet there tomorrow."

"You said your friend lives amid the Pyramids, Blanco. I didn't know that such habitation was permitted."

"How much do you know about Coba, Señor?"

"Not a great deal. I have never been there. I presume it's a place where a few crumbling pyramids are located."

Emilio Duarte was busy pouring tequila into two small glasses as he responded to El Blanco's question; otherwise he would have seen the look of intense hatred which spread across the albino's usually colorless features. Before he looked up from his task, his visitor's mask of impassiveness was once again in place.

"It is a bit more than that, Señor Duarte. It is an area of some thirty square miles, containing five small lakes and many pyramids. One of them is nearly 150 feet high and has a Mayan temple on its summit. At one time, Coba was the principal trade and cultural center of the Quintana Roo. It is still an important place in the Mayan and Aztec heritage."

"I'm sorry if I offended you, Blanco. I didn't intend to."

"I did not take offense, Señor."

Emilio reached across Padre Pedro's desk and handed his peculiar visitor a tray containing a glass of tequila, a pinch of salt, and a section of lemon. He retained an identical setup for himself. He lifted the glass of the fiery liquid in salute.

"To a safe and profitable journey, El Blanco."

Each man licked the salt, tossed down the tequila, and then sucked on the sour lemon, all the while grinning with pleasure.

"I see you have learned to appreciate some of our local customs," remarked El Blanco.

"A number of them seem to have grown on me, Blanco," laughed his host.

"Señor Duarte, will you drive your own automobile to Coba tomorrow, or use a different means of transportation?"

"I'm sure that if I coax it along and don't try to go too fast, the old relic will make it."

"Very well, Señor. I have a request. Please do not tell anyone about our agreement. Anything that concerns the Old Ones demands absolute silence. Since I do not dare to be seen with you in this village, I have drawn directions on a map that will guide you to Xcan. I will wait beside El Raton Moro Cantina on the plaza from eleven to twelve tomorrow night. If I am not there when you arrive, leave at once. Do not delay! If you are not there by midnight, I will leave. I will never contact you again, nor should you attempt to find me. That would be dangerous for both of us."

Emilio took the crude map, which El Blanco had drawn and examined it. The directions seemed clear and easy to follow.

"I agree to your terms, Blanco. I will be at the cantina in ample time. Now, please understand one thing. Together with the required number of pesos for you and your friend, I will also bring a very powerful pistol, one quite capable of blowing your head completely off your shoulders. At the first sign of trouble, whether you are responsible for it or not, I will kill you. Even if I die, so do you."

"You have made a believer of me, Señor Duarte. I am only a humble peluquero, a barber, not a warrior. Con su permiso, I will leave now and return to my temporary dwelling, under the safety of the night's dark blanket. Hasta mañana, Señor."

After the man left the rectory, Emilio returned to the Padre's study and reviewed the entire conversation in his mind. Either El Blanco was actually very frightened because he was telling the truth, or he was one of the Yucatan's finest actors.

Blanco had seemed genuinely concerned about the payment of his pesos. That was a definite plus. Also, he had

383

been adamant about telling no one else of their plans. That might be a plus, but it could also be a minus. If Blanco was what he claimed to be, his reluctance was understandable. And if not, he could not afford unnecessary witnesses.

Emilio considered confiding in Padre Pedro but rejected the notion. His mission might be dangerous, and it would be unfair to involve the priest more than necessary. He finally concluded that it was probably safe to go with El Blanco since Rosa Perez, the Padre's housekeeper, had seen him. Should he fail to return, she would be able to provide an accurate description of the unique individual to the police.

He poured another glass of tequila before opening a writing pad and unscrewing the top of his fountain pen. He slowly sipped the liquor as he wrote a short letter. He described his visitor's appearance and detailed the plan to which they had agreed. He made a complete list of the information he had gathered over the preceding months and asked that it be forwarded to Cardinal Cabrini, should he fail to return from his midnight rendezvous.

When he finished, he placed the note in an envelope and wrote: "To Be Opened in the Event of My Death." Confident that he had done everything possible, he left the note on the desk and went to bed. The next morning he rose at dawn, attended Mass, and then joined Padre Pedro for breakfast.

"You found the letter I left on your desk, Padre?"

"The one with the ominous inscription? I did. What prompted you to write it?"

"A little suspicion and a great deal of overcautiousness."

"Can you tell me any more at this time, Don Emilio?"

"Unfortunately not. When I return, I will share what may be a great adventure with you. If I am not back within three days, please open the letter."

"Very well, Don Emilio, although I am burning with curiosity. I will keep your mysterious communication here in my pocket and guard it with my life until you return."

As the priest finished speaking, Rosa Perez entered the room and placed before them a large platter of ranchos huevos, a spicy egg dish which was a favorite of both men. Then she waited until Padre Pedro had blessed the food before she spoke.

"Padre, the rope in the bell tower has fallen down. That is why Jorge Vasquez did not ring the bells for Mass this morning. Because of his broken foot, he could not climb up to fix it, but he thinks he can find someone else to do it for you."

"Is he still in the chapel, Rosa?"

"Yes, Padre."

"Good. Thank him for his concern and tell him I will replace the rope myself before we need the bells again at dusk."

"Also Padre, with your permission, my sister Rita has asked me to come to her home this afternoon for a short visit. If you do not object, I will go after I prepare your midday meal."

"I have many sick calls to make today, Rosa. I will not return until late afternoon. If you wish, you may go to Rita's home this morning and stay until suppertime."

"Gracias, Padre, that is what I will do. I will return in time to prepare a fine plump chicken for your supper. Please excuse me. I will give your message to Jorge Vasquez and go to Rita's."

"When are you planning to leave, Don Emilio?" asked the Padre.

"I must make some stops in this area to administer medicine before I leave. Then I will have several hours of travel ahead of me. I'd better leave by noon. Many thanks for your hospitality and all of your help, Padre. If all goes well, I'll see you in two or three days."

"Bueno, Don Emilio. Vaya con Dios."

➢

It was early afternoon when Rosa and her sister finished their lunch and went into Rita's living room to relax.

"Rita, that was one of the best meals you have ever made. You know how much I enjoy roast lamb."

"You always have. By the way, I have another treat for you. Someone recently sent me a special gift of coffee. Since I never drink coffee, I saved it for you. I would like to tell the ones who gave it to me how it was. Will you taste it for me?"

Eager to help her sister, Rosa agreed.

"Good, I'll put some in a pot to brew."

Rita went to the kitchen to prepare the coffee and returned a few moments later.

"What is new at the mission? Anything unusual going on with the Padre or his guest?"

"The most unusual thing that has happened recently was a visit last night from a very strange-looking man. He had snow-white hair, almost white skin, and little pink eyes. He was not a man one might easily forget."

"What did he want with the Padre?" asked Rita.

"He didn't want the Padre. He came to see Señor Duarte."

"Did he see him?"

"Yes, they talked in the Padre's study for over an hour."

"I wonder what he wanted?"

"I don't know, but I have a feeling that Señor Duarte is going somewhere to meet him today."

Rita excused herself and went to the kitchen. She returned a few moments later with a steaming cup of the special coffee that she handed to Rosa.

"Drink it while it's hot!" she urged.

Rosa took a sip of the hot liquid and discovered that it was quite bitter in spite of a great deal of sugar, which she could taste as well. She wrinkled her nose and drank some more.

"How is it, Rosa?" asked her sister.

"I'm not sure. It has an unusual taste."

"Finish it up and I'll get another cupful for you."

Rosa complied and handed the empty cup to Rita, who left the room once again and strode toward the kitchen, where she remained for several minutes.

When she returned, her sister's face was contorted with pain, and she was writhing in agony on the couch.

"Something is terribly wrong with the coffee, Rita. Who gave it to you?"

"Nothing is wrong with the coffee, Rosa. It is doing what it's supposed to do. It was a gift from the Old Ones. They sent it especially for you. They were sure you would be able to identify El Blanco, and they could not permit that. I am truly sorry, but as you can see, I had no choice. We must protect our secrets from outsiders."

"And to do that, you would willingly kill your own sister?" Rosa gasped in disbelief. "How long have you worked for these wicked Old Ones, Rita?" gasped her stricken sister.

"Since our days together at the mission school. It was they who arranged your employment with the Padre. Now, their foresight has been rewarded."

"I can't believe that you have poisoned me!" groaned Rosa.

"Again, I say that I'm sorry, but the Old Ones must be obeyed. We must protect our secrets. No price is too great."

Rosa lapsed into unconsciousness, slipped from the couch, and fell heavily to the floor. A moment later she shuddered for the last time and then lay still. Rita went to her front window and pulled down the shade. Minutes later, two men carrying a carpet knocked on her door. She opened it quickly and admitted the pair.

"Los Viejos will be pleased, Rita. You have done well," said the taller of the two men, gazing down at Rosa's sprawled form.

They moved the dead woman's limp body to the edge of the rug and then carefully rolled it up inside. Then they moved the roll to one side and spread the rug they had brought with them.

"Enjoy your beautiful new carpet, Señora," said the tall man.

Moments later, as Rita watched through her window, the pair loaded her old carpet into an ancient truck and drove off down the street.

A single tear emerged from the corner of Rita's right eye and coursed slowly down her cheek. Killing her only sister had been difficult. Rosa had been her best friend, as well as her sister, for nearly fifty years. Serving the ancient gods and their priests was sometimes difficult, she mused. But Rosa would have identified El Blanco to the police. She really had no other choice.

Chapter XXVI

➢

The Pyramids Of Coba

Quintana Roo Province
Northern Yucatan Peninsula
Mexico
January 9, 1942

Emilio Duarte lay in a clump of bushes on the outskirts of Xcan. It was 11:30 P.M. He had been in this place of concealment for over two hours. Peering out from beneath some low-hanging branches, he had maintained a constant surveillance of El Raton Moro Cantina.

Throughout the evening, foot traffic in and out of the double bat-wing doors had been almost constant. El Blanco had arrived about forty-five minutes earlier and seated himself on an idler's bench, which stood against the wall of the front porch. Several of the patrons nodded to him as they entered or left, but no one engaged him in prolonged conversation.

Satisfied that it was safe to approach the cantina, Emilio retraced his steps to the grove of trees where he had hidden the old Ford and then drove slowly into town. He turned into the narrow alley, which ran along the side of the cantina and stopped.

El Blanco came down the steps at once, opened the car door, and sat down on the seat next to Emilio.

"This is certainly a wonderful automobile, Señor Duarte," he remarked.

"Why do you say that?"

"The radiator is still cold, after many hours of driving."

Knowing that he had been caught in a deception, the Spaniard admitted that he had been watching the cantina from cover.

"You are very observant for a humble peluquero, Blanco."

"And you, Señor, are very careful for a misionario."

For a moment, Emilio was taken aback. The word misionario, in Spanish, usually referred to someone on a diplomatic mission. Then Emilio relaxed, assuming that El Blanco's reference was to his healing missions on behalf of Padre Pedro.

"How far do we have to drive?"

"We must continue down this road for an hour. It is nearly thirty miles. Then we must walk for the last two miles."

"Are you sure your friend will be there?"

"He will be there, never fear. Will you pay us as soon as I take you to him?"

"I will pay both of you as soon as I'm sure that he is a legitimate source of information."

"No one could ask for more, Señor."

Reassured once again of El Blanco's greed, Emilio relaxed.

"What is your friend's name?"

"He is called Sergio and he is a remendon, a bootmaker."

"Why do you wish to go to the city?"

"Neither remendones nor peluqueros are in great demand in this place. But in la Ciudad de Mexico, everyone needs fine boots and good-looking hair. So we will go there and become rich."

Emilio no longer felt concerned for his own safety but rather about the accuracy of the information he would receive from Sergio. Both of these men are desperate to leave the Yucatan, he decided, and they might be willing to resort to anything in order to accomplish those ambitions. Every word they uttered might well be a lie.

One of El Blanco's statements was certainly correct. It was exactly an hour later when they reached the turnoff that led to Coba. Fifty yards from the entrance, the old, narrow, rock-strewn road became impassable for vehicles. Unable to maneuver the old Ford around a jumble of boulders, Emilio simply parked it where it was.

"Stay in the middle of the trail," cautioned El Blanco as they began walking, "and watch out for snakes. I am glad to see you are wearing high boots."

For the next two miles, Emilio walked behind his guide with his eyes glued to the sides of the road. Thirty minutes later, as they drew abreast of a small, decrepit shack, a large, bearded man came around one of the corners and walked toward them.

As the man approached, Emilio detected the odor of tequila. At ten feet it was noticeable; at three feet it was overpowering. But his speech was not slurred as he spoke.

"Hola, Blanco. Buenos noches, Señor Duarte. Welcome to Coba."

"This is my friend Sergio, Señor Duarte."

"I'm glad we could meet, Sergio. Hopefully you will be able to help me."

"I bring you great tidings, Señor Duarte, news that will make you jump for joy."

"Please share it with me."

"As you can see, I have had a lot of tequila tonight, but not nearly as much as my drinking companion, who is now sleeping off the effects. When he wakes, he may be quite talkative. That man, Señor, is a messenger for the Old Ones."

"That is exciting news! You are fairly sure that the man will talk to me?"

"I am sure that you will learn a great deal tonight, Señor."

"Where is the messenger now?"

"He is asleep on the altar of the ancient temple."

"Where is the temple?"

391

Sergio waited for a few moments before he answered. Then, as they rounded the far end of a crumbling wall, he pointed skyward.

"Up there, Señor, on top of the Great Pyramid."

They had now reached the base of a steep flight of stone steps that led upward toward the pagan pyramid's dizzying summit. Each step was more than a foot high and less than six inches wide. The ancient stones were nearly obscured by long, green, slippery, jungle plant tendrils that sprouted from every stony crack and crevice. Emilio Duarte, sensing a pervasive presence of terrible evil, shuddered as he stood in the dim, eerie moonlight.

"Do we actually have to climb this man-made mountain?"

"Only if you wish to confront the messenger of the Old Ones."

Emilio turned to face El Blanco.

"Are you climbing up with us?"

"No, Señor Duarte, that was not part of our agreement."

"All right, Sergio, I am ready to try it if you are."

It was a long and arduous climb that required all of Emilio's determination and attention. Many years ago, while in college, he spent a summer in Switzerland and attempted to scale Mount Blanc. He learned then of his aversion to heights. He was not phobic nor did he suffer vertigo. He simply disliked high places. During the tortuous transit up the pyramid, he looked neither up nor down, preferring to rivet his attention on each individual step.

Since the entire pyramid was shrouded in darkness whenever a cloud obscured the moon, he had to rely on his sense of touch rather than sight. Such was the case when he reached the wide platform in front of the temple. For a moment, he did not realize that he was on the summit. This lack of knowledge proved to be his undoing as he was seized from behind and slammed, headfirst, into the rough temple wall, causing him to lose consciousness.

When he recovered his senses several minutes later, he was propped up in a corner of a small, dimly lighted room. The meager light, he saw, was provided by several coal-oil-burning lanterns, a pair of which hung upon each of the low walls, intermittently sputtering and spewing out thick clouds of black, noxious smoke.

Taking stock of his predicament, he realized that his pistol was gone, his money belt was missing, and his hands were bound securely behind his back. As his eyes adjusted to the dim light, he saw that he had been dragged inside the temple. He peered cautiously out from beneath hooded eyelids and discovered that the walls were covered with Mayan or Aztec carvings and drawings. Hanging on the walls, amidst the drawings, were sinister looking implements which reminded him of crude surgical instruments.

Emilio was lying against the back wall of the room. Directly across from him, parallel to the front wall, he saw what appeared to be a stone altar. Behind the altar sat three people wearing Aztec ceremonial masks. Stone benches ran for a short distance along both of the side walls. Upon these benches sat a number of individuals. Among them, Emilio recognized El Blanco, Sergio, and Rita Perez, the sister of Padre Pedro's housekeeper.

El Blanco rose from his seat, bowed reverently to each of the three masked figures, then turned and came toward Emilio. Blanco pulled him to his feet and then pushed the Spaniard to a position a few feet in front of the altar.

"Thank you for joining us, El Curandero," said a familiar and sarcastic voice behind the right-hand mask. "We are the Council of Three. You are here tonight because the Old Ones have decided to satisfy your rampant curiosity. It is an honor to welcome so distinguished a guest. Please comport yourself while we conclude another piece of urgent business."

El Blanco seized his arm once again and shoved Emilio toward one of the stone benches.

"Rita," said the center mask, "please come forward. We were very pleased with your performance this afternoon. Killing a relative, or any loved one for that matter, is never a pleasant duty, although from time to time we have all had to do it. You have been a good and loyal servant for many years.

"Unfortunately, our relationship cannot continue. After all of the misfortunes that transpired in Tunkas this afternoon, we feel that you have become a liability — or, if you prefer, a loose end. We simply cannot afford to allow you to live any longer. All of us are very sorry that it must end this way. We have always liked you. But we Old Ones can never shirk our duties."

As he finished speaking, Rita Perez began screaming.

"No! No! No! Don't kill me! No! No! No!"

Unmoved by her pleas, the Council of Three leader motioned to the two men who had delivered Rita's carpet and disposed of her sister's body. They seized the startled, struggling, screaming woman and dragged her to a table behind the altar. While one of them held her tightly, the other took down an implement from its position on the wall. When he was ready, he grasped a handful of Rita's hair and pulled back her head, exposing her throat to his whimsy. Although she continued to struggle and scream, the man managed to place the tool's cutting edge on her neck, then drew the blade quickly across her jugular vein, neatly severing it.

Before the gaping wound could spout blood, the executioner tilted her head forward once again and draped her lifeless body across the table, allowing the blood to empty into a handy trough which, evidently, the temple's designers had provided for that very purpose.

Emilio tried to fight down the nausea evoked by the helpless woman's heartless murder. This was a sample, he knew, of the pagan horror which terrorized the frightened people of the Yucatan and turned them into helpless, hopeless simpletons. He could have kicked himself for not being perceptive enough to grasp the enormity of the silent panic he had seen, or the complete control that paralyzing fear engendered.

The right-hand mask now signaled to El Blanco, and once again Emilio was pushed forward. From beneath the altar, the man withdrew a number of items and laid them out before him. Emilio saw his own pistol, his personal papers and passport, his letters of credit, and the letters of introduction from Cardinal Cabrini. He also saw his money belt, which still contained several dozen $20 gold pieces.

The most disturbing item of evidence, before the masked men, was the letter Emilio had written to the Cardinal. The letter he had entrusted to Padre Pedro. A communication, which the priest had pledged to protect with his life if, need be. He felt a sudden despair, knowing in his heart that his friend was dead. His Colt .45 pistol and two thousand pesos were the only things he had brought with him. Everything else had been locked up in the rectory. These fiends would have none of those other things if the Padre were still alive.

"What have you done to Padre Pedro, you blood-thirsty, pagan bastards?" he demanded defiantly.

"First of all," said the man in the center, "please understand that we abhor violence. It is distasteful to all of us. But you must realize that, at certain times, it is our only means of preservation."

"In answer to your question," said the mask with the familiar voice, "the Padre had a most unfortunate accident this afternoon. When he climbed up the bell tower to reconnect the rope, it seems he lost his balance and fell. The poor man broke his neck."

"The wrath of God will descend on all of you and mete out just vengeance for murdering a priest!" Emilio exploded. "No way in hell did that bell rope break by accident."

"No," left-hand mask laughed viciously, "it was no accident, and neither was the injury to the foot of Vasquez, the Padre's handyman."

"And now, I must be killed to protect your secrets, correct?"

"Of course!" said the familiar voice. "You must serve as an example to all those who still dare to defy us. But we will keep the promises we made to you. Before you die, you will learn much about us and our secrets. No one should die for nothing."

Turning away from his intended victim for a moment, he issued a warning to the individuals who were seated on the side benches.

"With the exception of Alboroto, Blanco, and Casquete, the rest of you may leave. Never forget what you have seen here tonight. Never forget what it means to challenge the power or the patience of the Old Ones. Never, never forget! Now go! Vamos!"

Minutes later, everyone except Blanco and the two executioners of Rita Perez were gone. The shorter of these two wore a black skullcap, which accounted for the name Casquete. The villainous facial appearance and menacing attitude of his partner in murder made it easy to believe that he was, as his name suggested, an agitator.

"With only seven of us left in the room," the center mask said to his companions, "it is time to unmask and relax, mis amigos."

As they stripped off the masks and laid them aside, Emilio understood why the muffled voice behind the right-hand mask sounded familiar. It belonged to his host at the birthday fiesta in Dzibilchaltun, Julio Verrano, the man who gave him the vial of the Tratamiento and mentioned the Old Ones for the first time!

"The people of the Yucatan will miss you when you are gone, Don Emilio. You have been very good to them. I think we might have been able to avoid killing the young priest if he had been alone. But such was not the case after you came here. You were getting too close to the old secrets. Alas, my friend, we have had to kill priests before. They always send out another padre to look after the needs of the people. But I fear that there will never be another Curandero. You have done us all a bad turn."

Emilio realized that there was almost no chance of making an escape, but he had learned long ago that situations, which appear hopeless often, change after a sufficient lapse of time. And so, he reached two quick decisions. First, he would not plead or beg for his life. That wouldn't work, and it would rob him of his dignity. Secondly, he would play upon Don Julio's pride and encourage him to talk.

"You ungrateful wretch, Julio! After I cured your daughter, Mercata, the least you can do is tell me about the Old Ones!" he demanded.

"It is a long story, Señor Duarte," replied Don Julio.

"I have plenty of time!" quipped the brave captive.

Don Julio smiled and continued.

"To understand the Old Ones, you must know our history. About 650 B.C., the first civilized people in the New World appeared. They were the Mayas of Mexico and Central America. This ancient people had a written language and a calendar more accurate than our own. They produced bountiful crops with advanced irrigation systems and developed amazingly accurate techniques in astronomy, mathematics, and construction. Some were talented artists and sculptors. Many of the drawings still visible on these walls are original Mayaglyphs. Hundreds of their temple-pyramids, if they still existed, would put those of ancient Egypt to shame."

He paused to give his statement time to sink in and continued.

"During the fifteen hundred years that their civilization endured, they also discovered a method of combining various herbs and fungi to create a substance that cures many ailments. It has always been called the Tratamiento. It stops pain and bleeding, but it does other things, too. Tell him of your brother, Blanco."

"Many years ago," began El Blanco, "when we were very young, my brother fell out of a tall tree. He did not move after that for several minutes. I ran home to fetch my parents, who rushed back to my brother's side. By then he was not breathing. His skin was as white as my own. My father could not feel his son's heart beating. We knew that he was dead and we were filled with sorrow. Just as my father lifted him in his arms, Don Julio appeared. He poured several drops of the Tratamiento into my brother's mouth, and moments later he came back to life."

"Of course," said Don Julio, picking up the narration, "the boy was not dead. But he was in a state of deep unconsciousness or perhaps a coma. Had the Tratamiento not revived him, he surely would have died. Undoubtedly, you experimented with the vial I gave you. I am sure that it worked for you as well."

"It did," Emilio admitted, playing for time. "It stopped the pain I have had for many years."

"Allow me to continue with your history lesson. By 900 A.D., Mayan power had dwindled and the Toltecs became dominant under their famous leader Quetzalcoatl, who established his capital here on the Yucatan Peninsula, at Chichen Itza. Toltecs remained in control and protected the Mayas' discoveries and secrets until the Aztecs came to power under Montezuma I, in 1450.

"Then in 1519 your countrymen, led by Hernando Cortez, came to our country and destroyed it. Many say they saved us. But we did not ask them to come, and we did not ask them to overwhelm us. When the Spanish conquerors came they tried to destroy everything that the ruling class of royal citizens had established during the past several hundred years. We were the ones who supported the emperors. We were the ones who chose the high priests. We were the ones who organized the Aztec warriors and led the revolt that nearly crushed those foreign invaders on the night you call La Noche de Triste. They thought they could destroy our will to resist by destroying our temples and our pyramids; but they were wrong. Control and influence became covert and more subtle, but we remained strong. As we are now, and always will be.

"Just before the Noche de Triste, the Old Ones discovered that the high priest of Tenochtitlan's main temple, a great fool named Attapa, had given the secret of the Tratamiento to the Spanish priest, Diego Garza. Of course, Attapa and his entire family were executed for such stupidity. You see, it has not only been your priests who have paid the price."

"How comforting!" retorted the defiant prisoner.

Don Julio ignored the interruption and continued.

"The Old Ones made certain that Padre Garza perished in the ensuing fight, but they did not know if he had told anyone else of the Tratamiento. When the Spaniards returned the next year, the other padre, Olmedo, tried desperately to locate the high priest and his family. This made the Old Ones certain that he knew enough to be curious, but did not have any Tratamiento or possess any worthwhile knowledge about it. Your own deep-seated curiosity seems to call into question that conclusion, reached so long ago. We will not ask you to enlighten us, for two reasons. First, you would certainly not tell the truth, and second, it does not matter anyway, as long as we remain strong and on guard.

"For as long as the world lasts, we Old Ones will continue to protect the secret of the Tratamiento and will always perpetuate our responsibilities as ruling class members to help the common people. We will stop at nothing to punish those who transgress against us, and we will ruthlessly kill any who trespass against us, or betray our rituals. It was the way of our ancestors, and it is our way as well."

"How are the reins of control passed down from one generation to the next?" Emilio asked, fighting to buy more time.

"Each of us appoints his own successor. Alboroto, Blanco, and Casquete are the ones we three have chosen.

"Well, Señor Duarte, it is a shame, but since we have kept our promise and told you about the Old Ones, we must now conclude our visit. I wish this were the time of our high holidays when we worship the ancient gods and offer human sacrifices. Your living heart would have been such a worthy gift to them. Of course, we no longer require the vast number of people that our ancestors once did, but good sacrificial victims are getting harder to find."

He smiled malevolently at Emilio and then signaled to the three eager protégés who came forward at once.

Emilio had seen abundant proof that these assassins were well schooled in their art and had ample experience. He also knew that they were used to victims who shrank from this blatant brutality. He decided that before he died, he would make at least two of the three suffer. Consequently, as Blanco reached out to seize his arm, Emilio moved back a full step. Then, as Blanco moved forward to follow him, his victim sprang forward and slammed his forehead into the face of the albino. His own skin split in the process, but he opened his eyes in time to see Blanco's nose flatten out and then burst in a fountain of blood. Whenever he looked in a mirror, the future Old One would remember this night, thought the gallant Spaniard with some satisfaction.

As El Blanco collapsed to the floor of the temple, in a bloody heap, Casquete threw all caution to the wind and leaped forward to subdue this troublesome intruder. The eager toady arrived just in time to receive a vicious kick to the groin from one of the high boots that Blanco had been so pleased to see Emilio wearing.

Since their henchmen were now writhing in pain and groaning, it was necessary for the Old Ones themselves to rush toward Alboroto and help him to push the smiling, victorious Emilio Duarte off of the high ledge and down to a martyr's death — while the Old Ones and their one remaining toady stood on the platform, trembling in the face of such courage.

➤

The following morning, when Padre Pedro did not appear for Mass, his parishioners, thinking that he might be ill, went next door to the rectory. When prolonged knocking on the front door failed to produce any response, they timidly entered the building and satisfied themselves that it was empty.

That was curious, they thought, since the Padre's old Ford, the car El Curandero had been driving, was parked next to the mission. But El Señor Duarte was nowhere to be found either.

Then Jorge Vasquez, the handy man, still hobbling along on crutches because of his broken foot, made a terrible discovery. In the bell tower, directly beneath the belfry, lay the body of Padre Pedro. Police, summoned immediately, questioned everyone who might be able to shed some light on the Padre's tragic death.

It was Jorge Vasquez who contributed the most important piece of information. He explained that the bell rope had broken the previous morning and, because of his fractured foot, he was unable to repair it. Instead, he reported the difficulty to the Padre, who decided to repair the rope himself.

"Well," said the police inspector, Don Pacho, who was in charge, "it was obviously just a sad accident. The Padre simply slipped and fell from the ladder. In the process, the poor man broke his neck and died. I don't see how it could have happened any other way."

He turned to his brother-in-law from Dzibilchaltun, Don Julio Verrano, who was in Tunkas this morning with his wife, Doña Iñez.

"Can you suggest any other explanation, Don Julio?"

"No, Don Pacho," replied his grief-stricken relative, "That must be how it happened. I will never understand why so many of the good ones are taken from us at such a young age. Rest assured that Doña Iñez and I will pray for him."

Pacho turned to Jorge.

"Have you seen Doña Rosa this morning?"

"No, Señor, I have not. I was so upset about the Padre that I did not even think about the Señora."

"Could she have spent the night somewhere else, Jorge?"

"The only possible place would be at the home of her sister, Rita. She lives in the small white house on the Calle de Delfin Verde. Rosa has no other close friends."

"I will drive by the house on the way back to the police building and see if Rita knows where Rosa is."

Pacho got into his vehicle and drove to the house owned by Rita Perez. When he determined that none of her neighbors were watching, he did not stop. Instead, he drove directly to the village hall.

He entered the building and went at once to the office of his supervisor.

"Jefe," he reported, "big trouble. Padre Pedro fell from the bell tower and broke his neck. His house guest, Señor Duarte, is also gone, and the Perez sisters are both missing."

"The Padre's death is a terrible blow, Pacho. But I'm sure the others will turn up in a day or two. You're not suggesting any connection between these events, are you? Or perhaps," he added sarcastically, "foul play by your imaginary Old Ones."

"Jefe, I am not suggesting anything. I am reporting what I know and only what I know. What do you want to do about this?"

"Send a telegram to Padre Pedro's superior in Mexico City. Notify the Rurales about the possibility of some missing persons, and sit in front of this big fan until the sun goes down and it cools off. Any more questions, Pacho?"

"No, Jefe. You are a marvel at making things clear!"

The lazy oaf was a marvel all right, thought Pacho, a marvel at looking the other way whenever trouble appeared.

Don Julio was right, he decided. If the average official was thrown into the sea with a hundred pounds of gold strapped to his back, he would show no concern until he had to make a choice of living or abandoning the gold.

Most of them would drown while they agonized over the decision.

One thing was certain: Jefe was totally brainwashed about the Old Ones. To him, they were about as believable as Santa Claus.

Pacho went to his desk and wrote out one telegram to Padre Pedro's superiors and a second one to the federal police, as directed by El Jefe. He left the building and, disdaining his car, decided to walk the two blocks to the telegraph office.

He strolled along the shady side of the street on this mild and pleasant morning, wondering who had disposed of the bodies of the Perez sisters and Duarte. Then he quickly dismissed such ideas from his head. It was not even safe to wonder, when the Old Ones were part of the equation. Don Julio was married to his sister Iñez, and that made him a close relative, but Julio was still as treacherous as a viper, blood or no blood. Pacho would simply do what he was told and keep his nose out of the Old Ones' affairs—a policy guaranteed to keep him healthy and make him very wealthy.

Late in the day, a hearse arrived from Campeche. The driver drove straight to the village morgue and claimed the body of Padre Pedro on behalf of his Order. The next day, after a solemn requiem Mass, the unfortunate young priest was laid to rest in a hail of tears that fell like spring rain.

➢

When Emilio Duarte failed to report back to Cardinal Cabrini, either by cable or letter, for over a month, the cleric knew that evil had befallen his emissary. Had he been alive, Emilio would have found a way of communicating. Even though a global war now raged, lines of reciprocation never closed between the Princes of the Church. The Cardinal wrote to his counterpart in Mexico City and requested any assistance that might help to locate his good friend and valued associate. "At least," he wrote, "I would like to know whether or not he is alive."

Three months passed before he received an answer.

Although they were not certain, it seemed that Emilio Duarte had stayed in the village of Tunkas with the local priest for several months. This young priest had fallen from a bell tower and been killed. According to trusted officials in Tunkas, on the same day the cleric's body was found, two sisters and a man, believed to be Emilio Duarte, disappeared. Although an intensive investigation was still underway, no clues as to the whereabouts of the missing persons had yet been found.

The letter went on to assure him that all possible pressure was being brought to bear on the authorities and that no stone would be left unturned in the continuing search for his friend. The communication ended with an extension of warmest personal regards from the Cardinal of Mexico.

True to their word, the Cardinal's staff in Mexico City sent periodic bulletins in reference to the investigation for the duration of the war and for a year beyond. By then, Cardinal Cabrini knew that it was an exercise in futility.

➢

In the summer of 1946, when the war-torn world had begun to return to normal, Cardinal Cabrini sent another investigator to pick up Emilio Duarte's trail in the village of Tunkas. Once a week, for the next two months, his operative called each Saturday evening on Trans-Atlantic cable. Each time his news was slightly more encouraging, until one Saturday when he reported his first real breakthrough. A man named Alboroto had offered to help him for a payment of a thousand pesos. "I'll call again tomorrow after the meeting and tell you all that I've learned," the man promised. The next day Cardinal Cabrini waited in vain beside his telephone for a call that never came, that day or any other day. Another investigator had disappeared.

➤

Ten more years elapsed before a third man went out to try his skill against the unknown. Cardinal Cabrini was reluctant to give his permission to still another candidate, but this one had a reputation for accomplishing the impossible and was convinced that he could succeed. The aging Cardinal, now in a state of dwindling health, was perhaps influenced as much by wishful thinking and the eager young man's exuberance, as he was by his heretofore perpetually sound logic. Whatever the reason, the young man went forth, never reported any progress, and was never heard from again.

Cardinal Cabrini was greatly depressed by the loss of this last representative. A project that had begun with such high hopes had come crashing down. For the disappointed Cardinal, it would never become a phoenix rising anew from its own flames.

➤

On October 2, 1958, the old Cardinal rose from a sickbed and journeyed to Rome to witness the consecration and installation of an old friend and protégé to the rank of bishop. The wonderful evening was spent amongst a multitude of life-long friends. As he prepared to leave the Vatican's Grand Hall, he felt a sharp pain in his chest. It was so severe that he collapsed. Loving hands lifted him very gently and placed him on a nearby sofa. A moment later, the Holy Father was at his side.

"Eminence, you gave me a scare, but then you always did have a flair for the dramatic," smiled Pope Pius XII.

"Holiness, I fear that this will be my last grand exit," grimaced his old friend.

"Is it that severe, Eminence?" asked the concerned Pontiff.

"Without any doubt, Holiness. Would you do me the inestimable honor of administering my Last Rites?"

"It is I who shall be honored, Eminence."

The Pontiff did as the Cardinal requested, then motioned the concerned bystanders away to share these final moments with his old friend.

"You have had a fine life and accomplished much, Luigi."

"You have done far more, and you have outlived me as well."

"Had you been elected to the Chair of St Peter, you would have done as well as I, perhaps better."

"I once thought so myself, Holiness. But now I know that I was wrong."

"In any case, I think Our Lord will be preparing a place for me at His Table very soon as well," said the Pope, squeezing his old friend's hand.

Another severe pain coursed through Cardinal Cabrini's body, and he shuddered once again. The Pope, knowing that the final moments were near, blessed him again and said, "Goodbye, Luigi, my dear friend."

"Goodbye, Eugenio, my dear friend."

The once worldly Cardinal looked over the Pontiff's shoulder and saw his protégé, the new Bishop of San Antonio. A young man, the Cardinal believed, who would also one day become a Prince of the Church.

Luigi Cardinal Cabrini rallied slightly and smiled at his young friend. Then he winked, smiled once more, and closed his eyes for the last time.

PART TEN

KEY TO AN ENIGMA

Chapter XXVII
➢
Antonio Garza

The Vatican
Rome, Italy
January 7, 1999

It was hard to believe that over forty years had passed since his consecration as bishop on the fateful night that his mentor, Luigi Cardinal Cabrini, had died. The old Cardinal certainly had been a prophet. Just two months ago, he had celebrated his own eightieth birthday, as well as his silver jubilee as Cardinal. He still clearly remembered Cardinal Cabrini's last night on earth, when Pope Pius XII had so accurately predicted his own death.

A death which occurred exactly one week later.

Perhaps, Emmanuel Cardinal Questa mused, we are all given such premonitions in our final days. But I am not ready for that, he thought; I still have too much to do.

He had very few regrets about his life, but he had one very persistent one. Perhaps, he thought, I set this appointment with today's guest to fulfill the dreams I had as a young seminarian, or to put them to rest once and for all.

The intercom on his desk buzzed, and he heard the voice of his secretary, Monsignor O'Reilly.

"Your visitor has arrived, Your Eminence. May I show him in?"

"Yes, Michael. Please do."

The two men who entered moments later could not have been more different in appearance. Monsignor Michael O'Reilly was quite tall and broad. His rugged Celtic features and flaming red hair made him look for all the world like the hard-nosed Irish rugby player he had been in the days before he answered God's call. His strength of faith and character, as well as his proficiency, were the principal reasons he held his important post.

The second man seemed shorter than his medium height, because of a very slender physique. His darkly handsome, finely chiseled features and delicate chin seemed almost wasted on a man. Cardinal Questa's gaze rested briefly on his visitor's slim, long-fingered, well-manicured hands, before ascending to look directly into a pair of steady, friendly, and confident dark eyes.

Cardinal Questa walked across the room and offered his hand. The guest dropped to one knee and bent to kiss the Cardinal's ring before he straightened up and smiled at the elderly cleric.

"Seeing you again, Your Eminence, is a great pleasure as well as a distinct honor."

"Thank you, Tony. It is good to see you again, too."

He turned to his secretary.

"Michael, this young man has had the ability to say exactly the right thing on every occasion for as long as I've known him."

When the Monsignor looked puzzled, the Cardinal continued.

"I'm sorry, Michael. I forgot that your assistant set up this meeting while you were on your annual Irish renewal, enjoying the craggy braes and gusty days on your beloved Aran Isles."

He smiled at his visitor.

"Tony, since Michael was not party to our correspondence, please tell him a bit about yourself and your family."

"I was born in San Antonio, Texas, Monsignor, hence the name. I am the youngest of seven brothers, born to parents with great respect for the higher education that they, themselves, had never been able to acquire. When each of my brothers and myself were born, my mother consecrated us to the Holy Spirit and prayed that we might be priests or, at least, well-educated men."

"All six of Antonio's brothers are now priests, Michael. All of them, at one time or another, worked for me while I was Bishop of San Antonio. The Garzas are famous throughout all of Texas and have been for hundreds of years. A Garza priest was the chaplain to the Alamo in 1836 while General Antonio Lopez de Santa Anna and his armies besieged it. Another Garza was a padre who ministered to the Conquistadors of Hernando Cortez."

"I remember those two Padre Garzas from my study of history, Eminence," recalled the Monsignor. "The Alamo's chaplain was also the confessor for Jim Bowie and his wife. Of course, I also know of your interest in the Padre Garza who served with Cortez."

"Your Eminence," Tony asked, "when you scheduled this audience with me, did you realize that today is the 515th anniversary of my ancestor's birth? He was born in Castile, on January 7, 1484."

"No, I didn't know, Tony, but I'm not really surprised. Such special days seem to follow me. Before you continue with your narrative, let me say to you, Monsignor, that our distinguished guest is really Dr. Antonio Garza. He holds a Ph.D. in History and is one of the world's most esteemed scholars in his field. Many years ago, when Tony was a stripling teenager, he shared his ambitions with me and I shared with him my curiosity about his famous ancestor. We struck a deal on that very day. I agreed to help in his quest for an education and he agreed to search for an answer to a very old mystery. His presence here today is, I hope, the culmination of many years of intensive research. Is it, Tony?"

"As you know, Eminence, I am at times painfully brutal in my desire to provide honest and complete answers."

The statement so obviously foreshadowed the negative comments that were about to follow that the Cardinal sagged in his chair. Antonio's research, he surmised, has ended in failure and he is ready to admit total defeat.

"I have completed all of my academic research, Your Eminence," Dr. Garza continued, "and I am now absolutely certain that I can solve the mystery. I'm so sure, that I have taken a six-month leave of absence from Texas State University to allow time for field research. I'm free until the first of July. When I realized how close I was to the end of our long search, I wanted to come here and share the good news with you. And, of course, I would never set out on this venture without receiving your blessing."

"This is wonderful news, Tony! How do you plan to proceed?" asked the excited cleric.

"I still have places to visit, people to see, and questions to ask. My itinerary includes stops in Spain, the Yucatan Peninsula, and perhaps Cuba before I return to America. Then I need to visit a number of other locations in several western states. Most of the puzzle's pieces are now in place, but some vital ones are still missing. I suppose I could solve the enigma without them, but for my peace of mind as well as for yours, I want to know the entire story. When I return, I hope to have all the parts of our fascinating mystery neatly arranged."

"Do you expect to encounter danger on your journey, Tony?" His Eminence was acutely aware that the same question had been asked by another concerned Cardinal sixty years earlier, and he remembered the unfortunate fate of the other investigators.

"Only fools rule out violence and danger, Eminence. I know exactly what I'm looking for, and I've formulated a good plan for success. However, I can't be certain of the people I'll meet or the conditions I'll face. I can only say that, because of a three-year stint in U.S. Special Forces, I'm trained in hand-to-hand combat, proficient with many types of weapons, and pretty good at covert operations. All things considered, I'm confident that I can take care of myself."

He paused and smiled at the two clergymen.

"Since I'm a former paratrooper, if I get into more trouble than I can handle, I'll just jump out of danger."

"You can make light of this, Tony, but I'm still concerned for your safety and cannot understand why you are not. As you know, several men have died in pursuit of this quest. What can I do to assist you? Do you need money? Letters of credibility? Do you need anything?"

"Eminence, I won't minimize the obvious danger, but I'm so eager to begin this journey that I can barely contain my excitement. I've always enjoyed reading about great adventures, but I'm tired of gliding over oceans on other people's balsa rafts or sailing across dense jungles on someone else's hot-air balloon. For the first time in my life, perhaps the only time, I'm going to embark on a great adventure of my own, and frankly, I'm dazzled by the prospect. And the fact that I'm looking for an ancient medical cure which has the potential to help all of mankind, really makes my adventure a sort of a quest for the Holy Grail." Tony paused and looked into the eyes of the anxious Cardinal. Then he continued.

"There are other reasons as well. I'm going on this quest to take something wonderful away from a group of selfish, vindictive people who have misused it for 500 years. There is too much suffering on this old, tortured planet to allow them to continue. I think the statement of Emilio Duarte, that you transcribed a half-century ago, was absolutely correct. He said that only a very small and tightly controlled group could keep such a secret for long. The fewer the confidants, the safer the secret. He was right! Poor Emilio's disappearance, and that of the other emissaries, give his observation even more validity."

A faraway, dreamy look crept into the Cardinal's dark eyes.

"I remember sitting across the table from Emilio Duarte on the day he made that observation. We were gathered at the residence of Cardinal Cabrini, late in the summer of 1941. Emilio left the following morning —

and disappeared a few months later. Not long after, Pearl Harbor was attacked and America entered the war, but the Cardinal was still able to acquire all the information that was available to the people in Mexico City. I thought then, and still believe now, that Emilio learned too much and was murdered."

"I agree, Eminence. I'm going to search through as many files and records as possible, in the cities and villages of Yucatan and the Quintana Roo, to see how many cases of missing persons I can discover. There may well be a traceable pattern."

"You have obviously done a good deal of planning, Tony, and are well prepared. I'll admit that I'm losing a good deal of my trepidation. But you still haven't answered my question concerning financial aid or any type of letters from me."

"A letter requesting all possible cooperation from religious or government officials might be extremely beneficial. I probably won't need it, but one can never tell. Financially, I'm fine. And who knows?" he laughed. "When I return, I may write a best-seller about my adventures and become rich."

"Very true," agreed the Cardinal. "Michael, skip the letters and prepare a complete set of Vatican credentials. As Tony says, he probably won't need them, but one can never tell."

Cardinal Questa and Dr. Garza relaxed in the comfortable study until the Monsignor returned. Then it was time for Tony to leave for the airport. Two hours later, he was winging toward the old-world charm of Granada and his rendezvous with destiny.

➢

What a marvelous time and place to be alive, thought a highly inspired Antonio Garza the next day as he left the peaceful solitude of the Granada Cathedral and stepped

413

back into the warm sunlight of a soft Iberian afternoon. The magnificent old city lay in splendor before him, sparkling like a bright jewel, framed against the background of the majestic, snow-clad Sierra Nevadas.

Granada had already become a very special city for him. That morning, after attending Mass, he walked back along the Gran Via de Colon to his hotel for breakfast and then returned to the cathedral in the Plaza de Pasiegas. There he spent a long time meditating in the Royal Chapel before the tomb of Isabel and Fernando, Los Reyes Catolicos.

The years had succeeded in slowly wearing away much of his grief and loneliness, but on this day his spirits plummeted and tears welled up in his eyes. Since he was in this place, he did not have to wonder why the melancholy mood had overtaken him.

Years ago, when he was in college, and preparing to follow in the wake of his brothers and enter the seminary, in the spring of his senior year he met Pamela Greenfield and underwent what the Sicilians call "a strike from the thunderbolt." Within two weeks, it was clear to both of them that love was here to stay and that marriage better follow as soon as possible. But there were obstacles on their road to blissful togetherness.

Pamela was an exchange student on a one-year sabbatical. She was frightfully British and a practicing Presbyterian. Whenever they examined their differences under the bright light of reason, the chances of ever having a lasting relationship seemed remote.

Knowing that they needed counsel, they went to see Antonio's oldest brother, Padre Fernando. He was very patient with the young English woman, answering all of her questions and explaining traditional Catholic doctrine. As their third meeting drew to a close, this one without Antonio, Padre Fernando gave her a book that he had cherished for many years. It was the story of Isabel and Fernando, the man for whom he had been named.

414

The following week, she returned to the Padre with the book and a request to be instructed in the Catholic Faith. On a Friday afternoon, six months later, she was baptized, made her first confession, and received First Holy Communion. The following day, she and Antonio wed and were, according to Padre Fernando, the most handsome couple he had ever joined in matrimony.

It was not until their honeymoon that Antonio discovered how important Isabel had been in Pamela's decision. "After all," she said to him, "all I have to do is help you bring forth a fruitful and happy marriage. Isabel had to help Fernando win back, unite, and defend an entire country. Isabel's life made me see my future clearly, and for that I will always love her and be eternally grateful to her."

How I wish Pamela could be here with me today, he thought.

Their life together had been fruitful and extremely happy, but so woefully short. Eighteen wonderful years, and then she was gone, racked and ravaged by the bone cancer that had taken her from him in her fortieth year. How sorry she had been to go and leave him and the girls. They were teenagers then. Now Barbara and Becky were married with children of their own, and Bridget was a member of a contemplative order of nuns in St. Louis.

I'm certain about one thing, he decided, as he rose to leave the Royal Chapel. Our Lord is being bombarded with prayers for the success of my mission by His Own Blessed Mother; by the great Catholic Queen, Isabel; and by my own beloved, Pamela. It's very difficult for me to withstand one insistent woman. No one, not even Our Lord, can hold out against three of them.

It was such a lovely afternoon that, after lunch, instead of driving his rental car, Antonio parked it at La Plaza Nueva and climbed the steep Hill of Gomerez. At the top, he rested beneath the Gate of Granadas, which marks the border between Granada and the Alhambra. This gate, built by order of Charles V, is far more than a symbolic line of demarcation, he thought. Here the city and its noises are left far behind as one enters a wonderful, pristine forest, where the only sounds are the murmur of the streams running down from the Alhambra.

He spent the balance of the day and early evening wandering about the immense grounds and reveling in such sites as the Plaza de los Aljibes, the Adarves Garden, the Watch Towers, the Red Tower, the Gate of Justice with its Moorish arch, and the Gate of Wine, which connects the Palace and the Fortress. He climbed the twenty-seven meters to the top of the Watch Tower and looked out at the panoramic splendor of Granada. He was sorry when visiting hours ended at dusk. He was also sorry that his schedule would permit no more sight-seeing. Tomorrow was a work day.

The following morning after Mass, Antonio did not return to his hotel. Instead, he walked directly to the museum and library, which were part of the cathedral complex. He stood politely near the front desk until the young woman working behind it turned to him and smiled.

"May I be of service, Señor?"

Antonio presented her with his Texas State University identity card but decided to withhold the Vatican credentials unless they were required to gain access to the rare document section. It quickly became apparent that such would not be the case.

"Dr. Garza, my name is Martina Salinas and this is a great honor. I'm enrolled in the graduate school pursuing a master's degree in World History. Your books and many of your articles have provided me with wonderful source material, particularly your insightful reviews of the Reconquista and the reigns of Charles V and Phillip II. Your works appear countless times in many of my bibliographies."

"I appreciate your gracious accolades, Senorita Salinas. I sometimes think that the only people who still study my works are my own students at Texas State." He smiled at

416

her and added, "Of course, they have to, since they're all part of my captive audience."

"You're being modest, Dr. Garza. Your works are brilliant. Most of my classmates are also in your debt. Please allow me to assist you in any possible way, and please call me Martina."

"Thank you, Martina. I'm currently engaged in a project that involves documents written during the era of the Conquistadors. Some of them were written or received by my own ancestors, one of whom was a grandee named Diego Garza. Previous research indicates that some of his letters are housed in your archives."

"They are, Dr. Garza. I'm familiar with the documents of Diego Garza. I used them as source material while I was conducting my own research and remember them because they're somewhat unusual."

"In what way do you find them unusual, Martina?"

"In his later years, the Grandee apparently discarded most of the correspondence that he'd accumulated during his lifetime. After he decided which documents were worthy of being preserved, he numbered them. Originally there were sixty-four inclusions. However, in our archives, only sixty-three remain. Somehow, one of the letters disappeared."

"Number 7!" said a smiling scholar to a startled student.

"How do you know that?" she queried.

"Because I have seen the letter in question. Hernando Cortez wrote it to the Grandee in 1520. It's been in the Vatican archives since 1527."

"The year of the Grandee's death," responded the knowledgeable young lady. "He died two weeks after his ninety-fifth birthday, on Christmas morning. I wonder if he sent the document to the Vatican, and if so, why?"

"Two excellent questions. Unfortunately, neither of them may ever be answered. By the way, Martina, what is the procedure for gaining access to the files?"

"Everything has been reproduced in the computer system. I will supply you with a personal data access code, which will allow you to search and find anything you, may require. Will one week of access be sufficient, Dr. Garza?"

"More than adequate, Martina, since regrettably I must leave Granada the day after tomorrow and go on to Toledo."

He spent the balance of the day perusing ancient records. The Grandee's were most interesting. One was a letter accepting him for training at the Royal Academy of Toledo in 1449. Another one appointed him to the service of King Henry IV of Castile in 1453. A third, written in 1469 by Henry IV, charged Captain Garza with the responsibility of protecting the life and person of his royal heir, Isabel.

One impressive document was a royal decree from Fernando and Isabel, issued on the day of his retirement in 1492, announcing his elevation to the rank of Grandee, providing for a generous lifetime income, and praising him for his years of loyal service. Attached to the decree was a tear-stained personal letter from Queen Isabel, thanking him for his devotion and protection and reminiscing about their first weeks together when he had saved her life on several harrowing occasions.

"Don Diego," she concluded, "during all of our years together, you have been my most loyal subject, my bravest protector, and my staunchest friend. May God always keep you near Him."

The simplest but most helpful document was a short, badly scrawled note from someone named José Mendoza, which Don Diego had received in 1472. In it, Señor Mendoza expressed his pleasure at the ascension of Isabel and Fernando to the throne and thanked Captain Garza for his continuing support of Los Reyes Catolicos.

"Eighteen years ago," he concluded, "I never dreamt the young man I served then would become the great man I honor now. Though few know the sword's secret, many know that one of Spain's great defenders wields it. Your humble servant, José Mendoza, E.E."

Antonio felt like jumping for joy. Here was actual proof that Cardinal Questa's deductions, made nearly sixty years ago, were correct. The letters "E.E." stood for Espadas Españas, Swords of Spain. It was the name of a company, which, for hundreds of years, was famous around the world for fine craftsmen. They were the legendary designers of the Toledo blade.

Mendoza not only had crafted the weapon; he had designed it as well. His allusion to the "sword's secret" must mean that he had added the hidden compartment at Garza's request. It also seemed to indicate that such a request—not to mention the compartment itself—was unusual.

His search through documents continued throughout the day but produced nothing else as significant as the Mendoza letter.

The following day, more to satisfy his curiosity than in hopes of discovering anything of real importance, he visited the tomb of the Great Grandee and, with the assistance of Martina Salinas, was able to arrange a personal tour of the Garza estate. Although the manor had been preserved as a museum for nearly five hundred years, the building was normally closed for refurbishing during the months of January and February.

One of the most interesting rooms in the old mansion was the library, filled as it was with many fascinating artifacts. One wall was lined with dozens of rare books. Some of them, printed only a few years after Herr Gutenberg and his German associates developed a system of movable type printing in the 1440's, were priceless.

The Grandee also seemed to have been a collector of swords. A wide variety of dueling foils, epees, broadswords, and sabres were mounted singly or in pairs and displayed on every wall of what Antonio presumed had been his study. On one wall, directly behind the grandee's long writing table, hung a handsome walnut rack with spaces for six swords. Beside each of them, a small engraved silver plaque, explaining the weapon's origin and date of presentation, had been installed.

The sword in the top position proclaimed that the weapon had been given to him when he entered the Royal Academy in 1449. The next one was a gift from the grateful citizens of Valladolid. King Henry IV had presented him with a magnificent sword in 1470, in recognition of his valorous service. Each sword was exquisite. All had hilts of gold or silver, and many of the scabbards were encrusted with jewels.

The sword that should have been in the third bracket was not there. However, its silver identification plaque was. It said:

DIEGO GARZA - ESPADAS ESPAÑAS - TOLEDO ESPAÑA - MCDLIV

Antonio remembered Señor Mendoza's letter without referring to his notes. The letter, written in 1472, referred to a sword with a secret, which he had crafted eighteen years before, in 1454. Now Antonio realized he had made another major discovery. Mendoza's letter was the first hard proof to support the conclusions that Emmanuel Questa had drawn from scant evidence back in the early 1940's. Antonio conjured up a mental image of a sheet containing Questa's original ten questions and answers. Questions about the Grandee, Padre Garza, Cabeza de Vaca, La Noche de Triste, and most of all the knife with its secret compartment. This small rectangle of engraved silver proved that the future Cardinal's deductions had been amazingly accurate. It was the glue that held all the pieces of the Garza mystery together.

➢

He left Granada early the next morning and arrived in Toledo in time for lunch. He rented an automobile at the airport and drove directly to El Museo de Armas (The Museum of Weapons).

One entire floor of this rambling building was dedicated to tracing the development of Toledo's high-quality steel production and the history of the blade-forging industry. A large section was filled with displays of prototype models, featuring the works of the world's finest crafters and designers of handheld weapons.

He was not surprised to learn that for over forty years, José Mendoza had been one of Toledo's most famous citizens. He was the leading innovator of his day, and a man that everyone else tried to emulate. Antonio smiled to himself at the thought of a sword designer being on the cutting edge of his profession.

Three of Don José's favorite features appeared in nearly all of the swords and knives that he created. Between the blade and the haft, he inserted a soft brass handguard, about the size and shape of a grown man's forefinger. It was obviously designed to catch, and momentarily hold, the sharp edge of an enemy blade. At the very top of the hilt, he usually added a triangularly-shaped brass tang extension. Between these two other signature features, Mendoza invariably built in a pair of slender, semicircular, parallel pieces of thin, strong steel. Aside from protecting the user's hand and lower arm, they appeared to provide a convenient method of battering the person of one's antagonist if one were so inclined. Although Antonio could not be certain, he would have wagered a sizable amount that the Grandee's sword, if it still existed, had all three of El Señor Mendoza's favorite features.

Since his flight from Madrid to Mexico City was scheduled for departure at 11:45 that evening, he was compelled to leave the museum in the late afternoon before he had been able to see a great many of the other interesting exhibits.

Most of Spain's rolling green hills were wrapped in winter's dappled white that sparkling afternoon as Antonio left Toledo and drove northeastward toward Madrid. Halfway toward his destination he stopped just north of the ancient city of Aranjuez, to dine at a quaint restaurant built on a terraced hillside overlooking the Rio Jarama.

His table was situated next to a window that faced westward and framed the vista of an orange sun sinking toward the waters of a dancing, rippling river. The lovely tableau, partially shielded by the branches of a weeping willow tree which grew just outside, was so reminiscent of the view of the Rio Grande that Pamela and he had enjoyed from their veranda in San Antonio that tears came to his eyes and, for a brief moment, blurred his vision. A dozen times each day, he remembered special times they had shared and wished that she were here. I have no desire to grow old without you, my love, he confided to her, struggling for composure.

In the background, mandolins strummed a gentle serenade as he enjoyed a tart and chilled Margarita before an excellent dinner of brook trout and a wonderful, dark Spanish beer. An hour later, feeling greatly refreshed and far less melancholy, he resumed his journey to Madrid.

➢

The Trans-Atlantic flight was even longer and more tedious than the average intercontinental journey. The head winds were stronger than forecast. The in-flight movie was boring, and he had forgotten to transfer a fairly interesting historical novel that he had begun reading from his suitcase to his briefcase.

He dozed off, but woke an hour later with the chronic headache that always seemed to accompany interrupted sleep in turbulent weather. He roused himself and struggled along the bouncing aisle toward the lavatory, reaching it just as the huge plane slammed into a maze of invisible and nearly impenetrable aerial barriers. Once inside the tiny, stainless steel room, he rested for a moment before combing his hair and dousing his face with cold water. He soon emerged but did not return to his seat. Instead, he sidled carefully from one perilous handhold to the next, eventually arriving at the cabin attendant's service center.

He ordered three tiny bottles of Crown Royal, one considerably larger bottle of ginger ale, and several ice cubes. All of these items quickly found their way into a tall glass, together with a large measure of anticipation. Ten minutes after he regained his seat, the only thing that remained was the glass. Everything else had disappeared, along with his restlessness.

He slept soundly throughout the rest of the night and did not stir until he was gently roused by a cheerful flight attendant. She announced that they would be landing in one hour and breakfast was currently being served, if he cared to make a selection. He did!

➤

Two hours later, he was again airborne, this time flying in the opposite direction. In Madrid, he had made a reservation on the morning commuter flight to Cancun with Mexicana Airlines.

Because of the Trans-Atlantic flight's late arrival in Mexico City, he was forced to scurry through customs and dash across the width of the airport to the departure gate, where he arrived weak-kneed and out of breath. Moments later, he was also red-faced with embarrassment after discovering that a feeder flight to Cancun departed every hour.

Since he estimated a stay of several days in the northern section of the Quintana Roo and the northeastern portion of the Yucatan, he decided to rent a three-room suite at La Carrousel, one of Cancun's most luxurious hotels.

Still weary from the frantic pace of the last few days, he spent the balance of the afternoon and early evening swimming in the crystal-clear ocean and relaxing on the soft, inviting sands.

After a light dinner, he retired and was asleep by 10:00 P.M.

The next morning he arose at dawn, finished breakfast by 7:00 A.M., and an hour later was driving a very comfortable Lincoln Mark VII rental car south along a sunlit oceanside highway. At Puerto Morelos, he swung away from the sea and angled inland toward the interior of the Quintana Roo. A short distance after the turn, a road sign assured him that it was eighty kilometers to the area that he had chosen as the starting point for his investigation into the mysteries of the Yucatan Peninsula and the ancient secrets of the Mayas and Aztecs: the Pyramids of Coba.

The heat of the day continued to increase as he drove. The car's handy outside temperature sensor informed him that beyond the tinted windows, the part of this world not cooled by the Lincoln's purring air conditioner was approaching one hundred degrees. The numerous heat waves rising from the road's boiling blacktop made him question the wisdom of being here. Then, in a sudden moment of clairvoyance, he realized that the temperature would soon be the least of his concerns.

Chapter XXVIII

➢

A Millennium Of Terror

Yucatan & Quintana Roo Provinces
Northern Yucatan Peninsula
Mexico
Spring, 1999

Dr. Antonio Garza arrived in Coba an hour later and spent the rest of the morning and early afternoon wandering about the area, picturing the thriving metropolis which had existed 2,500 years ago. One which had figured so prominently in the destiny of an ancient society.

Around each of the altars and in many other places, he sensed the pervasive presence of the countless spirits who, for over a thousand years, were sacrificed to hundreds of bloodthirsty pagan gods. It was the same feeling he had experienced when he visited a Civil War battlefield, walked upon the hallowed sands of Omaha Beach, or stood amid the markers of Flanders Field. It was a strange but special feeling, comprised of equal parts of sadness and awe. How right General Patton had been when he said, "Rains will wash away all of the blood and erase the other evidence which mark these fields of combat, but the eternal spirits of the warriors who strove and enjoined the battle will forever remain. Ten thousand years from now, the soldiers of new conflicts will know, however darkly, that others like themselves, fought and died here."

Of all the places he visited at Coba, the most eerie was the pagan temple, which sat atop the great pyramid. Soaring nearly 150 feet above the sun-baked plain, the ancient structure was an architectural marvel. As he prepared to ascend the narrow vine-tangled steps, he placed a hand on one of the stones and recoiled in horror as a feeling of foreboding came over him. When he had recovered his composure, he slowly mounted the steep, seemingly endless flight of stairs, feeling more insecure with each passing step. At last he reached the summit and stood beside the temple's entrance, awaiting the phenomenon that occurred at special times of the year.

As the sun reached a certain point in the midday sky, its rays gained access to a strangely shaped opening at the top of a Mayan obelisk, which protruded, from the temple roof. Then, for the next several minutes, an ever-lengthening shadow crept from the roof down the temple wall, inched its way across the narrow platform, dropping over the edge of the precipice, slithering slowly down each successive step, taking on the characteristics of a vaunted feathered serpent, just as the snake-worshiping designers of the obelisk had intended.

Antonio watched the age-old ritual of the slithering shadow until it reached its vanishing point; then he entered the temple. Within the dim interior, an absence of direct sunlight and the influence of a steady breeze through the many wall openings should have had a cooling effect; but they did not.

He gazed at ancient drawings, at ceremonial masks, and at the blood-carrying troughs along the bottom of each wall. He imagined how the unfortunates who were brought here to be sacrificed must have felt, especially the ones who were forced to witness the sufferings and hideous deaths of those who died before them. Many places on the floor and walls bore irregular smears and spatters, which Antonio knew to be bloodstains. Right here, he decided, I'm as close to hell on earth as I ever want to be.

He left the confines of the temple and felt as if a great burden had been lifted from his shoulders. Grasping the safety rope with a grip of iron, he backed down the steps to the ground.

A short distance from the pyramid steps, he saw an elderly lady sitting in the shade of a gaily striped red-white-and-green beach umbrella. She caught his eye and beckoned to him. As he approached her, she said, "I could not help noticing you, Señor. You are not like the usual tourists that frequent Coba. I detect about you the air of a scholar."

"I'm a writer, Señora. I'm here to gather additional material for a book I plan to write about the prevalent customs in various ancient civilizations, and the pressure those customs still exert on modern societies. I've finished my research on European cultures and have now begun on the Americas."

"How interesting," she purred. "My name is Mercata Verrano, and I would be pleased to assist you in any possible way. I have been visiting ruins in the Yucatan and Quintana Roo since my earliest childhood. For many years, my father, Don Julio, and my mother, Doña Iñez, worked very hard to safeguard what remains of Coba, Chichen Itza, and the other historical centers. They spent their lives protecting the heritage of Mayan and Aztec civilizations."

"I am honored that you would be willing to help me, Señora Verrano. How can I contact you?"

"I live on the outskirts of Dzibilchaltun. It is the only home I have ever known. Anyone can direct you to my dwelling."

Antonio thanked her again and then departed. It was amazing, he thought, how many harmless, lonely people one met in every corner of the world.

Mercata Verrano watched the stranger stroll toward the parking area. Many who knew her thought of Mercata as brutal, deadly, and unforgiving. But no one who really knew her would ever describe her as "harmless." Don Julio had taught her to be an excellent judge of character; and Mercata smelled a rat!

Something about that man, she deduced, just doesn't ring true. First of all, why had he not introduced himself? She had known other authors during her life, and everyone an author met was more than a person or even a friend. He or she was a potential reader! Also, this alleged author had made no effort to verify the extent of the knowledge she professed to have about the civilizations he claimed to be studying and preparing to write about.

How did he plan to write anything, she wondered, without a map of the area, a pad for jotting down notes, or a cassette machine for recording his observations? He might be an author, Mercata decided, but he is something else as well! And if he is not an author, why does he claim to be one? Certainly not to impress me! Undoubtedly, he thinks of me as a harmless old woman. Don Julio had taught her to follow her instincts; and at this moment, her instincts sensed danger.

She turned slightly to face the pyramid and beckoned toward a large, powerful-looking man with massive shoulders and a fleshy, pockmarked face. He left the shadow of the wall and came to her side, then stood waiting respectfully and expectantly.

Mercata could hear his labored breathing as he struggled to draw air into his lungs through his broad, flat nose. It had been broken so many times that finally it had failed to heal properly. That was a price that marginally successful boxers had to pay for their careers in the ring, Mercata supposed.

She smiled at him and said, "Embalador, did you see the man I was speaking with?"

"Si, Doña Mercata."

"I want you to follow him and find out all you can. Make a record of the places he visits. Tell me who he speaks with and find out what his conversations are about. Use any methods that you require — bribery, intimidation, anything! Do not let him see you or find out what you are about. Call me tonight after you know where he is staying, but only when you are sure he has retired for the night. If necessary, I will assign some others to help. Do you have any questions?"

"No, Doña Mercata, your orders are very clear."

"Very well, Embalador. I fear that this stranger may be very dangerous. Bring me answers, Embalador. We may have to kill him, but don't do it without my express permission."

Embalador walked quickly to his vehicle, a battered-looking Jeep Cherokee whose body had seen better days. What was less obvious was the world-class power plant that lurked under the dented and paint-splotched hood, an engine capable of pushing the Cherokee up to an honest hundred and forty miles per hour.

He left the parking area and drove at a sedate pace until the ruins of Coba were behind him and the open highway loomed ahead.

To be certain of overtaking the stranger's automobile, he pushed the Jeep hard for the first dozen miles, occasionally glancing at the speedometer needle which quivered near the one hundred mark.

He closed the gap rapidly and soon saw the black Lincoln, skimming over the road about a half mile ahead. He backed off on the accelerator and drifted down to a tame seventy-five. For the rest of the way into Xcan, he maintained the same interval so as not to alarm the stranger, or to provide Doña Mercata with a reason to find fault with him. A few minutes later, the covert caravan entered Xcan, and the dusty Lincoln pulled to a halt before El Raton Moro Cantina.

Antonio left the bright modern world when he left the luxury car and stepped into the dim past as he mounted the Raton Moro's creaking stairs. Pushing open the bat-wing doors, he strode into the tavern's dingy interior. His gaze fell upon a time-ravaged, barely legible sign that clung to the filthy wall behind the peeled and cracked mahogany bar. The faded lettering proclaimed that Pancho Villa had once spent an evening in El Raton Moro. From the looks of things, they hadn't cleaned up the place since he left. Somehow, Antonio doubted that an attempt to maintain a nostalgic atmosphere accounted for the building's deplorable condition.

Looking around the room, he decided that El Raton Moro would never be listed in the Michelin Tourist's Guide as a "Don't Miss This" location. Most of the patrons seemed to be a cross between the "sinister looking but good-at-heart banditos" of old-time Cisco Kid movies, and the panhandlers on New York City streets who wipe windshields with oily rags to coerce a few coins from intimidated motorists.

He ordered a Carta Blanca beer and continued his study of the Raton Moro's clientele. Mostly, though, he covertly watched the door in case he had been followed here from Coba's pyramids. For a reason he couldn't explain, something about Mercata Verrano had made him feel uneasy and suspicious. Perhaps it was only his imagination, but the eerie feeling persisted. A bartender with hanging jowls and a drooping mustache laid a frosted bottle and dust-covered glass on the bar before him and stood waiting to see what he would do. Garza disdainfully pushed the cracked container aside before lifting the bottle to his lips and taking a swig of the refreshing, ice-cold beer.

"No vaso, Señor?" the barman asked. (No glass, Mister?)

"Solamente por novatos y hermanitas!" Antonio replied. (They are only for beginners and sissies.)

The barman moved down to the far end of the bar and resumed his quiet conversation with a pair of elderly citizens, who made an elaborate show of ignoring the stranger. Antonio scrutinized each new arrival very carefully and was reasonably satisfied that he had not been followed. However, he delayed for several more minutes to make certain. While speaking with the old woman, he had carefully noted all of the idlers who lounged around the pyramid. None of that dozen or more were now in sight.

He drank the last of the beer, nodded to the bartender and his friends, and ambled back toward his Lincoln. Starting the engine, he rolled the windows down partway, and set the air conditioner on its maximum setting, all the while carefully looking out from under lowered brows in an effort to detect suspicious persons or behavior.

Satisfied that all was well, he rolled up the windows and sat for a few moments, luxuriating in the car's now-cool interior. Then he left the Cantina and drove toward the town square, which was less than a mile away. This time, he was fortunate enough to find a parking place beneath a large, shady tree. He locked the Lincoln and strolled along one of the four bench-lined lanes that led into the plaza and its cluster of municipal buildings. Old-fashioned hand-lettered signs pointed the way to the alcalde's office, the hall of records, the police department, and the jail.

He entered the department of records and spent the next few minutes establishing the same cover story, identity, and purpose that he had given Señora Verrano. Eventually, he wanted to gain access to the police files on missing persons in all the small towns and villages of the Quintana Roo and Yucatan. Particularly those of Tunkas. But in these early stages, patience was vitally important. Antonio had to convince any observers that his motives were completely innocent in order to eliminate any suspicion.

He presented to the clerk in charge of the records office an absolutely impossible-to-follow explanation, forcefully asserting that the keys to the study of any modern culture's evolvement, from its ancient pagan mores and on into the enlightenment stages of its progressive ages, depended heavily on certain obscure but traceable trends. To a great extent, he said, these indicators included male and female life expectancy, the rate of infant mortality, the size of families, and the dilution of heritage and culture which intermarriage inevitably brought with it.

Of nearly equal importance, he asserted, were the changing agronomistic tendencies made necessary by variable climatic conditions. Sometimes, he confided, types of prevalent diseases even changed because of the decrease in time-tested culturally ethnic nutritional levels. The strangest phenomena of all, he concluded, were the types of crimes and degrees of criminality, which a society in flux permitted.

Throughout this soliloquy, he was careful to excise anything of real relevance from his psychobabble. The more Antonio talked, the more confused the clerk became, but dutifully continued to nod. He was clearly relieved when his visitor said, "You see, do you not, Señor, how important it is to have access to information that others would find meaningless?"

"Of course, Señor! The reasons are perfectly clear!"

"I suppose that I will have to study the records of the police to obtain a part of the necessary information."

"If you need current files, Señor, you will have to have the consent of the alcalde. But at the end of three years, all files in the police office are sent over here for storage. That is the policy throughout all of Mexico—old files are accessible without consent."

Antonio could hardly believe his good fortune. He could negate the need of winning the confidence of the mayor or prefect of police in every town or village, and concentrate on records that were available to the general public. It was almost like having a library card and unlimited browsing privileges.

He spent the balance of the afternoon scanning records and making a mountain of notes, most of them meaningless.

A few minutes before 6:00 P.M., the posted closing time, he approached the clerk, whose name was Rico.

"Don Rico, I will be remaining in town for a few days. Can you recommend a place to stay?"

"I fear the choices are few, Don Antonio. The only truly fine place is El Palacio Amarillo. There you will find nice rooms and also very good food and wine."

"Wonderful. I'm extremely grateful for your help and patience. Perhaps if you have time, you could show me the way to El Palacio Amarillo and then join me for one of those good drinks."

"Con mucho gusto, mi amigo," smiled the grateful Rico.

➤

Three hours later, Rico was not smiling; he was choking. He was being held up against the rough adobe wall of his own house by the strong right hand of Embalador, whose long fingers nearly met at the back of Rico's scrawny neck. Rico's feet dangled eight inches above the ground, and his face had begun to turn purple.

Embalador was only following orders. He had been taught that friendly people often talk, but frightened people always do. He relaxed his iron grip just long enough to allow Rico three quick, desperate gasps of air before clamping his windpipe shut again. He smiled maliciously at the smaller man before attempting to speak and breathe at the same time through his fleshy mouth, a difficult feat made necessary by the crushed nose.

"Rico, I don't want to hurt you, but I need your help. I'm going to let you down now. Don't make any noise."

Embalador gave the frightened record clerk a few moments to regain his breath as well as his composure.

"What did the stranger want in your office this afternoon?"

"He wanted to look at some records," responded the frightened clerk.

"Estupido! Are you trying to make a fool of me? Or do you think I am already a fool? Of course he wanted to look at your records! You work in the record office. What kind of records did he want to look at?"

"All kinds of records. He is an author and needs different kinds of information on ancient cultures. He spent many years in Europe studying the Greeks and Romans and some others, and now he is comparing our Mayas and Aztecs with them. He asks questions about food and farming and climate and diseases and such things."

"Did he, by chance, ask about cures for these diseases?"

"No! He is concerned with diseases like plagues that wipe out large numbers of people."

Rico was so frightened of the huge ex-boxer that he would gladly have told him everything he knew. Perhaps because of his nearly paralyzing fear, he forgot the brief reference by the author to the investigation of criminality and the need for access to police records. Since Embalador did not specifically make reference to other records, the subject was never mentioned.

"Did the man tell you his name and say how long he will stay?"

"His name is Dr. Antonio Garza. He is a professor of History at Texas State University in San Antonio, and he is going to be in town for a few days."

"How do you know he is who he says he is?" asked the always suspicious Embalador.

"I saw his identification card from the university, and he loaned me a periodical in which he has written an article. I have it here in my house."

"Show it to me!"

Rico led his menacing guest around the corner of his small house and darted in the front door. A moment later he reappeared and thrust a magazine into the big man's hands.

It was a Spanish language edition of a quarterly journal called Ancient Worlds in Review. Dr. Antonio Garza had written one of the feature articles. The accompanying photograph was clearly that of the man he had been following throughout the day. Embalador leafed quickly through the book to be certain of its authenticity and then returned it to the record clerk.

"Everything seems to be all right for now," confided Señora Verrano's enforcer to a relieved Rico, "but I will meet with you each night until he is gone. I would be very unhappy if you did not keep me informed about things. You understand, don't you?"

"You can count on me, Embalador!"

434

"I am counting on you, Rico. I will see you here, tomorrow."

➢

Much later that night, Embalador arrived at the home of Mercata Verrano on the outskirts of Dzibilchaltun. She admitted him at once and preceded him into her small, spartan living room.

"What did you learn?" she demanded.

"The man is Dr. Antonio Garza. He teaches at the Texas State University and seems to be a well-known writer. I saw a story in a magazine that he wrote."

"What was the name of the magazine?" she queried.

"It is called Ancient Worlds in Review," he responded.

"Did you examine the article and the magazine closely?"

"Of course, Doña Mercata."

"Tell me about them."

"His article was called The Mysteries of Stonehenge, and it was quite long. Dr. Garza's picture was there, and there were also many photographs of ancient stones. The magazine was very thick and heavy. It had a lot of pages in it. Many other people had written stories about different things. The cover said, "Summer Quarter — 1998."

"Where is Dr. Garza staying?"

"He has a suite at the Palacio Amarillo. The desk clerk said he checked in for three days. Horca will watch him at night in the hotel, and Rico will stay on guard during the day."

"You have done well, Embalador. He may be what he claims to be after all, but I want you to continue to watch him. Check with your informers daily and keep me informed."

"I will, Doña Mercata. Is there anything else?"

"There certainly is. You bungled one of your other assignments completely. Luis Vasquez, that old fool who lives in Tunkas, must be killed. My sources at Chichen Itza tell me that he's ready to go to the police. Apparently, he didn't take your warning or the advice of his friends very seriously. As soon as I and the other members of the Council of Three decide on the fate of this Dr. Garza," Mercata continued, "we want Vasquez to die. Arrange an accident and leave his body where all those who harbor resentment against us will see it."

"Do you want this accident to happen near Tunkas, Doña?"

"Of course! Otherwise it will serve no great purpose. Plan the execution for the next few days. Be ready to move at once."

➢

Dr. Garza spent the next morning perusing files in Rico's record office. In the rear of the room was an old rolltop desk that was no longer being used. It was here that Antonio worked among tall piles of records. He pulled so many meaningless files out of so many different drawers and cabinets that neither Rico nor his clerk could possibly keep track of them all.

By late morning, after searching through hundreds of missing-persons records, he made a most startling discovery. It was so bizarre that at first he couldn't believe his eyes; but case after similar case eliminated all of his doubts.

At noon, Rico closed the office and went to lunch. Antonio declined an invitation to join him and left Xcan at once.

During the afternoon and for the balance of the next two days, he culled the files of Valladolid, Chemax, Tizimin, Panaba, and Rio Lagartos. In each of them, he continued his surreptitious examination and was almost certain that the disinterested clerks were unaware of the real purpose of his search. In every village, the evidence mounted.

After three days in the village, Antonio was glad to drive back to Cancun and his suite at La Carrousel. During all his days in Xcan and the surrounding towns, he had felt eyes on his back. It was an eerie feeling, reminiscent of other dangerous times.

In each record office, he had been able to research nearly one hundred years of missing-person files. Almost every one of those people simply disappeared, with no further trace! It was as if the earth had opened up and swallowed them.

An even more astonishing fact had come to light. More than 90% of the disappearances occurred shortly before the winter or summer solstice each year. For a week before June 22 and for a similar length of time before December 22, the entire area was clearly unsafe to live in.

The solstices had been important 500 years ago when Montezuma and the other Aztec leaders had decided to offer their insatiable, bloodthirsty gods more sacrifices than ever before. They began the slaughter at Tenochtitlan with 10,000 victims on 600 altars. By the end of the 1400's, the Aztecs were waging wars with their neighbors for the sole purpose of capturing ever more victims.

At the summer solstice in 1499, a column containing thousands of prisoners was herded into the plaza and prepared for execution. After each prisoner was stretched out on an altar, a high priest plunged a stone dagger into the victim's chest and hacked out his still beating heart. Seconds later, it was elaborately presented to the gods. So strong was the captors' control over the victims that no escape attempts were ever recorded.

But this, thought Antonio Garza, is 1999, not 1499. Things like that don't happen anymore. Human sacrifices are no longer offered to pagan gods! Or are they?

Suddenly he shuddered, and a feeling of utter dread froze his heart. He felt as though a mental door had opened, allowing his mind's eye to see an unspeakable horror which, until now, he had been unwilling to consider. He saw a sacrificial altar, like the ancient one on top of the pyramid, running red with fresh blood. But the vision was not of the past; it was of the present. He staggered to the nearest chair and fell into it, his knees no longer able to support him. His palms were damp and a sour sweat, borne of fear and frustration, coursed down his spine. He was also overwhelmed by a powerful sorrow, the likes of which he had known only twice before: once in the jungles of Southeast Asia, and again when his beloved Pamela lay dying.

"Oh Lord, no!" he cried aloud, slamming his fist down on his knee. But as difficult as it was to believe, he knew it was true. There were far too many missing persons in the Yucatan each year because many of them actually did become the victims of pagan sacrifices.

It is painfully obvious, Antonio realized, that a group of despicable people are doing far more than merely protecting an ancient medicine. They are still performing the same pagan rites that the Mayans and Aztecs enacted 500 years ago! To them, it was still 1499, and always would be!

Because of this startling discovery, he decided to leave the following morning and drive across the Yucatan Peninsula toward Merida. On the way, he would stop in two other important places and search for several more pieces of vital information.

At the same moment, many miles away, Mercata Verrano finally dismissed Antonio Garza from her mind and turned her thoughts to Luis Vasquez and the accident he would have the following night.

➢

Dusk was almost ready to descend the next evening as Antonio approached the outskirts of the sleepy hamlet of Tunkas. He had just slowed down to comply with the lower speed limit when he saw an old Jeep Cherokee parked at the side of the road a short distance ahead. The driver had left the cab and was bent over some sort of bundle that lay on the ground next to him.

Just at that moment, the Lincoln's automatic headlights snapped on. The driver immediately straightened up, vaulted into his Jeep, and sped away. Seconds later, Antonio parked next to the bundle in the place where the Jeep had been.

As he opened the door and stepped out, he heard a soft groan. The bundle of rags actually was the bloody and broken body of an elderly man.

Antonio knelt down beside him. "Can you hear me?" he asked.

"Yes. . . I hear you," came the slow and painful reply.

"Let me get you into my car. I'll take you to a hospital, or at least to the nearest medical aid."

"It is too late . . . for that, amigo. . . . If you . . . had not arrived when you did . . . I would be . . . dead by now."

"I don't understand."

"My name is . . . Luis Vasquez and . . . the Old Ones have . . . marked me for death. Embalador ran me down . . . with his Jeep . . . as I walked along the road. . . . He would have . . . finished me . . . with his hammer . . . if you had not seen him."

"Señor Vasquez, my name is Tony Garza, and I was sent here to investigate the many disappearances and to search for an ancient Aztec medicine that cures numerous illnesses. Can you help me?"

"All of my insides . . . were squashed . . . by Embalador's Jeep. I can . . . barely breathe . . . but I will tell you . . . all I can . . . in the time I have left."

He choked and coughed up a great gob of blood, then continued.

"It began . . . almost sixty years ago . . . when the evil man . . . who worked for Señor Verrano . . . named Casquete . . . started a fight . . . with my father . . . and broke his foot. . . . When Casquete took him . . . to the doctor . . . for a cast, . . . he was told that . . . if anyone found out . . . what had happened . . . he would be killed. . . . I was . . . only twelve years old . . . at the time . . . and did not learn the details . .

439

. until many years later . . . but I remember . . . the day after my father's foot was broken . . . our parish priest was killed . . . in an accident . . . and his housekeeper . . . disappeared along . . . with her sister . . . The same week . . . a houseguest . . .of the Padre . . . disappeared as well. Over the years . . . many other people . . . have also vanished . . . but nobody has the courage . . . to notice . . . they are gone."

He stopped talking and lay silently for several seconds.

"Last summer . . . on her way back . . . from a vacation in Cancun . . . my granddaughter disappeared. . . . My love for her . . . was stronger than my lifelong fear . . . but it took me . . . a while to muster up . . . my courage. . . . When I finally decided to act . . . the Old Ones . . .must have looked . . . into my mind . . . No sooner . . . do I go . . . (gasp) to the police . . . than I . . . am killed . . . (gasp) Not even . . . Tratamiento can . . . help . . . me now."

"Tratamiento?"

"The Aztec medicine . . . you seek . . . (gasp) I have carried some of it . . .(gasp) with me . . . (gasp) for many . . . years . . . If it was not broken . . . you will find it . . . . (gasp) (gasp) in my . . . poccckkk. . . . ."

Luis stared up into the stranger's compassionate eyes, his old, sun-wrinkled face contorted with pain, gurgled blood, gasped once more, managed a last strangled breath, and died.

Antonio traced the Sign of the Cross on the old man's forehead and whispered a prayer for the repose of his soul before reaching into the torn pocket that Luis had indicated. He withdrew a small jar, made from very thick glass topped with a cork stopper. Luis had been carrying it in the only pocket that was not crushed.

He shook the jar and discovered that the ounce or more of the clear liquid it contained had a syrupy consistency.

He removed the cork and placed the pad of his thumb across the opening, then inverted the jar. Almost at once, he felt a warm, then soothing sensation on his skin.

He lifted his thumb to his mouth and tasted a tiny amount of the substance. Tissues in his tongue reacted immediately. He felt a sharp, searing pain. Nothing pleasant about this sensation. It hurt. Momentarily, his heart rate even increased.

I'll bet Tratamiento would revive an unconscious person in a real hurry, Antonio thought, quickly putting the jar into his own pocket.

Since Luis' body lay just off the road, Antonio decided to leave it where it was after marking the location with a flare that he found in the trunk of his rental car. Then, as he drove toward the center of Tunkas, he made several important decisions.

On the western side of the town's small plaza, Antonio saw a large neon sign that said: POLICIA. He parked in an adjacent space, clearly reserved for those with official business and no others. He strode quickly toward the small, surprisingly modern police station and entered a well-lighted reception area.

A man wearing a gray, nondescript uniform sat behind a high desk.

"I wish to report an accident," Antonio began.

"What kind of accident?"

"An automobile accident."

"Was anyone hurt?"

"A man was killed."

"Who?"

"Look, officer, I was driving along the road and I saw a man lying next to the road. I stopped only long enough to be certain that he was dead. Then I came directly here. I have no idea who the man was."

"I am sorry, Señor. If you will have a seat over there, next to the far wall, I will call Chief Portero at his home. I am sure he will want to speak with you, personally."

As he sat on the hard, uncomfortable bench, Antonio reviewed his decision to conceal what he knew from the police about Luis Vasquez' death.

441

When he reconstructed the dead man's dying declaration, he vividly recalled his statement that as soon as he had gone to the police, the "Old Ones" had known about it. Antonio concluded that there had to be an informant within the ranks of the police department. Also, the name, "Old Ones," was much more than a simple identification. It conveyed an overwhelming feeling of prestige, power, and permanence.

Although he was convinced that his decision was the only practical one, Antonio still felt reluctant to hide certain facts from official investigators.

A few minutes later a large ponderous man, also wearing a dingy gray uniform, entered the room and came directly toward him.

"Señor, I am sorry you had to witness such a terrible accident. Please come into my office and give me the details."

The office was furnished with a bargain-catalog gray metal desk, three gray metal filing cabinets, and gray metal chairs, covered with a minimum of padding and cheap gray plastic.

The man indicated one of the chairs in front of the desk.

"Please sit down, Señor. I am Raoul Portero. And you are?"

"My name is Antonio Garza."

"Señor Garza," said the chief, withdrawing a long, yellow, official form from his desk. "Tell me what you saw."

"Actually, Chief Portero, I saw nothing other than a dead body beside the road."

"You told Officer Gomez that you saw an accident."

"Forgive me for correcting you, but I told Officer Gomez I wished to report an accident, not that I had witnessed one."

"Then how do you know that it was an accident?"

Antonio decided that this interview was not going well. Chief Portero might not look like a big city detective, but the man was no fool.

"I presumed it was an accident because the man was covered with blood and lying in a grotesque position. I assumed that the driver of the vehicle that struck the old man would come directly here and would have arrived before I did."

"Now you assume that the driver did not report this accident. Why, Señor Garza?"

"I don't understand your question, Chief Portero."

"I believe your words were: 'I assumed that the driver would come here.' Not — 'I assume that the driver came here.' That indicates to me, Señor Garza, that you no longer harbor that assumption. May I ask what logic you employed to come to that conclusion?"

This time, Antonio thought carefully before he began to speak.

"I reached that conclusion for two reasons, Chief. For one thing, Officer Gomez knew nothing about it. My report came as a complete surprise to him. Secondly, he said you were at home. If anyone had reported it, you would have been here, or on your way here, or on the way to the scene of the accident."

Antonio felt the first beads of perspiration break out on his forehead. He had almost said, "the scene of the crime," instead of "the scene of the accident." From his follow-up question, it was obvious that Raoul Portero had clearly seen his reaction.

"Is the room too warm for you, Señor? Or is it my questions?"

"Neither, Chief. It is simply unusual for me to find a body, or to be questioned by the police."

"You say this man was dead when you arrived. How did you make sure of that?"

"I parked next to him and felt his throat for a pulse."

"Did you see anyone else? Either on foot or in a vehicle?"

"When I was a long way up the road, I thought I saw taillights in the distance, but I was too far away to be certain. Also, my vision, in twilight conditions, is not what it once was."

"Well," said Tunkas' Chief of Police, "your powers of logic have not diminished. What do you do for a living, Señor Garza?"

"I teach History at Texas State University. I am also an author of articles and books about ancient civilizations."

"To what do we owe the honor of your visit?"

"I was merely passing through, on my way to Merida."

"I see. Tell me, Professor Garza, as a learned and logical man, what do you think happened out there this evening?"

"Well, to begin with, I'm an historian, not a detective."

"Perhaps," interrupted the Chief, "you missed your calling. You certainly have the logical mind to fit such a career."

"Logical minds are an asset in any career. I think the man was a victim of a hit-and-run driver. Maybe a young person who was just learning to drive, or perhaps an older person who simply panicked and drove away in fear. I suspect the driver may feel remorse and come in here at any moment."

"An interesting theory. Let's hope you are correct. Well, that's all for tonight, Señor Garza. Please remain in town until this unfortunate business is cleared up. Be so good as to call me once a day, and I will let you know when you can leave."

Chapter XXIX

➤

The Tangled Web

Yucatan Province
Yucatan Peninsula
Mexico
Spring, 1999

Antonio left the police building and walked back to his car, convinced that he had discovered the identity of the informer. Raoul Portero had neglected to do a number of things that any honest law enforcement official, as smart as he, most certainly would have done. Portero had accepted his claim that he was a History professor from Texas State without question. Neither a passport nor a visa had been required for validation. He had not even asked to see a lawman's favorite I.D., the driver's license. Why had he not checked any of these credentials? There was only one logical answer. He already knew all about his visitor!

If such were not the case, why would he presume that Antonio's version of the hit-and-run accident was true? How could Portero know that Antonio was not the perpetrator of the crime? Any competent investigator would have checked the automobile rental papers and then examined the vehicle itself for physical damage. There were simply too many pieces that didn't fit together.

Another mystery was Portero's insistent request that he remain in town for a few days. Again, he asked himself, why should I be required to stay if the Chief believes I've revealed everything I know? Perhaps I'll be detained until Embalador's organization grants permission for me to leave!

Bruce T. Clark

Not wishing to drive past the scene of Luis Vasquez' demise and perhaps implicate himself further, Antonio drove through the small town toward its western edge. There he found a small hotel called El Abrigo Seguro, the Safe Haven, where he secured a room for the night. Upon entering, he extinguished all of the lights and peeked through narrowly-parted drapes. On the far side of the parking area, he saw a man sitting inside an unlit Jeep Cherokee.

I wonder why I'm not surprised! Antonio thought.

Trained as he was in covert operations, Antonio realized at once that he was in no immediate danger from the silent watcher. Acutely aware of his need to relax and think clearly, he stripped off his soiled clothing and stepped into the shower. He stood there for some time, rotating and luxuriating under the thick, welcome stream of comforting water that tumbled down to soothe his sore muscles and lift the cobwebs from his mind.

Twenty minutes later, he once again extinguished the lights and plunged the room into total darkness. For a second time, he opened the drapes enough to create a narrow slit, wide enough to look through but insufficient to allow anyone to see inside. His timing could not have been better. He saw a small dark sedan being nosed into a parking place beside the Jeep, which had been backed in. Although he could see nothing but the occasional glow of a cigarette, he continued to watch the two vehicles for several minutes. Finally, his patience was rewarded. The Jeep pulled out of the parking area and left the driver of the sedan to his lonely vigil.

Antonio carefully closed the drapes and crept into bed without turning on any of the lights. He stretched out, pondered the strange turn of events, and wondered where Luis Vasquez's murderer had gone — if indeed he had been the driver of the Jeep.

Embalador certainly had been the driver of the Jeep. At that moment, he was sitting at a table in the main house of the large estate owned by Eduardo Peña, the member of the Council of Three who lived in Tunkas. Also present were Mercata Verrano, Tino Mallete (the third member of the Council), and Chief Raoul Portero, who was reading from his official notes.

"Garza said to Gomez... 'I stopped long enough to be certain that he was dead. Then I came directly here...' When he made that statement, Dr. Antonio Garza was lying. My question is, why?"

"Tell the Council why you believe he was lying," requested Mercata Verrano.

"Because the timing is all wrong. We know Embalador struck Luis Vasquez at 7:11, then turned his vehicle around and parked beside him. At 7:14, before he could be certain that the man was really dead, he was interrupted by the headlights of Garza's approaching car. Without taking a few extra seconds to be sure of his kill, he fled. Am I correct so far, Embalador?"

"Remember," Embalador said in an effort to defend himself, "that I hit him hard enough to kill a much younger and stronger man. I have killed enough people to know whether or not they are dead by the way they fall. Vasquez was dead. Also, I had to leave before Garza could identify my Jeep. When I pulled away, he was still too far off to see it clearly."

"Embalador," said the disdainful police chief, "everything you have just said is conjectural. You are certain of none of those things. Doña Mercata, do you wish me to pursue this, or should I go on with my Garza scenario?"

"Let's finish with Garza first. Please proceed."

"Garza parked next to the body of Luis Vasquez at 7:15 and, he says, remained beside it only long enough to be certain he was dead. Let's allow two minutes for that examination. Certainly, no one wishes to remain near a dead body any longer than necessary. It would then be 7:17.

"To drive from that place on the road to the town plaza, even at the posted speed limit, requires less than five minutes.

447

But since Garza is a stranger, I will allow him ten minutes to make that short trip. Ten minutes is far more than necessary because of the clearly marked directions to the police building. This would put the time at no later than 7:27.

"At that hour, parking is never a problem. Let us give this Good Samaritan three more minutes to park and enter the building. The time would then be 7:30. But Gomez logged Garza in at 7:57, not at 7:30, and his recordkeeping is always impeccable. I also believe Gomez because he called me at 8:00 sharp. What happened to those missing 27 minutes? Garza says he went directly to the police building as soon as he left the body! I believe him! I also believe that Luis Vasquez did not die until 27 minutes after Garza arrived on the scene! In which case, our friend Dr. Garza knows far too much to remain alive!"

"Are you not," asked Doña Mercata, "to some extent, engaging in the same sort of conjecture of which you accuse Embalador?"

"Perhaps, Doña, but my conjecture is rooted in fact, while Embalador's is based on fallacy."

"Please explain, Don Raoul," she encouraged.

"Three things bother me about Embalador's latest fiasco. He was close enough to positively identify a black Lincoln that was moving toward him through the dusk. An automobile, I might add, that he did not expect to see again. If he could identify a black Lincoln, Antonio Garza could certainly identify a green and brown Jeep, especially since he must have gotten quite close to the scene before Embalador was able to drive away.

"The next thing is Embalador's admission that he took a hammer with him when he left the Jeep. The hammer that he uses to finish off his targets. I believe that if he had been as certain of his kill as he claims, he would not have taken the hammer along. The fact that he did not then take the time to use it distresses me.

"The final item, and the one that worries me most, is the fact that for the last year his work has been very sloppy. If he were investigated by anyone less sympathetic than myself, he would be behind bars, or dangling from a gallows. He has become a very dangerous liability, Doña Mercata."

"Unfortunately for Embalador," Mercata agreed, "the Council of Three came to the same conclusion earlier this evening. It is unfortunate for us as well, because he has been our faithful worker for many years."

Before Embalador or anyone else in the room could move, La Señora Verrano withdrew a shiny, nickel-plated automatic pistol from beneath her shawl and fired three bullets into the former boxer's chest. BAM! ...... BAM! BAM! Concussions shook the room as hard-hitting, 250-grain chunks of lead slammed into fragile flesh. The force of the sledgchammer blows lifted the heavy body from its chair like a rag doll, and hurled it across the room.

Mercata Verrano looked down at the sprawled, bloody Embalador.

"I abhor violence! I always have! I particularly hate to kill people I like. Don Eduardo, my apologies for this unpleasantness. Don Raoul, please be good enough to dispose of the body at once, and kindly hide the Jeep until this trouble has been resolved."

She held the .45 caliber Colt pistol up for a moment before returning it to its hiding place.

"My father, Don Julio, gave me this weapon and taught me to use it over fifty years ago. It has never let me down."

She waited until Embalador's body had been dragged from the room before she spoke to the other members of the Council of Three.

"Señores, this situation with Dr. Garza is critical. We cannot kill a man of his stature unless we are certain there is no other alternative. His death would bring a multitude of troubles down around us. Perhaps more than we have ever before encountered."

When Raoul Portero returned a few minutes later, Mercata asked, "What are your recommendations for dealing with Antonio Garza?"

"Although I'm confident that my Garza scenario is correct, I can't be certain of it. Garza may have been so upset by the sight of Vasquez's body that he simply sat in his automobile for a few minutes. Many people, after similar experiences, cannot account for short spans of time. Their minds refuse to accept what their eyes have seen. Whether or not the sight of bodies emotionally disturbs him and blood is the big question. But I do know that during my interview with him, he was either very disturbed or he was lying. Before we do anything else, we must determine if he is working for someone else or really doing his own research."

"How will you go about that?" asked Don Eduardo.

"We must depend on Garza's immediate actions for our answer. If he communicates with anyone in the next few days and his message affects us adversely, he will have to die at once. If he does not make such a contact, we can allow him to live. But even then, he must be watched constantly until we are absolutely sure that our decision is the right one."

"If he is really going back to the university, as he told the desk clerk at the Palacio Amarillo, we may have to follow him for quite a long time," observed Mercata Verrano.

"Of course, you are right, Doña Mercata. The farther he is from the Yucatan, if a fatal accident should befall him, the more difficult it becomes to trace it back to us," added Portero.

"Who should we appoint to replace Embalador?" asked Mercata.

"Horca can replace him with no problem. Embalador's death will give Horca even more reason to exercise care and caution in the future. But I believe, Doña Mercata, that only one of our people is clever enough to handle Antonio Garza. We must use Asesino."

"You're right, Don Raoul. Asesino is the smartest agent and most competent assassin the Old Ones have ever had. All of the time and diligent effort we invested over the years,

450

turning Asesino into a brilliant operative and ruthless killing machine, has already been vindicated many times over." She stared directly at the other Council members and said, "Do you concur, Señores?"

Knowing better than to argue with Señora Verrano once she stated an opinion, both men nodded vigorously in agreement.

➢

The next morning, shortly after sunrise, Mercata Verrano sat in her small breakfast nook with "the smartest agent and most competent assassin the Old Ones had ever had."

Asesino certainly doesn't look like a ruthless killing machine, the old woman reflected, but like so many other things, looks are often deceiving. Smiling at her guest, she said, "I cannot overemphasize the importance of your new assignment. Antonio Garza is a brilliant, as well as a famous man. He is one of the very few people that we cannot eliminate with impunity."

The shrewd leader of the Council of Three paused for emphasis before continuing.

"Raoul and the other Council members agree that killing him must be a last resort. When he leaves the Yucatan, which we expect him to do very soon, his life or death becomes your sole responsibility. You will have to rely on your own instincts and judgment. If you feel that we have been compromised, or that he is dangerous to us, kill him at once."

"After the intensive training you and Don Raoul have given me for the past fifteen years, I should think you would trust my judgment and instincts completely."

"We do!" replied Mercata. "But I have always been a worrier. Especially about members of the family. Please be very careful!"

"I was born careful!" smiled the sweet-faced, heartless young killer. "Never fear! Nothing will happen that

451

I can't handle! I'll call often and keep you informed, Grandmother."

➢

Later that morning, Antonio visited Tunkas' record office and, as was his wont, surreptitiously examined a plethora of files in order to conceal his real objective.

He found a death certificate for Padre Pedro J. Constanzia, dated January 9, 1942, listing as his cause of death a broken neck, sustained in a fall.

Antonio minutely examined every police report, death notice, and missing-person file for the first six months of 1942, and found no mention of the disappearance of Emilio Duarte, nor of the sisters who, according to Luis Vasquez, had both vanished the same week the Padre died. Far from being surprised, he would have been astonished if any such files still existed. Tunkas' record office certainly had more than a reasonable number of unsolved missing-persons cases; but then, so did every other village on the Yucatan Peninsula.

Two ideas occurred to him. The first was a reaffirmation of his human sacrifice theory, while the second was more comforting. He reasoned that the ease with which the pagan perpetrators had acquired sacrificial victims over the years should soon become far more difficult. Computerized record-keeping, on an international level, would make all such methods of violence and murder nearly impossible. Never again would anyone simply disappear.

One of the clerks approached Antonio.

"Señor Garza, I have a message for you from Chief Portero. He would like to see you in his office as soon as possible."

"Thank you very much. I find it convenient to go at once."

Antonio spent the next few minutes collecting the files and records he had been examining and returning them

452

to their proper locations. He thanked the clerks again and then descended to the ground floor of the building, which housed the police offices and the jail. He entered the outer reception area and was pleasantly greeted by Officer Gomez.

"Thank you for coming so soon, Dr. Garza. Chief Portero is waiting for you in his office. Allow me to show you the way."

As Antonio entered the police chief's private office, Raoul Portero rose to greet him and indicated a chair.

"Dr. Garza, how good to see you again. I asked you to come downstairs to congratulate you."

"Congratulate me about what, Chief?"

"For so cleverly solving the hit and-run accident. You were correct in every one of your surmises. The driver of the Jeep that struck the poor man was a teenaged boy, so high on drugs that he never saw him. He says he felt a bump, but thought it was only a dog. Two of my officers have gone to Rio Lagartos to fetch him."

"That's impressive police work, Chief."

Raoul Portero studied the eyes of his guest intently.

"We're not as inept as some people believe. Now that it's over and his carelessness will have such a terrible effect on the life of that foolish young man, I suppose the only good thing to come out of this business is the fact that the victim didn't suffer."

"That is always a blessing," Antonio agreed.

"By the way, Señor Garza, did you take anything out of the victim's pockets?"

Antonio had been anticipating this question and was ready.

"No. I checked for a pulse, but not for identification. Have you been able to identify him?"

"Yes. He was a local man named Gordo Verrano. It is just that there was nothing at all on the body."

"I'm sorry, but I can't help you any further, Chief."

"You have helped us a great deal already, Dr. Garza. Well, you are free to go. Many thanks for your cooperation. Will you be remaining in our village for much longer?"

"No, I'll be driving to Merida early tomorrow morning."

"Once again, Señor, thank you for your assistance. Good luck with your research and, ultimately, with your entire project."

"Thank you, Chief, for your good wishes as well as for your kindness and consideration. Hasta luego."

After Antonio left his office, Raoul Portero sat pondering the man's fate. The hook he had tried to set, by calling the victim Verrano rather than Vasquez, had evoked a tiny but detectable reaction in Garza's eyes, but nothing of real significance. He was grateful that he was no longer responsible for keeping Garza in check. I'm glad, he decided, that Asesino has taken charge.

The following morning, soon after finishing breakfast, Antonio left Tunkas and drove toward Merida. On his way, he intended to check the official records of Dzibilchaltun and to accept Mercata Verrano's offer of hospitality. Ever since Luis Vasquez, in his final moments of life, had implicated a man named Verrano in the murder of Padre Constanza and the disappearance of Emilio Duarte, Antonio had wondered if Mercata Verrano might be related to that man. If she were, she might also be involved with the Old Ones. Her conduct at the Pyramids of Coba had been curious enough to make any scenario conceivable. He remembered the eerie feeling that he had experienced during their brief conversation. I may soon know for sure, he decided. Dzibilchaltun's missing-persons records might very well provide a key to everything.

> ➤

The ruins of Dzibilchaltun were not as famous as those of Coba or Chichen Itza, and only recently had Dzibilchaltun begun to approach the great numbers of annual tourists who had for so long descended upon the ruins of Mayapan and Tulum. But as he stood looking down from the highest remaining pyramid, Antonio realized that at its zenith, this ancient city must have been spectacular.

He visualized how it must have looked five hundred years before, and could almost understand the pagan inhabitants' commitment to maintain its splendor at any price. Unfortunately, they had chosen to enlist the aid of their gods and attempted to quench the insatiable blood lust of those deities by offering them an ever-increasing number of human sacrifices.

Antonio had arrived in the village an hour earlier and had no difficulty in locating the record office. However, experience with the clerks in other such places had taught him that their impatience with any interruption grew in direct proportion to the proximity of their approaching midday meal. Clerks who acted like docile lambs during most of the morning and again after lunch, all seemed to sprout vampires' fangs at 11:30 A.M. He decided to leave their collective tranquility intact and wait until midafternoon. Also, that would afford him some time to explore the ancient city.

He left the small village plaza and drove the short distance to the ruins. His timing was perfect. He was able to join a small group of tourists who were preparing to leave the visitor's center in the company of a local tour guide.

The party of guests included an elderly man and woman, two couples who were obviously newlyweds, and several younger people whom Antonio judged to be college students.

The last member of the group was a tall, slender, dusky woman who appeared to be in her early thirties, dressed in comfortable khaki walking shorts, matching shirt, and sturdy hiking boots. The only condescension she had made to femininity was a red ribbon tied around the shoulder-length ebony hair that framed her lovely face.

455

He noticed her full lips and flashing black eyes. Had he been asked to describe the unusual color of her skin, he would have said golden tan, but he decided there was no adjective that could truly do her justice. She would be an ideal model for a provider of sun-screen products, he mused. Many women would have spent a month's pay to look just like that as they lay on a tropical beach.

He was embarrassed when she looked directly at him and smiled.

Antonio could feel an aura of magnetism about her as she walked toward him, holding out her hands.

"Thank you, gallant sir, for making my efforts worthwhile."

When he looked puzzled she continued.

"I'm sorry, I didn't mean to sound mysterious. My name is Carla Cansino and I'm a petroleum geologist. My work takes me to many lonely places around the world. Sometimes, when I'm far from civilization, I'm tempted to forego the jogging and other daily exercises that I find so tedious. At such times I wonder why I bother. But the admiration I see in your eyes at this moment makes all my hard efforts worthwhile. For that, I thank you."

"I'm Antonio Garza, Señorita Cansino, and I don't make a habit of ogling beautiful women. But if a blind man learned that he had missed the sight of you standing here this morning, he would curse his darkness."

"What a pretty speech, Señor Garza. Are you a poet?"

"No, for nearly ten years I've thought of myself only as an historian and writer, but you've made me remember once again, and be very glad, that I am also a man. For that, I thank you."

"What a wonderful thing to remember," smiled the tantalizing Señorita Cansino, "for both of us."

Antonio smiled back at her, and realized he was still holding her hands. It was as though her touch had drained away his feelings of loneliness and replaced them with emotions he had not felt for many years.

She was certainly unique, he thought, or perhaps paradoxical was a more appropriate description. When he looked into her large, luminous black eyes, he felt sensations of peace and contentment. But her physical presence — the musicality of her voice — the lilt of her laughter — the exotic fragrance of her perfume, as it combined with the light coating of perspiration on her skin — transformed her into the most woman he had ever met.

She walked closely beside him as they toured the ruins and joined him on the long climb to the top of the highest pyramid where they shared the panoramic view. During those two exciting hours, they talked about the Mayas and Aztecs, progressed on to other ancient societies and civilizations, and finally to current events in the world. As these discussions evolved, he realized that Carla was a very intelligent woman, knowledgeable and well-read. Whenever she disagreed with one of his opinions, she did not hesitate to explain her point of view in a friendly and well-organized manner, using sound logic and good examples.

When the tour ended, he asked her to join him for lunch at a pleasant, nearby restaurant, an invitation she eagerly accepted. In the next two hours, they learned a great deal about each other over a pair of surprisingly good chef's salads, which in addition to fresh, crisp vegetables, featured chucks of spicy chicken. Before, during, and after lunch, they drank quantities of cold, frothy draft beer, quaffed from frosty mugs. They laughed a great deal and felt very much at ease in each other's company.

When Carla excused herself for a few moments, Antonio's memory drifted back to the dinner he had eaten at the quaint restaurant in Aranjuez, overlooking the Rio Jarama, and remembered his time of great sadness. Yet here I am, he thought, such a short time later, in the company of a woman I scarcely know, feeling happier and more content than I have for many years.

His jubilation would have been greatly dampened had

he known that Asesino, the deadly assassin, was nearby, observing him with interest and deciding on an appropriate course of action.

Carla returned to the table and Antonio asked, "What are your plans? Are you scheduled to start another project right away?"

"No, I have a month of accrued vacation time coming. I guess I'm a workaholic, Tony. I can never seem to relax."

"Isn't petroleum geology a rather unusual field for a woman?"

"It certainly was when I opted into it eighteen years ago. But that isn't true any longer. At the time of my decision, I didn't have much choice. But everything has worked out very well."

"You've really piqued my curiosity! Please tell me more."

"In the spring of my sophomore year, my father and mother died in an auto accident. For a while, I thought I would have to quit college, find a job, and support my younger sisters. But then good fortune intervened. A few weeks before that semester ended, corporate recruiters began to descend on Colorado University's School of Mines, attempting to obtain commitments from the juniors and seniors. Although I was only a nineteen-year-old sophomore, my faculty advisor scheduled several meetings for me with the various recruiters. Either the fact that I'm a woman, or because I was carrying a 4.0 average, persuaded three of them to offer immediate financial assistance in exchange for a long-term commitment from me."

She smiled at Tony before she continued.

"The Petrotex Corporation paid for my final two years of undergraduate work and advanced me enough money to support my sisters and myself. When I finished college, I went to work full-time, but under corporate sponsorship continued my post-graduate studies part time. Since then I've earned my Master's and Ph.D."

"I'm very impressed, Dr. Cansino."

"I'm awfully glad. I'm very impressed with you, too, Dr. Garza."

"Do you still work with the Petrotex Corporation?"

"I can't afford to leave. Each year, part of my earnings buy corporate stock, and my contributions are matched by the company. If I resign before age fifty-five, I retain my own half, but the balance reverts to the corporation. Seven years ago, I designed a system that allows petrographic surveys to be done from the air. It saves a great deal of time and money. Not only does it provide vast profits for Petrotex, but it means huge bonuses for me as well. If I work for them long enough, I'll be a very rich woman."

"Please forgive my bluntness in asking, Carla, but I would really like to know. Why is it that you have never been married?"

"I was married once for three whole months. Roger was also a geologist. He was tall, very handsome, extremely considerate, absolutely brilliant, and we were very much in love. A short time after our wedding he flew to Venezuela on a temporary assignment. One night, as he was inspecting an oil-drilling rig, the well blew up, killing him instantly. I was devastated for a long time. It's been ten years; but that awful hurt and loneliness still return sometimes. I've buried myself in my work and vowed never to fall in love again because I'm unwilling to endure even one day of that terrible, empty sorrow for anyone else. Forgive me for burdening you. I've never shared these thoughts before."

He reached across the table and took her hand in an attempt to console her.

"Where do you and your sisters live now, Carla?"

"One lives in Portland, Oregon and the other in Boston. I have a beautiful condo in Houston. I also own a ski chalet in Vail, Colorado, and a wonderful Jamaican beach house overlooking Black River Bay. But for about forty weeks every year," she laughed, "I'm a guest of some of the world's great families, the Marriotts, the Hiltons, and the Holidays. Or are the Holidays a family? All of this

Carta Blanca has made me a bit woozy. I think it's time to return to La Madera Flotante for a short swim and a long nap."

"Where is La Madera Flotante?"

"A few miles north of here, in Progreso. Right on the shore of the Bahia. You can follow me, and I'll show you the way."

"I have to do a bit of research and make a short visit to one of the local residents. Suppose I meet you at La Madera Flotante for dinner, about nine o'clock. Perhaps, if there are available rooms, you can make a reservation for me."

"That sounds great to me, Tony. I'll expect you at nine."

They left the restaurant and he drove her back to her rental car, which had been left at the ruins. When they arrived, Antonio insisted that Carla remain in his Lincoln while he unlocked her rental, rolled the windows down partway to allow the boiling air to escape, and flipped the air conditioner switch to its highest setting. Certain that everything possible had been done to insure her comfort, he slid out of the car just as she approached.

Before entering the quickly cooling compartment, Carla placed a hand on his shoulder and kissed him lightly on the corner of the mouth.

"Are you trying to make me fall in love with you, Dr. Garza? Because if you are, I think you may succeed. Please don't be late, Tony. I'm beginning to miss you already. Before you arrive this evening, I'll try to arrange a nice surprise for you."

She hugged him once more, obviously enjoying the encirclement of his arms. Then she climbed into her automobile and drove away, leaving him to puzzle happily over her surprise and wonder how so much could have happened in such a short time.

By the time he reached the records office, all the clerks had settled into their normal late afternoon routines. It was simple to enlist their aid in gaining access to the files and diverting attention away from his real purpose. By the time the office closed two hours later, he had seen every record and finished his examination. Dzibilchaltun's vital statistics had provided the key he had hoped to find. There were no missing persons files. In the past seventy-five years, not a single one of the village's inhabitants had disappeared. Tony wasn't surprised. He had been anticipating such a phenomenon.

He thought again of Mercata Verrano. Something about the old woman had touched off his mental alarm system during his visit to Coba. Perhaps it had been the condescending tone Mercata Verrano used with him, or her brief reference to the lifelong struggles of her beatific parents to protect the ancient building sites of the Mayas, Toltecs, and Aztecs, and to perpetuate their collective cultural heritage. Feelings of disquiet had been growing ever since that encounter.

He decided that if Mercata Verrano and her parents really were members of a secret, bloodthirsty cult, they could promote the success of their organization, as well as their own safety and survival, only by establishing a code of silence around themselves and their covert activities. He also reasoned that the price the Old Ones paid for that secrecy and silence was the exemption of all local people and their close relatives from inclusion in the sacrificial rites. The constant threat of being victimized, and the prospect of becoming a human sacrifice, eliminated any possibility of the code of silence being broken. It guaranteed to the Verranos and their cohorts the complete, lasting cooperation of the locals. Complete submission and silence were one's only guarantees for continued existence. That blanket of immunity had not covered Vasquez and his granddaughter because they lived in Tunkas and had no close family ties in Dzibilchaltun.

Records of Dzibilchaltun proved that it was the only village in the area that was immune to the problem of missing persons, the only village immune to the scourge of human sacrifice. That was certainly enough circumstantial evidence to support his cult theory and to make the Verrano family members prime suspects. His initial research complete, it was now time to fit the next piece of the puzzle into place. It was time to visit Mercata Verrano.

He stopped at a small service plaza and filled his gas tank, then asked the clerk-cashier for directions to the home of Señora Verrano. The young man, who until then had been very helpful and friendly, underwent an instant transformation. His body stiffened and his expression became uneasy and somber. He averted his eyes and conveyed the directions his customer sought as quickly as possible. Scant seconds after he handed Tony the change from his purchases, he hurried away.

Eager to discover whether a mere mention of the Verrano name evoked the same bizarre reaction in other village residents, he stopped and asked for directions at two more places. At each location, he saw distinct signs of fear and resignation. These people seemed to be completely intimidated.

He pulled to the far edge of the last shopping center parking lot and stopped in the deep shadow being cast by a thick clump of trees. Here the black Lincoln would be as invisible as a stealth bomber to any casual observer looking out from beneath the glare of the plaza's bright lights. He switched off the ignition and sat for several minutes, taking stock of his situation. He began by dividing his newly acquired knowledge into three categories.

He considered first what the Old Ones knew about his recent discoveries. They knew he was conducting old file searches in record offices. They knew he had found the body of Luis Vasquez, and that he had seen a Jeep pulling away from the scene. He was sure of that point because Raoul Portero had carefully mentioned it during his explanation of the hit-and-run driver's apprehension.

In the second category he listed information that they didn't know. He had no reason to believe that they yet knew why he was perusing the old files. They didn't know that Luis Vasquez had lived long enough to tell him a great deal. They didn't know he had discovered that they were called the Old Ones, or that the Aztec medicine was called Tratamiento. Nor did they know about his knowledge of Embalador and his hammer. They couldn't know he had uncovered evidence of continuing sacrifices demanded by their bloody cult. Most of all, they didn't know the two most important things. They were unaware of his knowledge of Vasquez's murder and, of course, they didn't know that he had a small sample of the Tratamiento in his possession.

The third and last category contained information that could lead to his assassination, if the Old Ones discovered he had it. Perhaps just his knowledge of the name Old Ones was enough. Certainly he would be assassinated for his possession of the Tratamiento. Also, because he had proof of their many murderous activities and their long history of human sacrifices. His suspicions about the probable involvement of Mercata Verrano and her parents would undoubtedly make him a candidate for extinction. Finally, he reasoned that although the Old Ones might suspect many things, they could prove nothing with certainty except his possession of the Tratamiento. If they did prove that, it would become his immediate death warrant.

He dismissed all thoughts of throwing the small sample away. Any modern laboratory could analyze the substance and determine not only the components but also their proportions. Once the composition was known, if the Tratamiento could not be recreated from natural materials, chemists might still be able to manufacture it from synthetic ones.

Since he could not possibly dispose of the Tratamiento, he decided to disguise it as something else. From a small traveling bag, which lay on the back seat, he removed his shaving kit. He unzipped a compartment and withdrew a small brown bottle, held closed by a screw-off top containing an eye dropper.

Antonio had suffered from chronic ear infections for many years and was forced to use this special medicine after immersion in any type of water. Salt water or fresh, it made no difference; the infections persisted whenever he did not insert the ear drops, both before and after any type of swimming. He unscrewed the top and emptied the medicine on the ground, shaking the tiny vial to expel every drop, and then blowing into it until the residue evaporated. He carefully poured the Tratamiento from Vasquez's vial into the medicine bottle, screwed back the top, and replaced it in the zippered place. He decided to keep the original vial for the time being and dispose of it in some safe place on the way to Mercata Verrano's home.

Later, as he drove along the road, he found an ideal spot where the road crossed a deep ravine. He threw the container out of the car window and over the bridge railing into the thick shrubbery far below. A short time later, he left the main road and turned into the twisting country lane, which led to the old woman's property.

As he drove, he put the final touches on the plan he had decided to adopt. The more he thought of it, the more appealing it became, for personal as well as professional reasons.

Two miles down the lane, from the store clerk's description, he recognized the Verrano driveway by the giant pair of stone jaguars that guarded Mercata's sanctuary. As soon as he passed by this brace of granite felines, a bank of security lights snapped on and made the entire area as bright as day. He continued down the long, narrow entryway and finally stopped beside the house's large veranda, where Mercata Verrano sat happily rocking in a huge old chair.

"This is a pleasant surprise," she said, as he approached her. "You're the gentleman I met in Coba. The historical writer. Forgive an old woman's poor memory. I don't recall your name."

This old woman could easily give lessons in covert operations, thought a wary Antonio. He gave her a friendly smile.

"Good evening, Señora Verrano. I'm Antonio Garza."

"Of course, Señor Garza. Now I remember. A hundred thousand pardons for my forgetfulness. How thoughtful of you to accept my invitation to visit. How is your project going, and how can I help you?"

"To be perfectly honest, Señora, I have just begun to scratch the surface. I still have many more weeks of research to do. But alas, I must interrupt this project for a while."

"Oh?" queried a visibly concerned Mercata Verrano. "What has happened?"

"I make my living as a university professor and by writing freelance articles for history magazines and periodicals. In most cases there's no guarantee that my material ever will be published. But occasionally I'm offered a commission by a magazine or a specific organization to write a special article, or to provide material for one of their esoteric projects. Those offers are often be quite lucrative."

"And you have recently received such an offer?" asked Mercata.

"Just this afternoon, Señora. I made a routine call to my literary agent and discovered that an offer was made this morning."

"How exciting for you! I hope you'll be paid well and enjoy the assignment, Señor Garza."

"Thank you, Señora. To a college professor, the offer seems extremely generous, and the subject is of great interest to me."

"I'm very glad for you. Can you tell me more about it?"

"Of course. The publication is American Heritage magazine. Next winter's issue will feature the ten historical events which the editors consider to be the most significant in the perpetuation of America's manifest destiny."

"Although I certainly don't think of myself as a scholar, I am fairly well educated. I should think that narrowing such a vast array of possibilities down to a mere ten would be nearly impossible," commented Mercata.

"Of course, Señora, every historian's list would be different because all of us have pet theories, but I don't believe the basic inclusions would vary that much. For example, some of the events I might choose are the discovery of gold in California, the wanderlust created in so many veterans by the Civil War, and the establishment of the transcontinental railroad. Perhaps most important is the fact that, unlike citizens of most Old World cultures, succeeding generations of Americans have never been prone to settle down near their ancestral homesteads. They have always been eager to see the other side of the mountain."

"Now I understand why people enjoy reading your material. You make everything sound so simple, yet it is very interesting. What will your part in this undertaking be?" Mercata inquired.

"The subject I have been assigned is the ouster of the Native Americans to make room for the great waves of immigrants. Of course, the principal act, which spelled doom for all American Indians, was the Sioux and Cheyenne's Pyrrhic Victory over Custer and the Seventh Cavalry. That single act, more than any other, led to the ultimate destruction of the red man and his nomadic way of life by intensifying America's hue and cry against them. I intend to visit that battlefield as well as several others. My objective will be to gather inspiration as well as material. Perhaps I can use the article to awaken readers to the continuing sorry plight of so many Indians. They have been treated in a shameful fashion."

"That's true of many conquered peoples," said Mercata. "More so in my own country than anywhere else. I fear that Mexico will always be forced to endure as a monetary and cultural weakling."

"When I return, after my assignment with American Heritage is completed, perhaps you could assist me in bringing to light some of the more blatant atrocities that have been perpetrated against the Mexican people. Very often, when people are made aware of injustice, they feel compelled to fight against it."

"I think that is often true, Señor Garza. Please forgive me, I'm being a poor hostess. May I offer you a cold beer, a cola, or a tall glass of iced tea?"

"The tea would be most welcome, Señora."

She excused herself and walked into the house. Even while she was gone Antonio remained alert and did not relax his vigilant posture. A few minutes later, she returned with two icy tumblers, filled with ice cubes and a bright amber liquid, and set them on a small table between their chairs.

"I have always preferred iced tea to any other beverage," she said.

"This tastes like Red Zinger," commented her sipping guest, praying that it did not contain poison.

"I'm impressed, Don Antonio. That is just what it is. By the way, have you been enjoying the sights of the Yucatan?"

"I regret to say, Doña Mercata, that all of them have not been pleasant."

"Why? What has happened?" asked an indulgent Señora Verrano.

"As I was driving through the village of Tunkas, I discovered a dead body. The victim of a hit-and-run driver, according to the chief of police. An old man had nearly been squashed by a vehicle, which ran him down. Yesterday Chief Portero told me that he had discovered the identity of the victim and had apprehended the culprit. He said the poor man's name was Gordo Verrano. I was concerned that Señor Verrano might be one of your relatives."

"Thank you for your concern, Don Antonio. Gordo was my distant cousin. Perhaps it is just as well that the poor old man is gone. He lost his wife two years ago to a heart attack, and recently his granddaughter died in a drowning accident. He may have been so overwrought with grief that he wandered into the path of the vehicle. Life can be very hard for elderly people, Don Antonio."

"You're right, Doña Mercata. Death can often be a blessing."

"How soon will you be leaving us?" she asked sweetly.

"In the next day or two, Doña. I'm going up to Progreso tonight, to enjoy the ocean for a little while, then I'll be flying back to the States. I'll return to the Yucatan in six or eight weeks, and contact you as soon as I arrive."

He rose and placed his empty tea glass on the table.

"Again, Doña, I appreciate your hospitality and your help. Until I next see you, hasta luego y vaya con Dios."

"Hasta luego, Don Antonio. You are always welcome in my home."

As soon as Antonio drove away, Mercata went to the telephone and pressed a speed-dial key. Seconds later she was speaking with Asesino.

"Antonio Garza just left my house. He claims to be returning to the States very soon to begin work on a new assignment. At this moment, I believe he's heading for Progreso. It's imperative that you never lose sight of him. He is very friendly and very intelligent, but something about him bothers me. I simply cannot make myself trust the man."

"At the ruins this afternoon," responded Asesino, "Garza met a beautiful woman. He seemed to be very attracted to her. Did he happen to mention her at any time?"

"No, he didn't, but that is not a surprise. Affairs of the heart are hardly the concern of an old woman. Although I can certainly see why many women might find Antonio Garza attractive. Follow him wherever he goes and keep me informed."

"As I have said many times before, don't worry. I can handle any situation that might arise. Good night, Grandmother."

As Antonio drove toward Progreso, he had mixed

feelings about his meeting with Mercata. His brain told him she had accepted his story, but his instincts tended to reject any such notion. Part of the story was true. He did have a contract with American Heritage to produce the article he had described for their winter quarter, but the maximum amount of time required, from start to finish, would only be about four weeks. So, he had originally planned to research and write the article in early autumn. He was certain that this portion of his narrative had been convincing, because he had given the assignment a great deal of thought.

Yet Antonio still had an overwhelming feeling that the old woman suspected his motives. The most disturbing thing was that, more often than not, his instincts were correct. He remembered the famous Winston Churchill quotation about a mystery being carefully wrapped in an enigma. That, he decided, was a perfect description of Mercata Verrano. Nonetheless, their interview had proved conclusively that she was implicated in the murder of Luis Vasquez. Why else would she have spun a false tale about her distant cousin, the nonexistent Gordo Verrano?

He saw the bright glare of fast-approaching headlights in his rearview mirror and was greatly relieved when a large white sedan pulled around him and sped off into the night. He realized he had been half-expecting a strange-looking Jeep and its menacing driver, who often wielded a deadly hammer. He shivered and thought, "I felt a lot safer in the Mekong Delta than I do here. At least in Southeast Asia, when you went into Badman's Territory, you knew where you stood — everyone wanted to kill you, not just a select few." He shuddered again as his thoughts returned to Mercata and her henchmen, like Embalador. The astonishing thing about them was their cavalier attitude toward abduction and murder. They stomp on a person as indifferently as I would stomp on a bug.

His last thought before he forced his mind away from the Old Ones and their murderous escapades was Mercata's appearance. At times during the evening, when the veranda lights had illuminated one part of her face and cast the rest in shadow, she reminded him of somebody else. Someone he knew. The resemblance was vivid!

He racked his brain but was unable to figure out who that other person might be.

He decided to relax and concentrate on more pleasant thoughts for the balance of the trip. The winning entry in any current contest for pleasant thoughts was obvious. Carla Cansino won every blue ribbon. He wondered again about the surprise she was planning and smiled to himself. I'm behaving like a small boy who expects a special toy for Christmas, he thought. Carla is special, all right, but she's no toy. She's smart, sensual, and beautiful, and I am very much attracted to her. I'm also extremely vulnerable. Go slowly, he told himself.

He arrived in Progreso a short time later and followed the signs to La Madera Flotante, which was built, as Carla had said, on a low sandy bluff overlooking the blue expanse of the Bahia. Designed to resemble an old windjammer sailing ship, it looked inviting and restful. He parked near the front entrance, entered the bright, impressive lobby, and walked toward the front desk.

"Oh, yes, Dr. Garza," said the clerk, "we expected you. You are in Suite 123. Dr. Cansino will meet you in the dining room at 9:00. While you are with us, please call if you need anything."

Tony found Suite 123 to be spacious and luxurious. He removed his soiled clothing and spent a long time under a warm, soothing shower. Greatly refreshed, he set his travel alarm for 8:30, then stretched out on the bed and took a short nap. He awoke, feeling quite anxious and even a bit nervous. He dressed in a very formal dinner jacket, replete with a red carnation, and, at the stroke of 9:00, entered the dining room and saw Carla sitting in the soft candlelight, looking incredibly beautiful.

Chapter XXX
➢
Carla Cansino

The Northern Yucatan Peninsula &
The Western United States
Late Spring, 1999

As he approached her table, his knees began to shake so violently that it made walking difficult.

"You look absolutely wonderful," he said, smiling down at her. "Your radiance takes my breath away."

"I made a special effort to look nice. You know, I haven't dressed for a man in many years. But I did tonight because I wanted to please you. We both deserve to relax, have fun, and enjoy each other's company."

He took her hand and kissed it, savoring the same mystically exciting fragrance on her skin that he found so appealing earlier in the day. He reluctantly released her fingers and sat down opposite her. She smiled at him and said, "I called the wine steward this afternoon and ordered several bottles of champagne. I insisted that he provide us with his last four bottles of Dom 1964. They're the first part of your special surprise."

"I'm more than surprised. I'm flabbergasted. I would not have believed that four bottles of 1964 Dom Perignon existed any longer, in all of Mexico. They must have been very expensive."

"Please allow me to spoil and pamper both of us in my own way. For the first time in a long time, I'm glad I can afford such luxuries. I never indulge myself when I'm alone."

"The greatest luxury I can imagine is being here with you."

471

"I feel the same way, Tony. But I don't understand how all of this can be happening so quickly. I have another present for you that expresses our mutual feelings far more eloquently than I can with mere words. I had two special gifts made today. One for each of us. They should be delivered shortly."

They enjoyed an excellent meal and then raised toasts to each other and to all the romantic evenings they hoped to share. For they were falling in love, and the world was theirs.

When the last drop of the Dom Perignon had been savored, they strolled hand in hand into La Madera Flotante's lovely tropical garden overlooking the moonlit sea, and watched as the Bahia added to their feelings of romance by sending a chorus line of tiny, silver-tipped wavelets dancing in to caress the shore. *Carla is right, he thought. All of this is crazy. I haven't had a real interest in any woman since Pamela died. Now here I am, drowning in waves of romance.*

He turned her toward him, cupped her chin gently in his hand, and raised her lips to meet his own. It was as though a bolt of lightning had struck them. Their physical awakening was immediate. His arms dropped and encircled her in a tight embrace. Bodies blended together, as lips sought lips in an increasingly daring and imploring fashion. That which moments before had been a romantic interlude now bordered on uncontrolled passion. Tony could feel a runaway desire mounting within him, but it was Carla who suddenly wrenched herself out of his arms and spun away.

"Tony, this isn't right, or fair, to either of us. We've just met. And please don't ask me what I want at this moment, because I desperately want you. But we can seldom have what we want. The right choice is always the hardest because it requires strength; the wrong one permits weakness. I want our relationship to be very special, and I know you do, too. It must be based on more than physical

472

pleasure. Please, Tony, please help me. If we can't be strong for ourselves, let's try to be strong for each other."

➢

Since the mixture of fragrances, arising from the abundance of exotic tropical plants and flowers, seemed to be acting on them like an aphrodisiac, they decided to leave the garden and wander along the beach.

They left their shoes inside Carla's pool cabana and pottered along the water's edge for well over a mile, smiling and holding hands and enjoying the antics of a pair of frisky sandpipers who ran just ahead of them, searching for sandy treasures that only they and their feathered kind can covet.

As they moved along, anytime a small rogue wave roiled up and churned ashore, Carla would yelp with delight and go scurrying up the beach ahead of it, as though she were being pursued by a band of brigands. She reminded Tony of a seven-year-old urchin rather than a highly successful thirty-seven-year-old woman. For a few happy moments, she shed all of her worldly burdens and became a carefree child. As they walked back toward the hotel, she found a sand dollar and declared their first nocturnal adventure together a complete success.

Their first stop as they entered the lobby was at the desk. When the clerk saw them approaching, he reached into a hidden recess and withdrew a small, brightly wrapped package. He handed it, with a triumphant flourish, to Carla.

"Here is the parcel you've been expecting, Dr. Cansino. The messenger arrived with it less than ten minutes ago."

Carla thanked him and then, taking Tony by the hand, led him across the lobby toward the most secluded and private corner in the huge room, an inviting area made more so by a dozen stately potted palms that, for all the world, seemed to be stretching up to reach the bank of skylights sixty feet above. They sat close together on a comfortable, oversized couch, fronted by a long walnut coffee table, and Carla eagerly opened the package. She withdrew a pair of identical boxes from within and shook them. Then she placed one on the table and handed the other to Tony.

"Perhaps I'm a hopeless romantic, Tony; but I couldn't allow this very special day to slip away from us. I think I have found a way to freeze this moment in time."

He opened the small but surprisingly heavy box and withdrew a beautifully crafted identification bracelet. On the outer surface the engraver had etched Antonio Garza in a classic-style script. On the inside, their first names and the date were engraved. Around the letters and figures was carved a feathered serpent coiled into the shape of a heart.

Carla opened the second box and handed another bracelet to Tony. It was a smaller, lighter version of his own. She extended her arm.

"Please put it on for me, Tony."

After he had complied, she clasped the other one around Tony's wrist and kissed him gently.

"Our lives are joined by these symbolic circles of gold. Since we met here in the heartland of the Mayas and Aztecs, I decided that the feathered serpents would be most appropriate."

"Beautiful and extremely appropriate, Carina [Loved One]."

They strolled through the lobby and settled into a pair of wicker chairs on the hotel's festooned back patio. Surrounded by craggy cactus and plump piñatas, they enjoyed piña coladas and listened to the dramatic music of a flamenco guitarist. The musician left his tiny stage a half hour later, and a low rumble of conversation began to fill the room.

"As the senior member of this organization," Tony said, "I've made an executive decision. In order to fulfill a contractual obligation with American Heritage magazine,

474

I'll have to leave here in a few days, so I can visit a number of locations in the western U.S. Although a portion of my time will be spent rifling through documents and artifacts, mostly I'll be touring old battlefields and museums. Places that you would find very interesting."

He paused for a moment and observed the pleased smile that was slowly creeping across her happy face.

"Since you have a month of vacation time coming, I propose that you join me for as long as you can before you go back to being Dr. Cansino."

She paused for several moments before she replied.

"Enamorado [Sweetheart], your idea is wonderful and I will eagerly agree, on one condition. When I'm near you, you shatter all of my resolve and good intentions; so I ask you once more to remember that we must be strong for each other. To be lovers would be thrilling and enjoyable, and for a little while we might seem to be very happy. But that would only be an illusion. Truly falling in love is so much more than that. It is also true or false, right or wrong, sharing or taking. You told me once that you're old-fashioned. I guess I am too. I want us to share a wonderful love affair, not a selfish relationship based on lust alone."

Tony squeezed her hand and nodded in agreement, thinking how fortunate and blessed he had been to find such a terrific lady after so many years of loneliness.

Two days later, they took a commuter flight to Mexico City and after a short stopover, continued on to Albuquerque, New Mexico.

Tony rented a luxury automobile, and for the next two weeks they toured through parts of New Mexico, Arizona, Oklahoma, and finally south, into Texas. Although Tony had originally conceived this trip as a means of throwing the Old Ones off the track, as the days passed it became increasingly important for other reasons as well. It became an exciting adventure for two desperately lonely people, both of whom were blissfully content to be in the company of the other.

During those days they visited Adobe Walls, where Kit Carson had headquartered during the Navajo War of 1864 and also where a big Kiowa and Comanche war party besieged a group of buffalo hunters ten years later. They toured other battle sites where Apache, Navajo, Arapahoe, and Southern Cheyenne warriors had battled great odds against Eighth Cavalry troopers and Texas Rangers — where many tribesmen had eventually been brought to bay and exterminated in the numerous canyons, arroyos, and mesas that dotted the stark, inhospitable landscape.

They saw the Staked Plains and toured Forts Bascom, Union, and Sill. They saw, too, the reservations at Darlington and Anadarko, and all the other places where General Sheridan had tried to turn bad Indians into good ones in the late 1860's and on into the middle 70's during the Red River War. They looked down from the heights above the site of the Battle of Palo Duro Canyon and at the scene of the Buffalo Wallow Fight. Everywhere they looked, they found other places where Indians from every Plains tribe, alone or in bands, both large and small, made their own last stands rather than surrender their freedom to make way for America's inevitable western expansion.

It was a somber pair of wanderers who returned to Carla's condo in Houston for an overnight stay, before flying on to their final destination, the Custer Battlefield and Museum. They would remain there for the balance of the week.

For their fourth week together, Carla had suggested a camping trip into one of the Colorado or Wyoming wilderness areas. Tony, who had had his fill of tent-living in the military, had less than enthusiastically agreed.

➢

Back in her Yucatanian lair, Mercata Verrano was eager for some definitive information. Asesino had contacted her several times during the preceding two weeks, but had nothing concrete to report. They agreed that the possibility of danger to the Old Ones from Antonio Garza was decreasing. So was the potential need to assassinate him. But the old woman was still not ready to drop the surveillance. She ordered Asesino to stay on the assignment and to keep her informed.

➢

It was nearly 10 A.M. on the morning after their arrival in Houston when Carla tapped on the door of the guest room.

"Tony, are you awake?"

She received an unintelligible babble as a reply, so she continued, "Get up, you lazybones. I've spent the last hour and a half swimming and now I'm ready for breakfast. I'll start cooking the steaks while you shower. Hurry up, or I'm liable to eat both of these great looking filets and all of the eggs."

Ten minutes later, Tony walked out onto the condo's terrace just as Carla transferred the last of the food from a serving cart to a glass-topped table. She was dressed in a brief, off-white outfit, which resembled a tennis dress. The contrast between her bright costume and her dusky skin was dazzling.

"Carina, you look good enough to eat in that outfit. I don't know whether to start on you or the steak."

She stretched up on tiptoe, as was her custom, and delivered a quick kiss to his check.

"Better start on the steak," Carla purred. "It's sizzling."

"So am I!" Tony assured her, releasing her from his embrace.

Over breakfast, they discussed the various places they could camp after they left the Custer historical area.

"I'm sure there are a multitude of sites," Tony guaranteed. "Also, the local folks will gladly help us select a good location."

"You're right, Tony. We're going to find a great place and have a terrific time. As of this minute, I will stop worrying."

She relaxed for a moment and took a sip from her coffee cup.

"Did you bring the prescription for your ear medicine?"

"Yes," said a suddenly nervous Antonio Garza. "There's one in the small zipper pocket of my shaving kit. Why do you ask?"

"When I unpacked your things last night, I noticed an unusual bottle in your shaving kit. I was so curious that I read the instructions and discovered its purpose. I borrowed the medicine this morning and took it down to the pool with me. I was sure you wouldn't mind. I sometimes get earache after I swim, so I decided to see if it would help me. I put five drops in my ear as the prescription indicated, but something must be wrong with the medicine. It made my ear feel like it was on fire. I couldn't wash it out quickly enough. Fortunately, I only put the drops in one ear. It isn't supposed to feel like that, is it, Tony?"

"No, Carina, of course not!" her suddenly crushed and deflated guest replied. "I'm sorry that you suffered such discomfort. What did you do with the bottle?" he asked casually. "I need the prescription label to get it refilled."

"I'm sorry, Tony. I threw it into the trash can beside the pool exit. I'll run right down and see if I can find it."

"I'll go," Tony said quickly. "I need to get some exercise after that big breakfast, anyway. I'll be right back."

Tony could feel a huge knot of anxiety building up in his stomach. He thought of the many lives that had been given up to protect the precious medicine. He had failed Luis Vasquez. He had allowed his vigilance to be diverted by foolish dreams about his wonderful future with Carla, and he had grown careless. I should be horsewhipped, he thought, as he raced down the hall.

He didn't wait for the elevator; instead, he took the stairs two at a time. When he reached the bottom of the last flight, he burst through the door, dashed quickly across the lobby, and ran onto the surrounding apron of the large swimming pool. He could hardly believe that his clever hiding place had been discovered and that the Tratamiento had, inadvertently, been thrown away. Please Lord, he prayed as he ran, let it still be there. What can I do if it isn't, he wondered? I was so fortunate to get it. It simply has to be there!!!

But it was not.

Every trash receptacle around the pool had been emptied. Not even a scrap of paper remained in any of the large, wire mesh containers. Tony rushed back through the building toward the doorman, his heart sinking.

"What happens to the trash that's emptied out of the pool-side receptacles?" he asked the gold-and-maroon-liveried guard. "I think I may have dropped my keys into one of them by mistake!"

"Oh? I'm sorry to hear that, sir! Every couple of hours those containers are emptied into the big dumpster behind our building, and the dumpster is emptied early every morning. Unfortunately, the trash pickup for today has already been done. The truck left about fifteen minutes ago. I'm awfully sorry, sir!

Tony thanked the doorman and turned away.

How can I explain such stupidity to Cardinal Questa? Antonio suddenly wondered. What can I say to a man who is counting on me so heavily? He shuddered as he thought, I'll simply have to return to the Yucatan and start again. There must be somebody, somewhere, that I can persuade to help me and rid himself of the threat of the Old Ones. The loss of the Tratamiento was certainly a devastating blow, but he couldn't let it deter him. His mission was much too important! He had risen above misfortune many times before. He would simply have to do so again, or die trying. I suppose, he thought, the precious medicine is riding along in a trash truck on its way to a disposal site. No doubt it will never be seen again.

479

But Tony was wrong. The tiny bottle of Tratamiento was not in the trash, nor was it likely to ever be lost again. At that very moment, the vial lay in the palm of Asesino's hand. Asesino was sure that when Mercata Verrano was informed of this morning's discovery, the small, brown, eye-droppered bottle would become Antonio Garza's death warrant.

➢

Late that afternoon, Mercata Verrano received a call that she had been anticipating. She learned about the vial of Tratamiento and of Antonio Garza's dismay when he was unable to recover the container from the trash.

"Do you believe there can now be any doubt about his duplicity, or his purpose?" Mercata asked.

"No, none at all. I kept watch on the trash container, and he nearly had a stroke when he saw that the bottle was gone. He knows more than we can afford to let anyone know."

"You're right. He must be killed. Where are you now?"

"At the Houston airport. Ready to board a flight. Garza and Carla Cansino are flying to Billings, Montana."

"You must make his death look like an accident!"

"I always make them look like accidents, Grandmother!"

"It would be good if you didn't have to involve Carla Cansino; but if she must be eliminated, don't hesitate. Nothing must stand in your way. Garza is much too dangerous. He must die. It's too bad we didn't have this information while he was here. It's so much harder outside of the areas we control since we must rely on well-planned, deadly accidents. Call me when you have a plan."

➢

The flight to Billings was smooth and uneventful. Tony and Carla ate dinner at Gussick's Restaurant, famous for its succulent prime rib. Then they retired to their respective rooms.

Well after 3:00 A.M., Tony was still tossing and turning, his mind in a turmoil over the loss of the Tratamiento and the thought of having to return to the perils of the Yucatan peninsula. The next morning he arose early and, operating within the narrow confines of a sleepless fog, went to meet Carla. Having grown tired of rich food, they breakfasted on simple stacks of silver-dollar-sized blueberry pancakes.

Tony arranged for an automobile and, at 8:00 A.M., they crossed over the Yellowstone River and began the beautiful fifty-five-mile drive along Interstate 90 to the Custer Battlefield.

The next week was filled with magic for both of them as they toured the battlefield and visited the memorials of a handful of famous men, as well as the final resting places of hundreds of other soldiers who were not well known and never would be. They saw the heights that had once been defended by the troops of Reno and Benteen. They stood atop Battle Ridge and the crest of Custer Hill and looked down from Weir Point and Calhoun Hill. They were able to walk along the Medicine Tail Coulee and gaze across the ford where many brave men had died one sultry June afternoon.

Wherever they went and wherever they stood, they were never far from places that had known both total triumph and devastating defeat, excited elation and utter despair. Many times each day Tony thought he heard the echoes of bugles and the sounds of pounding hoofs. He heard the screams of agony and frustration that emerged from many graves and reached across a century and more. Whispers of torment, borne on broken promises and unfulfilled dreams, were present, too. For paradoxically, the Sioux and Cheyenne lost by winning; while Custer,

481

in death, finally achieved his avowed purpose of bringing the Plains Indians to their knees.

Tony wondered how sad the Boy General might be if he could see the humiliation and sadness that his last battle had brought to an entire race of people who deserved a far better fate.

The Custer Museum, with more than twenty thousand artifacts and exhibits, was a historian's treasure trove. Antonio would have needed several weeks to examine all of the displays. But it was not the museum or any other official source that yielded his best piece of information. It was an ancient Crow Indian named Henry Walking Bear, whom he arranged to meet one day while Carla went shopping.

Henry had inherited his interest in historical events from his father, who was an army scout with General Terry in 1876 and had been among the first to reach the battlefield on June 27. Henry Walking Bear, like his famous father, was a leading expert on the Little Bighorn and all the other Indian Wars.

In addition to a vast array of memorabilia, the Walking Bear family had spent over a hundred years communicating with other Custer historians as well as actual survivors of the battle and their relatives. It was Antonio's question about various weapons that chanced to provide the missing piece to an ancient puzzle.

"Did you know," Henry asked, "that Charles De Rudio was the only officer to carry his sword into the Little Bighorn battle?"

"No, I didn't," Tony responded. "Custer ordered that all the swords be left behind, did he not?"

"Indeed, he did! De Rudio apparently disobeyed that order. As a matter of fact, he found part of another sword under the body of his friend, Myles Keogh. De Rudio sent it to Keogh's widow with her husband's uniform and a lock of his hair. Megan Keogh was kind enough to send a copy of De Rudio's letter to my father, back in 1889. Give me a minute and I'll get it for you."

Henry Walking Bear returned a few moments later with an airtight plastic letter holder which contained an age-yellowed sheet of paper, both sides of which were covered by a spiky, feminine handwriting.

"As you can see, Dr. Garza, despite our careful handling, the letter is beginning to show its one hundred ten years."

Tony took the artifact from a gnarled, blue-veined hand, only fifteen years younger than Megan's letter, and began to read. It was postmarked July 5, 1876, and had been written at Fort Abraham Lincoln, in the Dakota Territory. The letter conveyed news of the battle and word of Myles Keogh's death, together with Charles De Rudio's profound sympathies and words of comfort to the widow. He assured her that Myles had died quickly and had not undergone any unnecessary suffering.

"Knowing Myles as well as I did," De Rudio wrote, "I'm certain that he died with dignity, after performing his duty flawlessly."

He went on to say that he was sending a box containing Myles' uniform and a lock of his hair. He gently reminded her that Myles had spoken often about donating his military possessions for permanent display in the Swiss Guards' Hall of the Vatican.

In his final paragraph, perhaps written to divert the widow from her grief, De Rudio changed the subject. He was sending her, along with his other effects, a weapon, which Myles had captured on the battlefield. Although it had been reduced to the size of a knife, it had originally been a fine sword. De Rudio assured her that an inscription on the four hundred twenty-two-year-old blade supported his conclusion. It said:

TOLEDO ESPAÑA - MCDLIV

Some of the features which had been built into the weapon, De Rudio wrote, like the parallel handguards, triangular brass tang, and particularly the hooked point, reminded him of two knife-swords that he and Myles had once seen in Cuba at the Museo de Armas y Hojas de Espadas. De Rudio closed his letter by offering any type of help that his friend's widow might require.

Megan Keogh had faithfully copied De Rudio's entire letter and added a postscript: "I did send all of my husband's weapons and equipment to the Vatican as he requested. I also sent the Spanish knife, which Charles forwarded, to me. As far as I know, everything will remain there on display in the Hall of the Papal Guards."

Tony handed the letter back to its owner. "That is a wonderful artifact, Mr. Walking Bear," he said. "Thank you for sharing it with me. Unfortunately, I must excuse myself now. I appreciate your hospitality more than I can say, and I hope that I may be allowed to return again at some future time."

Tony left the old man's home in a state of amazement, scarcely able to contain his excitement. His mind drifted back to another building — a mansion in Granada, Spain — and a room which contained a handsome walnut sword rack — a rack with one missing sword.

He visualized a silver plaque on the shining walnut that read:

DIEGO GARZA - ESPADAS ESPAÑAS - TOLEDO ESPAÑA - MCDLIV

He left Henry Walking Bear's ranch house yard, and drove for about a mile before parking on the roadside under a shady tree. It was time to organize his thoughts and compute the percentages. Dr. Antonio Garza now shifted his great knowledge of history and his logical mind into high gear.

The weapon De Rudio had described had been made in Toledo in 1454 and could only have been crafted by José Mendoza, since all of his signature features were included. How many fine swords could Toledo's best weaponeer have made in one year using 1454 technology? he wondered. More than one per month would have been impossible, he finally decided. After all, he reasoned, as late as 1830, it had taken James Black almost two weeks to craft the famous knife for Jim Bowie. Therefore, twelve swords per year was undoubtedly an extremely generous estimate.

Next, he asked himself, of the twelve swords Mendoza had crafted in 1454, how many might have made their way across the ocean to the new world? Of equal importance was the fact that the weapon sent to the Vatican had been found on the Little Bighorn Battlefield, in one of the northwestern states.

Historically, the Sioux and their allies, the Cheyenne and Arapahoe, most frequently fought against their bitterest enemies, and nearest neighbors, the Pawnee. Whenever they strayed from the normal pattern, a variety of tactical reasons compelled them to raid either toward the west or the south. Their westerly forays were almost always very shallow in scope. He couldn't remember a single warpath that had carried the Sioux beyond the Bitterroot Mountains. Even their farthest western sweeps still left them hundreds of miles away from those areas frequented by any of the tribes who dwelt along the Pacific coast. No, he decided, the Mendoza weapon could not have come to Montana from the west.

On the other hand, although such assaults were rare, the Sioux occasionally raided deep into the heartlands of Kiowa, Comanche, Apache, and other tribes of the Southern Great Plains. Centuries later tribal storytellers were still recounting the awesome ferocity of these skirmishes. But the bloody battles had not been one-sided, Tony reflected. Very often, the Sioux' line of retreat could be followed by the bones of their dead. But then most long-running wars were quid pro quo. He pulled his mind back from the brink of the daydream, and returned to his systematic summation.

The chance of more than one of the twelve weapons forged by José Mendoza in 1454 appearing on the Custer Battlefield, after four centuries, was remote.

The Mendoza sword, one of the original twelve, must have been brought to the Powder River country from the south. The south meant Mexico, and Mexico meant one of the Spaniards who came to conquer the Aztecs in 1519 or 1520, with a sword that was already sixty-five years old!

The second part of his mental scenario was equally valid.

Chances of more than one of those twelve unique weapons existing in the small forces of Cortez or Narvaez must be a million to one. The weapon Megan Keogh sent to the Vatican, he concluded, had to be the Sword of the Garzas.

Obviously, his course was clear. Before returning for another dangerous mission in the Yucatan to search for another sample of Tratamiento, he must determine whether the sword was still at the Vatican Museum. If so, he would go to the Museo de Armas y Hojas de Espadas in Havana and find the swords Charles De Rudio had written about, in the hope that they might provide a key to José Mendoza's secret compartments. Not until he returned to the Vatican with a solution to the baffling enigma, or until he was able to open the sword's hilt, would he know if it actually was the Garzas' weapon. Additionally, after some 500 years, the material on which Padre Garza had recorded his precious formula might well have turned to useless dust!

In any case, he would be unable to determine any of those things until the following week, since early tomorrow morning he and Carla were departing for their camping trip. She had been extremely patient but was obviously anxious to get started. His afternoon of discovery had put Tony in a much happier frame of mind. He was finally ready to relax and enjoy their vacation.

Chapter XXXI

➢

The Golden Hoard

Yellowstone & Bighorn Rivers
Wyoming & Montana Wilderness
Late Spring, 1999

He found her lying beside the motel pool, enjoying the last rays of a late afternoon sun. He went forward as quietly as possible until he reached her side, then bent down and stroked her smoothly tanned back for a moment before kissing her ear.

"Hi, Darlin'," she cooed, without turning around.

"How did you know it was me?" Tony laughingly inquired.

"I didn't," she purred teasingly.

She flipped over onto her back and stretched her long arms lovingly around his neck, drawing him down to her and hugging so tightly that he grunted.

"I hope you didn't mind going without me this afternoon, Tony. I arranged for our equipment and heard about a neat camping spot. It even has a buried treasure! I'll show you the map at dinner. Why don't you run up and put on your swimsuit? We have plenty of time, and the water feels wonderful."

When he returned a few minutes later, she was sitting at a poolside table under a beach umbrella with a bowl of salted peanuts and a big pitcher of mimosas, the wonderful combination of champagne and orange juice to which she had introduced him.

"How did you guess I was dreaming about peanuts and mimosas?" he asked.

"Two reasons. First of all, I'm a female witch doctor and read minds. Second, and more important, I always want to please you because I love you so very much."

She took his hand in both of hers and nibbled on each of his knuckles before rubbing her soft cheek gently against them.

"Lady, if you're looking for new ways to jolt my self-control, you're on the right track. You asked me to help you be strong, but you bewitch me with your little games. Please don't try to make me hungry for something besides mimosas and peanuts."

"I'm sorry, Enamorado. I didn't mean to strain your resolve."

"Carla, feeling toward each other as we do, it's time for us to think about getting married."

"I have been thinking about it, Tony. We're going to have a lovely time camping and then we'll be separated for a few weeks. I think both of those things will go a long way toward helping us chart our future together."

She sat quietly for a moment, gazing into his eyes.

"You make me want to be near you all the time; but I know I must have some time alone, to think. You have a strange, hypnotic power over me, Tony, but neither of us can afford to make a mistake. This marriage must be forever."

"You're right. The next few weeks will tell us a great deal. Let's take that swim and then go to dinner. I can't wait to see your treasure map."

Sometime later, as they enjoyed their after-dinner drinks, Carla produced a small map and spread it out on the table.

"There is quite a story connected with this map. I'll give you the highlights. The treasure is called Custer's Legacy because in June 1876, before the wounded from the Little Bighorn battles could be brought aboard the rescue vessel, a large cargo of gold had to be unloaded. The captain and the pilot of this riverboat, called the Far West, hid the gold before they ferried the wounded men down the Bighorn, Yellowstone, and Missouri Rivers to the hospital at Fort Abraham Lincoln."

"I remember reading something about that many years ago," Tony recalled. "Was the gold ever recovered?"

"That's the best part," continued Carla. "Captain Grant Marsh and his friend, David Campbell, returned to retrieve the gold a short time later, but vanished before they could do so. There was substantial evidence to indicate that they had drowned in quicksand, but no one really knows for sure."

She indicated a place on the map as she continued.

"Marsh and Campbell left General Terry's encampment here, at the junction of the Yellowstone and Bighorn Rivers one evening, just after dark, to make sure their gold had not been disturbed. They expected to be back aboard the Far West within a couple of hours, but were never seen again."

"And the legend still persists that the gold was never found?" queried Tony. "How could that be possible?"

"Maybe it was found and maybe it wasn't, but nobody has ever admitted finding it."

As usual, Tony's logical mind went to work.

"If they were going to walk to the gold cache and planned to return within a couple of hours, the feasible search area is very small. Since a large river bisects the circle, one-half of the circle can be eliminated immediately."

Tony withdrew a small notepad and pen from his jacket pocket and drew a rough circle, divided in half by a line representing the river.

"In terrain with any appreciable growth of underbrush, it's impossible to hike more than four miles in an hour. Since they intended to return in two hours, only one hour could be spent on their outward leg. Therefore, their hiding place had to be within a semicircle with a four-mile radius, using the confluence of the rivers as the base point of the radius."

Below his diagram, Tony scribbled an equation.

"The entire zone of feasibility is just over twenty-five square miles. It's difficult to believe that in an area that size, such a valuable treasure has not been found for nearly a century and a quarter!"

"What do you think the chances are that it's still there?" Carla asked.

"Almost none!" he rejoined. "About the same as the odds of finding a lady like you at the site of a Mayan ruin!"

"So, it is possible?"

"I suppose," he responded, "but if you're selling shares in a gold-retrieval company, I'll pass up all of my stock options."

"Since we're going to camp on the western bank of the Bighorn, just south of the Yellowstone, we'll be within your feasibility zone, won't we?"

"About as close to the middle of it as we can get."

"Well then," Carla teased, "we might as well recover the treasure!"

"Why not!" he chuckled, "I could use a few extra tons of gold. How about you?"

➢

It was nearly dusk five days later as Tony and Carla sat beside a small fire cooking their evening meal. They had spent the better part of the past four days hiking over, under, around, and through the rocky hills and sharp cliffs, low hanging branches and Spanish moss, fallen trees and bramble bushes, as well as some of the worst foot-trapping undergrowth and ankle-wrenching terrain Tony had ever seen. He grinned at Carla.

"I think you're right about the treasure still being here. Before I saw this place, I decided that no twenty-five square mile area could possibly conceal a hoard of gold for a hundred and twenty-five years. After tramping over this

490

ground for the past few days, I'm convinced that the gold might not be found for the next hundred and twenty-five thousand years!"

"Don't despair so quickly," laughed Carla. "We still have three more days. Maybe we'll stumble onto the treasure by then."

An hour later, just as they finished dinner, Carla's paging device sounded. She dived quickly into her tent and Tony heard her yell, "Curses and more curses! Damn it to hell and back!"

She emerged from the low, green nylon structure a minute later, with her hand extended toward him. In it, she held her pager with its tiny screen that blinked - 44 - 44 - 44.

"What does 44 mean?" he asked.

"It means the end of our vacation and my immediate return to Houston," she told him sadly. "A signal 44 is in the 'worst possible calamity' category. Something critical that needs my attention at once. The corporate people know how important these days are to me and wouldn't have called me otherwise."

"It's time to go back to being a successful geologist, Dr. Cansino. I'll help you pack and drive you to the airport. We can be there in less than an hour."

"What will you do now, Tony? Go back to the university?"

"Not for a few days, at least. It's so peaceful and quiet here that I think I'll begin writing my article. Between my notes and cassette recordings, I can get most of it done. Then I'll need to make two additional stops before I finish the manuscript. Since the first draft isn't due until July 1, I'll have almost a full month to get it to American Heritage. Call me at Texas State as soon after that as you can." He hugged her tightly.

"I'll miss you, Carina. You've become very dear to me."

Sadly, Tony and Carla collected all of her possessions, packed them into the car, and drove directly to the airport.

Her flight left at eleven o'clock, and it was a disconsolate writer who returned to the campsite on the Bighorn River and slipped into his sleeping bag shortly after midnight. He lay awake for a long time, thinking about his relationship with Carla. He was strongly attracted to her, that was for sure, but he had begun to have an eerie feeling that he might be falling in love with the woman he wanted her to be rather than the woman she was. Some of the things she said and did simply did not fit the image she tried to portray. *Perhaps I find fault with Carla because I want her to be just like Pamela, and that's impossible.* He fell asleep wishing that much of his life had been different.

He was just finishing breakfast the following morning when he spied a young man walking along the riverbank toward his camp. As he drew near, Tony could see that the hiker was in his middle or late twenties and that he moved with the easy grace of a well-conditioned athlete. His extremely dark complexion seemed to add charm to a countenance that most people would have described as sweet-faced. He waved to Tony as he drew near.

"The smell of that coffee has been driving me crazy for the last mile," he called.

"The pot's still half full," Tony responded. "Pull up a campstool and help yourself."

The young man dropped his knapsack next to Tony's tent before settling down near the fire and pouring a cup of the coffee. He took a long drink, and then smiled broadly in appreciation.

"Thanks, amigo, you make a great cup of coffee. Are you camping all alone?"

"A friend was here with me until last night, but an emergency arose, and she had to leave suddenly. By the by, I'm Tony Garza."

The visitor extended his hand.

"My name is Chico Montoya. Are you a writer, Mr. Garza?"

"Yes, as a matter of fact I am. How did you know?"

"I noticed that a laptop computer was set up in your tent. Trust me when I say that we get a lot more treasure hunters than we do writers out here."

"For some reason, I assumed that you were not from this area. Do you live nearby?"

"No. I live in Colorado. I come from a family of Mexican immigrants who were brought north to harvest sugar beets over a century ago. I'm a throwback to my ancestors from Durango. If I put on a tilma and a pair of sandals, I could easily pass for a peon. I'm familiar with this area because I've been coming up here once or twice each month for several years. It's a great getaway, and someday I may even find Custer's Legacy. The thought of recovering eighteen tons of gold has always intrigued me."

"Do you think it's still here?" Tony asked.

"Quien sabe? Who knows? But it was here in 1876. I've spent a great deal of time researching the activities of Grant Marsh and David Campbell, so I know exactly what they did when they hid the gold. But I've come to believe that they threw out a red herring when they said it would take a couple of hours for them to check on the gold and return to the Far West."

"Why would they do that?" Tony queried. "Didn't they make that statement to Kevin McCarthy, the man who had given them the gold consignment? Why would they want to mislead him?"

"I don't think they did it to mislead McCarthy. But they made the statement while they were visiting him in a hospital tent. At that time, a number of other people were also present. I think they may have said it to throw eavesdroppers off the track."

"Perhaps," Tony persisted, "but weren't they going to recover the gold in the next day or two, as soon as they could organize a work party and transport it back aboard the Far West?"

"Sure. But let me ask you this. If the gold cache had been discovered in the meantime, how many forty-pound sacks of gold could a determined man, or group of men, have carried off in that day or two?"

"I see your point," Tony agreed. "Gold seems to make most men greedy and ruthless, as well as determined. You mentioned forty-pound sacks?"

"Yes. The gold was transported in 900 elkhide sacks, each of which weighed forty pounds."

"That's 36,000 pounds of gold!" Tony computed. "Also, hiding 900 bags would be backbreaking work and would require a great deal of space!"

"Far less space than you might think, since gold dust is so dense and heavy," Chico said. " But you're right about the hard work. They couldn't have done it without McCarthy's mules."

When Tony looked quizzically at him, Chico continued.

"McCarthy left nine of his mules in this area when he and his men attempted to escape from the Indians. Ten days later, all of the animals were still grazing nearby, so Marsh and Campbell used them to carry the gold in from the Far West. Each round trip took less than an hour. That's why I believe the gold cache is much closer to the Yellowstone than many people believe, and it's why I think Marsh's comment about needing two hours was a ruse."

"That sounds like a plausible theory," Tony agreed. "I hope it permits you to find the gold one of these days."

"I fear," lamented Chico Montoya, "that the treasure may never be found. If it is, it will probably be because of a stroke of blind luck."

He finished his coffee and rose, then retrieved his knapsack and draped it over his shoulders.

"Thanks for the hospitality, amigo. I hope you enjoy the rest of your stay in this country of futile golden dreams. Be grateful that you're a writer and not a frustrated treasure hunter."

He waved good-bye and resumed his walk along the riverbank.

Tony washed the pans and dishes he had used for breakfast and then sat down at his computer to begin the article. Ten minutes later, the side of the tent was suddenly torn apart by a high-powered rifle bullet that whizzed past his head. It plowed its way through the opposite wall and screamed off into the distance, just as the sound of an explosion finally reached his ears.

Tony's reaction was typical of any combat veteran. He dropped to the ground and rolled behind his duffel bags, the only objects in the tent that offered any sort of protection or concealment. That one came closer to killing me than anything in Vietnam, he thought. It was probably a careless varmint hunter who snapped off a round at a cougar or a coyote, with no thought to the consequences if his shot missed. The damned fool will probably never realize how close he came to killing someone. A few inches to the right, and Theresa Garza's seventh son would have been one dead pigeon.

He stayed under cover for the next several minutes, making sure that no more shots would be fired. So confident was the former Green Beret in his clandestine operations skills that he never gave thought to the possibility that the shot might have been fired, not by a careless hunter, but by a deadly assassin. He lay still, listening intently to each sound, that strange, keen sixth sense developed by every warrior now fully operational once again.

At last he left the security of the tent and shuffled slowly out toward his small cooking fire, peering cautiously about as he walked. The last of his morning coffee was being kept warm by the small flame that remained. He squatted beside the fire and, still continuing to listen carefully and peer about, he took a large metal mug in his still trembling hands, filled it half-full with the strong, murky, black liquid, added a huge spoonful of sugar and laced the mixture with an inch of bourbon before he nervously began to sip it. The strong brew tasted wonderful, and he hoped it might begin to splice his frayed nerve endings back together.

He sat for several minutes, nursing the potent mixture. When it was gone, he poured all that was left in the pot into his mug, ladled in even more sugar and an even more generous helping of bourbon. Half an hour later, the mug had been drained for the second time, and his nerves were once again steady. However, the home remedy for nerve-steadying had severely diminished his resolve to work. He decided to take a walk and return to his writing after lunch.

Instead of following the riverbank, as he and Carla had been doing, he decided to walk westward, away from the Bighorn toward a small granite mesa that rose abruptly out of the flat brushy plain that surrounded it. From the top of the mesa, he might even be able to see a place from which the shot could have been fired.

It was a hike of less than a mile, but it took more than half an hour to cover the distance, as the fates conspired against him. While he walked, the temperature and humidity rose and his sense of purpose declined, as alcohol began to exit through his heavily perspiring pores.

As he approached the small mesa, he discovered that the steep sides curled sharply upward to form a ten-foot-deep canyon within the confines of a humpbacked ridge. The upper end of the canyon was closed by a cairn, the lower end by a sheer stone wall. A natural spring, hidden deep within the cairn, sent a constant torrent of water gushing down to merge with a rill that circled the base of the rocks. The waters joined forces at a point just above this natural catchment that a thousand-year flow of water had carved along the length of the hogback ridge's summit.

As he climbed up one of the ridge's steep, stony side walls, Tony saw that a small but deep pool had been impounded by the high stone wall at the lower end of the canyon. It reminded him of a friend's expensive pool in San Antonio — thirty feet long, twelve feet wide, and ten feet deep, made to look as if it were a gift from nature. But this one really had been built by nature.

A deep pool, fed by the waters of two tiny streams that joined forces, tarried briefly in this rocky arroyo, then went cascading down over the basin's spillway before hurrying on to a rendezvous with the Bighorn River.

Tony looked across the crystal-clear pool of water to the opposite side of the canyon, twenty feet away. Just beyond that rocky rim was an area ten feet wide and flat as a table top. Just beyond that perfectly level stretch of ground was another deep gully, similar to the one directly below him, but without a water supply. It was a wadi, wet in the rainy season, but otherwise dry as the Sahara Desert. Even from this distance, Tony could see watermarks high up on the rocks of the other gully. How strange, he thought! Long ago that side was the waterway and this side the wadi. He wondered how the original stream had been diverted.

His attention returned to the natural pool below him. On the gravel bottom, about ten feet from the basin's upper end, lay a huge granite boulder which Tony guessed might weigh a ton or more. Fifteen feet away lay a similar granite boulder, two-thirds as large. Between the two boulders, a well-whiskered catfish was doggedly trying to make a meal out of a small, silvery fish. Tony laughed in surprise when he noticed that an unusual pattern of dots along the smaller fish's side formed a perfect numeral 2. The only fish I ever saw, he thought, that had his own number.

He gazed down for several minutes, fascinated by the catfish's persistence as it swam resolutely back and forth between the two boulders. Little number 2 is going to get worn out swimming away from that big fellow, Tony thought. Suddenly he made a startling observation. The number 2 fish wasn't swimming between the boulders. Number 2 simply disappeared under the bottom of one of them and suddenly reappeared next to the other boulder. The significance of his discovery jolted Tony. The smaller fish has to be swimming back and forth, but he's doing it in a different environment. He's swimming in a subterranean stream, one that runs beneath the surface of this one that I can see.

As he watched, the small fish appeared once again beside the downstream boulder. As soon as the catfish saw his quarry, he darted after him, at which point number 2 fled back under his rock. Moments later, while the foolish catfish maintained a weary vigil at the downstream boulder, his tiny quarry popped out from beneath the upstream boulder, having traversed his subterranean escape route once again.

The significance of the watery scenario suddenly dawned on Tony. Good Lord, he thought, that little fish may well have shown me the secret hiding place of the long lost gold cache! He began to think very logically, using a system he had devised long ago as a young history student. He called it "the what ifs."

What if the gold had been hidden in this canyon before the course of the stream had been altered? What if, while this side was the wadi, 900 bags of gold had been dropped down into a dry cave? A cave that had, at some point, become the subterranean waterway that it was now. What if, using the nine McCarthy mules in tandem, Marsh and Campbell had toppled the granite boulders over the canyon's rims, down into the gully, and then dragged them into position over the cave's two openings?

All of his conclusions, he decided, were logical and feasible. Had it not been for the tiny fish with the number 2, the cave's secret entrances might have remained hidden forever. How ingenious those two men had been! Tony thought. The chances of anyone dragging away two huge boulders were almost nonexistent, even before the wadi became a streambed. Once that happened, the odds dropped to zero.

Suddenly another thought crowded away all others. I'd better get out of here, he decided. Perhaps I can return after dark on a stealth mission. He slid down the steep slope and began walking rapidly back toward his campsite, wondering for the first time if the shot that had whizzed past his ear earlier had really been an accident after all.

➢

At the same moment, far away in the village of Dzibilchaltun, Mercata Verrano's phone rang. She picked it up and asked, "Is it over?"

"No, dammit," Asesino responded. "Somehow I missed him. I do not believe it! I fired a target rifle from less than two hundred yards away and missed! He was a few feet away from the tent wall that I shot through. The tough nylon deflected the bullet just enough to make it miss."

"That is really unfortunate!" Mercata commiserated. "I really liked the stray-bullet scenario. Well, Asesino, so much for careless hunters shooting people by accident. Both of our other plans are good. Will you try again today?"

"No," Asesino responded. "He probably believes this morning's shot was an accident; but he'll be extra cautious for the next day or two. I want to catch him off guard."

"Of course," Mercata agreed, "but don't you think it will be far easier to kill him in that isolated area than when he returns to an urban location?"

"I honestly don't know," the sweet-faced killer responded, "but I do know that an assassin's most important weapon is patience. I'll wait for as long as I must to make it look like an accident. Only as a last resort will I do otherwise. I've been at this business for a long time, and last resorts rarely happen. Hopefully, they won't now. Don't worry, Grandmother. I'll get this done for you."

➢

It was nearly dusk when Tony left his camp on the riverbank and strolled casually back toward the granite mesa. He had spent the past several hours excitedly but diligently working on his manuscript, and had accomplished a great deal. One fourth of the first draft was tucked away in the memory of his computer.

He had discarded the jeans he had worn all day, and was clad now in swimming trunks. A big beach towel was draped over one shoulder and a pair of diving goggles was tucked into his waistband. He reasoned that no one who might be watching would be suspicious of a tired man going for a cooling swim at the end of a hot day. Also, it made more sense for him to swim in a clear pristine pool than to risk the dangerous flotsam that occasionally clogged the Bighorn's waters.

His Special Forces training had taught him to be completely comfortable and competent in any aquatic situation. So he felt secure in his ability to perform the task that lay ahead. The diving goggles would certainly make things easier. He had carried them with him ever since his optician, Dr. Melton, suggested that he wear them whenever he swam in chlorinated water.

For the second time that day, his hands were trembling as he scaled the canyon wall and gazed down into the depths of what he hoped would be a treasure trove. As he sat at the water's edge, he saw his little friend with the number 2 and several of his relatives cavorting about in the pool.

Before entering the water he prayed, "Lord, if the gold is here, give me the will and the way to find it. And of greatest importance, Lord, give me the wisdom to use this great fortune for the good of all of Your people."

The catfish was nowhere to be seen. He probably became so disgusted, thought Tony, that he threw himself over the edge of the spillway. No doubt he'll find easier meals in the rivers.

He slipped down into the pool but did not put on his goggles until he was completely below the level of the surrounding rocks. No point in inviting trouble, he thought. He paused for a moment before he dove, steeling himself in case he found no evidence to support his theory. During the day he had convinced himself that, although this tiny canyon could certainly be the hiding place of the golden hoard, it was far more likely that it was not. There were probably a thousand other such places in the area that would never be found.

Well, he thought, there's no point in waiting. I might as well get this over with. He inhaled deeply several times in order to expand his lungs to their maximum capacity and held each breath for as long as possible before slowly exhaling. When he adjusted to the new breathing cycle, he held the last deep breath, pushed himself away from the wall, and swam down toward the larger of the two boulders.

He examined the huge rock carefully and ran his fingertips around a portion of its base before a lack of oxygen forced him to the surface. He repeated this procedure several more times, but discovered nothing except several minute openings, barely large enough to accommodate number 2 and his friends. A bit discouraged but not surprised, he finally swam back to the edge of the pool, removed his goggles and hoisted himself up onto the rocks. But he could not rest for long, since the sun was already sinking below the western horizon. He dropped back into the pool, readjusted the goggles, took his deep breaths, and dove again, this time toward the smaller of the two boulders.

He ran his fingers along the base of the granite that couldn't be seen from above and encountered an alien object. He pulled himself downward along the boulder's face as far as possible and brought his eyes into line with its base. He saw a small crack radiating up from the bottom of the rock and the gravel that surrounded it. The rush of water surging out of the crack carried out with it a wavering object that resembled a shoelace.

Again Tony needed to resurface and rest for a moment. When he returned to his scrutiny, he saw that it was not a shoelace, but a much thicker piece of rawhide thong. He tugged on it gently and was thrilled as more and more of the thong gradually came into view. He rose for air, then returned at once. He pulled until six or eight inches of the leather dangled in his hand before he felt resistance. Something was holding the opposite end of the object that was preventing it from sliding through the small opening. It was now so dark that he could no longer see. By touch alone, he carefully and patiently worked the rawhide out of the crack and finally brought it to the surface.

The entire process had taken over an hour. He was shaking with exertion as well as anticipation as he slid once again down the steep slope and walked quickly, but cautiously, through the pitch-blackness toward his camp, the prize carefully wrapped inside his towel.

Entering his tent, he pulled on a pair of coveralls to the dismay of thousands of mosquitoes, then pushed a switch that controlled four lanterns and flooded the nylon cave with light. He sat at his computer table and began to examine the still-wet lump of rawhide. In the bright light, he could see that it was the neck of a bag, tied together by the knotted thong that he had seen poking out through the crack in the boulder.

He spread several paper towels on the table before him and placed the remnant of the bag on them. Then he patiently began to loosen the swollen knots that had been in place for many years. He discovered that there were actually two separate thongs. One was tied tightly around the top of the bag's neck; the other secured its base. Between them was a space of about four inches.

It took him several minutes to untie the wet, stubborn knots. Once they were loose, he took the neck of the bag and turned it inside out. And there, on the wet rawhide, as well as on the white paper towels, he saw a profusion of glittering specks of gold that had been trapped inside the neck between the thongs for the last century and a quarter.

He had found the Custer Legacy!

He was so shocked by the spectacle before him that for the next few moments he sat riveted to his chair, his eyes locked on the collection of tiny, golden grains. He said a short prayer of thanksgiving and then, for one of the few times in his entire life, he totally lost control. He jumped up and down, then he raced out of the tent, dancing a lively jig and even howling up at the blasé moon.

His lively antics soon tired him out, and he was forced to sit down and rest. While waiting for his breath to return and his heart to stop pounding, he computed the value of 18 tons of gold, at current prices. When he decided on $200,000,000, he jumped up once again and began a series of leaps that would have stirred the soul of any leprechaun.

How incredible, he thought, that so many of God's blessings have been showered down on me. First meeting Carla, then discovering the location of the Garzas' sword in the Vatican museum and, finally, finding a fantastic fortune in gold.

Well, he decided, there are several things I must do and two I can't afford to do. I have to go about my business as though nothing has changed. I'll leave here tomorrow, go on to Cuba, visit the Museo de Armas y Hojas de Espadas, and examine the Mendoza swords. When I've finished in Havana, I'll return to the Vatican and share all of God's great blessings with Cardinal Questa. What wonderful presents to bring to that saintly old man! The one thing I don't dare do is return to the canyon of gold. I can't be stupid or careless, as I was with the Tratamiento. I'm glad no one was here to see me tonight. From now on, I'll use better judgment.

But Antonio Garza was wrong. A deadly visitor had seen him celebrating. The man was not present when Tony left for his swim, but he had been waiting across the river when he returned.

"I'll be damned," thought the observer. "That lucky fo⟨ must have stumbled onto Custer's gold! Well, that's ju fine! When the Guardians get him, he'll have two choi⟨ He can talk, or he can die!"

Chapter XXXII
➢
See How They Run

Yellowstone & Bighorn Rivers
Wyoming & Montana Wilderness
Late Spring, 1999

It was as black as the bottom of a coal mine at two o'clock the next morning when four men climbed a small, wooded hill and entered a rickety-looking old building that a hundred years earlier had been a line shack. Even then, it had been a barely acceptable place for cowboys to spend an occasional night as they patrolled their far-flung fence lines.

Shortly after World War I, the building, along with a few acres of land that surrounded it, was purchased by a group of men calling themselves The Guardians. They claimed to be the protectors of the nation's natural resources and often extolled the virtues of good conservation. But the organization's real purpose was to search continually for the lost treasure known as the Custer Legacy. They also maintained surveillance on all others who looked for the gold. The old line shack was perfect for their needs since it was located on the opposite side of the Yellowstone, almost directly across from the mouth of the Bighorn.

The old building's interior was the antithesis of its exterior. The floors were covered with colorful braided rugs and filled with a variety of comfortable furnishings. But the four men now gathered in the shack were anything but comfortable as they sat in the light of a flickering kerosene lamp.

The face of the man who appeared to be the leader was as red as a beet. A bulging purple vein in his neck looked as if it were ready to pop as he bellowed at the youngest of the other men.

"You were ordered to be in position before dark, Rudy. If you hadn't been late, you would have seen where Garza went. If you had seen him leave, we would finally know where in the hell that damned gold is buried. Rudy, you're a moron!"

"What was I supposed to do when my tire blew out? I changed it as fast as I could. What would you have done, Bull?"

Bull sneered at Rudy before he disdainfully replied.

"I, along with every other non-moron in the world, would have come up here a couple of hours before it got dark. Then, if my pickup broke down, I still would have gotten here in plenty o' time. Why is it that every time I trust you to do something you foul it up?"

"I always do my best, Bull! I always do my very best!"

"I believe you, Rudy, and that scares me worse than anything. Sittin' here and knowin' just how damned bad your best is!"

"Bull, me and Frolic didn't come up here in the middle of the night to hear you jabber at Rudy," interrupted Pinto Peters. "Let's figure out what we need to do to get Garza's attention."

"It's just too damned bad that fancy woman o' his left him high and dry. I could'a slapped her inta next week and back, and then that slick hombre would'a sung like a bird," laughed the huge man they called Frolic.

"Thanks to Rudy the Moron," lamented Bull once again, "we've got to try to sweat it out of him."

Rudy picked up the remnant of the old elkhide bag that Tony had retrieved from the bottom of the pool. Although traces of gold dust still clung to the rawhide, all signs of moisture had long since disappeared, thereby offering the Guardians no clue to its former watery hiding place.

"If I hadn't sneaked up to his tent and heared him snorin' and swiped that thing off his table, we still wouldn't know fer sure if he had found the gold," Rudy said in a defensive manner. "Let's just go over there and rough him up. Let's make him tell us whar it is, Bull. We kin do thet."

"How do we explain roughin' him up when he goes to the local sheriff, or worse, the state cops? Did ya ever think of that?"

"Hold on a minute here, Bull. This time Rudy may have a good idea," interposed Pinto Peters. "I think maybe we kin git this here feller to cut us a deal that we kin live with."

"This I gotta hear!" sneered the dubious Bull.

"If you'll shut yer mouth and open yer ears for the next two minutes, I'll explain it to ya."

The others all leaned forward in their chairs and listened intently as Pinto Peters' voice dropped to a low-pitched, conspiratorial whisper.

"At first light me 'n Frolic will go see Garza. We'll tell him we know that he's found the gold and that we want to make a deal with him. If he'll tell us, he gets ten million dollars and a chance to live a normal life. If not, Frolic will kill him on the spot. I'd rather lose the gold fer good than let some fancy pants dude get away with it, you kin bet on that."

"What if he agrees now and then tries to double-cross us later?" asked the still doubtful Bull.

"Simple answer to that," Pinto Peters assured him. "We'll chop off one of his fingers to make damned sure he gits the message. Every time he looks at the stump, he'll git the message all over again. He has to believe that we won't hesitate to kill him, even for one heartbeat, if'n he ever crosses us."

"I like it!" declared a suddenly enthusiastic Bull. "Let's go ahead with the plan as soon as it gets light!"

"Some of the other Guardians might not like all this rough stuff," cautioned a somber Rudy. "They might think this is goin' too far."

"Well, it's just too damned bad if a handful of pansies don't like the idea. How 'bout you, Rudy? How do you vote?" asked the menacing Bull.

"Oh hell, Bull, you know me, I'm easy. I think it's a great plan. I'm all for it," the suddenly affable Rudy assured him.

"All right then," confirmed Pinto Peters. "At first light, me 'n Frolic will go down and take care of Garza, while the two o' you guard the trail along the river from both directions. We sure don't need no witnesses hornin' in on this git together."

➢

Three hours later, just as dawn's first light began creeping across the eastern sky, Pinto Peters and Frolic, hatchets in hand, moved soundlessly up the bank toward the silent camp. Everything seemed to be just as it had been in the dark of night when Rudy had rushed away clutching the rawhide remnant. As the two deadly stalkers burst into the tent, ready to seize and throttle its inhabitant, they immediately discovered that at least one thing was different — Antonio Garza was gone.

The Guardians hadn't missed him by very much. A few minutes earlier, pain from a severe leg cramp had jolted Tony out of a deep sleep. He sat up, swung his feet to the ground, and massaged the muscles until the ache subsided. By then he was wide awake.

He rose and went to the folding table that held his laptop computer, his notes, a canteen, and a variety of other small items. He poured a cup of water and stood stock-still, staring dumbly down at the objects on the table. The elkhide bag was missing! It had been lying right here in plain sight and now it was gone. He searched below the table in vain. The bag had been stolen!

A shudder ran down his spine as he realized that his discovery of the golden hoard was no longer a secret. Someone else was aware that he had found the $200,000,000 gold cache. Vast multitudes of people had been killed for much less.

He quickly recalled the lesson he had learned in the jungles of Southeast Asia two and a half decades earlier. When something is not as you know it should be, don't look for an explanation — get away! When you're confronted with a possible life-threatening situation, don't rationalize — get away. Don't wait. Don't worry. Just get away!

It was this decision to act at once that saved at least one of his fingers, and perhaps his life. Tony stuffed his computer, wallet, pocket secretary, and several other items into a heavy canvas bag and fled at once. Moving at a brisk trot, he made his way along the riverbank trail to a clearing nearly a mile away where his rental car was parked. He reached it at the same moment that his would-be assailants burst into the empty tent.

He jumped into the seat and quickly started the car. A short drive brought him to the end of the rough, wooded trail where he moved out of the trees and up onto the highway. "I'm safe now," he thought, blithely unaware that he had just begun a journey that would ultimately become as bizarre as any ever seen on The Twilight Zone.

As he drove westward toward Billings, Tony was too distracted to appreciate the beauty of the countryside, the sparkling Yellowstone River on his right, and the breathtaking hills and canyons on his left. Wherever he looked, he would have found further evidence of the Ultimate Artist's handiwork, but he was so upset and nervous that he saw none of this, and he was not prepared for trouble when it erupted.

He had just entered a long stretch of highway, which followed a natural curve around a high hill. Here engineers had triumphed over every obstacle nature had thrown in their path by ingeniously carving a roadbed directly into the middle of the mountain's sheer face. The upper flank of the mountainside guarded the southern boundary of the resultant road as it rose almost straight up. Beyond the wide roadway, the mountain's abrupt drop-off continued. The edge of this lower cliff on the road's northern perimeter began only five feet from the driving surface and barely three feet beyond a heavy steel guardrail. Any driver unfortunate enough to miss this final measure of protection would plunge off the mountainside and begin a short, exciting, but fatal trip down the dizzying heights to the rocky riverbank far below.

This morning, had he not been pondering the loss of his gold-bag remnant, Tony realized later, he would have been thundering along the highway at his usual seventy-five or eighty miles per hour and, in short order, might well have died in a fiery crash.

Fortunately, the speedometer was only hovering near 50 when the big car suddenly dipped its right front corner and dived violently into the ground. Tony was thrown forward and down, but was held in place by the seat belt. An instant later, he saw the front tire and wheel separate from the automobile, go careening wildly past the guardrail, and disappear over the embankment. The bottom of the front bumper struck the road surface again — hard — then rebounded and smacked it for a third time, even harder.

The steel rotor, now without either wheel or tire to protect it, began skipping across the concrete like a flat stone skipping over water. On one such downward skip, the rotor's bare, sharp steel caught solidly and spun the car around, slewing it across the entire width of the pavement. There the undamaged left side smashed against the granite of the mountain so violently that the car rebounded almost at once and slid back toward the more hazardous side of the road, the one that overlooked the river.

For a second time, the right rear end snuggled tightly up against the guardrail. Now, with the back bumper scraping along the sturdy barrier, the front end was forced into a parallel position. It was only then that the car finally broke free from its guardian's grip. It spun halfway around for the last time and slid down the road backwards, while slowly being ground to a halt by the smashed, flattened rotor, which had by now become a very efficient anchor. The wrecked car finally came to rest on the wrong side of the road, tilted slightly forward, with its right side hard against the stony face of the mountain.

Tony was shaking and in shock. He had just begun to collect his thoughts and inventory his aching body for damage, when a highway patrol cruiser swooped in next to him, its roof lights flashing a silent warning.

Jumping out of his cruiser, a trooper rushed to Tony's side and called through the smashed window.

"Are you hurt, sir?"

"I hurt all over, but I can't tell if anything is broken."

He suddenly noticed that the entire front of his jacket was covered with blood.

"Can you tell where all of the blood is coming from, Officer?"

"Yes, sir," came the concerned and courteous reply. "Your chin is split open. Apply pressure against it until I can get you out of there and perform first aid. An ambulance is on the way."

Tony applied pressure to his chin with his right hand, and pushed against the driver's door with his left, but failed to budge it.

"This door is stuck!" He called to the officer whose name tag said: EVANS.

"It's jammed, but I think we can get it open with a pry bar."

Officer Evans opened the trunk of his patrol car and extracted a long, heavy steel bar. This he inserted between the driver's door and the car's frame, and forced it forward. A moment later, a two-inch crack appeared as the door squeaked open on its twisted hinges. Continuing to exert pressure, Evans managed to force the door open wide enough for Tony to struggle out.

It was then that Tony noticed how badly swollen and painful his left ankle had become.

"Don't try to walk on that pickle barrel until you've had it x-rayed," said Evans. "It may be broken. Even if it isn't, you'll be getting around on crutches for the next couple of weeks."

Evans brought his first-aid kit and asked Tony to turn his head to the left without moving his body any more than necessary. Officer Evans cleaned the gash in the victim's chin and pulled it closed with a butterfly bandage. Just then the ambulance arrived.

"That'll work until they put the stitches in. Give me your driver's license and rental agreement, and I'll wait here for the tow truck." He examined the documents and then helped the medics to transport Tony to the ambulance. As he turned away he said, "I'll see you at the hospital, Dr. Garza. For now, just relax and be grateful you're alive. When that wheel cut loose, I didn't think you had a chance of surviving the accident."

But Tony knew it had been no accident. Wheels and tires were checked last night when he refueled after taking Carla to the airport. Someone had obviously tried to kill him! He wondered again how much of an accident the stray bullet through his tent had been.

It was late morning before the wrecked auto could be hooked to a tow truck and hauled to the International Car Rental agency at the Billings Airport where Asesino was waiting.

A few minutes later, as the wrecker driver left the agency office, the deadly assassin entered and approached the clerk who stood behind the counter.

"Here are the keys and paperwork for my rental car. I noticed the wrecked car as I drove up. I hope no one was killed in that accident?"

"Fortunately not. According to the accident report, the driver was by himself. He wound up with a sprained ankle and a split chin, but no other injuries. If he had been going faster, or if he had been driving a smaller car, he probably would have been killed."

"Oh, hell," Asesino said suddenly. "I just remembered an errand I need to do. Give me the keys and hold on to that paperwork for a couple of hours. I'll be back later."

511

Half an hour later, Mercata Verrano's phone rang.

"Hola," said the grandmotherly leader of Los Viejos.

"He's still alive! That incredibly lucky man is still alive!"

"Why didn't the plan work?" Mercata asked.

"The first part of it worked fine. I removed three of the lug nuts from his car's right front wheel late last night. Once he started along the highway this morning, it was just a matter of time before the remaining two nuts sheared off and threw the whole wheel into the river. According to the accident report the rental clerk left lying on his desk, five miles after Garza started driving, that's exactly what happened. The wheel flew off as I thought it would. But instead of flipping into the river, the car apparently slid and smashed its way for several hundred yards, bouncing between the cliffs on one side and the guardrail on the other. In the process, it was almost completely demolished. But it protected Garza! He came out of a crash that would have killed anyone else with only a couple of minor injuries. I know, because I just heard a news report on the radio. The doctors are insisting that he remain in the hospital overnight for observation, but they plan to release him in the morning."

"Where is he going from there?" Mercata asked.

"I don't have the slightest idea," Asesino replied. "But I'll stay on his trail and arrange to be aboard whatever flight he departs on. I also have another problem."

"A serious one?" asked the voice from the Yucatan.

"It could become serious. They recovered the car's wheel. It's lying in the trunk. Three of the holes in the aluminum wheel are perfectly round, the other two are oval, made so by the pressure on the two lug nuts before they were sheared off. Anyone with half a brain will be able to see the evidence of sabotage, and then Garza will know someone is determined to kill him. I must be extra careful not to call attention to myself. Don't worry, Grandmother, I'll work it all out. Antonio Garza is as good as dead. I'll call you back as soon as I know anything more."

➤

A few miles away, Tony Garza lay in a hospital bed shivering. Feelings of foreboding and impending doom had seized him soon after he had been brought into this sterile room. Two attempts on his life — the stray bullet yesterday, then the car today — had triggered cold, vivid mental re-creations of many life-threatening situations in Southeast Asia. He had heard about such flashbacks, but had never given them much credence until now. He felt like a man who doesn't believe in ghosts until he suddenly encounters one. His old ghosts from Vietnam had finally caught up with him, and they were frighteningly real.

Although he had eaten nothing for the past twelve hours, he wasn't hungry. When the x-rays were finished and the examinations completed, he was able to choke down a half cup of black coffee, while his ankle was being fitted with an air splint. He sent back an untouched luncheon tray at noon and declined offers of juice throughout the afternoon. At dinnertime, he drank more coffee and tried to eat a bowl of chicken soup but was unable to digest it. During the hours of evening, he contented himself by nibbling tiny morsels of dry toast, fearing to test his stomach again.

He dozed fitfully throughout the night and awakened often, haunted by visions of old comrades screaming and bleeding and dying. He heard the thundering staccato of rifle fire, the sound of exploding mortar shells, and the rumble of Apache gunships. He felt himself being pulled down once again into the inky black steamy jungle darkness that had nearly spelled doom a quarter of a century earlier; and he was afraid that this time, he might not be able to struggle out of the cold, clammy, fatal embrace of uncontrollable terror.

➤

The following morning, although his feelings of apprehension and dread still persisted, he was able to eat two scrambled eggs and a piece of toast. As he finished, Dr. Calvin Moss entered.

"I'm glad to see you're eating something. Are you feeling a bit better?" he inquired.

"My chin feels like it's been used for a punching bag. But the air splint is making my ankle feel much better. How long should I continue to wear it?"

"You've suffered a very severe sprain. I would recommend that you use crutches for the next two weeks and continue to rely on the air splint until you can move your foot in every direction without any sensation of pain. I realize that it's cumbersome and makes walking difficult, but it is the best thing for you right now. By the way, have you felt any emotional or psychological stress since the accident?"

Tony was shocked by the question.

"Why do you ask? Are there outward signs?"

"A few. Emotional trauma is actually quite common after an experience such as yours, although most people are ashamed to admit it. It's called Post-Traumatic Stress. Or simply PTS."

"I guess I must be one of them," Tony confessed. "I've been having flashbacks of Vietnam all night. My stomach is upset. My palms are sweating and I have the shakes." He tried to grin as he added, "Other than that, I'm fine."

"Have you ever had these flashbacks or feelings before?"

"Yes, for a few months after I got back from Nam, but nothing since then. And never anything this intense or frightening."

"These dreams will probably revert to the recessive mode very quickly. If they don't begin to lessen in severity and frequency within a week or two, psychotherapy may be required to quell them. However, as with most traumatic experiences, I think the problems will be resolved by the passage of time."

"That's encouraging. I don't mind admitting that my emotional and mental states were starting to worry me."

"Yesterday you mentioned that you were on a leave of absence from Texas State University until the end of the month. And also that you have some additional research to complete in Cuba before that. Instead of flying across the country and plunging directly into your research, why don't you consider driving at a leisurely pace to the East Coast, or at least a part of the way there, and just relaxing for a week or two? I think a stint of peace, quiet, and seclusion might be the perfect solution to your current problems. Well, I've signed your release forms. You're free to leave us whenever you're ready."

"Dr. Moss, I appreciate your professionalism and your cheerful bedside manner. I think I may just follow your advice and drive part of the way. Perhaps as far as one of the cities on the Mississippi."

Tony extended a still unsteady hand.

"If we don't meet again, Doctor, many thanks for everything."

It was late morning before Tony had finished with the normal red tape and was ready to leave the hospital. He hailed a taxi and arrived at the airport a short time later. He arranged for a credit to be issued on the air ticket that he no longer intended to use and then strode through the terminal to the counter of International Car Rentals where a friendly clerk greeted him.

"It's good to see you up and about again, Dr. Garza. Please accept my congratulations on your narrow escape."

"Thank you," Tony replied. "Are you willing to risk leasing another vehicle to me?"

"Of course," chuckled the clerk." Freak accidents are just like lightning; they don't strike twice. Now that you've had yours, you're probably a better risk than most people."

"I certainly hope you're right. This time, I'd like to rent either a Lincoln or a Caddy."

"Is it for local use, Dr. Garza? If so, both are available."

"No," Tony told him, "as a matter of fact, I might drive it quite a long distance. Perhaps as far as Florida."

"I have only one of each of those big cars here at this time, Dr. Garza, so I can't release them. But I do have three Park Avenues. You can have your choice. They tell me the Park is a great highway car, easy handling and very comfortable. I have a gold one with less than 1,000 miles on it."

"That sounds fine," Tony assured him. "Is it serviced and ready to go?"

"Of course!" the clerk replied defensively, accepting Tony's credit card. "This is International."

Minutes later, he ushered Tony out to the parking lot. They performed a walk-around inspection, making certain that there was no unrecorded damage. When the circuit was complete, he indicated a block on the rental agreement, which signified that such an inspection had been done and asked his customer to initial it.

The clerk stood back and gazed admiringly at the shiny Buick.

"She sure is a beauty, Dr. Garza. I hope you'll enjoy it. By the way, our radio dispatcher just reported a stalled car blocking the on-ramp to Route 90, West."

"I appreciate your concern," Tony told him. "But the Park Avenue and I are heading in the opposite direction. Have a good day."

The clerk returned to his station and found a customer waiting for him.

"I want to return the car I have and rent that silver Camaro Z-28. I have a long way to go and I need to do this in a hurry."

"Of course," the clerk replied. "The Camaro is available for long distance. All I have to do is enter the new car's I.D. into the computer and change your rental rate. The whole thing will only take a couple of minutes."

True to his word, the clerk completed the transaction in short order and then conducted the lessee on the obligatory inspection.

As they walked around the sporty vehicle, the International employee noticed a small scrape on the rear quarter panel and stopped to make note of it on his records. The customer, however, continued on toward the front of the Camaro, covertly withdrew a wallet from a pocket, bent down, and feigned finding it beneath the Z-28 before exclaiming, "This wallet belongs to someone named Antonio Garza. He must have dropped it."

"I'll bet he did," the clerk agreed. "He just left a few minutes ago in a gold Park Avenue."

"If you know which way he went, I'll chase after him and try to return it."

"That would be terrific," beamed the grateful clerk. "He's going to be heading east on Route 90. If you can't catch him, he may be a long way from here before he misses it. It's sure nice of you to go to so much trouble."

"It's really not that much trouble. I'm going that way myself. Now, don't you worry," smiled the eager Asesino. "I have no intention of letting Antonio Garza get away."

A few minutes later, as the Camaro flashed along the broad Interstate Highway, the sweet-faced assassin picked up the old leather wallet and broke into great peals of laughter.

The lost wallet trick was terrific. Over the years, it had been the entrance key to restricted sections of airports, limited-access conferences, intensive care units of hospitals, and many other places marked No Trespassing, No Admittance, and Keep Out. The old wallet was more valuable than the Rosetta Stone.

➤

Twenty miles later, Asesino saw a gold Park Avenue with an International Rental sticker. It was Garza. The cautious killer slowed down and retreated for over half a mile before sliding into a space between an old pickup truck and a new Ford Bronco.

517

Behind the wheel of the old pickup, the driver watched the sleek Camaro slip nimbly in ahead of him. A shadow of longing covered his face and a light of love appeared in his eyes. For one brief moment, he looked as boyish and innocent as a freckle-faced Tom Sawyer watching Becky Thatcher at the church social.

"Check that Z-car out, Bull," he exclaimed to his companion. "There's three hundred ponies pullin' that peppy-payload."

"Rudy," growled Bull, as he often did, "you're a moron. You must memorize every damned ad that comes on the idiot box. You spend half your time looking at hotrod magazines and the other half repeating stupid slogans. Can't you ever say anything original?"

"Sure I can," Rudy assured him. "I say new stuff almost every day. I did a good job of following this Garza fellow, didn't I?"

"Yeah," Bull admitted, "you did a first-class job all right."

"How come, do ya suppose, he didn't take the plane, after all?"

"I dunno. Maybe he remembered that he needed to do somethin' down the road a piece. Are Pinto and Frolic gittin' too far ahead of us in the Bronco?"

Rudy swerved over next to the center lane and craned his neck far to the left before reporting.

"I kin see 'em up there, just ahead of that randy, racin' rig."

Once again, Bull shook with exasperation.

"Rudy, don't you start up with me, again. You're gonna git out and walk if you keep talkin' that trash!"

Bull soon dozed off and missed the pleasure of hearing Rudy singing commercial jingles with inane lyrics, as he drove along the Little Bighorn, and then as the road lifted out of the valley and climbed toward the heart of the Rosebud and Wolf Mountains.

For the next three hours, this strange caravan whizzed along Route 90, with each of its bizarre participants minding his own business and ignoring the other players with an elaborate, blasé nonchalance.

Tony Garza, still in the throes of Post-Trumatic Stress, led the way, his shaking hands glued to the steering wheel, forcing himself to disregard anything that might interfere with his hopes of quickly snapping out of his deep depression. Asesino and the Guardians, for the present, were content to regard the fact that they had been traveling in a convoy as a coincidence.

They were well into the wilds of Wyoming when the Park Avenue slowed down and swung into a rest area. The Bronco and the pickup truck pulled in as well, and parked together some distance away from the Buick. The Camaro, however, flashed past the oasis without pausing and disappeared over the horizon, on toward the Black Hills which still lay many miles away.

The four Guardians clambered out of their vehicles, then stood between them, plotting a new strategy.

"I was glad to see that Camaro go on," said Pinto Peters. "I was beginnin' to think we might have a competitor for the gold."

"Yeah," agreed Bull, "I was gettin' worried myself. If Garza was payin' any kind of attention, he saw it go on, too. We can't keep followin' him with both of these vehicles. He's bound to get suspicious. Pinto, you and Frolic trail him when he leaves. Me and Rudy will wait awhile and stay a ways behind. We'll just keep comin' on down the road until you call us. If'n you can't get us on the CB, use the cellular phone. Garza will feel a lot better if two o' the three chase cars drop out. If we're still taggin' him tomorrow, we kin switch, and me and Rudy will take over in the pickup. O.K. Does everybody agree with the plan?"

They all nodded in assent just as the Buick backed out of its parking slot and headed once again for the interstate. A minute later, the Bronco, with Pinto and Frolic on board, followed it.

More than a mile ahead, at a point where the road ascended a steep grade, Asesino saw Antonio Garza return to the highway as well. The professional assassin, with far more skill and experience than the amateur Guardians, had stood beside the swift Camaro and watched the rest area through powerful binoculars.

It was a scene that would be repeated at every interchange. The Z-28 and its clever driver would wait until the Park Avenue had passed beyond the off-ramp and then scurry on to the next exit. Should Tony Garza quit the highway at any point, Asesino would instantly make a U-turn and go in immediate pursuit. This was a system of covert surveillance, which eliminated any possibility that the target might realize he was being shadowed. The new plan required one additional change. One that would be handled at each overnight stop. That first stop came in Rapid City, South Dakota.

➢

His nerves jumpier than ever after his many hours of driving, Tony checked into a motel, took a quick shower and fell exhausted into bed, with no thought of food. Often, during those fretful hours of the night, he awoke, drenched in sweat and shaking with fear as the result of a remembered firefight, a patrol gone wrong, or a Viet Cong ambush, with its blood and gore and terror. But most of all, in these dreams, it was the faces of war's helpless victims that haunted him, the children and the elderly who stared pleadingly out at him from the deep shadows in the corners of his mind and silently asked: Why can't you help us? And despite his fear and dread, he reached out to them, but they were always too far away.

And so he dozed fitfully throughout the long restless hours of darkness, a modern-day knight errant. A gentle and compliant man by nature, once easygoing and adaptable, reshaped as a gladiator by war, now driven by the debt, which he felt he owed the world. A debt incurred because he had lived while so many others had died. A debt that he hoped his present mission would finally permit him to mark "paid in full."

➤

Across the street, at a far less classy motel, the Guardians telephoned a local delivery service and devoured four large Meat Lover's pizzas while they watched a Colorado Rockies game on TV. During the entire evening, Rudy and Frolic took turns keeping watch on the Park Avenue. Even during the night, rather than chance losing contact with Garza, all four shared the sentry duty.

➤

Asesino had pulled off the highway at Rapid City's most easterly exit, since that location offered the widest selection of national motels, and parked in a place that permitted a clear view of each of the motels as well as the off-ramp. Minutes later, Garza's Park Avenue drove past, followed soon after by the Bronco and pickup truck from the afternoon convoy.

After determining where Garza would register, the killer's next stop had been the local International Car Rental agency. There the flashy Camaro was exchanged for a rather nondescript, mouse-colored Toyota.

Asesino ate a leisurely dinner at the fine restaurant next to Antonio Garza's motel. From the dining room window, the Park Avenue was in full view. An hour later, the assassin strolled across the parking area to the motel and registered for a luxury suite.

Handing over the key, the desk clerked asked, "Is there any other service that I may offer you?"

"Yes, I think there might be. Has my friend Antonio Garza checked in yet?"

The clerk scanned his computer data.

"Yes, he has. He checked in about an hour ago."

"Oh, that's great," the stony killer replied. "I wasn't sure he would make it. Tomorrow is Tony's birthday and a few of us are planning a little surprise breakfast party for him before he leaves town. Would you give me a call as soon as he comes down to begin breakfast or, heaven forbid, when he gets ready to check out? We certainly would be grateful for your help. Tony's a great guy, and we sure wouldn't want to miss celebrating his birthday with him."

"Of course! I'll be glad to help. I wish I had friends as nice as you."

The assassin smiled at the clerk and turned away, secure in the knowledge that if you were clever enough, you could always get a good night's sleep. Even on the night before a kill.

➢

But the next day was not to be the day of the kill — nor the next, or the next. For nearly three weeks, no opportunities arose, either for the Guardians' confrontation and attempted intimidation, or for Asesino's assassination. One faction that threatened a finger and another that imperiled a life. One willing to maim to learn a secret; the other eager to kill to protect one.

Throughout all those days and the thousands of miles, their intended victim was never in a place where the Guardians could accost him or killed by Asesino, unless the perpetrator was willing to sacrifice freedom or self in return. Although the Guardians were still unaware of Asesino's presence, the opposite was not true. The assassin had been cognizant of their presence since the first morning in Rapid City, but had not been able to determine their reason for following Garza.

Antonio was slowly recovering from his Post-Trumatic Stress, but was still far from being the normal, confident,

522

self-reliant individual that he had always been. He still looked suspiciously at everyone and was never able to relax completely. Since the day of the last attempt on his life, he had aged dramatically. He had lost a great deal of weight, and whenever he looked in a mirror, he saw a man that appeared to carry the miseries of the world on his shoulders. Only Dr. Moss's assurance that the condition was temporary and could be cured with psychotherapy kept him going.

It was late afternoon on the first day of summer when Antonio Garza and his entourage arrived in Miami and drove directly to the airport. The other three vehicles parked at a considerable distance from Garza's Park Avenue and had to hustle to keep him in sight as he hurried into the terminal. Pinto Peters entered the building, but Asesino remained outside, watching Tony through the big glass windows as he went to the desk of Cuba Libre Airlines.

Cuba Libre had been inaugurated several weeks earlier after the new democratic government became firmly entrenched. For the first time in nearly forty years, regular commercial flights shuttled back and forth between Miami and Havana.

Pinto Peters was in the line next to Tony and had no trouble hearing him book a reservation on the evening flight. When he got to the desk, Pinto bought four cash tickets on the same flight.

Asesino watched as Tony left the terminal and walked back to the Park Avenue. Confident that he was going to return the rental car, the clever killer once again "found" Antonio Garza's wallet and took it to the Cuba Libre counter. Since a public address announcement failed to engender a response, Asesino, by offering to return the lost property, was able to determine the proper flight and acquire a seat in the first-class section.

Three hours later, the hunted and the hunters were in the air over open ocean on a short trip to a deadly rendezvous.

Although there were over a hundred passengers on the flight, only ten of them were seated in the first-class section located in the forward area of the aircraft. The four boisterous ones were young representatives from the same small manufacturing company in the Midwest. Their collective enthusiasm and eager anticipation of outlandish success reminded Tony of Professor Harold Hill, the Music Man, as he prepared to descend on the citizens of River City, certain that he could sell a boys' band to the stiff-necked Hawkeyes. Just behind this happy-go-lucky group sat two sedate, older men, obviously business executives, who worked on their laptop computers during the entire trip.

The last man wore casual clothes and dozed throughout most of the flight. He had thick, bushy black hair, a bristling beard and a wide mustache. Tony stared at this young man for a long time after he boarded in an effort to identify him. He racked his memory for nearly an hour without success before finally coming up with a remote possibility. The upper half of the man's face, particularly his eyes, reminded Tony of Chico Montoya, the hiker who had shared his morning coffee at the Yellowstone campsite. But that was impossible, he decided; the thick whiskers appeared to be real, and Montoya could not have grown such a full beard in so short a time. Well, Tony thought, it had been an interesting speculation, and he had managed to get his mind off his problems for a little while. He ordered a drink and continued his study of the other passengers.

At the very front of the cabin sat a woman hunched over in her seat, her black nun's habit and veil pulled tightly about her. She did not get up during the flight, nor did she doze. She spent the time concentrating on a Bible, which she held on her lap, turning each page slowly and lovingly. Tony found it difficult to adjust to the idea of nuns travelling alone. While he was growing up, they had traveled in pairs whenever they left the protection of the mother house or mission. Why they had discarded this age-old practice,

524

designed to provide an additional degree of safety in a society that was far less stable and far more immoral than ever before, was to him a puzzlement.

His attention turned to the last group of people in first-class, a pert and pretty young woman who sat directly across the aisle from him with her two merry, and blond daughters. Tony guessed them to be three and four. They looked so much like Pamela and their own girls at the same ages that, for a moment, tears sprang into his eyes. But the little family was so cheerful and happy that he smiled at them, remembering all of the good years and blocking out the sadness.

As he sipped his drink, he tried to relax by thinking about Carla and the wonderful life they would have together. She would, he decided, supply the strength and love he needed to get his troubled emotions under control. He was surely a lucky man.

➢

When they landed at the Havana Airport, they were required to undergo one of the strictest customs inspections Tony could remember. Fortunately, there were nearly as many officials as there were passengers.

From there, Tony went to the crowded car rental desk. When he reached the front of the line, all he needed to do was leave an enormous deposit and agree to a huge daily rate in order to rent the best available car, a 1955 Chevrolet Bel Air which the man assured him had excellent secondhand recapped tires.

He left the airport and began driving toward the city. A short distance down the road, he was pleased and surprised to find a pleasant modern motel, which advertised fine food at competitive prices, satellite television from Miami, air conditioning, and an Olympic-sized swimming pool.

He registered in a lobby, reminiscent of the Moro Castle, and was nearly overwhelmed by the staff's serious efforts to make him comfortable. He followed a talkative bellhop to his spacious and well-ordered room, which was air conditioned and which did have American television. Yes, replied the friendly young man in response to his question, the restaurant was open until midnight; however, grill orders had to be in by 11:30. He showered, dressed in fresh clothing, and then strolled past the pool on the way to the restaurant, finding that it was indeed Olympic in size.

There would be a twenty-minute wait for a table, the affable hostess told him; but if he would care to wait in the bar and order a drink, she would come for him as soon as it was ready.

He perched on a comfortable stool in the bar, the motif of which, like the rest of the motel, resembled an ancient Moorish castle. One entered across a tiny drawbridge, which spanned a tiny moat, guarded by empty suits of Conquistadors' armor. Inside the room were models of galleons, archaic sailing maps of fifteenth-century oceans, and a great array of paintings. At each end of the solid teak bar, a smoothbore naval cannon stood ready to repel boarders, or perhaps, to discourage anyone from disturbing an atmosphere that had been so carefully contrived.

To determine whether or not the alcoholic beverage supply lines had been reopened, Tony ordered a Crown Royal and ginger ale and was pleasantly surprised when the distinctively-shaped bottle seemed to materialize magically in the bartender's hand. He was equally surprised and pleased when he tasted the drink and noted that the heavy, cut-glass container held a healthy knock of the premium liquor. He had learned long ago that a well-made drink was almost always the herald of an excellent dinner.

The bartender had just placed a second drink before him when the hostess appeared at his elbow. His table was ready, and she would be happy to carry his drink to the table for him when he was ready. He dropped a ten-dollar bill on the bar and signaled to the bartender to keep the change, then followed the hostess into a pleasant, candlelit dining room that reminded him of Carla and their first dinner together in Progreso. Only ten more days, he consoled himself, and we'll be together again.

How much had happened since they had parted. How pleased Carla would be with his success. He could hardly wait to tell her and Cardinal Questa about the Garza sword and the Tratamiento. Maybe Carla would be willing to quit the life of a petroleum geologist and help him to set up a charitable foundation to administer the riches from the Custer Legacy. His eyes took on a dreamy look as he pictured himself and Carla working side-by-side for many years, fighting together to make the world a better place. But these were decisions that he wanted the Cardinal to share in.

The rare roastbeef dinner, enhanced by excellent draft beer, was everything that he could have hoped for. It was a far happier and more stable Antonio Garza who returned to his room that night and fell asleep almost as soon as he lay down. Although he awoke at times, he enjoyed his best night's rest in over a month.

Chapter XXXIII
➢
The Last Assassin

Havana, Cuba
Early Summer, 1999

The next morning, although he still had some of the holdover symptoms from his Post-Traumatic Stress, he felt for the first time as though he had begun to emerge from the doldrums and was finally on the road to recovery.

He obtained a street map of Havana at the desk and plotted the best route to the Museo de Armas y Hojas de Espada as he ate a hurried breakfast. He left as soon as he finished his meal and arrived at the museum a short time later, barely able to control his excitement at finally being able to see the two José Mendoza weapons with their hidden compartments, which the museo had on display. Once inside, he purchased a ticket and began to walk slowly from room to room. His absolute disbelief grew with each step. For on most of the walls and in many glass cases, printed cards described artifacts that were no longer there! In one small case, an old, faded, handprinted card proclaimed:

**THESE WEAPONS CRAFTED BY JOSÉ MENDOZA
AT TOLEDO, ESPAÑA - MCDLV**

How ironic as well as painful, he thought. Two of the Mendoza weapons had lain here. Both had been made only one year after the Garza sword had been fashioned. It was a crushing blow to come so close and see his plans dashed on the rocky shores of futility.

He almost wished that the old card was not here to taunt him. He should have suspected such damage in Cuba!

At the end of the long room, he saw a sign on a closed door, which identified it as the entrance to the office of the curator. He knocked, and a female voice from within bade him enter. When he did so, he saw an attractive woman sitting behind a cluttered desk.

"Hello. I'm Kitty Delgado, the curator. May I assist you?"

"I'm Tony Garza from Texas State University, and I can see how busy you are. I'll try to be brief. I noticed that a great many of the artifacts are missing, and I wondered why?"

"They've been gone for many years, Señor Garza. The Museo was looted forty years ago during the takeover in 1959. Although the Castro government was very helpful in assisting our personnel, many of the finest and most rare pieces were never recovered."

"I'm particularly interested in the two weapons crafted by José Mendoza of Espadas Españas in 1455. I finally traced them here after a thirty-year search in many parts of North America. I think they may hold the key to an ancient mystery."

"I wish I had time to learn more, Señor Garza. The only person who can provide you with a complete history of those weapons is our former curator, Cesare Castellani. He has always had a great interest in Toledo blades, especially those of José Mendoza. He may well be the world's most knowledgeable man on that subject."

"I wonder if it might be possible to visit Señor Castellani?" asked the suddenly hopeful historian.

"I'll phone and see if he's willing to meet with a kindred spirit."

She returned a few minutes later.

"He is busy all day today, Señor. But he would be happy to see you tomorrow afternoon about one o'clock, if that is convenient."

"That would be wonderful, Señora!"

"Fine. I'll call Señor Castellani and tell him to expect you. Before you go, I'll draw a map for you. One cannot drive all the way to his home since he lives in a historic section of the city where wheeled vehicles of any kind are prohibited. Regardless of the direction from which you approach, it is still necessary to walk for quite some distance along bumpy old cobblestone streets and narrow alleys. But the whole area is extremely interesting. I'm sure you will thoroughly enjoy your walk."

Tony spent the remaining daylight hours touring crowded shops and markets that had been inaccessible for the past four decades. Everywhere he went, he found the Cubans to be warm and friendly, as well as eager to exchange their goods and services for Yankee dollars. He returned to his motel in the early evening, where he enjoyed another excellent dinner and a second good night's sleep. The next day, shortly after lunch, he set out for the Casa de Castellani.

He parked the old Chevy as close to the cobblestone section as possible and followed his map toward the old man's house, unaware that a short distance behind him, Asesino and the Guardians were following. They had been unable to isolate their quarry the day before as he toured the teeming streets of the city, but today would be different. Today, Antonio Garza was venturing into an area that might well have been made for foul play, or murder.

Cesare Castellani's home was surrounded by a high stone wall, inside of which every inch of space not required for the house was covered by a profusion of flowers, plants, and shrubs. Walking toward the door, he was dazzled by the rainbow of colors provided by Castellani's botanical bombast. A spry man wearing a bright Hawaiian shirt answered his knock.

"Hello. Is Señor Castellani here? I have an appointment with him. My name is Tony Garza."

"I'm Cesare Castellani," said the surprisingly young-looking octogenarian. "There is no need to introduce yourself, Dr. Garza. I have been reading your historical articles for many years. I am an archaeologist by doctoral degree, a historian by choice, and perhaps as you have already noticed, a botanist by avocation. Kitty tells me that you are embroiled in a fascinating mystery."

"I've been immersed in it for many years. I was hopeful that the Mendoza weapons at the Museo might provide a vital link in an historical chain of events."

"Come out to my garden and tell me about the mystery. I have just tapped a fresh keg of icy beer. Can I count on you to help me finish it off before it goes flat?"

"With the utmost pleasure, Dr. Castellani."

"Please, Tony, call me Cesare."

When they were settled in the shade of a lovely arbor, the courtly host patted his guest on the arm.

"Now Tony, tell me everything. We have the rest of the day, so please take your time. I hope you'll allow me to ask questions as the story unfolds."

"Of course, Cesare. To completely understand the mystery, we must trace it back to 1454, to the day when one of my ancestors, a man named Don Diego Garza, a man who was destined to become the protector of Queen Isabel, ordered a sword to be made by the finest craftsman at Espadas Españas, José Mendoza."

For the next three hours, Tony shared all that he had learned about the Grandee and his sword. He traced the Grandee's lifelong defense of King Henry and Los Reyes Catolicos. He told of Padre Garza and the part he had played in the history of the Mendoza sword, of the Padre's pious life, his time with Hernando Cortez, and of his holy death. Tony recounted the story of the Aztecs' secret medicine and information about Padre Garza's discovery of the secret. He told of Cabeza de Vaca, and the part the sword had played in his defense, as he wandered an unexplored continent. He praised the contributions of

Cardinal Cabrini and explained the part that Cardinal Questa had played, uncovering the mystery for the first time as a young seminarian. He detailed the unfortunate disappearance of Emilio Duarte and of all the other brave men who had gone forth to follow a dream. He shared the great joy he had felt when he visited the home of Henry Walking Bear and for the first time learned of the presence of a 1454 Mendoza weapon on the Custer battlefield. He relived the exhilaration he had experienced when he learned about the two Mendoza knives at the Museo in Havana from Charles De Rudio's letter to Megan Keogh. He told Cesare about his firm belief that the Garza weapon, at this very moment, might well lie within the walls of the Vatican. He ended the long story by recounting all that he had discovered about the Old Ones and their trail of terror. He spoke of everything — except his discovery of the Custer Legacy.

"So, I'm convinced, Cesare," he said in conclusion, "that Megan Keogh sent the Garza sword-knife to the Vatican Museum and that the ancient formula still lies concealed in some type of secret compartment. I was hopeful that the weapons once housed in your museum would provide the answer to Mendoza's swords."

"You've done a masterful job of following a trail of nebulous clues, Tony. Señor Conan Doyle would have been proud of you. A worthy search such as yours deserves to be rewarded, and I am very happy to be able to provide that reward."

He heaved himself to his feet and started toward the house.

"Draw each of us another draft beer while I'm gone, Tony. I'll only be away for a few minutes."

True to his word, Cesare soon returned carrying a very old, small, square wooden box. Its hammered copper hinges glistened in the sun.

"Before I open this, allow me to tell you a story. Over five hundred years ago, even the finest swords were made with inferior steel. The best blades produced in Toledo, and that meant the best in the world, tended to break under stress. Therefore, many of the swords that left the continent of Europe and arrived here in the New World were eventually broken. But that was not the end of them. Many of the swords were brought back to metalsmiths in Cuba, who converted them into fine fighting knives. Mendoza's weapons, which the Museo had on display for many years, were such conversions. In all probability, the sword of the Garzas was transformed into the knife of Cabeza de Vaca right here in Havana."

He pulled the box off the table and cradled it in his lap.

"In 1959, on the morning after the Museo was pillaged, I arrived before anyone else and was horrified by the devastation. Anything that the mob didn't covet, it destroyed. The first artifacts I checked were the Mendoza weapons. One of them had been wrenched apart and ruined, but I was astonished to find the second one completely intact. I picked up the pieces of the weapon that had been demolished, as well as the one, which a quirk of fate had left unharmed. I put them both into a box and carried them quickly out of danger. During the next two years I studied the parts from that ruined weapon and Mendoza's design techniques, which were eons ahead of his time. I tried thousands of different possible combinations until I found the secret of the hidden compartments. Tony, this box has held those weapons for the past forty years."

He opened the box lovingly and withdrew a knife with a blade less than a foot long, reshaped and sharpened to a razor's edge. The rest of the knife was obviously by Mendoza. Here were the parallel steel protectors; the brass finger-shaped guard just above the blade, designed to temporarily catch and hold an enemy knife; and, finally, the strange triangular brass tang at the top of the hilt. At the bottom of the box, Tony saw the parts that had once been the other Mendoza weapon. Cesare handed him the undamaged knife.

"Have you ever held a Mendoza weapon before?"

"No, Cesare. The only ones I ever saw were locked away under glass in Spain."

"All right. Let me show you José Mendoza's ingenious system. Take the knife and try to open the hilt. Since you know what all the others who held it did not know, it should be easy for you."

Tony took the knife and examined it closely. Then he shook it, this way and that, pressed one thing, pulled another, and tried to rotate the various parts, all to no avail. He finally looked up at Cesare in defeat.

"I'm stumped. I can't do it."

"If the other knife had not been destroyed, I think the secret might have remained hidden forever. It opens only when each part of a clever combination is worked in a precise order. Begin by placing the knife on your thigh and pressing down against the parallel guards with your forearm. Continue to apply pressure and twist the small brass handguard above the blade clockwise for a quarter turn. Then press downward on the triangular tang at the top of the hilt, and turn it counterclockwise for a quarter turn.

"Now release the pressure on the parallel guards, but continue the sequence with the handguard and tang. Rotate another quarter turn on each. Next turn the knife onto its side. Now, instead of pressing the parallel guards apart, push them toward each other. Turn the handguard a final half turn, completing its rotation, then finish the full circle with the triangular tang. Finally, holding the blade securely between your knees, press downward on the brass guard, as you pull upward on the triangular tang."

As Tony completed the final step of the sequence, the entire hilt assembly, comprised of the parallel guards, the small brass handguard, and the triangular tang, lifted off in his hand.

"It's an incredibly intricate and ingenious system. Eight catches and eight latches around the top and bottom perimeters of the hilt, which must be worked in order. If any of the steps are done out of sequence, the entire mechanism snaps shut and must be started over. Is it any wonder the secret compartments were never found?"

"I'm not sure that I could do this again," Tony told him. "You may have helped to make the dreams of myself and many others come true. Is there anything I can do for you in return?"

"Not unless you happen to have ten million spare dollars lying around. Now that Cuba has a chance to revive and prosper, I would like Havana to have a real centerpiece once again. But it will take many dollars to make the Museo de Armas y Hojas de Espada a place to be proud of. Unlike your dream, my friend, I fear that mine will never come true."

"Don't be so sure, Cesare. Let me ask you something. Would you rent me the Mendoza knife for the next twelve months? If you say yes, I will return it at the end of one year, along with a certified check for ten million dollars."

"Of course you may borrow the knife, Tony. But don't play tricks on an old war-horse."

He stared probingly into Tony's eyes and made a startling discovery.

"You aren't joking, are you? How can you do such a thing?"

"I'm not joking, Cesare! I mean every word. Where the money will come from I can't tell you yet. However, it will be a legal donation. Do we have a deal?"

"We have a deal! I'll start making up a list of available artifacts at once! If you promise to return here next summer, I'll promise to stay alive to greet you! Let's have one more beer to celebrate our collective good fortune before you go. All things considered, it has been a very good day. You have given an old man new life!"

➤

A short time later, Tony left the home of his new but staunch friend and walked back toward the old Chevy. The warm glow in his heart was every bit as real as the Mendoza knife in his belt.

He had walked about a third of the way back to the car when a pair of menacing-looking men suddenly walked out from between two houses and confronted him. He spun back in the opposite direction and found two more of the same ilk. Cesare had told him that this area was free from thugs, at least until sundown, but these four didn't look like Cubans. They were dressed like Americans. When the biggest man spoke, Tony's suspicions were confirmed.

"We want to talk to you, Garza."

Tony was convinced of two things. First, he could not afford to show fear. Next, he had to get to the narrow doorway of a small house that lay close at hand, between himself and his assailants. He continued walking purposefully ahead. After what seemed an eternity, he ducked gratefully into the shelter of the doorway. Here they could reach him only one at a time, unless they had guns, in which case it wouldn't matter. Otherwise, they would be facing a former Green Beret armed with one of the most formidable fighting knives ever crafted.

Once again, the biggest of his antagonists spoke.

"I said, we want to talk to you, Garza."

"It's Dr. Garza, and you'll have to speak to me through my agent. I never converse with people I don't like, or who smell bad. Unfortunately, all four of you fit both those categories."

"You don't seem to understand, Buddy," said one of the rogues who had been behind him. "There's a lot of us and only one of you. You're badly outnumbered."

"How absolutely frightening," Tony snarled sarcastically. "All right, it's time that you bozos understood something. I'm not your 'buddy,' and if you're pretending to be tough guys, you're doing a miserable job of it. But, I've decided to listen to your message. One of you may come to within ten feet of this doorway. While he's up here, you other three better stand very still."

He pulled the Mendoza knife from his waistband and brandished it before continuing.

"If any of you idiots threaten me, at any time, in any way, I'll split the first gizzard I can reach. If you don't believe that, try me. If you don't like my terms, get out."

The Guardians quickly conferred; Pinto Peters came forward and attempted to open negotiations.

"Look, Dr. Garza. We don't want to harm you, but we know you found the gold and we want to work out a deal."

"Why should I make any kind of a deal? With anyone?"

"Because the Guardians have watched over that gold for a long time, and we don't think it's fair for you to have it. What we're willing to do is give you $10,000,000 and never bother you again, if you'll lead us to the gold cache."

"And if I refuse?"

"We'll have to kill you. If the Guardians can't have it, we wouldn't let you live to enjoy it neither."

"All right, listen up. I'm only going to say this once. I don't know who you people are; but I'll soon have $200,000,000, and the ability to find out. I reject your stupid offer. However, you have made me see the need to buy some life insurance. Before my death can occur, due to any outside influence, I'm going to place the sum of $10,000,000 in a trust account and offer a cash bounty to any person or group that kills anyone who is a current member, a former member, or anyone suspected of ever having been a member, of the Guardians. Do you understand me?"

"I understand Garza. But this thing ain't over yet. Not by a whole jugful, it ain't."

"For your sake, I hope it is. If anything ever happens to me, little man, one million out of those ten is going to be the bounty on you, personally. Even if everybody else lives, you'll die! Now, scram!"

Stunned by this sudden turn of events, Pinto Peters turned on his heel and walked back toward his confederates. A trembling Antonio Garza slunk as far back in the doorway as he could get. His ferocious bravado had cost him all of the ground that he had regained on his Post-Traumatic Stress, and, understandably, this experience had triggered a fresh wave of anxiety.

He felt that he had handled the situation as well as it could be handled and that if the Guardians made another attempt to intimidate or harm him, their effort would come very soon, before his warning had sunk into their brains. To give them time to think, he waited in the doorway for a few minutes before resuming his walk.

Even then, he did not go directly toward his car, but took a circuitous route. Therefore, he was astonished when, suddenly, the biggest of his enemies jumped out at him from behind a fence, a short-bladed knife clinched in his hand.

"Let's see how brave you are now, Garza!" Frolic shouted, storming toward him, swishing the knife before him as he came.

Tony, in an attempt to avoid the man's rush, dodged to his left, putting all of his weight on his still weak ankle, which gave way. In severe pain he staggered backwards, just in time to feel new pain as his enemy's blade sliced deeply into his thigh. Knowing that with two injured legs he was no match for his far quicker and stronger opponent, Tony decided to close with the big man before he could bring his weapon to bear again. Switching the Mendoza knife to his left hand, he lunged forward and encircled his enemy's neck with his right arm, swinging him around toward the waiting blade of the Spanish knife, a move that reversed their positions. At that instant, a muffled shot rang out and his powerful assailant slumped to the ground, his back covered with blood from a bullet which had severed his spine and killed him instantly.

Before the hidden sniper could fire a second shot, Tony dove behind a fence. The same fence that minutes earlier had concealed the man who now lay dead. He limped along the length of the structure, fully aware that the bullet had been meant for him. The other Guardians would never have risked shooting their confederate, certainly not when his battle had nearly been won. More importantly, one second before that shot was fired, it was his own back that had been turned toward the building from which the fatal bullet had come.

As he lurched along, he looked for the other three Guardians. Then he realized that they had probably separated in order to set up four different ambushes. It was merely a coincidence that their most lethal assailant had confronted him.

Finally reaching the comparative safety of his car, he climbed painfully into the driver's seat of the old Chevy. His hands were shaking so violently that it took three attempts to insert the ignition key in the slot. As soon as the ancient engine leaped into life, he depressed the accelerator, and rushed away from the mayhem and murder. As the old car gathered speed, Tony began to tremble from shock. He pressed down as hard as possible on the wound in his leg, in an effort to control the bleeding.

As he drove carefully along, he pondered all of the recent events. He concluded that an assassin sent by Mercata Verrano or one of the other Old Ones must have fired the shot. Since the three remaining Guardians could be eliminated as suspects in any such attack, the Old Ones were the only ones with a possible motive. Besides, he reasoned, the Guardians needed him to live until he could talk! The Old Ones needed him to die before he could talk! But why now, Tony wondered? Why had the Old Ones only now marked him for death?

Suddenly his eyes opened wide in recognition and resignation! What if the trash collectors had not picked up the tiny bottle of Tratamiento that Carla had thrown away? What if it had been found by one of the Old Ones' agents? If so, he would have been marked for death from that moment. That would explain all the recent attempts

539

on his life. The shot that had ripped through his tent had come before his discovery of the gold, so that could not have been the Guardians. Once again, logic dictated that the Guardians needed to keep him alive until they learned his secret, while the Old Ones needed to kill him before he could expose theirs.

For now, he felt far more confident in his chances with the gold seekers. They were, after all, amateurs. After they thought about his ultimatum, they would decide that certain death awaited them if they persisted. As he pulled into the emergency entrance of a hospital, he theorized that sudden death might also await the Old Ones' professional assassins who did not persist in their assignments, or who failed to successfully complete any mission.

I have to leave Havana as soon as possible, he decided, and fly to Rome. Vietnam had taught him that the winners never let their enemies corner them in unfamiliar territory. He had lived through those deadly days in a hostile jungle because he had been able to outthink the Viet Cong. To survive now, he would have to outsmart the Old Ones' assassins.

He staggered from the old Chevy toward the emergency room entrance of the hospital, but was met some distance from it by a young, wheelchair-pushing orderly who raced forward to intercept him. In his hand, Tony carried his ankle air splint. Fortunately, he had left it in the car rather than at the hotel.

A compassionate, elderly female doctor reinstalled and adjusted the splint, then quickly began cleansing the gash in his thigh.

"How did this happen, Señor?" she asked.

"What do you think did it?" he countered.

"I know what did it! I asked how it happened."

"I was sharpening a sickle blade. It slipped and cut my leg."

"Exactly as I thought, Señor Smith," she replied, fixing him with a steady gaze that betrayed a slight hint of amusement. "You are fortunate it isn't a knife wound, Señor Smith. If it were, an official report would have to be filed, and you would be detained until the police were satisfied."

"I certainly am fortunate, Dr. Estrella, to have you here to treat me. I'm beginning to understand just how lucky I am."

She carefully aligned the lips of the wound and stitched them together with an easy show of proficiency.

"You've lost some blood, Señor Smith, and suffered some torn muscles. I'm going to bandage your thigh to make a minimal amount of walking possible. Mind you, I said possible, not comfortable. You'll have some pain in that wound and greatly hampered mobility for the next week or two. Stay off your feet as much as you can. I'll give you a dozen pain pills. They are very potent. Take one, and only one, when the pain becomes severe. I have decided against a transfusion. If you drink plenty of water and juices, you'll replace the blood naturally within the next forty-eight hours."

When she had finished attending to his needs, she said, "Go down this corridor to room #1, the last door on your left. It is just inside the exit to the parking lot. Rest for as long as you wish before leaving. If you feel dizzy, come back at once to see me. Please use the front half of the room only. The body of a coronary victim who passed away a short time ago is still in the back of the room. A mortician will be here in about an hour to claim the body."

"Thank you, for everything, Dr. Estrella. I am truly grateful. I wish there were something I could do for you in return."

"There is something, Señor Smith. Just be careful of that wound and get well as quickly as possible."

With that she smiled, then she turned and walked away.

Tony dropped back into the wheelchair and propelled himself toward the room at the end of the hall. He entered and closed the door behind him. On a bed, positioned against the opposite wall, lay the body of a heavy set, middle-aged man. On a table beside him lay everything that a priest would need to administer the last rites of the church. The hospital chaplain would probably appear at any moment, Tony thought, to retrieve his possessions.

He went into the bathroom to refresh himself and realized that there were no paper towels. Certain that there must be a supply of them somewhere, he opened the closet and was astonished to find a cleric's clothing. On the floor, he also saw a small suitcase, containing a set of vestments, various stoles, and a Mass kit. The dead man had been a priest!

Tony went to the small bedside table and found, among the other things, a wallet and an identity card. The dead man was forty-eight-year-old Father Guido Andolini. He must have been visiting the sick when he had the coronary, Tony decided. Well, I'm sure he's with Our Lord by now. Suddenly he had a stroke of genius. Tony Garza, history scholar, would remain here in this room with the dead priest for as long as possible. From the hospital, dressed in a suit of clothes slightly too large for him, Padre Antonio Garza, priest, would emerge. I have a U.S. passport and travel visas, he reasoned. But I also have Vatican documents that afford me total and complete diplomatic immunity.

He would not fly to Rome tomorrow, as his advance reservations indicated. How could he? Tony Garza was staying in the hospital. He would not return to his room. He would simply leave his extra clothing and his few personal possessions at the motel. When he did not return, they would automatically bill him. Padre Garza, on the other hand, would fly to Atlanta tonight. From there, the Cardinal's envoy would leave, later tonight or tomorrow, for Rome. It would take an extremely enterprising assassin to follow all the jumps in time, place, and identities. The plan was so fiendishly clever that Tony, or rather Padre Antonio, would have danced with joy had his legs not hurt so much.

Fifteen minutes later a middle-aged priest, carrying a small travelling bag, left the hospital and hobbled toward a waiting taxi, nodding to the faithful and waving a figure eight Sign of the Cross to everyone in sight.

During the trip to the airport, he watched the traffic behind him, while the driver speeded up, slowed down, and switched lanes, without apparent rhyme or reason. At one point, they even doubled back for several blocks before proceeding, to see if anyone would follow them. But throughout the entire trip, he saw nothing that looked like a chase car. Maybe I've managed to shake them off, he hoped.

His clerical garb and Vatican credentials were accepted without question and he was able to obtain a seat on a flight to Atlanta, scheduled to leave an hour later. He spent that hour in the V.I.P. lounge. Still troubled by the terrors of the day, as well as by the constant pain emanating from his thigh and ankle, he refused to eat, but did accept a cup of black coffee.

➢

By the time he arrived in Atlanta, he had begun to feel much better about his chances of survival. During the flight from Havana, he had walked from the first-class section all the way back to the tail, peering furtively at each passenger. Several of them looked a bit sinister; but none of the three remaining Guardians were aboard. He saw only one other passenger who had been on the flight to Havana two nights earlier.

Inside the mammoth Atlanta terminal, he boarded one of the trams and rode to the next concourse. Just before the shuttle's doors were slammed shut, in preparation to proceed to the next stop, he hurried out of one car and boarded another, which was bound in the opposite direction. After repeating the procedure twice more, and observing no efforts to follow him, he left the terminal and took a taxi directly to the Airport Inn.

An hour later he fell into a restless sleep. Although he awoke on several occasions, he was able to control his nerves, knowing that by the same time tomorrow, he would be safely back in the Vatican, his great adventure over.

The next morning he decided not to tempt fate, or assassins, more than necessary. Rather than leave the safety of his room, he called room service and ordered scrambled eggs, toast, and a large pot of coffee. While he waited, he telephoned TransOcean Airways and secured a reservation on the crowded evening flight to Rome. As only two seats were left, in order to claim one of them he was forced to reveal that he was the personal emissary of Cardinal Questa, travelling under diplomatic immunity.

The TransOcean evening flight was scheduled to depart at 7:00 P.M. Since the flight's duration was eight hours, and another five hours would be lost crossing into the European time zones, touchdown in Rome would be at 8:00 A.M.

Perhaps in time to join Cardinal Questa for breakfast!

His seat on the plane was confirmed, so he did not need to be at the departure gate until twenty minutes before takeoff. If the taxi picked him up at 6:15, the timing would be perfect. He did not venture out of his room for the remainder of the day. At noon, he ordered a light lunch and another pot of coffee, then returned to his laptop computer and the business of finishing the article for American Heritage.

At 5:15, he called the motel's front desk.

"Good afternoon. This is Padre Garza in room 244. As you may have noticed yesterday, I'm partially crippled. I would like to have a bellman bring a wheelchair to my room at 6:10. And please have a taxi waiting at the motel's service entrance at 6:15 to take me to the terminal. I know vanity is unworthy in a priest; but I dislike having anyone stare at me in a wheelchair."

"Please don't apologize, Padre. I understand exactly how you feel. You may count on me to take care of everything. Is there anything else that you require?"

"No," replied the temporary cleric, "other than sending a copy of my credit card receipts to the address which I provided."

"No problem there, Padre. If I don't see you before you go, thank you for choosing our motel and please enjoy your flight."

He hung up, delighted with this bit of subterfuge à la James Bond. He was confident that the Guardians would now give up, since they knew about his plan for a $10,000,000 reprisal, and because they had experienced the violent death of one of their members. But he had no such feelings about the Old Ones. No, he thought, I must continue my efforts to throw their assassins off the track.

His carefully orchestrated plans unfolded without a flaw, and as the giant 747 lifted off the runway, he was confident that he had eluded all pursuit and was finally in the clear. An hour later he was not so sure, when he spotted a familiar figure, one that had been present on each of his last two flights. He tried to convince himself that it was just a coincidence, a one-in-a-hundred chance, but all the while his instincts shouted: BEWARE.

As he painfully descended from the plane the next morning, he looked for the suspicious figure, but to no avail. He scanned the passengers as they queued up at the customs counter, again with no success. Since his new status produced special treatment, he was able to clear customs and reach the waiting taxis before the others. He tottered to the first cab in line and slid into the back seat. The taxi driver shuttled him about the city for the next two hours. They made random stops in every quarter and went around in circles several times in an effort to elude pursuit. He finally quit the taxi half a mile from St. Peter's Square.

In hopes that his clerical garb would allow him to blend into the crowd and offer additional protection, he tugged his wide-brimmed hat well down over his eyes and pulled his dark, loose-fitting cloak about him. Satisfied that he had done his best, he began a trudging transit down a narrow street toward the square, on the far side of which lay the Vatican gate and safety.

As he neared the end of the street, he paused in the shadows of an ancient building and looked furtively about. He was glad to stop, even for a moment. The pain emanating from the wound inflicted two days earlier was becoming unbearable. Thank God, he thought, once I cross the square, I'll finally be safe.

As he rested, he mused about the coincidence of finishing his journey on June 25, a day that had been so important in many other years, starting nearly five centuries ago. Custer's death, Padre Garza's discovery, and much more had occurred on June 25. He was grateful that soon he would be able to share the burden of these awesome secrets with Cardinal Questa. Sole knowledge of the Tratamiento and the Custer Legacy was too much for one man to carry.

He continued to peer suspiciously at each approaching figure, still alert to impending danger. To reassure himself, he reached into his heavy canvas bag and fingered the Mendoza knife. As he touched it, a feeling of foreboding enveloped him. How foolish, he thought; premonitions of impending doom should be reserved for superstitious old women.

By sheer force of will, he pushed himself erect, shouldered his bag and, leaving the security of the shadows, resumed his painful, trudging walk, still glancing fretfully about him as he crossed the crowded sunlit square. After what seemed to him a very long way, he reached the opposite side and paused beside a gate. A gate that meant the end of his long but now successful journey.

He reached forward to ring the bell, but as he did, he saw an ominous shadow and suddenly felt a sharp pain course through his back. With utter disappointment and frustration, he pitched forward as the remaining strength drained from his tortured body, his arms too weak to cushion his fall. An instant later, his pack was roughly ripped from his shoulder. Over the thunderous roaring in his ears he heard a new sound, the rush of approaching footsteps. With his last ounce of strength, he turned his head and looked up into the concerned face of a Swiss Guard. With his last conscious breath, Antonio Garza whispered, "Tell the Cardinal I found it."

Epilogue

➢

And Justice For All

The Vatican
Rome, Italy
June 25, 1999

When Tony revived, he was lying on a hospital bed, surrounded by three men. Two of them were Cardinal Questa and his secretary, Monsignor O'Reilly. The third man wore a white coat and had a stethoscope draped around his neck.

"It's wonderful to see you, Tony!" the Cardinal said, gently squeezing his wounded friend's hand in a gesture of compassion and relief. "I've prayed for you, and worried about you, and felt very guilty about sending you on such a dangerous mission. You've obviously undergone a great number of hardships in the past few months. But unlike all of the others, you have returned to us. And," he added joyfully, "according to the message you whispered to the guard, we must all thank God for the success of your mission as well as for your safe return."

"Eminence," Tony said, "not even you can begin to realize how much we have to thank God for!"

"The doctor tells me that you have several wounds and injuries in addition to the one you received an hour ago. A wound, praise God, which is not serious. Before you go to your other patients, Doctor, would you explain to Tony what happened?"

"His Eminence is correct, Dr. Garza. The wound is not serious. I presume that you were wearing some type of backpack with very wide, thick shoulder straps. Am I correct?" asked the doctor.

"That's right. How did you know?" Tony queried in return.

"As the knife descended, instead of entering your back, the blade obviously struck something that impeded its progress. Otherwise it probably would have plunged into your body and killed you. I concluded that the webbing of a pack strap would have been in an ideal location to prevent that from happening. The blade penetrated your flesh enough to be extremely painful and produce shock, but the puncture was not of sufficient depth to be serious. I have already sutured it. If you were not given a tetanus shot as part of any of your recent treatments, I'll give you one now."

"I had one two days ago," Tony assured him.

"I concluded that as well. The closure of your thigh wound is a real work of art. Don't get up for a while. Whether you realize it or not, you're in a state of complete exhaustion."

The doctor departed to complete his rounds, leaving Cardinal Questa and Monsignor O'Reilly alone with Tony.

"The Swiss Guard came rushing inside," the Cardinal explained, "shouting that there was a wounded man at the gate, proclaiming that he had 'found it.' When Michael heard him, he thought it might be you. So we both came at once to investigate. And there you were! We've all been very concerned about you, Tony. How do you feel?"

"The doctor is right. I am completely exhausted. I've packed a lifetime of adventures into the past five and a half months. But I'm also extremely happy. I discovered the answer to the Garza puzzle; I uncovered an organization which still offers human sacrifices; I stumbled onto a $200,000,000 fortune in gold, known as the Custer Legacy, which I believe God gave to us at this time, Eminence, because all of mankind needs our help so desperately!" He hesitated for several moments before concluding in an almost skeptical tone. "In addition to everything else, I think I'm falling in love again."

"That's wonderful, Tony! If you're able, please start at the very beginning and tell us everything!"

Just then a messenger entered the room and handed a note to Monsignor O'Reilly, who read it and said, "Police officials have captured your assailant, Tony, and recovered your knapsack. They want to know if you would like a face-to-face meeting with the prisoner, here in the Vatican. I'm to call them back as soon as possible with your answer."

"After he chased me halfway around the world and made several attempts on my life? Of course I want to meet him! Also, Monsignor, with the Cardinal's permission, would you please call the Vatican Museum? Ask the curator to go to the Papal Guards Hall and remove the old Spanish knife from the Myles Keogh and Charles De Rudio exhibit and bring it here. In case there is more than one knife, I need the one with MCDLIV inscribed on the blade."

Monsignor O'Reilly returned a few minutes later and informed Tony that he had left a message for the curator, who was at lunch, and that the police would bring the assassin to Cardinal Questa's office in three hours. He also brought along a flagon of brandy and three heavy, cut-glass snifters.

For the next two hours, Tony shared his adventures as well as the brandy. One gave him chills, the other a warm, rosy feeling.

As the saga unfolded, both of his listeners shook their heads in amazement. Just as he began to relate the story of his interview with Henry Walking Bear, which led to his discovery of the Garza weapon's present location, there came a knock on the door, and the museum curator entered with the Spanish knife. Tony's heart almost exploded with joy as, at last, he held the fine old weapon and read the inscription:

TOLEDO ESPAÑA - MCDLIV

Not until this moment had he been certain that he would ever see the historic weapon. There were more than a few tears in his eyes as he cradled it gently in his hands and ran his fingertips slowly over the time-worn letters. Tony handed the precious artifact to the Cardinal.

"I present you with the Garza sword, Your Eminence. The one you have hoped to find for the past sixty years. A sword that has protected its secret since La Noche de Triste."

Cardinal Questa was so overcome with emotion that he could only smile sadly, nod, and remember. His memory swept him back to the first week of 1941, to a long-forgotten winter afternoon. He saw himself, as a young seminarian, standing in front of a large display case that contained artifacts of Myles Keogh and Charles De Rudio, gathered up after the Battle of the Little Bighorn. How well he recalled the ancient knife that had held his attention for so long on that afternoon of yesteryear. The wondrous knife that he now held in his own trembling hands. How terribly ironic that Emilio Duarte and the others had died so unnecessarily, searching for something that lay hidden away, right under their noses, in the safety of the Vatican Museum. How he wished his mentor, Cardinal Cabrini, could be with them now to share this final triumph. He was roused from his reverie by the sound of Tony's voice.

"At one time, the secret of a great Aztec medicine was hidden within this weapon's secret chamber," Tony said confidently. "I'm certain that it still is. However, the material on which it was written may have long since disintegrated and turned to dust. Say a special prayer, Eminence, that such was not the case. I've seen for myself the Tratamiento's ability to aid healing. It would be a great blessing for many people. But if the formula is lost, we may never recover it. Those who control this secret have, for hundreds of years, demonstrated a willingness to kill in order to keep it."

Monsignor O'Reilly took the weapon from the Cardinal and examined it carefully before handing it back to Tony.

"This is truly wonderful craftsmanship! No one would suspect that any type of hidden chamber existed in this beautiful knife."

551

"Thank heaven, no one ever did, Monsignor!" Tony responded. "Let's hope that José Mendoza didn't decide to use a different combination for each of the swords he created."

With a feeling of reverential awe, Tony took the weapon and laid it on his leg, the way Cesare Castellani had demonstrated. He paused for several moments, thinking about other hands that had held it. Hands of men who had helped to shape history. The brave hands of the Grandee and the blest hands of Padre Garza. The capable hands of Cabeza de Vaca and those of the many Indian warriors who had carried this knife into so many long-forgotten battles. He wondered about the Sioux or Cheyenne who had used the weapon at the Little Bighorn and wondered how he had lived and how he had died. Tony was suddenly sad that he would never know more about that warrior or any of the men who, for the past five hundred years, had helped to forge the destiny of America.

After saying a silent prayer for guidance, Tony carefully followed the first seven steps in the sequence he had memorized. Finally uttering a brief final prayer of hope, Tony clamped the blade securely between his knees and steeled himself before the eighth and final step. Pushing down on the brass guard, he pulled upward on the tang and, as if by magic, the hilt came off in his hand.

He peered inside the hilt. Something was inside! He reached cautiously into the opening and tested the composition of the material. His finger did not encounter flimsy papyrus or tapa cloth, as he had expected it might. No! What he felt was strong, solid metal. Tony slowly and carefully withdrew a scroll, made from thinly hammered gold. Countless warriors in incalculable numbers of battles had wielded a scroll that had lain hidden for nearly five centuries, while the weapon that concealed it. The satin-smooth steel blade that now glowed in the soft lamplight had been tempered in José Mendoza's steeling fires, but quenched in the blood of a thousand enemies. What tales it would tell if it could only speak, Tony thought once again.

Cardinal Questa slowly and delicately unrolled the ancient golden scroll, and spread it out. The others gathered about him and stared in amazement at the clarity of the printing, as well as the list of ingredients that were described and explained.

Tratamiento consisted of six different components. They were identified by the Aztec name, and next to each was a pictograph drawing of that specific ingredient. Beside each drawing, Padre Garza had printed the Spanish word for the substance. Below the descriptive section were two additional sections. On the middle one was etched:

Item 1. One measure of Hawthorn Berries.

Item 2. One measure of Red/Orange Tree Mold.

Item 3. One measure of Blue/Green Lichens.

Item 4. One measure of Wood Ashes. (Potash)

Item 5. Two measures of Yucca Cactus Juice and Pulp.

Item 6. Four measures of ground Cayenne Peppers.

The final section explained how to combine and blend the mixture and concluded with an instruction to shake it vigorously each day for three months until aging and fermenting brought it to full potency.

"So that's what makes up the Tratamiento," marveled Tony. "That accounts for a quick rush of blood to an area where it's applied. Each one of those ingredients has been hailed, at one time or another, as a wonder drug. I'm amazed that the Aztecs discovered them so long ago. With your permission, Eminence, I will now arrange for the Tratamiento to be manufactured and given to all who need it."

Just then, there was a knock at the door, and a uniformed police officer entered.

"Good evening, Your Eminence, Monsignor O'Reilly, Dr. Garza. Whenever you're ready, the prisoner is outside in the hallway."

Tony looked past the man and saw a figure in the dim light. He was chagrined, but not shocked, to see the nun who had been on several flights with him. Her veil was still pulled tightly about her face, though a lock of hair poked out beneath her coif.

"That old woman is Tony's assailant?" asked Cardinal Questa incredulously.

"Yes, Eminence, but she's not just any woman, and she's not old. She is the most dangerous assassin in the world since Carlos the Jackal retired," the police official assured him. "Do not be deceived by the makeup, the phony hair, and the carefully drawn age lines. Beneath that nun's habit is a much younger woman."

The official left the study and walked into the hall. A moment later, he returned with his prisoner. As he followed her into the room, he suddenly pulled off the veil, the coif, and the wig with one swift motion.

"Here is your assailant, Dr. Garza!" he declared triumphantly.

Tony's eyes opened wide with astonishment.

"Good Lord," he stammered, "it's Carla! I can't believe this!"

"Believe it, Dr. Garza!" said the policeman. "You are very, very lucky to be alive! She doesn't miss very many of her targets. Carla Cansino is only one of her many aliases. She uses Carla when she's a petroleum geologist from Houston."

"Isn't she really a petroleum geologist?" Tony asked weakly.

"No more than you are an astronaut. Let me say this again, Dr. Garza. This woman is the most dangerous and cunning assassin in the world! She has a dozen different identities. Her code name is Asesino. Her only business is killing, and she's very good at it! It has also made her very rich. We suspect that she charges as much as a million dollars for each assassination. We believe that her real name is Artesta Verrano."

Tony's heart was in his throat as he struggled to control his emotions. This couldn't be true! It had to be a nightmare!

"Can I see her alone for a few minutes?" he asked.

"I'll give you fifteen minutes," the police officer responded. "Then she's going back to a jail cell, where she belongs!"

"Can't you take some of those restraints off of her? Don't you think cuffing her, hand and foot, to a chain around her waist, is a little extreme?"

"No, Dr. Garza, I don't! After we cornered her and took away all of her weapons, she managed to send two more of my men to the hospital. She's a martial arts expert. She can kill you with her hands, her feet, or even her teeth. I don't think she's trussed up too much! In fact, I don't feel very comfortable about leaving you alone with her. I'm going to lay my policeman's riot whistle here on this desk. If you get into trouble, or if she makes you so disgusted that you never want to see her again, just blow the whistle and I'll hurry back."

When the Cardinal, the police official, and all the others had left the room, Tony said, "I'm sorry about your troubles, Carla."

"Call me, Artesta. Or, for that matter, Asesino. Most of my friends do. You have nothing to feel sorry about. You did a good job of playing a lovesick idiot and helping me in all of my assassination attempts. I still can't believe that I missed you so damned many times. You must have nine lives."

"You're apparently related to Mercata Verrano."

"She's my grandmother."

"Do she and the other Old Ones really pay you to kill people?"

For an instant her eyes flashed in amazement in response to his use of the name "Old Ones" and his awareness of Mercata Verrano's involvement, but she quickly recovered her composure.

"I don't charge my own grandmother. What kind of woman do you think I am?"

Tony couldn't believe his ears! The beautiful, intelligent, sensitive woman he had fallen in love with had never really existed! She was only a facade for this callous, evil, brutal monster. The very antithesis of everything that Carla Cansino had seemed to be.

"Our relationship never meant anything to you, did it?"

"Any relationship you thought we had existed only in your mind."

"I can't believe your callousness," he said sadly. "And I can't believe I was so naive. I guess I was never more than an amusing diversion for you."

"Don't flatter yourself," she hissed. "You weren't even a good diversion. You were never anything but a target."

Tony shuddered in disgust and revulsion.

"You're a terrific actress! You really had me fooled! But the deception that you practiced on me is harmless and petty compared to the horror being orchestrated by your grandmother and the other diabolical savages. Their bloodthirsty cult must be obliterated. What gives Mercata Verrano and the Old Ones a right to destroy the lives of innocent people? The right to decide who shall be sacrificed in their insane rituals? The Old Ones are a cancerous growth that must be cut out and destroyed. I'm going to make their annihilation my first priority!"

"You're even more naive than I imagined!" she sneered. "Grandmother and the Old Ones have reestablished the ancient empire. They have enormous power and influence, as well as fabulous wealth. They'll prove that by securing my quick release from prison. They simply can't be stopped. Anyone foolish enough to challenge their authority would need a private army to go into Mexico and fight a battle of nerves in every single village and town the Old Ones control. That army would need a leader with an immense fortune and a total commitment. You'll certainly never fill that bill! You'll always be an insignificant penny-ante player, making a few dollars with your stupid magazine articles and your pathetic teaching job. In a million years you couldn't dig up enough money, or muster enough determination, to make a dent in the Old Ones' empire!" she concluded smugly.

"You couldn't be more wrong! But it's ironic that you should use the words dig up. Before the police come back, I want to share some interesting news. While I was wandering about on the Yellowstone, I managed to dig up part of the Custer Legacy. About an hour ago, we recovered Padre Garza's original formula for Tratamiento. Every single element needed to defeat the Old Ones is falling into place. Very soon, their evil empire will exist only as a horrible memory! While you sit in your jail cell, paying for a lifetime of brutal murders, I'll be decimating the Old Ones. The treasure will be used to finish the battle against the evils of your bloodthirsty pagan gods. We will finally end the struggle that Hernando Cortez began nearly five hundred years ago."

Asesino gave an impatient shrug, but Garza quickly continued.

"I'm not through! Far from it. There is an amazing irony in all of this, Asesino. Cortez and the others went to Mexico to spread the word of God. There they found demonic idols and endless human sacrifices. They found devil-worshippers who waged war for the sole purpose of obtaining a continuous supply of victims. To the ancient Aztecs, these human beings had no value until the moment of death. They chose to ignore the bounty of life that God had given them. They were even blessed with a wonderful medicine that cured their ills and enriched their lives. They responded by hiding the Tratamiento away from everyone except a chosen few.

"Then one day a gentle, caring, and humble Catholic priest won the gratitude of a fierce, bloodthirsty Aztec priest, who reluctantly, I'm sure, shared that great gift of life. History tells us that one of those priests died protecting the secret, while the other died for not protecting it. For the last five hundred years, the Old Ones and those who preceded them have murdered to hide the secret of Tratamiento, and to suppress the descendants of their original victims. Now, after nearly five centuries, the miracle cure that generations of these cutthroats sought to keep for themselves to increase their own power will become the instrument of their destruction. The Church has finally reclaimed the reward that one of her sons won for her many years ago—a great prize that will be used to help people everywhere in the world."

She stared at him in sudden, startled, wide-eyed amazement.

"The final irony is the major role that you, the offspring of those evil ones, have played in their destruction.

"You've taught me a valuable lesson. You've made me realize that I can't afford to waste another minute. Asesino, it's time to stamp out the evil and misery that you and the Old Ones have created. It's time for both of us to repay the people of this sad old world. I plan to do my share with the miraculous formula and the golden Custer Legacy!"

Filled with new determination and resolve, he turned his back on her, and blew the whistle.

Appendix A:
➤
The Writing of The Custer Legacy

Nearly sixty years ago I became a history buff. That love has given me a lifelong passport to many exciting places on their most important days. During those six decades, my tour guides have been the world's finest storytellers. Like Antonio Garza, I too have glided across the blue Pacific on a balsa raft, scaled the heights of Mt. Everest, roped to a sure-footed Sherpa guide, and angled my Dauntless divebomber down toward a menacing enemy aircraft carrier during the Battle of Midway. History has taught me a great deal about the world and its people, both as a student and as a teacher; but it is historical fiction that has claimed the allegiance of my heart of hearts.

Naming all of the literary spellbinders who helped to turn me into an avid reader during those years is impossible. Suffice to say that they shared two common characteristics. Each one took the time and made the effort to clothe the characters that his fertile imagination had created in suits of carefully researched historical facts. And after their novels had ended and the final arcane curtain had fallen, my favorite authors shared a special moment of magic with the readers and allowed us to go backstage to their world of creativity. Such is the purpose of this piece.

The major players in *The Custer Legacy* are fictitious, but most of the supporting cast members were real. I have portrayed them as honestly and fairly as possible. My fictional friends are patterned after actual people or composites of known prototypes.

During the reign of Isabel and Fernando, for example, the man identified as the Grandee, Don Diego Garza, did not exist, but someone like him certainly did. For over twenty years, he kept Los Reyes Catolicos safe from harm. Obviously his grandson, Padre Diego Garza, is also fictitious. But, for hundreds of years the Garza family was famous for its priests. One of them, as Emmanuel Questa recalled, served as a chaplain to the Alamo before it fell to Santa Anna in 1836. Of course, Cortez, Narvaez, Father Olmedo and Cabeza de Vaca all lived. Just as obviously, the Aztec High Priest, Attapa, and his son, Curco, did not; but their historical counterparts were real. Frighteningly real.

Kevin McCarthy and his parents are my fictional friends, as are Catherine Gerot and her brother, Geofrey. A fine young man who fought and died in Vietnam inspired Geofrey's character. The lovely Catherine, with her blond hair, green eyes and rapier wit is a tribute to one of the best friends I have ever had. Pamela Greenfield is fictional, but the beautiful, vivacious, delightful lady she symbolizes once lived. She, too, died in her fortieth year and left a loving husband and three daughters. On life's lighter side, gamblers like Kerry Kelly traveled on riverboats for many years and made excellent incomes, living on jacks and queens.

Fire Hawk and White Wolf are fictional, as is Little Fawn, but the Sioux were blessed with many great warriors, like White Wolf, and herbal healers, like Little Fawn. A small number of white men really did become adopted members of various tribes and found their hosts to be fair and just. Although a few became traitors, most were as devoted and loyal as Fire Hawk. But the Plains Indians could be brutal and savage, too, as Red Fern's pauperism and death reveals.

Villain and Stork are fictional, but their Green Beret role models will recognize themselves. The episode of Jumping Frog, Chipmunk, and the human head came from a personal experience in an Alaskan Indian village in 1959 when two small boys actually did acquire what was, to them, such a wonderful and unique trophy.

With very few exceptions, the Indians and soldiers described in the Battle of the Little Bighorn and the other firefights are real. All of Custer's troop commanders and the other Seventh Cavalry personnel who drift into the story were actual people who fought and died. Crazy Horse will always be one of our country's greatest heroes and finest cavalry leaders. His mismanaged and tragic personal life, as well as the stigma connected with his removal as one of the Lakota Shirt Wearers, may disqualify him from the lofty moral pedestal on which role models must stand; but his tactical and strategical skills were brilliant. Crazy Horse was never conquered. When he surrendered at Fort Robinson, in May 1877, it was for the good of his people, not because he was beaten. I believe that his story of the Sioux' tree of life truly typifies the beliefs of this great, inspirational leader.

Sitting Bull, Red Cloud, Young Man Afraid of His Horses, Gall, American Horse, and most of the other Sioux were real; so were the Cheyennes: Bobtail Horse, Roman Nose, and Black Kettle. Sitting Bull's adopted son, Frank Grouard, the Grabber, was an actual person who did betray the Sioux. After several years of warrior training, he became the army's most dependable Indian scout. His treachery led to the deaths of hundreds of his former allies.

For the past 120 years, historians and self-styled military analysts have tried to find scapegoats for the Little Bighorn. At one time or another, every senior officer involved with the operation has been blamed. I have sought only to award credit, not to fix responsibility or point fingers.

Beecher's Island, Chivington's raid at Sand Creek, Custer's at the Washita, and the famous "Last Stand" are described as fairly and accurately as the narrative allows. So too are the Wagon Box Fight and Crazy Horse's defeat of W. J. Fetterman and his eighty men, where, incidentally, there actually were no survivors.

Captain Grant Marsh and Pilot David Campbell were real men and actual heroes. Marsh became a legend in his own time. His dash of 710 miles in 54 hours, with Reno's wounded, along the Bighorn, Yellowstone, and Missouri, established a speed record which has never been equaled on those rivers. Grant Marsh's life and times are extolled in a wonderful book by Joseph Mills Hanson entitled Conquest of the Missouri, published by McClurg & Co. in 1909. My apologies to the kindly captain for terminating him in 1876, when he actually lived until 1916. I took the liberty of rearranging his life in the hope that his part in *The Custer Legacy* might awaken a new interest in this remarkable riverman's career.

Every major historical event that I have described actually happened. Only one of them was placed out of sequence. That was Custer's raid on Black Kettle's village at the Washita River. In the story it occurs in late August 1868, when, in fact, it actually happened three months later, at the end of November. The flow of the story demanded that the chronology be changed.

Anyone who has ever participated in mortal combat knows that war and violent death are neither pretty nor glamorous. Some of my scenes vividly depict this harsh and cruel world — the crusty, deadly world where every warrior is forced to exist. But in *The Custer Legacy*, there is no immorality or needless violence. While it is true that some of my characters die violent and painful deaths, all of them, whether real or fictional, die with dignity.

Since the day that a caveman found the first shiny gold nugget and gave it to his woman, who smiled her gap-toothed grin and said "pretty" or its equivalent in cave jargon, desire for this glittering metal has persisted. So have legends about large rich caches searched for, found, then lost again. For many years, one legend concerned the Custer gold depicted in our story. Was this tale of great riches part of western lore, or only a western lure? Like the answers to so many historical mysteries, the solution to this one will probably never be known for sure. The veils of time are simply too difficult to pierce. But the real treasures of such legends are the golden dreams they spin in imaginations of wise men, not in dreams of gold that clog the minds of greedy fools.

How real is the Aztecs' cure? To be sure, I employed literary license in describing the many attributes of "Tratamiento." However, the principal ingredient, capsaicin (extract of cayenne peppers), really works. It rushes blood to a location faster than anything I have ever used. As a result, it does relieve pain, eliminate numbness, and generally improve the healing process. As with all other remedies, please consult a physician before trying this or any other medicine!

Finally, let me say that *The Custer Legacy* is a fictional work, with a primary goal of entertainment. Although I have striven for accuracy, the book is not meant to be used as a historical text. I have already authored a plethora of material for that purpose.

So ends our first fictional journey through history together. We have spanned half the millennium and circled half the globe. It has been a long, complex and, I hope, exciting trip. Along the way we've touched the lives of many people, long since dead, most of whom have been my friends for over fifty years. I have tried to relate their stories with understanding, love, and compassion.

Appendix B:
➤
Important Dates and Events

1454 - Diego Garza, a future Grandee of Spain, commissions a sword to be made for him by Espadas Españas' finest craftsman, José Mendoza.

1519 - The Grandee gives the sword to his namesake grandson, the priest, Padre Diego Garza, who will soon join Hernando Cortez in his conquest of Mexico.

1520 - In June, Padre Garza is given an Aztec wonder drug. In July, the now-broken sword passes into the hands of Alvar Nuñez, known as Cabeza de Vaca, at La Noche de Triste.

1530 - Cabeza de Vaca loses the sword-knife after a fight with a Comanche warrior.

1854 - The sword-knife is recovered from the body of a slain Comanche by a Sioux warrior named White Wolf.

1867 - White Wolf gives the sword-knife to his friend, Fire Hawk, when he becomes a Sioux warrior.

1876 - The sword-knife is lost after the Battle of the Little Bighorn. So is an eighteen-ton shipment of gold.

1877 - Word of the golden treasure leaks out, and a century-long gold hunt begins.

1939 - A young American, studying at the Pontifical College of Rome, finds evidence of the ancient Aztec medicine, and a desperate search begins.

1941 - Emilio Duarte, a soldier of fortune, goes to Mexico to begin the search in the land of the Aztecs.

1999 - Antonio Garza, a former Green Beret skilled in covert operations, goes back to the Yucatan peninsula to pick up the search.

Appendix C:
➤
15TH, 16TH, 19TH & 20TH Century Players

The Fifteenth and Sixteenth Century Players

Queen Isabel and King Fernando — Los Reyes Catolicos (The Catholic Majesties). Barely out of their teens when they ascended the throne, they brought unity and justice out of chaos.

Don Diego Garza — Grandee of Granada. The man who kept Queen Isabel safe for twenty three difficult and dangerous years. He is the original owner of the wondrous Garza sword.

Padre Diego Garza — Grandson of the Grandee. One of the priests who joins the Conquistadors on their conquest of Mexico in 1519. A peaceful and gentle man, thrust into the middle of a fight for an empire. A man who learns an ancient Aztec secret.

Hernando Cortez — The great captain from Castile. The man most responsible for taking away the devil's favorite playground and conquering an evil society that demanded a hundred thousand human sacrifices each year.

The Nineteenth Century Players

Kevin McCarthy — A hot blooded Irish immigrant who survives the perils of the Civil War, only to be thrust into other deadly dangers in the post war western United States. He is as eager to claim his share of the American Dream as he is to win the hand of a fiery French Canadian beauty.

Catherine Gerot — A golden haired, green eyed product of a strict Catholic convent education. Confined throughout much of her life, she is eager to challenge the world on her own terms before settling down.

Clayton Forrester — 1858 graduate of V.M.I. and Jeb Stuart's chief of skirmishers during the Civil War—a war that cost him his family and everything he held dear. The sole survivor of the Fetterman Massacre in December 1866, he is a man convinced that the Plains Indians are brutal, murderous heathens. Why then does he forsake the white man's civilized world and become "Fire Hawk," a great Sioux warrior and adopted son of Crazy Horse?

Little Fawn — A young Indian woman, skilled in the ways of herbal healing. She loves Fire Hawk with all of the heart that is not hers to give. She is a White Sun Woman, sworn to forsake marriage to better serve her people. Will commitment or passion prevail?

White Wolf — Fire Hawk's tribal blood brother. A tenacious fighter who takes great pride in killing his antagonists. He teaches Fire Hawk the ways of a Sioux warrior and swears that one day before they die they will stand together to defeat General Custer and many of the Sioux' other mortal enemies.

Crazy Horse — Great chief of the Oglalas and the hero of every Sioux and Cheyenne warrior. The foster father of Fire Hawk, he will fight for his people until he is murdered.

Brevet General George A. Custer — Fallen from grace because of public scandal. Recently chastised by President U.S. Grant. He desperately needs the recognition of national headlines, and willing to

Bruce T. Clark

> purchase them by slaughtering Indians—men, women, or children, it matters not.

The Twentieth Century Players

Emmanuel Questa — A young American, who is studying at the Pontifical College of Rome when World War II erupts in 1939. He discovers a clue to an Aztec secret, which has been hidden for the past 400 years.

Luigi Cardinal Cabrini — A Prince of the Catholic Church who lost in his bid to become Pope by two votes. He vows the next election will be different. Can a successful search for the Aztec secret become the bridge for this ambitious Cardinal to the Chair of St. Peter?

Emilio Duarte — A good hearted soldier of fortune, hired by Cardinal Cabrini to find the Aztec secret and to pave a way to the papacy. He finds far more than he bargains for in the dangerous Yucatan Peninsula.

Antonio Garza — Descendant of the earlier Garzas and former Green Beret, skilled in covert operations. A modern knight errant, still grieving for his wife after eight years, and feeling guilty about the victims of the Vietnam War after twenty five. He is on a mission of mercy for yet another Catholic Cardinal. A dangerous mission, which may mark his self imposed debt to the world, "paid in full." To succeed he must outwit two deadly organizations.

Carla Cansino — A highly successful petroleum geologist from Houston, Texas. Beautiful and alluring, she is the only woman to spark Tony Garza's interest since the death of his wife. Will she wait until he finishes his dangerous mission? And if so, what price will she demand for her favors?

ACKNOWLEDGMENTS

I'm amused when people say, "Someday, I'm going to write a book, too." Of course, it's a well-intentioned, offhand remark, uttered as readily as, "I'm going to the barbecue tonight," or "We're going to Florida for our vacation." But should the truth be told, writing requires endless dedication, and a great deal of assistance from others. I guess that had I not undergone above-the-knee amputation, in the spring of 1994, I never would have mustered the patience or the determination that is required. But enough of that. Now is the time to focus on the large measures of assistance that I have received. Help for which I shall always be grateful.

Thanks first and foremost to Our Blessed Lord for giving me my faith, my spirit, and whatever talent I may possess. Thanks to each of my family members for your strength and support so freely given, and your warm love so boundlessly shared. Thank you to so many others for the enthusiasm and courage you helped to build in this "arrogant, old crippled guy."

Although it's difficult for me to single out a few, where so many should be, I do want to mention and offer thanks to several very special people. To Martha Brown, for always having time to chat, and to her daughter, P. J. Galligan, for her cheerful and patient proofreading. To Mitch Kalpakgian, for so many helpful suggestions. To Robin Janton, for teaching me about frontier weaponry. To Bob Harkness, for sharing his amazing Indian lore. To Doug Hollingsworth, Front Royal's Mr. Goodwrench, for his expertise on cars and their idiosyncrasies. To Father Robert Hermley for his guidance in Catholic doctrine, and verbal tours of Rome; and to Father Constantine Bellisarius, for his clever insightfulness. To Green Beret and American hero, John Garcia, for those picturesque looks at his native Yucatan and its pyramids that he shared with me so long ago. To Captain Allan Bates, the legendary designer of the riverboat *Natchez Belle*, for his input on side-wheelers and life on the rivers. And to Jack E. Custer, riverboat historian, for his data on similar subjects. Thanks to my helpful, cheerful, and enthusiastic assistants: Robin Hibl, Therese Elliot, and Juanita Konechne. To the Smithsonian Institute's Dr. Cesare Marino, for sharing his great knowledge of the Plains Indians. A very special thank you to Pam Gruber for being the most important part of our long and wonderful friendship; for introducing me to the works and worlds of Robert Ludlum and John MacDonald; and most of all for sharing so many great eggs Benedict and mimosa breakfasts. To my production overseer, Patrick Karcher, who baled me out so often. He made me understand how the settlers felt when the cavalry came to their rescue. To Ed and Amy Eldredge, at Four Winds Publishing, for their faith in *The Custer Legacy* and their encouragement.

Finally to Patrick Keats, actor, teacher, director, dialogtician, editor, and friend extraordinaire. Perhaps *The Custer Legacy* could have been written without him, but for the life of me, I can't figure out how.

A very wise person once said that a truly wealthy man measures his riches, not by stacking his gold, but by counting his friends. To each of you, whether or not you are on this short list, please believe that I cherish your friendship. You've made me one of the world's richest men.

Another Adventure

Please plan to join me once again in the pages of *The Castro Conspiracy*. It's 1960 and Fidel Castro has been in power for three months.

So far, he has seized $700,000 of American businessmen's assets. Every Mafia casino has been closed, and over a billion dollars of mob money has been confiscated. Sam Giancana and other Mafia bigwigs are extremely unhappy with Fidel. They are looking for a way to get even. So are the Americans, many of whom have been forced to flee to safety.

Castro has already executed seven hundred Cuban citizens who dared to object to his murderous regime. There are no rights in Cuba other than those granted by Fidel Castro and his henchmen. Murder and mayhem are the order of the day. The burning question is, what can be done to stop Castro?

On March 17th, President Eisenhower gives his permission for the C.I.A.'s Allen Dulles and Richard Bissell, to develop a small, covert, anti-Castro operation. A thousand Cuban refugees will be recruited and trained as guerrilla fighters and saboteurs. When they're ready, they'll be infiltrated back into Cuba, where they'll begin a series of raids designed to upset, and eventually overthrow, the Castro regime.

In the pages of *The Castro Conspiracy* we'll meet the U.S. Marine and Special Forces personnel who train those men. We'll visit them in their Central American mountain and jungle training camps.

Then we'll watch as the 1960 Presidential Election puts a reluctant commander-in-chief in the White House, and see the entire, carefully orchestrated, covert operation fall apart.

We'll attend dozens of secret meetings conducted by the CIA, FBI, and the CFR. At those meetings we'll finally discover why Operation Trinidad, a small, easily controlled and plausible incursion, a plan that was almost certain to succeed, was turned into the over-zealous, overly ambitious, and impossible to control fiasco that the Bay of Pigs Invasion eventually became.

We'll meet the Kennedy family and the Castros, along with the deadly Mafia hitmen who are recruited to kill Castro. Washington insiders and Hollywood stars will be on display. Along the way we'll watch men who willingly risk their lives to achieve success, and women who willingly use their wiles to keep them from gaining that success.

We'll get to know Jack Kennedy, a man who desperately wants the Cuban Invasion to succeed, and John F. Kennedy, a president who desperately can't afford to allow it to. And we'll be present when he cancels American air support—the decision that spelled doom for the invasion and every Cuba Freedom Fighter.

We'll spend three frightening days in the middle of the Bay of Pigs Invasion, and eighteen frustrating months in its aftermath—fighting and dying on the beaches—running and hiding in the swamps—sweating and suffering in the prisons. And wondering, always wondering, why the Americanos deserted us?

We'll see the Cuban Missile Crisis through the eyes of the men who lived it. Part of our time will be spent in America's Oval Office—another part in Russia's Kremlin—and the rest of our days at the UN. And we'll discover how close America came to the brink of World War III during that historic October fortnight—and learn, perhaps for the first time, why the Cuban Missile Crisis was John F. Kennedy's finest hour.

In the first half of 1963, we'll sit in on meetings with war profiteers and Old Guard G-men—with double-crossed Mafia dons, and desperate Castro supporters—the four groups of men that cannot permit President Kennedy to live one day longer than necessary!

We'll meet Phyllis McGuire and other "show biz folks," and we'll get to know the dupes who had starring roles in the Kennedy Assassination—Jack Ruby and Lee Harvey Oswald.

We'll be present at the final and deadly negotiations with Carlos, the Jackal, when he agrees to assassinate the American President, and we'll eavesdrop when the Jackal hires three other "professional shooters," so that there will be no slip-ups in Texas.

And finally, we'll be in Dallas with Jack and Jackie on that fatal Friday in November, and we'll relive the shock and sorrow of a grieving nation.

After three years of research and writing, *The Castro Conspiracy* is now available.

Bruce T. Clark
Front Royal, Va.
October 15, 2000

"The Custer Legacy is an absolutely amazing book. It is historically accurate and brilliantly presented. The creativity and writing style are truly captivating."

Dr. Cesare Marino, Director,
Book of North American Indians,
Smithsonian Institute.

"The Custer Legacy is spellbinding, ingenious, and intense. The final two hundred pages move like a runaway freight train to reach an incredible ending."

Dr. Mitch Kalpakgian,
English Department,
Simpson College

"The Custer Legacy is rich historical fare with a broad spectrum of times and cultures, characters that ring true, and a story that fascinates and satisfies."

Father Constantine Belisarius,
Contributing Historian,
Encyclopedia Americana.

"The Custer Legacy is an historical novel in the tradition of James Michener and Sir Walter Scott. Broad and panoramic in scope, it contains two baffling mysteries in need of solutions, and a host of dynamic and unforgettable characters."

Dr. Patrick Keats,
Professor of English Literature,
Christendom College.

"The Custer Legacy lures you into an historical adventure mixed with mystery and romance. Delightful and exciting reading."

Paul Galligan,
Past-President
Catholic Women's Guild.

Review of The Custer Legacy

The Custer Legacy is epic in scope, part historical novel and part mystery thriller. First it takes you back, briefly but memorably, to the 1520's Mexico: the Mexico of Cortez, Montezuma, and the Aztecs. There, a magnificent Toledo sword and Aztec wonder drug are both lost in the heat of battle, seemingly for all times.

But re-appear they do: in the western United States of the late 1860's, shortly after the Civil War has ended. Then come the stirring adventures of Clayton Forrester, a former Confederate Cavalry officer, and Kevin McCarthy, a colorful Irish immigrant who pursues the beautiful Catherine Gerot even as he attempts to carve a fortune out of a savage, danger-filled frontier.

Also present are such larger-than-life figures as George Armstrong Custer, Sitting Bull, and the Sioux cavalry genius Crazy Horse. Novelist/Historian Bruce T. Clark presents great western battles such as the Wagon Box Fight, Siege at Beecher's Island, and Custer's Last Stand with painstaking authenticity as well as a marvelous brand of runaway excitement.

In the final, equally exciting section of the novel, Clark brings the action up to the twentieth century. Here, Vatican- sponsored investigators discover that the key to the Aztec enigma is intertwined with a legendary hoard of gold that was lost after Custer's Little Bighorn defeat. The detectives, however, are not the only ones searching for the twin treasures. Pitted against them are murderous agents of two other organizations, both intent on recovering the gold, and the even greater prize that awaits those who control the world's medical future.

About the Author

Bruce T. Clark a Who's Who Historian, has had a sixty year love affair with America's past. He has been a teacher, lecturer, and radio talk show host since his return from military service in 1962. Prior to leg amputation in 1994, he was a six-handicap golfer. "I always found time for golf," he muses, "but never seemed to have enough time to share any of the historical mystery stories that have crowded into my imagination for so long. I hope people think I'm a good storyteller, because I've become a lousy golfer." A growing legion of avid fans are hopeful that *The Custer Legacy* is only the first of many exciting mystery/history novels.

Mr. Clark and his wife of forty-seven years, Dr. Mary Kay Clark, the founder and director of Seton Home Study School, are the proud parents of seven sons, and grandparents of thirty-one. They all reside in the historically rich Shenandoah Valley of Virginia.